WALTER SCOTT

ANNE OF GEIERSTEIN

Elibron Classics
www.elibron.com

Elibron Classics series.

© 2006 Adamant Media Corporation.

ISBN 0-543-90116-5 (paperback)
ISBN 0-543-90115-7 (hardcover)

This Elibron Classics book contains the complete text of the
edition published in 1868 by Ticknor and Fields, Boston.

CONTENTS

> What! Will the aspiring blood of Lancastor
> Sink in the ground?
>
> SHAKSPEARE

INTRODUCTION —— (1831.)

This novel was written at a time when circumstances did not place within my reach the stores of a library tolerably rich in historical works, and especially the memoirs of the middle ages, amidst which I had been accustomed to pursue the composition of my fictitious narratives. In other words, it was chiefly the work of leisure hours in Edinburgh, not of quiet mornings in the country. In consequence of trusting to a memory, strongly tenacious certainly, but not less capricious in its efforts, I have to confess on this occasion more violations of accuracy in historical details, than can perhaps be alleged against others of my novels. In truth, often as I have been complimented on the strength of my memory, I have through life been entitled to adopt old Beattie of Meikledale's answer to his parish minister when eulogizing him with respect to the same faculty. "No, Doctor," said the honest border-laird. "I have no command of my memory; it only retains what happens to hit my fancy, and like enough, sir, if you were to preach to me for a couple of hours on end, I might be unable at the close of the discourse to remember one word of it." Perhaps there are few men whose memory serves them with equal fidelity as to many different classes of subjects; but I am sorry to say, that while mine has rarely failed me as to any snatch of verse or trait of character that had once interested my fancy, it has generally been a frail support, not only as to names, and dates, and other minute technicalities of history, but as to many more important things.

I hope this apology will suffice for one mistake which has been pointed out to me by the descendant of one of the persons introduced in this story, and who complains with reason that I have made a peasant deputy of the ancestor of a distinguished and noble family, none of whom ever declined from the high rank, to which, as far as my pen trenched on it, I now beg leave to restore them. The name of the person who figures as deputy of Soleure in these pages, was always, it seems, as it is now, that of a patrician house. I am reminded by the same correspondent of another slip, probably of less consequence. The Emperor of the days my novel refers to, though the representative of that Leopold who fell in the great battle of Sempach, never set up any pretensions against the liberties of the gallant Swiss, but, on the contrary, treated with uniform prudence and forbearance, such of that nation as had established their independence, and with wise, as well as generous kindness, others who still continued to acknowledge fealty to the imperial crown. Errors of this sort, however trivial, ought never, in my opinion, to be pointed out to an author, without meeting with a candid and respectful acknowledgment.

With regard to a general subject of great curiosity and interest, in the eyes at least of all antiquarian students, upon which I have touched at some length in this narrative, I mean the *Vehmic* tribunals of Westphalia, a name so awful in men's ears during many centuries, and which, through the genius of Goethe, has again been revived in public fancy with a full share of its ancient terrors, I am bound to state my opinion, that a wholly new and most important light has been thrown upon this matter since Anne of Geierstein first appeared, by the elaborate researches of my ingenious friend, Mr. Francis Palgrave[1], whose proof-sheets, containing the passages I allude to, have been kindly forwarded to me, and whose complete work will be before the public ere this Introduction can pass through the press.

"In Germany," says this very learned writer, "there existed a singular jurisdiction which claimed a *direct descent from the Pagan policy and mystic ritual of the earliest Teutons.*

"We learn from the historians of Saxony, that the 'Frey Feld gericht,' or Free Field Court of Corbey, was, in Pagan times, under the supremacy of the Priests of the Eresburgh, the Temple which contained the Irminsule, or pillar of Irmin. After the conversion of the people, the possessions of the temple were conferred by Louis the Pious upon the Abbey which arose upon its site. The court was composed of sixteen persons, who held their offices for life. The senior member presided as the Gerefa or Graff; the junior performed the humbler duties of 'Frohner', or summoner; the remaining fourteen acted as the Echevins, and by them all judgments were pronounced or declared. When any one

---

[1] Now Sir Francis Palgrave.

of these died, a new member was elected by the Priests, from amongst the twenty-two septs or families inhabiting the Gau or district, and who included all the hereditary occupants of the soil. Afterwards, the selection was made by the Monks, but always with the assent of the Graff and of the 'Frohner.'

"The seat of judgment, the King's seat, or 'Königsstuhl,' was always established on the greensward; and we collect from the context, that the tribunal was also raised or appointed in the common fields of the Gau, for the purpose of deciding disputes relating to the land within its precinct. Such a 'King's seat' was a plot sixteen feet in length, and sixteen feet in breadth; and when the ground was first consecrated, the Frohner dug a grave in the centre, into which each of the Free Echevins threw a handful of ashes, a coal, and a tile. If any doubt arose whether a place of judgment had been duly hallowed, the Judges sought for the tokens. If they were not found, then all the judgments which had been given became null and void. It was also of the very essence of the Court, that it should be held beneath the sky, and by the light of the sun. All the ancient Teutonic judicial assemblies were held in the open air; but some relics of solar worship may, perhaps, be traced in the usage and in the language of this tribunal. The forms adopted in the Free Field Court also betray a singular affinity to the doctrines of the British Bards respecting their Gorseddau, or Conventions, which were 'always held in the open air, in the eye of the light, and in face of the sun.'[2]

"When a criminal was to be judged, or a cause to be decided, the Graff and the Free Echevins assembled around the 'Königsstuhl;' and the 'Frohner,' having proclaimed silence, opened the proceedings by reciting the following rhymes: —

> "Sir Graff, with permission,
>   I beg you to say,
> According to law, and without delay,
>   If I your Knave,
>   Who judgment crave,
>   With your good grace,
> Upon the King's seat this seat may place.

---

[2] Owen Pugh's Elegies of Lewarch Hen, Pref. p. 46. — The place of these meetings was set apart by forming a circle of stones round the *Maen Gorsedd,* or Stone of the Gorsedd.

"To this address the Graff replied: —

> "While the sun shines with even light
> Upon Masters and Knaves, I shall declare
> The law of might, according to right.
> Place the King's seat true and square,
> Let even measure, for justice' sake,
> Be given in sight of God and man,
> That the plaintiff his complaint may make,
> And the defendant answer, — if he can.

"In conformity to this permission, the 'Frohner' placed the seat of judgment in the middle of the plot, and then he spake for the second time: —

> "Sir Graff; Master brave,
> I remind you of your honour, here,
> And moreover that I am your Knave;
> Tell me, therefore, for law sincere,
> If these mete-wands are even and sure,
> Fit for the rich and fit for the poor,
> Both to measure land and condition;
> Tell me as you would eschew perdition.

"And so speaking, he laid the mete-wand on the ground.

The Graff then began to try the measure, by placing his right foot against the wand, and he was followed by the other Free Echevins in rank and order, according to seniority. The length of the mete-wand being thus proved, the Frohner spake for the third time: —

> "Sir Graff, I ask by permission,
> If I with your mete-wand may mete
> Openly, and without displeasure,
> Here the king's free judgment seat.

"And the Graff replied: —

> "I permit right,
> And I forbid wrong,
> Under the pains and penalties
> That to the old known laws belong.

"Now was the time of measuring the mystic plot; it was measured by the mete-wand along and athwart, and when the dimensions were found to be true, the Graff placed himself in the

seat of judgment, and gave the charge to the assembled Free
Echevins, warning them to pronounce judgment, according to
right and justice.

> "On this day, with common consent,
> And under the clear firmament,
> A free field court is established here
> In the open eye of day;
> Enter soberly, ye who may.
> The seat in its place is pight,
> The mete-wand is found to be right;
> Declare your judgments without delay:
> And let the doom be truly given,
> Whilst yet the Sun shines bright in heaven.

"Judgment was given by the Free Echevins according to
plurality of voices."

After observing that the author of Anne of Geierstein had,
by what he calls a "very excusable poetical license," transferred
something of these judicial rhymes from the Free Field Court of
the Abbey of Corbey, to the Free Vehmic Tribunals of Westphalia, Mr. Palgrave proceeds to correct many vulgar errors, in
which, the novel he remarks on no doubt had shared, with respect to the actual constitution of those last-named courts. "The
protocols of their proceedings," he says, "do not altogether realize the popular idea of their terrors and tyranny." It may be allowed to me to question whether the mere protocols of such
tribunals are quite enough to annul all the import of tradition respecting them; but in the following details there is no doubt
much that will instruct the antiquarian, as well as amuse the
popular reader.

"The Court," says Mr. Palgrave, "was held with known and
notorious publicity beneath the 'eye of light;' and the sentences,
though speedy and severe, were founded upon a regular system
of established jurisprudence, not so strange, even to England, as
it may at first sight appear.

"Westphalia, according to its ancient constitution, was divided into districts called 'Freygraffschafften,' each of which
usually contained one, and sometimes many, Vehmic tribunals,
whose boundaries were accurately defined. The right of the
'Stuhlherr,' or Lord, was of a feudal nature, and could be transferred by the ordinary modes of alienation; and if the Lord did

not choose to act in his own person, he nominated a 'Freigraff' to execute the office in his stead. The court itself was composed of 'Freyschöppfen,' Scabini, or Echevins, nominated by the Graff, and who were divided into two classes: the ordinary, and the 'Wissenden' or 'Witan,' who were admitted under a strict and singular bond of secrecy.

"The initiation of these, the participators in all the mysteries of the tribunal, could only take place upon the 'red earth,' or within the limits of the ancient Duchy of Westphalia. Bareheaded and ungirt, the candidate is conducted before the dread tribunal. He is interrogated as to his qualifications, or rattier as to the absence of any disqualification. He must be free born, a Teuton, and clear of any accusation cognizable by the tribunal of which he is to become a member. — If the answers are satisfactory, he then takes the oath, swearing by the Holy Law, that he will conceal the secrets of the Holy Vehme from wife and child — from father and mother — from sister and brother — from fire and water — from every creature upon which the sun shines, or upon which the rain falls — from every being between earth and heaven.

"Another clause relates to his active duties. He further swears, that he will 'say forth' to the tribunal all crimes or offences which fall beneath the secret ban of the Emperor, which he knows to be true, or which he has heard from trustworthy report; and that he will not forbear to do so, for love nor for loathing, for gold nor for silver nor precious stones. — This oath being imposed upon him, the new Freischöpff was then intrusted with the secrets of the Vehmic tribunal. He received the password, by which he was to know his fellows, and the grip or sign by which they recognised each other in silence; and he was warned of the terrible punishment awaiting the perjured brother. — If he discloses the secrets of the Court, he is to expect that he will be suddenly seized by the ministers of vengeance. His eyes are bound, he is cast down on the soil, his tongue is torn out through the back of his neck — and he is then to be hanged seven times higher than any other criminal. And whether restrained by the fear of punishment, or by the stronger ties of mystery, no instance was ever known of any violation of the secrets of the tribunal.

"Thus connected by an invisible bond, the members of the

'Holy Vehme' became extremely numerous. In the fourteenth century, the league contained upwards of one hundred thousand members. Persons of every rank sought to be associated to this powerful community, and to participate in the immunities which the brethren possessed. Princes were eager to allow their ministers to become the members of this mysterious and holy alliance; and the cities of the Empire were equally anxious to enrol their magistrates in the Vehmic union.

"The supreme government of the Vehmic tribunals was vested in the great or general Chapter, composed of the Freegraves and all the other initiated members, high and low. Over this assembly the Emperor might preside in person, but more usually by his deputy, the Stadtholder of the ancient Duchy of Westphalia; an office, which, after the fall of Henry the Lion, Duke of Brunswick, was annexed to the Archbishopric of Cologne.

"Before the general Chapter, all the members were liable to account for their acts. And it appears that the 'Freegraves' reported the proceedings which had taken place within their jurisdictions in the course of the year. Unworthy members were expelled, or sustained a severer punishment. Statutes, or 'Reformations,' as they were called, were here enacted for the regulation of the Courts, and the amendment of any abuses; and new and unforeseen cases, for which the existing laws did not provide a remedy, received their determination in the Vehmic Parliament.

"As the Echevins were of two classes, uninitiated and initiated, so the Vehmic Courts had also a twofold character; the 'Offenbare Ding' was an Open Court or Folkmoot; but the 'Heimliche Acht' was the far-famed Secret Tribunal.

"The first was held three times in each year. According to the ancient Teutonic usage, it usually assembled on Tuesday, anciently called 'Dingstag,' or court-day, as well as 'Dienstag,' or serving-day, the first open or working-day after the two great weekly festivals of Sunday and Moon-day. Here all the householders of the district, whether free or bond, attended as suitors. The 'Offenbare Ding' exercised a civil jurisdiction: and in this Folkmoot appeared any complainant or appellant who sought to obtain the aid of the Vehmic tribunal, in those cases when it did not possess that summary jurisdiction from which it has obtained such fearful celebrity. Here also the suitors of the district made presentments or 'wroge,' as they are termed, of any offences committed within their knowledge, and which were to be punished by the Graff and Echevins.

"The criminal jurisdiction of the Vehmic Tribunal took the widest range. The 'Vehme' could punish mere slander and contumely. Any violation of the Ten Commandments was to be restrained by the Echevins. Secret crimes, not to be proved by the ordinary testimony of witnesses, such as magic, witchcraft, and poison, were particularly to be restrained by the Vehmic Judges; and they sometimes designated their jurisdiction as comprehending every offence against the honour of man or the precepts of religion. Such a definition, if definition it can be called, evidently allowed them to bring every action of which an individual might complain, within the scope of their tribunals. The forcible usurpation of land became an offence against the 'Vehme.' And if the property of an humble individual was occupied by the proud Burghers of the Hanse, the power of the Defendants might afford a reasonable excuse for the interference of the Vehmic power.

"The Echevins, as Conservators of the Ban of the Empire, were bound to make constant circuits within their districts, by night and by day. If they could apprehend a thief, a murderer, or the perpetrator of any other heinous crime in possession of the 'mainour,' or in the very act — or if his own mouth confessed the deed, they hung him upon the next tree. But to render this execution legal, the following requisites were necessary: — Fresh suit, or the apprehension and execution of the offender before daybreak or nightfall; — the visible evidence of the crime; and, lastly, that three Echevins, at least, should seize the offender, testify against him, and judge of the recent deed.

"If, without any certain accuser, and without the indication of crime, an individual was strongly and vehemently suspected; or when the nature of the offence was such as that its proof could only rest upon opinion and presumption, the offender then became subject to what the German jurists term the inquisitorial proceeding; it became the duty of the Echevin to denounce the 'Leumund,' or manifest evil fame, to the secret tribunal. If the Echevins and the Freygraff were satisfied with the presentment, either from their own knowledge, or from the information of their compeer, the offender was said to be 'verfämbt;' — his life was forfeited; and wherever he was found by the brethren of the tribunal, they executed him without the slightest delay or mercy. An offender who had escaped from the Echevins was liable to the same punishment; and such also was the doom of the party who, after having been summoned pursuant to an appeal preferred in open court, made default in appearing. But one of the 'Wissenden' was in no respect liable to the summary process, or to the inquisitorial proceeding, unless he had revealed the secrets of the Court. He was presumed to be a true man; and if accused upon vehement suspicion, or 'Leumund,' the same presumption or evil repute, which was fatal to the uninitiated, might he entirely rebutted by the compurgatory oath of the free Echevin. If a party, accused by appeal, did not shun investigation, he appeared in the open court, and defended himself according to the ordinary rules of law. If he absconded, or if the evidence or presumptions were against him, the accusation then came before the Judges of the Secret Court, who pronounced the doom. The accusatorial process, as it was termed, was also, in many cases, brought in the first instance before the 'Heimliche Acht.' Proceeding upon the examination of witnesses, it possessed no peculiar character, and its forms were those of the ordinary courts of justice. It was only in this manner that one of the 'Wissenden,' or Witan, could be tried; and the privilege of being exempted from the summary process, or from the effects of the 'Leumund,' appears to have been one of the reasons which induced so many of those who did not tread the 'red earth' to seek to be included in the Vehmic bond.

"There was no mystery in the assembly of the Heimliche Acht. Under the oak, or under the lime-tree, the Judges assembled in broad daylight, and before the eye of heaven; but the tribunal derived its name from the precautions which were taken, for the purpose of preventing any disclosure of its proceedings which might enable the offender to escape the vengeance of the Vehme. Hence, the fearful oath of secrecy which bound the Echevins. And if any stranger was found present in the Court, the unlucky intruder instantly forfeited his life as a punishment for his temerity. If the presentment or denunciation did chance to become known to the offender, the law allowed him a right of appeal. But the permission was of very little utility, it was a profitless boon, for the Vehmic Judges always laboured to conceal the judgment from the hapless criminal, who seldom was aware of his sentence until his neck was encircled by the halter.

"Charlemagne, according to the traditions of Westphalia, was the founder of the Vehmic tribunal; and it was supposed that he instituted the Court for the purpose of coercing the Saxons, ever ready to relapse into the idolatry from which they had been reclaimed, not by persuasion, but by the sword. This opinion, however, is not confirmed either by documentary evidence or by contemporary historians. And if we examine the proceedings of the Vehmic tribunal, we shall see that, in principle, it differs in no essential character from the summary jurisdiction exercised in the townships and hundreds of Anglo-Saxon England. Amongst us, the thief or the robber was equally liable to summary punishment, if apprehended by the men of the township; and the same rules disqualified them from proceeding to summary execution. An English outlaw was exactly in the situation of him who had escaped from the hands of the Echevins, or who had failed to appear before the Vehmic Court: he was condemned unheard, nor was he confronted with his accusers. The inquisitorial proceedings, as they are termed by the German jurists, are identical with our ancient presentments. Presumptions are substituted for proofs, and general opinion holds the place of a responsible accuser. He who was untrue to all the people in the Saxon age, or liable to the malecredence of the inquest at a subsequent period, was scarcely more fortunate than he who was branded as 'Leumund' by the Vehmic law.

"In cases of open delict and of outlawry, there was substantially no difference whatever between the English and the Vehmic proceedings. But in the inquisitorial process, the delinquent was allowed, according to our older code, to run the risk of the ordeal. He was accused by or before the Hundred, or the Thanes of the Wapentake; and his own oath cleared him, if a true man; but he 'bore the iron' if unable to avail himself of the credit derived from a good and fair reputation. The same course may have been originally adopted in Westphalia; for the 'Wissend,' when accused, could exculpate himself by his compurgatory oath, being presumed to be of good fame; and it is, therefore, probable that an uninitiated offender, standing a stage lower in character and credibility, was allowed the last resort of the ordeal. But when the 'Judgment of God' was abolished by the decrees of the Church, it did not occur to the Vehmic Judges to put the offender upon his second trial by the visne, which now forms the distinguishing characteristic of the English law, and he was at once considered as condemned. The Heimliche Acht is a presentment not traversable by the offender.

"*The Vehmic Tribunals can only be considered as the original jurisdictions of the 'Old Saxons,' which survived the subjugation of their country. The singular and mystic forms of initiation, the system of enigmatical phrases, the use of the signs and symbols of recognition, may probably be ascribed to the period when the whole system was united to the worship of the Deities of Vengeance, and when the sentence was promulgated by the Doomsmen, assembled, like the Asi of old, before the altars of Thor or Woden.* Of this connexion with ancient pagan policy, so clearly to be traced in the Icelandic Courts, the English territorial jurisdictions offer some very faint vestiges; but the mystery had long been dispersed, and the whole system passed into the ordinary machinery of the law.

"As to the Vehmic Tribunals, it is acknowledged, that in a truly barbarous age and country, their proceedings, however violent, were not without utility. Their severe and secret vengeance often deterred the rapacity of the noble robber, and protected the humble suppliant; the extent, and even the abuse, of their authority was in some measure justified in an Empire divided into numerous independent jurisdictions, and not subjected to any paramount tribunal, able to administer impartial justice to the oppressed. But as the times improved, the Vehmic tribunals degenerated. The Echevins, chosen from the inferior ranks, did not possess any personal consideration. Opposed by the opulent cities of the Hanse, and objects of the suspicion and the enmity of the powerful aristocracy, the tribunals of some districts were abolished by law, and others took the form of ordinary territorial jurisdictions; the greater number fell into desuetude. Yet, as late as the middle of the eighteenth century, a few Vehmic tribunals existed in name, though, as it may be easily supposed, without possessing any remnant of their pristine power." — PALGRAVE *on the Rise and Progress of the English Commonwealth. Proofs and Illustrations,* p.157.

I have marked *by italic letters* the most important passage of the above quotation. The view it contains seems to me to have every appearance of truth and justice — and if such should, on maturer investigation, turn out to be the fact, it will certainly confer no small honour on an English scholar to have discovered the key to a mystery, which had long exercised in vain the laborious and profound students of German antiquity.

There are probably several other points on which I ought to have embraced this opportunity of enlarging; but the necessity of preparing for an excursion to foreign countries, in quest of health and strength, that have been for some time sinking, makes me cut short my address upon the present occasion.

Although I had never been in Switzerland, and numerous mistakes must of course have occurred in my attempts to describe the local scenery of that romantic region, I must not conclude without a statement highly gratifying to myself, that the work met with a reception of more than usual cordiality among the descendants of the Alpine heroes whose manners I had ventured to treat of; and I have in particular to express my thanks to the several Swiss gentlemen who have, since the novel was published, enriched my little collection of armour with specimens of the huge weapon that sheared the lances of the Austrian chivalry at Sempach, and was employed with equal success on the bloody days of Granson and Morat. Of the ancient double-handed *espadons* of the Switzer, I have, in this way, received, I think, not less than six, in excellent preservation, from as many different individuals, who thus testified their general approbation of these pages. They are not the less interesting, that gigantic swords, of nearly the same pattern and dimensions, were employed in their conflicts with the bold knights and men-at-arms of England, by Wallace, and the sturdy foot-soldiers who, under his guidance, laid the foundations of Scottish independence.

The reader who wishes to examine with attention the historical events of the period which the novel embraces, will find ample means of doing so, in the valuable works of Zschokké and M. de Barante — which last author's account of the Dukes of Burgundy is among the most valuable of recent accessions of European literature — and in the new Parisian edition of Froissart, which has not as yet attracted so much attention in this country as it well deserves to do.

W. S.

ABBOTSFORD, *Sept.* 17,1831.

CHAPTER I

The mists boil up around the glaciers; clouds
Rise curling fast beneath me, white and sulphurous,
Like foam from the roused ocean.*   *
*   *   *   *   I am giddy.

MANFRED.

The course of four centuries has well-nigh elapsed since the series of events which are related in the following chapters, took place on the Continent. The records which contained the outlines of the history, and might be referred to as proof of its veracity, were long preserved in the superb library of the Monastery of Saint Gall, but perished, with many of the literary treasures of that establishment, when the convent was plundered by the French revolutionary armies. The events are fixed by historical dale, to the middle of the fifteenth century — that important period, when chivalry still shone with a setting ray, soon about to be totally obscured; in some countries, by the establishment of free institutions, in others, by that of arbitrary power, which alike rendered useless the interference of those self-endowed redressers of wrongs, whose only warrant of authority was the sword.

Amid the general light which had recently shone upon Europe, France, Burgundy, and Italy, but more especially Austria, had been made acquainted with the character of a people, of whose very existence they had before been scarcely conscious. It is true, that the inhabitants of those countries which lie in the vicinity of the Alps, that immense barrier, were not ignorant, that notwithstanding their rugged and desolate appearance, the secluded valleys which winded among those gigantic mountains nourished a race of hunters and shepherds; men, who, living in a state of primeval simplicity, compelled from the soil a subsistence gained by severe labour, followed the chase over the most savage precipices and through the darkest pine forests, or drove their cattle to spots which afforded them a scanty pasturage, even in the vicinage of eternal snows. But the existence of such a people, or rather of a number of small communities who followed nearly the same poor and hardy course of life, had seemed to the rich and powerful princes in the neighbourhood a matter of as little consequence, as it is to the stately herds which repose in a fertile meadow, that a few half-starved goats find their scanty food among the rocks which overlook their rich domain.

But wonder and attention began to be attracted towards these mountaineers, about the middle of the fourteenth century, when reports were spread abroad of severe contests, in which the German chivalry, endeavouring to suppress insurrections among their Alpine vassals, had sustained repeated and bloody defeats, although having on their side numbers and discipline, and the advantage of the most perfect military equipment then known and confided in. Great was the wonder that cavalry, which made the only efficient part of the feudal armies of these ages, should be routed by men on foot; that warriors sheathed in complete steel should be overpowered by naked peasants who wore no defensive armour, and were irregularly provided with pikes, halberds, and clubs, for the purpose of attack; above all, it seemed a species of miracle, that knights and nobles of the highest birth should be defeated by mountaineers and shepherds. But the repeated victories of the Swiss at Laupen, Sempach, and on other less distinguished occasions, plainly intimated that a new principle of civil organization, as well as of military movements, had arisen amid the stormy regions of Helvetia.

Still, although the decisive victories which obtained liberty for the Swiss Cantons, as well as the spirit of resolution and wisdom with which the members of the little confederation had maintained themselves against the utmost exertions of Austria, had spread their fame abroad through all the neighbouring countries; and although they themselves were conscious of the character and actual power which repeated victories had acquired for themselves and their country, yet down to the middle of the fifteenth century, and at a later date, the Swiss retained in a great measure the wisdom, moderation, and simplicity of their ancient manners; so much so, that those who were intrusted with the command of the troops of the Republic in battle, were wont to resume the shepherd's staff when they laid down the truncheon, and, like the Roman dictators, to retire to complete equality with their fellow-citizens, from the eminence of military command to which their talents, and the call of their country, had raised them.

It is, then, in the Forest Cantons of Switzerland, in the autumn of 1474, while these districts were in the rude and simple state we have described, that our tale opens.

Two travellers, one considerably past the prime of life, the other probably two or three-and-twenty years old, had passed the night at the little town of Lucerne, the capital of the Swiss state of the same name, and beautifully situated on the lake of the Four Cantons. Their dress and character seemed those of merchants of a higher class, and while they themselves journeyed on foot, the character of the country rendering that by far the most easy mode of pursuing their route, a young peasant lad, from the Italian side of the Alps, followed them with a sumpter mule, laden apparently with men's wares and baggage, which he sometimes mounted, but more frequently led by the bridle.

The travellers were uncommonly fine-looking men, and seemed connected by some very near relationship, — probably that of father and son; for at the little inn where they lodged on the preceding evening, the great deference and respect paid by the younger to the elder, had not escaped the observation of the natives, who, like other sequestered beings, were curious in proportion to the limited means of information which they possessed. They observed also, that the merchants, under pretence of haste, declined opening their bales, or proposing traffic to the inhabitants of Lucerne, alleging in excuse, that they had no commodities fitted for the market. The females of the town were the more displeased with the reserve of the mercantile travellers, because they were given to understand, that it was occasioned by the wares in which they dealt being too costly to find customers among the Helvetian mountains; for it had transpired by means of their attendant, that the strangers had visited Venice, and had there made many purchases of rich commodities, which were brought from India and Egypt to that celebrated emporium, as to the common mart of the Western World, and thence dispersed into all quarters of Europe. Now the Swiss maidens had of late made the discovery that gauds and gems were fair to look upon, and though without the hope of being able to possess themselves of such ornaments, they felt a natural desire to review and handle the rich stores of the merchants, and some displeasure at being prevented from doing so.

It was also observed, that though the strangers were sufficiently courteous in their demeanour, they did not evince that studious anxiety to please, displayed by the travelling pedlars or merchants of Lombardy or Savoy, by whom the inhabitants of the mountains were occasionally visited; and who had been more frequent in their rounds of late years, since the spoils of victory had invested the Swiss with some wealth, and had taught many of them new wants. Those peripatetic traders were civil and assiduous, as their calling required; but the new visitors seemed men who were indifferent to traffic, or at least to such slender gains as could be gathered in Switzerland.

Curiosity was further excited by the circumstance, that they spoke to each other in a language which was certainly neither German, Italian, nor French, but from which an old man serving in the cabaret, who had once been as far as Paris, supposed they might be English; a people of whom it was only known in these mountains, that they were a fierce insular race, at war with the French for many years, and a large body of whom had long since invaded the Forest Cantons, and sustained such a defeat in the valley of Russwyl, as was well remembered by the gray-haired men of Lucerne, who received the tale from their fathers.

The lad who attended the strangers was soon ascertained to be a youth from the Grison country, who acted as their guide, so far as his knowledge of the mountains permitted. He said they designed to go to Bâle, but seemed desirous to travel by circuitous and unfrequented routes. The circumstances just mentioned increased the general desire to know more of the travellers and of their merchandise. Not a bale, however, was unpacked, and the merchants, leaving Lucerne next morning, resumed their toilsome journey, preferring a circuitous route and bad roads, through the peaceful cantons of Switzerland, to encountering the exactions and rapine of the robber chivalry of Germany, who, like so many sovereigns, made war each at his own pleasure, and levied tolls and taxes on every one who passed their domains of a mile's breadth with all the insolence of petty tyranny.

For several hours after leaving Lucerne, the journey of our travellers was successfully prosecuted. The road, though precipitous and difficult, was rendered interesting by those splendid phenomena, which no country exhibits in a more astonishing manner than the mountains of Switzerland, where the rocky pass, the verdant valley, the broad lake, and the rushing torrent, the attributes of other hills as well as these, are interspersed with the magnificent and yet fearful horrors of the glaciers, a feature peculiar to themselves.

It was not an age in which the beauties or grandeur of a landscape made much impression either on the minds of those who travelled through the country, or who resided in it. To the latter, the objects, however dignified, were familiar, and associated with daily habits and with daily toil; and the former saw, perhaps, more terror than beauty in the wild region through which they passed, and were rather solicitous to get safe to their night's quarters, than to comment on the grandeur of the scenes which lay between them and their place of rest. Yet our merchants, as they proceeded on their journey, could not help being strongly impressed by the character of the scenery around them. Their road lay along the side of the lake, at times level and close on its very margin, at times rising to a great height on the side of the mountain, and winding along the verge of precipices which sunk down to the water as sharp and sheer as the wall of a castle descending upon the ditch which defends it. At other times it traversed spots of a milder character, — delightful green slopes, and lowly retired valleys, affording both pasturage and arable ground, sometimes watered by small streams, which winded by the hamlet of wooden huts with their fantastic little church and steeple, meandered round the orchard and the mount of vines, and murmuring gently as they flowed, found a quiet passage into the lake.

"That stream, Arthur," said the elder traveller, as with one consent they stopped to gaze on such a scene as I have described, "resembles the life of a good and a happy man."

"And the brook, which hurries itself headlong down yon distant hill, marking its course by a streak of white foam," answered Arthur, — "what does that resemble?"

"That of a brave and unfortunate one," replied his father.

"The torrent for me," said Arthur; "a headlong course which no human force can oppose, and then let it be as brief as it is glorious."

"It is a young man's thought," replied his father; "but I am well aware that it is so rooted in thy heart, that nothing but the rude hand of adversity can pluck it up."

"As yet the root clings fast to my heart's strings," said the young man; "and methinks adversity's hand hath had a fair grasp of it."

"You speak, my son, of what you little understand," said his father. "Know, that till the middle of life be passed, men scarce distinguish true prosperity from adversity, or rather they court as the favours of fortune what they should more justly regard as the marks of her displeasure. Look at yonder mountain, which wears on its shaggy brow a diadem of clouds, now raised and now depressed, while the sun glances upon, but is unable to dispel it; — a child might believe it to be a crown of glory — a man knows it to be the signal of tempest."

Arthur followed the direction of his father's eye to the dark and shadowy eminence of Mount Pilatre.

"Is the mist on yonder wild mountain so ominous then?" asked the young man.

"Demand of Antonio," said his father; "he will tell you the legend."

The young merchant addressed himself to the Swiss lad who acted as their attendant, desiring to know the name of the gloomy height, which, in that quarter, seems the leviathan of the huge congregation of mountains assembled about Lucerne.

The lad crossed himself devoutly, as he recounted the popular legend, that the wicked Pontius Pilate, Proconsul of Judea, had here found the termination of his impious life; having, after spending years in the recesses of that mountain which bears his name, at length, in remorse and despair rather than in penitence, plunged into the dismal lake which occupies the summit. Whether water refused to do the executioner's duty upon such a wretch, or whether, his body being drowned, his vexed spirit continued to haunt the place where he committed suicide, Antonio did not pretend to explain. But a form was, often, he said, seen to emerge from the gloomy waters, and go through the action of one washing his hands; and when he did so, dark clouds of mist gathered first round the bosom of the Infernal Lake, (such it had been styled of old,) and then wrapping the whole upper part of the mountain in darkness, presaged a tempest or hurricane, which was sure to follow in a short space. He added, that the evil spirit was peculiarly exasperated at the audacity of such strangers as ascended the mountain to gaze at his place of punishment, and that, in consequence, the magistrates of Lucerne had prohibited any one from approaching Mount Pilatre, under severe penalties. Antonio once more crossed himself as he finished his legend in which act of devotion he was imitated by his hearers, too good Catholics to entertain any doubt of the truth of the story.

"How the accursed heathen scowls upon us!" said the younger of the merchants, while the cloud darkened and seemed to settle on the brow of Mount Pilatre. "*Vade retro; —* be thou defied, sinner!"

A rising wind, rather heard than felt, seemed to groan forth, in the tone of a dying lion, the acceptance of the suffering spirit to the rash challenge of the young Englishman. The mountain was seen to send down its rugged sides thick wreaths of heaving mist, which, rolling through the rugged chasms that seamed the grisly hill, resembled torrents of rushing lava pouring down from a volcano. The ridgy precipices, which formed the sides of these huge ravines, showed their splintery and rugged edges over the vapour, as if dividing from each other the descending streams of mist which rolled around them. As a strong contrast to this gloomy and threatening scene, the more distant mountain range of Righi shone brilliant with all the hues of an autumnal sun.

While the travellers watched this striking and varied contrast, which resembled an approaching combat betwixt the powers of Light and Darkness, their guide, in his mixed jargon of Italian and German, exhorted them to make haste on their journey. The village to which he proposed to conduct them, he said, was yet distant, the road bad, and difficult to find, and if the Evil One (looking to Mount Pilatre, and crossing himself) should send his darkness upon the valley, the path would be both doubtful and dangerous. The travellers, thus admonished, gathered the capes of their cloaks close round their throats, pulled their bonnets resolvedly over their brows, drew the buckle of the broad belts which fastened their mantles, and each with a mountain staff in his hand, well shod with an iron spike, they pursued their journey, with unabated strength and undaunted spirit.

With every step the scenes around them appeared to change. Each mountain, as if its firm and immutable form were flexible and varying, altered in appearance, like that of a shadowy apparition, as the position of the strangers relative to them changed with their motions, and as the mist, which continued slowly, though constantly to descend, influenced the rugged aspect of the hills and valleys which it shrouded with its vapoury mantle. The nature of their progress, too, never direct, but winding by a narrow path along the sinuosities of the valley, and making many a circuit round precipices and other obstacles which it was impossible to surmount, added to the wild variety of a journey, in which, at last, the travellers totally lost any vague idea which they had previously entertained concerning the direction in which the road led them.

"I would," said the elder, "we had that mystical needle which mariners talk of, that points ever to the north, and enables them to keep their way on the waters, when there is neither cape nor headland, sun, moon, nor stars, nor any mark in heaven or earth to tell them how to steer."

"It would scarce avail us among these mountains," answered the youth; "for though that wonderful needle may keep its point to the northern Pole-star, when it is on a flat surface like the sea, it is not to be thought it would do so when these huge mountains arise like walls, betwixt the steel and the object of its sympathy."

"I fear me," replied the father, "we shall find our guide, who has been growing hourly more stupid since he left his own valley, as useless as you suppose the compass would be among the hills of this wild country. — Canst tell, my boy," said he, addressing Antonio in bad Italian, "if we be in the road we purposed?"

"If it please Saint Antonio" — said the guide, who was obviously too much confused to answer the question directly.

"And that water, half covered with mist, which glimmers through the fog, at the foot of this huge black precipice — is it still a part of the Lake of Lucerne, or have we lighted upon another since we ascended that last hill?"

Antonio could only answer that they ought to be on the Lake of Lucerne still, and that he hoped that what they saw below them was only a winding branch of the same sheet of water. But he could say nothing with certainty.

"Dog of an Italian!" exclaimed the younger traveller, "thou deservest to have thy bones broken, for undertaking a charge which thou art as incapable to perform, as thou art to guide us to heaven!"

"Peace, Arthur," said his father; "if you frighten the lad, he runs off, and we lose the small advantage we might have by his knowledge; if you use your baton, he rewards you with the stab of a knife, — for such is the humour of a revengeful Lombard. Either way, you are marred instead of helped. — Hark thee hither, my boy," he continued, in his indifferent Italian, "be not afraid of that hot youngster, whom I will not permit to injure thee; but tell me, if thou canst, the names of the villages by which we are to make our journey to-day?"

The gentle mode in which the elder traveller spoke reassured the lad, who had been somewhat alarmed at the harsh tone and menacing expressions of his younger companion; and he poured forth, in his patois, a flood of names, in which the German guttural sounds were strangely intermixed with the soft accents of the Italian, but which carried to the hearer no intelligible information concerning the object of his question; so that at length he was forced to conclude, "Even lead on, in Our Lady's name, or in Saint Antonio's, if you like it better; we shall but lose time, I see, in trying to understand each other."

They moved on as before, with this difference, that the guide, leading the mule, now went first, and was followed by the other two, whose motions he had formerly directed by calling to them from behind. The clouds meantime became thicker and thicker, and the mist, which had at first been a thin vapour, began now to descend in the form of a small thick rain, which gathered like dew upon the capotes of the travellers. Distant rustling and groaning sounds were heard among the remote mountains, similar to those by which the Evil Spirit of Mount Pilatre had seemed to announce the storm. The boy again pressed his companions to advance, but at the same time threw impediments in the way of their doing so, by the slowness and indecision which he showed in leading them on.

Having proceeded in this manner for three or four miles, which uncertainty rendered doubly tedious, the travellers were at length engaged in a narrow path, running along the verge of a precipice. Beneath was water but of what description they could not ascertain. The wind, indeed, which began to be felt in sudden gusts, sometimes swept aside the mist so completely as to show the waves glimmering below; but whether they were those of the same lake on which their morning journey had commenced, whether it was another and separate sheet of water of a similar character, or whether it was a river or large brook, the view afforded was too indistinct to determine. Thus far was certain, that they were not on the shores of the Lake of Lucerne, where it displays its usual expanse of waters; for the same hurricane gusts which showed them water in the bottom of the glen, gave them a transient view of the opposite side, at what exact distance they could not well discern, but near enough to show tall abrupt rocks and shaggy pine-trees, here united in groups, and there singly anchored among the cliffs which overhung the water. This was a more distinct landscape than the farther side of the lake would have offered, had they been on the right road.

Hitherto the path, though steep and rugged, was plainly enough indicated, and showed traces of having been used both by riders and foot passengers. But suddenly, as Antonio with the loaded mule had reached a projecting eminence, around the peak of which the path made a sharp turn, he stopped short, with his usual exclamation, addressed to his patron saint. It appeared to Arthur that the mule shared the terrors of the guide; for it started back, put forwards its fore-feet separate from each other, and seemed, by the attitude which it assumed, to intimate a determination to resist every proposal to advance, at the same time expressing horror and fear at the prospect which lay before it.

Arthur pressed forward, not only from curiosity, but that he might if possible bear the brunt of any danger before his father came up to share it. In less time than we have taken to tell the story, the young man stood beside Antonio and the mule, upon a platform of rock on which the road seemed absolutely to terminate, and from the farther side of which a precipice sunk sheer down, to what depth the mist did not permit him to discern, but certainly uninterrupted for more than three hundred feet.

The blank expression which overcast the visage of the younger traveller, and traces of which might be discerned in the physiognomy of the beast of burden, announced alarm and mortification at this unexpected, and, as it seemed, insurmountable obstacle. Nor did the looks of the father, who presently after came up to the same spot, convey either hope or comfort. He stood with the others gazing on the misty gulf beneath them, and looking all around, but in vain, for some continuation of the path, which certainly had never been originally designed to terminate in this summary manner. As they stood uncertain what to do next, the son in vain attempting to discover some mode of passing onward, and the father about to propose that they should return by the road which had brought them hither, a loud howl of the wind, more wild than they had yet heard, swept down the valley. All being aware of the danger of being hurled from the precarious station which they occupied, snatched at bushes and rocks by which to secure themselves, and even the poor mule seemed to steady itself in order to withstand the approaching hurricane. The gust came with such unexpected fury that it appeared to the travellers to shake the very rock on which they stood, and would have swept them from its surface like so many dry leaves, had it not been for the momentary precautions which they had taken for their safety. But as the wind rushed down the glen, it completely removed for the space of three or four minutes the veil of mist which former gusts had only served to agitate or discompose, and showed them the nature and cause of the interruption which they had met with so unexpectedly.

The rapid but correct eye of Arthur was then able to ascertain that the path, after leaving the platform of rock on which they stood, had originally passed upwards in the same direction along the edge of a steep bank of earth, which had then formed the upper covering of a stratum of precipitous rocks. But it had chanced, in some of the convulsions of nature which take place in those wild regions, where she works upon a scale so formidable, that the earth had made a slip, or almost a precipitous descent, from the rock, and been hurled downwards with the path, which was traced along the top, and with bushes, trees, or whatever grew upon it, into the channel of the stream; for such they could now discern the water beneath them to be, and not a lake or an arm of a lake, as they had hitherto supposed.

The immediate cause of this phenomenon might probably have been an earthquake, not unfrequent in that country. The bank of earth, now a confused mass of ruins inverted in its fall, showed some trees growing in a horizontal position, and others, which, having pitched on their heads in their descent, were at once inverted and shattered to pieces, and lay a sport to the streams of the river which they had heretofore covered with gloomy shadow. The gaunt precipice which remained behind, like the skeleton of some huge monster divested of its flesh, formed the wall of a fearful abyss, resembling the face of a newly wrought quarry, more dismal of aspect from the rawness of its recent formation, and from its being as yet uncovered with any of the vegetation with which, nature speedily mantles over the bare surface even of her sternest crags and precipices.

Besides remarking these appearances, which tended to show that this interruption of the road had been of recent occurrence, Arthur was able to observe, on the further side of the river, higher up the valley, and rising out of the pine forests, interspersed with rocks, a square building of considerable height, like the ruins of a Gothic tower. He pointed out this remarkable object to Antonio, and demanded if he knew it; justly conjecturing that, from the peculiarity of the site, it was a landmark not easily to be forgotten by any who had seen it before. Accordingly, it was gladly and promptly recognised by the lad, who called cheerfully out, that the place was Geierstein, that is, as he explained it, the Rock of the Vultures. He knew it, he said, by the old tower, as well as by a huge pinnacle of rock which arose near it, almost in the form of a steeple, to the top of which the lammer-geier (one of the largest birds of prey known to exist) had in former days transported the child of an ancient lord of the castle. He proceeded to recount the vow which was made by the Knight of Geierstein to our Lady of Einsiedlen; and, while he spoke, the castle, rocks, woods, and precipices, again faded in mist. But as he concluded his wonderful narrative with the miracle which restored the infant again to its father's arms, he cried out suddenly, "Look to yourselves — the storm! — the storm!" It came accordingly, and sweeping the mist before it, again bestowed on the travellers a view of the horrors around them.

"Ay!" quoth Antonio, triumphantly, as the gust abated, "old Pontius loves little to hear of Our Lady of Einsiedlen; but she will keep her own with him — Ave Maria!"

"That tower," said the young traveller, "seems uninhabited. I can descry no smoke, and the battlement appears ruinous."

"It has not been inhabited for many a day," answered the guide. "But I would I were at it for all that. Honest Arnold Biederman, the Landamman" (chief magistrate) "of the Canton of Unterwalden, dwells near, and, I warrant you, distressed strangers will not want the best that cupboard and cellar can find them, wherever he holds rule."

"I have heard of him," said the elder traveller, whom Antonio had been taught to call Seignor Philipson; "a good and hospitable man, and one who enjoys deserved weight with his countrymen."

"You have spoken him right, Seignor," answered the guide; "and I would we could reach his house, where you should be sure of hospitable treatment, and a good direction for your next day's journey. But how we are to get to the Vulture's Castle, unless we had wings like the vulture, is a question hard to answer."

Arthur replied by a daring proposal, which the reader will find in the next chapter.

CHAPTER II

———— Away with me.
The clouds grow thicker — there — now lean on me.
Place your foot here — here, take this staff, and cling
A moment to that shrub — now, give me your hand.
 *   *   *   *   *   *
The chalet will be gain'd in half an hour.

MANFRED.

After surveying the desolate scene as accurately as the stormy state of the atmosphere would permit, the younger of the travellers observed, "In any other country, I should say the tempest begins to abate; but what to expert in this land of desolation, it were rash to decide. If the apostate spirit of Pilate be actually on the blast, these lingering and more distant howls seem to intimate that he is returning to his place of punishment. The pathway has sunk with the ground on which it was traced — I can see part of it lying down in the abyss, marking, as with a streak of clay, yonder mass of earth and stone. But I think it possible, with your permission, my father, that I could still scramble forward along the edge of the precipice till I come in sight of the habitation which the lad tells us of. If there be actually such a one, there must be an access to it somewhere; and if I cannot find the path out, I can at least make a signal to those who dwell near the Vulture's Nest yonder, and obtain some friendly guidance."

"I cannot consent to your incurring such a risk," said his father; "let the lad go forward, if he can and will. He is mountain-bred, and I will reward him richly."

But Antonio declined the proposal absolutely and decidedly. "I am mountain-bred," he said, "but I am no chamois hunter; and I have no wings to transport me from cliff to cliff, like a raven — gold is not worth life."

"And God forbid," said Seignor Philipson, "that I should tempt thee to weigh them against each other! — Go on, then, my son, — I follow thee."

"Under your favour, dearest sir, no," replied the young man; "it is enough to endanger the life of one — and mine, far the most worthless, should, by all the rules of wisdom as well as nature, be put first in hazard."

"No, Arthur," replied his father, in a determined voice; "no, my son — I have survived much, but I will not survive thee."

"I fear not for the issue, father, if you permit me to go alone; but I cannot — dare not — undertake a task so perilous, if you persist in attempting to share it, with no better aid than mine. While I endeavoured to make a new advance, I should be ever looking back to see how you might attain the station which I was about to leave — And bethink you, dearest father, that if I fall, I fall an unregarded thing, of as little moment as the stone or tree which has toppled headlong down before me. But you — should your foot slip, or your hand fail, bethink you what and how much must needs fall with you!"

"Thou art right, my child," said the father. "I still have that which binds me to life, even though I were to lose in thee all that is dear to me. — Our Lady and Our Lady's Knight bless thee and prosper thee, my child! Thy foot is young, thy hand is strong — thou hast not climbed Plynlimmon in vain. Be bold, but be wary — remember there is a man who, failing thee, has but one act of duty to bind him to the earth, and, that discharged, will soon follow thee."

The young man accordingly prepared for his journey, and, stripping himself of his cumbrous cloak, showed his well-proportioned limbs in a jerkin of gray cloth, which sat close to his person. The father's resolution gave way when his son turned round to bid him farewell. He recalled his permission, and in a peremptory tone forbade him to proceed. But, without listening to the prohibition, Arthur had commenced his perilous adventure. Descending from the platform on which he stood, by the boughs of an old ash-tree, which thrust itself out of the cleft of a rock, the youth was enabled to gain, though at great risk, a narrow ledge, the very brink of the precipice, by creeping along which he hoped to pass on till he made himself heard or seen from the habitation, of whose existence the guide had informed him. His situation, as he pursued this bold purpose, appeared so precarious, that even the hired attendant hardly dared to draw breath as he gazed on him. The ledge which supported him seemed to grow so narrow as he passed along it, as to become altogether invisible, while sometimes with his face to the precipice, sometimes looking forward, sometimes glancing his eyes upward, but never venturing to cast a look below, lest his brain should grow giddy at a sight so appalling, he wound his way onward. To his father and the attendant, who beheld his progress, it was less that of a man advancing in the ordinary manner, and resting by aught connected with the firm earth, than that of an insect crawling along the face of a perpendicular wall, of whose progressive movement we are indeed sensible, but cannot perceive the means of its support. And bitterly, most bitterly, did the miserable parent now lament, that he had not persisted in his purpose to encounter the baffling and even perilous measure of retracing his steps to the habitation of the preceding night. He should then, at least, have partaken the fate of the son of his love.

Meanwhile, the young man's spirits were strongly braced for the performance of his perilous task. He laid a powerful restraint on his imagination, which in general was sufficiently active, and refused to listen, even for an instant, to any of the horrible insinuations by which fancy augments actual danger. He endeavoured manfully to reduce all around him to the scale of right reason, as the best support of true courage. "This ledge of rock," he urged to himself, "is but narrow, yet it has breadth enough to support me; these cliffs and crevices in the surface are small and distant, but the one affords as secure a resting-place to my feet, the other as available a grasp to my hands, as if I stood on a platform of a cubit broad, and rested my arm on a balustrade of marble. My safety, therefore, depends on myself. If I move with decision, step firmly, and hold fast, what signifies how near I am to the mouth of an abyss?"

Thus estimating the extent of his danger by the measure of sound sense and reality, and supported by some degree of practice in such exercise, the brave youth went forward on his awful journey, step by step, winning his way with a caution, and fortitude, and presence of mind, which alone could have saved him from instant destruction. At length he gained a point where a projecting rock formed the angle of the precipice, so far as it had been visible to him from the platform. This, therefore, was the critical point of his undertaking; but it was also the most perilous part of it. The rock projected more than six feet forward over the torrent, which he heard raging at the depth of a hundred yards beneath, with a noise like subterranean thunder. He examined the spot with the utmost care, and was led by the existence of shrubs, grass, and even stunted trees, to believe that this rock marked thy farthest extent of the slip or slide of earth, and that, could he but turn round the angle of which it was the termination, he might hope to attain the continuation of the path which had been so strangely interrupted by this convulsion of nature. But the crag jutted out so much as to afford no possibility of passing either under or around it; and as it rose several feet above the position which Arthur had attained, it was no easy matter to climb over it. This was, however, the course which he chose, as the only mode of surmounting what he hoped might prove the last obstacle to his voyage of discovery. A projecting tree afforded him the means of raising and swinging himself up to the top of the crag. But he had scarcely planted himself on it, had scarcely a moment to congratulate himself, on seeing, amid a wild chaos of cliffs and wood, the gloomy ruins of Geierstein, with smoke arising, and indicating something like a human habitation beside them, when, to his extreme terror, he felt the huge cliff on which he stood tremble, stoop slowly forward, and gradually sink from its position. Projecting as it was, and shaken as its equilibrium had been by the recent earthquake, it lay now so insecurely poised, that its balance was entirely destroyed, even by the addition of the young man's weight.

Aroused by the imminence of the danger, Arthur, by an instinctive attempt at self-preservation, drew cautiously back from the falling crag into the tree by which he had ascended, and turned his head back as if spellbound, to watch the descent of the fatal rock from which he had just retreated. It tottered for two or three seconds, as if uncertain which way to fall; and had it taken a sidelong direction, must have dashed the adventurer from his place of refuge, or borne both the tree and him headlong down into the river. After a moment of horrible uncertainty, the power of gravitation determined a direct and forward descent. Down went the huge fragment, which must have weighed at least twenty tons, rending and splintering in its precipitate course the trees and bushes which it encountered, and settling at length in the channel of the torrent with a din equal to the discharge of a hundred pieces of artillery. The sound was reëchoed from bank to bank, from precipice to precipice, with emulative thunders; nor was the tumult silent till it rose into the region of eternal snows, which, equally insensible to terrestrial sounds, and unfavourable to animal life, heard the roar in their majestic solitude, but suffered it to die away without a responsive voice.

What, in the meanwhile, were the thoughts of the distracted father, who saw the ponderous rock descend, but could not mark whether his only son had borne it company in its dreadful fall! His first impulse was to rush forward along the face of the precipice, which he had seen Arthur so lately traverse; and when the lad Antonio withheld him, by throwing his arms around him, he turned on the guide with the fury of a bear which had been robbed of her cubs.

"Unhand me, base peasant," he exclaimed, "or thou diest on the spot!"

"Alas!" said the poor boy, dropping on his knees before him, "I, too, have a father!"

The appeal went to the heart of the traveller, who instantly let the lad go, and holding up his hands and lifting his eyes towards heaven, said, in accents of the deepest agony, mingled with devout resignation, "*Fiat voluntus tua!* — he was my last, and loveliest, and best beloved, and most worthy of my love; and yonder," he added, "yonder over the glen soar the birds of prey, who are to feast on his young blood. — But I will see him once more," exclaimed the miserable parent, as the huge carrion vulture floated past him on the thick air, — "I will see my Arthur once more, ere the wolf and the eagle mangle him — I will see all of him that earth still holds. Detain me not — but abide here, and watch me as I advance. If I fall, as is most likely, I charge you to take the sealed papers, which you will find in the valise, and carry them to the person to whom they are addressed, with the least possible delay. There is money enough in the purse to bury me with my poor boy, and to cause masses be said for our souls, and yet leave you a rich recompense for your journey."

The honest Swiss lad, obtuse in his understanding, but kind and faithful in his disposition, blubbered as his employer spoke, and, afraid to offer farther remonstrance or opposition, saw his temporary master prepare himself to traverse the same fatal precipice, over the verge of which his ill-fated son had seemed to pass to the fate which, with all the wildness of a parent's anguish, his father was hastening to share.

Suddenly there was heard from beyond the fatal angle from which the mass of stone had been displaced by Arthur's rash ascent, the loud hoarse sound of one of those huge horns, made out of the spoils of the urus, or wild bull, of Switzerland, which in ancient times announced the terrors of the charge of these mountaineers, and, indeed, served them in war instead of all musical instruments.

"Hold, sir, hold!" exclaimed the Grison, "yonder is a signal from Geierstein. Some one will presently come to our assistance, and show us the safer way to seek for your son — And look you — at yon green bush that is glimmering through the mist, Saint Antonio preserve me, as I see a white cloth displayed there! — it is just beyond the point where the rock fell."

The father endeavoured to fix his eyes on the spot, but they filled so fast with tears, that they could not discern the object which the guide pointed out. — "It is all in vain," he said, dashing the tears from his eyes — "I shall never see more of him than his lifeless remains!"

"You will — you will see him in life!" said the Grison, "Saint Antonio wills it so — See, the white cloth waves again!"

"Some remnant of his garments," said the despairing father, — "some wretched memorial of his fate. — No, my eyes see it not — I have beheld the fall of my house — would that the vultures of these crags had rather torn them from their sockets!"

"Yet look again," said the Swiss; "the cloth hangs not loose upon a bough — I can see that it is raised on the end of a staff, and is distinctly waved to and fro. Your son makes a signal that he is safe."

"And if it be so," said the traveller, clasping his hands together, "blessed be the eyes that see it, and the tongue that tells it! If we find my son, and find him alive, this day shall be a lucky one for thee too."

"Nay," answered the lad, "I only ask that you will abide still, and act by counsel, and I will hold myself quit for nay services. Only it is not creditable to an honest lad to have people lose themselves by their own wilfulness; for the blame, after all, is sure to fall upon the guide, as if he could prevent old Pontius from shaking the mist from his brow, or banks of earth from slipping down into the valley at a time, or young harebrained gallants from walking upon precipices as narrow as the edge of a knife, or madmen, whose gray hairs might make them wiser, from drawing daggers like bravoes in Lombardy."

Thus the guide ran on, and in that vein he might have long continued, for Seignor Philipson heard him not. Each throb of his pulse, each thought of his heart, was directed towards thy object which the lad referred to as a signal of his son's safety. He became at length satisfied that the signal was actually waved by a human hand; and, as eager in the glow of reviving hope, as he had of late been under the influence of desperate grief, he again prepared for the attempt of advancing towards his son, and assisting him, if possible, in regaining a place of safety. But the entreaties and reiterated assurances of his guide induced him to pause."

"Are you fit," he said, "to go on the crag? Can you repeat your Credo and Ave without missing or misplacing a word? for without that, our old men say your neck, had you a score of them, would be in danger. — Is your eye clear, and your feet firm? — I trow the one streams like a fountain, and the other shakes like the aspen which overhangs it! Rest here till those arrive who are far more able to give your son help than either you or I are. I judge by the fashion of his blowing, that yonder is the horn of the Goodman of Geierstein, Arnold Biederman. He hath seen your son's danger, and is even now providing for his safety and ours. There are cases in which the aid of one stranger, well acquainted with the country, is worth that of three brothers, who know not the crags."

"But if yonder horn really sounded a signal," said the traveller, "how chanced it that my son replied not?"

"And if he did so, as is most likely he did," rejoined the Grison, "how should we have heard him? The bugle of Uri itself sounded amid these horrible dins of water and tempest like the reed of a shepherd boy; and how think you we should hear the holloa of a man?"

"Yet, methinks," said Seignor Philipson, "I do hear something amid this roar of elements which is like a human voice — but it is not Arthur's."

"I wot well, no," answered the Grison; "that is a woman's voice. The maidens will converse with each other in that manner, from cliff to cliff, through storm and tempest, were there a mile between."

"Now, Heaven be praised for this providential relief!" said Seignor Philipson; "I trust we shall yet see this dreadful day safely ended. I will holloa in answer."

He attempted to do so, but, inexperienced in the art of

making himself heard in such a country, he pitched his voice in the same key with that of the roar of wave and wind; so that, even at twenty yards from the place where he was speaking, it must have been totally indistinguishable from that of the elemental war around them. The lad smiled at his patron's ineffectual attempts, and then raised his voice himself in a high, wild, and prolonged scream, which, while produced with apparently much less effort than that of the Englishman, was nevertheless a distinct sound, separated from others by the key to which it was pitched, and was probably audible to a very considerable distance. It was presently answered by distant cries of the same nature, which gradually approached the platform, bringing renovated hope to the anxious traveller.

If the distress of the father rendered his condition an object of deep compassion, that of the son, at the same moment, was sufficiently perilous. We have already stated, that Arthur Philipson had commenced his precarious journey along the precipice, with all the coolness, resolution, and unshaken determination of mind, which was most essential to a task where all must depend upon firmness of nerve. But the formidable accident which checked his onward progress, was of a character so dreadful, as made him feel all the bitterness of a death, instant, horrible, and, as it seemed, inevitable. The solid rock had trembled and rent beneath his footsteps, and although, by an effort rather mechanical than voluntary, he had withdrawn himself from the instant ruin attending its descent, he felt as if the better part of him, his firmness of mind and strength of body, had been rent away with the descending rock, as it fell thundering, with clouds of dust and smoke, into the torrents and whirlpools of the vexed gulf beneath. In fact, the seaman swept from the deck of a wrecked vessel, drenched in the waves, and battered against the rocks on the shore, does not differ more from the same mariner, when, at the commencement of the gale, he stood upon the deck of his favourite ship, proud of her strength and his own dexterity, than Arthur, when commencing his journey, from the same Arthur, while clinging to the decayed trunk of an old tree, from which, suspended between heaven and earth, he saw the fall of the crag which he had so nearly accompanied. The effects of his terror, indeed, were physical as well as moral, for a thousand colours played before his eyes; he was attacked by a sick dizziness, and deprived at once of the obedience of those limbs which had hitherto served him so admirably; his arms and hands, as if no longer at his own command, now clung to the branches of the tree, with a cramp-like tenacity over which he seemed to possess no power, and now trembled in a state of such complete nervous relaxation, as led him to fear that they were becoming unable to support him longer in his position.

An incident, in itself trifling, added to the distress occasioned by this alienation of his powers. All living things in the neighbourhood had, as might be supposed, been startled by the tremendous fall to which his progress had given occasion. Flights of owls, bats, and other birds of darkness, compelled to betake themselves to the air, had lost no time in returning into their bowers of ivy, or the harbour afforded them by the rifts and holes of the neighbouring rocks. One of this ill-omened flight chanced to be a lammer-geier, or Alpine vulture, a bird larger and more voracious than the eagle himself, and which Arthur had not been accustomed to see, or at least to look upon closely. With the instinct of most birds of prey, it is the custom of this creature, when gorged with food, to assume some station of inaccessible security, and there remain stationary and motionless for days together, till the work of digestion has been accomplished, and activity returns with the pressure of appetite. Disturbed from such a state of repose, one of these terrific birds had risen from the ravine to which the species gives its name, and having circled unwillingly round, with a ghastly scream and a flagging wing, it had sunk down upon the pinnacle of a crag, not four yards from the tree in which Arthur held his precarious station. Although still in some degree stupefied by torpor, it seemed encouraged by the motionless state of the young man to suppose him dead, or dying, and sat there and gazed at him, without displaying any of that apprehension which the fiercest animals usually entertain from the vicinity of man.

As Arthur, endeavouring to shake off the incapacitating effects of his panic fear, raised his eyes to look gradually and cautiously around, he encountered those of the voracious and obscene bird, whose head and neck denuded of feathers, her eyes surrounded by an iris of an orange tawny colour, and a position more horizontal than erect, distinguished her as much from the noble carriage and graceful proportions of the eagle, as those of the lion place him in the ranks of creation above the gaunt, ravenous, grisly, yet dastard wolf.

As if arrested by a charm, the eyes of young Philipson remained bent on this ill-omened and ill-favoured bird, without his having the power to remove them. The apprehension of dangers, ideal as well as real, weighed upon his weakened mind, disabled as it was by the circumstances of his situation. The near approach of a creature, not more loathsome to the human race, than averse to come within their reach, seemed as ominous as it was unusual. Why did it gaze on him with such glaring earnestness, projecting its disgusting form, as if presently to alight upon his person? The foul bird, was she the demon of the place to which her name referred; and did she come to exult, that an intruder on her haunts seemed involved amid their perils, with little hope or chance of deliverance? Or was it a native vulture of the rocks, whose sagacity foresaw that the rash traveller was soon destined to become its victim? Could the creature, whose senses are said to be so acute, argue from circumstances the stranger's approaching death, and wait, like a raven or hooded crow by a dying sheep, for the earliest opportunity to commence her ravenous banquet? Was he doomed to feel its beak and talons before his heart's blood should cease to beat? Had he already lost the dignity of humanity, the awe which the being formed in the image of his Maker, inspires into all inferior creatures?

Apprehensions so painful served more than all that reason could suggest, to renew in some degree the elasticity of the young man's mind. By waving his handkerchief, using, however, the greatest precaution in his movements, he succeeded in scaring the vulture from his vicinity. It rose from its resting-place, screaming harshly and dolefully, and sailed on its expanded pinions to seek a place of more undisturbed repose, while the adventurous traveller felt a sensible pleasure at being relieved of its disgusting presence.

With more collected ideas, the young man, who could obtain, from his position, a partial view of the platform he had left, endeavoured to testify his safety to his father, by displaying, as high as he could, the banner by which he had chased off the vulture. Like them, too, he heard, but at a less distance, the burst of the great Swiss horn, which seemed to announce some near succour. He replied by shouting and waving his flag, to direct assistance to the spot where it was so much required; and, re-calling his faculties, which had almost deserted him, he laboured mentally to recover hope, and with hope the means and motive for exertion.

A faithful Catholic, he eagerly recommended himself in prayer to Our Lady of Einsiedlen, and, making vows of propitiation, besought her intercession, that he might be delivered from his dreadful condition. "Or, gracious Lady!" he concluded his orison, "if it is my doom to lose my life like a hunted fox amidst this savage wilderness of tottering crags, restore at least my natural sense of patience and courage, and let not one who has lived like a man, though a sinful one, meet death like a timid hare!"

Having devoutly recommended himself to that Protectress, of whom the legends of the Catholic Church form a picture so amiable, Arthur, though every nerve still shook with his late agitation, and his heart throbbed with a violence that threatened to suffocate him, turned his thoughts and observation to the means of effecting his escape. But, as he looked around him, he became more and more sensible how much he was enervated by the bodily injuries and the mental agony which he had sustained during his late peril. He could not, by any effort of which he was capable, fix his giddy and bewildered eyes on the scene around him; — they seemed to reel till the landscape danced along with them, and a motley chaos of thickets and tall cliffs, which interposed between him and the ruinous Castle of Geierstein, mixed and whirled round in such confusion, that nothing, save the consciousness that such an idea was the suggestion of partial insanity, prevented him from throwing himself from the tree, as if to join the wild dance to which his disturbed brain had given motion.

"Heaven be my protection!" said the unfortunate young man, closing his eyes, in hopes, by abstracting himself from the terrors of his situation, to compose his too active imagination, "my senses are abandoning me!"

He became still more convinced that this was the case, when a female voice, in a high-pitched but eminently musical accent, was heard at no great distance, as if calling to him. He opened his eyes once more, raised his head, and looked towards the place from whence the sounds seemed to come, though far from being certain that they existed saving in his own disordered imagination. The vision which appeared had almost confirmed him in the opinion that his mind was unsettled, and his senses in no state to serve him accurately.

Upon the very summit of a pyramidical rock that rose out of the depth of the valley, was seen a female figure, so obscured by mist, that only the outline could be traced. The form, reflected against the sky, appeared rather the undefined lineaments of a spirit than of a mortal maiden; for her person seemed as light, and scarcely more opaque, than the thin cloud that surrounded her pedestal. Arthur's first belief was, that the Virgin had heard his vows, and had descended in person to his rescue; and he was about to recite his Ave Maria, when the voice again called to him with the singular shrill modulation of the mountain haloo, by which the natives of the Alps can hold conference with each other from one mountain ridge to another, across ravines of great depth and width.

While he debated how to address this unexpected apparition, it disappeared from the point which it at first occupied, and presently after became again visible, perched on the cliff out of which projected the tree in which Arthur had taken refuge. Her personal appearance, as well as her dress, made it then apparent that she was a maiden of those mountains, familiar with their dangerous paths. He saw that a beautiful young woman stood before him, who regarded him with a mixture of pity and wonder.

"Stranger," she at length said, "who are you, and whence come you?"

"I am a stranger, maiden, as you justly term me," answered the young man, raising himself as well as he could. "I left Lucerne this morning, with my father and a guide. I parted with them not three furlongs from hence. May it please you, gentle maiden, to warn them of my safety, for I know my father will be in despair upon my account?"

"Willingly," said the maiden; "but I think my uncle, or some one of my kinsmen, must have already found them, and will prove faithful guides. Can I not aid you? — are you wounded? — are you hurt? We were alarmed by the fall of a rock — ay, and yonder it lies, a mass of no ordinary size."

As the Swiss maiden spoke thus, she approached so close to the verge of the precipice, and looked with such indifference into the gulf, that the sympathy which connects the actor and spectator upon such occasions brought back the sickness and vertigo from which Arthur had just recovered, and he sunk back into his former more recumbent posture with something like a faint groan.

"You are then ill" said the maiden, who observed him turn pale — "Where and what is the harm you have received?"

"None, gentle maiden, saving some bruises of little import; but my head turns, and my heart grows sick, when I see you so near the verge of the cliff."

"Is that all?" replied the Swiss maiden. — "Know, stranger, that I do not stand on my uncle's hearth with more security than I have stood upon precipices, compared to which this is a child's leap. You, too, stranger, if, as I judge from the traces, you have come along the edge of the precipice which the earth-slide hath laid bare, ought to be far beyond such weakness, since surely you must be well entitled to call yourself a cragsman."

"I might have called myself so half an hour since," answered Arthur; "but I think I shall hardly venture to assume the name in future."

"Be not downcast," said his kind adviser, "for a passing qualm, which will at times cloud the spirit and dazzle the eyesight of the bravest and most experienced. Raise yourself upon the trunk of the tree, and advance closer to the rock out of which it grows. Observe the place well. It is easy for you, when you have attained the lower part of the projecting stem, to gain by one bold step the solid rock upon which I stand; after which there is no danger or difficulty worthy of mention to a young man, whose limbs are whole, and whose courage is active."

"My limbs are indeed sound," replied the youth; "but I am ashamed to think how much my courage is broken. Yet I will not disgrace the interest you have taken in an unhappy wanderer, by listening longer to the dastardly suggestions of a feeling, which till to-day has been a stranger to my bosom."

The maiden looked on him anxiously, and with much interest, as, raising himself cautiously, and moving along the trunk of the tree, which lay nearly horizontal from the rock, and seemed to bend as he changed his posture, the youth at length stood upright, within what, on level ground, had been but an extended stride to the cliff on which the Swiss maiden stood. But instead of being a step to be taken on the level and firm earth, it was one which must cross a dark abyss, at the bottom of which a torrent surged and boiled with incredible fury. Arthur's knees knocked against each other, his feet became of lead, and seemed no longer at his command; and he experienced, in a stronger degree than ever, that unnerving influence, which those who have been overwhelmed by it in a situation of like peril never can forget, and which others, happily strangers to its power, may have difficulty even in comprehending.

The young woman discerned his emotion, and foresaw its probable consequences. As the only mode in her power to restore his confidence, she sprung lightly from the rock to the stem of the tree, on which she alighted with the ease and security of a bird, and in the same instant back to the cliff; and extending her hand to the stranger, "My arm," she said, "is but a slight balustrade; yet do but step forward with resolution, and you will find it as secure as the battlement of Berne." But shame now overcame terror so much, that Arthur, declining assistance which he could not have accepted without feeling lowered in his own eyes, took heart of grace, and successfully achieved the formidable step which placed him upon the same cliff with his kind assistant.

To seize her hand and raise it to his lips, in affectionate token of gratitude and respect, was naturally the youth's first action; nor was it possible for the maiden to have prevented him from doing so, without assuming a degree of prudery foreign to her character, and occasioning a ceremonious debate upon a matter of no great consequence, where the scene of action was a rock scarce five feet long by three in width, and which looked down upon a torrent roaring some hundred feet below.

CHAPTER III

Cursed be the gold and silver, which persuade
Weak man to follow far fatiguing trade.
The lily, peace, outshines the silver store,
And life is dearer than the golden ore.
Yet money tempts us o'er the desert brown,
To every distant mart and wealthy town.

HASSAN, OR THE CAMEL-DRIVER.

Arthur Philipson, and Anne of Geierstein, thug placed together in a situation which brought them into the closest possible contiguity, felt a slight degree of embarrassment; the young man, doubtless, from the fear of being judged a poltroon in the eyes of the maiden by whom he had been rescued, and the young woman, perhaps, in consequence of the exertion she had made, or a sense of being placed suddenly in a situation of such proximity to the youth whose life she had probably saved.

"And now, maiden," said Arthur, "I must repair to my father. The life which I owe to your assistance, can scarce be called welcome to me, unless I am permitted to hasten to his rescue."

He was here interrupted by another bugle-blast, which seemed to come from the quarter in which the elder Philipson and his guide had been left by their young and daring companion. Arthur looked in that direction; but the platform, which he had seen but imperfectly from the tree, when he was perched in that place of refuge, was invisible from the rock on which they now stood.

"It would cost me nothing to step back on yonder root," said the young woman, "to spy from thence whether I could see aught of your friends. But I am convinced they are under safer guidance than either yours or mine; for the horn announces that my uncle, or some of my young kinsmen have reached them. They are by this time on their way to the Geierstein, to which, with your permission, I will become your guide; for you may be assured that my uncle Arnold will not allow you to pass farther today; and we shall but lose time by endeavouring to find your friends, who, situated where you say you left them, will reach the Geierstein sooner than we shall. Follow me, then, or I must suppose you weary of my guidance."

"Sooner suppose me weary of the life which your guidance has in all probability saved," replied Arthur, and prepared to attend her; at the same time taking a view of her dress and person, which confirmed the satisfaction he had in following such a conductor, and which we shall take the liberty to detail somewhat more minutely than he could do at that time.

An upper vest, neither so close as to display the person, a habit forbidden by the sumptuary laws of the canton, nor so loose as to be an encumbrance in walking or climbing, covered a close tunic of a different colour, and came down beneath the middle of the leg, but suffered the ankle, in all its fine proportions, to be completely visible. The foot was defended by a sandal, the point of which was turned upwards, and the crossings and knots of the strings, which secured it on the front of the leg, were garnished with silver rings. The upper vest was gathered round the middle by a sash of parti-coloured silk, ornamented with twisted threads of gold; while the tunic, open at the throat, permitted the shape and exquisite whiteness of a well-formed neck to be visible at the collar, and for an inch or two beneath. The small portion of the throat and bosom thus exposed, was even more brilliantly fair than was promised by the countenance, which last bore some marks of having been freely exposed to the sun and air, by no means in a degree to diminish its beauty, but just so far as to show that the maiden possessed the health which is purchased by habits of rural exercise. Her long fair hair fell down in a profusion of curls on each side of a face, whose blue eyes, lovely features, and dignified simplicity of expression implied at once a character of gentleness, and of the self-relying resolution of a mind too virtuous to suspect evil, and too noble to fear it. Above these locks, beauty's natural and most beseeming ornament — or rather, I should say, amongst them — was placed the small bonnet, which, from its size, little answered the purpose of protecting the head, but served to exercise the ingenuity of the fair wearer, who had not failed, according to the prevailing custom of the mountain maidens, to decorate the tiny cap with a heron's feather, and the then unusual luxury of a small and thin chain of gold, long enough to encircle the cap four or five times, and having the ends secured under a broad medal of the same costly metal.

I have only to add, that the stature of the young person was something above the common size, and that the whole contour of her form, without being in the slightest degree masculine, resembled that of Minerva, rather than the proud beauties of Juno, or the yielding graces of Venus. The noble brow, the well-formed and active limbs, the firm and yet light step — above all, the total absence of any thing resembling the consciousness of personal beauty, and the open and candid look, which seemed desirous of knowing nothing that was hidden, and conscious that she herself had nothing to hide, were traits not unworthy of the goddess of wisdom and of chastity.

The road which the young Englishman pursued, under the guidance of this beautiful young woman, was difficult and unequal, but could not be termed dangerous, at least in comparison to those precipices over which Arthur had recently passed. It was, in fact, a continuation of the path which the slip or slide of earth, so often mentioned, had interrupted; and although it had sustained damage in several places at the period of the same earthquake, yet there were marks of these having been already repaired in such a rude manner as made the way sufficient for the necessary intercourse of a people so indifferent as the Swiss to smooth or level paths. The maiden also gave Arthur to understand, that the present road took a circuit for the purpose of gaining that on which he was lately travelling, and that if he and his companions had turned off at the place where this new track united with the old pathway, they would have escaped the danger which had attended their keeping the road by the verge of the precipice.

The path which they now pursued was rather averted from the torrent, though still within hearing of its sullen thunders, which seemed to increase as they ascended parallel to its course, till suddenly the road, turning short, and directing itself straight upon the old castle, brought them within sight of one of the most splendid and awful scenes of that mountainous region.

The ancient tower of Geierstein, though neither extensive, nor distinguished by architectural ornament, possessed an air of terrible dignity by its position on the very verge of the opposite bank of the torrent, which, just at the angle of the rock on which the ruins are situated, falls sheer over a cascade of nearly a hundred feet in height, and then rushes down the defile, through a trough of living rock, which perhaps its waves have been deepening since time itself had a commencement. Facing, and at the same time looking down upon this eternal roar of waters, stood the old tower, built so close to the verge of the precipice, that the buttresses with which the architect had strengthened the foundation, seemed a part of the solid rock itself, and a continuation of its perpendicular ascent. As usual throughout Europe in the feudal times, the principal part of the building was a massive square pile, the decayed summit of which was rendered picturesque, by flanking turrets of different sizes and heights, some round, some angular, some ruinous, some tolerably entire, varying the outline of the building as seen against the stormy sky.

A projecting sallyport, descending by a flight of steps from the tower, had in former times given access to a bridge connecting the castle with that side of the stream on which Arthur Philipson and his fair guide now stood. A single arch, or rather one rib of an arch, consisting of single stones, still remained, and spanned the river immediately in front of the waterfall. In former times this arch had served for the support of a wooden drawbridge, of more convenient breadth, and of such length and weight as must have been rather unmanageable, had it not been lowered on some solid resting-place. It is true the device was attended with this inconvenience, that even when the drawbridge was up there remained a possibility of approaching the castle gate by means of this narrow rib of stone. But as it was not above eighteen inches broad, and could only admit the daring foe who should traverse it, to a doorway regularly defended by gate and portcullis, and having flanking turrets and projections from which stories, darts, melted lead, and scalding water, might be poured down on the soldiery who should venture to approach Geierstein by this precarious access, the possibility of such an attempt was not considered as diminishing the security of the garrison.

In the time we treat of, the castle being entirely ruined and dismantled, and the door, drawbridge, and portcullis gone, the dilapidated gateway, and the slender arch which connected the two sides of the stream, were used as a means of communication between the banks of the river, by the inhabitants of the neighbourhood, whom habit had familiarized with the dangerous nature of the passage.

Arthur Philipson had, in the meantime, like a good bow

when new strung, regained the elasticity of feeling and character which was natural to him. It was not, indeed, with perfect composure that he followed his guide, as she tripped lightly over the narrow arch, composed of rugged stones, and rendered wet and slippery with the perpetual drizzle of the mist issuing from the neighbouring cascade. Nor was it without apprehension that he found himself performing this perilous feat in the neighbourhood of the waterfall itself, whose deafening roar he could not exclude from his ears, though he took care not to turn his head towards its terrors, lest his brain should again be dizzied by the tumult of the waters as they shot forward from the precipice above, and plunged themselves into what seemed the fathomless gulf below. But notwithstanding these feelings of agitation, the natural shame to show cowardice where a beautiful young female exhibited so much indifference, and the desire to regain his character in the eyes of his guide, prevented Arthur from again giving way to the appalling feelings by which ho had been overwhelmed a short time before. Stepping firmly on, yet cautiously supporting himself with his piked staff, he traced the light footsteps of his guide along the bridge of dread, and followed her through the ruined sallyport, to which they ascended by stairs which were equally dilapidated.

The gateway admitted them into a mass of ruins, formerly a sort of court-yard to the donjon, which rose in gloomy dignity above the wreck of what had been works destined for external defence, or buildings for internal accommodation. They quickly passed through these ruins, over which vegetation had thrown a wild mantle of ivy, and other creeping shrubs, and issued from them through the main gate of the castle into one of those spots in which Nature often embosoms her sweetest charms, in the midst of districts chiefly characterised by waste and desolation.

The Castle, in this aspect also, rose considerably above the neighbouring ground, but the elevation of the site, which towards the torrent was an abrupt rock, was on this side a steep eminence, which had been scarped like a modern glacis, to render the building more secure. It was now covered with young trees and bushes, out of which the tower itself seemed to rise in ruined dignity. Beyond this hanging thicket the view was of a very different character. A piece of ground, amounting to more than a hundred acres, seemed scooped out of the rocks and mountains, which, retaining the same savage character with the tract in which the travellers had been that morning bewildered, enclosed, and as it were defended, a limited space of a mild and fertile character. The surface of this little domain was considerably varied, but its general aspect was a gentle slope to the south-west.

The principal object which it presented was a large house composed of huge logs, without any pretence to form or symmetry, but indicating, by the smoke which arose from it, as well as the extent of the neighbouring offices, and the improved and cultivated character of the fields around, that it was the abode, not of splendour certainly, but of ease and competence. An orchard of thriving fruit-trees extended to the southward of the dwelling. Groves of walnut and chestnut grew in stately array, and even a vineyard, of three or four acres, showed that the cultivation of the grape was understood and practised. It is now universal in Switzerland, but was, in those early days, almost exclusively confined to a few more fortunate proprietors, who had the rare advantage of uniting intelligence with opulent, or at least easy circumstances.

There were fair ranges of pasture-fields, into which the fine race of cattle which constitute the pride and wealth of the Swiss mountaineers, had been brought down from the more Alpine grazings where they had fed during the summer, to be near shelter and protection when the autumnal storms might be expected. On some selected spots, the lambs of the last season fed in plenty and security, and in others, huge trees, the natural growth of the soil, were suffered to remain, from motives of convenience probably, that they might be at hand when timber was required for domestic use, but giving, at the same time, a woodland character to a scene otherwise agricultural. Through this mountain-paradise the course of a small brook might be traced, now showing itself to the sun, which had by this time dispelled the fogs, now intimating its course, by its gently sloping banks, clothed in some places with lofty trees, or concealing itself under thickets of hawthorn and nut bushes. This stream, by a devious and gentle course, which seemed to indicate a reluctance to leave this quiet region, found its way at length out of the sequestered domain, and, like a youth hurrying from the gay and tranquil sports of boyhood into the wild career of active life, finally united itself with the boisterous torrent, which, breaking down tumultuously from the mountains, shook the ancient Tower of Geierstein, as it rolled down the adjacent rock, and then rushed howling through the defile in which our youthful traveller had well-nigh lost his life.

Eager as the younger Philipson was to rejoin his father, he could not help pausing for a moment to wonder how so much beauty should be found amid such scenes of horror, and to look back on the Tower of Geierstein, and on the huge cliff from which it derived its name, as if to ascertain, by the sight of these distinguished landmarks, that he was actually in the neighbourhood of the savage wild where he had encountered so much danger and terror. Yet so narrow were the limits of this cultivated farm, that it hardly required such a retrospect to satisfy the spectator that the spot susceptible of human industry, and on which it seemed that a considerable degree of labour had been bestowed, bore a very small proportion to the wilderness in which it was situated. It was on all sides surrounded by lofty hills, in some places rising into walls of rock, in others clothed with dark and savage forests of the pine and the larch, of primeval antiquity. Above these, from the eminence on which the tower was situated, could be seen the almost rosy hue in which an immense glacier threw back the sun; and, still higher over the frozen surface of that icy sea, arose, in silent dignity, the pale peaks of those countless mountains, on which the snow eternally rests.

What we have taken some time to describe, occupied young Philipson only for one or two hurried minutes; for on a sloping lawn, which was in front of the farm-house, as the mansion might be properly styled, he saw five or six persons, the foremost of whom, from his gait, his dress, and the form of his cap, he could easily distinguish as the parent whom he hardly expected at one time to have again beheld.

He followed, therefore, his conductress with a glad step, as she led the way down the steep ascent on which the ruined tower was situated. They approached the group whom Arthur had noticed, the foremost of which was his father, who hastily came forward to meet him, in company with another person, of advanced age, and stature well-nigh gigantic, and who, from his simple yet majestic bearing, seemed the worthy countryman of William Tell, Staufbacher, Winkelried, and other Swiss worthies, whose stout hearts and hardy arms had, in the preceding age, vindicated against countless hosts their personal liberty, and the Independence of their country.

With a natural courtesy, as if to spare the father and son many witnesses to a meeting which must be attended with emotion, the Landamman himself, in walking forward with the elder Philipson, signed to those by whom he was attended, all of whom seemed young men, to remain behind: — they remained accordingly, examining, as it seemed, the guide Antonio, upon the adventures of the strangers. Anne, the conductress of Arthur Philipson, bad but time to say to him, "Yonder old man is my uncle, Arnold Biederman, and these young men are my kinsmen," when the former, with the elder traveller, were close before them. The Landamman, with the same propriety of feeling which he had before displayed, signed to his niece to move a little aside; yet while requiring from her an account of her morning's expedition, he watched the interview of the father and son with as much curiosity as his natural sense of complaisance permitted him to testify. It was of a character different from what he had expected.

We have already described the elder Philipson as a father devotedly attached to his son, ready to rush on death when he had expected to lose him, and equally overjoyed at heart, doubtless, to see him again restored to his affections. It might have been therefore expected, that the father and son would have rushed into each other's arms, and such probably was the scene which Arnold Biederman expected to hare witnessed.

But the English traveller, in common with many of his countrymen, covered keen and quick feelings with much appearance of coldness and reserve, and thought it a weakness to give unlimited sway even to the influence of the most amiable and most natural emotions. Eminently handsome in youth, his countenance, still fine in his more advanced years, had an expression which intimated an unwillingness either to yield to passion or encourage confidence. His pace, when he first beheld his son, had been quickened by the natural wish to meet him; but he slackened it as they drew near to each other, and when they met, said in a tone rather of censure and admonition than affection, — "Arthur, may the Saints forgive the pain thou hast this day given me."

"Amen," said the youth. "I must need pardon since I have given you pain. Believe, however, that I acted for the best."

"It is well, Arthur, that in acting for the best, according to your forward will, you have not encountered the worst."

"That I have not," answered the son, with the same devoted and patient submission, "is owing to this maiden," printing to Anne, who stood at a few paces' distance, desirous perhaps of avoiding to witness the reproof of the father, which might seem to her rather ill-timed and unreasonable.

"To the maiden my thanks shall be rendered," said his father, "when I can study how to pay them in an adequate manner; but is it well or comely, think you, that you should receive from a maiden the succour which it is your duty as a man to extend to the weaker sex?"

Arthur held down his head and blushed deeply, while Arnold Biederman, sympathizing with his feelings, stepped forward and mingled in the conversation.

"Never be abashed, my young guest, that you have been indebted for aught of counsel or assistance to a maiden of Unterwalden. Know that the freedom of their country owes no less to the firmness and wisdom of her daughters than to that of her sons. — And you, my elder guest, who have, I judge, seen many years, and various lands, must have often known examples how the strong are saved by the help of the weak, the proud by the aid of the humble."

"I have at least learned," said the Englishman, "to debate no point unnecessarily with the host who has kindly harboured me;" and after one glance at his son, which seemed to kindle with the fondest affection, he resumed, as the party turned back towards the house, a conversation which he had been maintaining with his new acquaintance before Arthur and the maiden had joined them.

Arthur had in the meantime an opportunity of observing the figure and features of their Swiss landlord, which, I have already hinted, exhibited a primeval simplicity mixed with a certain rude dignity, arising out of its masculine and unaffected character.

The dress did not greatly differ in form from the habit of the female which we have described. It consisted of an upper frock, shaped like the modern shirt, and only open at the bosom, worn above a tunic or under doublet. But the man's vest was considerably shorter in the skirts, which did not come lower down than the kilt of the Scottish Highlander; a species of boots or buskins rose above the knee, and the person was thus entirely clothed. A bonnet made of the fur of the marten, and garnished with a silver medal, was the only part of the dress which displayed any thing like ornament; the broad belt which gathered the garment together, was of buff leather, secured by a large brass buckle.

But the figure of him who wore this homely attire, which seemed almost wholly composed of the fleeces of the mountain sheep, and the spoils of animals of the chase, would have commanded respect wherever the wearer had presented himself, especially in those warlike days, when men were judged of according to the promising or unpromising qualities of their thews and sinews. To those, who looked at Arnold Biederman in this point of view, he displayed the size and form, the broad shoulders and prominent muscles, of a Hercules. But to such as looked rather at his countenance, the steady sagacious features, open front, large blue eyes, and deliberate resolution which it expressed, more resembled the character of the fabled King of Gods and Men. He was attended by several sons and relatives, young men, among whom he walked, receiving, as his undeniable due, respect and obedience, similar to that which a herd of deer are observed to render to the monarch stag.

While Arnold Biederman walked and spoke with the elder stranger, the young men seemed closely to scrutinize Arthur, and occasionally interrogated in whispers their relation Anne, receiving from her brief and impatient answers, which rather excited than appeased the vein of merriment in which the mountaineers indulged, very much, as it seemed to the young Englishman, at the expense of their guest. To feel himself exposed to derision was not softened by the reflection, that in such a society, it would probably be attached to all who could not tread on the edge of a precipice with a step as firm and undismayed as if they walked the street of a city. However unreasonable ridicule may be, it is always unpleasing to be subjected to it, but more particularly is it distressing to a young man, where beauty is a listener. It was some consolation to Arthur that he thought the maiden certainly did not enjoy the jest, and seemed by word and look to reprove the rudeness of her companions; but this he feared was only from a sense of humanity.

"She, too, must despise me," he thought, "though civility, unknown to these ill-taught boors, has enabled her to conceal contempt under the guise of pity. She can but judge of me from that which she has seen — if she could know me better," (such was his proud thought,) "she might perhaps rank me more highly."

As the travellers entered the habitation of Arnold Biederman, they found preparations made in a large apartment, which served the purpose of general accommodation, for a homely but plentiful meal. A glance round the walls showed the implements of agriculture and the chase; but the eyes of the elder Philipson rested upon a leathern corselet, a long heavy halberd, and a two-handed sword, which were displayed as a sort of trophy. Near these, but covered with dust, unfurbished and neglected, hung a helmet, with a visor, such as was used by knights and men-at-arms. The golden garland, or coronal twisted around it, though sorely tarnished, indicated noble birth and rank; and the crest, which was a vulture of the species which gave name to the old castle and its adjacent cliff, suggested various conjectures to the English guest, who, acquainted in a great measure with the history of the Swiss revolution, made little doubt that in this relic he saw some trophy of the ancient warfare between the inhabitants of these mountains, and the feudal lord to whom they had of yore appertained.

A summons to the hospitable board disturbed the train of the English merchant's reflections, and a large company, comprising the whole inhabitants of every description that lived under Biederman's roof, sat down to a plentiful repast of goat's flesh, fish, preparations of milk of various kinds, cheese, and, for the upper mess, the venison of a young chamois. The Landamman himself did the honours of the table with great kindness and simplicity, and urged the strangers to show, by their appetite, that they thought themselves as welcome as he desired to make them. During the repast, he carried on a conversation with his elder guest, while the younger people at table, as well as the menials, ate in modesty and silence. Ere the dinner was finished, a figure crossed on the outside of the large window which lighted the eating hall, the sight of which seemed to occasion a lively sensation among such as observed it.

"Who passed?" said old Biederman to those seated opposite

to the window.

"It is our cousin, Rudolph of Donnerhugel," answered one of Arnold's sons eagerly.

The annunciation seemed to give great pleasure to the younger part of the company, especially the sons of the Landamman; while the head of the family only said, with a grave, calm voice, — "Your kinsman is welcome — tell him so, and let him come hither."

Two or three arose for this purpose, as if there had been a contention among them who should do the honours of the house to the new guest. He entered presently; a young man, unusually tall, well-proportioned and active, with a quantity of dark-brown locks curling around his face, together with mustaches of the same, or rather a still darker hue. His cap was small, considering the quantity of his thickly clustering hair, and rather might be said to hang upon one side of his head than to cover it. His clothes were of the same form and general fashion as those of Arnold, but made of much finer cloth, the manufacture of the German loom, and ornamented in a rich and fanciful manner. One sleeve of his vest was dark green, curiously laced and embroidered with devices in silver, while the rest of the garment was scarlet. His sash was twisted and netted with gold, and besides answering the purpose of a belt, by securing the upper garment round his waist, sustained a silver-hilted poniard. His finery was completed by boots, the tips of which were so long as to turn upwards with a peak, after a prevailing fashion in the Middle Ages. A golden chain hung round his neck, and sustained a large medallion of the same metal.

This young gallant was instantly surrounded by the race of Biederman, among whom he appeared to be considered as the model upon which the Swiss youth ought to build themselves, and whose gait, opinions, dress, and manners, all ought to follow, who would keep pace with the fashion of the day, in which he reigned an acknowledged and unrivalled example.

By two persons in the company, however, it seemed to Arthur Philipson, that this young man was received with less distinguished marks of regard than those with which he was hailed by the general voice of the youths present. Arnold Biederman himself was at least no way warm in welcoming the young Bernese, for such was Rudolph's country. The young man drew from his bosom a sealed packet, which he delivered to the Landamman with demonstrations of great respect, and seemed to expect that Arnold, when he had broken the seal and perused the contents, would say something to him on the subject. But the patriarch only bade him be seated, and partake of their meal, and Rudolph found a place accordingly next to Anne of Geierstein, which was yielded to him by one of the sons of Arnold with ready courtesy.

It seemed also to the observant young Englishman, that the new comer was received with marked coldness by the maiden, to whom he appeared eager and solicitous to pay his compliments, by whose side he had contrived to seat himself at the well-furnished board, and to whom he seemed more anxious to recommend himself, than to partake of the food which it offered. He observed the gallant whisper her, and look towards him. Anne gave a very brief reply, but one of the young Biedermans, who sat on his other hand, was probably more communicative, as the youths both laughed, and the maiden again seemed disconcerted, and blushed with displeasure.

"Had I either of these sons of the mountain," thought young Philipson, "upon six yards of level greensward, if there be so much flat ground in this country, methinks I were more likely to spoil their mirth, than to furnish food for it. It is as marvellous to see such conceited boors under the same roof with so courteous and amiable a damsel, as it would be to see one of their shaggy bears dance a rigadoon with a maiden like the daughter of our host. Well, I need not concern myself more than I can help about her beauty or their breeding, since morning will separate me from them for ever."

As these reflections passed through the young guest's mind, the father of the family called for a cup of wine, and having required the two strangers to pledge him in a maple cup of considerable size, he sent a similar goblet to Rudolph Donnerhugel. "Yet you," he said, "kinsman, are used to more highly flavoured wine than the half-ripened grapes of Geierstein can supply. — Would you think it, sir merchant," he continued, addressing Philipson, "there are burghers of Berne who send for wine, for their own drinking, both to France and Germany?"

"My kinsman disapproves of that," replied Rudolph; "yet every place is not blessed with vineyards like Geierstein, which produces all that heart and eye can desire." This was said with a glance at his fair companion, who did not appear to take the compliment, while the envoy of Berne proceeded: — "But our wealthier burghers, having some superfluous crowns, think it no extravagance to barter them for a goblet of better wine than our own mountains car produce. But we will be more frugal when we have at our disposal tuns of the wine of Burgundy, for the mere trouble of transporting them."

"How mean you by that, cousin Rudolph?" said Arnold Biederman.

"Methinks, respected kinsman," answered the Bernese, "your letters must have told you that our Diet is likely to declare war against Burgundy?"

"All? and you know, then, the contents of my letters?" said Arnold; "another mark how times are changed at Berne, and with the Diet of Switzerland. When did all her gray-haired statesmen die, that our allies should have brought beardless boys into their councils?"

"The Senate of Berne, and the Diet of the Confederacy," said the young man, partly abashed, partly in vindication of what he had before spoken, "allow the young men to know their purposes, since it is they by whom they must be executed. The head which thinks, may well confide in the hand that strikes."

"Not till the moment of dealing the blow, young man," said Arnold Biederman, sternly. "What kind of counsellor is he who talks loosely the secrets of state affairs before women and strangers? Go, Rudolph, and all of ye, and try by manly exercises which is best fitted to serve your country, rather than give your judgment upon her measures. — Hold, young man," he continued, addressing Arthur, who had arisen, "this does not apply to you, who are unused to mountain travel, and require rest after it."

"Under your favour, sir, not so," said the elder stranger. "We hold in England, that the best refreshment after we have been exhausted by one species of exercise, is to betake ourselves to another; as riding, for example, affords more relief to one fatigued by walking, than a bed of down would. So, if your young men will permit, my son will join their exercises."

"He will find them rough playmates," answered the Switzer; "but be it at your pleasure."

The young men went out accordingly to the open lawn in

front of the house. Anne of Geierstein and some females of the household, sat down on a bank to judge which performed best, and shouts, loud laughing, and all that announces the riot of juvenile spirits occupied by manly sports, was soon after heard by the two seniors, as they sat together in the hall. The master of the house resumed the wine-flask, and having filled the cup of his guest, poured the remainder into his own.

"At an age, worthy stranger," he said, "when the blood grows colder, and the feelings heavier, a moderate cup of wine brings back light thoughts, and makes the limbs supple. Yet, I almost wish that Noah had never planted the grape, when of late years I have seen with my own eyes my countrymen swill wine like very Germans, till they were like gorged swine, incapable of sense, thought, or motion."

"It is a vice," said the Englishman, "which I have observed gains ground in your country, where within a century I have heard it was totally unknown."

"It was so," said the Swiss, "for wine was seldom made at home, and never imported from abroad; for indeed none possessed the means of purchasing that, or aught else, which our valleys produce not. But our wars and our victories have gained us wealth as well as fame; and in the poor thoughts of one Switzer at least, we had been better without both, had we not also gained liberty by the same exertion. It is something, however, that commerce may occasionally send into our remote mountains a sensible visitor like yourself, worthy guest, whose discourse shows him to be a man of sagacity and discernment; for though I love not the increasing taste for trinkets and gewgaws which you merchants introduce, yet I acknowledge that we simple mountaineers learn from men like you more of the world around us, than we could acquire by our own exertions. You are bound, you say, to Bâle, and thence to the Duke of Burgundy's leaguer?"

"I am so, my worthy host" — said the merchant, "that is, providing I can perform my journey with safety."

"Your safety, good friend, may be assured, if you list to tarry for two or three days; for in that space I shall myself take the journey, and with such an escort as will prevent any risk of danger. You will find in me a sure and faithful guide, and I shall learn from you much of other countries, which it concerns me to know better than I do. Is it a bargain?"

"The proposal is too much to my advantage to be refused," said the Englishman; "but may I ask the purpose of your journey?"

"I chid yonder boy but now," answered Biederman, "for speaking on public affairs without reflection, and before the whole family; but our tidings and my errand seed not be concealed from a considerate person like you, who must indeed soon learn it from public rumour. You know doubtless the mutual hatred which subsists between Louis XI. of France, and Charles of Burgundy, whom men call the Bold; and having seen these countries, as I understand from your former discourse, you are probably well aware of the various contending interests, which, besides the personal hatred of the sovereigns, make them irreconcilable enemies. Now Louis, whom the world cannot match for craft and subtlety, is using all his influence, by distributions of large sums amongst some of the counsellors of our neighbours of Berne, by pouring treasures into the exchequer of that state itself, by holding out the bait of emolument to the old men, and encouraging the violence of the young, to urge the Bernese into a war with the Duke. Charles, on the other hand, is acting, as he frequently does, exactly as Louis could have wished. Our neighbours and allies of Berne do not, like us of the Forest Cantons, confine themselves to pasture or agriculture, but carry on considerable commerce; which the Duke of Burgundy has in various instances interrupted, by the exactions and violence of his officers in the frontier towns, as is doubtless well known to you."

"Unquestionably," answered the merchant; "they are universally regarded as vexatious."

"You will not then be surprised, that, solicited by the one sovereign, and aggrieved by the other, proud of past victories, and ambitious of additional power, Berne and the City Cantons of our Confederacy, whose representatives, from their superior wealth and better education, have more to say in our Diet than we of the Forests, should be bent upon war, from which it has hitherto happened that the Republic has always derived victory, wealth, and increase of territory."

"Ay, worthy host, and of glory," said Philipson, interrupting him with some enthusiasm; "I wonder not that the brave youths of your states are willing to thrust themselves upon new wars, since their past victories have been so brilliant and so far famed."

"You are no wise merchant, kind guest," answered the host, "if you regard success in former desperate undertakings as an encouragement to future rashness. Let us make a better use of past victories. When we fought for our liberties God blessed our arms; but will he do so if we fight either for aggrandizement or for the gold of France?"

"Your doubt is just," said the merchant, more sedately; "but suppose you draw the sword to put an end to the vexatious exactions of Burgundy?"

"Hear me, good friend," answered the Switzer; "it may be that we of the Forest Cantons think too little of those matters of trade, which so much engross the attention of the burghers of Berne. Yet we will not desert our neighbours and allies in a just quarrel; and it is well-nigh settled that a deputation shall be sent to the Duke of Burgundy to request redress. In this embassy the General Diet now assembled at Berne have requested that I should take some share; and hence the journey in which I propose that you should accompany me."

"It will be much to ray satisfaction to travel in your company, worthy host," said the Englishman. "But, as I am a true roan, methinks your port and figure resemble an envoy of defiance rather than a messenger of peace."

"And I too might say," replied the Switzer, "that your language and sentiments, my honoured guest, rather belong to the sword than the measuring wand."

"I was bred to the sword, worthy sir, before I took the clothyard in my hand," replied Philipson, smiling, "and it may be I am still more partial to my old trade than wisdom would altogether recommend."

"I thought so," said Arnold; "but then you fought most likely under your country's banners against a foreign and national enemy; and in that case I will admit that war has something in it which elevates the heart above the due sense it should entertain of the calamity inflicted and endured by God's creatures on each side. But the warfare in which I was engaged had no such gilding. It was the miserable war of Zurich, where Switzers levelled their pikes against the bosoms of their own countrymen; and quarter was asked and refused in the same kindly mountain language. From such remembrances, your warlike recollections are probably free."

The merchant hung down his head and pressed his forehead with his hand, as one to whom the most painful thoughts were suddenly recalled.

"Alas!" he said, "I deserve to feel the pain which your words inflict. What nation can know the woes of England that has not felt them — what eye can estimate them which has not seen a land torn and bleeding with the strife of two desperate factions; battles fought in every province; plains heaped with slain, and scaffolds drenched in blood! Even in your quiet valleys, methinks, you may have heard of the Civil Wars of England?"

"I do indeed bethink me," said the Switzer, "that England had lost her possessions in France during many years of bloody internal wars concerning the colour of a rose — was it not? — But these are ended."

"For the present," answered Philipson, "it would seem so."

As he spoke, there was a knock at the door; the master of the house said, "Come in;" the door opened, and, with the reverence which was expected from young persons towards their elders in those pastoral regions, the fine form of Anne of Geierstein presented itself.

CHAPTER IV

And now the well-known bow the roaster bore,
Turn'd on all sides, and view'd it o'er and o'er,
Whilst some deriding, "How he turns the bow!
Some other like It sure the man must know:
Or else would copy — or in bows he deals;
Perhaps he makes them, or perhaps he steals."
POPE'S HOMER'S ODYSSEY.

The fair maiden approached with the half-bashful half-important look which sits so well on a young housekeeper, when she is at once proud and ashamed of the matronly duties she is called upon to discharge, and whispered something in her uncle's ear.

"And could not the idle-pated boys have brought their own errand — what is it they want that they cannot ask themselves, but must send thee to beg it for them? Had it been any thing reasonable, I should have heard it dinned into my ears by forty voices, so modest are our Swiss youths become now-a-days." She stooped forward, and again whispered in his ear, as he fondly stroked her curling tresses with his ample hand, and replied, "The bow of Buttisholz, my dear? why the youths surely are not grown stronger since last year, when none of them could bend it? But yonder it hangs with its three arrows. Who is the wise champion that is challenger at a game where he is sure to be foiled?"

"It is this gentleman's son, sir," said the maiden, "who, not being able to contend with my cousins in running, leaping, hurling the bar, or pitching the stone, has challenged them to ride, or to shoot with the English longbow."

"To ride," said the venerable Swiss, "were difficult, where there are no horses, and no level ground to career upon if there were. But an English bow he shall have, since we happen to possess one. Take it to the young men, my niece, with the three arrows, and say to them from me, that he who bends it will do more than William Tell, or the renowned Staufbacher, could have done."

As the maiden went to take the weapon from the place where it hung amid the group of arms which Philipson had formerly remarked, the English merchant observed, "that were the minstrels of his land to assign her occupation, so fair a maiden should be bow-bearer to none but the little blind god Cupid."

"I will have nothing of the blind god Cupid," said Arnold, hastily, yet half laughing at the same time; "we have been deafened with the foolery of minstrels and strolling minnesingers, ever since the wandering knaves have found there were pence to be gathered among us. A Swiss maiden should only sing Albert Ischudi's ballads, or the merry lay of the going out and return of the cows to and from the mountain pastures."

While he spoke, the damsel had selected from the arms a bow of extraordinary strength, considerably above six feet in length, with three shafts of a cloth-yard long. Philipson asked to look at the weapons, and examined them closely. "It is a tough piece of yew," he said. "I should know it, since I have dealt in such commodities in my time; but when I was of Arthur's age, I could have bent it as easily as a boy bends a willow."

"We are too old to boast like boys," said Arnold Biederman, with something of a reproving glance at his companion. "Carry the bow to thy kinsmen, Anne, and let him who can bend it, say he beat Arnold Biederman." As he spoke, he turned his eyes on the spare, yet muscular figure of the Englishman, then again glanced down on his own stately person.

"You must remember, good my host," said Philipson, "that weapons are wielded not by strength, but by art and sleight of hand. What most I wonder at, is to see in this place a bow made by Matthew of Doncaster, a bowyer who lived at least a hundred years ago, remarkable for the great toughness and strength of the weapons which he made, and which are now become somewhat unmanageable, even by an English yeoman."

"How are you assured of the maker's name, worthy guest?" replied the Swiss.

"By old Matthew's mark," answered the Englishman, "and his initials cut upon the bow. I wonder not a little to find such a weapon here, and in such good preservation."

"It has been regularly waxed, oiled, and kept in good order," said the Landamman, "being preserved as a trophy of a memorable day. It would but grieve you to recount its early history, since it was taken in a day fatal to your country."

"My country," said the Englishman, composedly, "has gained so many victories, that her children may well afford to hear of a single defeat. But I knew not that the English ever warred in Switzerland."

"Not precisely as a nation," answered Biederman; "but it was in my grandsire's days, that a large body of roving soldiers, composed of men from almost all countries, but especially Englishmen, Normans, and Gascons, poured down on the Argau, and the districts adjacent. They were headed by a great warrior called Ingelram de Couci, who pretended some claims upon the Duke of Austria; to satisfy which, he ravaged indifferently the Austrian territory, and that of our Confederacy. His soldiers were hired warriors — Free Companions they called themselves — that seemed to belong to no country, and were as brave in the fight as they were cruel in their depredations. Some pause in the constant wars betwixt France and England had deprived many of those bands of their ordinary employment, and battle being their element, they came to seek it among our valleys. The air seemed on fire with the blaze of their armour, and the very sun was darkened at the flight of their arrows. They did us much evil, and we sustained the loss of more than one battle. But we met them at Buttisholz, and mingled the blood of many a rider (noble, as they were called and esteemed) with that of their horses. The huge mound that covers the bones of man and steed, is still called the English Barrow."

Philipson was silent for a minute or two, and then replied, "Then let them sleep in peace. If they did wrong, they paid for it with their lives; and that is all the ransom that mortal man can render for his transgressions. — Heaven pardon their souls!"

"Amen," replied the Landamman, "and those of all brave men! — My grandsire was at the battle, and was held to have demeaned himself like a good soldier; and this bow has been ever since carefully preserved in our family. There is a prophecy about it, but I hold it not worthy of remark."

Philipson was about to inquire farther, but was interrupted by a loud cry of surprise and astonishment from without.

"I must out," said Biederman, "and see what these wild lads are doing. It is not now as formerly in this land, when the young dared not judge for themselves, till the old man's voice had been heard."

He went forth from the lodge, followed by his guest. The company who had witnessed the games were all talking, shouting, and disputing in the same breath; while Arthur Philipson stood a little apart from the rest, leaning on the unbent bow with apparent indifference. At the sight of the Landamman all were silent.

"What means this unwonted clamour?" he said, raising a voice to which all were accustomed to listen with reverence. — "Rudiger," addressing the eldest of his sons, "has the young stranger bent the bow?"

"He has, father," said Rudiger; "and he has hit the mark. Three such shots were never shot by William Tell."

"It was chance — pure chance," said the young Swiss from Berne. "No human skill could have done it, much less a puny lad, baffled in all besides that he attempted among us."

"But what *has* been done?" said the Landamman. — "Nay, speak not all at once! — Anne of Geierstein, thou hast more sense and breeding than these boys — tell me how the game has gone." The maiden seemed a little confused at this appeal, but answered with a composed and downcast look, —

"The mark was, as usual, a pigeon to a pole. All the young men, except the stranger, had practised at it with the cross-bow and long-bow, without hitting it. When I brought out the bow of Buttisholz, I offered it first to my kinsmen. None would accept of it, saying, respected uncle, that a task too great for you, must be far too difficult for them."

"They said well," answered Arnold Biederman; "and the stranger, did he string the bow?"

"He did, my uncle; but first he wrote something on a piece of paper, and placed it in my hands."

"And did he shoot and hit the mark?" continued the surprised Switzer.

"He first," said the maiden, "removed the pole a hundred yards farther than the post where it stood."

"Singular!" said the Landamman, "that is double the usual distance."

"He then drew the bow," continued the maiden, "and shot off, one after another, with incredible rapidity, the three arrows which he had stuck into his belt. The first cleft the pole, the second cut the string, the third killed the poor bird as it rose into the air."

"By Saint Mary of Einsiedlen," said the old man, looking

up in amaze, "if your eyes really saw this, they saw such archery as was never before witnessed in the Forest States!"

"I say nay to that, my revered kinsman," replied Rudolph Donnerhugel, whose vexation was apparent; "it was mere chance, if not illusion or witchery."

"What say'st thou of it thyself, Arthur," said his father, half smiling; "was thy success by chance or skill?"

"My father," said the young man, "I need not tell you that I have done but an ordinary feat for an English bow-man. Nor do I speak to gratify that misproud and ignorant young man. But to our worthy lost end his family, I make answer. This youth charges me with having deluded men's eyes, or hit the mark by chance. For illusion, yonder is the pierced pole, the severed string, and the slain bird, they will endure sight and handling; and, besides, if that fair maiden will open the note which I put into her hand, she will find evidence to assure you, that even before I drew the bow, I had fixed upon the three marks which I designed to aim at."

"Produce the scroll, good niece," said her uncle, "and end the controversy."

"Nay, under your favour, my worthy host," said Arthur, "it is but some foolish rhymes addressed to the maiden's own eye."

"And under your favour, sir," said the Landamman, "whatsoever is fit for my niece's eyes may greet my ears."

He took the scroll from the maiden, who blushed deeply when she resigned it. The character in which it was written was so fine, that the Landamman in surprise exclaimed, "No clerk of Saint Gall could have written more fairly. — Strange," he again repeated, "that a hand which could draw so true a bow, should have the cunning to form characters so fair." He then exclaimed anew, "Ha! verses, by Our Lady! What, have we minstrels disguised as traders?" He then opened the scroll, and read the following lines: —

> If I hit mast, and line, and bird,
> An English archer keeps his word.
> Ah! maiden, didst thou aim at me,
> A single glance were worth the three.

"Here is rare rhyming, my worthy guest," said the Landamman, shaking his head; "fine words to make foolish maidens fain. But do not excuse it; it is your country fashion, and we know how to treat it as such." And without further allusion to the concluding couplet, the reading of which threw the poet as well as the object of the verses into some discomposure, he added gravely, "You must now allow, Rudolph Donnerhugel, that the stranger has fairly attained the three marks which he proposed to himself."

"That he has attained them is plain," answered the party to whom the appeal was made; "but that he has done this fairly may be doubted, if there are such things as witchery and magic in this world."

"Shame, shame, Rudolph!" said the Landamman; "can spleen and envy have weight with so brave a man as you, from whom my sons ought to learn temperance, forbearance, and candour, as well as manly courage and dexterity?"

The Bernese coloured high under this rebuke, to which he ventured not to attempt a reply.

"To your sports till sunset, my children," continued Arnold; "while I and my worthy friend occupy our time with a walk, for which the evening is now favourable."

"Methinks," said the English merchant, "I should like to visit the ruins of yonder castle, situated by the waterfall. There is something of melancholy dignity in such a scene which reconciles us to the misfortunes of our own time, by showing that our ancestors, who were perhaps more intelligent or more powerful, have nevertheless, in their days, encountered cares and distresses similar to those which we now groan under."

"Have with you, my worthy sir," replied his host; "there will be time also upon the road to talk of things that you should know."

The slow step of the two elderly men carried them by degrees from the limits of the lawn, where shout, and laugh, and halloo, were again revived. Young Philipson, whose success as an archer had obliterated all recollection of former failure, made other attempts to mingle in the manly pastimes of the country, and gained a considerable portion of applause. The young men who had but lately been so ready to join in ridiculing him, now began to consider him as a person to be looked up and appealed to while Rudolph Donnerhugel saw with resentment that he was no longer without a rival in the opinion of his male cousins, perhaps of his kinswoman also. The proud young Swiss reflected with bitterness that he had fallen under the Landamman's displeasure, declined in reputation with his companions, of whom he had been hitherto the leader, and even hazarded a more mortifying disappointment, all, as his swelling heart expressed it, through the means of a stranger stripling, of neither blood nor fame, who could not step from one rock to another without the encouragement of a girl.

In this irritated mood, he drew near the young Englishman, and while he seemed to address him on the chances of the sports which were still proceeding, he conveyed, in a whisper, matter of a far different tendency. Striking Arthur's shoulder with the frank bluntness of a mountaineer, he said aloud: "Yonder bolt of Ernest whistled through the air like a falcon when she stoops down the wind!" And then proceeded in a deep low voice, "You merchants sell gloves — do you ever deal in single gauntlets, or only in pairs?"

"I *sell* no single glove," said Arthur, instantly apprehending him, and sufficiently disposed to resent the scornful looks of the Bernese champion during the time of their meal, and his having but lately imputed his successful shooting to chance or sorcery, — "I *sell* no single glove, sir, but never refuse to exchange one."

"You are apt, I see," said Rudolph; "look at the players while I speak, or our purpose will be suspected — You are quicker, I say, of apprehension than I expected. If we exchange our gloves, how shall each redeem his own?"

"With our good swords," said Arthur Philipson.

"In armour, or as we stand?"

"Even as we stand," said Arthur. "I have no better garment of proof than this doublet — no other weapon than my sword; and these, Sir Switzer, I hold enough for the purpose. — Name time and place."

"The old castle-court at Geierstein," replied Rudolph; "the time sunrise; — but we are watched. — I have lost my wager, stranger," he added, speaking aloud, and in an indifferent tone of voice, "since Ulrick has made a cast beyond Ernest. — There is my glove, in token I shall not forget the flask of wine."

"And there is mine," said Arthur, "in token I will drink it

with you merrily."

Thus, amid the peaceful though rough sports of their companions, did these two hot-headed youths contrive to indulge their hostile inclinations towards each other, by settling a meeting of deadly purpose.

CHAPTER V

——————— I was one
Who loved the greenwood bank and lowing herd,
The russet prize, the lowly peasant's life,
Season'd with sweet content, more than the halls
Where revellers feast to fever-height. Believe me,
There ne'er was poison mix'd in maple bowl.

ANONYMOUS.

Leaving the young persons engaged with their sports, the Landamman of Unterwalden and the elder Philipson walked on in company, conversing chiefly on the political relations of France, England, and Burgundy, until the conversation was changed as they entered the gate of the old castle-yard of Geierstein, where arose the lonely and dismantled keep, surrounded by the ruins of other buildings.

"This has been a proud and a strong habitation in its time," said Philipson.

"They were a proud and powerful race who held it," replied the Landamman. "The Counts of Geierstein have a history which runs back to the times of the old Helvetians, and their deeds are reported to have matched their antiquity. But all earthly grandeur has an end, and free men tread the ruins of their feudal castle, at the most distant sight of whose turrets serfs were formerly obliged to vail their bonnets, if they would escape the chastisement of contumacious rebels."

"I observe," said the merchant, "engraved on a stone under yonder turret, the crest, I conceive, of the last family, a vulture perched on a rock, descriptive, doubtless, of the word Geierstein."

"It is the ancient cognizance of the family," replied Arnold Biederman, "and, as you say, expresses the name of the castle, being the same with that of the knights who so long held it."

"I also remarked in your hall," continued the merchant, "a helmet bearing the same crest or cognizance. It is, I suppose, a trophy of the triumph of the Swiss peasants over the nobles of Geierstein, as the English bow is preserved in remembrance of the battle of Buttisholz?"

"And you, fair sir," replied the Landamman, "would, I perceive, from the prejudices of your education, regard the one victory with as unpleasant feelings as the other? — Strange, that the veneration for rank should be rooted even in the minds of those who have no claim to share it! But clear up your downcast brows, my worthy guest, and be assured that though many a proud baron's castle, when Switzerland threw off the bonds of feudal slavery, was plundered and destroyed by the just vengeance of an incensed people, such was not the lot of Geierstein. The blood of the old possessors of these towers still flows in the veins of him by whom these lands are occupied."

"What am I to understand by that, Sir Landamman?" said Philipson. "Are not you yourself the occupant of this place?"

"And you think, probably," answered Arnold, "because I live like the other shepherds, wear homespun gray, and hold the plough with my own hands, I cannot be descended from a line of ancient nobility? This land holds many such gentle peasants, Sir Merchant; nor is there a more ancient nobility than that of which the remains are to be found in my native country. But they have voluntarily resigned the oppressive part of their feudal power, and are no longer regarded as wolves amongst the flock, but as sagacious mastiffs, who attend the sheep in time of peace, and are prompt in their defence when war threatens our community."

"But," repeated the merchant, who could not yet reconcile himself to the idea. that his plain and peasant-seeming host was a man of distinguished birth, "you bear not the name, worthy sir, of your fathers — They were, you say, the Counts of Geierstein, and you are" ——

"Arnold Biederman, at your command," answered the magistrate. "But know, — if the knowledge can make you sup with more sense of dignity or comfort, — I need but put on yonder old helmet, or, if that were too much trouble, I have only to stick a falcon's feather into my cap, and call myself Arnold, Count of Geierstein. No man could gainsay me — though whether it would become my Lord Count to drive his bullocks to the pasture, and whether his Excellency the High and Well-born, could, without derogation, sow a field or reap it, are questions which should be settled beforehand. I see you are confounded, my respected guest, at my degeneracy; but the state of my family is very soon explained.

"My lordly fathers ruled this same domain of Geierstein, which in their time was very extensive, much after the mode of feudal barons — that is, they were sometimes the protectors and patrons, but oftener the oppressors of their subjects. But when my grandfather, Heinrich of Geierstein, flourished, he not only joined the Confederates to repel Ingelram de Couci, and his roving bands, as I already told you, but, when the wars with Austria were renewed, and many of his degree joined with the boat of the Emperor Leopold, my ancestor adopted the opposite side, fought in front of the Confederates, and contributed by his skill and valour to the decisive victory at Sempach, in which Leopold lost his life, and the flower of Austrian chivalry fell around him. My father, Count Williewald, followed the same course, both from inclination and policy. He united himself closely with the state of Unterwalden, became a citizen of the Confederacy, and distinguished himself so much, that he was chosen Landamman of the Republic. He had two sons, — myself, and a younger brother, Albert; and possessed, as he felt himself, of a species of double character, he was desirous, perhaps unwisely, (if I may censure the purpose of a deceased parent,) that one of his sons should succeed him in his Lordship of Geierstein, and the other support the less ostentatious, though not in my thought less honourable condition, of a free citizen of Unterwalden, possessing such influence among his equals in the Canton as might be acquired by his father's merits and his own. When Albert was twelve years old, our father took us on a short excursion to Germany, where the form, pomp, and magnificence which we witnessed, made a very different impression on the mind of my brother and on my own. What appeared to Albert the consummation of earthly splendour, seemed to me a weary display of tiresome and useless ceremonials. Our father explained his purpose, and offered to me, as his eldest son, the large estate belonging to Geierstein, reserving such a portion of the most fertile ground, as might make my brother one of the wealthiest citizens, in a district where competence is esteemed wealth. The tears gushed from Albert's eyes — 'And must my brother,' he said, 'be a noble Count, honoured and followed by vassals and attendants, and I a homespun peasant among the gray-bearded shepherds of Unterwalden? — No, father — I respect your will — but I will not sacrifice my own rights. Geierstein is a fief held of the empire, and the laws entitle me to my equal half of the lands. If my brother be Count of Geierstein, I am not the less

Count Albert of Geierstein; and I will appeal to the Emperor, rather than that the arbitrary will of one ancestor, though he be my father, shall cancel in me the rank and rights which I have derived from a hundred.' My father was greatly incensed. 'Go,' he said, 'proud boy, give the enemy of thy country a pretext to interfere in her affairs — appeal to the will of a foreign prince from the pleasure of thy father. Go, but never again look me in the face, and dread my eternal malediction!' Albert was about to reply with vehemence, when I entreated him to be silent, and hear me speak. I had, I said, all my life loved the mountain better than the plain; had been more pleased to walk than to ride; more proud to contend with shepherds in their sports, than with nobles in the lists; and happier in the village dance than among the feasts of the German nobles. 'Let me, therefore,' I said, 'be a citizen of the republic of Unterwalden; you will relieve me of a thousand cares; and let my brother Albert wear the coronet and bear the honours of Geierstein.' After some farther discussion, my father was at length contented to adopt my proposal, in order to attain the object which he had so much at heart. Albert was declared heir of his castle and his rank, by the title of Count Albert of Geierstein; and I was placed in possession of these fields and fertile meadows amidst which my house is situated, and my neighbours called me Arnold Biederman."

"And if Biederman," said the merchant, "means, as I understand the word, a man of worth, candour, and generosity, I know none on whom the epithet could be so justly conferred. Yet let me observe, that I praise the conduct, which, in your circumstances, I could not have bowed my spirit to practise. Proceed, I pray you, with the history of your house, if the recital be not painful to you."

"I have little more to say," replied the Landamman. "My father died soon after the settlement of his estate in the manner I have told you. My brother had other possessions in Swabia and Westphalia, and seldom visited his paternal castle, which was chiefly occupied by a seneschal, a man so obnoxious to the vassals of the family, that but for the protection afforded by my near residence, and relationship with his lord, he would have been plucked out of the Vulture's Nest, and treated with as little ceremony as if he had been the vulture himself. Neither, to say the truth, did my brother's occasional visits to Geierstein afford his vassals much relief, or acquire any popularity for himself. He heard with the ears and saw with the eyes of his cruel and interested steward, Ital Schreckenwald, and would not listen even to my interference and admonition. Indeed, though he always demeaned himself with personal kindness towards me, I believe he considered me as a dull and poor-spirited clown, who had disgraced my noble blood by my mean propensities. He showed contempt on every occasion for the prejudices of his countrymen, and particularly by wearing a peacock's feather in public, and causing his followers to display the same badge, though the cognizance of the House of Austria, and so unpopular in this country, that men have been put to death for no better reason than for carrying it in their caps. In the meantime I was married to my Bertha, now a saint in Heaven, by whom I had six stately sons, five of whom you saw surrounding my table this day. Albert also married. His wife was a lady of rank in Westphalia, but his bridal-bed was less fruitful; he had only one daughter, Anne of Geierstein. Then came on the wars between the city of Zurich and our Forest Cantons, in which so much blood was shed, and when our brethren of Zurich were so ill advised as to embrace the alliance of Austria. Their Emperor strained every nerve to avail himself of the favourable opportunity afforded by the disunion of the Swiss; and engaged all with whom he had influence to second his efforts. With my brother he was but too successful; for Albert not only took arms in the Emperor's cause, but admitted into the strong fortress of Geierstein a band of Austrian soldiers, with whom the wicked Ital Schreckenwald laid waste the whole country, excepting my little patrimony."

"It came to a severe pass with you, my worthy host," said the merchant, "since you were to decide against the cause of your country or that of your brother."

"I did not hesitate," continued Arnold Biederman. "My brother was in the Emperor's army, and I was not therefore reduced to act personally against him; but I denounced war against the robbers and thieves with whom Schreckenwald had filled my father's house. It was waged with various fortune. The seneschal, during my absence, burnt down my house, and slew my youngest son, who died, alas! in defence of his father's hearth. It is little to add that my lands were wasted and my flocks destroyed. On the other hand, I succeeded, with help of a body of the peasants of

Unterwalden, in storming the Castle of Geierstein. It was offered back to me by the Confederates; but I had no desire to sully the fair cause in which I had assumed arms, by enriching myself at the expense of my brother; and besides, to have dwelt in that guarded hold would have been a penance to one, the sole protectors of whose house of late years had been a latch and a shepherd's cur. The castle was therefore dismantled, as you see, by order of the ciders of the Canton; and I even think, that considering the uses it was too often put to, I look with more pleasure on the rugged remains of Geierstein, than I ever did when it was entire, and apparently impregnable."

"I can understand your feelings," said the Englishman, "though I repeat, my virtue would not perhaps have extended so far beyond the circle of my family affections. — Your brother, what said he to your patriotic exertions?"

"He was, as I learnt," answered the Landamman, "dreadfully incensed, having no doubt been informed that I had taken his castle with a view to my own aggrandizement. He even swore he would renounce my kindred, seek me through the battle, and slay me with his own hand. We were, in fact, both at the battle of Freyenbach, but my brother was prevented from attempting the execution of his vindictive purpose by a wound from an arrow, which occasioned his being carried out of the mêlée. I was afterwards in the bloody and melancholy fight at Mount Herzel, and that other onslaught at the Chapel of St. Jacob, which brought our brethren of Zurich to terms, and reduced Austria once more to the necessity of making peace with us. After this war of thirteen years, the Diet passed sentence of banishment for life on my brother Albert, and would have deprived him of his possessions, but forbore in consideration of what they thought my good service. When the sentence was intimated to the Count of Geierstein, he returned an answer of defiance; yet a singular circumstance showed us not long afterwards that he retained an attachment to his country, and amidst his resentment against me his brother, did justice to my unaltered affection for him."

"I would pledge my credit," said the merchant, "that what follows relates to yonder fair maiden, your niece?"

"You guess rightly," said the Landamman. "For some time we heard, though indistinctly, (for we have, as you know, but little communication with foreign countries,) that my brother was high in favour at the court of the Emperor, but latterly that he had fallen under suspicion, and, in the course of some of those revolutions common at the courts of princes, had been driven into exile. It was shortly after this news, and, as I think, more than seven years ago, that I was returning from hunting on the further side of the river, had passed the narrow bridge as usual, and was walking through the court-yard which we have lately left," (for their walk was now turned homeward,) "when a voice said in the German language, 'Uncle, have compassion upon me!' As I looked around, I beheld a girl of ten years old approach timidly from the shelter of the ruins, and kneel down at my feet. 'Uncle, spare my life,' she said, holding up her little hands in the act of supplication, while mortal terror was painted upon her countenance. — 'Am I your uncle, little maiden?' said I; 'and if I am, why should you fear me?' — 'because you are the head of the wicked and base clowns who delight to spill noble blood,' replied the girl, with a courage which surprised me. — 'What is your name, my little maiden?' said I; 'and who, having planted in your mind opinions so unfavourable to your kinsman, has brought you hither, to see if he resembles the picture you have received of him?' — 'It was Ital Schreckenwald that brought me hither,' said the girl, only half comprehending the nature of my question. — 'Ital Schreckenwald?' I repeated, shocked at the name of a wretch I have so much reason to hate. A voice from the ruins, like that of a sullen echo from the grave, answered, 'Ital Schreckenwald!' and the caitiff issued from his place of concealment, and stood before me, with that singular indifference to danger which he unites to his atrocity of character. I had my spiked mountain-staff in my hand — What should I have done — or what would you have done, under like circumstances?"

"I would have laid him on the earth, with his skull shivered like an icicle!" said the Englishman, fiercely.

"I had well-nigh done so," replied the Swiss, "but he was unarmed, a messenger from my brother, and therefore no object of revenge. His own undismayed and audacious conduct contributed to save him. 'Let the vassal of the noble and high-born Count of Geierstein hear the words of his master, and let him look that they are obeyed,' said the insolent ruffian. 'Doff thy cap, and listen; for though the voice is mine, the words are those of the noble Count.' — 'God and man know,' replied I, 'if I owe my brother respect or homage — it is much, if, in respect for him, I defer paying to his messenger the meed I dearly owe him. Proceed with thy tale, and rid me of thy hateful presence.' — 'Albert Count of Geierstein, thy lord and my lord,' proceeded Schreckenwald, 'having on his hand wars, and other affairs of weight, sends his daughter the Countess Anne, to thy charge, and graces thee so far as to intrust to thee her support and nurture, until it shall suit his purposes to require her back from thee; and he desires that thou apply to her maintenance the rents and profits of the lands of Geierstein, which thou hast usurped from him.' — 'Ital Schreckenwald,' I replied, 'I will not stop to ask if this mode of addressing me be according to my brother's directions, or thine own insolent pleasure. If circumstances have, as thou sayest, deprived my niece of her natural protector, I will be to her as a father, nor shall she want aught which I have to give her. The lands of Geierstein are forfeited to the state, the castle is ruinous, as thou seest, and it is much of thy crimes that the house of my fathers is desolate. But where I dwell Anne of Geierstein shall dwell, as my children fare, shall she fare, and she shall be to me as a daughter. And now thou hast thine errand — Go hence, if thou lovest thy life; for it is unsafe parleying with the father, when thy hands are stained with the blood of the son.' The wretch retired as I spoke, but took his leave with his usual determined insolence of manner. — 'Farewell,' he said, 'Count of the Plough and Harrow — farewell, noble companion of paltry burghers!' He disappeared, and released me from the strong temptation under which I laboured, and which urged me to stain with his blood the place which had witnessed his cruelty and his crimes. I conveyed my niece to my house, and soon convinced her that I was her sincere friend. I inured her, as if she had been my daughter, to all our mountain exercises; and while she excels in these the damsels of the district, there burst from her such sparkles of sense and courage, mingled with delicacy, as belong not — I must needs own the truth — to the simple maidens of these wild hills, but relish of a nobler stem, and higher breeding. Yet they are so happily mixed with simplicity and courtesy, that Anne of Geierstein is justly considered as the pride of the district; nor do I doubt but that, if she should make a worthy choice of a husband, the state would assign her a large dower out of her father's possessions, since it is not our maxim to punish the child for the faults of the parent."

"It will naturally be your anxious desire, my worthy host," replied the Englishman, "to secure to your niece, in whose praises I have deep cause to join with a grateful voice, such a suitable match as her birth and expectations, but above all her merit, demand."

"It is, my good guest," said the Landamman, "that which hath often occupied my thoughts. The over-near relationship prohibits what would have been my most earnest desire, the hope of seeing her wedded to one of my own sons. This young man, Rudolph Donnerhugel, is brave, and highly esteemed by his fellow-citizens; but more ambitious, and more desirous of distinction, than I would desire for my niece's companion through life. His temper is violent, though his heart, I trust, is good. But I am like to be unpleasantly released from all care on this score, since my brother, having, as it seemed, forgotten Anne for seven years and upwards, has, by a letter, which I have lately received, demanded that she shall be restored to him. — You can read, my worthy sir, for your profession requires it. See, here is the scroll, coldly worded, but far less unkindly than his unbrotherly message by Ital Schreckenwald — Read it, I pray you, aloud."

The merchant read accordingly.

"Brother — I thank you for the care you have taken of my daughter, for she has been in safety when she would otherwise have been in peril, and kindly used, when she would have been in hardship. I now entreat you to restore her to me, and trust that she will come with the virtues which become a woman in every station, and a disposition to lay aside the habits of a Swiss villager for the graces of a high-born maiden. — Adieu. I thank you once more for your care, and would repay it were it in my power; but you need nothing I can give, having renounced the rank to which you were born, and made your nest on the ground, where the storm passes over you. I rest your brother,

"GEIERSTEIN."

"It is addressed 'to Count Arnold of Geierstein, called Arnold Biederman.' A postscript requires you to send the maiden to the court of the Duke of Burgundy. — This, good sir, appears to me the language of a haughty man, divided betwixt the recollection of old offence and recent obligation. The speech of his messenger was that of a malicious vassal, desirous of venting his own spite under pretence of doing his lord's errand."

"I so receive both," replied Arnold Biederman.

"And do you intend," continued the merchant, "to resign this beautiful and interesting creature to the conduct of her father, wilful as he seems to be, without knowing what his condition is, or what his power of protecting her?"

The Landamman hastened to reply. "The tie which unites the parent to the child, is the earliest and the most hallowed that binds the human race. The difficulty of her travelling in safety has hitherto prevented my attempting to carry my brother's instructions into execution. But as I am now likely to journey in person towards the court of Charles, I have determined that Anne shall accompany me; and as I will myself converse with my brother, whom I have not seen for many years, I shall learn his purpose respecting his daughter, and it may be I may prevail on Albert to suffer her to remain under my charge. — And now, sir, having told you of my family affairs at some greater length than was necessary, I must crave your attention as a wise man, to what farther I have to say. You know the disposition which young men and women naturally have to talk, jest, and sport with each other, out of which practice arise often more serious attachments, which they call loving *par amours*. I trust, if we are to travel together, you will so school your young man as to make him aware that Anne of Geierstein cannot, with propriety on her part, be made the object of his thoughts or attentions."

The merchant coloured with resentment, or something like it. "I asked not to join your company, Sir Landamman — it was you who requested mine," he said; "if my son and I have since become in any respect the objects of your suspicion, we will gladly pursue our way separately."

"Nay, be not angry, worthy guest," said the Landamman; "we Switzers do not rashly harbour suspicions; and, that we may not harbour them, we speak respecting the circumstances out of which they might arise, more plainly than is the wont of more civilized countries. When I proposed to you to be my companion on the journey, to speak the truth, though it may displease a father's ear, I regarded your son as a soft, faint-hearted youth, who was, as yet at least, too timid and milky-blooded to attract either respect or regard from the maidens. But a few hours have presented him to us in the character of such a one as is sure to interest them. He has accomplished the emprise of the bow, long thought unattainable, and with which a popular report connects an idle prophecy. He has wit to make verses, and knows doubtless how to recommend himself by other accomplishments which bind young persons to each other, though they are lightly esteemed by men whose beards are mixed with gray, like yours, friend merchant, and mine own. Now, you must be aware, that since my brother broke terms with me, simply for preferring the freedom of a Swiss citizen to the tawdry and servile condition of a German courtier, he will not approve of any one looking towards his daughter who hath not the advantage of noble blood, or who hath, what he would call, debased himself by attention to merchandise, to the cultivation of land — in a word, to any art that is useful. Should your son love Anne of Geierstein, he prepares for himself danger and disappointment. And, now you know the whole, — I ask you, Do we travel together or apart?"

"Even as ye list, my worthy host," said Philipson, in an indifferent tone; "for me, I can but say that such an attachment as you speak of would be as contrary to my wishes as to those of your brother, or what I suppose are your own. Arthur Philipson has duties to perform totally inconsistent with his playing the gentle bachelor to any maiden in Switzerland, take Germany to boot, whether of high or low degree. He is an obedient son, besides — hath never seriously disobeyed my commands, and I will have an eye upon his motions."

"Enough, my friend," said the Landamman; "we travel together, then, and I willingly keep my original purpose, being both pleased and instructed by your discourse."

Then changing the conversation, he began to ask whether his acquaintance thought that the league entered into by the King of England and the Duke of Burgundy would continue stable. "We hear much," continued the Swiss, "of the immense army with which King Edward proposes the recovery of the English dominions in France."

"I am well aware," said Philipson, "that nothing can be so popular in my country as the invasion of France, and the attempt to reconquer Normandy, Maine, and Gascony, the ancient appanages of our English crown. But I greatly doubt whether the voluptuous usurper, who now calls himself king, will be graced by Heaven with success in such an adventure. This Fourth Edward is brave indeed, and has gained every battle in which he drew his sword, and they have been many in number. But since he readied, through a bloody path, to the summit of his ambition, he has shown himself rather a sensual debauchee than a valiant knight; and it is my firm belief, that not even the chance of recovering all the fair dominions which were lost during the civil wars excited by his ambitious house, will tempt him to exchange the soft beds of London, with sheets of silk and pillows of down, and the music of a dying lute to lull him to rest, for the turf of France and the reveille of an alarm trumpet."

"It is the better for us should it prove so," said the Landamman; "for if England and Burgundy were to dismember France, as in our fathers' days was nearly accomplished, Duke Charles would then have leisure to exhaust his long-hoarded vengeance against our Confederacy."

As they conversed thus, they attained once more the lawn in front of Arnold Biederman's mansion, where the contention of the young men had given place to the dance performed by the young persons of both sexes. The dance was led by Anne of Geierstein, and the youthful stranger; which, although it was the most natural arrangement, where the one was a guest, and the other represented the mistress of the family, occasioned the Landamman's exchanging a glance with the elder Philipson, as if it had held some relation to the suspicions he had recently expressed.

But so soon as her uncle and his elder guest appeared, Anne of Geierstein took the earliest opportunity of a pause to break off the dance, and to enter into conversation with her kinsman, as if on the domestic affairs under her attendance. Philipson observed, that his host listened seriously to his niece's communication; and nodding in his frank manner, seemed to intimate that her request should receive a favourable consideration.

The family were presently afterwards summoned to attend the evening meal, which consisted chiefly of the excellent fish afforded by the neighbouring streams and lakes. A large cup, containing what was called the *schlaf-trunk*, or sleeping drink, then went round, which was first quaffed by the master of the household, then modestly tasted by the maiden, next pledged by the two strangers, and finally emptied by the rest of the company. Such were then the sober manners of the Swiss, afterwards much corrupted by their intercourse with more luxurious regions. The guests were conducted to the sleeping apartments, where Philipson and young Arthur occupied the same couch, and shortly after the whole inhabitants of the household were locked in sound repose.

CHAPTER VI

When we two meet, we meet like rushing torrents;
Like warring winds, like names from various points,
That mate each others fury — there is nought
Of elemental strife, were fiends to guide it,
Can match the wrath of man.

FRENAUD.

The elder of our two travellers, though a strong man and familiar with fatigue, slept sounder and longer than usual on the morning which was now beginning to dawn, but his son Arthur had that upon his mind which early interrupted his repose.

The encounter with the bold Switzer, a chosen man of a renowned race of warriors, was an engagement, which, in the opinion of the period in which he lived, was not to be delayed or broken. He left his father's side, avoiding as much as possible the risk of disturbing him, though even in that case the circumstance would not have excited any attention, as he was in the habit of rising early, in order to make preparations for the day's journey, to see that the guide was on his duty, and that the mule had his provender, and to discharge similar offices which might otherwise have given trouble to his father. The old man, however, fatigued with the exertions of the preceding day, slept, as we have said, more soundly than his wont, and Arthur, arming himself with his good sword, sallied out to the lawn in front of the Landamman's dwelling, amid the magic dawn of a beautiful harvest morning in the Swiss mountains.

The sun was just about to kiss the top of the most gigantic of that race of Titans, though the long shadows still lay on the rough grass, which, crisped under the young man's feet, with a strong intimation of frost. But Arthur looked not round on the landscape, however lovely, which lay waiting one flash from the orb of day to start into brilliant existence. He drew the belt of his trusty sword which he was in the act of fastening when he left the house, and ere he had secured the buckle, he was many paces on his way towards the place where he was to use it.

It was still the custom of that military period, to regard a summons to combat as a sacred engagement, preferable to all others which could be formed; and stifling whatever inward feelings of reluctance Nature might oppose to the dictates of

fashion, the step of a gallant to the place of encounter was required to be as free and ready, as if he had been going to a bridal.
I do not know whether this alacrity was altogether real on the
part of Arthur Philipson; but if it were otherwise, neither his look
nor pace betrayed the secret.

Having hastily traversed the fields and groves which separated the Landamman's residence from the old castle of Geierstein, he entered the court-yard from the side where the castle
overlooked the land; and nearly in the same instant his almost
gigantic antagonist, who looked yet more tall and burly by the
pale morning light than he had seemed the preceding evening,
appeared ascending from the precarious bridge beside the torrent, having reached Geierstein by a different route from that
pursued by the Englishman.

The young champion of Berne had hanging along his back
one of those huge two-handed swords, the blade of which measured five feet, and which were wielded with both hands. These
were almost universally used by the Swiss; for, besides the impression which such weapons were calculated to make upon the
array of the German men-at-arms, whose armour was impenetrable to lighter swords, they were also well calculated to defend
mountain passes, where the great bodily strength and agility of
those who bore them, enabled the combatants, in spite of their
weight and length, to use them with much address and effect.
One of these gigantic swords hung round Rudolph Donnerhugel's neck, the point rattling against his heel, and the handle
extending itself over his left shoulder, considerably above his
head. He carried another in his hand.

"Thou art punctual," he called out to Arthur Philipson in a
voice which was distinctly heard above the roar of the waterfall,
which it seemed to rival in sullen force. "But I judged thou
wouldst come without a two-handed sword. There is my kinsman
Ernest's," he said, throwing on the ground the weapon which he
carried, with the hilt towards the young Englishman. "Look,
stranger, that thou disgrace it not, for my kinsman will never
forgive me if thou dost. Or thou mayst have mine if thou likest it
better."

The Englishman looked at the weapon with some surprise,
to the use of which he was totally unaccustomed.

"The challenger," he said, "in all countries where honour is known, accepts the arms of the challenged."

"He who fights on a Swiss mountain, fights with a Swiss brand," answered Rudolph. "Think you our hands are made to handle penknives?"

"Nor are ours made to wield scythes," said Arthur; and muttered betwixt his teeth, as he looked at the sword, which the Swiss continued to offer him — "*Usum non habeo*, I have not proved the weapon."

"Do you repent the bargain you have made?" said the Swiss; "if so, cry craven, and return in safety. Speak plainly, instead of prattling Latin like a clerk or a shaven monk."

"No, proud man," replied the Englishman, "I ask thee no forbearance. I thought but of a combat between a shepherd and a giant, in which God gave the victory to him who had worse odds of weapons than falls to my lot to-day. I will fight as I stand; my own good sword shall serve my need now, as it has done before."

"Content! — But blame not me who offered thee equality of weapons," said the mountaineer. "And now hear me. This is a fight for life or death — yon waterfall sounds the alarum for our conflict. — Yes, old bellower," he continued, looking back, "it is long since thou hast heard the noise of battle; — and look at it ere we begin, stranger, for if you fall, I will commit your body to its waters."

"And if thou fall'st, proud Swiss," answered Arthur, "as well I trust thy presumption leads to destruction, I will have thee buried in the church at Einsiedlen, where the priests shall sing masses for thy soul — thy two-handed sword shall be displayed above thy grave, and a scroll shall tell the passenger, Here lies a bear's cub of Berne, slain by Arthur the Englishman."

"The stone is not in Switzerland, rocky as it is," said Rudolph, scornfully, "that shall bear that inscription. Prepare thyself for battle."

The Englishman cast a calm and deliberate glance around the scene of action — a court-yard, partly open, partly encumbered with ruins, in less and larger masses.

"Methinks," said he to himself, "a master of his weapon, with the instructions of Bottaferma of Florence in his remembrance, a light heart, a good blade, a firm hand, and a just cause, might make up a worse odds than two feet of steel."

Thinking thus, and imprinting on his mind, as much as the time would permit, every circumstance of the locality around him which promised advantage in the combat, and taking his station in the middle of the courtyard, where the ground was entirely clear, he flung his cloak from him, and drew his sword.

Rudolph had at first believed that his foreign antagonist was an effeminate youth, who would be swept from before him at the first flourish of his tremendous weapon. But the firm and watchful attitude assumed by the young man, reminded the Swiss of the deficiencies of his own unwieldy implement, and made him determine to avoid any precipitation which might give advantage to an enemy who seemed both daring and vigilant. He unsheathed his huge sword, by drawing it over the left shoulder, an operation which required some little time, and might have offered formidable advantage to his antagonist, had Arthur's sense of honour permitted him to begin the attack ere it was completed. The Englishman remained firm, however, until the Swiss, displaying his bright brand to the morning sun, made three or four nourishes as if to prove its weight, and the facility with which he wielded it — then stood firm within sword-stroke of his adversary, grasping his weapon with both hands, and advancing it a little before his body, with the blade pointed straight upwards. The Englishman, on the contrary, carried his sword in one hand, holding it across his face in a horizontal position, so as to be at once ready to strike, thrust, or parry.

"Strike, Englishman!" said the Switzer, after they had confronted each other in this manner for about a minute.

"The longest sword should strike first," said Arthur; and the words had not left his mouth, when the Swiss sword rose, and descended with a rapidity which, the weight and size of the weapon considered, appeared portentous. No parry, however dexterously interposed, could have baffled the ruinous descent of that dreadful weapon, by which the champion of Berne had hoped at once to begin the battle and end it. But young Philipson had not over-estimated the justice of his own eye, or the activity of his limbs. Ere the blade descended, a sudden spring to one side carried him from beneath its heavy sway, and before the Swiss could again raise his sword aloft, he received a wound, though a slight one, upon the left arm. Irritated at the failure and at the wound, the Switzer heaved up his sword once more, and availing himself of a strength corresponding to his size, he discharged towards his adversary a succession of blows, downright, athwart, horizontal, and from left to right, with such surprising strength and velocity, that it required all the address of the young Englishman, by parrying, shifting, eluding, or retreating, to evade a storm, of which every individual blow seemed sufficient to cleave a solid rock. The Englishman was compelled to give ground, now bark wards, now swerving to the one side or the other, now availing himself of the fragments of the ruins, but watching all the while, with the utmost composure, the moment when the strength of his enraged enemy might become somewhat exhausted, or when by some improvident or furious blow he might again lay himself open to a close attack. The latter of these advantages had nearly occurred, for in the middle of his headlong charge, the Switzer stumbled over a large stone concealed among the long grass, and ere he could recover himself, received a severe blow across the head from his antagonist. It lighted upon his bonnet, the lining of which enclosed a small steel cap, so that he escaped unwounded, and springing up, renewed the battle with unabated fury, though it seemed to the young Englishman with breath somewhat short, and blows dealt with more caution.

They were still contending with equal fortune, when a stern voice, rising over the clash of swords, as well as the roar of waters, called out in a commanding tone, "On your lives, forbear!"

The two combatants sunk the points of their swords, not very sorry perhaps for the interruption of a strife which must otherwise have had a deadly termination. They looked round, and the Landamman stood before them, with anger frowning on his broad and expressive forehead.

"How now, boys!" he said; "are you guests of Arnold Biederman, and do you dishonour his house by acts of violence more becoming the wolves of the mountains, than beings to whom the great Creator has given a form after his own likeness, and an immortal soul to be saved by penance and repentance?"

"Arthur," said the elder Philipson, who had come up at the same time with their host, "what frenzy is this? Are your duties of so light and heedless a nature, as to give time and place for quarrels and combats with every idle boor who chances to be boastful at once and bull-headed?"

The young men, whose strife had ceased at the entrance of these unexpected spectators, stood looking at each other, and resting on their swords.

"Rudolph Donnerhugel," said the Landamman, "give thy sword to me — to me, the owner of this ground, the master of this family, and magistrate of the canton."

"And which is more," answered Rudolph submissively, "to you who are Arnold Biederman, at whose command every native of these mountains draws his sword or sheathes it."

He gave his two-handed sword to the Landamman.

"Now, by my honest word," said Biederman, "it is the same with which thy father Stephen fought so gloriously at Sempach, abreast with the famous De Winkelried! Shame it is, that it should be drawn on a helpless stranger. — And you, young sir," continued the Swiss, addressing Arthur, while his father said at the same time, "Young man, yield up your sword to the Landamman."

"It shall not need, sir," replied the young Englishman, "since, for my part, I hold our strife at an end. This gallant gentleman called me hither, on a trial as I conceive, of courage; I can give my unqualified testimony to his gallantry and swordmanship; and as I trust he will say nothing to the shame of my manhood, I think our strife has lasted long enough for the purpose which gave rise to it."

"Too long for me," said Rudolph, frankly; "the green sleeve of my doublet, which I wore of that colour out of my love to the Forest Cantons, is now stained into as dirty a crimson as could have been done by any dyer in Ypres or Ghent. But I heartily forgive the brave stranger who has spoiled my jerkin, and given its master a lesson he will not soon forget. Had all Englishmen been like your guest, worthy kinsman, methinks the mound at Buttisholz had hardly risen so high."

"Cousin Rudolph," said the Landamman, smoothing his brow as his kinsman spoke, "I have ever thought thee as generous as thou art harebrained and quarrel-some; and you, my young guest, may rely, that when a Swiss says the quarrel is over, there is no chance of its being renewed. We are not like the men of the valleys to the eastward, who nurse revenge as if it were a favourite child. And now, join hands, my children, and let us forget this foolish feud."

"Here is my hand, brave stranger," said Donnerhugel; "thou hast taught me a trick of fence, and when we have broken our fast, we will, by your leave, to the forest, where I will teach you a trick of woodcraft in return. When your foot hath half the experience of your hand, and your eye hath gained a portion of the steadiness of your heart, you will not find many hunters to match you."

Arthur, with all the ready confidence of youth, readily embraced a proposition so frankly made, and before they reached the house, various subjects of sport were eagerly discussed between them, with as much cordiality as if no disturbance of their concord had taken place.

"Now this," said the Landamman, "is as it should be. I am ever ready to forgive the headlong impetuosity of our youth, if they will be but manly and open in their reconciliation, and bear their heart on their tongue, as a true Swiss should."

"These two youths had made but wild work of it, however," said Philipson, "had not your care, my worthy host, learned of their rendezvous, and called me to assist in breaking their purpose. May I ask how it came to your knowledge so opportunely?"

"It was e'en through means of my domestic fairy," answered Arnold Biederman, "who seems born for the good luck of my family, — I mean my niece, Anne, who had observed a glove exchanged betwixt the two young braggadocios, and heard them mention Geierstein and break of day. O, sir, it is much to see a woman's sharpness of wit! it would have been long enough ere any of my thick-headed sons had shown themselves so apprehensive."

"I think I see our propitious protectress peeping at us from yonder high ground," said Philipson; "but it seems as if she would willingly observe us without being seen in return."

"Ay," said the Landamman, "she has been looking out to see that there has been no hurt done; and now, I warrant me, the foolish girl is ashamed of having shown such a laudable degree of interest in a matter of the kind."

"Methinks," said the Englishman, "I would willingly return my thanks, in your presence, to the fair maiden to whom I have been so highly indebted."

"There can be no better time than the present," said the

Landamman; and he sent through the groves the maiden's name, in one of those shrilly accented tones which we have already noticed.

Anne of Geierstein, as Philipson had before observed, was stationed upon a knoll at some distance, and concealed, as she thought, from notice, by a screen of brushwood. She started at her uncle's summons, therefore, but presently obeyed it; and avoiding the young men, who passed on foremost, she joined the Landamman and Philipson, by a circuitous path through the woods.

"My worthy friend and guest would speak with you, Anne," said the Landamman, so soon as the morning greeting had been exchanged. The Swiss maiden coloured over brow as well as cheek, when Philipson, with a grace which seemed beyond his calling, addressed her in these words: —

"It happens sometimes to us merchants, my fair young friend, that we are unlucky enough not to possess means for the instant defraying of our debts; but he is justly held amongst us as the meanest of mankind who does not acknowledge them. Accept, therefore, the thanks of a father, whose son your courage, only yesterday, saved from destruction, and whom your prudence has, this very morning, rescued from a great danger. And grieve me not, by refusing to wear these ear-rings," he added, producing a small jewel-case, which he opened as he spoke; "they are, it is true, only of pearls, but they have not been thought unworthy the ears of a countess" ——

"And must, therefore," said the old Landamman, "show misplaced on the person of a Swiss maiden of Unterwalden; for such and no more is my niece Anne while she resides in my solitude. Methinks, good Master Philipson, you display less than your usual judgment in matching the quality of your gifts with the rank of her on whom they are bestowed — as a merchant, too, you should remember that large guerdons will lighten your gains."

"Let me crave your pardon, my good host," answered the Englishman, "while I reply, that at least I have consulted my own sense of the obligation under which I labour, and have chosen, out of what I have at my free disposal, that which I thought might best express it. I trust the host whom I have found hitherto so kind, will pot prevent this young maiden from accepting what

92

is at least not unbecoming the rank she is born to; and you will judge me unjustly if you think me capable of doing either myself or you the wrong, of offering any token of a value beyond what I can well spare." The Landamman took the jewel-case into his own hand.

"I have ever set my countenance," he said, "against gaudy gems, which are leading us daily farther astray from the simplicity of our fathers and mothers. — And yet," he added with a good-humoured smile, and holding one of the ear-rings close to his relation's face, "the ornaments do set off the wench rarely, and they say girls have more pleasure in wearing such toys than gray-haired men can comprehend. Wherefore, dear Anne, as thou hast deserved a dearer trust in a greater matter, I refer thee entirely to thine own wisdom, to accept of our good friend's costly present, and wear it or not as thou thinkest fit."

"Since such is your pleasure, my best friend and kinsman," said the young maiden, blushing as she spoke, "I will not give pain to our valued guest, by refusing what he desires so earnestly that I should accept; but, by his leave, good uncle, and yours, I will bestow these splendid ear-rings on the shrine of Our Lady of Einsiedlen, to express our general gratitude to her protecting favour, which has been around us in the terrors of yesterday's storm, and the alarms of this morning's discord."

"By Our Lady, the wench speaks sensibly!" said the Landamman; "and her wisdom has applied the bounty well, my good guest, to bespeak prayers for thy family and mine, and for the general peace of Unterwalden. — Go to, Anne, thou shalt have a necklace of jet at next shearing-feast, if our fleeces bear any price in the market."

CHAPTER VII

Let him who will not proffer'd peace receive,
Be sated with the plagues which war can give;
And well thy hatred of the peace is known,
If now thy soul reject the friendship shown.

HOOLE'S Tasso.

The confidence betwixt the Landamman and the English merchant appeared to increase during the course of a few busy days, which occurred before that appointed for the commencement of their journey to the Court of Charles of Burgundy. The state of Europe, and of the Helvetian Confederacy, has been already alluded to; but, for the distinct explanation of our story, may be here briefly recapitulated.

In the interval of a week, whilst the English travellers remained at Geierstein, meetings or diets were held, as well of the City Cantons of the Confederacy, as of those of the Forest. The former, aggrieved by the taxes imposed on their commerce by the Duke of Burgundy, rendered yet more intolerable by the violence of the agents whom he employed in such oppression, were eager for war, in which they had hitherto uniformly found victory and wealth. Many of them were also privately instigated to arms by the largesses of Louis XI., who spared neither intrigues nor gold to effect a breach betwixt these dauntless Confederate's and his formidable enemy, Charles the Bold.

On the other hand, there were many reasons which appeared to render it impolitic for the Switzers to engage in war with one of the most wealthy, most obstinate, and most powerful princes in Europe, — for such unquestionably was Charles of Burgundy, — without the existence of some strong reason affecting their own honour and independence. Every day brought fresh intelligence from the interior, that Edward the Fourth of England had entered into a strict and intimate alliance, offensive and defensive, with the Duke of Burgundy, and that it was the purpose of the English King, renowned for his numerous victories over the rival House of Lancaster, by which, after various reverses, he had obtained undisputed possession of the throne, to re-assert his claims to those provinces of France, so long held by his ancestors. It seemed as if this alone were wanting to his fame; and that, having subdued his internal enemies, he now turned his

eyes to the regaining of those rich and valuable foreign possessions which had been lost during the administration of the feeble
Henry VI., and the civil discords so dreadfully prosecuted in the
wars of the White and Red Roses. It was universally known, that
throughout England generally, the loss of the French provinces
was felt as a national degradation; and that not only the nobility
who had in consequence been deprived of the large fiefs which
they had held in Normandy, Gascony, Maine, and Anjou, but the
warlike gentry, accustomed to gain both fame and wealth at the
expense of France, and the fiery yeomanry, whose bows had decided so many fatal battles, were as eager to renew the conflict,
as their ancestors of Cressy, Poitiers, and Agincourt, had been to
follow their sovereign to the fields of victory, on which their
deeds had conferred deathless renown.

The latest and most authentic intelligence bore, that the
King of England was on the point of passing to France in person,
(an invasion rendered easy by his possession of Calais,) with an
army superior in numbers and discipline to any with which an
English monarch had ever before entered that kingdom; that all
the hostile preparations were completed, and that the arrival of
Edward might instantly be expected; whilst the powerful co-
operation of the Duke of Burgundy, and the assistance of numerous disaffected French noblemen in the provinces which had
been so long under the English dominion, threatened a fearful
issue of the war to Louis XI., sagacious, wise, and powerful, as
that prince unquestionably was.

It would no doubt have been the wisest policy of Charles of
Burgundy, when thus engaging in an alliance against his most
formidable neighbour, and hereditary as well as personal enemy,
to have avoided all cause of quarrel with the Helvetian Confederacy, a poor but most warlike people, who already had been
taught by repeated successes, to feel that their hardy infantry
could, if necessary, engage on terms of equality, or even of advantage, the flower of that chivalry, which had hitherto been
considered as forming the strength of European battle. But the
measures of Charles, whom fortune had opposed to the most astucious and politic monarch of his time, were always dictated by
passionate feeling and impulse, rather than by a judicious consideration of the circumstances in which he stood. Haughty,
proud, and uncompromising, though neither destitute of honour

nor generosity, he despised and hated what he termed the paltry associations of herdsmen and shepherds, united with a few towns which subsisted chiefly by commerce; and instead of courting the Helvetian Cantons, like his crafty enemy, or at least affording them no ostensible pretence of quarrel, he omitted no opportunity of showing the disregard and contempt in which he held their upstart consequence, and of evincing the secret longing which he entertained to take vengeance upon them for the quantity of noble blood which they had shed, and to compensate the repeated successes they had gained over the feudal lords, of whom he imagined himself the destined avenger.

The Duke of Burgundy's possessions in the Alsatian territory afforded him many opportunities for wreaking his displeasure upon the Swiss League. The little castle and town of Ferette, lying within ten or eleven miles of Bâle, served as a thoroughfare to the traffic of Berne and Soleure, the two principal towns of the Confederation. In this place the Duke posted a governor, or seneschal, who was also an administrator of the revenue, and seemed born on purpose to be the plague and scourge of his republican neighbours.

Archibald von Hagenbach was a German noble, whose possessions lay in Swabia, and was universally esteemed one of the fiercest and most lawless of that frontier nobility, known by the name of Robber-knights, and Robber-counts. These dignitaries, because they held their fiefs of the Holy Roman Empire, claimed as complete sovereignty within their territories of a mile square, as any reigning prince of Germany in his more extended dominions. They levied tolls and taxes on strangers, and imprisoned, tried, and executed those who, as they alleged, had committed offences within their petty domains. But especially, and in further exercise of their seignorial privileges, they made war on each other, and on the Free Cities of the Empire, attacking and plundering without mercy the caravans, or large trains of wagons, by which the internal commerce of Germany was carried on.

A succession of injuries done and received by Archibald of Hagenbach, who had been one of the fiercest sticklers for this privilege of *faustrecht*, or club-law, as it may be termed, had ended in his being obliged, though somewhat advanced in life, to leave a country where his tenure of existence was become extremely precarious, and to engage in the service of the Duke of

Burgundy, who willingly employed him, as he was a man of high descent and proved valour, and not the less, perhaps, that he was sure to find in a man of Hagenbach's fierce, rapacious, and haughty disposition, the unscrupulous executioner of whatsoever severities it might be his master's pleasure to enjoin.

The traders of Berne and Soleure, accordingly, made loud and violent complaints of Hagenbach's exactions. The impositions laid on commodities which passed through his district of La Ferette, to whatever place they might be ultimately bound, were arbitrarily increased, and the merchants and traders who hesitated to make instant payment of what was demanded, were exposed to imprisonment and personal punishment. The commercial towns of Germany appealed to the Duke against this iniquitous conduct on the part of the Governor of La Ferette, and requested of his Grace's goodness that he would withdraw Von Hagenbach from their neighbourhood; but the Duke treated their complaints with contempt. The Swiss League carried their remonstrances higher, and required that justice should be done on the Governor of La Ferette, as having offended against the law of nations; but they were equally unable to attract attention or obtain redress.

At length the Dict of the Confederation devotion send the solemn deputation which has been repeatedly mentioned. One or two of these envoys joined with the calm and prudent Arnold Biederman, in the hope that so solemn a measure might open the eyes of the Duke to the wicked injustice of his representative; others among the deputies, having no such peaceful views, were determined, by this resolute remonstrance, to pave the way for hostilities.

Arnold Biederman was an especial advocate for peace, while its preservation was compatible with national independence, and the honour of the Confederacy; but the younger Philipson soon discovered that the Landamman alone, of all his family, cherished these moderate views. The opinion of his sons had been swayed and seduced by the impetuous eloquence and overbearing influence of Rudolph of Donnerhugel, who, by some feats of peculiar gallantry, and the consideration due to the merit of his ancestors, had acquired an influence in the councils of his native canton, and with the youth of the League in general, beyond what was usually yielded by these wise republicans to men of his early age. Arthur, who was now an acceptable and welcome companion of all their hunting parties and other sports, heard nothing among the young men but anticipations of war, rendered delightful by the hopes of booty and of distinction, which were to be obtained by the Switzers. The feats of their ancestors against the Germans had been so wonderful as to realize the fabulous victories of romance; and while the present race possessed the same hardy limbs, and the same inflexible courage, they eagerly anticipated the same distinguished success. When the Governor of La Ferette was mentioned in the conversation, he was usually spoken of as the bandog of Burgundy, or the Alsatian mastiff; and intimations were openly given, that if his course were not instantly checked by his master, and he himself withdrawn from the frontiers of Switzerland, Archibald of Hagenbach would find his fortress no protection from the awakened indignation of the wronged inhabitants of Soleure, and particularly of those of Berne.

This general disposition to war among the young Switzers was reported to the elder Philipson by his son, and led him at one time to hesitate whether he ought not rather to resume all the inconveniences and dangers of a journey, accompanied only by Arthur, than run the risk of the quarrels in which he might be involved by the unruly conduct of these fierce mountain youths, after they should have left their own frontiers. Such an event would have had, in a peculiar degree, the effect of destroying every purpose of his journey; but respected as Arnold Biederman was by his family and countrymen, the English merchant concluded, upon the whole, that his influence would be able to restrain his companions until the great question of peace or war should be determined, and especially until they should have discharged their commission by obtaining an audience of the Duke of Burgundy, and after this he should be separated from their society, and not liable to be engaged in any responsibility for their ulterior measures.

After a delay of about ten days, the deputation commissioned to remonstrate with the Duke on the aggressions and exactions of Archibald of Hagenbach, at length assembled at Geierstein, from whence the members were to journey forth together. They were three in number, besides the young Bernese, and the Landamman of Unterwalden. One was, like Arnold, a proprietor from the Forest Cantons, wearing a dress scarcely handsomer than that of a common herdsman, but distinguished by the beauty and size of his long silvery beard. His name was Nicholas Bonstetten. Melchior Sturmthal, banner-bearer of Berne, a man of middle age, and a soldier of distinguished courage, with Adam Zimmerman, a burgess of Soleure, who was considerably older, completed the number of the envoys.

Each was dressed after his best fashion; but notwithstanding that the severe eye of Arnold Biederman censured one or two silver belt-buckles, as well as a chain of the same metal, which decorated the portly person of the burgess of Soleure, it seemed that a powerful and victorious people, for such the Swiss were now to be esteemed, were never represented by an embassy of such patriarchal simplicity. The deputies travelled on foot, with their piked staves in their hands, like pilgrims bound for some place of devotion. Two mules, which bore their little stock of baggage, were led by young lads, sons or cousins of members of the embassy, who had obtained permission, in this manner, to get such a glance of the world beyond the mountains as this journey promised to afford.

But although their retinue was small, so far as respected either state or personal attendance and accommodation, the dangerous circumstances of the times, and the very unsettled state of the country beyond their own territories, did not permit men charged with affairs of such importance to travel without a guard. Even the danger arising from the wolves, which, when pinched by the approach of winter, have been known to descend from their mountain fastnesses into open villages, such as those the travellers might choose to quarter in, rendered the presence of some escort necessary; and the bands of deserters from various services, who formed parties of banditti on the frontiers of Alsatia and Germany, combined to recommend such a precaution.

Accordingly, about twenty of the selected youth from the various Swiss cantons, including Rudiger, Ernest, and Sigismund, Arnold's three eldest sons, attended upon the deputation; they did not, however, observe any military order, or march close or near to the patriarchal train. On the contrary, they formed hunting parties of five or six together, who explored the rocks, woods, and passes of the mountains, through which the envoys journeyed. Their slower pace allowed the active young men, who were accompanied by their large shaggy dogs, full time to destroy wolves and bears, or occasionally to surprise a chamois among the cliffs; while the hunters, even while in pursuit of their sport, were careful to examine such places as might afford opportunity for ambush, and thus ascertained the safety of the party whom they escorted more securely than if they had attended close on their train. A peculiar note on the huge Swiss bugle, before described, formed of the horn of the mountain bull, was the signal agreed upon for collecting in a body should danger occur. Rudolph Donnerhugel, so much younger than his brethren in the same important commission, took the command of this mountain bodyguard, whom he usually accompanied in their sportive excursions. In point of arms they were well provided, bearing two-handed swords, long partisans and spears, as well as both cross and long bows, short cutlasses, and huntsmen's knives. The heavier weapons, as impeding their activity, were carried with the baggage, but were ready to be assumed on the slightest alarm.

Arthur Philipson, like his late antagonist, naturally preferred the company and sports of the younger men, to the grave conversation and slow pace of the fathers of the mountain commonwealth. There was, however, one temptation to loiter with the baggage, which, had other circumstances permitted, might have reconciled the young Englishman to forego the opportunities of sport which the Swiss youth so eagerly sought after, and endure the slow pace and grave conversation of the elders of the party. In a word, Anne of Geierstein, accompanied by a Swiss girl her attendant, travelled in the rear of the deputation.

The two females were mounted upon asses, whose slow step hardly kept pace with the baggage mules; and it may be fairly suspected that Arthur Philipson, in requital of the important services which he had received from that beautiful and interesting young woman, would have deemed it no extreme hardship to have afforded her occasionally his assistance on the journey, and the advantage of his conversation to relieve the tediousness of the way. But he dared not presume to offer attentions which the customs of the country did not seem to permit, since they were not attempted by any of the maiden's cousins, or even by Rudolph Donnerhugel, who certainly had hitherto appeared to neglect no opportunity to recommend himself to his fair cousin. Besides, Arthur had reflection enough to be convinced, that in yielding to the feelings which impelled him to cultivate the acquaintance of this amiable young person, he would certainly incur the serious displeasure of his father, and probably also that of her uncle, by whose hospitality they had profited, and whose safe-conduct they were in the act of enjoying.

The young Englishman, therefore, pursued the same amusements which interested the other young men of the party, managing only, as frequently as their halts permitted, to venture upon offering to the maiden such marks of courtesy as could afford no room for remark or censure. And his character as a sportsman being now well established, he sometimes permitted himself, even when the game was afoot, to loiter in the vicinity of the path on which he could at least mark the flutter of the gray wimple of Anne of Geierstein, and the outline of the form which it shrouded. This indolence, as it seemed, was not unfavourably construed by his companions, being only accounted an indifference to the less noble or less dangerous game; for when the object was a bear, wolf, or other animal of prey, no spear, cutlass, or bow of the party, not even those of Rudolph Donnerhugel, were so prompt in the chase as those of the young Englishman.

Meantime, the elder Philipson had other and more serious subjects of consideration. He was a man, as the reader must have already seen, of much acquaintance with the world, in which he had acted parts different from that which he now sustained. Former feelings were recalled and awakened, by the view of sports familiar to his early years. The clamour of the hounds, echoing from the wild hills and dark forests through which they travelled; the sight of the gallant young huntsmen, appearing, as they brought the object of their chase to bay, amid airy cliffs and profound precipices, which seemed impervious to the human foot; the sounds of halloo and horn reverberating from hill to hill, had more than once well-nigh impelled him to take a share in the hazardous but animating amusement, which, next to war, was then in most parts of Europe the most serious occupation of life. But the feeling was transient, and he became yet more deeply interested in studying the manners and opinions of the persons with whom he was travelling.

They seemed to be all coloured with the same downright

and blunt simplicity which characterized Arnold Biederman, although it was in none of them elevated by the same dignity of thought or profound sagacity. In speaking of the political state of their country, they affected no secrecy; and although, with the exception of Rudolph, their own young men were not admitted into their councils, the exclusion seemed only adopted with a view to the necessary subordination of youth to age, and not for the purpose of observing any mystery. In the presence of the elder Philipson, they freely discussed the pretensions of the Duke of Burgundy, the means which their country possessed of maintaining her independence, and the firm resolution of the Helvetian League to bid defiance to the utmost force the world could bring against it, rather than submit to the slightest insult. In other respects, their views appeared wise and moderate, although both the Banneret of Berne, and the consequential Burgher of Soleure, seemed to hold the consequences of war more lightly than they were viewed by the cautious Landamman of Unterwalden, and his venerable companion, Nicholas Bonstetten, who subscribed to all his opinions.

It frequently happened, that, quitting these subjects, the conversation turned on such as were less attractive to their fellow-traveller. The signs of the weather, the comparative fertility of recent seasons, the most advantageous mode of managing their orchards and rearing their crops, though interesting to the mountaineers themselves, gave Philipson slender amusement; and notwithstanding that the excellent Meinherr Zimmerman of Soleure would fain have joined with him in conversation respecting trade and merchandise, yet the Englishman, who dealt in articles of small bulk and considerable value, and traversed sea and land to carry on his traffic, could find few mutual topics to discuss with the Swiss trader, whose commerce only extended into the neighbouring districts of Burgundy and Germany, and whose goods consisted of coarse woollen cloths, fustian, hides, peltry, and such ordinary articles.

But, ever and anon, while the Switzers were discussing some paltry interests of trade, or describing some process of rude cultivation, or speaking of blights in grain, and the murrain amongst cattle, with all the dull minuteness of petty farmers and traders met at a country fair, a well-known spot would recall the name and story of a battle in which some of them had served, (for there were none of the party who had not been repeatedly in arms,) and the military details, which in other countries were only the theme of knights and squires who had acted their part in them, or of learned clerks who laboured to record them, were, in this singular region, the familiar and intimate subjects of discussion with men whose peaceful occupations seemed to place them at an immeasurable distance from the profession of a soldier. This led the Englishman to think of the ancient inhabitants of Rome, where the plough was so readily exchanged for the sword, and the cultivation of a rude farm for the management of public affairs. He hinted this resemblance to the Landamman, who was naturally gratified with the compliment to his country, but presently replied, — "May Heaven continue among us the homebred virtues of the Romans, and preserve us from their lust of conquest and love of foreign luxuries!"

The slow pace of the travellers, with various causes of delay which it is unnecessary to dwell upon, occasioned the deputation spending two nights on the road before they reached Bâle. The small towns or villages in which they quartered, received them with such marks of respectful hospitality as they had the means to bestow, and their arrival was a signal for a little feast, with which the heads of the community uniformly regaled them.

On such occasions, while the elders of the village entertained the deputies of the Confederation, the young men of the escort were provided for by those of their own age, several of whom, usually aware of their approach, were accustomed to join in the chase of the day, and made the strangers acquainted with the spots where game was most plenty.

These feasts were never prolonged to excess, and the most special dainties which composed them were kids, lambs, and game, the produce of the mountains. Yet it seemed both to Arthur Philipson and his father, that the advantages of good cheer were more prized by the Banneret of Berne and the Burgess of Soleure, than by their host the Landamman, and the Deputy of Schwitz. There was no excess committed, as we have already said; but the deputies first mentioned obviously understood the art of selecting the choicest morsels, and were connoisseurs in the good wine, chiefly of foreign growth, with which they freely washed it down. Arnold was too wise to censure what he had no means of amending; he contented himself by observing in his own person a rigorous diet, living indeed almost entirely upon vegetables and fair water, in which he was closely imitated by the old gray-bearded Nicholas Bonstetten, who seemed to make it his principal object to follow the Landamman's example in every thing.

It was, as we have already said, the third day after the commencement of their journey, before the Swiss deputation reached the vicinity of Bâle, in which city, then one of the largest in the south-western extremity of Germany, they proposed taking up their abode for the evening, nothing doubting a friendly reception. The town, it is true, was not then, nor till about thirty years afterwards, a part of the Swiss Confederation, to which it was only joined in 1501; but it was a Free Imperial City, connected with Berne, Soleure, Lucerne, and other towns of Switzerland, by mutual interests, and constant intercourse. It was the object of the deputation to negotiate, if possible, a peace, which could not be more useful to themselves than to the city of Bâle, considering the interruptions of commerce which must be occasioned by a rupture between the Duke of Burgundy and the Cantons, and the great advantage which that city would derive by preserving a neutrality, situated as it was betwixt these two hostile powers.

They anticipated therefore, as welcome a reception from the authorities of Bâle, as they had received while in the bounds of their own Confederation, since the interests of that city were so deeply concerned in the objects of their mission. — The next chapter will show how far these expectations were realized.

CHAPTER VIII

They saw that city, welcoming the Rhine.
As from his mountain heritage he bursts,
As purposed proud Orgetorix of yore,
Leaving the desert region of the hills,
To lord it o'er the fertile plains of Gaul.

HELVETIA.

The eyes of the English travellers, wearied with a succession of wild mountainous scenery, now gazed with pleasure upon a country still indeed irregular and hilly in its surface, but capable of high cultivation, and adorned with corn-fields and vineyards. The Rhine, a broad and large river, poured its gray stream in a huge sweep through the landscape, and divided into two portions the city of Bâle, which is situated on its banks. The southern part, to which the path of the Swiss deputies conducted them, displayed the celebrated cathedral, and the lofty terrace which runs in front of it, and seemed to remind the travellers that they now approached a country in which the operations of man could make themselves distinguished even among the works of nature, instead of being lost, as the fate of the most splendid efforts of human labour must have been, among those tremendous mountains which they had so lately traversed.

They were yet a mile from the entrance of the city, when the party was met by one of the magistrates, attended by two or three citizens mounted on mules, the velvet housings of which expressed wealth and quality. They greeted the Landamman of Unterwalden and his party in a respectful manner, and the latter prepared themselves to hear and make a suitable reply to, the hospitable invitation which they naturally expected to receive.

The message of the community of Bâle was, however, diametrically opposite to what they had anticipated. It was delivered with a good deal of diffidence and hesitation by the functionary who met them, and who certainly, while discharging his commission, did not appear to consider it as the most respectable which he might have borne. There were many professions of the most profound and fraternal regard for the cities of the Helvetian League, with whom the orator of Bâle declared his own state to be united in friendship and interests. But he ended by intimating, that, on account of certain cogent and weighty reasons, which should be satisfactorily explained at more leisure, the free city of Bâle could not, this evening, receive within its walls the highly respected deputies, who were travelling at the command of the Helvetian Diet, to the court of the Duke of Burgundy.

Philipson marked with much interest the effect which this most unexpected intimation produced on the members of the embassage. Rudolph Donnerhugel, who had joined their company as they approached Bâle, appeared less surprised than his associates, and, while he remained perfectly silent, seemed rather anxious to penetrate their sentiments, than disposed to express his own. It was not the first time the sagacious merchant had observed, that this bold and fiery young man could, when his purposes required it, place a strong constraint upon the natural impetuosity of his temper. For the others, the Banneret's brow darkened; the face of the Burgess of Soleure became flushed like the moon when rising in the north-west; the gray-bearded Deputy of Schwitz looked anxiously on Arnold Biederman; and the Landamman himself seemed more moved than was usual in a person of his equanimity. At length, he replied to the functionary of Bâle, in a voice somewhat altered by his feelings: —

"This is a singular message to the Deputies of the Swiss Confederacy, bound as we are upon an amicable mission, on which depends the interest of the good citizens of Bâle, whom we have always treated as our good friends, and who still profess to be so. The shelter of their roofs, the protection of their walls, the wonted intercourse of hospitality, is what no friendly state hath a right to refuse to the inhabitants of another."

"Nor is it with their will that the community of Bâle refuse it, worthy Landamman," replied the magistrate. "Not you alone, and your worthy associates, but your escort, and your very beasts of burden, should be entertained with all the kindness which the citizens of Bâle could bestow — But we act under constraint."

"And by whom exercised?" said the Banneret, bursting out into passion. "Has the Emperor Sigismund profited so little by the example of his predecessors" ——

"The Emperor," replied the delegate of Bâle, interrupting the Banneret, "is a well-intentioned and peaceful monarch, as he has been ever; but — there are Burgundian troops, of late, marched into the Sundgaw, and messages have been sent to our state from Count Archibald of Hagenbach."

"Enough said," replied the Landamman. "Draw not farther the veil from a weakness for which you blush. I comprehend you entirely. Bâle lies too near the citadel of La Ferette to permit its citizens to consult their own inclinations. — Brother, we see where your difficulty lies — we pity you — and we forgive your inhospitality."

"Nay, but hear me to an end, worthy Landamman," answered the magistrate. "There is here in the vicinity an old hunting-seat of the Counts of Falkenstein, called Graffs-lust,[3] which, though ruinous, yet may afford better lodgings than the open air, and is capable of some defence — though Heaven forbid that any one should dare to intrude upon your repose! And hark ye hither, my worthy friends; — if you find in the old place some refreshments, as wine, beer, and the like, use them without scruple, for they are there for your accommodation."

"I do not refuse to occupy a place of security," said the Landamman; "for although the causing us to be excluded from Bâle may be only done in the spirit of petty insolence and malice, yet it may also, for what we can tell, be connected with some purpose of violence. Your provisions we thank you for; but we will not, with my consent, feed at the cost of friends, who are ashamed to own us unless by stealth."

"One thing more, my worthy sir," said the official of Bâle — "You have a maiden in company, who, I presume to think, is your daughter. There is but rough accommodation where you are going, even for men; — for women there is little better, though what we could we have done to arrange matters as well as may be. But rather let your daughter go with us back to Bâle, where my dame will be a mother to her till next morning, when I will bring her to your camp in safety. We promised to shut our gates against the men of the Confederacy, but the women were not mentioned."

"You are subtle casuists, you men of Bâle," answered the Landamman; "but know, that from the time in which the Helvetians sallied forth to encounter Cæsar down to the present

---

[3] Graffs-lust — *i.e.*, Count's-delight.

hour, the women of Switzerland, in the press of danger, have had their abode in the camp of their fathers, brothers, and husbands, and sought no farther safety than they might find in the courage of their relations. We have enough of men to protect our women, and my niece shall remain with us, and take the fate which Heaven may send us."

"Adieu, then, worthy friend," said the magistrate of Bâle; "it grieves me to part with you thus, but evil fate will have it so. Yonder grassy avenue will conduct you to the old hunting-seat, where Heaven send that you may pass a quiet night; for, apart from other risks, men say that these ruins have no good name. Will you yet permit your niece, since such the young person is, to pass to Bâle for the night in my company?"

"If we are disturbed by beings like ourselves," said Arnold Biederman, "we have strong arms, and heavy partisans; if we should be visited, as your words would imply, by those of a different description, we have, or should have, good consciences, and confidence in Heaven. — Good friends, my brethren on this embassy, have I spoken your sentiments as well as mine own?"

The other deputies intimated their assent to what their companion had said, and the citizens of Bâle took a courteous farewell of their guests, endeavouring, by the excess of civility, to atone for their deficiency in effective hospitality. After their departure, Rudolph was the first to express his sense of their pusillanimous behaviour, on which he had been silent during their presence. "Coward dogs!" he said; "may the Butcher of Burgundy flay the very skins from them with his exactions, to teach them to disown old friendships, rather than abide the lightest blast of a tyrant's anger!"

"And not even their own tyrant either," said another of the group, — for several of the young men had gathered round their seniors, to hear the welcome which they expected from the magistrates of Bâle.

"No," replied Ernest, one of Arnold Biederman's sons, "they do not pretend that their own prince the Emperor hath interfered with them; but a word of the Duke of Burgundy, which should be no more to them than a breath of wind from the west, is sufficient to stir them to such brutal inhospitality. It were well to march to the city, and compel them at the sword's point to give us shelter."

A murmur of applause arose amongst the youth around, which awakened the displeasure of Arnold Biederman.

"Did I hear," he said, "the tongue of a son of mine, or was it that of a brutish Lanz-knecht,[4] who has no pleasure but in battle or violence? Where is the modesty of the youth of Switzerland, who were wont to wait the signal for action till it pleased the elders of the canton to give it, and were as gentle as maidens till the voice of their patriarchs bade them be bold as lions?"

"I meant no harm, father," said Ernest, abashed with this rebuke, "far less any slight towards you; but I must needs say" —

"Say not a word, my son," replied Arnold, "but leave our camp to-morrow by break of day; and, as thou takest thy way back to Geierstein, to which I command thine instant return, remember, that he is not fit to visit strange countries, who cannot rule his tongue before his own countrymen, and to his own father."

The Banneret of Berne, the Burgess of Soleure, even the long-bearded Deputy from Schwitz, endeavoured to intercede for the offender, and obtain a remission of his banishment; but it was in vain.

"No, my good friends and brethren, no," replied Arnold. "These young men require an example; and though I am grieved in one sense that the offence has chanced within my own family, yet I am pleased in another light, that the delinquent should be one over whom I can exercise full authority, without suspicion of partiality. — Ernest, my son, thou hast heard my commands: Return to Geierstein with the morning's light, and let me find thee an altered man when I return thither."

The young Swiss, who was evidently much hurt and shocked at this public affront, placed one knee on the ground, and kissed his father's right hand, while Arnold, without the slightest sign of anger, bestowed his blessing upon him; and Ernest, without a word of remonstrance, fell into the rear of the party. The deputation then proceeded down the avenue which had been pointed out to them, and at the bottom of which arose the massy ruins of Graffs-lust; but there was not enough of day-

---

[4] A private soldier of the German infantry.

light remaining to discern their exact form. They could observe as they drew nearer, and as the night became darker, that three or four windows were lighted up, while the rest of the front remained obscured in gloom. When they arrived at the place, they perceived it was surrounded by a large and deep moat, the sullen surface of which reflected, though faintly, the glimmer of the lights within.

CHAPTER IX

Francisco. — Give you good-night.

Marcellus. — O, farewell, honest soldier.
Who hath relieved you?

Francisco. — Give you good-night; Bernardo hath
my place

HAMLET.

The first occupation of our travellers was to find the means of crossing the moat; and they were not long of discovering the *tête-du-pont* on which the drawbridge, when lowered, had formerly rested. The bridge itself had been long decayed, but a temporary passage of fir-trees and planks had been constructed, apparently very lately, which admitted them to the chief entrance of the castle. On entering it, they found a wicket opening under the archway, which, glimmering with light, served to guide them to a hall prepared evidently for their accommodation as well as circumstances had admitted of.

A large fire of well-seasoned wood burned blithely in the chimney, and had been maintained so long there that the air of the hall, notwithstanding its great size and somewhat ruinous aspect, felt mild and genial. There was also at the end of the apartment, a stack of wood, large enough to maintain the fire had they been to remain there a week. Two or three long tables in the hall stood covered and ready for their reception; and, on looking more closely, several large hampers were found in a corner, containing cold provisions of every kind, prepared with great care, for their immediate use. The eyes of the good Burgess of Soleure twinkled when he beheld the young men in the act of transferring the supper from the hampers, and arranging it on the table.

"Well," said he, "these poor men of Bâle have saved their character; since, if they have fallen short in welcome, they have abounded in good cheer."

"Ah, friend!" said Arnold Biederman, "the absence of the landlord is a great deduction from the entertainment. Better half an apple from the hand of your host, than a bridal feast without his company."

"We owe them the less for their banquet," said the Banneret.

"But, from the doubtful language they held, I should judge it meet to keep a strong guard to-night, and even that some of our young men should, from time to time, patrol around the old ruins. The place is strong and defensible, and so far our thanks are due to those who have acted as our quarter-masters. We will, however, with your permission, my honoured brethren, examine the house within, and then arrange regular guards and patrols. — To your duty then, young men, and search these ruins carefully, — they may, perchance, contain more than ourselves; for we are now near one who, like a pilfering fox, moves more willingly by night than by day, and seeks his prey amidst ruins and wildernesses rather than in the open field."

All agreed to this proposal. The young men took torches, of which a good provision had been left for their use, and made a strict search through the ruins.

The greater part of the castle was much more wasted and ruinous than the portion which the citizens of Bâle seemed to have destined for the accommodation of the embassy. Some parts were roofless, and the whole desolate. The glare of light — the gleam of arms — the sound of the human voice, and echoes of mortal tread, startled from their dark recesses bats, owls, and other birds of ill omen, the usual inhabitants of such time-worn edifices, whose flight through the desolate chambers repeatedly occasioned alarm amongst those who heard the noise without seeing the cause, and shouts of laughter when it became known. They discovered that the deep moat surrounded their place of retreat on all sides, and of course that they were in safety against any attack which could be made from without, except it was attempted by the main entrance, which it was easy to barricade, and guard with sentinels. They also ascertained by strict search, that though it was possible an individual might be concealed amid such a waste of ruins, yet it was altogether impossible that any number which might be formidable to so large a party as their own, could have remained there without a certainty of discovery. These particulars were reported to the Banneret, who directed Donnerhugel to take charge of a body of six of the young men, such as he should himself choose, to patrol on the outside of the building till the first cock-crowing, and at that hour to return to the castle, when the same number were to take the duty till morning dawned, and then be relieved in their turn.

Rudolph declared his own intention to remain on guard the whole night; and as he was equally remarkable for vigilance as for strength and courage, the external watch was considered as safely provided for, it being settled that, in case of any sudden encounter, the deep and hoarse sound of the Swiss bugle should be the signal for sending support to the patrolling party.

Within side the castle, the precautions were taken with equal vigilance. A sentinel, to be relieved every two hours, was appointed to take post at the principal gate, and other two kept watch on the other side of the castle, although the moat appeared to ensure safety in that quarter.

These precautions being taken, the remainder of the party sat down to refresh themselves, the deputies occupying the upper part of the hall, while those of their escort modestly arranged themselves in the lower end of the same large apartment. Quantities of hay and straw, which were left piled in the wide castle, were put to the purpose for which undoubtedly they had been destined by the citizens of Bâle, and, with the aid of cloaks and mantles, were judged excellent good bedding by a hardy race, who, in war or the chase, were often well satisfied with a much worse night's lair.

The attention of the Bâlese had even gone so far as to provide for Anne of Geierstein separate accommodation, more suitable to her use than that assigned to the men of the party. An apartment, which had probably been the buttery of the castle, entered from the hall, and had also a doorway leading out into a passage connected with the ruins; but this last had hastily, yet carefully, been built up with large hewn stones taken from the ruins; without mortar, indeed, or any other cement, but so well secured by their own weight, that an attempt to displace them must have alarmed not only any one who might be in the apartment itself, but also those who were in the hall adjacent, or indeed in any part of the castle. In the small room thus carefully arranged and secured, there were two pallet-beds and a large fire, which blazed on the hearth, and gave warmth and comfort to the apartment. Even the means of devotion were not forgotten, a small crucifix of bronze being hung over a table, on which lay a breviary.

Those who first discovered this little place of retreat, came back loud in praise of the delicacy of the citizens of Bâle, who, while preparing for the general accommodation of the strangers, had not failed to provide separately and peculiarly for that of their female companion.

Arnold Biederman felt the kindness of this conduct. "We should pity our friends of Bâle, and not nourish resentment against them," he said. "They have stretched their kindness towards us as far as their personal apprehensions permitted; and that is saying no small matter for them, my masters, for no passion is so unutterably selfish as that of fear. — Anne, my love, thou art fatigued. Go to the retreat provided for you, and Lizette shall bring you from this abundant mass of provisions what will be fittest for your evening meal."

So saying, he led his niece into the little bedroom, and, looking round with an air of complacency, wished her good repose; but there was something on the maiden's brow which seemed to augur that her uncle's wishes would not be fulfilled. From the moment she had left Switzerland, her looks had become clouded; her intercourse with those who approached her had grown more brief and rare; her whole appearance was marked with secret anxiety or secret sorrow. This did not escape her uncle, who naturally imputed it to the pain of parting from him, which was probably soon to take place, and to her regret at leaving the tranquil spot in which so many years of her youth had been spent.

But Anne of Geierstein had no sooner entered the apartment, than her whole frame trembled violently, and the colour leaving her cheeks entirely, she sunk down on one of the pallets, where, resting her elbows on her knees, and pressing her hands on her forehead, she rather resembled a person borne down by mental distress, or oppressed by some severe illness, than one who, tired with a journey, was in haste to betake herself to needful rest. Arnold was not quick-sighted as to the many sources of female passion. He saw that his niece suffered; but imputing it only to the causes already mentioned, augmented by the hysterical effects often produced by fatigue, he gently blamed her for having departed from her character of a Swiss maiden ere she was yet out of reach of a Swiss breeze of wind.

"Thou must not let the dames of Germany or Flanders think that our daughters have degenerated from their mothers; else must we fight the battles of Sempach and Laupen over again, to convince the Emperor, and this haughty Duke of Burgundy, that our men are of the same mettle with their forefathers. And as for our parting, I do not fear it. My brother is a Count of the Empire, indeed, and therefore he roust needs satisfy himself that every thing over which he possesses any title shall be at his command, and sends for thee to prove his right of doing so. But I know him well: He will no sooner be satisfied that he may command thy attendance at pleasure, than he will concern himself about thee no more. Thee? Alas! poor thing, in what couldst thou aid his courtly intrigues and ambitious plans? No, no — thou art not for the noble Count's purpose, and must be content to trudge back to rule the dairy at Geierstein, and be the darling of thine old peasant-like uncle."

"Would to God we were there even now!" said the maiden, in a tone of wretchedness which she strove in vain to conceal or suppress.

"That may hardly be till we have executed the purpose which brought us hither," said the literal Landamman. "But lay thee on thy pallet, Anne — take a morsel of food, and three drops of wine, and thou wilt wake to-morrow, as gay as on a Swiss holiday when the pipe sounds the réveille."

Anne was now able to plead a severe headach, and declining all refreshment, which she declared herself incapable of tasting, she bade her uncle good-night. She then desired Lizette to get some food for herself, cautioning her, as she returned, to make as little noise as possible, and not to break her repose if she should have the good fortune to fall asleep. Arnold Biederman then kissed his niece, and returned to the hall, where his colleagues in office were impatient to commence an attack on the provisions which were in readiness; to which the escort of young men, diminished by the patrols and sentinels, were no less disposed than their seniors.

The signal of assault was given by the Deputy from Schwitz, the eldest of the party, pronouncing in patriarchal form a benediction over the meal. The travellers then commenced their operations with a vivacity, which showed that the uncertainty whether they should get any food, and the delays which had occurred in arranging themselves in their quarters, had infinitely increased their appetites. Even the Landamman, whose moderation sometimes approached to abstinence, seemed that night in a more genial humour than ordinary. His friend of Schwitz, after his example, ate, drank, and spoke more than usual; while the rest of the deputies pushed their meal to the verge of a carousal. The elder Philipson marked the scene with an attentive and anxious eye, confining his applications to the wine-cup to such pledges as the politeness of the times called upon him to reply to. His son had left the hall just as the banquet began, in the manner which we are now to relate.

Arthur had proposed to himself to join the youths who were to perform the duty of sentinels within, or patrols on the outside of their place of repose, and had indeed made some arrangement for that purpose with Sigismund, the third of the Landamman's sons. But while about to steal a parting glance at Anne of Geierstein, before offering his service as he proposed, there appeared on her brow such a deep and solemn expression, as diverted his thoughts from every other subject, excepting the anxious doubts as to what could possibly have given rise to such a change. The placid openness of brow; the eye which expressed conscious and fearless innocence; the lips which, seconded by a look as frank as her words, seemed ever ready to speak, in kindness and in confidence, that which the heart dictated, were for the moment entirely changed in character and expression, and in a degree and manner for which no ordinary cause could satisfactorily account. Fatigue might have banished the rose from the maiden's beautiful complexion, and sickness or pain might have dimmed her eye and clouded her brow. But the look of deep dejection with which she fixed her eyes at times on the ground, and the startled and terrified glance which she cast around her at other intervals, must have had their rise in some different source. Neither could illness or weariness explain the manner in which her lips were contracted or compressed together, like one who makes up her mind to act or be hold something that is fearful, or account for the tremor which seemed at times to steal over her insensibly, though by a strong effort she was able at intervals to throw it off. For this change of expression there must be in the heart some deeply melancholy and afflicting cause. What could that cause be?

It is dangerous for youth to behold beauty in the pomp of all her charms, with every look bent upon conquest — more dangerous to see her in the hour of unaffected and unapprehensive ease and simplicity, yielding herself to the graceful whim of the moment, and as willing to be pleased as desirous of pleasing. There are minds which may be still more affected by gazing on beauty in sorrow, and feeling that pity, that desire of comforting the lovely mourner, which the poet has described as so nearly akin to love. But to a spirit of that romantic and adventurous cast which the Middle Ages frequently produced, the sight of a young and amiable person evidently in a state of terror and suffering, which had no visible cause, was perhaps still more impressive than beauty, in her pride, her tenderness, or her sorrow. Such sentiments, it must be remembered, were not confined to the highest ranks only, but might then be found in all classes of society which were raised above the mere peasant or artisan. Young Philipson gazed on Anne of Geierstein with such intense curiosity, mingled with pity and tenderness, that the bustling scene around him seemed to vanish from his eyes, and leave no one in the noisy hall save himself and the object of his interest.

What could it be that so evidently oppressed and almost quailed a spirit so well balanced, and a courage so well tempered, when, being guarded by the swords of the bravest men perhaps to be found in Europe, and lodged in a place of strength, even the most timid of her sex might have found confidence? Surely if an attack were to be made upon them, the clamour of a conflict in such circumstances could scarce be more terrific than the roar of those cataracts which he had seen her despise? At least, he thought, she ought to be aware that there is ONE, who is bound by friendship and gratitude to fight to the death in her defence. Would to heaven, he continued in the same reverie, it were possible to convey to her, without sign or speech, the assurance of my unalterable resolution to protect her in the worst of perils! — As such thoughts streamed through his mind, Anne raised her eyes in one of those fits of deep feeling which seemed to overwhelm her; and, while she cast them round the hall, with a look of apprehension, as if she expected to see amid the well-known companions of her journey some strange and unwelcome apparition, they encountered the fixed and anxious gaze of young Philipson. They were instantly bent on the ground, while a deep blush showed how much she was conscious of having attracted his attention by her previous deportment.

Arthur, on his part, with equal consciousness, blushed as

deeply as the maiden herself, and drew himself back from her observation. But when Anne rose up, and was escorted by her uncle to her bedchamber, in the manner we have already mentioned, it seemed to Philipson as if she had carried with her from the apartment the lights with which it was illuminated, and left it in the twilight melancholy of some funeral hall. His deep musings were pursuing the subject which occupied them thus anxiously, when the manly voice of Donnerhugel spoke close in his ear —

"What, comrade, has our journey to-day fatigued you so much that you go to sleep upon your feet?"

"Now Heaven forbid, Hauptman," said the Englishman, starting from his reverie, and addressing Rudolph by this name, (signifying Captain, or literally Head-man,) which the youth of the expedition had by unanimous consent bestowed on him, — "Heaven forbid I should sleep, if there be aught like action in the wind."

"Where dost thou propose to be at cock-crow?" said the Swiss.

"Where duty shall call me, or your experience, noble Hauptman, shall appoint," replied Arthur. — "But, with your leave, I purposed to take Sigismund's guard on the bridge till midnight or morning dawn. He still feels the sprain which he received in his spring after yonder chamois, and I persuaded him to take some uninterrupted rest, as the best mode of restoring his strength."

"He will do well to keep his counsel then," again whispered Donnerhugel; "the old Landamman is not a man to make allowances for mishaps, when they interfere with duty. Those who are under his orders should have as few brains as a bull, as strong limbs as a bear, and be as impossible as lead or iron to all the casualties of life, and all the weaknesses of humanity."

Arthur replied in the same tone: — "I have been the Landamman's guest for some time, and have seen no specimens of any such rigid discipline."

"You are a stranger," said the Swiss, "and the old man has too much hospitality to lay you under the least restraint. You are a volunteer, too, in whatever share you choose to take in our sports or our military duty; and, therefore, when I ask you to walk abroad with me at the first cock-crowing, it is only in the event that such exercise shall entirely consist with your own pleasure."

"I consider myself as under your command for the time," said Philipson; "but, not to bandy courtesy, at cock-crow I shall be relieved from my watch on the drawbridge, and will be by that time glad to exchange the post for a more extended walk."

"Do you not choose more of this fatiguing, and probably unnecessary duty, than may befit your strength?" said Rudolph.

"I take no more than you do," said Arthur, "as you propose not to take rest till morning."

"True," answered Donnerhugel, "but I am a Swiss."

"And I," answered Philipson, quickly, "am an Englishman."

"I did not mean what I said in the sense you take it," said Rudolph, laughing; "I only meant, that I am more interested in this matter than you can be, who are a stranger to the cause in which we are personally engaged."

"I am a stranger, no doubt," replied Arthur; "but a stranger who has enjoyed your hospitality, and who, therefore, claims a right, while with you, to a share in your labours and dangers."

"Be it so," said Rudolph Donnerhugel. "I shall have finished my first rounds at the hour when the sentinels at the castle are relieved, and shall be ready to recommence them in your good company."

"Content," said the Englishman. "And now I will to my post, for I suspect Sigismund is blaming me already, as oblivious of my promise."

They hastened together to the gate, where Sigismund willingly yielded up his weapon and his guard to young Philipson, confirming the idea sometimes entertained of him, that he was the most indolent and least spirited of the family of Geierstein. Rudolph could not suppress his displeasure.

"What would the Landamman say," he demanded, "if he saw thee thus quietly yield up post and partisan to a stranger?"

"He would say I did well," answered the young man, nothing daunted; "for he is for ever reminding us to let the stranger have his own way in every thing; and English Arthur stands on this bridge by his own wish, and no asking of mine. — Therefore, kind Arthur, since thou wilt barter warm straw and a sound sleep for frosty air and a clear moonlight, I make thee welcome with all my heart. Hear your duty: You are to stop all who enter, or attempt to enter, or till they give the password. If they are strangers, you must give alarm. But you will suffer such of our friends as are known to you to pass outwards, without challenge or alarm, because the deputation may find occasion to send messengers abroad."

"A murrain on thee, thou lazy losel!" said Rudolph — "Thou art the only sluggard of thy kin."

"Then am I the only wise man of them all," said the youth. — "Hark ye, brave Hauptman, ye have supped this evening, — have ye not?"

"It is a point of wisdom, ye owl," answered the Bernese, "not to go into the forest fasting."

"If it is wisdom to eat when we are hungry," answered Sigismund, "there can be no folly in sleeping when we are weary." So saying, and after a desperate yawn or two, the relieved sentinel halted off, giving full effect to the sprain of which he complained.

"Yet there is strength in those loitering limbs, and valour in that indolent and sluggish spirit," said Rudolph to the Englishman. "But it is time that I, who censure others, should betake me to my own task. — Hither, comrades of the watch, hither."

The Bernese accompanied these words with a whistle which brought from within six young men, whom he had previously chosen for the duty, and who, after a hurried supper, now waited his summons. One or two of them had large bloodhounds or lyme-dogs, which, though usually employed in the pursuit of animals of chase, were also excellent for discovering ambuscades, in which duty their services were now to be employed. One of these animals was held in a leash, by the person who, forming the advance of the party, went about twenty yards in front of them; a second was the property of Donnerhugel himself, who had the creature singularly under command. Three of his companions attended him closely, and the two others followed, one of whom bore a horn, of the Bernese wild bull, by way of bugle. This little party crossed the moat by the temporary bridge, and moved on to the verge of the forest, which lay adjacent to the castle, and the skirts of which were most likely to conceal any ambuscade that could be apprehended. The moon was now up, and near the full, so that Arthur, from the elevation on which the castle stood, could trace their slow, cautious march, amid the broad silver light, until they were lost in the depths of the forest.

When this object had ceased to occupy his eyes, the thoughts of his lonely watch again returned to Anne of Geierstein, and to the singular expression of distress and apprehension which had that evening clouded her beautiful features. Then the blush which had chased, for the moment, paleness and terror from her countenance, at the instant his eyes encountered hers — was it anger — was it modesty — was it some softer feeling, more gentle than the one, more tender than the other? Young Philipson, who, like Chaucer's Squire, was "as modest as a maid," almost trembled to give to that look the favourable interpretation, which a more self-satisfied gallant would have applied to it without scruple. No hue of rising or setting day was ever so lovely in the eyes of the young man, as that blush was in his recollection; nor did ever enthusiastic visionary, or poetical dreamer, find out so many fanciful forma in the clouds, as Arthur divined various interpretations from the indications of interest which had passed over the beautiful countenance of the Swiss maiden.

In the meantime, the thought suddenly burst on his reverie, that it could little concern him what was the cause of the perturbation she had exhibited. They had met at no distant period for the first time, — they must soon part for ever. She could be nothing more to him than the remembrance of a beautiful vision, and he could have no other part in her memory save as a stranger from a foreign land, who had been a sojourner for a season in her uncle's house, but whom she could never expect to see again. When this idea intruded on the train of romantic visions which agitated him, it was like the sharp stroke of the harpoon, which awakens the whale from slumbering torpidity into violent action. The gateway in which the young soldier kept his watch seemed suddenly too narrow for him. He rushed across the temporary bridge, and hastily traversed a short space of ground in front of the *tête-du-pont*, or defensive work, on which its outer extremity rested.

Here for a time he paced the narrow extent to which he was confined by his duty as a sentinel, with long and rapid strides, as if he had been engaged by vow to take the greatest possible quantity of exercise upon that limited space of ground. His exertion, however, produced the effect of in some degree composing his mind, recalling him to himself, and reminding him of the numerous reasons which prohibited his fixing his attention, much more his affections, upon this young person, however fascinating she was.

I have surely, he thought, as he slackened his pace, and shouldered his heavy partisan, sense enough left to recollect my condition and my duties — to think of my father, to whom I am all in all — and to think also on the dishonour which must accrue to me, were I capable of winning the affections of a frank-hearted and confiding girl, to whom I could never do justice by dedicating my life to return them. "No," he said to himself, "she will soon forget me, and I will study to remember her no otherwise than I would a pleasing dream, which hath for a moment crossed a night of perils and dangers, such as my life seems doomed to be."

As he spoke, he stopped short in his walk, and as he rested on his weapon, a tear rose unbidden to his eye, and stole down his cheek without being wiped away. But he combated this gentler mood of passion as he had formerly battled with that which was of a wilder and more desperate character. Shaking off the dejection and sinking of spirit which he felt creeping upon him, he resumed, at the same time, the air and attitude of an attentive sentinel, and recalled his mind to the duties of his watch, which, in the tumult of his feelings, he had almost forgotten. But what was his astonishment, when, an he looked out on the clear landscape, there passed from the bridge towards the forest, crossing him in the broad moonlight, the living and moving likeness of Anne of Geierstein!

CHAPTER X

We know not when we sleep nor when we wake.
Visions distinct and perfect cross our eye,
Which to the slumberer seem realities;
And while they waked, some men have seen such sights
As set at nought the evidence of sense.
And left them well persuaded they were dreaming.

ANONYMOUS.

The apparition of Anne of Geierstein crossed her lover —
her admirer, at least, we must call him — within shorter time
than we can tell the story. But it was distinct, perfect, and undoubted. In the very instant when the young Englishman, shaking off his fond despondency, raised his head to look out upon
the scene of his watch, she came from the nearer end of the
bridge, crossing the path of the sentinel, upon whom she did not
even cast a look, and passed with a rapid yet steady pace towards
the verge of the woodland.

It would have been natural, though Arthur had been directed
not to challenge persons who left the castle, but only such as
might approach it, that he should nevertheless, had it only been
in mere civility, have held some communication, however slight,
with the maiden as she crossed his post. But the suddenness of
her appearance took from him for the instant both speech and
motion. It seemed as if his own imagination had raised up a
phantom, presenting to his outward senses the form and features
which engrossed his mind; and he was silent, partly at least from
the idea, that what he gazed upon was immaterial, and not of this
world.

It would have been no less natural that Anne of Geierstein
should have in some manner acknowledged the person who had
spent a considerable time under the game roof with her, had been
often her partner in the dance, and her companion in the field;
but she did not evince the slightest token of recognition, nor even
look towards him as she passed; her eye was on the wood, to
which she advanced swiftly and steadily, and she was hidden by
its boughs ere Arthur had recollected himself sufficiently to determine what to do.

His first feeling was anger at himself for suffering her to
pass unquestioned, when it might well chance, that upon any

errand which called her forth at so extraordinary a time and place, he might have been enabled to afford her assistance, or at least advice. This sentiment was for a short time so predominant, that he ran towards the place where he had seen the skirt of her dress disappear, and whispering her name as loud as the fear of alarming the castle permitted, conjured her to return, and hear him but for a few brief moments. No answer, however, was returned; and when the branches of the trees began to darken over his head and to intercept the moonlight, he recollected that he was leaving his post, and exposing his fellow-travellers, who were trusting in his vigilance, to the danger of surprise.

He hastened, therefore, back to the castle gate, with matter for deeper and more inextricable doubt and anxiety, than had occupied him during the commencement of his watch. He asked himself in vain, with what purpose that modest young maiden, whose manners were frank, but whose conduct had always seemed so delicate and reserved, could sally forth at midnight, like a damsel-errant in romance, when she was in a strange country and suspicious neighbourhood; yet he rejected, as he would have shrunk from blasphemy, any interpretation which could have thrown censure upon Anne of Geierstein. No, nothing was she capable of doing for which a friend could have to blush. But connecting her previous agitation with the extraordinary fact of her leaving the castle, alone and defenceless, at such an hour, Arthur necessarily concluded it must argue some cogent reason, and, as was most likely, of an unpleasant nature. — "I will watch her return," he internally uttered, "and, if she will give me an opportunity, I will convey to her the assurance that there is one faithful bosom in her neighbourhood, which is bound in honour and gratitude to pour out every drop of its blood, if by doing so it can protect her from the slightest inconvenience. This is no silly flight of romance, for which common sense has a right to reproach me, it is only what I ought to do, what I must do, or forego every claim to be termed a man of honesty or honour."

Yet scarce did the young man think himself anchored on a resolution which seemed unobjectionable, than his thoughts were again adrift. He reflected that Anne might have a desire to visit the neighbouring town of Bâle, to which she had been invited the day before, and where her uncle had friends. It was indeed an uncommon hour to select for such a purpose; but Arthur was aware that the Swiss maidens feared neither solitary walks nor late hours, and that Anne would have walked among her own hills by moonlight much farther than the distance betwixt their place of encampment and Bâle, to see a sick friend, or for any similar purpose. To press himself on her confidence, then, might be impertinence, not kindness and as she had passed him without taking the slightest notice of his presence, it was evident she did not mean voluntarily to make him her confidant; and probably she was involved in no difficulties where his aid could be useful. In that case, the duty of a gentleman was to permit her to return as she had gone forth, unnoticed and unquestioned, leaving it with herself to hold communication with him or not as she should choose.

Another idea, belonging to the age, also passed through his mind, though it made no strong impression upon it. This form, so perfectly resembling Anne of Geierstein, might be a deception of the sight, or it might be one of those fantastic apparitions, concerning which there were so many tales told in all countries, and of which Switzerland and Germany had, as Arthur well knew, their full share. The internal and undefinable feelings which restrained him from accosting the maiden, as might have been natural for him to have done, are easily explained, on the supposition that his mortal frame shrunk from an encounter with a being of a different nature. There had also been some expressions of the magistrate of Bâle, which might apply to the castle's being liable to be haunted by beings from another world. But though the general belief in such ghostly apparitions prevented the Englishman from being positively incredulous on the subject, yet the instructions of his father, a man of great intrepidity and distinguished good sense, had taught him to be extremely unwilling to refer any thing to supernatural interferences, which was capable of explanation by ordinary rules; and he therefore shook off, without difficulty, any feelings of superstitious fear, which for an instant connected itself with his nocturnal adventure. He resolved finally to suppress all disquieting conjecture on the subject, and to await firmly, if not patiently, the return of the fair vision, which, if it should not fully explain the mystery, seemed at least to afford the only chance of throwing light upon it.

Fixed, therefore, in purpose, he traversed the walk which his duty permitted, with his eyes fixed on the part of the forest where he had seen the beloved form disappear, and forgetful for the moment that his watch had any other purpose than to observe her return. But from this abstraction of mind he was roused by a distant sound in the forest, which seemed the clash of armour. Recalled at once to a sense of his duty, and its importance to his father and his fellow-travellers, Arthur planted himself on the temporary bridge, where a stand could best be made, and turned both eyes and ears to watch for approaching danger. The sound of arms and footsteps came nearer — spears and helmets advanced from the greenwood glade, and twinkled in the moonlight. But the stately form of Rudolph Donnerhugel, marching in front, was easily recognised, and announced to our sentinel the return of the patrol. Upon their approach to the bridge, the challenge, and interchange of sign and countersign, which is usual on such occasions, took place in due form; and as Rudolph's party filed off one after another into the castle, he commanded them to wake their companions, with whom he intended to renew the patrol, and at the same time to send a relief to Arthur Philipson, whose watch on the bridge was now ended. This last fact was confirmed by the deep and distant toll of the Minster clock from the town of Bâle, which, prolonging its sullen sound over field and forest, announced that midnight was past.

"And now, comrade," continued Rudolph to the Englishman, "have the cold air and long watch determined thee to retire to food and rest, or dost thou still hold the intention of partaking our rounds?"

In very truth, it would have been Arthur's choice to have remained in the place where he was, for the purpose of watching Anne of Geierstein's return from her mysterious excursion. He could not easily have found an excuse for this, however, and he was unwilling to give the haughty Donnerhugel the least suspicion that he was inferior in hardihood, or in the power of enduring fatigue, to any of the tall mountaineers, whose companion he chanced to be for the present. He did not, therefore, indulge even a moment's hesitation; but while he restored the borrowed partisan to the sluggish Sigismund, who came from the castle yawning and stretching himself like one whose slumbers had been broken by no welcome summons, when they were deepest and sweetest, he acquainted Rudolph that he retained his purpose of partaking in his reconnoitring duty. They were speedily joined by the rest of the patrolling party, amongst whom was Rudiger, the eldest son of the Landamman of Unterwalden; and when, led by the Bernese champion, they had reached the skirts of the forest, Rudolph commanded three of them to attend Rudiger Biederman.

"Thou wilt make thy round to the left side," said the Bernese; "I will draw off to the right — see thou keepest a good look-out, and we will meet merrily at the place appointed. Take one of the hounds with you. I will keep Wolf-fanger, who will open on a Burgundian as readily as on a bear."

Rudiger moved off with his party to the left, according to the directions received; and Rudolph, having sent forward one of his number in front, and stationed another in the rear, commanded the third to follow himself and Arthur Philipson, who thus constituted the main body of the patrol. Having intimated to their immediate attendant to keep at such distance as to allow them freedom of conversation, Rudolph addressed the Englishman with the familiarity which their recent friendship had created. — "And now, King Arthur, what thinks the Majesty of England of our Helvetian youth? Could they win guerdon in tilt or tourney, thinkest thou, noble prince? Or would they rank but amongst the coward knights of Cornouailles?"[5]

"For tilt and tourney I cannot answer," said Arthur, summoning up his spirits to reply, "because I never beheld one of you mounted on a steed, or having spear in rest. But if strong limbs and stout hearts are to be considered, I would match you Swiss gallants with those of any country in the universe, where manhood is to be looked for, whether it be in heart or hand."

"Thou speakest us fair; and, young Englishman," said Rudolph, "know that we think as highly of thee, of which I will presently afford thee a proof. Thou talkedst but now of horses. I know but little of them; yet I judge thou wouldst not buy a steed which thou hadst only seen covered with trappings, or encumbered with saddle and bridle, but wouldst desire to look at him when stripped, and in his natural state of freedom?"

"Ay, marry, would I," said Arthur. "Thou hast spoken on that as if thou hadst been born in a district called Yorkshire,

---

[5] The chivalry of Cornwall are generally undervalued in the Norman-French romances. The cause is difficult to discover.

which men call the merriest part of merry England."

"Then I tell thee," said Rudolph Donnerhugel, "that thou hast seen our Swiss youth but half, since thou hast observed them as yet only in their submissive attendance upon the elders of their Cantons, or, at most, in their mountain sports, which, though they may show men's outward strength and activity, can throw no light on the spirit and disposition by which that strength and activity are to be guided and directed in matters of high enterprise."

The Swiss probably designed that these remarks should excite the curiosity of the stranger. But the Englishman had the image, look, and form of Anne of Geierstein, as she had passed him in the silent hours of his watch, too constantly before him, to enter willingly upon a subject of conversation totally foreign to what agitated his mind. He, therefore, only compelled himself to reply in civility, that he had no doubt his esteem for the Swiss, both aged and young, would increase in proportion with his more intimate knowledge of the nation.

He was then silent; and Donnerhugel, disappointed, perhaps, at having failed to excite his curiosity, walked also in silence by his side. Arthur, meanwhile, was considering with himself whether he should mention to his companion the circumstance which occupied his own mind, in the hope that the kinsman of Anne of Geierstein, and ancient friend of her house, might be able to throw some light on the subject.

But he felt within his mind an insurmountable objection to converse with the Swiss on a subject in which Anne was concerned. That Rudolph made pretensions to her favour could hardly be doubted; and though Arthur, had the question been put to him, must in common consistency have resigned all competition on the subject still he could not bear to think on the possibility of his rival's success, and would not willingly have endured to hear him pronounce her name.

Perhaps it was owing to this secret irritability that Arthur, though he made every effort to conceal and to overcome the sensation, still felt a secret dislike to Rudolph Donnerhugel, whose frank, but somewhat coarse familiarity, was mingled with a certain air of protection and patronage, which the Englishman thought was by no means called for. He met the openness of the Bernese, indeed, with equal frankness, but he was ever and anon tempted to reject or repel the tone of superiority by which it was accompanied. The circumstances of their duel had given the Swiss no ground for such triumph; nor did Arthur feel himself included in that roll of the Swiss youth, over whom Rudolph exercised domination, by general consent. So little did Philipson relish this affectation of superiority, that the poor jest, that termed him King Arthur, although quite indifferent to him when applied by any of the Biedermans, was rather offensive when Rudolph took the same liberty; so that he often found himself in the awkward condition of one who is internally irritated, without having any outward manner of testifying it with propriety. Undoubtedly, the root of all this tacit dislike to the young Bernese was a feeling of rivalry; but it was a feeling which Arthur dared not avow even to himself. It was sufficiently powerful, however, to suppress the slight inclination he had felt to speak with Rudolph on the passage of the night which had most interested him; and as the topic of conversation introduced by his companion had been suffered to drop, they walked on side by side in silence, "with the beard on the shoulder," as the Spaniard says — looking round, that is, on all hands; and thus performing the duty of a vigilant watch.

At length, after they had walked nearly a mile through forest and field, making a circuit around the ruins of Grafts-lust, of such an extent as to leave no room for an ambush betwixt them and the place, the old hound, led by the vidette who was foremost, stopped, and uttered a low growl.

"Flow now, Wolf-fanger!" said Rudolph, advancing. — "What, old fellow! dost thou not know friends from foes? Come, what sayest thou, on better thoughts? — Thou must not lose character in thy old age — try it again."

The dog raised his head, snuffed the air all around, as if he understood what his master had said, then shook his head and tail, as if answering to his voice.

"Why, there it is now," said Donnerhugel, patting the animal's shaggy back; "second thoughts are worth gold; thou seest it is a friend after all."

The dog again shook his tail, and moved forward with the same unconcern as before; Rudolph fell back into his place, and his companion said to him —

"We are about to meet Rudiger and our companions I suppose, and the dog hears their footsteps, though we cannot."

"It can scarcely yet be Rudiger," said the Bernese; "his walk around the castle is of a wider circumference than ours. Some one approaches, however, for Wolf-fanger is again dissatisfied. — Look sharply out on all sides."

As Rudolph gave his party the word to be on the alert, they reached an open glade, in which were scattered, at considerable distance from each other, some old pine-trees of gigantic size, which seemed yet huger and blacker than ordinary, from their broad sable tops and shattered branches being displayed against the clear and white moonlight.

"We shall here at least," said the Swiss, "have the advantage of seeing clearly whatever approaches. But I judge," said he, after looking around for a minute, "it is but some wolf or deer that has crossed our path, and the scent disturbs the hound. — Hold — stop — yes, it must be so; he goes on."

The dog accordingly proceeded, after having given some signs of doubt, uncertainty, and even anxiety. Apparently, however, he became reconciled to what had disturbed him, and proceeded once more in the ordinary manner.

"This is singular!" said Arthur Philipson; "and, to my thinking, I saw an object close by yonder patch of thicket, where, as well as I can guess, a few thorn and hazel bushes surround the stems of four or five large trees."

"My eye has been on that very thicket for these five minutes past, and I saw nothing," said Rudolph.

"Nay, but," answered the young Englishman, "I saw the object, whatever it was, while you were engaged in attending to the dog. And by your permission, I will forward and examine the spot."

"Were you, strictly speaking, under my command," said Donnerhugel, "I would command you to keep your place. If they be foes, it is essential that we should remain together. But you are a volunteer in our watch, and therefore may use your freedom."

"I thank you," answered Arthur, and sprung quickly forward.

He felt, indeed, at the moment, that he was not acting courteously as an individual, nor perhaps correctly as a soldier; and that he ought to have rendered obedience, for the time, to the captain of the party in which he had enlisted himself. But, on the other hand, the object which he had seen, though at a distance and imperfectly, seemed to bear a resemblance to the retiring form of Anne of Geierstein, as she had vanished from his eyes, an hour or two before, under the cover of the forest; and his ungovernable curiosity to ascertain whether it might not be the maiden in person, allowed him to listen to no other consideration.

Ere Rudolph had spoken out his few words of reply, Arthur was half-way to the thicket. It was, as it had seemed at a distance, of small extent, and not fitted to hide any person who did not actually couch down amongst the dwarf bushes and underwood. Any thing white, also, which bore the human size and form, must, he thought, have been discovered among the dark-red stems and swarthy-coloured bushes which were before him. These observations were mingled with other thoughts. If it was Anne of Geierstein whom he had a second time seen, she must have left the more open path, desirous probably of avoiding notice; and what right or title had he to direct upon her the observation of the patrol? He had, he thought, observed, that, in general, the maiden rather repelled than encouraged the attentions of Rudolph Donnerhugel; or, where it would have been discourteous to have rejected them entirely, that she endured without encouraging them. What, then, could be the propriety of his intruding upon her private walk, singular, indeed, from time and place, but which, on that account, she might be more desirous to keep secret from the observation of one who was disagreeable to her? Nay, was it not possible that Rudolph might derive advantage to his otherwise unacceptable suit, by possessing the knowledge of something which the maiden desired to be concealed?

As these thoughts pressed upon him, Arthur made a pause, with his eyes fixed on the thicket, from which he was now scarce thirty yards distant; and although scrutinizing it with all the keen accuracy which his uncertainty and anxiety dictated, he was actuated by a strong feeling that it would be wisest to turn back to his companions, and report to Rudolph that his eyes had deceived him.

But while he was yet undecided whether to advance or return, the object which he had seen became again visible on the verge of the thicket, and advanced straight towards him, bearing, as on the former occasion, the exact dress and figure of Anne of Geierstein! This vision — for the time, place, and suddenness of the appearance, made it seem rather an illusion than a reality — struck Arthur with surprise which amounted to terror. The figure passed within a spear's length, unchallenged by him, and giving not the slightest sign of recognition; and, directing its course to the right hand of Rudolph, and the two or three who were with him, was again lost among the broken ground and bushes.

Once more the young man was reduced to a state of the most inextricable doubt; nor was he roused from the stupor into which he was thrown, till the voice of the Bernese sounded in his ear, —

"Why, how now, King Arthur — art thou asleep, or art thou wounded?"

"Neither," said Philipson, collecting himself; "only much surprised."

"Surprised? and at what, most royal" ——

"Forbear foolery," said Arthur, somewhat sternly, "and answer as thou art a man — Did she not meet thee? — didst thou not see her?"

"See her! — see whom?" said Donnerhugel. "I saw no one. And I could have sworn you had seen no one either, for I had you in my eye the whole time of your absence, excepting two or three moments. If you saw aught, why gave you not the alarm?"

"Because it was only a woman," answered Arthur faintly.

"Only a woman!" repeated Rudolph, in a tone of contempt. "By my honest word, King Arthur, if I had not seen pretty flashes of valour fly from thee at times, I should be apt to think that thou hadst only a woman's courage thyself. Strange, that a shadow by night, or a precipice in the day, should quell so bold a spirit as thou hast often shown" ——

"And as I will ever show, when occasion demands it," interrupted the Englishman, with recovered spirit. "But I swear to you, that if I be now daunted, it is by no merely earthly fears that my mind hath been for a moment subdued."

"Let us proceed on our walk," said Rudolph; "we must not neglect the safety of our friends. This appearance, of which thou speakest, may be but a trick to interrupt our duty."

They moved on through the moonlight glades. A minute's

reflection restored young Philipson to his full recollection, and with that to the painful consciousness that he had played a ridiculous and unworthy part in the presence of the person, whom (of the male sex, at least) he would the very last have chosen as a witness of his weakness.

He ran hastily over the relations which stood betwixt himself, Donnerhugel, the Landamman, his niece, and the rest of that family; and, contrary to the opinion which he had entertained but a short while before, settled in his own mind that it was his duty to mention to the immediate leader under whom he had placed himself, the appearance which he had twice observed in the course of that night's duty. There might be family circumstances, — the payment of a vow, perhaps, or some such reason, — which might render intelligible to her connexions the behaviour of this young lady. Besides, he was for the present a soldier on duty, and these mysteries might be fraught with evils to be anticipated or guarded against; in either case, his companions were entitled to he made aware of what he had seen. It must be supposed that this resolution was adopted when the sense of duty, and of shame for the weakness which he had exhibited, had for the moment subdued Arthur's personal feelings towards Anne of Geierstein, — feelings, also, liable to be chilled by the mysterious uncertainty which the events of that evening had cast, like a thick mist, around the object of them.

While the Englishman's reflections were taking this turn, his captain or companion, after a silence of several minutes, at length addressed him.

"I believe," he said, "my dear comrade, that, as being at present your officer, I have some title to hear from you the report of what you have just now seen, since it must be something of importance which could so strongly agitate a mind so firm as yours. But if, in your own opinion it consists with the general safety to delay your report of what you have seen until we return to the castle, and then to deliver it to the private ear of the Landamman, you have only to intimate your purpose; and, far from urging you to place confidence in me personally, though I hope I am not undeserving of it, I will authorize your leaving us, and returning instantly to the castle."

This proposal touched him to whom it was made exactly in the right place. An absolute demand of his confidence might perhaps have been declined; the tone of moderate request and conciliation fell presently in with the Englishman's own reflections.

"I am sensible," he said, "Hauptman, that I ought to mention to you that which I have seen to-night; but on the first occasion, it did not fall within my duty to do so; and, now that I have a second time witnessed the same appearance, I have felt for these few seconds so much surprised at what I have seen, that even yet I can scarce find words to express it."

"As I cannot guess what you may have to say," replied the Bernese, "I must beseech you to be explicit. We are but poor readers of riddles, we thick-headed Switzers."

"Yet it is but a riddle which I have to place before you, Rudolph Donnerhugel," answered the Englishman, "and a riddle which is far beyond my own guessing at." He then proceeded, though not without hesitation, "While you were performing your first patrol amongst the ruins, a female crossed the bridge from within the castle, walked by my post without saying a single word, and vanished under the shadows of the forest."

"Ha!" exclaimed Donnerhugel, and made no farther answer.

Arthur proceeded. "Within these five minutes, the same female form passed me a second time, issuing from the little thicket and clump of firs, and disappeared without exchanging a word. Know, farther, this apparition bore the form, face, gait, and dress of your kinswoman. Anne of Geierstein."

"Singular enough," said Rudolph, in a tone of incredulity. "I must not, I suppose, dispute your word, for you would receive doubt on my part as a mortal injury — such is your northern chivalry. Yet, let me say, I have eyes as well as you, and I scarce think they quitted you for a minute. We were not fifty yards from the place where I found you standing in amazement. How, therefore, should not we also have seen that which you say and think you saw?"

"To that I can give no answer," said Arthur. "Perhaps your eyes were not exactly turned upon me during the short space in which I saw this form — Perhaps it might be visible — as they say fantastic appearances sometimes are — to only one person at a time."

"You suppose, then, that the appearance was imaginary, or fantastic?" said the Bernese.

"Can I tell you?" replied the Englishman. "The Church gives its warrant that there are such things; and surely it is more natural to believe this apparition to be an illusion, than to suppose that Anne of Geierstein, a gentle and well-nurtured maiden, should be traversing the woods at this wild hour, when safety and propriety so strongly recommend her being within doors."

"There is much in what you say," said Rudolph; "and yet there are stories afloat, though few care to mention them, which seem to allege that Anne of Geierstein is not altogether such as other maidens; and that she has been met with, in body and spirit, where she could hardly have come by her own unassisted efforts."

"Ha!" said Arthur; "so young, so beautiful, and already in league with the destroyer of mankind? It is impossible."

"I said not so," replied the Bernese; "nor have I leisure at present to explain my meaning more fully. As we return to the Castle of Graffs-lust, I may have an opportunity to tell you more. But I chiefly brought you on this patrol to introduce you to some friends, whom you will be pleased to know, and who desire your acquaintance; and it is here I expect to meet them."

So saying, he turned round the projecting corner of a rock, and an unexpected scene was presented to the eyes of the young Englishman.

In a sort of nook, or corner, screened by the rocky projection, there burned a large fire of wood, and around it sat, reclined, or lay, twelve or fifteen young men in the Swiss garb, but decorated with ornaments and embroidery, which reflected back the light of the fire. The same red gleam was returned by silver wine-cups, which circulated from hand to hand with the flasks which filled them. Arthur could also observe the relics of a banquet, to which due honour seemed to have been lately rendered.

The revellers started joyfully up at the sight of Donnerhugel and his companions, and saluted him, easily distinguished as he was by his stature, by the title of Captain, warmly and exultingly uttered, while, at the same time, every tendency to noisy acclamation was cautiously suppressed. The zeal indicated that Rudolph came most welcome — the caution that he came in secret, and was to be received with mystery.

To the general greeting he answered, — "I thank you my brave comrades. Has Rudiger yet reached you?"

"Thou see'st he has not," said one of the party; "had it been so, we would have detained him here till your coming, brave Captain."

"He has loitered on his patrol," said the Bernese. "We too were delayed, yet we are here before him. I bring with me, comrades, the brave Englishman, whom I mentioned to you as a desirable associate in our daring purpose."

"He is welcome, most welcome to us," said a young man, whose richly embroidered dress of azure blue gave him an air of authority; "most welcome is he, if he brings with him a heart and a hand to serve our noble task."

"For both I will be responsible," said Rudolph. "Pass the wine-cup, then, to the success of our glorious enterprise, and the health of this our new associate!"

While they were replenishing the cups with wine of a quality far superior to any which Arthur had yet tasted in these regions, he thought it right, before engaging himself in the pledge, to learn the secret object of the association which seemed desirous of adopting him.

"Before I engage my poor services to you, fair sirs, since it pleases you to desire them, permit me," he said, "to ask the purpose and character of the undertaking in which they are to be employed?"

"Shouldst thou have brought him hither," said the cavalier in blue to Rudolph, "without satisfying him and thyself on that point?"

"Care not thou about it, Lawrenz," replied the Bernese; "I know my man. — Be it known, then, to you, my good friend," he continued, addressing the Englishman, "that my comrades and I are determined at once to declare the freedom of the Swiss commerce, and to resist to the death, if it be necessary, all unlawful and extortionate demands on the part of our neighbours."

"I understand so much," said the young Englishman, "and that the present deputation proceeds to the Duke of Burgundy with remonstrances to that effect."

"Hear me," replied Rudolph. "The question is like to be brought to a bloody determination long ere we see the Duke of Burgundy's most august and most gracious countenance. That his influence should be used to exclude us from Bâle, a neutral town, and pertaining to the empire, gives us cause to expect the worst reception when we enter his own dominions. We have even reason to think that we might have suffered from his hatred already, but for the vigilance of the ward which we have kept. Horsemen, from the direction of La Ferette, have this night reconnoitred our posts; and had they not found us prepared, we had, without question, been attacked in our quarters. But since we have escaped to-night, we must take care for to-morrow. For this purpose, a number of the bravest youth of the city of Bâle, incensed at the pusillanimity of their magistrates, are determined to join us, in order to wipe away the disgrace which the cowardly inhospitality of their magistracy has brought on their native place."

"That we will do ere the sun, that will rise two hours hence, shall sink into the western sky," said the cavalier in blue; and those around joined him in stern assent.

"Gentle sirs," replied Arthur, when there was a pause, "let me remind you, that the embassy which you attend is a peaceful one, and that those who act as its escort ought to avoid any thing which can augment the differences which it comes to reconcile. You cannot expect to receive offence in the Duke's dominions, the privileges of envoys being respected in all civilized countries; and you will, I am sure, desire to offer none."

"We may be subjected to insult, however," replied the Bernese, "and that through your concerns, Arthur Philipson, and those of thy father."

"I understand you not," replied Philipson.

"Your father," answered Donnerhugel, "is a merchant, and bears with him wares of small bulk but high value?"

"He does so," answered Arthur; "and what of that?"

"Marry," answered Rudolph, "that if it be not better looked to, the Bandog of Burgundy is like to fall heir to a large proportion of your silks, satins, and jewellery work."

"Silks, satins, and jewels!" exclaimed another of the revellers; "such wares will not pass toll-free where Archibald of Hagenbach hath authority."

"Fair sirs," resumed Arthur, after a moment's consideration, "these wares are my father's property, not mine; and it is for him, not me, to pronounce how much of them he might be content to part with in the way of toll, rather than give occasion to a fray, in which his companions, who have received him into their society, must be exposed to injury as well as himself. I can only say, that he has weighty affairs at the court of Burgundy, which must render him desirous of reaching it in peace with all men; and it is my private belief that rather than incur the loss and danger of a broil with the garrison of La Ferette, he would be contented to sacrifice all the property which he has at present with him. Therefore, I must request of you, gentlemen, a space to consult his pleasure on this occasion; assuring you, that if it be his will to resist the payment of these duties to Burgundy, you shall find in me one who is fully determined to fight to the last drop of his blood."

"Good King Arthur," said Rudolph; "thou art a dutiful observer of the Fifth Commandment, and thy days shall be long in the land. Do not suppose us neglectful of the same duty, although, for the present, we conceive ourselves bound, in the first place, to attend to the weal of our country, the common parent of our fathers and ourselves. But as you know our profound respect for the Landamman, you need not fear that we shall willingly offer him offence, by rashly engaging in hostilities, or without some weighty reason; and an attempt to plunder his guest would have been met, on his part, with resistance to the death. I had hoped to find both you and your father prompt enough to resent such a gross injury. Nevertheless, if your father inclines to present his fleece to be shorn by Archibald of Hagenbach, whose scissors, he will find, clip pretty closely, it would be unnecessary and uncivil in us to interpose. Meantime, you have the advantage of knowing, that in case the Governor of La Ferette should be disposed to strip you of skin as well as fleece, there are more men close at hand than you looked for, whom you will find both able and willing to render you prompt assistance."

"On these terms," said the Englishman, "I make my acknowledgments to these gentlemen of Bâle, or whatever other country hath sent them forth, and pledge them in a brotherly cup to our farther and more intimate acquaintance."

"Health and prosperity to the United Cantons, and their friends!" answered the Blue Cavalier. "And death and confusion to all besides."

The cups were replenished; and instead of a shout of applause, the young men around testified their devoted determination to the cause which was thus announced, by grasping each other's hands, and then brandishing their weapons with a fierce yet noiseless gesture.

"Thus," said Rudolph Donnerhugel, "our illustrious ancestors, the fathers of Swiss independence, met in the immortal field of Rutli, between Uri and Unterwalden. Thus they swore to each other, under the blue firmament of heaven, that they would restore the liberty of their oppressed country; and history can tell how well they kept their word."

"And she shall record," said the Blue Cavalier, "how well the present Switzers can preserve the freedom which their fathers won. — Proceed in your rounds, good Rudolph, and be assured, that at the signal of the Hauptman, the soldiers will not be far absent; — all is arranged as formerly, unless you have new orders to give us."

"Hark thee hither, Lawrenz," said Rudolph to the Blue Cavalier, — and Arthur could hear him say, — "Beware, my friend, that the Rhine wine be not abused; — if there is too much provision of it, manage to destroy the flasks; — a mule may stumble, thou knowest, or so. Give not way to Rudiger in this. He is grown a wine-bibber since he joined us. We must bring both heart and hand to what may be done to-morrow." — They then whispered so low that Arthur could hear nothing of their farther conference, and bid each other adieu, after clasping hands, as if they were renewing some solemn pledge of union.

Rudolph and his party then moved forward, and were scarce out of sight of their new associates, when the vidette, or foremost of their patrol, gave the signal of alarm. Arthur's heart leaped to his lips — "It is Anne of Geierstein!" he said, internally.

"The dogs are silent," said the Bernese. "Those who approach must be the companions of our watch."

They proved, accordingly, to be Rudiger and his party, who, halting on the appearance of their comrades, made and underwent a formal challenge; such advance had the Swiss already made in military discipline, which was but little and rudely studied by the infantry in other parts of Europe. Arthur could hear Rudolph take his friend Rudiger to task for not meeting him at the halting-place appointed. "It leads to new revelry on your arrival," he said, "and to-morrow must find us cool and determined."

"Cool as an icicle, noble Hauptman," answered the son of

the Landamman, "and determined as the rock it hangs upon."

Rudolph again recommended temperance, and the young Biederman promised compliance. The two parties passed each other with friendly though silent greeting; and there was soon a considerable distance between them.

The country was more open on the side of the castle, around which their duty now led them, than where it lay opposite to the principal gate. The glades were broad, the trees thinly scattered over pasture land, and there were no thickets, ravines, or similar places of ambush, so that the eye might, in the clear moonlight, well command the country.

"Here," said Rudolph, "we may judge ourselves secure enough for some conference; and therefore may I ask thee, Arthur of England, now thou hast seen us more closely, what thinkest thou of the Switzer youth? If thou hast learned less than I could have wished, thank thine own uncommunicative temper, which retired in some degree from our confidence."

"Only in so far as I could not have answered, and therefore ought not to have received it," said Arthur.

"The judgment I have been enabled to form amounts, in few words, to this: Your purposes are lofty and noble as your mountains; but the stranger from the low country is not accustomed to tread the circuitous path by which you ascend them. My foot has been always accustomed to move straight forward upon the greensward."

"You speak in riddles," answered the Bernese.

"Not so," returned the Englishman. "I think you ought plainly to mention to your seniors, (the nominal leaders of young men who seem well disposed to take their own road,) that you expect an attack in the neighbourhood of La Ferette, and hope for assistance from some of the townsmen of Bâle."

"Ay, truly," answered Donnerhugel; "and the Landamman would stop his journey till he dispatched a messenger for a safe-conduct to the Duke of Burgundy; and should he grant it, there were an end of all hope of war."

"True," replied Arthur; "but the Landamman would thereby obtain his own principal object, and the sole purpose of the mission — that is, the establishment of peace."

"Peace — peace?" answered the Bernese, hastily. "Were my wishes alone to be opposed to those of Arnold Biederman, I know so much of his honour and faith, I respect so highly his valour and patriotism, that at his voice I would sheathe my sword, even if my most mortal enemy stood before me. But mine is not the single wish of a single man; the whole of my canton, and that of Soleure, are determined on war. It was by war, noble war, that our fathers came forth from the house of their captivity — it was by war, successful and glorious war, that a race, who had been held scarce so much worth thinking on as the oxen which they goaded, emerged at once into liberty and consequence, and were honoured because they were feared, as much as they had been formerly despised because they were unresisting."

"This may be all very true," said the young Englishman; "but, in my opinion, the object of your mission has been determined by your Diet or House of Commons. They have resolved to send you with others as messengers of peace; but you are secretly blowing the coals of war; and while all, or most of your senior colleagues are setting out to-morrow in expectation of a peaceful journey, you stand prepared for a combat, and look for the means of giving cause for it."

"And is it not well that I do stand so prepared?" answered Rudolph. "If our reception in Burgundy's dependencies be peaceful, as you say the rest of the deputation expect, my precautions will be needless; but at least they can do no harm. If it prove otherwise, I shall be the means of averting a great misfortune from my colleagues, my kinsman Arnold Biederman, my fair cousin Anne, your father, yourself — from all of us in short, who are joyously travelling together."

Arthur shook his head. "There is something in all this," he said, "which I understand not, and will not seek to understand. I only pray that you will not make toy father's concerns the subject of breaking truce; it may, as you hint, involve the Landamman in a quarrel, which he might otherwise have avoided. I am sure my father will never forgive it."

"I have pledged my word," said Rudolph, "already to that effect. But if he should like the usage of the Bandog of Burgundy less than you seem to apprehend he will, there is no harm in your knowing, that, in time of need, he may be well and actively supported."

"I am greatly obliged by the assurance," replied the Englishman.

"And thou mayest thyself, my friend," continued Rudolph, "take a warning from what thou hast heard: Men go not to a bridal in armour, nor to a brawl in silken doublet."

"I will be clad to meet the worst," said Arthur; "and for that purpose I will don a light hauberk of well-tempered steel, proof against spear or arrow; and I thank you for your kindly counsel."

"Nay, thank not me," said Rudolph; "I were ill deserving to be a leader did I not make those who are to follow me — more especially so trusty a follower as thou art — aware of the time when they should buckle on their armour, and prepare for hard blows."

Here the conversation paused for a moment or two, neither of the speakers being entirely contented with his companion, although neither pressed any further remark.

The Bernese, judging from the feelings which he had seen predominate among the traders of his own country, had entertained little doubt that the Englishman, finding himself powerfully supported in point of force, would have caught at the opportunity to resist paying the exorbitant imposts with which he was threatened at the next town, which would probably, without any effort on Rudolph's part, have led to breaking off the truce on the part of Arnold Biederman himself, and to an instant declaration of hostilities. On the other hand, young Philipson could not understand or approve of Donnerhugel's conduct, who, himself a member of a peaceful deputation, seemed to be animated with the purpose of seizing an opportunity to kindle the flames of war.

Occupied by these various reflections, they walked side by side for some time without speaking together, until Rudolph broke silence.

"Your curiosity is then ended, Sir Englishman," said he, "respecting the apparition of Anne of Geierstein?"

"Far from it," replied Philipson; "but I would unwillingly intrude any questions on you while you are busy with the duties of your patrol."

"That may be considered as over," said the Bernese, "for there is not a bush near us to cover a Burgundian knave, and a glance around us from time to time is all that is now needful to prevent surprise. And so, listen while I tell a tale, never sung or

144

harped in hall or bower, and which, I begin to think, deserves as much credit, at least, as is due to the Tales of the Round Table, which ancient troubadours and minne-singers dole out to us as the authentic chronicles of your renowned namesake.

"Of Anne's ancestors on the male side of the house," continued Rudolph, "I dare say you have heard enough, and are well aware how they dwelt in the old walls at Geierstein beside the cascade, grinding their vassals, devouring the substance of their less powerful neighbours, and plundering the goods of the travellers whom ill luck sent within ken of the vulture's eyry, the one year; and in the next, wearying the shrines for mercy for their trespasses, overwhelming the priests with the wealth which they showered upon them, and, finally, vowing vows, and making pilgrimages, sometimes as palmers, sometimes as crusaders, as far as Jerusalem itself, to atone for the iniquities which they had committed without hesitation or struggle of conscience."

"Such, I have understood," replied the young Englishman, "was the history of the house of Geierstein, till Arnold, or his immediate ancestors, exchanged the lance for the sheep-hook."

"But it is said," replied the Bernese, "that the powerful and wealthy Barons of Arnheim, of Swabia, whose only female descendant became the wife to Count Albert of Geierstein, and the mother of this young person, whom Swiss call simply Anne, and Germans Countess Anne of Geierstein, were nobles of a different caste. They did not restrict their lives within the limits of sinning and repenting, — of plundering harmless peasants, and pampering fat monks; but were distinguished for something more than building castles with dungeons and folter-kammers, or torture-chambers, and founding monasteries with Galilees and Refectories.

"These same Barons of Arnheim were men who strove to enlarge the boundaries of human knowledge, and converted their castle into a species of college, where there were more ancient volumes than the monks have piled together in the library of St. Gall. Nor were their studies in books alone. Deep buried in their private laboratories, they attained secrets which were afterwards transmitted through the race from father to son, and were supposed to have approached nearly to the deepest recesses of alchymy. The report of their wisdom and their wealth was often brought to the Imperial footstool; and in the frequent disputes which the Emperors maintained with the Popes of old, it is said they were encouraged, if not instigated, by the counsels of the Barons of Arnheim, and supported by their treasures. It was, perhaps, such a course of politics, joined to the unusual and mysterious studies which the family of Arnheim so long pursued, which excited against them the generally received opinion, that they were assisted in their superhuman researches by supernatural influences. The priests were active in forwarding this cry against men, who, perhaps, had no other fault than that of being wiser than themselves.

" 'Look what guests,' they said, 'are received in the halls of Arnheim! Let a Christian knight, crippled in war with the Saracens, present himself on the drawbridge, he is guerdoned with a crust and a cup of wine, and required to pass on his way. If a palmer, redolent of the sanctity acquired by his recent visits to the most holy shrines, and by the sacred relics which attest and reward his toil, approach the unhallowed walls, the warder bends his crossbow, and the porter shuts the gate, as if the wandering saint brought the plague with him from Palestine. But comes there a gray-bearded, glib-tongued Greek, with his parchment scrolls, the very letters of which are painful to Christian eyes — comes there a Jewish Rabbin, with his Talmud and Cabala — comes there a swarthy sunburnt Moor, who can boast of having read the language of the Stars in Chaldea, the cradle of astrological science — Lo, the wandering impostor or sorcerer occupies the highest seat at the Baron of Arnheim's board, shares with him the labours of the alembic and the furnace, learns from him mystic knowledge, like that of which our first parents participated to the overthrow of their race, and requites it with lessons more dreadful than he receives, till the profane host has added to his hoard of unholy wisdom, all that the pagan visitor can communicate. And these things are done in Almain, which is called the Holy Roman Empire, of which so many priests are princes! — they are done, and neither ban nor monition is issued against a race of sorcerers, who, from age to age, go on triumphing in their necromancy!'

"Such arguments, which were echoed from mitred Abbots to the cell of Anchorites, seem, nevertheless, to have made little impression on the Imperial council. But they served to excite the zeal of many a Baron and Free Count of the Empire, who were taught by them to esteem a war or feud with the Barons of Arnheim as partaking of the nature, and entitled to the immunities, of a crusade against the enemies of the Faith, and to regard an attack upon these obnoxious potentates, as a mode of clearing off their deep scores with the Christian Church. But the Lords of Arnheim, though not seeking for quarrel, were by no means unwarlike, or averse to maintaining their own defence. Some, on the contrary, belonging to this obnoxious race, were not the less distinguished as gallant knights and good men-at-arms. They were, besides, wealthy, secured and strengthened by great alliances, and in an eminent degree wise and provident. This the parties who assailed them learned to their cost.

"The confederacies formed against the Lords of Arnheim were broken up; the attacks which their enemies meditated were anticipated and disconcerted; and those who employed actual violence were repelled with signal loss to the assailants; until at length an impression was produced in their neighbourhood, that by their accurate information concerning meditated violence, and their extraordinary powers of resisting and defeating it, the obnoxious Barons must have brought to their defence means which merely human force was incapable of overthrowing; so that, becoming as much feared as hated, they were suffered for the last generation to remain unmolested. And this was the rather the case, that the numerous vassals of this great house were perfectly satisfied with their feudal superiors, abundantly ready to rise in their defence, and disposed to believe, that, whether their lords were sorcerers or no, their own condition would not be mended by exchanging their government, either for the rule of the crusaders in this holy warfare, or that of the churchmen by whom it was instigated. The race of these barons ended in Herman von Arnheim, the maternal grandfather of Anne of Geierstein. He was buried with his helmet, sword, and shield, as is the German custom with the last male of a noble family.

"But he left an only daughter, Sybilla of Arnheim, to inherit a considerable portion of his estate; and I never heard that the strong imputation of sorcery which attached to her house, prevented numerous applications, from persons of the highest distinction in the Empire, to her legal guardian the Emperor, for the rich heiress's hand in marriage. Albert of Geierstein, however, though an exile, obtained the preference. He was gallant and handsome, which recommended him to Sybilla; and the Emperor, bent at the time on the vain idea of recovering his authority in the Swiss mountains, was desirous to show himself generous to Albert, whom he considered as a fugitive from his country for espousing the Imperial cause. You may thus see, most noble King Arthur, that Anne of Geierstein, the only child of their marriage, descends from no ordinary stock; and that circumstances in which she may be concerned, are not to be explained or judged of so easily, or upon the same grounds of reasoning, as in the case of ordinary persons."

"By my honest word, Sir Rudolph of Donnerhugel," said Arthur, studiously labouring to keep a command upon his feelings, "I can see nothing in your narrative, and understand nothing from it, unless it be, that because in Germany, as in other countries, there have been fools who have annexed the idea of witchcraft and sorcery to the possession of knowledge and wisdom, you are therefore disposed to stigmatize a young maiden, who has always been respected and beloved by those around her, as a disciple of arts which, I trust, are as uncommon as unlawful."

Rudolph paused ere he replied.

"I could have wished," he said, "that you had been satisfied with the general character of Anne of Geierstein's maternal family, as offering some circumstances which may account for what you have, according to your own report, this night witnessed, and I am really unwilling to go into more particular details. To no one can Anne of Geierstein's fame be so dear as to me. I am, after her uncle's family, her nearest relative, and had she remained in Switzerland, or should she, as is most probable, return thither after the present visit to her father, perhaps our connexion might be drawn yet closer. This has, indeed, only been prevented by certain prejudices of her uncle's respecting her father's authority, and the nearness of our relationship, which, however, comes within reach of a license very frequently obtained. But I only mention these things, to show you how much more tender I must necessarily hold Anne of Geierstein's reputation, than it is possible for you to do, being a stranger, known to her but a short while since, and soon to part with her, as I understand your purpose, for ever."

The turn taken in this kind of apology irritated Arthur so

highly, that it required all the reasons which recommended coolness, to enable him to answer with assumed composure.

"I can have no ground, Sir Hauptman," he said, "to challenge any opinion which you may entertain of a young person with whom you are so closely connected, as you appear to be with Anne of Geierstein. I only wonder that, with such regard for tier as your relationship implies, you should be disposed to receive, on popular and trivial traditions, a belief which must injuriously affect your kinswoman, more especially one with whom you intimate a wish to form a still more close connexion. Bethink you, sir, that in all Christian lands, the imputation of sorcery is the most foul which can be thrown on Christian man or woman."

"And I am so far from intimating such an imputation," said Rudolph, somewhat fiercely, "that, by the good sword I wear, he that dared give breath to such a thought against Anne of Geierstein, must undergo my challenge, and take my life, or lose his own. But the question is not whether the maiden herself practises sorcery, which he who avers had better get ready his tomb, and provide for his soul's safety; the doubt lies here, whether, as the descendant of a family, whose relations with the unseen world are reported to have been of the closest degree, elfish and fantastical beings may not have power to imitate her form, and to present her appearance where she is not personally present — in fine, whether they have permission to play at her expense fantastical tricks, which they cannot exercise over other mortals, whose forefathers have ever regulated their lives by the rules of the Church, and died in regular communion with it. And as I sincerely desire to retain your esteem, I have no objection to communicate to you more particular circumstances respecting her genealogy, confirming the idea I have now expressed. But you will understand they are of the most private nature, and that I expect secrecy under the strictest personal penalty."

"I shall be silent, sir," replied the young Englishman, still struggling with suppressed passion, "on every thing respecting the character of a maiden whom I am bound to respect so highly. But the fear of no man's displeasure can add a feather's weight to the guarantee of my own honour."

"Be it so," said Rudolph; "it is not my wish to awake angry feelings; but I am desirous, both for the sake of your good opinion, which I value, and also for the plainer explanation of what I have darkly intimated, to communicate to you what otherwise I would much rather have left untold."

"You must be guided by your own sense of what is necessary and proper in the case," answered Philipson; "but remember I press not on your confidence for the communication of any thing that ought to remain secret, far less where that young lady is the subject."

Rudolph answered, after a minute's pause, — "Thou hast seen and heard too much, Arthur, not to learn the whole, or at least all that I know, or apprehend on the mysterious subject. It is impossible but the circumstances must at times recur to your recollection, and I am desirous that you should possess all the information necessary to understand them as clearly as the nature of the facts will permit. We have yet, keeping leftward to view the bog, upwards of a mile to make ere the circuit of the castle is accomplished. It will afford leisure enough for the tale I have to tell."

"Speak on — I listen!" answered the Englishman, divided between his desire to know all that it was possible to learn concerning Anne of Geierstein, and his dislike to hear her name pronounced with such pretensions as those of Donnerhugel, together with the revival of his original prejudices against the gigantic Swiss, whose manners, always blunt, nearly to coarseness, seemed now marked by assumed superiority and presumption. Arthur listened, however, to his wild tale, and the interest which he took in it soon overpowered all other sensations.

CHAPTER XI

DONNERHUGEL'S NARRATIVE

These be the adept's doctrines — every element
Is peopled with its separate race of spirits.
The airy Sylphs on the blue ether float;
Deep in the earthy cavern skulks the Gnome;
The sea-green Naiad skims the ocean-billow,
And the fierce fire is yet a friendly home
To its peculiar sprite — the Salamander.

ANONYMOUS.

I told you, (said Rudolph,) that the Lords of Arnheim, though from father to son they were notoriously addicted to secret studies, were, nevertheless, like the other German nobles, followers of war and the chase. This was peculiarly the case with Anne's maternal grandfather, Herman of Arnheim, who prided himself on possessing a splendid stud of horses, and one steed in particular, the noblest ever known in these circles of Germany. I should make wild work were I to attempt a description of such an animal, so I will content myself with saying his colour was jet-black, without a hair of white either on his face or feet. For this reason, and the wildness of his disposition, his master had termed him Apollyon; a circumstance which was secretly considered as tending to sanction the evil reports which touched the house of Arnheim, being, it was said, the naming of a favourite animal after a foul fiend.

It chanced, one November day, that the Baron had been hunting in the forest, and did not reach home till nightfall. There were no guests with him, for, as I hinted to you before, the Castle of Arnheim seldom received any other than those from whom its inhabitants hoped to gain augmentation of knowledge. The Baron was seated alone in his hall, illuminated with cressets and torches. His one hand held a volume covered with characters unintelligible to all save himself. The other rested on the marble table, on which was placed a flask of Tokay wine. A page stood in respectful attendance near the bottom of the large and dim apartment, and no sound was heard save that of the night wind, when it sighed mournfully through the rusty coats of mail, and waved the tattered banners which were the tapestry of the feudal hall. At once the footstep of a person was heard ascending the stairs in haste and trepidation; the door of the hall was thrown violently open, and, terrified to a degree of ecstasy, Caspar, the head of the Baron's stable, or his master of horse, stumbled up almost to the foot of the table at which his lord was seated, with the exclamation in his mouth, —

"My lord, my lord, a fiend is in the stable!"

"What means this folly?" said the Baron, arising, surprised and displeased at an interruption so unusual.

"Let me endure your displeasure," said Caspar, "If I speak not truth! Apollyon" ——

Here he paused.

"Speak out, thou frightened fool," said the Baron; "is my horse sick, or injured?"

The master of the stalls again gasped forth the word, "Apollyon!"

"Say on," said the Baron; "were Apollyon in presence personally, it were nothing to shake a brave man's mind."

"The devil," answered the master of the horse, "is in Apollyon's stall!"

"Fool!" exclaimed the nobleman, snatching a torch from the wall; "what is it that could have turned thy brain in such silly fashion? Things like thee, that are born to serve us, should hold their brains on a firmer tenure, for our sakes, if not for that of their worthless selves."

As he spoke, he descended to the court of the castle, to visit the stately range of stables which occupied all the lower part of the quadrangle on one side. He entered, where fifty gallant steeds stood in rows, on each side of the ample hall. At the side of each stall hung the weapons of offence and defence of a man-at-arms, as bright as constant attention could make them, together with the buff-coat which formed the trooper's under garment. The Baron, followed by one or two of the domestics, who had assembled full of astonishment at the unusual alarm, hastened up to the head of the stable betwixt the rows of steeds. As he approached the stall of his favourite horse, which was the uppermost of the right-hand row, the gallant steed neither neighed, nor shook his head, nor stamped with his foot, nor gave the usual signs of joy at his lord's approach; a faint moaning, as if he implored assistance, was the only acknowledgment he gave of the

Baron's presence.

Sir Herman held up the torch, and discovered that there was indeed a tall dark figure standing in the stall, resting his hand on the horse's shoulder. "Who art thou," said the Baron, "and what dost thou here?"

"I seek refuge and hospitality," replied the stranger; "and I conjure thee to grant it me, by the shoulder of thy horse, and by the edge of thy sword, and so as they may never fail thee when thy need is at the utmost!"

"Thou art, then, a brother of the Sacred Fire," said Baron Herman of Arnheim; "and I may not refuse thee the refuge which thou requirest of me, after the ritual of the Persian Magi. From whom, and for what length of time, dost thou crave my protection?"

"From those," replied the stranger, "who shall arrive in quest of me before the morning cock shall crow, and for the full space of a year and a day from this period."

"I may not refuse thee," said the Baron, "consistently with my oath and my honour. For a year and a day I will be thy pledge, and thou shalt share with me roof and chamber, wine and food. But thou, too, must obey the law of Zoroaster, which, as it says, Let the Stronger protect the weaker brother, says also, let the Wiser instruct the brother who hath less knowledge. I am the stronger, and thou shalt be safe under my protection; but thou art the wiser, and must instruct me in the more secret mysteries."

"You mock your servant," said the stranger visitor; "but if aught is known to Dannischemend which can avail Herman, his instructions shall be as those of a father to a son."

"Come forth, then, from thy place of refuge," said the Baron of Arnheim. "I swear to thee by the sacred fire which lives without terrestrial fuel, and by the fraternity which is betwixt us, and by the shoulder of my horse, and the edge of my good sword, I will be thy warrand for a year and a day, if so far my power shall extend."

The stranger came forth accordingly; and those who saw the singularity of his appearance, scarce wondered at the fears of Caspar, the stall-master, when he found such a person in the stable, by what mode of entrance he was unable to conceive. When he reached the lighted hall, to which the Baron conducted him, as he would have done a welcome and honoured guest, the stranger appeared to be very tall, and of a dignified aspect. His dress was Asiatic, being a long black caftan, or gown, like that worn by Armenians, and a lofty square cap, covered with the wool of Astracan lambs. Every article of the dress was black, which gave relief to the long white beard, that flowed down over his bosom. His gown was fastened by a sash of black silk network, in which, instead of a poniard or sword, was stuck a silver case, containing writing materials, and a roll of parchment. The only ornament of his apparel consisted in a large ruby of uncommon brilliancy, which, when he approached the light, seemed to glow with such liveliness, as if the gem itself had emitted the rays which it only reflected back. To the offer of refreshment the stranger replied, "Bread I may not eat, water shall not moisten my lips, until the avenger shall have passed by the threshold."

The Baron commanded the lamps to be trimmed, and fresh torches to be lighted, and sending his whole household to rest, remained seated in the hall along with the stranger, his suppliant. At the dead hour of midnight, the gates of the castle were shaken as by a whirlwind, and a voice, as of a herald, was heard to demand a herald's lawful prisoner, Dannischemend, the son of Hali. The warder then heard a lower window of the hall thrown open, and could distinguish his master's voice addressing the person who had thus summoned the castle. But the night was so dark that he might not see the speakers, and the language which they used was either entirely foreign, or so largely interspersed with strange words, that he could not understand a syllable which they said. Scarce five minutes had elapsed, when he who was without again elevated his voice as before, and said in German, "For a year and a day, then, I forbear my forfeiture; — but coming for it when that time shall elapse, I come for my right, and will no longer be withstood."

From that period, Dannischemend, the Persian, was a constant guest at the castle of Arnheim, and, indeed, never for any visible purpose crossed the drawbridge. His amusements, or studies, seemed centred in the library of the castle, and in the laboratory, where the Baron sometimes toiled in conjunction with him for many hours together. The inhabitants of the castle could find no fault in the Magus, or Persian, excepting his apparently dispensing with the ordinances of religion, since he neither went to mass nor confession, nor attended upon other religious ceremonies. The chaplain did indeed profess himself satisfied with the state of the stranger's conscience; but it had been long suspected, that the worthy ecclesiastic held his easy office on the very reasonable condition of approving the principles, and asserting the orthodoxy, of all guests whom the Baron invited to share his hospitality.

It was observed that Dannischemend was rigid in paying his devotions, by prostrating himself in the first rays of the rising sun, and that he constructed a silver lamp of the most beautiful proportions, which he placed on a pedestal, representing a truncated column of marble, having its base sculptured with hieroglyphical imagery. With what essences he fed this flame was unknown to all, unless perhaps to the Baron; but the flame was more steady, pure, and lustrous, than any which was ever seen, excepting the sun of heaven itself; and it was generally believed that the Magian made it an object of worship in the absence of that blessed luminary. Nothing else was observed of him, unless that his morals seemed severe, his gravity extreme, his general mode of life very temperate, and his fasts and vigils of frequent recurrence. Except on particular occasions, he spoke to no one of the castle but the Baron; but as he had money, and was liberal, he was regarded by the domestics with awe indeed, but without fear or dislike.

Winter was succeeded by spring, summer brought her flowers, and autumn her fruits, which ripened and were fading, when a foot-page, who sometimes attended them in the laboratory to render manual assistance when required, heard the Persian say to the Baron of Arnheim, "You will do well, my son, to mark my words; for my lessons to you are drawing to an end, and there is no power on earth which can longer postpone my fate."

"Alas, my master!" said the Baron, "and must I then lose the benefit of your direction, just when your guiding hand becomes necessary to place me on the very pinnacle of the temple of wisdom?"

"Be not discouraged, my son," answered the sage; "I will bequeath the task of perfecting you in your studies to my daughter, who will come hither on purpose. But remember, if you value the permanence of your family, look not upon her as aught else than a helpmate in your studies; for if you forget the instructress in the beauty of the maiden, you will be buried with your sword and your shield, as the last male of your house; and farther evil, believe me, will arise; for such alliances never come to a happy issue, of which my own is an example. — But hush, we are observed."

The household of the castle of Arnheim having but few things to interest them, were the more eager observers of those which came under their notice; and when the termination of the period when the Persian was to receive shelter in the castle began to approach, some of the inmates, under various pretexts, but which resolved into very terror, absconded, while others held themselves in expectation of some striking and terrible catastrophe. None such, however, took place; and, on the expected anniversary, long ere the witching hour of midnight, Dannischemend terminated his visit in the castle of Arnheim, by riding away from the gate in the guise of an ordinary traveller. The Baron had meantime taken leave of his tutor with many marks of regret, and some which amounted even to sorrow. The sage Persian comforted him by a long whisper, of which the last part only was heard, — "By the first beam of sunshine she will be with you. Be kind to her, but not over kind." He then departed, and was never again seen or heard of in the vicinity of Arnheim.

The Baron was observed during all the day after the departure of the stranger to be particularly melancholy. He remained, contrary to his custom, in the great hall, and neither visited the library nor the laboratory, where he could no longer enjoy the company of his departed instructor. At dawn of the ensuing morning. Sir Herman summoned his page, and, contrary to his habits, which used to be rather careless in respect of apparel, he dressed himself with great accuracy; and, as he was in the prime of life, and of a noble figure, he had reason to be satisfied with his appearance. Having performed his toilet, he waited till the sun had just appeared above the horizon, and, taking from the table the key of the laboratory, which the page believed must have lain there all night, he walked thither, followed by his attendant. At the door, the Baron made a pause, and seemed at one time to doubt whether he should not send away the page, at another to hesitate whether he should open the door, as one might do who expected some strange sight within. He pulled up resolution, however, turned the key, threw the door open, and entered. The page followed close behind his master, and was astonished to the point of extreme terror at what he beheld, although the sight, however extraordinary, had in it nothing save what was agreeable and lovely.

The silver lamp was extinguished, or removed from its pedestal, where stood in place of it a most beautiful female figure in the Persian costume, in which the colour of pink predominated. But she wore no turban or headdress of any kind, saving a blue ribbon drawn through her auburn hair, and secured by a gold clasp, the outer side of which was ornamented by a superb opal, which, amid the changing lights peculiar to that gem, displayed internally a slight tinge of red like a spark of fire.

The figure of this young person was rather under the middle size, but perfectly well formed; the Eastern dress, with the wide trowsers gathered round the ankles, made visible the smallest and most beautiful feet which had ever been seen, while hands and arms of the most perfect symmetry were partly seen from under the folds of the robe. The little lady's countenance was of a lively and expressive character, in which spirit and wit seemed to predominate; and the quick dark eye, with its beautifully formed eyebrow, seemed to presage the arch remark, to which the rosy and half smiling lip appeared ready to give utterance.

The pedestal on which she stood, or rather was perched, would have appeared unsafe had any figure heavier than her own been placed there. But, however she had been transported thither, she seemed to rest on it as lightly and safely as a linnet, when it has dropped from the sky on the tendril of a rose-bud. The first beam of the rising sun, falling through a window directly opposite to the pedestal, increased the effect of this beautiful figure, which remained as motionless as if it had been carved in marble. She only expressed her sense of the Baron of Arnheim's presence by something of a quicker respiration, and a deep blush, accompanied by a alight smile.

Whatever reason the Baron of Arnheim might have for expecting to see some such object as now exhibited its actual presence, the degree of beauty which it presented was so much beyond his expectation, that for an instant he stood without breath or motion. At once, however, he seemed to recollect that it was his duty to welcome the fair stranger to his castle, and to relieve her from her precarious situation. He stepped forward accordingly with the words of welcome on his tongue, and was extending his arms to lift her from the pedestal, which was nearly six feet high; but the light and active stranger merely accepted the support of his hand, and descended on the floor as light and as safe as if she had been formed of gossamer. It was, indeed, only by the momentary pressure of her little hand, that the Baron of Arnheim was finally made sensible that he had to do with a being of flesh and blood.

"I am come as I have been commanded," she said, looking around her. "You must expect a strict and diligent mistress, and I hope for the credit of an attentive pupil."

After the arrival of this singular and interesting being in the castle of Arnheim, various alterations took place within the interior of the household. A lady of high rank and small fortune, the respectable widow of a Count of the Empire, who was the Baron's blood relation, received and accepted an invitation to preside over her kinsman's domestic affairs, and remove, by her countenance, any suspicions which might arise from the presence of Hermione, as the beautiful Persian was generally called.

The Countess Waldstetten carried her complaisance so far, as to be present on almost all occasions, whether in the laboratory or library, when the Baron of Arnheim received lessons from, or pursued studies with, the young and lovely tutor who had been thus strangely substituted for the aged Magus. If this lady's report was to be trusted, their pursuits were of a most extraordinary nature, and the results which she sometimes witnessed, were such as to create fear as well as surprise. But she strongly vindicated them from practising unlawful arts, or overstepping the boundaries of natural science.

A better judge of such matters, the Bishop of Bamberg himself, made a visit to Arnheim, on purpose to witness the wisdom of which so much was reported through the whole Rhine-country. He conversed with Hermione, and found her deeply impressed with the truths of religion, and so perfectly acquainted with its doctrines, that he compared her to a doctor of theology in the dress of an Eastern dancing-girl. When asked regarding her knowledge of languages and science, he answered, that he had been attracted to Arnheim by the most extravagant reports on these points, but that he must return, confessing "the half thereof had not been told unto him."

In consequence of this indisputable testimony, the sinister reports which had been occasioned by the singular appearance of the fair stranger, were in a great measure lulled to sleep, especially as her amiable manners won the involuntary good-will of every one that approached her.

Meantime a marked alteration began to take place in the interviews between the lovely tutor and her pupil. These were conducted with the same caution as before, and never, so far as could be observed, took place without the presence of the Countess of Waldstetten, or some other third person of respectability. But the scenes of these meetings were no longer the scholar's library, or the chemist's laboratory; — the gardens, the groves, were resorted to for amusement, and parties of hunting and fishing, with evenings spent in the dance, seemed to announce that the studies of wisdom were for a time abandoned for the pursuits of pleasure. It was not difficult to guess the meaning of this; the Baron of Arnheim and his fair guest, speaking a language different from all others, could enjoy their private conversation, even amid all the tumult of gaiety around them; and no one was surprised to hear it formally announced, after a few weeks of gaiety, that the fair Persian was to be wedded to the Baron of Arnheim.

The manners of this fascinating young person were so pleasing, her conversation so animated, her wit so keen, yet so well tempered with good nature and modesty, that, notwithstanding her unknown origin, her high fortune attracted less envy than might have been expected in a case so singular. Above all, her generosity amazed and won the hearts of all the young persons who approached her. Her wealth seemed to be measureless, for the many rich jewels which she distributed among her fair friends would otherwise have left her without ornaments for herself. These good qualities, her liberality above all, together with a simplicity of thought and character, which formed a beautiful contrast to the depth of acquired knowledge which she was well known to possess, — these, and her total want of ostentation, made her superiority be pardoned among her companions. Still there was notice taken of some peculiarities, exaggerated perhaps by envy, which seemed to draw a mystical distinction between the beautiful Hermione and the mere mortals with whom she lived and conversed.

In the merry dance she was so unrivalled in lightness and

agility, that her performance seemed that of an aerial being. She could, without suffering from her exertion, continue the pleasure till she had tired out the most active revellers; and even the young Duke of Hochspringen, who was reckoned the most indefatigable at that exercise in Germany, having been her partner for half an hour, was compelled to break off the dance, and throw himself, totally exhausted, on a couch, exclaiming, he had been dancing not with a woman, but with an *ignis fatuus.*

Other whispers averred, that while she played with her young companions in the labyrinth and mazes of the castle gardens at hide-and-seek, or similar games of activity, she became animated with the same supernatural alertness which was supposed to inspire her in the dance. She appeared amongst her companions, and vanished from them, with a degree of rapidity which was inconceivable; and hedges, treillage, or such like obstructions, were surmounted by her in a manner which the most vigilant eye could not detect; for, after being observed on the side of the barrier at one instant, in another she was beheld close beside the spectator.

In such moments, when her eyes sparkled, her cheeks reddened, and her whole frame became animated, it was pretended that the opal clasp amid her tresses, the ornament which she never laid aside, shot forth the little spark, or tongue of flame, which it always displayed, with an increased vivacity. In the same manner, if in the half-darkened hall the conversation of Hermione became unusually animated, it was believed that the jewel became brilliant, and even displayed a twinkling and flashing gleam which seemed to be emitted by the gem itself, and not produced in the usual manner, by the reflection of some external light. Her maidens were also heard to surmise, that when their mistress was agitated by any hasty or brief resentment, (the only weakness of temper which she was sometimes observed to display,) they could observe dark-red sparks flash from the mystic brooch, as if it sympathized with the wearer's emotions. The women who attended on her toilet farther reported that this gem was never removed but for a few minutes, when the Baroness's hair was combed out; that she was unusually pensive and silent during the time it was laid aside, and particularly apprehensive when any liquid was brought near it. Even in the use of holy water at the door of the church, she was observed to omit the sign of the cross on the forehead, for fear, it was supposed, of the water touching the valued jewel.

These singular reports did not prevent the marriage of the Baron of Arnheim from proceeding as had been arranged. It was celebrated in the usual form, and with the utmost splendour, and the young couple seemed to commence a life of happiness rarely to be found on earth. In the course of twelve months, the lovely Baroness presented her husband with a daughter, which was to be christened Sybilla, after the Count's mother. As the health of the child was excellent, the ceremony was postponed till the recovery of the mother from her confinement; many were invited to be present on the occasion, and the castle was thronged with company.

It happened, that amongst the guests was an old lady, notorious for playing in private society the part of a malicious fairy in a minstrel's tale. This was the Baroness of Steinfeldt, famous in the neighbourhood for her insatiable curiosity and overweening pride. She had not been many days in the castle, ere, by the aid of a female attendant, who acted as an intelligencer, she had made herself mistress of all that was heard, said, or suspected, concerning the peculiarities of the Baroness Hermione. It was on the morning of the day appointed for the christening, while the whole company were assembled in the hall, and waiting till the Baroness should appear, to pass with them to the chapel, that there arose between the censorious and haughty dame whom we have just mentioned, and the Countess Waldstetten, a violent discussion concerning some point of disputed precedence. It was referred to the Baron von Arnheim, who decided in favour of the Countess. Madame de Steinfeldt instantly ordered her palfrey to be prepared, and her attendants to mount.

"I leave this place," she said, "which a good Christian ought never to have entered; I leave a house of which the master is a sorcerer, the mistress a demon who dares not cross her brow with holy water, and their trencher companion one, who for a wretched pittance is willing to act as matchmaker between a wizard and an incarnate fiend!"

She then departed with rage in her countenance, and spite in her heart.

The Baron of Arnheim then stepped forward, and demanded of the knights and gentlemen around, if there were any among them who would dare to make good with his sword the infamous falsehoods thrown upon himself, his spouse, and his kinswoman.

There was a general answer, utterly refusing to defend the Baroness of Steinfeldt's words in so bad a cause, and universally testifying the belief of the company that she spoke in the spirit of calumny and falsehood.

"Then let that lie fall to the ground, which no man of courage will hold up," said the Baron of Arnheim; "only, all who are here this morning shall be satisfied whether the Baroness Hermione doth or doth not share the rites of Christianity."

The Countess of Waldstetten made anxious signs to him while he spoke thus; and when the crowd permitted her to approach near him, she was heard to whisper, "O, be not rash! try no experiment! there is something mysterious about that opal talisman; be prudent, and let the matter pass by."

The Baron, who was in a more towering passion than well became the wisdom to which he made pretence — although it will be perhaps allowed, that an affront so public, and in such a time and place, was enough to shake the prudence of the most staid, and the philosophy of the most wise — answered sternly and briefly, "Are you, too, such a fool?" and retained his purpose.

The Baroness of Arnheim at this moment entered the hall, looking just so pale from her late confinement, as to render her lovely countenance more interesting, if less animated, than usual. Having paid her compliments to the assembled company, with the most graceful and condescending attention, she was beginning to inquire why Madame de Steinfeldt was not present, when her husband made the signal for the company to move forward to the chapel, and lent the Baroness his arm to bring up the rear. The chapel was nearly filled by the splendid company, and all eyes were bent on their host and hostess, as they entered the place of devotion immediately after four young ladies, who supported the infant babe in a light and beautiful litter.

As they passed the threshold, the Baron dipt his finger in the font-stone, and offered holy water to his lady, who accepted it, as usual, by touching his finger with her own. But then, as if to confute the calumnies of the malevolent lady of Steinfeldt, with an air of sportive familiarity which was rather unwarranted by the time and place, he flirted on her beautiful forehead a drop or two of the moisture which remained on his own hand. The opal, on which one of these drops had lighted, shot out a brilliant spark like a falling star, and became the instant afterwards lightless and colourless as a common pebble, while the beautiful Baroness sunk on the floor of the chapel with a deep sigh of pain. All crowded around her in dismay. The unfortunate Hermione was raised from the ground, and conveyed to her chamber; and so much did her countenance and pulse alter, within the short time necessary to do this, that those who looked upon her pronounced her a dying woman. She was no sooner in her own apartment than she requested to be left alone with her husband. He remained an hour in the room, and when he came out he locked and double locked the door behind him. He then betook himself to the chapel, and remained shore for an hour or more, prostrated before the altar.

In the meantime most of the guests had dispersed in dismay; though some abode out of courtesy or curiosity. There was a general sense of impropriety in suffering the door of the sick lady's apartment to remain locked; but, alarmed at the whole circumstances of her illness, it was some time ere any one dared disturb the devotions of the Baron. At length medical aid arrived, and the Countess of Waldstetten took upon her to demand the key. She spoke more than once to a man, who seemed incapable of hearing, at least of understanding what she said. At length he gave her the key, and added sternly, as he did so, that all aid was unavailing, and that it was his pleasure that all strangers should leave the castle. There were few who inclined to stay, when, upon opening the door of the chamber in which the Baroness had been deposited little more than two hours before, no traces of her could be discovered, unless that there was about a handful of light gray ashes, like such as might have been produced by burning fine paper, found on the bed where she had been laid. A solemn funeral was nevertheless performed, with masses, and all other spiritual rites, for the soul of the high and noble Lady Hermione of Arnheim; and it was exactly on that same day three years that the Baron himself was laid in the grave of the same chapel of Arnheim, with sword, shield, and helmet, as the last male of his family.

Here the Swiss paused, for they were approaching the bridge of the castle of Graffs-lust.

CHAPTER XII

—— Believe me, sir,
It carries a rare form — But 'tis a spirit.

THE TEMPEST.

There was a short silence after the Bernese had concluded his singular tale. Arthur Philipson's attention had been gradually and intensely attracted by a story, which was too much in unison with the received ideas of the age to be encountered by the unhesitating incredulity with which it must have been heard in later and more enlightened times.

He was also considerably struck by the manner in which it had been told by the narrator, whom he had hitherto only regarded in the light of a rude huntsman or soldier; whereas he now allowed Donnerhugel credit for a more extensive acquaintance with the general manners of the world than he had previously anticipated. The Swiss rose in his opinion as a man of talent, but without making the slightest progress in his affections. "The swash-buckler," he said to himself, "has brains, as well as brawn and bones, and is fitter for the office of commanding others than I formerly thought him." Then, turning to his companion, he thanked him for the tale, which had shortened the way in so interesting a manner.

"And it is from this singular marriage," he continued, "that Anne of Geierstein derives her origin?"

"Her mother," answered the Swiss, "was Sybilla of Arnheim, the infant at whose christening the mother died — disappeared — or whatever you may list to call it. The barony of Arnheim, being a male fief, reverted to the Emperor. The castle has never been inhabited since the death of the last lord; and has, as I have heard, become in some sort ruinous. The occupations of its ancient proprietors, and, above all, the catastrophe of its last inhabitant, have been thought to render it no eligible place of residence."

"Did there appear any thing preternatural," said the Englishman, "about the young Baroness, who married the brother of the Landamman?"

"So far as I have heard," replied Rudolph, "there were strange stories. It was said that the nurses, at the dead of night, have seen Hermione, the last Baroness of Arnheim, stand weeping by the side of the child's cradle, and other things to the same purpose. But here I speak from less correct information than that from which I drew my former narrative."

"And since the credibility of a story, not very probable in itself, must needs be granted, or withheld, according to the evidence on which it is given, may I ask you," said Arthur, "to tell me what is the authority on which you have so much reliance?"

"Willingly," answered the Swiss. "Know that Theodore Donnerhugel, the favourite page of the last Baron of Arnheim, was my father's brother. Upon his master's death, he retired to his native town of Berne, and most of his time was employed in training me up to arms and martial exercises, as well according to the fashion of Germany as of Switzerland, for he was master of all. He witnessed with his own eyes, and heard with his own ears, great part of the melancholy and mysterious events which I have detailed to you. Should you ever visit Berne, you may see the good old man."

"You think, then," said Arthur, "that the appearance which I have this night seen is connected with the mysterious marriage of Anne of Geierstein's grandfather?"

"Nay," replied Rudolph, "think not that I can lay down any positive explanation of a thing so strange. I can only say, that unless I did you the injustice to disbelieve your testimony respecting the apparition of this evening, I know no way to account for it, except by remembering that there is a portion of the young lady's blood which is thought not to be derived from the race of Adam, but more or less directly from one of those elementary spirits which have been talked of both in ancient and modern times. But I may be mistaken. We will see how she bears herself in the morning, and whether she carries in her looks the weariness and paleness of a midnight watcher. If she doth not, we may be authorized in thinking, either that your eyes have strangely deceived you, or that they have been cheated by some spectral appearance, which is not of this world."

To this the young Englishman attempted no reply, nor was there time for any; for they were immediately afterwards challenged by the sentinel from the drawbridge.

The question, "Who goes there?" was twice satisfactorily answered, before Sigismund would admit the patrol to cross the drawbridge.

"Ass and mule that thou art," said Rudolph, "what was the meaning of thy delay?"

"Ass and mule thyself, Hauptman!" said the Swiss, in answer to this objurgation. "I have been surprised by a goblin on my post once to-night already, and I have got so much experience upon that matter, that I will not easily be caught a second time."

"What goblin, thou fool," said Donnerhugel; "would be idle enough to play his gambols at the expense of so very poor an animal as thou art?"

"Thou art as cross as my father, Hauptman," replied Sigismund, "who cries fool and blockhead at every word I speak; and yet I have lips, teeth, and tongue to speak with, just like other folk."

"We will not contest the matter, Sigismund," said Rudolph. "It is clear, that if thou dost differ from other people, it is in a particular which thou canst be hardly expected to find out or acknowledge. But what, in the name of simplicity, is it which hath alarmed thee on thy post?"

"Marry, thus it was, Hauptman," returned Sigismund Biederman. "I was something tired, you see, with looking up at the broad moon, and thinking what in the universe it could be made of, and how we came to see it just as well here as at home, this place being so many miles from Geierstein. I was tired, I say, of this and other perplexing thoughts, so I drew my fur cap down over my ears, for I promise you the wind blew shrill; and then I planted myself firm on my feet, with one of my legs a little advanced, and both my hands resting on my partisan, which I placed upright before me to rest upon; and so I shut mine eyes."

"Shut thine eyes, Sigismund, and thou upon thy watch!" exclaimed Donnerhugel.

"Care not thou for that," answered Sigismund; "I kept my ears open. And yet it was to little purpose, for something came upon the bridge with a step as stealthy as that of a mouse. I looked up with a start at the moment it was opposite to me, and when I looked up — whom think you I saw?"

"Some fool like thyself," said Rudolph, at the same time pressing Philipson's foot to make him attend to the answer; a hint which, is little necessary, since he waited for it in the utmost agitation. Out it came at last.

"By Saint Mark, it was our own Anne of Geierstein!"

"It is impossible!" replied the Bernese.

"I should have said so too," quoth Sigismund, "for I had peeped into her bedroom before she went thither, and it was so bedizened that a queen or a princess might have slept in it; and why should the wench get out of her good quarters, with all her friends about her to guard her, and go out to wander in the forest?"

"May be," said Rudolph, "she only looked from the bridge to see how the night waned."

"No," said Sigismund; "she was returning from the forest. I saw her when she reached the end of the bridge, and thought of striking at her, conceiving it to be the devil in her likeness. But I remembered my halberd is no birch switch to chastise boys and girls with; and had I done Anne any harm, you would all have been angry with me, and, to speak truth, I should have been ill pleased with myself; for although she doth make a jest of me now and then, yet it were a dull house ours were we to lose Anne."

"Ass," answered the Bernese, "didst thou speak to this form, or goblin as you call it?"

"Indeed I did not, Captain Wiseacre. My father is ever angry with me when I speak without thinking, and I could not at that particular moment think on any thing to the purpose. Neither was there time to think, for she passed me like a snowflake upon a whirlwind. I marched into the castle after her, however, calling on her by name so the sleepers were awakened, and men flew to their arms, and there was as much confusion as if Archibald of Hagenbach had been among us with sword and pike. And who should come out of her little bedroom, as much startled and as much in a bustle as any of us, but Mrs. Anne herself! And as she protested she had never left her room that night, why I, Sigismund Biederman, was made to stand the whole blame, as if I could prevent people's ghosts from walking. But I told her my mind when I saw them all so set against me. 'And, Mistress Anne,' quoth I, 'it's well known the kindred you come of; and, after this fair notice, if you send any of your double-gangers[6] to

---

[6] Double-walkers, a name in Germany for those aërial duplicates of humanity who represent the features and appearance of other living persons.

me, let them put iron skull-caps on their heads, for I will give them the length and weight of a Swiss halberd, come in what shape they list.' However, they all cried, 'Shame on me!' and my father drove me out again, with as little remorse as if I had been the old house-dog, which had stolen in from his watch to the fireside."

The Bernese replied, with an air of coldness approaching to contempt, "You have slept on your watch, Sigismund, a high military offence, and you have dreamed while you slept. You were in good luck that the Landamman did not suspect your negligence, or, instead of being sent back to your duty like a lazy watch-dog, you might have been scourged back like a faithless one to your kennel at Geierstein, as chanced to poor Ernest for a less matter."

"Ernest has not yet gone back though," said Sigismund, "and I think he may pass as far into Burgundy as we shall do in this journey. I pray you, however, Hauptman, to treat me not dog-like, but as a man, and send some one to relieve me, instead of prating here in the cold night air. If there be any thing to do to-morrow, as I well guess there may, a mouthful of food, and a minute of sleep, will be but a fitting preparative, and I have stood watch here these two mortal hours."

With that the young giant yawned portentously, as if to enforce the reasons of his appeal.

"A mouthful and a minute?" said Rudolph, — "a roasted ox, and a lethargy like that of the Seven Sleepers would scarce restore you to the use of your refreshed and waking senses. But I am your friend, Sigismund, and you are secure in my favourable report; you shall be instantly relieved, that you may sleep, if it be possible, without disturbances from dreams. — Pass on, young men," (addressing the others, who by this time had come up,) "and go to your rest; Arthur of England and I will report to the Landamman and the Banneret the account of our patrol."

The patrol accordingly entered the castle, and were soon heard joining their slumbering companions. Rudolph Donner-hugel seized Arthur's arm, and, while they went towards the hall, whispered in his ear, —

"These are strange passages! — How think you we should report them to the deputation?"

"That I must refer to yourself," said Arthur; "you are the

captain of our watch. I have done my duty in telling you what I saw — or thought I saw — it is for you to judge how far it is fitting to communicate it to the Landamman; only, as it concerns the honour of his family, to his ear alone I think it should be confided."

"I see no occasion for that," said the Bernese, hastily; "it cannot affect or interest our general safety. But I may take occasion hereafter to speak with Anne on this subject."

This latter hint gave as much pain to Arthur, as the general proposal of silence on an affair so delicate had afforded him satisfaction. But his uneasiness was of a kind which he felt it necessary to suppress, and he therefore replied with as much composure as he could assume: —

"You will act, Sir Hauptman, as your sense of duty and delicacy shall dictate. For me, I shall be silent on what you call the strange passages of the night, rendered doubly wonderful by the report of Sigismund Biederman."

"And also on what you have seen and heard concerning our auxiliaries of Berne?" said Rudolph.

"On that I shall certainly be silent," said Arthur; "unless thus far, that I mean to communicate to my father the risk of his baggage being liable to examination and seizure at La Ferette."

"It is needless," said Rudolph; "I will answer with head and hand for the safety of every thing belonging to him."

"I thank you in his name," said Arthur; "but we are peaceful travellers, to whom it must be much more desirable to avoid a broil, than to give occasion for one, even when secure of coming out of it triumphantly."

"These are the sentiments of a merchant, but not of a soldier," said Rudolph, in a cold and displeased tone; "but the matter is your own, and you must act in it as you think best. Only remember, if you go to La Ferette without our assistance, you hazard both goods and life."

They entered, as he spoke, the apartment of their fellow-travellers. The companions of their patrol had already laid themselves down amongst their sleeping comrades at the lower end of the room. The Landamman and the Bannerman of Berne heard Donnerhugel make a report, that his patrol, both before and after midnight, had been made in safety, and without any encounter which expressed either danger or suspicion. The Bernese then wrapped him in his cloak, and, lying down on the straw, with that happy indifference to accommodation, and promptitude to seize the moment of repose, which is acquired by a life of vigilance and hardship, was in a few minutes fast asleep.

Arthur remained on foot but a little longer, to dart an earnest look on the door of Anne of Geierstein's apartment, and to reflect on the wonderful occurrences of the evening. But they formed a chaotic mystery, for which he could see no clew, and the necessity of holding instant communication with his father compelled him forcibly to turn his thoughts in that direction. He was obliged to observe caution and secrecy in accomplishing his purpose. For this he laid himself down beside his parent, whose couch, with the hospitality which he had experienced from the beginning of his intercourse with the kind-hearted Swiss, had been arranged in what was thought the most convenient place of the apartment, and somewhat apart from all others. He slept sound, but awoke at the touch of his son, who whispered to him in English, for the greater precaution, that he had important tidings for his private ear.

"An attack on our post?" — said the elder Philipson "must we take to our weapons?"

"Not now," said Arthur; "and I pray of you not to rise or make alarm — this matter concerns us alone."

"Tell it instantly, my son," replied his father; "you speak to one too much used to danger to be startled at it."

"It is a case for your wisdom to consider," said Arthur. "I had information while upon the patrol, that the Governor of La Ferette will unquestionably seize upon your baggage and merchandise, under pretext of levying dues claimed by the Duke of Burgundy. I have also been informed that our escort of Swiss youth are determined to resist this exaction, and conceive themselves possessed of the numbers and means sufficient to do so successfully."

"By St. George, that must not be!" said the elder Philipson; "it would be an evil requital to the true-hearted Landamman, to give the fiery Duke a pretext for that war which the excellent old man is so anxiously desirous to avoid, if it be possible. Any exactions, however unreasonable, I will gladly pay. But to have my papers seized on were utter ruin. I partly feared this, and it made me unwilling to join myself to the Landamman's party. We must now break off from it. This rapacious governor will not surely lay hands on the deputation which seeks his master's court under protection of the law of nations; but I can easily see how he might make our presence with them a pretext for quarrel, which will equally suit his own avaricious spirit and the humour of these fiery young men, who are seeking for matter of offence. This shall not be taken for our sake. We will separate ourselves from the deputies, and remain behind till they are passed on. If this De Hagenbach be not the most unreasonable of men, I will find a way to content him so far as we are individually concerned. Meanwhile, I will instantly wake the Landamman," he said, "and acquaint him with our purpose."

This was immediately done, for Philipson was not slow in the execution of his resolutions. In a minute he was standing by the side of Arnold Biederman, who, raised on his elbow, was listening to his communication, while, over the shoulder of the Landamman, rose the head and long beard of the deputy from Schwitz, his large clear blue eyes gleaming from beneath a fur cap, bent on the Englishman's face, but stealing a glance aside now and then to mark the impression which what was said made upon his colleague.

"Good friend and host," said the elder Philipson, "we have heard for a certainty that our poor merchandise will be subjected to taxation or seizure on our passage through La Ferette, and I would gladly avoid all cause of quarrel for your sake as well as our own."

"You do not doubt that we can and will protect you?" replied the Landamman. "I tell you, Englishman, that the guest of a Swiss is as safe by his side as an eaglet under the wing of its dam; and to leave us because danger approaches, is but a poor compliment to our courage or constancy. I am desirous of peace; but not the Duke of Burgundy himself should wrong a guest of mine, so far as my power might prevent it."

At this the deputy from Schwitz clenched a fist like a bull's knuckles, and showed it above the shoulders of his friend.

"It is even to avoid this, my worthy host," replied Philipson, "that I intend to separate from your friendly company sooner than I desire or purposed. Bethink you, my brave and worthy host, you are an ambassador seeking a national peace, I a trader seeking private gain. War, or quarrels which may cause war, are alike ruinous to your purpose and mine. I confess to you frankly, that I am willing and able to pay a large ransom, and when you are departed I will negotiate for the amount. I will abide in the town of Bâle till I have made fair terms with Archibald de Hagenbach; and even if he is the avaricious extortioner you describe him, he will be somewhat moderate with me rather than run the risk of losing his booty entirely, by my turning back, or taking another route."

"You speak wisely, Sir Englishman," said the Landamman; "and I thank you for recalling my duty to my remembrance. But you must not, nevertheless, be exposed to danger. So soon as we move forward, the country will be again open to the devastations of the Burgundian Riders and Lanz-knecht, who will sweep the roads in every direction. The people of Bâle are unhappily too timorous to protect you; they would yield you up upon the Governor's first hint; and for justice or lenity, you might as well expect it in hell as from Hagenbach."

"There are conjurations, it is said, that can make hell itself tremble," said Philipson; "and I have means to propitiate even this De Hagenbach, providing I can get to private speech with him. But, I own, I can expect nothing from his wild riders, but to be put to death for the value of my cloak."

"If that be the case," said the Landamman, "and if you must needs separate from us, for which I deny not that you have alleged wise and worthy reasons, wherefore should you not leave Graffs-lust two hours before us. The roads will be safe, as our escort is expected; and you will probably, if you travel early, find De Hagenbach sober, and as capable as he ever is of hearing reason — that is, of perceiving his own interest. But, after his breakfast is washed down with Rhinewein, which he drinks every morning before he hears mass, his fury blinds even his avarice."

"All I want, in order to execute this scheme," said Philipson, "is the loan of a mule to carry my valise, which is packed up with your baggage."

"Take the she-mule," said the Landamman; "she belongs to my brother here from Schwitz; he will gladly bestow her on thee."

"If she were worth twenty crowns, and my comrade Arnold desired me to do so," said the old whiteboard.

"I will accept her as a loan with gratitude," said the Englishman. "But how can you dispense with the use of the creature? You have only one left."

"We can easily supply our want from Bâle," said the Landamman. "Nay, we can make this little delay serve your purpose, Sir Englishman. I named for our time of departure the first hour after daybreak; we will postpone it to the second hour, which will give us enough of time to get a horse or mule, and you, Sir Philipson, space to reach La Ferette, where I trust you will have achieved your business with De Hagenbach to your contentment, and will join company again with us as we travel through Burgundy."

"If our mutual objects will permit our travelling together, worthy Landamman," answered the merchant, "I shall esteem myself most happy in becoming the partner of your journey. — And now resume the repose which I have interrupted."

"God bless you, wise and true-hearted man," said the Landamman, rising and embracing the Englishman. "Should we never meet again, I will still remember the merchant who neglected thoughts of gain, that he might keep the path of wisdom and rectitude. I know not another who would not have risked the shedding a lake of blood to save five ounces of gold. — Farewell thou, too, gallant young man. Thou hast learned among us to keep thy foot firm while on the edge of a Helvetian crag, but none can teach thee so well as thy father, to keep an upright path among the morasses and precipices of human life."

He then embraced and took a kind farewell of his friends, in which, as usual, he was imitated by his friend of Schwitz, who swept with his long beard the right and left cheeks of both the Englishmen, and again made them heartily welcome to the use of his mule. All then once more composed themselves to rest, for the space which remained before the appearance of the autumnal dawn.

CHAPTER XIII

The enmity and discord, which of late
Sprung from the rancorous outrage of your Duke
To merchants, our well-dealing countrymen, —
Who, wanting guilders to redeem their lives,
Have seal'd his rigorous statutes with their bloods,
Excludes all pity from our threatining looks.
COMEDY OF ERRORS.

The dawn had scarce begun to touch the distant horizon, when Arthur Philipson was on foot to prepare for his father's departure and his own, which, as arranged on the preceding night, was to take place two hours before the Landamman and his attendants proposed to leave the ruinous castle of Graffs-lust. It was no difficult matter for him to separate the neatly arranged packages which contained his father's effects, from the clumsy bundles in which the baggage of the Swiss was deposited. The one set of mails was made up with the neatness of men accustomed to long and perilous journeys; the other, with the rude carelessness of those who rarely left their home, and who were altogether inexperienced.

A servant of the Landamman assisted Arthur in this task, and in placing his father's baggage on the mule belonging to the bearded deputy from Schwitz. From this man also he received instructions concerning the road from Graffs-lust to Brisach, (the chief citadel of La Ferette,) which was too plain and direct to render it likely that they should incur any risk of losing their way, as had befallen them when travelling on the Swiss mountains. Every thing being now prepared for their departure, the young Englishman awakened his father, and acquainted him that all was ready. He then retired towards the chimney, while his father, according to his daily custom, repeated the prayer of St. Julian, the patron of travellers, and adjusted his dress for the journey.

It will not be wondered at, that, while the father went through his devotions, and equipped himself for travel, Arthur, with his heart full of what he had seen of Anne of Geierstein for some time before, and his brain dizzy with the recollection of the incidents of the preceding night, should have kept his eyes riveted on the door of the sleeping apartment at which he had last seen that young person disappear; that is, unless the pale, and seemingly fantastic form, which had twice crossed him so strangely, should prove no wandering spirit of the elements, but the living substance of the person whose appearance it bore. So eager was his curiosity on this subject, that he strained his eyes to the utmost, as if it had been possible for them to have penetrated through wood and walls into the chamber of the slumbering maiden, in order to discover whether her eye or cheek bore any mark that she had last night been a watcher or a wanderer.

"But that was the proof to which Rudolph appealed," he said, internally, "and Rudolph alone will have the opportunity of remarking the result. Who knows what advantage my communication may give him in his suit with yonder lovely creature? And what must she think of me, save as one light of thought and loose of tongue, to whom nothing extraordinary can chance, but he must hasten to babble it into the ears of those who are nearest to him at the moment? I would my tongue had been palsied ere I said a syllable to yonder proud, yet wily prize-fighter! I shall never see her more — that is to be counted for certain. I shall never know the true interpretation of those mysteries which hang around her. But to think I may have prated something tending to throw her into the power of yonder ferocious boor, will be a subject of remorse to me while I live."

Here he was startled out of his reverie by the voice of his father. "Why, how now, boy; art thou waking, Arthur, or sleeping on thy feet from the fatigue of last night's service?"

"Not so, my father," answered Arthur, at once recollecting himself. "Somewhat drowsy, perhaps; but the fresh morning air will soon put that to flight."

Walking with precaution through the group of sleepers who lay around, the elder Philipson, when they had gained the door of the apartment, turned back, and, looking on the straw couch which the large form of the Landamman, and the silvery beard of his constant companion, touched by the earliest beams of light, distinguished as that of Arnold Biederman, he muttered between his lips an involuntary adieu.

"Farewell, mirror of ancient faith and integrity — farewell, noble Arnold — farewell, soul of truth and candour — to whom cowardice, selfishness, and falsehood, are alike unknown!"

And farewell, thought his son, to the loveliest, and most

candid, yet most mysterious of maidens! — But the adieu, as may well be believed, was not, like that of his father, expressed in words.

They were soon after on the outside of the gate. The Swiss domestic was liberally recompensed, and charged with a thousand kind words of farewell and of remembrance to the Landamman from his English guests, mingled with hopes and wishes that they might soon meet again in the Burgundian territory. The young man then took the bridle of the mule, and led the animal forward on their journey at an easy pace, his father walking by his side.

After a silence of some minutes, the elder Philipson addressed Arthur. "I fear me," he said, "we shall see the worthy Landamman no more. The youths who attend him are bent upon taking offence — the Duke of Burgundy will not fail, I fear, to give them ample occasion — and the peace which the excellent man desires for the land of his fathers, will be shipwrecked ere they reach the Duke's presence; though even were it otherwise, how the proudest prince in Europe will brook the moody looks of burgesses and peasants, (so will Charles of Burgundy term the friends we have parted from,) is a question too easily answered. A war, fatal to the interests of all concerned, save Louis of France, will certainly take place; and dreadful must be the contest if the ranks of the Burgundian chivalry shall encounter those iron sons of the mountains, before whom so many of the Austrian nobility have been repeatedly prostrated."

"I am so much convinced of the truth of what you say, my father," replied Arthur, "that I judge even this day will not pass over without a breach of truce. I have already put on my shirt of mail, in case we should meet bad company betwixt Grafts-lust and Brisach; and I would to Heaven that you would observe the same precaution. It will not delay our journey, and I confess to you, that I, at least, will travel with much greater consciousness of safety should you do so."

"I understand you, my son," replied the elder Philipson. "But I am a peaceful traveller in the Duke of Burgundy's territories, and must not willingly suppose, that while under the shadow of his banner, I must guard myself against banditti, as if I were in the wilds of Palestine. As for the authority of his officers, and the extent of their exactions, I need not tell you that they are, in our circumstances, things to be submitted to without grief or grudging."

Leaving the two travellers to journey towards Brisach at their leisure, I must transport my readers to the eastern gate of that small town, which, situated on an eminence, had a commanding prospect on every side, but especially towards Bâle. It did not properly make a part of the dominions of the Duke of Burgundy, but had been placed in his hands in pawn or in pledge, for the repayment of a considerable sum of money, due to Charles by the Emperor Sigismund of Austria, to whom the seigniory of the place belonged in property. But the town lay so conveniently for distressing the commerce of the Swiss, and inflicting on that people, whom he at once hated and despised, similar marks of his malevolence, as to encourage a general opinion, that the Duke of Burgundy, the implacable and unreasonable enemy of these mountaineers, would never listen to any terms of redemption, however equitable or advantageous, which might have the effect of restoring to the Emperor an advanced post, of such consequence to the gratification of his dislike, as Brisach.

The situation of the little town was in itself strong, but the fortifications which surrounded it were barely sufficient to repel any sudden attack, and not adequate to resist for any length of time a formal siege. The morning beams had shone on the spire of the church for more than an hour, when a tall, thin, elderly man, wrapt in a morning gown, over which was buckled a broad belt, supporting on the left side a sword, on the right a dagger, approached the barbican of the eastern gate. His bonnet displayed a feather, which, or the tail of a fox in lieu of it, was the emblem of gentle blood throughout all Germany, and a badge highly prized by those who had a right to wear it.

The small party of soldiers who had kept watch there during the course of the preceding night, and supplied sentinels both for ward and outlook, took arms on the appearance of this individual, and drew themselves up in the form of a guard, which receives with military reverence an officer of importance. Archibald de Hagenbach's countenance, for it was the Governor himself, expressed that settled peevishness and ill temper which characterize the morning hours of a valetudinary debauchee. His head throbbed, his pulse was feverish, and his cheek was pale, —

symptoms of his having spent the last night, as was his usual custom, amid wine-stoups and flagons. Judging from the haste with which his soldiers fell into their ranks, and the awe and silence which reigned among them, it appeared that they were accustomed to expect and dread his ill humour on such occasions. He glanced at them, accordingly, an inquisitive and dissatisfied look. as if he sought something on which to vent his peevishness, and then asked for the "loitering dog Kilian."

Kilian presently made his appearance, a stout hard-favoured man-at-arms, a Bavarian by birth, and by rank the personal squire of the Governor.

"What news of the Swiss churls, Kilian?" demanded Archibald de Hagenbach. "They should, by their thrifty habits, have been on the road two hours since. Have the peasant-clods presumed to ape the manners of gentlemen, and stuck by the flask till cock-crow?"

"By my faith, it may well be," answered Kilian; "the burghers of Bâle gave them full means of carousal."

"How, Kilian? — They dared not offer hospitality to the Swiss drove of bullocks, after the charge we sent them to the contrary?"

"Nay, the Bâlese received them not into the town," replied the squire; "but I learned, by sure espial, that they afforded them means of quartering at Graffs-lust, which was furnished with many a fair gammon and pasty, to speak nought of flasks of Rhine wine, barrels of beer, and stoups of strong waters."

"The Bâlese shall answer this, Kilian," said the Governor; "do they think I am for ever to be thrusting myself between the Duke and his pleasure on their behalf? — The fat porkers have presumed too much since we accepted some trifling gifts at their hands, more for gracing of them, than for any advantage we could make of their paltry donations. Was it not the wine from Bâle which we were obliged to drink out in pint goblets, lest it should become sour before morning?"

"It was drunk out, and in pint goblets too," said Kilian; "so much I can well remember."

"Why, go to, then," said the Governor; "they shall know, these beasts of Bâle, that I hold myself no way obliged by such donations as these, and that my remembrance of the wines which I carouse, rests no longer than the headache, which the mixtures they drug me with never fail of late years to leave behind, for the next morning's pastime."

"Your excellency," replied the squire, "will make it, then, a quarrel between the Duke of Burgundy and the city of Bâle, that they gave this indirect degree of comfort and assistance to the Swiss deputation?"

"Ay, marry will I," said De Hagenbach, "unless there be wise men among them, who shall show me good reasons for protecting them. — Oh, the Bâlese do not know our Noble Duke, nor the gift he hath for chastising the gutter-blooded citizens of a free town. Thou canst tell them, Kilian, as well as any man, how he dealt with the villains of Liege, when they would needs be pragmatical."

"I will apprize them of the matter," said Kilian, "when opportunity shall serve, and I trust I shall find them in a temper disposed to cultivate your honourable friendship."

"Nay, if it is the same to them, it is quite indifferent to me, Kilian," continued the Governor; "but, methinks, whole and sound throats are worth some purchase, were it only to swallow black-puddings and schwarz-beer, to say nothing of Westphalian hams and Nierensteiner — I say, a slashed throat is a useless thing, Kilian."

"I will make the fat citizens to understand their danger, and the necessity of making interest," answered Kilian. "Sure, I am not now to learn how to turn the ball into your excellency's lap."

"You speak well," said Sir Archibald; "but how chanced it thou hast so little to say to the Switzers' leaguer? I should have thought an old trooper like thee would have made their pinions flutter amidst the good cheer thou tellest me of."

"I might as well have annoyed an angry hedgehog with my bare finger," said Kilian. "I surveyed Graffs-lust myself; — there were sentinels on the castle walls, a sentinel on the bridge, besides a regular patrol of these Swiss fellows who kept strict watch. So that there was nothing to be done; otherwise, knowing your excellency's ancient quarrel, I would have had a hit at them, when they should never have known who hurt them. — I will tell you, however, fairly, that these churls are acquiring better knowledge in the art of war than the best Ritter knight."

"Well, they will be the better worth the looking after when they arrive," said De Hagenbach; "they come forth in state doubtless, with all their finery, their wives' chains of silver, their own medals, and rings of lead and copper. — Ah, the base hinds! they are unworthy that a man of noble blood should ease them of their trash!"

"There is better ware among them, if my intelligence hath not deceived me," replied Kilian; "there are merchants" ——

"Pshaw! the packhorses of Berne and Soleure," said the Governor, "with their paltry lumber! — cloth too coarse to make covers for horses of any breeding, and linen that is more like hair-cloth than any composition of flax. I will strip them, however, were it but to vex the knaves. What! not content with claiming to be treated like an independent people, and sending forth deputies and embassies forsooth, they expect, I warrant, to make the indemnities of ambassadors cover the introduction of a cargo of their contraband commodities, and thus insult the noble Duke of Burgundy, and cheat him at the same time? But De Hagenbach is neither knight nor gentleman if he allow them to pass unchallenged."

"And they are better worth being stopped," said Kilian, "than your excellency supposes; for they have English merchants along with them, and under their protection."

"English merchants!" exclaimed De Hagenbach, his eyes sparkling with joy; "English merchants, Kilian! Men talk of Cathay and Ind, where there are mines of silver, and gold, and diamonds; but on the faith of a gentleman, I believe these brutish Islanders have the caves of treasure wholly within their own foggy land! And then the variety of their rich merchandise, — Ha, Kilian! is it a long train of mules — a jolly tinkling team? — By Our Lady's glove! the sound of it is already jingling in my ears, more musically than all the harps of all the minnesingers at Heilbron!"

"Nay, my lord, there is no great train," replied the squire; — "only two men, as I am given to understand, with scarce so much baggage as loads a mule; but, it is said, of infinite value, silk and samite, lace and furs, pearls and jewellery-work — perfumes from the East, and gold-work from Venice."

"Raptures and paradise! say not a word more," exclaimed the rapacious knight of Hagenbach; "they are all our own, Kilian! Why, these are the very men I have dreamed of twice a-week for this month past — ay, two men of middle stature, or somewhat under it — with smooth, round, fair, comely visages, having stomachs as plump as partridges, and purses as plump as their stomachs — Ha, what sayst thou to my dream, Kilian?"

"Only, that, to be quite soothfast," answered the squire, "it should have included the presence of a score, or thereabouts, of sturdy young giants as ever climbed cliff, or carried bolt to whistle at a chamois — a lusty plump of clubs, bills, and partisans, such as make shields crack like oaten cakes and helmets ring like church-bells."

"The better, knave, the better!" exclaimed the Governor rubbing his hands. "English pedlars to plunder! Swiss bullies to beat into submission! I wot well, we can have nothing of the Helvetian swine save their beastly bristles — it is lucky they bring the-e two island sheep along with them. But we must get ready our boar-spears, and clear the clipping-pens for exercise of our craft — Here, Lieutenant Schonfeldt!"

An officer stepped forth.

"How many men are here on duty?"

"About sixty," replied the officer. "Twenty out on parties in different directions, and there may be forty or fifty in their quarters."

"Order them all under arms instantly; — hark ye, not by trumpet or bugle, but by warning them individually in their quarters, to draw to arms as quietly as possible, and rendezvous here at the eastern gate. Tell the villains there is booty to be gained, and they shall have their share."

"On these terms," said Schonfeldt, "they will walk over a spider's web without startling the insect that wove it. I will collect them without loss of an instant."

"I tell thee, Kilian," continued the exulting commandant, again speaking apart with his confidential attendant, "nothing could come so luckily as the chance of this onslaught. Duke Charles desires to affront the Swiss, — not, look you, that he cares to act towards them by his own direct orders, in such a manner as might be termed a breach of public faith towards a peaceful embassy; but the gallant follower who shall save his prince the scandal of such an affair, and whose actions may be termed a mistake or misapprehension, shall, I warrant you, be accounted to have done knightly service. Perchance a frown may be passed upon him in public, but in private the Duke will know how to esteem him. — Why standest thou so silent, man, and what ails thy ugly ill-looking aspect? Thou art not afraid of twenty Switzer boys, and we at the head of such a band of spears?"

"The Swiss," answered Kilian, "will give and take good blows; yet I have no fear of them. But I like not that we should trust too much to Duke Charles. That he would be, in the first instance, pleased with any dishonour done the Swiss is likely enough; but if, as your excellency hints, he finds it afterwards convenient to disown the action, he is a prince likely to give a lively colour to his disavowal by hanging up the actors."

"Pshaw!" said the commandant, "I know where I stand. Such a trick were like enough to be played by Louis of France, but it is foreign to the blunt character of our Bold one of Burgundy. — Why the devil stand'st thou still, man, simpering like an ape at a roasted chestnut, which he thinks too warm for his fingers?"

"Your excellency is wise as well as warlike," said the esquire, "and it is not for me to contest your pleasure. But this peaceful embassy — these English merchants — if Charles goes to war with Louis, as the rumour is current, what he should most of all desire is the neutrality of Switzerland, and the assistance of England, whose King is crossing the sea with a great army. Now you, Sir Archibald of Hagenbach, may well do that in the course of this very morning, which will put the Confederated Cantons in arms against Charles, and turn the English from allies into enemies."

"I care not," said the commandant; "I know the Duke's humour well, and if he, the master of so many provinces, is willing to risk them in a self-willed frolic, what is it to Archibald de Hagenbach, who has not a foot of land to lose in the cause?"

"But you have life, my lord," said the esquire.

"Ay, life!" replied the knight; "a paltry right to exist, which I have been ready to stake every day of my life for dollars — ay, and for creutzers — and think you I will hesitate to pledge it for broad-pieces, jewels of the East, and goldsmith's work of Venice? No, Kilian; these English must be eased of their bales, that Archibald de Hagenbach may drink a purer flask than their thin Moselle, and wear a brocade doublet instead of greasy velvet. Nor is it less necessary that Kilian should have a seemly new jerkin, with a purse of ducats to jingle at his girdle."

"By my faith," said Kilian, "that last argument hath disarmed my scruples, and I give up the point, since it ill befits me to dispute with your excellency."

"To the work then," said his leader. "But stay — we must first take the Church along with us. The priest of Saint Paul's hath been moody of late, and spread abroad strange things from the pulpit, as if we were little better than common pillagers and robbers. Nay, he hath had the insolence to warn me, as he termed it, twice, in strange form. It were well to break the growling mastiff's bald head; but since that might be ill taken by the Duke, the next point of wisdom is to fling him a bone."

"He may be a dangerous enemy," said the squire, dubiously; "his power is great with the people."

"Tush!" replied Hagenbach, "I know how to disarm the shaveling. Send to him, and tell him to come hither to speak, with me. Meanwhile, have all our force under arms; let the barbican and barrier be well-manned with archers; station spearmen in the houses on each hand of the gateway; and let the street be barricaded with carts, well bound together, but placed as if they had been there by accident — place a body of determined fellows in these carts, and behind them. So soon as the merchants and their mules enter, (for that is the main point,) up with your drawbridge, down with the portcullis, send a volley of arrows among those who are without, if they make any scuffle; disarm and secure those who have entered, and are cooped up between the barricade before, and the ambush behind and around them — And *then*, Kilian" ——

"And then," said his esquire, "shall we, like merry Free Companions, be knuckle deep in the English budgets" ——

"And, like jovial hunters," replied the knight, "elbow-deep in Swiss blood."

"The game will stand at bay though," answered Kilian. "They are led by that Donnerhugel whom we have heard of, whom they call the Young Bear of Berne. They will turn to their defence."

"The better, man — wouldst thou kill sheep rather than hunt wolves? Besides, our toils are set, and the whole garrison shall assist. Shame on thee, Kilian, thou wert not wont to have so many scruples!"

"Nor have I now," said Kilian. "But these Swiss bills, and two-handed swords of the breadth of four inches, are no child's play. — And then, if you call all our garrison to the attack, to whom will your excellency intrust the defence of the other gates, and the circuit of the walls?"

"Lock, bolt, and chain up the gates," replied the Governor, "and bring the keys hither. There shall no one leave the place till this affair is over. Let some score of the citizens take arms for the duty of guarding the walls; and look they discharge it well, or I will lay a fine on them which they shall discharge to purpose."

"They will grumble," said Kilian. "They say, that not being the Duke's subjects, though the place is impledged to his Grace, they are not liable to military service."

"They lie! the cowardly slaves," answered De Hagenbach. "If I have not employed them much hitherto, it is because I scorn their assistance; nor would I now use their help, were it for any thing save to keep a watch, by looking out straight before them. Let them obey, as they respect their property, persons, and families."

A deep voice behind them repeated the emphatic language of Scripture, — "I have seen the wicked man flourish in his power even like unto a laurel, but I returned and he was not — yea, I sought him, but he was not to be found."

Sir Archibald de Hagenbach turned sternly, and encountered the dark and ominous looks of the Priest of Saint Paul's, dressed in the vestments of his order.

"We are busy, father," said the Governor, "and will hear your preachment another time."

"I come by your summons, Sir Governor," said the priest, "or I had not intruded myself, where I well knew my preachments, if you term them so, will do no good."

"O, I crave your mercy, reverend father," said De Hagenbach. "Yes, it is true that I did send for you, to desire your prayers and kind intercession with Our Lady and Saint Paul, in some transactions which are likely to occur this morning, and in which, as the Lombard says, I do espy *roba di guadagno*."

"Sir Archibald," answered the priest calmly, "I well hope and trust that you do not forget the nature of the glorified Saints so far as to ask them for their blessing upon such exploits as you have been too oft engaged in since your arrival amongst us — an event which of itself gave token of the Divine anger. Nay, lot me say, humble as I am, that decency to a servant of the altar should check you from proposing to me to put up prayers for the success of pillage and robbery."

"I understand you, father," said the rapacious Governor, "and you shall see I do. While you are the Duke's subject, you must by your office put up your prayers for his success in matters that are fairly managed. — You acknowledge this with a graceful bend of your reverend head? — Well, then, I will be as reasonable as you are. Say we desire the intercession of the good Saints, and of you, their pious orator, in something a little out of the ordinary path, and, if you will, somewhat of a doubtful complexion, — are we entitled to ask you or them for their pains and trouble without a just consideration? Surely, no. Therefore I vow and solemnly promise, that if I have good fortune in this morning's adventure, Saint Paul shall have an altar-cloth and a basin of silver, large or little, as my booty will permit — Our Lady a web of satin for a full suit, with a necklace of pearl for holidays — and thou, priest, some twenty pieces of broad English gold, for acting as go-between betwixt ourselves and the blessed Apostles, whom we acknowledge ourselves unworthy to negotiate with in our profane person. And now, Sir Priest, do we understand each other, for I have little time to lose? I know you have hard thoughts of me, but you see the devil is not quite so horrible as he is painted."

"Do we understand each other?" answered the Black Priest of Saint Paul's, repeating the Governor's question — "Alas, no! and I fear me we never shall. Hast thou never heard the words spoken by the holy hermit, Berchtold of Offringen, to the implacable Queen Agnes, who had revenged with such dreadful severity the assassination of her father, the Emperor Albert."

"Not I," returned the knight; "I have neither studied the chronicles of emperors, nor the legends of hermits; and, therefore, Sir Priest, an you like not my proposal, let us have no farther words on the matter. I am unwont to press my favours, or to deal with priests who require entreaty, when gifts are held out to them."

"Hear yet the words of the holy man," said the priest. "The time may come, and that shortly, when you would gladly desire to hear what you scornfully reject."

"Speak on, but be brief," said Archibald de Hagenbach; "and know, though thou mayest terrify or cajole the multitude, thou now speakest to one whose resolution is fixed far beyond the power of thy eloquence to melt."

"Know, then," said the Priest of Saint Paul's, "that Agnes, daughter of the murdered Albert, after shedding oceans of blood in avenging his bloody death, founded at length the rich abbey of Königsfeldt; and, that it might have a superior claim to renowned sanctity, made a pilgrimage in person to the cell of the holy hermit, and besought of him to honour her abbey by taking up his residence there. But what was his reply? — Mark it, and tremble. 'Begone, ruthless woman!' said the holy man; 'God will not be served with blood-guiltiness, and rejects the gifts which are obtained by violence and robbery. The Almighty loves mercy, justice, and humanity, and by the lovers of these only will he be worshipped.' — And now, Archibald of Hagenbach, once, twice, thrice, hast thou had warning. Live as becomes a man on whom sentence is passed, and who must expect execution."

Having spoken these words with a menacing tone and frowning aspect, the Priest of Saint Paul's turned away from the Governor, whose first impulse was to command him to be arrested. But when he recollected the serious consequences which attached to the laying violent hands on a priest, he suffered him to depart in peace, conscious that his own unpopularity might render any attempt to revenge himself an act of great rashness. He called, therefore, for a beaker of Burgundy, in which he swallowed down his displeasure, and had just returned to Kilian the cup, which he had drained to the bottom, when the warden winded a blast from the watch-tower, which betokened the arrival of strangers at the gate of the city.

CHAPTER XIV

I will resist such entertainment, till
My enemy has more power.

THE TEMPEST.

"That blast was but feebly blown," said De Hagenbach, ascending to the ramparts, from which he could see what passed on the outside of the gate; "who approaches, Kilian?"

The trusty squire was hastening to meet him with the news.

"Two men, with a mule, an it please your excellency; and merchants I presume them to be."

"Merchants? 'sdeath, villain! pedlars you mean. Heard ever man of English merchants tramping it on foot, with no more baggage than one mule can manage to carry? They must be beggarly Bohemians, or those whom the French people call Escossais. The knaves! they shall pay with the pining of their paunches for the poverty of their purses."

"Do not be too hasty, an please your excellency," quoth the squire; "small budgets hold rich goods. But rich or poor, they are our men, at least they have all the marks; the elder, well-sized, and dark-visaged, may write fifty and five years, a beard somewhat grizzled; — the younger some two-and-twenty, taller than the first, and a well-favoured lad, with a smooth chin, and light-brown mustaches."

"Let them be admitted," said the Governor, turning back in order again to descend to the street, "and bring them into the folter-kammer of the toll-house."

So saying, he betook himself to the place appointed, which was an apartment in the large tower that protected the eastern gateway, in which were deposited the rack, with various other instruments of torture, which the cruel and rapacious Governor was in the habit of applying to such prisoners from whom he was desirous of extorting either booty or information. He entered the apartment, which was dimly lighted, and had a lofty Gothic roof which could be but imperfectly seen, while nooses and cords hanging down from thence, announced a fearful connexion with various implements of rusted iron that hung round the walls, or lay scattered on the floor.

A faint stream of light, through one of the numerous and

narrow slits, or shot-holes, with which the walls were garnished, fell directly upon the person and visage of a tall swarthy man, seated in what, but for the partial illumination, would have been an obscure corner of this evil-boding apartment. His features were regular, and even handsome, but of a character peculiarly stern and sinister. This person's dress was a cloak of scarlet; his head was bare, and surrounded by shaggy locks of black, which time had partly grizzled. He was busily employed in furbishing and burnishing a broad two-handed sword, of a peculiar shape, and considerably shorter than the weapons of that kind which we have described as used by the Swiss. He was so deeply engaged in his task, that he started as the heavy door opened with a jarring noise, and the sword, escaping from his hold, rolled on the stone-floor with a heavy clash.

"Ha! Scharfgerichter," said the Knight, as he entered the folter-kammer, "thou art preparing for thy duty?"

"It would ill become your excellency's servant," answered the man, in a harsh deep tone, "to be found idle. But the prisoner is not far off, as I can judge by the fall of my sword, which infallibly announces the presence of him who shall feel its edge."

"The prisoners are at hand, Francis," replied the Governor; "but thy omen has deceived thee for once. They are fellows for whom a good rope will suffice, and thy sword drinks only noble blood."

"The worse for Francis Steinernherz," replied the official in scarlet; "I trusted that your excellency, who have ever been a bountiful patron, should this day have made me noble."

"Noble!" said the Governor; "thou art mad — thou noble! The common executioner!"

"And wherefore not, Sir Archibald de Hagenbach? I think the name of Francis Steinernherz *von* Blut-acker will suit nobility, being fairly and legally won, as well as another. Nay, do not stare on me thus. If one of my profession shall do his grim office on nine men of noble birth, with the same weapon, and with a single blow to each patient, hath he not a right to his freedom from taxes, and his nobility by patent?"

"So says the law," said Sir Archibald, after reflecting for a moment, — "but rather more in scorn than seriously, I should judge, since no one was ever known to claim the benefit of it."

"The prouder boast for him," said the functionary, "that

shall be the first to demand the honours due to a sharp sword and a clean stroke. I, Francis Steinernherz, will be the first noble of my profession, when I shall have dispatched one more knight of the Empire."

"Thou hast been ever in *my* service, hast thou not?" demanded De Hagenbach.

"Under what other master," replied the executioner, "could I have enjoyed such constant practice? I have executed your decrees on condemned sinners since I could swing a scourge, lift a crow-bar, or wield this trusty weapon; and who can say I ever failed of my first blow, or needed to deal a second? Tristrem of the Hospital, and his famous assistants, Petit André, and Trois Eschelles, are novices compared with me, in the use of the noble and knightly sword. Marry, I should be ashamed to match myself with them in the field practice with bowstring and dagger; these are no feats worthy of a Christian man who would rise to honour and nobility."

"Thou art a fellow of excellent address, and I do not deny it," replied De Hagenbach. "But it cannot be — I trust it cannot be — that when noble blood is becoming scarce in the land, and proud churls are lording it over knights and barons, I myself should have caused so much to be spilled?"

"I will number the patients to your excellency by name and title," said Francis, drawing out a scroll of parchment, and reading with a commentary as he went on, — "There was Count William of Elvershoe — he was my assay-piece, a sweet youth, and died most like a Christian."

"I remember — he was indeed a most smart youth, and courted my mistress," said Sir Archibald.

"He died on St. Jude's, in the year of grace 1455," said the executioner.

"Go on — but name no dates," said the Governor.

"Sir Miles of Stockenborg" ——

"He drove off my cattle," observed his excellency.

"Sir Louis of Riesenfeldt" — continued the executioner.

"He made love to my wife," commented the Governor.

"The three Jung-herrn of Lammerbourg — you made their father, the Count, childless in one day."

"And he made me landless," said Sir Archibald, "so that account is settled. — Thou needest read no farther," he continued;

"I admit thy record, though it is written in letters somewhat of the reddest. I had counted these three young gentlemen as one execution."

"You did me the greater wrong," said Francis; "they cost three good separate blows of this good sword."

"Be it so, and God be with their souls," said Hagenbach. "But thy ambition must go to sleep for a while, Scharfgerichter, for the stuff that came hither to-day is for dungeon and cord, or perhaps a touch of the rack or strappado — there is no honour to win on them."

"The worse luck mine," said the executioner. "I had dreamed so surely that your honour had made me noble; — and then the fall of my sword?"

"Take a bowl of wine, and forget your auguries."

"With your honour's permission, no," said the executioner; "to drink before noon were to endanger the nicety of my hand."

"Be silent, then, and mind your duty," said De Hagenbach.

Francis took up his sheathless sword, wiped the dust reverently from it, and withdrew into a corner of the chamber, where he stood leaning with his hands on the pommel of the fatal weapon.

Almost immediately afterwards, Kilian entered at the head of five or six soldiers, conducting the two Philipsons, whose arms were tied down with cords.

"Approach me a chair," said the Governor, and took his place gravely beside a table, on which stood writing materials.

"Who are these men, Kilian, and wherefore are they bound?"

"So please your excellency," said Kilian, with a deep respect of manner, which entirely differed from the tone, approaching to familiarity, with which he communicated with his master in private, "we thought it well that these two strangers should not appear armed in your gracious presence; and when we required of them to surrender their weapons at the gate, as is the custom of the garrison, this young gallant must needs offer resistance. I admit he gave up his weapon at his father's command."

"It is false!" exclaimed young Philipson; but his father making a sign to him to be silent, he obeyed instantly.

"Noble sir," said the elder Philipson, "we are strangers, and unacquainted with the rules of this citadel; we are Englishmen, and unaccustomed to submit to personal mishandling; we trust you will have excuse for us, when we found ourselves, without any explanation of the cause, rudely seized on by we knew not whom. My son, who is young and unthinking, did partly draw his weapon, but desisted at my command, without having altogether unsheathed his sword, far less made a blow. For myself, I am a merchant, accustomed to submit to the laws and customs of the countries in which I traffic; I am in the territories of the Duke of Burgundy, and I know his laws and customs must be just and equitable. He is the powerful and faithful ally of England, and I fear nothing while under his banner."

"Hem! hem!" replied De Hagenbach, a little disconcerted by the Englishman's composure, and perhaps recollecting, that, unless his passions were awakened, (as in the case of the Swiss, whom he detested,) Charles of Burgundy deserved the character of a just though severe prince — "Fair words are well, but hardly make amends for foul actions. You have drawn swords in riot, and opposition to the Duke's soldiers, when obeying the mandates which regulate their watch."

"Surely, sir," answered Philipson, "this is a severe construction of a most natural action. But, in a word, if you are disposed to be rigorous, the simple action of drawing, or attempting to draw, a sword in a garrison town, is only punishable by pecuniary fine, and such we must pay, if it be your will."

"Now, here is a silly sheep," said Kilian to the executioner, beside whom he had stationed himself, somewhat apart from the group, "who voluntarily offers his own fleece to the clipper."

"It will scarcely serve as a ransom for his throat, Sir Squire," answered Francis Steinernherz; "for, look you, I dreamed last night that our master made me noble, and I knew by the fall of my sword that this is the man by whom I am to mount to gentility. I must this very day deal on him with my good sword."

"Why, thou ambitious fool," said the esquire, "this is no noble, but an island pedlar — a mere English citizen."

"Thou art deceived," said the executioner, "and hast never looked on men when they are about to die."

"Have I not?" said the squire. "Have I not looked on five pitched fields, besides skirmishes and ambuscades innumerable!"

"That tries not the courage," said the Scharfgerichter. "All men will fight when pitched against each other. So will the most paltry curs — so will the dunghill fowls. But he is brave and noble who can look on a scaffold and a block, a priest to give him absolution, and the headsman and good sword which is to mow him down in his strength, as he would look upon things indifferent; and such a man is that whom we now behold."

"Yes," answered Kilian, "but that man looks not on such an apparatus — he only sees our illustrious patron, Sir Archibald de Hagenbach."

"And he who looks upon Sir Archibald," said the executioner, "being, as yonder man assuredly is, a person of sense and apprehension, looks he not upon sword and headsman? Assuredly that prisoner apprehends as much, and being so composed as he is under such conviction, it shows him to be a nobleman by blood, or may I myself never win nobility!"

"Our master will come to compromise with him, I judge," replied Kilian; "he looks smilingly on him."

"Never trust to me then," said the man in scarlet; "there is a glance in Sir Archibald's eye which betokens blood, as surely as the dog-star bodes pestilence."

While these dependents of Sir Archibald de Hagenbach were thus conversing apart, their master had engaged the prisoners in a long train of captious interrogatories concerning their business in Switzerland, their connexion with the Landamman, and the cause of their travelling into Burgundy, to all which the senior Philipson gave direct and plain answers, excepting to the last. He was going, he said, into Burgundy, for the purpose of his traffic, — his wares were at the disposal of the Governor, who might detain all, or any part of them, as he might be disposed to make himself answerable to his master. But his business with the Duke was of a private nature, respecting some particular matters of commerce, in which others as well as he himself were interested. To the Duke alone, he declared, would he communicate the affair; and he pressed it strongly on the Governor, that if he should sustain any damage in his own person or that of lug son, the Duke's severe displeasure would be the inevitable consequence.

De Hagenbach was evidently much embarrassed by the

steady tone of his prisoner, and more than once held council with the bottle, his never-failing oracle in cases of extreme difficulty. Philipson had readily surrendered to the Governor a list or invoice of his merchandise, which was of so inviting a character, that Sir Archibald absolutely gloated over it. After remaining in deep meditation for some time, he raised his head, and spoke thus: —

"You must be well aware, Sir Merchant, that it is the Duke's pleasure that no Swiss merchandise shall pass through his territories; and that, nevertheless, you having been, by your own account, some time in that country, and having also accompanied a body of men calling themselves Swiss Deputies, I am authorized to believe that these valuable articles are rather the property of those persons, than of a single individual of so poor an appearance as yourself, and that should I demand pecuniary satisfaction, three hundred pieces of gold would not be an extravagant fine for so bold a practice; and you might wander where you will with the rest of your wares, so you bring them not into Burgundy."

"But it is to Burgundy, and to the Duke's presence, that I am expressly bound," said the Englishman. "If I go not thither my journey is wrecked, and the Duke's displeasure is certain to light on those who may molest me. For I make your excellency aware, that your gracious Prince already knows of my journey, and will make strict inquiry where and by whom I have been intercepted."

Again the Governor was silent, endeavouring to decide how he might best reconcile the gratification of his rapacity with precaution for his safety. After a few minutes' consideration he again addressed his prisoner.

"Thou art very positive in thy tale, my good friend; but my orders are equally so to exclude merchandise coming from Switzerland. What if I put thy mule and baggage under arrest?"

"I cannot withstand your power, my lord, to do what you will. I will in that case go to the Duke's footstool, and do my errand there."

"Ay, and my errand also," answered the Governor. "That is, thou wilt carry thy complaint to the Duke against the Governor of La Ferette, for executing his orders too strictly?"

"On my life and honest word," answered the Englishman, "I

will make no complaint. Leave me but my ready money, without which I can hardly travel to the Duke's court, and I will look no more after these goods and wares than the stag looks after the antlers which he shed last year."

Again the Governor of La Ferette looked doubtful, and shook his head.

"Men in such a case as yours," he said, "cannot be trusted; nor, to say truth, is it reasonable to expect they should be trustworthy. — These same wares, designed for the Duke's private hand, in what do they consist?"

"They are under seal," replied the Englishman.

"They are of rare value, doubtless?" continued the Governor.

"I cannot tell," answered the elder Philipson; "I know the Duke sets great store by them. But your excellency knows, that great princes sometimes place a high value on trifles."

"Bear you them about you?" said the Governor. "Take heed how you answer — Look around you on these engines, which can bring a dumb man to speak, and consider I have the power to employ them!"

"And I the courage to support their worst infliction," answered Philipson, with the same impenetrable coolness which he had maintained throughout the whole conference.

"Remember, also," said Hagenbach, "that I can have your person searched as thoroughly as your mails and budgets."

"I do remember that I am wholly in thy power; and, that I may leave thee no excuse for employing force on a peaceful traveller, I will own to you," said Philipson, "that I have the Duke's packet in the bosom of my doublet."

"Bring it forth," answered the Governor.

"My hands are tied, both in honour and literally," said the Englishman.

"Pluck it from his bosom, Kilian," said Sir Archibald; "let us see this gear he talks of."

"Could resistance avail," replied the stout merchant, "you should pluck forth my heart first. But I pray all who are present to observe, that the seals are every one whole and unbroken at this moment when it is forcibly taken from my person."

As he spoke thus he looked around on the soldiers, whose presence De Hagenbach had perhaps forgotten.

"How, dog!" said Sir Archibald, giving way to his passion, "would you stir up mutiny among my men-at-arms? — Kilian, let the soldiers wait without."

So saying, he hastily placed under cover of his own robe the small but remarkably well-secured packet, which Kilian had taken from the merchant's person. The soldiers withdrew, lingering, however, and looking back, like children brought away from a show before its final conclusion.

"So, fellow!" again began De Hagenbach, "we are now more private. Wilt thou deal more on the level with me, and tell me what this packet is, and whence it comes?"

"Could all your garrison be crowded into this room, I can only answer as before. — The contents I do not precisely know — the person by whom it was sent I am determined not to name."

"Perhaps your son," said the Governor, "may be more compliant."

"He cannot tell you that, of which he is himself ignorant," answered the merchant.

"Perchance the rack may make you both find your tongues; — and we will try it on the young fellow first, Kilian, since thou knowest we have seen men shrink from beholding the wrenched joints of their children, that would have committed their own old sinews to the stretching with much endurance."

"You may make the trial," said Arthur, "and Heaven will give me strength to endure" ——

"And me courage to behold," added his father.

All this while the Governor was turning and returning the little packet in his hand, curiously inspecting every fold, and regretting, doubtless, in secret, that a few patches of wax, placed under an envelope of crimson satin, and ligatures of twisted silk cord, should prevent his eager eyes from ascertaining the nature of the treasure which he doubted not it concealed. At length he again called in the soldiers, and delivered up the two prisoners to their charge, commanding that they should be kept safely, and in separate holds, and that the father, in particular, should be most carefully looked after.

"I take you all here to witness," exclaimed the elder Philipson, despising the menacing signs of De Hagenbach, "that the Governor detains from me a packet, addressed to his most gracious lord and master, the Duke of Burgundy."

De Hagenbach actually foamed at the mouth with passion.

"And should I *not* detain it?" he exclaimed, in a voice inarticulate with rage. "May there not be some foul practice against the life of our most gracious sovereign, by poison or otherwise, in this suspicious packet, brought by a most suspicious bearer? Have we never heard of poisons which do their work by the smell? And shall we, who keep the gate, as I may say, of his Grace of Burgundy's dominions, give access to what may rob Europe of its pride of chivalry, Burgundy of its prince, and Flanders of her father? — No! Away with these miscreants, soldiers — down to the lowest dungeons with them — keep them separate, and watch them carefully. This treasonable practice has been meditated with the connivance of Berne and Soleure."

Thus Sir Archibald de Hagenbach raved, with a raised voice and inflamed countenance, lashing himself as it were into passion, until the steps of the soldiers, and the clash of their arms, as they retired with the prisoners, were no longer audible. His complexion, when these had ceased, waxed paler than was natural to him — his brow was furrowed with anxious wrinkles — and his voice became lower and more hesitating than ordinary, as, turning to his esquire, he said, "Kilian, we stand upon a slippery plank, with a raging torrent beneath us — What is to be done?"

"Marry, to move forward with a resolved yet prudent step," answered the crafty Kilian. "It is unlucky that all these fellows should have seen the packet, and heard the appeal of yonder iron-nerved trader. But this ill luck has befallen us, and the packet having been in your excellency's hands, you will have all the credit of having broken the seals; for, though you leave them as entire as the moment they were impressed, it will only be supposed they have been ingeniously replaced. Let us see what are the contents, before we determine what is to be done with them. They must be of rare value, since the churl merchant was well contented to leave behind all his rich mule's-load of merchandise, so that this precious packet might pass unexamined."

"They may be papers on some political matter. Many such, and of high importance, pass secretly between Edward of England and our bold Duke." Such was the reply of De Hagenbach.

"If they be papers of consequence to the Duke," answered Kilian, "we can forward them to Dijon. — Or they may be such as Louis of France would purchase with their weight, of gold."

"For shame, Kilian," said the Knight; "wouldst thou have me betray my master's secrets to the King of France? Sooner would I lay my head on the block."

"Indeed? And yet your excellency hesitates not to" ——

Here the squire stopped, apparently for fear of giving offence, by affixing a name too broad and intelligible to the practices of his patron.

"To plunder the Duke, thou wouldst say, thou impudent slave! And, saying so, thou wouldst be as dull as thou wert wont to be," answered De Hagenbach. "I partake, indeed, in the plunder which the Duke takes from aliens; and reason good. Even so the hound and the hawk have their share of the quarry they bring down — ay, and the lion's share, too, unless the huntsman or falconer be all the nearer to them. Such are the perquisites of my rank; and the Duke, who placed me here for the gratification of his resentment and the bettering of my fortune, does not grudge them to a faithful servant. And, indeed, I may term myself, in so far as this territory of La Ferette extends, the Duke's full representative, or, as it may be termed, ALTER EGO — and, thereupon, I will open this packet, which, being addressed to him, is thereby equally addressed to me."

Having thus in a manner talked himself up to an idea of his own high authority, he cut the strings of the packet which he had all this while held in his hand, and, undoing the outer coverings, produced a very small case made of sandal-wood.

"The contents," he said, "had need to be valuable, as they he in so little compass."

So saying, he pressed the spring, and the casket, opening, displayed a necklace of diamonds, distinguished by brilliancy and size, and apparently of extraordinary value. The eyes of the avaricious Governor, and his no less rapacious attendant, were so dazzled with the unusual splendour, that for some time they could express nothing save joy and surprise.

"Ay, marry, sir," said Kilian, "the obstinate old knave had reasons for his hardihood. My own joints should have stood a strain or two ere I surrendered such sparklers as these. — And now, Sir Archibald, may your trusty follower ask you how this booty is to be divided between the Duke and his Governor, according to the most approved rules of garrison towns?"

"Faith, we will suppose the garrison stormed, Kilian; and, in a storm, thou knowest, the first finder takes all — with due consideration always of his trusty followers."

"As myself, for example," said Kilian.

"Ay, and myself, for example," answered a voice, which sounded like the echo of the esquire's words, from the remote corner of the ancient apartment.

" 'Sdeath! we are overheard," exclaimed the Governor, starting, and laying his hand on his dagger.

"Only by a faithful follower, as the worthy esquire observes," said the executioner, moving slowly forward.

"Villain, how didst thou dare watch me?" said Sir Archibald de Hagenbach.

"Trouble not yourself for that, sir," said Kilian. "Honest Steinernherz has no tongue to speak, or ear to hear, save according to your pleasure. Indeed, we must shortly have taken him into our counsels, seeing these men must be dealt upon, and that speedily."

"Indeed!" said De Hagenbach; "I had thought they might be spared."

"To tell the Duke of Burgundy how the Governor of La Ferette accounts to his treasurer for the duties and forfeitures at his custom-house?" demanded Kilian.

" 'Tis true," said the Knight: "dead men have neither teeth nor tongue — they bite not, and they tell no tales. Thou wilt take order with them, Scharfgerichter."

"I will, my lord," answered the executioner, "on condition that, if this must be in the way of dungeon execution, which I call cellar practice, my privilege to claim nobility shall be saved and reserved to me, and the execution shall be declared to be as effectual to my claim, as it might have been if the blow had been dealt in broad daylight, with my honourable blade of office."

De Hagenbach stared at the executioner, as not understanding what he meant; on which Kilian took occasion to explain, that the Scharfgerichter was strongly impressed, from the free and dauntless conduct of the elder prisoner, that he was a man of noble blood, from whose decapitation he would himself derive all the advantages proposed to the headsman who should execute his function on nine men of illustrious extraction.

"He may be right," said Sir Archibald, "for here is a slip of parchment, commending the bearer of this carcanet to the Duke, desiring him to accept it as a true token from one well known to him, and to give the bearer full credence in all that he should say on the part of those by whom he is sent."

"By whom is the note signed, if I may make bold to ask?" said Kilian.

"There is no name — the Duke must be supposed to collect that information from the gems, or perhaps the handwriting."

"On neither of which he is likely to have a speedy opportunity of exercising his ingenuity," said Kilian.

De Hagenbach looked at the diamonds, and smiled darkly. The Scharfgerichter, encouraged by the familiarity into which he had in a manner forced himself, returned to his plea, and insisted on the nobility of the supposed merchant. Such a trust, and such a letter of unlimited credence, could never, he contended, be intrusted to a man meanly born.[7]

"Thou art deceived, thou fool," said the Knight; "kings now use the lowest tools to do their dearest offices. Louis has set the example of putting his barber, and the valets of his chamber, to do the work formerly intrusted to dukes and peers; and other monarchs begin to think that it is better, in choosing their agents for important affairs, to judge rather by the quality of men's brains than that of their blood. And as for the stately look and bold bearing which distinguish yonder fellow in the eyes of cravens like thee, it belongs to his country, not his rank. Thou thinkest it is in England as in Flanders, where a city-bred burgher of Ghent, Liege, or Ypres, is as distinct an animal from a knight of Hainault, as a Flanders-waggon-horse from a Spanish jennet. But thou art deceived. England has many a merchant as haughty of heart, and as prompt of hand, as any noble-born son of her rich bosom. But be not dejected, thou foolish man; do thy business well on this merchant, and we shall presently have on our hands the Landamman of Unterwalden, who, though a churl by his choice, is yet a nobleman by blood, and shall, by his well-deserved death, aid thee to get rid of the peasant slough which thou art so weary of."

"Were not your excellency better adjourn these men's fate,"

---

[7] Louis XI. was probably the first King of France who flung aside all affectation of choosing his ministers from among the nobility. He often placed men of mean birth in situations of the highest trust.

said Kilian, "till you hear something of them from the Swiss prisoners whom we shall presently have in our power?"

"Be it as you will," said Hagenbach, waving his hand, as if putting aside some disagreeable task. "But let all be finished ere I hear of it again."

The stern satellites bowed obedience, and the deadly conclave broke up; their chief carefully securing the valuable gems, which he was willing to purchase at the expense of treachery to the sovereign in whose employment he had enlisted himself, as well as the blood of two innocent men. Yet with a weakness of mind not uncommon to great criminals, he shrunk from the thoughts of his own baseness and cruelty, and endeavoured to banish the feeling of dishonour from his mind, by devolving the immediate execution of his villainy upon his subordinate agents.

CHAPTER XV

And this place our forefathers built for man!

OLD PLAY.

The dungeon in which the younger Philipson was immured, was one of those gloomy caverns which cry shame on the inhumanity of our ancestors. They seem to have been almost insensible to the distinction betwixt innocence and guilt, as the consequences of mere accusation must have been far more severe in those days, than is in our own that species of imprisonment which is adjudged as an express punishment for crime.

The cell of Arthur Philipson was of considerable length, but dark and narrow, and dug out of the solid rock upon which the tower was founded. A small lamp was allowed him, not however, without some grumbling, but his arms were still kept bound; and when he asked for a draught of water, one of the grim satellites, by whom he was thrust into this cell, answered surlily, that he might endure his thirst for all the time his life was likely to last — a gloomy response, which augured that his privations would continue as long as his life, yet neither be of long duration. By the dim lamp he had groped his way to a bench, or rough seat, cut in the rock; and, as his eyes got gradually accustomed to the obscurity of the region in which he was immured, he became aware of a ghastly cleft in the floor of his dungeon, somewhat resembling the opening of a draw-well, but irregular in its aperture, and apparently the mouth of a gulf of Nature's conformation, slightly assisted by the labour of human art.

"Here, then, is my death-bed," he said, "and that gulf perhaps the grave which yawns for my remains! Nay, I have heard of prisoners being plunged into such horrid abysses while they were yet alive, to die at leisure, crushed with wounds, their groans unheard, and their fate unpitied!"

He approached his head to the dismal cavity, and heard, as at a great depth, the sound of a sullen, and, as it seemed, subterranean stream. The sunless waves appeared murmuring for their victim. Death is dreadful at all ages; but in the first springtide of youth, with all the feelings of enjoyment afloat, and eager for gratification, to be snatched forcibly from the banquet to which the individual has but just sat down, is peculiarly appalling, even when the change comes in the ordinary course of nature. But to sit, like young Philipson, on the brink of the subterranean abyss, and ruminate in horrid doubt concerning the mode in which death was to be inflicted, was a situation which might break the spirit of the boldest; and the unfortunate captive was wholly unable to suppress the natural tears that flowed from his eyes in torrents, and which his bound arms did not permit him to wipe away. We have already noticed, that although a gallant young man in aught of danger which was to be faced and overcome by active exertion, the youth was strongly imaginative, and sensitive to a powerful extent to all those exaggerations, which, in a situation of helpless uncertainty, fancy lends to district the soul of him who must passively expect an approaching evil.

Yet the feelings of Arthur Philipson were not selfish. They reverted to his father, whose just and noble character was as much formed to attract veneration, as his unceasing paternal care and affection to excite love and gratitude. He, too, was in the hands of remorseless villains, who were determined to conceal robbery by secret murder — he, too, undaunted in so many dangers, resolute in so many encounters, lay hound and defenceless, exposed to the dagger of the meanest stabber. Arthur remembered, too, the giddy peak of the rock near Geierstein, and the grim vulture which claimed him as its prey. Here was no angel to burst through the mist, and marshal him on a path of safety — here the darkness was subterranean and eternal, saving when the captive should behold the knife of the ruffian flash against the lamp, which lent him light to aim the fatal blow. This agony of mind lasted until the feelings of the unhappy prisoner arose to ecstasy. He started up, and struggled so hard to free himself of his bonds, that it seemed they should have fallen from him as from the arms of the mighty Nazarene. But the cords were of too firm a texture; and, after a violent and unavailing struggle, in which the ligatures seemed to enter his flesh, the prisoner lost his balance, and, while the feeling thrilled through him that he was tumbling backward into the subterranean abyss, he fell to the ground with great force.

Fortunately he escaped the danger which in his agony he apprehended, but so narrowly, that his head struck against the low and broken fence with which the mouth of the horrible pit was partly surrounded. Here he lay stunned and motionless, and, as the lamp was extinguished in his fall, immersed in absolute and total darkness. He was recalled to sensation by a jarring noise.

"They come — they come — the murderers! Oh, Lady of Mercy! and oh, gracious Heaven, forgive my transgressions!"

He looked up, and observed, with dazzled eyes, that a dark form approached him, with a knife in one hand, and a torch in the other. He might well have seemed the man who was to do the last deed upon the unhappy prisoner, if he had come alone. But he came not alone — his torch gleamed upon the white dress of a female, which was so much illuminated by it, that Arthur could discover a form, and had even a glimpse of features, never to be forgotten, though now seen under circumstances least of all to be expected. The prisoner's unutterable astonishment impressed him with a degree of awe which overcame even his personal fear — "Can these things be?" was his muttered reflection; "has she really the power of an elementary spirit? has she conjured up this earthlike and dark demon to concur with her in my deliverance?"

It appeared as if his guess were real; for the figure in black, giving the light to Anne of Geierstein, or at least the form which bore her perfect resemblance, stooped over the prisoner, and cut the cord that bound his arms, with so much dispatch, that it seemed as if it fell from his person at a touch. Arthur's first attempt to arise was unsuccessful, and a second time it was the hand of Anne of Geierstein — a living hand, sensible to touch as to sight — which aided to raise and to support him, as it had formerly done when the tormented waters of the river thundered at their feet. Her touch produced an effect far beyond that of the slight personal aid which the maiden's strength could have rendered. Courage was restored to his heart, vigour and animation to his benumbed and bruised limbs; such influence does the human mind, when excited to energy, possess over the infirmities of the human body. He was about to address Anne in accents of the deepest gratitude. But the accents died away on his tongue, when the mysterious female, laying her finger on her lips, made him a sign to be silent, and at the same time beckoned him to follow her. He obeyed in silent amazement. They passed the entrance of the melancholy dungeon, and through one or two short but intricate passages, which, cut out of the rock in some places, and built in others with hewn stone of the same kind, probably led to holds similar to that in which Arthur was so lately a captive.

The recollection that his father might be immured in some such horrid cell as he himself had just quitted, induced Arthur to pause as they reached the bottom of a small winding staircase, which conducted apparently from this region of the building.

"Come," he said, "dearest Anne, lead me to his deliverance! I must not leave my father."

She shook her head impatiently, and beckoned him on.

"If your power extends not to save my father's life, I will remain and save him or die! — Anne, dearest Anne" ——

She answered not, but her companion replied, in a deep voice, not unsuitable to his appearance, "Speak, young man, to those who are permitted to answer you; or rather, be silent, and listen to my instructions, which direct to the only course which can bring thy father to freedom and safety."

They ascended the stair, Anne of Geierstein going first; while Arthur, who followed close behind, could not help thinking that her form gave existence to a part of the light which her garment reflected from the torch. This was probably the effect of the superstitious belief impressed on his mind by Rudolph's tale respecting her mother, and which was confirmed by her sudden appearance in a place and situation where she was so little to have been expected. He had not much time, however, to speculate upon her appearance or demeanour, for, mounting the stair with a lighter pace than he was able at the time to follow closely, she was no longer to be seen when he reached the landing-place. But whether she had melted into the air, or turned aside into some other passage, he was not permitted a moment's leisure to examine.

"Here lies your way," said his sable guide; and at the same time dashing out the light, and seizing Philipson by the arm, he led him along a dark gallery of considerable length. The young man was not without some momentary misgivings while he recollected the ominous looks of his conductor, and that he was armed with a dagger, or knife, which he could plunge of a sudden into his bosom. But he could not bring himself to dread treachery from any one whom he had seen in company with Anne of Geierstein; and in his heart he demanded her pardon for the fear which had flashed across him, and resigned himself to the guidance of his companion, who advanced with hasty but light footsteps, and cautioned him by a whisper to do the same.

"Our journey," he at length said, "ends here."

As he spoke, a door gave way and admitted them into a gloomy Gothic apartment, furnished with large oaken presses, apparently filled with books and manuscripts. As Arthur looked round, with eyes dazzled with the sudden gleam of daylight from which he had been for some time excluded, the door by which they had entered disappeared. This, however, did not greatly surprise him, who judged that, being formed in appearance to correspond with the presses around the entrance which they had used, it could not when shut be distinguished from them; a device sometimes then practised, as indeed it often is at the present day. He had now a full view of his deliverer, who, when seen by daylight, showed only the vestments and features of a clergyman, without any of that expression of supernatural horror, which the partial light and the melancholy appearance of all in the dungeon had combined to impress on him.

Young Philipson once more breathed with freedom, as one awakened from a hideous dream; and the supernatural qualities with which his imagination had invested Anne of Geierstein having begun to vanish, he addressed his deliverer thus: — "That I may testify my thanks, holy father, where they are so especially due, let me inquire of you if Anne of Geierstein" ——

"Speak of that which pertains to your house and family," answered the priest, as briefly as before. "Hast thou so soon forgot thy father's danger?"

"By heavens, no!" replied the youth; "tell me but how to act for his deliverance, and thou shalt see how a son can fight for a parent!"

"It is well, for it is needful," said the priest. "Don thou this vestment and follow me."

The vestment presented was the gown and hood of a novice.

"Draw the cowl over thy face," said the priest, "and return no answer to any man who meets thee. I will say thou art under a vow. — May Heaven forgive the unworthy tyrant who imposes on us the necessity of such profane dissimulation! Follow me close and near — beware that you speak not."

The business of disguise was soon accomplished, and the Priest of St. Paul's, for such he was, moving on, Arthur followed him a pace or two behind, assuming as well as he could the modest step and humble demeanour of a spiritual novice. On leaving the library, or study, and descending a short stair, he found himself in the street of Brisach. Irresistibly tempted to look back, he had only time, however, to see that the house he had left was a very small building of a Gothic character, on the one side of which rose the church of St. Paul's, and on the other the stern black gate-house, or entrance-tower.

"Follow me, Melchior," said the deep voice of the priest; and his keen eyes were at the same time fixed upon the supposed novice, with a look which instantly recalled Arthur to a sense of his situation.

They passed along, nobody noticing them, unless to greet the priest with a silent obeisance, or muttered phrase of salutation, until, having nearly gained the middle of the village, the guide turned abruptly off from the street, and moving northward by a short lane, reached a flight of steps, which, as usual in fortified towns, led to the banquette or walk behind the parapet, which was of the old Gothic fashion, flanked with towers from space to space, of different forms and various heights at different angles.

There were sentinels on the walls; but the watch, as it seemed, was kept not by regular soldiers, but by burghers, with spears, or swords, in their hands. The first whom they passed said to the priest, in a half whispered tone, "Holds our purpose?"

"It holds," replied the Priest of St. Paul's. — "Benedicite!"

"*Deo Gratias!*" replied the armed citizen, and continued his walk upon the battlements.

The other sentinels seemed to avoid them; for they disappeared when they came near, or passed them without looking, or seeming to observe them. At last their walk brought them to an ancient turret, which raised its head above the wall, and in which there was a small door opening from the battlement. It was in a corner, distinct from and uncommanded by any of the angles of the fortification. In a well-guarded fortress, such a point ought to have had a sentinel for its special protection, but no one was there upon duty.

"Now mark me," said the priest, "for your father's life, and, it may be, that of many a man besides, depends upon your attention, and no less upon your dispatch. — You can run? — You can leap?"

"I feel no weariness, father, since you freed me," answered Arthur; "and the dun deer that I have often chased shall not beat me in such a wager."

"Observe, then," replied the Black Priest of St. Paul's, "this turret contains a staircase, which descends to a small sallyport. I will give you entrance to it — The sallyport is barred on the inside, but not locked. It will give you access to the moat, which is almost entirely dry. On crossing it, you will find yourself in the circuit of the outer barriers. You may see sentinels, but they will not see you — speak not to them, but make your way over the palisade as you can. I trust you can climb over an undefended rampart?"

"I have surmounted a defended one," said Arthur. "What is my next charge? — All this is easy."

"You will see a species of thicket, or stretch of low bushes — make for it with all speed. When you are there, turn to the eastward; but beware, while holding that course, that you are not seen by the Burgundian Free Companions, who are on watch on that part of the walls. A volley of arrows, and the sally of a body of cavalry in pursuit, will be the consequence, if they get sight of you; and their eyes are those of the eagle, that spy the carnage afar off."

"I will be heedful," said the young Englishman.

"You will find," continued the priest, "upon the outer side of the thicket a path, or rather a sheep-track, which, sweeping at some distance from the walls, will conduct you at last into the road leading from Brisach to Bâle. Hasten forward to meet the Swiss who are advancing. Tell them your father's hours are counted, and that they must press on if they would save him; and say to Rudolph Donnerhugel, in especial, that the Black Priest of Saint Paul's waits to bestow upon him his blessing at the northern sallyport. Dost thou understand me?"

"Perfectly," answered the young man.

The Priest of Saint Paul's then pushed open the low-browed gate of the turret, and Arthur was about to precipitate himself down the stair which opened before him.

"Stay yet a moment," said the Priest, "and doff the novice's habit, which can only encumber thee."

Arthur in a trice threw it from him, and was again about to

start.

"Stay yet a moment longer," continued the Black Priest. "This gown may be a tell-tale — Stay, therefore, and help me to pull off my upper garment."

Inwardly glowing with impatience, Arthur yet saw the necessity of obeying his guide; and when he had pulled the long and loose upper vestment from the old man, he stood before him in a cassock of black serge, befitting his order and profession, but begirt, not with a suitable sash such as clergymen wear, but with a most uncanonical buff-belt, supporting a short two-edged sword, calculated alike to stab and to smite.

"Give me now the novice's habit," said the venerable father, "and over that I will put the priestly vestment. Since for the present I have some tokens of the laity about me, it is fitting it should be covered with a double portion of the clerical habit."

As he spoke thus he smiled grimly; and his smile had something more frightful and withering than the stern frown, which suited better with his features, and was their usual expression.

"And now," said he, "what does the fool tarry for, when life and death are in his speed?"

The young messenger waited not a second hint, but at once descended the stairs, as if it had been by a single step, found the portal, as the priest had said, only secured by bars on the inside, offering little resistance save from their rusted state, which made it difficult to draw them. Arthur succeeded, however, and found himself at the side of the moat, which presented a green and marshy appearance. Without stopping to examine whether it was deep or shallow, and almost without being sensible of the tenacity of the morass, the young Englishman forced his way through it and attained the opposite side, without attracting the attention of two worthy burghers of Brisach, who were the guardians of the barriers. One of them indeed was deeply employed in the perusal of some profane chronicle, or religious legend; the other was as anxiously engaged in examining the margin of the moat, in search of eels, perhaps, or frogs, for he wore over hid shoulder a scrip for securing some such amphibious booty.

Seeing that, as the priest foretold, he had nothing to apprehend from the vigilance of the sentinels, Arthur dashed at the palisade, in hope to catch hold of the top of the stockade, and so to clear it by one bold leap. He overrated his powers of activity, however, or they were diminished by his recent bonds and imprisonment. He fell lightly backward on the ground, and as he got to his feet, became aware of the presence of a soldier, in yellow and blue, the livery of De Hagenbach, who came running towards him, crying to the slothful and unobservant sentinels, "Alarm! — alarm! — you lazy swine! Stop the dog, or you are both dead men."

The fisherman, who was on the further side, laid down his eel-spear, drew his sword, and flourishing it over his head, advanced towards Philipson with very moderate haste. The student was yet more unfortunate, for, in his hurry to fold up his book and attend to his duty, he contrived to throw himself (inadvertently, doubtless,) full in the soldier's way. The latter, who was running at top speed, encountered the burgher with a severe shock which threw both down; but the citizen being a solid and substantial man, lay still where he fell, while the other, less weighty, and probably less prepared for the collision, lost his balance and the command of his limbs at once, and, rolling over the edge of the moat, was immersed in the mud and marsh. The fisher and the student went with deliberate speed to assist the unexpected and unwelcome partner of their watch; while Arthur, stimulated by the imminent sense of danger, sprung at the barrier with more address and vigour than before, and, succeeding in his leap, made, as he had been directed, with his utmost speed for the covert of the adjacent bushes. He reached them without hearing any alarm from the walls. But he was conscious that his situation had become extremely precarious, since his escape from the town was known to one man at least, who would not fail to give the alarm in case he was able to extricate himself from the marsh, — a feat, however, in which it seemed to Arthur that the armed citizens were likely to prove rather his apparent than actual assistants. While such thoughts shot across his mind, they served to augment his natural speed of foot, so that in less space than could have been thought possible, he reached the thinner extremity of the thicket, whence, as intimated by the Black Priest, he could see the eastern tower and the adjoining battlements of the town, —

"With hostile faces throng'd, and fiery arms."

It required, at the same time, some address on the part of the fugitive, to keep so much under shelter as to prevent himself from being seen in his turn by those whom he saw so plainly. He therefore expected every moment to hear a bugle wind, or to behold that bustle and commotion among the defenders, which might prognosticate a sally. Neither, however, took place, and heedfully observing the footpath, or track, which the priest had pointed out to him, young Philipson wheeled his course out of sight of the guarded towers, and soon falling into the public and frequented road, by which his father and he had approached the town in the morning, he had the happiness, by the dust and flash of arms, to see a small body of armed men advancing towards Brisach, whom he justly concluded to be the van of the Swiss deputation.

He soon met the party, which consisted of about ten men, with Rudolph Donnerhugel at their head. The figure of Philipson, covered with mud, and in some places stained with blood, (for his fall in the dungeon had cost him a slight wound,) attracted the wonder of every one, who crowded around to hear the news. Rudolph alone appeared unmoved. Like the visage on the ancient statues of Hercules, the physiognomy of the bulky Bernese was large and massive, having an air of indifferent and almost sullen composure, which did not change but in moments of the fiercest agitation.

He listened without emotion to the breathless tale of Arthur Philipson, that his father was in prison, and adjudged to death.

"And what else did you expect?" said the Bernese, coldly. "Were you not warned? It had been easy to have foreseen the misfortune, but it may be impossible to prevent it."

"I own — I own," said Arthur, wringing his hands, "that you were wise, and that we were foolish. — But oh! do not think of our folly, in the moment of our extremity! Be the gallant and generous champion which your Cantons proclaim you — give us your aid in this deadly strait!"

"But how, or in what manner?" said Rudolph, still hesitating. "We have dismissed the Bâlese, who were willing to have given assistance, so much did your dutiful example weigh with us. We are now scarce above a score of men — how can you ask us to attack a garrison town, secured by fortifications, and where there are six times our number?"

"You have friends within the fortifications," replied Arthur — "I am sure you have. Hark in your ear — The Black Priest sent to you — to you, Rudolph Donnerhugel of Berne — that he waits to give you his blessing at the northern sallyport."

"Ay, doubtless," said Rudolph, shaking himself free of Arthur's attempt to engage him in private conference, and speaking so that all around might hear him, "there is little doubt on't; I will find a priest at the northern sallyport to confess and absolve me, and a block, axe, and headsman, to strike my throat asunder when he has done. But I will scarce put the neck of my father's son into such risk. If they assassinate an English pedlar, who has never offended them, what will they do with the Bear of Berne, whose fangs and talons Archibald de Hagenbach has felt ere now?"

Young Philipson at these words clasped his hands together, and held them up to Heaven, as one who abandons hope, excepting from thence. The tears started to his eyes, and, clenching his hands and setting his teeth, he turned his back abruptly upon the Swiss.

"What means this passion?" said Rudolph. "Whither would you now?"

"To rescue my father, or perish with him," said Arthur; and was about to run wildly back to La Ferette, when a strong but kindly grasp detained him.

"Tarry a little till I tie my garter," said Sigismund Biederman, "and I will go with you, King Arthur."

"You, oaf?" exclaimed Rudolph, "you — and without orders?"

"Why, look you, cousin Rudolph," said the youth, continuing, with great composure, to fasten his garter, which, after the fashion of the time, was somewhat intricately secured — "you are always telling us that we are Swiss and freemen; and what is the advantage of being a freeman, if one is not at liberty to do what he has a mind? You are my Hauptman, look you, so long as it pleases me, and no longer."

"And why shouldst thou desert me now, thou fool? Why at this minute, of all other minutes in the year?" demanded the Bernese.

"Look you," replied the insubordinate follower, "I have hunted with Arthur for this month past, and I love him — he never called me fool or idiot, because my thoughts came slower, may be, and something duller, than those of other folk. And I love his father — the old man gave me this baldric and this horn, which I warrant cost many a kreutzer. He told me, too, not to be discouraged, for that it was better to think justly than to think fast, and that I had sense enough for the one if not for the other. And the kind old man is now in Hagenbach's butcher-shambles! — But we will free him, Arthur, if two men may. Thou shalt see me fight, while steel blade and ashen shaft will hold together."

So saying, he shook in the air his enormous partisan, which quivered in his grasp like a slip of willow. Indeed, if Iniquity was to be struck down like an ox, there was not one in that chosen band more likely to perform the feat than Sigismund; for though somewhat shorter in stature than his brethren, and of a less animated spirit, yet his breadth of shoulders and strength of muscles were enormous, and if thoroughly aroused and disposed for the contest, which was very rarely the case, perhaps Rudolph himself might, as far as sheer force went, have had difficulty in matching him.

Truth of sentiment and energy of expression always produce an effect on natural and generous characters. Several of the youths around began to exclaim, that Sigismund said well; that if the old man had put himself in danger it was because he thought more of the success of their negotiation than of his own safety, and had taken himself from under their protection, rather than involve them in quarrels on his account. "We are the more bound," they said, "to see him unscathed; and we will do so."

"Peace! all you wiseacres," said Rudolph, looking round with an air of superiority; "and you, Arthur of England, pass on to the Landamman, who is close behind; you know he is our chief commander, he is no less your father's sincere friend, and whatever he may determine in your father's favour, you will find most ready executors of his pleasure in all of us."

His companions appeared to concur in this advice, and young Philipson saw that his own compliance with the recommendation was indispensable. Indeed, although he still suspected that the Bernese, by his various intrigues, as well with the Swiss youth as with those of Bâle, and, as might be inferred from the Priest of Saint Paul's, by communication even within the town of La Ferette, possessed the greater power of assisting him at such a conjuncture; yet he trusted far more in the simple candour and perfect faith of Arnold Biederman, and pressed forward to tell to him his mournful tale, and crave his assistance.

From the top of a bank which he reached in a few minutes after he parted from Rudolph and the advanced guard, he saw beneath him the venerable Landamman and his associates, accompanied by a few of the youths who no longer were dispersed upon the flanks of the party, but attended on them closely, and in military array, as men prepared to repel any sudden attack.

Behind came a mule or two with baggage, together with the animals which, in the ordinary course of their march, supported Anne of Geierstein and her attendant. Both were occupied by female figures as usual, and to the best of Arthur's ken, the foremost had the well-known dress of Anne, from the gray mantle to a small heron's plume, which, since entering Germany, she had worn in compliance with the custom of the country, and in evidence of her rank as a maiden of birth and distinction. Yet, if the youth's eyes brought him true tidings at present, what was the character of their former information, when, scarce more than half an hour since, they had beheld, in the subterranean dungeon of Brisach, the same form which they now rested upon, in circumstances so very different! The feeling excited by this thought was powerful, but it was momentary, like the lightning which blazes through a midnight sky, which is but just seen ere it vanishes into darkness. Or rather, the wonder excited by this marvellous incident, only maintained its ground in his thoughts, by allying itself with the anxiety for his father's safety, which was their predominant occupation.

"If there be indeed a spirit," he said, "which wears that beautiful form, it must be beneficent as well as lovely, and will extend to my far more deserving father the protection which his son has twice experienced."

But ere he had time to prosecute such a thought farther, he had met the Landamman and his party. Here his appearance and his condition excited the same surprise as they had formerly occasioned to Rudolph and the vanguard. To the repeated interrogatories of the Landamman, he gave a brief account of his own imprisonment, and of his escape, of which he suffered the whole glory to rest with the Black Priest of St. Paul's, without mentioning one word of the more interesting female apparition, by which he had been attended and assisted in his charitable task. On another point also Arthur was silent. He saw no propriety in communicating to Arnold Biederman the message which the priest had addressed to Rudolph's ear alone. Whether good should come of it or no, he held sacred the obligation of silence imposed upon him by a man from whom he had just received the most important assistance.

The Landamman was struck dumb for a moment, with Borrow and surprise, at the news which he heard. The elder Philipson had gained his respect, as well by the purity and steadiness of the principles which he expressed, as by the extent and depth of his information, which was peculiarly valuable and interesting to the Switzer, who felt his admirable judgment considerably fettered for want of that knowledge of countries, times, and manners, with which his English friend often supplied him.

"Let us press forward," he said to the Banneret of Berne, and the other deputies; "let us offer our mediation betwixt the tyrant De Hagenbach and our friend, whose life is in danger. He must listen to us, for I know his master expects to see this Philipson at his court. the old man hinted to me so much. As we are possessed of such a secret, Archibald de Hagenbach will not dare to brave our vengeance, since we might easily send to Duke Charles information how the Governor of La Ferette abuses his power, in matters where not only the Swiss, but where the Duke himself is concerned."

"Under your reverend favour, my worthy sir," answered the Banneret of Berne, "we are Swiss Deputies, and go to represent the injuries of Switzerland alone. If we embroil ourselves with the quarrels of strangers, we shall find it more difficult to settle advantageously those of our own country; and if the Duke should, by this villainy done upon English merchants, bring upon him the resentment of the English monarch, such breach will only render it more a matter of peremptory necessity for him to make a treaty advantageous to the Swiss Cantons."

There was so much worldly policy in this advice, that Adam Zimmerman of Soleure instantly expressed his assent, with the additional argument, that their brother Biederman had told them, scarce two hours before, how these English merchants had, by his advice and their own free desire, parted company with them that morning, on purpose that they might not involve the Deputies in the quarrels which might be raised by the Governor's exactions on his merchandise.

"Now, what advantage," he said, "shall we derive from this same parting of company, supposing, as my brother seems to urge, we are still to consider this Englishman's interest as if he were our fellow traveller, and under our especial protection?"

This personal reasoning pinched the Landamman somewhat closely, for he had but a short while before descanted on the generosity of the elder Philipson, who had freely exposed himself to danger, rather than that he should embarrass their negotiation by remaining one of their company; and it completely shook the fealty of the white-bearded Nicolas Bonstetten, whose eyes wandered from the face of Zimmerman, which expressed triumphant confidence in his argument, to that of his friend the Landamman, which was rather more embarrassed than usual.

"Brethren," said Arnold at length with firmness and animation, "I erred in priding myself upon the worldly policy which I taught to you this morning. This man is not of our country, doubtless, but he is of our blood — a copy of the common Creator's image — and the more worthy of being called so, as he is a man of integrity and worth. We might not, without grievous sin, pass such a person, being in danger, without affording him relief, even if he lay accidentally by the side of our path; much less should we abandon him if the danger has been incurred in our own cause, and that we might escape the net in which he is himself caught. Be not, therefore, downcast — We do God's will in succouring an oppressed man. If we succeed by mild means, as I trust we shall, we do a good action at a cheap rate; — if not, God can assert the cause of humanity by the hands of few as well as many."

"If such is your opinion," said the Bannerman of Berne, "not a man here will shrink from you. For me, I pleaded against my own inclinations when I advised you to avoid a breach with the Burgundian. But as a soldier, I must needs say, I would rather fight the garrison, were they double the number they talk of, in a fair field, than undertake to storm their defences."

"Nay," said the Landamman, "I sincerely hope we shall both enter and depart from the town of Brisach, without deviating from the pacific character with which our mission from the Diet invests us."

CHAPTER XVI

For Somerset, off with his guilty head.

THIRD PART OF HENRY VI.

The Governor of La Ferette stood on the battlements of the eastern entrance-tower of his fortress, and looked out on the road to Bâle, when first the vanguard of the Swiss mission, then the centre and rear, appeared in the distance. At the same moment the van halting, the main body closed with it, white the females and baggage, and mules in the rear, moved in their turn up to the main body, and the whole were united in one group.

A messenger then stepped forth, and winded one of those tremendous horns, the spoils of the wild bulls, so numerous in the Canton of Uri, that they are supposed to have given rise to its name.

"They demand admittance," said the esquire.

"They shall have it," answered Sir Archibald de Hagenbach. "Marry, how they may pass out again, is another and a deeper question."

"Think yet a moment, noble sir," continued the esquire. "Bethink you, these Switzers are very fiends in fight, and have, besides, no booty to repay the conquest — some paltry chains of good copper, perchance, or adulterated silver. You have knocked out the marrow — do not damage your teeth by trying to grind the bone."

"Thou art a fool, Kilian," answered De Hagenbach, "and it may be a coward besides. The approach of some score, or at most some score and a half, of Swiss partisans, makes thee draw in thy horns like a snail at a child's finger! Mine are strong and inflexible as those of the Urus, of whom they talk so much, and on which they blow so boldly. Keep in mind, thou timid creature, that if the Swiss Deputies, as they presume to call themselves, are permitted to pass free, they carry to the Duke stories of merchants bound to his court, and fraught with precious commodities, specially addressed to his Grace! Charles has then at once to endure the presence of the ambassadors, whom he contemns and hates, and learns by them that the Governor of La Ferette, permitting such to pass, has nevertheless presumed to stop those whom he would full gladly see; for what prince would not blithely welcome such a casket as that which we have taken from yonder strolling English pedlar?"

"I see not how the assault on these ambassadors will mend your excellency's plea for despoiling the Englishmen," said Kilian.

"Because thou art a blind mole, Kilian," answered his chief. "If Burgundy hears of a ruffle between my garrison and the mountain churls, whom he scorns, and yet hates, it will drown all notice of the two pedlars who have perished in the fray. If after-inquiry should come, an hour's ride transports me with my confidants into the Imperial dominions, where, though the Emperor be a spiritless fool, the rich prize I have found on these islanders will ensure me a good reception."

"I will stick by your excellency to the last," returned the esquire; "and you shall yourself witness, that if a fool, I am at least no coward."

"I never thought thee such when it came to hand-blows," said De Hagenbach; "but in policy thou art timid and irresolute. Hand me mine armour, Kilian, and beware thou brace it well. The Swiss pikes and swords are no wasp stings."

"May your excellency wear it with honour and profit," said Kilian; and, according to the duty of his office, he buckled upon his principal the complete panoply of a knight of the empire. "Your purpose of assaulting the Swiss then holds firm," said Kilian. "But what pretext will your excellency assign?"

"Let me alone," said Archibald de Hagenbach, "to take one, or to make one. Do you only have Schonfeldt and the soldiers on their stations. And remember the words are — 'Burgundy to the Rescue.' When these words are first spoken, let the soldiers show themselves — when repeated, let them fall on. And now that I am accoutred, away to the churls and admit them."

Kilian bowed and withdrew.

The bugle of the Switzers had repeatedly emitted its angry roar, exasperated by the delay of nearly half an hour, without an answer from the guarded gate of Brisach; and every blast declared, by the prolonged echoes which it awakened, the increased impatience of those who summoned the town. At length the portcullis arose, the gate opened, the drawbridge fell, and Kilian, in the equipage of a man-at-arms arrayed for fight, rode forth on an ambling palfrey.

"What bold men are ye, sirs, who are here in arms before the fortress of Brisach, appertaining in right and seignorie to the thrice noble Duke of Burgundy and Lorraine, and garrisoned for his cause and interest by the excellent Sir Archibald, Lord of Hagenbach, Knight of the most Holy Roman Empire?"

"So please you, Sir Enquire," said the Landamman, "for such I conjecture you to be by the feather in your bonnet, we are here with no hostile intentions; though armed, as you see, to defend us in a perilous journey, where we are something unsafe by day, and cannot always repose by night in places of security. But our arms have no offensive purpose; if they had such, our numbers had not been so few as you see them."

"What then is your character and purpose?" said Kilian, who had learned to use, in his master's absence, the lordly and insolent tone of the Governor himself.

"We are Delegates," answered the Landamman, in a calm and even tone of voice, without appearing to take offence at, or to observe, the insolent demeanour of the esquire, "from the Free and Confederated Cantons of the Swiss States and provinces, and from the good town of Soleure, who are accredited from our Diet of Legislature to travel to the presence of his Grace the Duke of Burgundy, on an errand of high importance to both countries, and with a hope of establishing with your master's lord — I mean with the noble Duke of Burgundy — a sure and steadfast peace, upon such terms as shall be to the mutual honour and advantage of both countries, and to avert disputes, and the effusion of Christian blood, which may otherwise be shed for want of timely and good understanding."

"Show me your letters of credence," said the esquire.

"Under your forgiveness, Sir Esquire," replied the Landamman, "it will be time enough to exhibit these, when we are admitted to the presence of your master the Governor."

"That is as much as to say, wilful will to it. It is well, my masters; and yet you may take this advice from Kilian of Kersberg. It is sometimes better to reel backwards than to run forwards. — My master, and my master's master, are more ticklish persons than the dealers of Bâle, to whom you sell your cheeses. Home, honest men, home! your way lies before you, and you are fairly warned."

"We thank thee for thy counsel," said the Landamman, interrupting the Banneret of Berne, who had commenced an angry reply, "supposing it kindly meant; if not, an uncivil jest is like an overcharged gun, which recoils on the cannoneer. Our road lies onward through Brisach, and onward we propose to go, and take such hap as that which we may find before us."

"Go onward then, in the devil's name," said the squire, who had entertained some hope of deterring them from pursuing their journey, but found himself effectually foiled.

The Switzers entered the town, and, stopped by the barricade of cars which the Governor had formed across the street, at about twenty yards from the gate, they drew themselves up in military order, with their little body formed into three lines, the two females and the fathers of the deputation being in the centre. The little phalanx presented a double front, one to each side of the street, while the centre line faced so as to move forward, and only waited for the removal of the barricade in order to do so. But while they stood thus inactive, a knight in complete armour appeared from a side door of the great tower, under the arch of which they had entered into the town. His visor was raised, and he walked along the front of the little line formed by the Swiss, with a stern and frowning aspect.

"Who are you," he said, "who have thus far intruded yourselves in arms into a Burgundian garrison?"

"With your excellency's leave," said the Landamman, "we are men who come on a peaceful errand, though we carry arms for our own defence. Deputies we are from the towns of Berne and Soleure, the Cantons of Uri, Schwitz, and Unterwalden, come to adjust matters of importance with the gracious Duke of Burgundy and Lorraine."

"What towns, what cantons?" said the Governor of La Ferette. "I have heard no such names among the Free Cities of Germany. — Berne, truly! when became Berne a free state?"

"Since the twenty-first day of June," said Arnold Biederman, "in the year of grace one thousand three hundred and thirty-nine, on which day the battle of Laupen was fought."

"Away, vain old man," said the Knight; "thinkest thou that such idle boasts can avail thee here? We have heard, indeed, of some insurgent villages and communities among the Alps, and how they rebelled against the Emperor, and by the advantage of fastnesses, ambuscades, and lurking-places, how they have murdered some knights and gentlemen sent against them by the Duke of Austria; but we little thought that such paltry townships and insignificant bands of mutineers had the insolence to term themselves Free States, and propose to enter into negotiation as such with a mighty prince like Charles of Burgundy."

"May it please your excellency," replied the Landamman, with perfect temper, "your own laws of chivalry declare, that if the stronger wrong the weaker, or the noble does injury to the less gentle, the very act levels distinctions between them, and the doer of an injury becomes bound to give condign satisfaction, of such kind as the wronged party shall demand."

"Hence to thy hills, churl!" exclaimed the haughty Knight; "there comb thy beard and roast thy chestnuts. What! because a few rats and mice find retreat among the walls and wainscoting of our dwelling-houses, shall we therefore allow them to intrude their disgusting presence, and their airs of freedom and independence, into our personal presence? No, we will rather crush them beneath the heel of our ironshod boots."

"We are not men to be trodden on," said Arnold Biederman, calmly; "those who have attempted it have found us stumbling-blocks. Lay, Sir Knight, lay aside for an instant this haughty language, which can only lead to warfare, and listen to the words of peace. Dismiss our comrade, the English merchant Philipson, on whom you have this morning laid unlawful hands; let him pay a moderate sum for his ransom, and we, who are bound instantly to the Duke's presence, will bear a fair report to him of his Governor of La Ferette."

"You will be so generous, will you!" said Sir Archibald, in a tone of ridicule. "And what pledge shall I have that you will favour me so kindly as you propose?"

"The word of a man who never broke his promise," answered the stoical Landamman.

"Insolent hind!" replied the Knight, "dost thou stipulate? *thou* offer thy paltry word as a pledge betwixt the Duke of Burgundy and Archibald de Hagenbach? Know that ye go not to Burgundy at all, or you go thither with fetters on your hands and halters round your necks. — So ho, Burgundy to the Rescue!"

Instantly as he spoke, the soldiers showed themselves before, behind, and around the narrow space where the Swiss had drawn themselves up. The battlements of the town were lined with men, others presented themselves at the doors of each house in the street, prepared to sally, and, at the windows, prepared to shoot, as well with guns as with bows and crossbows. The soldiers who defended the barricade also started up, and seemed ready to dispute the passage in front. The little band, encompassed and over-matched, but neither startled nor disheartened, stood to their arms. The centre rank under the Landamman prepared to force their way over the barricade. The two fronts stood back to back, ready to dispute the street with those that should issue from the houses. It could not fail to prove a work of no small blood and toil to subdue this handful of determined men, even with five times their number. Some sense of this, perhaps, made Sir Archibald delay giving the signal for onset, when suddenly behind arose a cry of "Treason, treason!"

A soldier, covered with mud, rushed before the Governor, and said, in hurried accents, that, as he endeavoured to stop a prisoner who had made his escape some short time since, he had been seized by the burghers of the town, and well-nigh drowned in the moat. He added, that the citizens were even now admitting the enemy into the place.

"Kilian," said the Knight, "take two score of men — hasten to the northern sallyport; stab, cut down, or throw from the battlements whomsoever you meet in arms, townsmen or strangers. Leave me to settle with these peasants by fair means or foul."

But ere Kilian could obey his master's commands, a shout arose in the rear, where they cried, "Bâle! Bâle! — Freedom! freedom! — The day is our own!"

Onward came the youth of Bâle, who had not been at such a distance but that Rudolph had contrived to recall them — onward came many Swiss who had hovered around the embassy, holding themselves in readiness for such a piece of service; and onward came the armed citizens of La Ferette, who, compelled to take arms and mount guard by the tyranny of De Hagenbach, had availed themselves of the opportunity to admit the Bâlese, at the sallyport through which Philipson had lately made his escape.

The garrison, somewhat discouraged before by the firm aspect of the Swiss who had held their numbers at defiance, were totally disconcerted by this new and unexpected insurrection. Most of them prepared rather to fly than to fight, and they threw themselves in numbers from the walls, as the best chance of escaping. Kilian and some others, whom pride prevented from flying, and despair from asking quarter, fought with fury, and were killed on the spot. In the midst of this confusion the Landamman kept his own bands unmoved, permitting them to take no share in the action, save to repel such violence as was offered to them.

"Stand fast all!" sounded the deep voice of Arnold Biederman along their little body. "Where is Rudolph? — Save lives, but take none. — Why, how now, Arthur Philipson! stand fast, I say."

"I cannot stand fast," said Arthur, who was in the act of leaving the ranks. "I must seek my father in the dungeons; they may be slaying him in this confusion while I stand idle here."

"By Our Lady of Einsiedlen, you say well," answered the Landamman; "that I should have forgot my noble guest! I will help thee to search for him, Arthur — the affray seems well-nigh ended. — Ho, there, Sir Banneret, worthy Adam Zimmerman, my good friend Nicholas Bonstetten, keep our men standing firm — Have nothing to do with this affray, but leave the men of Bâle to answer their own deeds. I return in a few minutes."

So saying, he hurried after Arthur Philipson, whose recollection conducted him, with sufficient accuracy, to the head of the dungeon stairs. There they met an ill-looking man clad in a buff jerkin, who bore at his girdle a bunch of rusted keys, which intimated the nature of his calling.

"Show me the prison of the English merchant," said Arthur Philipson, "or thou diest by my hand!"

"Which of them desire you to see?" answered the official: — "the old man, or the young one?"

"The old," said young Philipson. "His son has escaped thee."

"Enter here then, gentlemen," said the jailer, undoing the spring-bolt of a heavy door.

At the upper end of the apartment lay the man they came to seek for, who was instantly raised from the ground, and loaded with their embraces.

"My dear father!" — "My worthy guest!" said his son and friend at the same moment, "how fares it with you?"

"Well," answered the elder Philipson, "if you, my friend, and son, come, as I judge from your arms and countenance, as conquerors, and at liberty — ill, if you come to share my prison-house."

"Have no fear of that," said the Landamman; "we have been in danger, but are remarkably delivered. — Your evil lair has be-numbed you. Lean on me, my noble guest, and let me assist you to better quarters."

Here he was interrupted by a heavy clash, as it seemed, of iron, and differing from the distant roar of the popular tumult, which they still heard from the open street, as men hear the deep voice of a remote and tempestuous ocean.

"By Saint Peter of the fetters!" said Arthur, who instantly discovered the cause of the sound, "the jailer has cast the door to the staple, or it has escaped his grasp. The spring-lock has closed upon us, and we cannot be liberated saving from the outside. — Ho, jailer dog! villain! open the door, or thou diest!"

"He is probably out of hearing of your threats," said the elder Philipson, "and your cries avail you nothing. But are you sure the Swiss are in possession of the town?"

"We are peaceful occupants of it," answered the Landam-man, "though without a blow given on our side."

"Why then," said the Englishman, "your followers will soon find you out. Arthur and I are paltry ciphers, and our absence might easily pass over unobserved; but you are too important a figure not to be missed and looked after, when the sum of your number is taken."

"I well hope it will prove so," said the Landamman, "though methinks I show but scurvily, shut up here like a cat in a cup-board, when he has been stealing cream. — Arthur, my brave boy, dost thou see no means of shooting back the bolt?"

Arthur, who had been minutely examining the lock, replied in the negative; and added, that they must take patience perforce, and arm themselves to wait calmly their deliverance, which they could do nothing to accelerate.

Arnold Biederman, however, felt somewhat severely the neglect of his sons and companions.

"All my youths, uncertain whether I am alive or dead, are taking the opportunity of my absence, doubtless, for pillage and license — and the politic Rudolph, I presume, cares not if I should never reappear on the stage — the Banneret, and the white-bearded fool Bonstetten, who calls me his friend — every neighbour has deserted me — and yet they know that I am anx-ious for the safety of the most insignificant of them all, as dearer to me than my own. By heavens! it looks like stratagem; and shows as if the rash young men desired to get rid of a rule too regular and peaceful to be pleasing to those who are eager for war and conquest."

The Landamman, fretted out of his usual serenity of temper, and afraid of the misbehaviour of his countrymen in his absence, thus reflected upon his friends and companions, while the distant noise soon died away into the most absolute and total silence.

"What is to do now?" said Arthur Philipson. "I trust they will take the opportunity of quiet to go through the roll-call, and inquire then who are amissing."

It seemed as if the young man's wish had some efficacy, for he had scarce uttered it before the lock was turned, and the door set ajar by some one who escaped up stairs from behind it, before those who were set at liberty could obtain a glance of their deliverer.

"It is the jailer, doubtless," said the Landamman, "who may be apprehensive, as he has some reason, that we might prove more incensed at our detention in the dungeon, than grateful for our deliverance."

As they spoke thus, they ascended the narrow stairs, and issued from the door of the Gate-house tower, where a singular spectacle awaited them. The Swiss Deputies, and their escort, still remained standing fast and firm on the very spot where Hagenbach had proposed to assail them. A few of the late Governor's soldiers, disarmed, and cowering from the rage of a multitude of the citizens, who now filled the streets, stood with downcast looks behind the phalanx of the mountaineers, as their safest place of retreat. But this was not all.

The cars, so lately placed to obstruct the passage of the street, were now joined together, and served to support a platform, or scaffold, which had been hastily constructed of planks. On this was placed a chair, in which sat a tall man, with his head, neck, and shoulders bare, the rest of his body clothed in bright armour. His countenance was as pale as death, yet young Philipson recognised the hard-hearted Governor, Sir Archibald de Hagenbach. He appeared to be bound to the chair. On his right, and close beside him, stood the Priest of Saint Paul's, muttering prayers, with his breviary in his hand; while, on his left, and somewhat behind the captive, appeared a tall man, attired in red, and leaning with both hands on the naked sword, which has been described on a former occasion. The instant that Arnold Biederman appeared, and before the Landamman could open his lips to demand the meaning of what he saw, the priest drew back, the executioner stepped forward, the sword was brandished, the blow was struck, and the victim's head rolled on the scaffold. A general acclamation and clapping of hands, like that by which a crowded theatre approves of some well-graced performer, followed this feat of dexterity. While the headless corpse shot streams from the arteries, which were drunk up by the saw-dust that strewed the scaffold, the executioner gracefully presented himself alternately at the four corners of the stage, modestly bowing, as the multitude greeted him with cheers of approbation.

"Nobles, knights, gentlemen of free-born blood, and good citizens," he said, "who have assisted at this act of high justice, I pray you to bear me witness that this judgment hath been executed after the form of the sentence, at one blow, and without stroke missed or repeated."

The acclamations were reiterated.

"Long live our Scharfgerichter Steineinherz, and many a tyrant may he do his duty on!"

"Noble friends," said the executioner, with the deepest obeisance, "I have yet another word to say, and it must be a proud one. — God be gracious to the soul of this good and noble knight, Sir Archibald de Hagenbach. He was the patron of my youth, and my guide to the path of honour. Eight steps have I made towards freedom and nobility on the heads of freeborn knights and nobles, who have fallen by his authority and command; and the ninth, by which I have attained it, is upon his own, in grateful memory of which I will expend this purse of gold, which but an hour since he bestowed on me, in masses for his soul. Gentlemen, noble friends, and now my equals, La Ferette has lost a nobleman, and gained one. Our Lady be gracious to the departed knight, Sir Archibald de Hagenbach, and bless and prosper the progress of Stephen Steinernherz von Blut-sacker, now free and noble of right!"[8]

---

[8] There is abundant evidence, that, in the middle ages, the office of public executioner was esteemed highly honourable all over Germany. It still is, in such parts of that country as retain the old custom of execution by stroke of sword, very far from being held discreditable to the extent to which we carry

our feelings on the subject, and which exposed the magistrates of a Scotch town, — I rather think no less a one than Glasgow, — to a good deal of ridicule, when they advertised, some few years ago, on occasion of the death of their hangman, that "none but persons of respectable character" need apply for the vacant situation. At this day, in China, in Persia, and probably in other Oriental kingdoms, the Chief Executioner is one of the great officers of state, and is as proud of the emblem of his fatal duty, as any European Lord Chamberlain of his Golden Key.

The circumstances of the strange trial and execution of the Knight of Hagenbach are detailed minutely by M. de Barante, from contemporary M S. documents; and the reader will be gratified with a specimen of that writer's narrative. A translation is also given for the benefit of many of my kind readers.

"De toutes parts on était accourus par milliers pour assister au procès de ce cruel gouverneur, tant la haine était grande contre lui. De sa prison, il entendait retentir sur le pont le pas des chevaux, et s'enquérait à son geôlier de ceux qui arrivaient: soit pour être ses juges, soit pour être témoins de son supplice. Parfois le geôlier répondait, 'Ce sont des étrangers; je ne les connais pas.' 'Ne sont-ce pas,' disait le prisonnier, 'des gens assez mal vêtus, de haute taille, de forte apparence, montés sur des chevaux aux courtes oreilles?' et si le geôlier répondait: 'Oui.' — 'Ah ce sont les Suisses,' s'écriait Hagenbach; 'Mon Dieu, ayez pitié de moi!' et il se rappelait toutes les insultes qu'il leur avait faites, toutes ses insolences envers eux. Il pensait, muis trop tard, que c'était leur alliance avec la maison d'Autriche qui était cause de sa perte. Le 4 Mai, 1474, après avoir été mis à la question, il fut, à la diligence d'Hermann d'Eptingen, gouverneur pour l'archiduc, amené devant ses juges, sur la place publique de Brisach. Sa contenance était ferme et d'un homme qui ne craint pas la mort. Henri Iselin de Bâle porta la parole au nom d'Hermann d'Eptingen, agissant pour le seigneur du pays. Il parla à peu près en ces termes: 'Pierre de Hagenbach, chevalier, maître d'hôtel de Monseigneur le Duc de Bourgogne, et son gouverneur dans le pays de Sératte et Haute Alsace, aurait dû respecter les privilèges réservés par l'acte d'engagement; mais il n'a pas moins frotté aux pieds les lois de Dieu et des hommes, que les droits jurés et garantis au pays. Il a fait mettre à mort sans jugement quatre honnêtes bourgeois de Sératte; il a depouillé la ville de Brisach de sa juridiction, et y a établi juges et consuls de son choix; il a rompu et dispersé les communautés de la bourgeoisie et des métiers; il a levé des impôts par sa seule volonté; il a, contre toutes les lois, logé chez les habitans des gens de guerre — Lombards, Français, Picards, ou Flamands; et a favorisé leur désordres et pillages. Il leur a même commandé d'égorger leurs hôtes durant la nuit, et avait fait préparer, pour y embarquer les femmes et les enfans, des bateaux qui devaient être submergés dans le Rhin. Enfin lors même qu'il rejetterait de telles cruautés sur les ordres qu'il a reçus, comment pourrait il s'excuser d'avoir fait violence et outrage à l'honneur de tant de filles et femmes, et même de saintes religieuses?'

"D'autres accusations furent portées dans les interrogatoires; et des temoins attestèrent les violences faites aux gens de Mulhausen et aux marchands de Bâle.

"Pour suivre toutes les formes de la justice, on avait donné un avocat à l'accusé. 'Messire Pierre de Hagenbach,' dit-il, 'ne reconnait d'autre juge et d'autre seigneur que Monseigneur le Duc de Bourgogne, dont il avait commission, et recevait les commandemens. Il n'avait nul droit de contrôler les ordres qu'il était chargé d'exécuter; et son devoir était d'obéir. Ne sait-on pas quelle soumission les gens de guerre doivent à leur seigneur et maitre? Croit-on que le landvogt de Monseigneur le Duc eût à lui remontrer et à lui résister? Et monseigneur n'a-t-il pas ensuite, par sa présence, confirmé et ratifié tout ce qui avait été fait en son nom? Si des impôts ont été demandés, c'est qu'il avait besoin d'argent. Pour les recueillir, il a bien fallu punir ceux qui se refusaient à payer. C'est ce que Monseigneur le Duc, et même l'empereur, quand ils sont venus, ont reconnu nécessaire. Le logement des gens de guerre était aussi la suite des ordres du Duc. Quant à la juridiction de Brisach; ne landvogt pouvait-il souffrir cette résistance? Enfin, dans une affaire si grave, où il y va de la vie, convient-il de produire comme un véritable grief, le dernier dont à parlé l'accusateur? Parmi ceux qui écoutent, y en a-t-il un seul qui puisse se vanter de ne pas avoir saisi les occasions de se divertir! N'est-il pas clair que Messire de Hagenbach a seulement profité de la bonne volonté de quelques femmes ou filles; ou, pour mettre les choses au pis, qu'il n'a exercé d'autre contrainte envers elles qu'au moyen de son bon argent?'

"Les juges siégèrent-long temps sur leur tribunal. Douze heures entières passèrent sans que l'affaire fût terminée. Le Sire de Hagenbach, toujours ferme et calme, n'allégua d'autres défenses, d'autres excuses, que celles qu'il avait donné déjà sous la torture — les ordres et la volonté de son seigneur, qui était son seul juge, et le seul qui pût lui demander compte.

"Enfin, à sept heures du soir, à la clarté des flambeaux, les juges, après avoir déclaré qu'à eux appartenait le droit de prononcer sur les crimes imputés au landvogt, le firent rappeler; et rendirent leur sentence qui le condamna à mort. Il ne s'émeut pas davantage; et demanda pour toute grace d'avoir seulement la tête tranchée. Huit bourreaux des diverses villes se présentèrent pour exécuter l'arrêt. Celui de Colmar, qui passait pour le plus adroit, fut préféré. Avant de le conduire à l'échafaud, les seize chevaliers qui faisaient partie des juges requirent que Messire de Hagenbach fût dégradé de sa dignité de chevalier et de tous ses honneurs. Pour lors s'avança Gaspard Hurter, héraut de l'empereur; et il dit: 'Pierre de Hagenbach, il me déplaît grandement que vous ayez si mal employé votre vie mortelle: de sorte qu'il convient que vous perdiez non-seulement la dignité et ordre de chevalerie, mais aussi la vie. Votre devoir était de rendre la justice, de protéger la veuve et l'orphelin; de respecter les femmes et les filles, d'honorer les saints prétres; de vous opposer à toute injuste violence; et, au contraire, vous avez commis tout ce que vous deviez empêcher. Ayant ainsi forfait au noble ordre de chevalerie, et aux sermens que vous aviez jurés, les chevaliers ici présens m'ont enjoint de vous en ôter les insignes. Ne les voyant pas sur vous en ce moment, je vous proclame indigne chevalier de Saint George, au nom et à l'honneur duquel on vous avait autrefois honoré de l'ordre de chevalerie.' Puis s'avança Hermann d'Eptingen:

Puis qu'on vient de te dégrader de chevalerie, je te dépouille de ton sollier, chaîne d'or, anneau, poignard, éperon, gantelet.' Il les lui prit et lui en frappa le visage, et ajouta: 'Chevaliers, et vous qui désirez le devenir, j'espère que cette punition publique vous servira d'exemple, et que vous vivrez dans la crainte de Dieu, noblement et vaillamment, selon la dignité de la chevalerie et l'honneur de votre nom.' Enfin, le prévôt d'Einsilheim et maréchal de cette commission de juges se leva, et s'adressant au bourreau, lui dit: 'Faites selon la justice.'

"Tous les juges montèrent à cheval ainsi qu'Hermann d'Eptingen. Au milieu d'eux marchait Pierre de Hagenbach, entre deux prêtres. C'était pendant la nuit. Des torches éclairaient la marche; une foule immense se pressait autour de ce triste cortège. Le condamné s'entretenait avec son confesseur d'un air pieux et recueilli, mais ferme; se recommandant aussi aux prières de tous ceux qui l'entouraient. Arrivé dans une prairie devant la porte de la ville, il monta sur l'échafaud d'un pas assuré; puis élevant la voix: —

" 'Je n'ai pas peur de la mort,' dit-il; 'encore que je ne l'attendisse pas de cette sorte, mais bien les armes à la main; que je plains c'est tout le sang que le mien fera couler. Monseigneur ne laissera point ce jour sans vengeance pour moi. Je ne regrette ni ma vie, ni mon corps. J'étais homme — priez pour moi.' Il s'entretint encore un instant avec son confesseur, présenta la tête et reçut le coup."— M. DE BARANTE, tom. x. p. 197.

TRANSLATIONS

"Such was the detestation in which this cruel governor was held, that multitudes flocked in from all quarters to be present at his trial. He heard from his prison the bridge re-echo with the tread of horses, and would ask of his jailer respecting those who were arriving, whether they might be his judges, or those desirous of witnessing his punishment. Sometimes the jailer would answer, 'These are strangers whom I know not.' — 'Are not they,' said the prisoner, 'men meanly clad, tall in stature, and of bold mien, mounted on short-eared horses?' And if the jailer answered in the affirmative, 'Ah, these are the Swiss,' cried Hagenbach. 'My God, have mercy on me!' and he recalled to mind all the insults and cruelties he had heaped upon them. He considered, but too late, that their alliance with the house of Austria had been his destruction.

"On the 4th of May, 1474, after being put to the torture, he was brought before his judges in the public square of Brisach, at the instance of Hermann d'Eptingen, who governed for the Archduke. His countenance was firm, as one who fears not death. Henry Iselin of Bâle first spoke in the name of Hermann d'Eptingen, who acted for the lord of the country. He proceeded in nearly these terms: —'Peter de Hagenbach, knight, steward of my lord the Duke of Burgundy, and his governor in the country of Seratte and Haute Alsace, was bound to observe the privileges reserved by act of compact, but he has alike trampled under foot the laws of God and man, and the rights which have been guaranteed by oath to the country. He has caused four worshipful burgesses of Seratte to be put to death without trial; he has spoiled the city of Brisach, and established there judges and consuls chosen by himself; he has broken and dispersed the various communities of burghers and craftsmen; he has levied imposts of his own will; contrary to every law, he has quartered upon the inhabitants soldiers of various countries, Lombards, French, men of Picardy and Flemings, and has encouraged them in pillage and disorder; he has even commanded these men to butcher their hosts during night, and had caused boats to be prepared to embark therein women and children to be sunk in the Rhine. Finally, should he plead the orders which he had received as an excuse for these cruelties, how can he clear himself of having dishonoured so many women and maidens, even those under religious vows?'

"Other accusations were brought against him by examination, and witnesses proved outrages committed on the people of Mulhausen, and the merchants of Bâle.

"That every form of justice might be observed, an advocate was appointed to defend the accused. 'Messire Peter de Hagenbach,' said he, 'recognises no other judge or master than my lord the Duke of Burgundy, whose commission he bore, and whose orders he received. He had no control over the orders he was charged to execute; — his duty was to obey. Who is ignorant of the submission due by military retainers to their lord and master? Can any one believe that the landvogt of my lord the Duke could remonstrate with or resist him? And has not my lord confirmed and ratified by his presence all acts done in his name? If imposts have been levied, it was because he had need of money; to obtain it, it was necessary to punish those who refused payment; this proceeding my lord the Duke, and the Emperor himself, when present, have considered as expedient. The quartering of soldiers was also in accordance with the orders of the Duke. With respect to the jurisdiction of Brisach, could the landvogt permit any resistance from that quarter? To conclude, in so serious an affair, — one which touches the life of the prisoner, — can the last accusation be really considered a grievance? Among all those who hear me, is there one man who can say he has never committed similar imprudences? Is it not evident that Messire de Hagenbach has only taken advantage of the good-will of some girls and women, or, at the worst, that his money was the only restraint imposed upon them?'

"The judges sat for a long time on the tribunal. Twelve hours elapsed before the termination of the trial. The Knight of Hagenbach, always calm and undaunted, brought forward no other defence or excuse than what he had before given when under the torture: viz., the orders and will of his lord, who alone was his judge, and who alone could demand an explanation. At length, at seven in the evening, and by the light of torches, the judges, after having declared it their province to pronounce judgment on the crimes of which the landvogt was accused, caused him to be called before them, and delivered their sentence condemning him to death. He betrayed no emotion, and only demanded, as a favour, that he should be beheaded. Eight executioners, of various towns, presented themselves to execute the sentence; the one belonging to Colmar, who was accounted the most expert, was preferred.

"Before conducting him to the scaffold, the sixteen knights, who acted as judges, required that Messire de Hagenbach should be degraded from the dignity of knight, and from all his honours. Then advanced Caspar Hurter, herald of the Emperor, and said: 'Peter de Hagenbach, I deeply deplore that you have so employed your mortal life, that you must lose not only the dignity and honour of knighthood, but your life also. Your duty was to render justice, to protect the widow and orphan, to respect women and maidens, to honour the holy priests, to oppose every unjust outrage; but you have yourself committed what you ought to have opposed in others. Having broken, therefore, the oaths which you have sworn, and having forfeited the noble order of knighthood, the knights here present have enjoined me to deprive you of its insignia. Not per-

With that he took the feather out of the cap of the deceased, which, soiled with the blood of the wearer, lay near his body upon the scaffold, and, putting it into his own official bonnet, received the homage of the crowd in loud huzzas, which were partly in earnest, partly in ridicule of such an unusual transformation.

Arnold Biederman at length found breath, which the extremity of surprise had at first denied him. Indeed, the whole execution had passed much too rapidly for the possibility of his interference.

"Who has dared to act this tragedy?" he said indignantly; "And by what right has it taken place?"

A cavalier, richly dressed in blue, replied to the question —

"The free citizens of Bâle have acted for themselves, as the fathers of Swiss liberty set them an example; and the tyrant, De Hagenbach, has fallen by the same right which put to death the tyrant Geysler. We bore with him till his cup was brimming over, and then we bore no longer."

"I say not but that he deserved death," replied the Landam-

---

ceiving them on your person at this moment, I proclaim you unworthy Knight of St. George, in whose name and honour you were formerly admitted in the order of knighthood.' Then Hermann d'Eptingen advanced. Since you are degraded from knighthood, I deprive you of your collar, gold chain, ring, poniard, spur, and gauntlet.' He then took them from him, and, striking him on the face, added: —'Knights, and you who aspire to that honour, I trust this public punishment will serve as an example to you, and that you will live in the fear of God, nobly and valiantly, in accordance with the dignity of knighthood, and the honour of your name.' At last the provost of Einselheim, and marshal of that commission of judges, arose, and addressing himself to the executioner, —'Let justice be done.'

"All the judges, along with Hermann d'Eptingen, mounted on horseback; in the midst of them walked Peter de Hagenbach between two priests. It was night, and they marched by the light of torches; an immense crowd pressed around this sad procession. The prisoner conversed with his confessor, with pious, collected, and firm demeanour, recommending himself to the prayers of the spectators. On arriving at a meadow without the gate of the town, he mounted the scaffold with a firm step, and elevating his voice, exclaimed: —

" 'I fear not death, I have always expected it; not, indeed, in this manner, but with arms in my hand. I regret alone the blood which mine will cause to be shed; my lord will not permit this day to pass unavenged. I regret neither my life nor body. I was a man — pray for me!' He conversed an instant more with his confessor, presented his head, and received the blow." — M. DE BARANTE, tom. x. p. 197.

man; "but for your own sake and for ours, you should have forborne him till the Duke's pleasure was known."

"What tell you us of the Duke?" answered Laurenz Neipperg, the same blue cavalier whom Arthur had seen at the secret rendezvous of the Bálese youth, in company with Rudolph, — "Why talk you of Burgundy to us, who are none of his subjects? The Emperor, our only rightful lord, had no title to pawn the town and fortifications of La Ferette, being as it is a dependency of Bâle, to the prejudice of our free city. He might have pledged the revenue indeed; and supposing him to have done so, the debt has been paid twice over by the exactions levied by yonder oppressor, who has now received his due. But pass on, Landamman of Unterwalden. If our actions displease you, abjure them at the footstool of the Duke of Burgundy; but, in doing so, abjure the memory of William Tell, and Staufbacher, of Furst, and Melchtal, the fathers of Swiss freedom."

"You speak truth," said the Landamman; "but it is in an ill-chosen and unhappy time. Patience would have remedied your evils, which none felt more deeply, or would have redressed more willingly, than I. But O, imprudent young man, you have thrown aside the modesty of your age, and the subjection you owe to your elders. William Tell and his brethren were men of years and judgment, husbands and fathers, having a right to be heard in council, and to be foremost in action. Enough — I leave it with the fathers and senators of your own city, to acknowledge or to reprove your actions. — But you, my friends — you, Banneret of Berne — you, Rudolph — above all, you, Nicholas Bonstetten, my comrade and my friend, why did you not take this miserable man under your protection? The action would have shown Burgundy, that we were slandered by those who have declared us desirous of seeking a quarrel with him, or of inciting his subjects to revolt. Now, all these prejudices will be confirmed in the minds of men naturally more tenacious of evil impressions than of those which are favourable."

"As I live by bread, good gossip and neighbour," answered Nicholas Bonstetten, "I thought to obey your injunctions to a tittle; so much so, that I once thought of breaking in and protecting the man, when Rudolph Donnerhugel reminded me, that your last orders were, to stand firm, and let the men of Bâle answer for their own actions; and surely, said I to myself, my gossip Arnold knows better than all of us what is fitting to be done."

"Ah, Rudolph, Rudolph," said the Landamman, looking on him with a displeased countenance, "wert thou not ashamed thus to deceive an old man?"

"To say I deceived him is a hard charge; but from you, Landamman," answered the Bernese, with his usual deference, "I can bear any thing. I will only say, that, being a member of this embassy, I am obliged to think, and to give my opinion as such, especially when he is not present who is wise enough to lead and direct us all."

"Thy words are always fair, Rudolph," replied Arnold Biederman, "and I trust so is thy meaning. Yet there are times when I somewhat doubt it. — But let disputes pass, and let me have your advice, my friends; and for that purpose go we where it may best profit us, even to the church, where we will first return our thanks for our deliverance from assassination, and then hold counsel what next is to be done."

The Landamman led the way, accordingly, to the church of St. Paul's, while his companions and associates followed in their order. This gave Rudolph, who, as youngest, suffered the others to precede him, an opportunity to beckon to him the Landamman's eldest son, Rudiger, and whisper to him to get rid of the two English merchants.

"Away with them, my dear Rudiger, by fair means, if possible; but away with them directly. Thy father is besotted with these two English pedlars, and will listen to no other counsel; and thou and I know, dearest Rudiger, that such men as these are unfit to give laws to free-born Switzers. Get the trumpery they have been robbed of, or as much of it as is extant, together as fast as thou canst, and send them a-travelling in Heaven's name."

Rudiger nodded intelligently, and went to offer his services to expedite the departure of the elder Philipson. He found the sagacious merchant as desirous to escape from the scene of confusion now presented in the town, as the young Swiss could be to urge his departure. He only waited to recover the casket of which Du Hagenbach had possessed himself, and Rudiger Biederman set on foot a strict search after it, which was the more likely to be successful, that the simplicity of the Swiss prevented them from setting the true value upon its contents. A strict and hasty search was immediately instituted, both on the person of the dead De

Hagenbach, on which the precious packet was not to be found, and on all who had approached him at his execution, or were supposed to enjoy his confidence.

Young Arthur Philipson would gladly have availed himself of a few moments to bid farewell to Anne of Geierstein. But the gray wimple was no longer seen in the ranks of the Switzers, and it was reasonable to think, that, in the confusion which followed the execution of De Hagenbach, and the retreat of the leaders of the little battalion, she had made her escape into some of the adjacent houses, while the soldiers around her, no longer restrained by the presence of their chiefs, had dispersed, some to search for the goods of which the Englishmen had been despoiled, others doubtless to mingle with and join in the rejoicings of the victorious youths of Bâle, and of those burghers of La Ferette by whom the fortifications of the town had been so gently surrendered.

The cry amongst them was universal, that Brisach, so long considered as the curb of the Swiss confederates, and the barrier against their commerce, should henceforth be garrisoned, as their protection against the encroachments and exactions of the Duke of Burgundy and his officers. The whole town was in a wild but joyful jubilee, while the citizens vied with each other in offering to the Swiss every species of refreshment, and the youths who attended upon the mission hurried gaily, and in triumph, to profit by the circumstances, which had so unexpectedly converted the ambuscade so treacherously laid for them, into a genial and joyous reception.

Amid this scene of confusion, it was impossible for Arthur to quit his father, even to satisfy the feelings which induced him to wish for a few moments at his own disposal. Sad, thoughtful, and sorrowful, amid the general joy, he remained with the parent whom he had so much reason to love and honour, to assist him in securing and placing on their mule the various packages and bales which the honest Switzers had recovered after the death of De Hagenbach, and which they emulated each other in bringing to their rightful owner; while they were with difficulty prevailed on to accept the guerdon which the Englishman, from the means which he had still left upon his person, was disposed not merely to offer, but to force upon the restorers of his property, and which, in their rude and simple ideas, seemed greatly to exceed the value of what they had recovered for him.

This scene had scarcely lasted ten or fifteen minutes, when Rudolph Donnerhugel approached the elder Philipson, and in a tone of great courtesy invited him to join the council of the Chiefs of the Embassy of the Swiss Cantons, who, he said, were desirous of having the advantage of his experience upon some important questions respecting their conduct on these unexpected occurrences.

"See to our affairs, Arthur, and stir not from the spot on which I leave you," said Philipson to his son. "Look especially after the sealed packet of which I was so infamously and illegally robbed; its recovery is of the utmost consequence."

So speaking, he instantly prepared himself to attend he Bernese, who, in a confidential manner, whispered, as he went arm-in-arm with him towards the church of St. Paul's —

"I think a man of your wisdom will scarce advise us to trust ourselves to the mood of the Duke of Burgundy, when he has received such an injury as the loss of this fortress, and the execution of his officer. You, at least, would be too judicious to afford us any farther the advantage of your company and society, since to do so would be wilfully to engage in our shipwreck."

"I will give my best advice," answered Philipson, "when I shall be more particularly acquainted with the circumstances under which it is asked of me."

Rudolph muttered an oath, or angry exclamation, and led Philipson to the church without farther argument.

In a small chapel adjoining to the church, and dedicated to St. Magnus the Martyr, the four deputies were assembled in close conclave around the shrine in which the sainted hero stood, armed as when he lived. The Priest of St. Paul's was also present, and seemed to interest himself deeply in the debate which was taking place. When Philipson entered, all were for a moment silent, until the Landamman addressed him thus: — "Seignor Philipson, we esteem you a man far travelled, well versed in the manners of foreign lands, and acquainted with the conditions of this Duke Charles of Burgundy; you are therefore fit to advise us in a matter of great weight. You know with what anxiety we go on this mission for peace with the Duke; you also know what has this day happened, which may probably be represented to Charles in the worst colours; — would you advise us in such a case, to proceed to the Duke's presence, with the odium of this action attached to us; or should we do better to return home, and prepare for war with Burgundy?"

"How do your own opinions stand on the subject?" said the cautious Englishman.

"We are divided," answered the Banneret of Berne. — "I have borne the banner of Berne against her foes for thirty years; I am more willing to carry it against the lances of the knights of Hainault, and Lorraine, than to undergo the rude treatment which we must look to meet at the footstool of the Duke."

"We put our heads in the lion's mouth if we go forward," said Zimmerman of Soleure: — "my opinion is, that we draw back."

"I would not advise retreat," said Rudolph Donnerhugel, "were my life alone concerned; but the Landamman of Unterwalden is the father of the United Cantons, and it would be parricide if I consented to put his life in peril. My advice is, that we return, and that the Confederacy stand on their defence."

"My opinion is different," said Arnold Biederman; "nor will I forgive any man, who, whether in sincere or feigned friendship, places my poor life in the scale with the advantage of the Cantons. If we go forward, we risk our heads — be it so. But if we turn back, we involve our country in war with a power of the first magnitude in Europe. Worthy citizens! you are brave in fight, — show your fortitude as boldly now; and let us not hesitate to incur such personal danger as may attend ourselves, if by doing so we can gain a chance of peace for our country."

"I think and vote with my neighbour and gossip, Arnold Biederman," said the laconic deputy from Schwitz.

"You hear how we are divided in opinion," said the Landamman to Philipson; "What is your opinion?"

"I would first ask of you," said the Englishman, "what has been your part in the storming of a town occupied by the Duke's forces, and putting to death his Governor?"

"So help me Heaven!" said the Landamman, "as I knew not of any purpose of storming the town until it unexpectedly took place."

"And for the execution of De Hagenbach," said the Black Priest, "I swear to you, stranger, by my holy order, that it took place under the direction of a competent court, whose sentence Charles of Burgundy himself is bound to respect, and whose proceedings the Deputies of the Swiss mission could neither have advanced nor retarded."

"If such be the case, and if you can really prove yourselves free of these proceedings," answered Philipson, "which must needs be highly resented by the Duke of Burgundy, I would advise you by all means to proceed upon your journey; with the certainty that you will obtain from that prince a just and impartial hearing, and it may be a favourable answer. I know Charles of Burgundy; I may even say that, our different ranks and walks of life considered, I know him well. He will be deeply incensed by the first tidings of what has here chanced, which he will no doubt interpret to your disfavour. But if, in the course of investigation, you are able to clear yourselves of these foul imputations, a sense of his own injustice may perhaps turn the balance in your favour; and in that case, he will rush from the excess of censure into that of indulgence. But your cause must be firmly stated to the Duke, by some tongue better acquainted with the language of courts than yours; and such a friendly interpreter might I have proved to you, had I not been plundered of the valuable packet which I bore with me in order to present to the Duke, and in testimony of my commission to him."

"A paltry fetch," whispered Donnerhugel to the Banneret, "that the trader may obtain from us satisfaction for the goods of which he has been plundered."

The Landamman himself was perhaps for a moment of the same opinion.

"Merchant," he said, "we hold ourselves bound to make good to you, — that is, if our substance can effect it, — whatever loss you may have sustained, trusting to our protection."

"Ay, that we will," said the old man of Schwitz, "should it cost us twenty zechins to make it good."

"To your guarantee of immunity I can have no claim," said Philipson, "seeing I parted company with you before I sustained any loss. And I regret the loss, not so much for its value, although that is greater than you may fancy; but chiefly because, that the contents of the casket I bore being a token betwixt a person of considerable importance and the Duke of Burgundy, I shall not, I fear, now that I am deprived of them, receive from his grace that credence which I desire, both for my own sake and yours. Without them, and speaking only in the person of a private traveller, I may not take upon me as I might have done, when using the names of the persons whose mandates I carried."

"This important packet," said the Landamman, "shall be most rigorously sought for, and carefully re-delivered to thee. For ourselves, not a Swiss of us knows the value of its contents; so that if they are in the hands of any of our men, they will be returned of course as baubles, upon which they set no value."

As he spoke, there was a knocking at the door of the chapel. Rudolph, who stood nearest to it, having held some communication with those without, observed with a smile, which he instantly repressed, lest it had given offence to Arnold Biederman, — "It is Sigismund, the good youth — Shall I admit him to our council?"

"To what purpose, poor simple lad?" said his father, with a sorrowful smile.

"Yet let me undo the door," said Philipson; "he is anxious to enter, and perhaps he brings news. I have observed, Landamman, that the young man, though with slowness of ideas and expression, is strong in his principles, and sometimes happy in his conceptions."

He admitted Sigismund accordingly; while Arnold Biederman felt, on the one hand, the soothing compliment which Philipson had paid to a boy, certainly the dullest of his family, and, on the other, feared some public display of his son's infirmity, or lack of understanding. Sigismund, however, seemed all confidence; and he certainly had reason to be so, since, as the shortest mode of explanation, he presented to Philipson the necklace of diamonds, with the casket in which it had been deposited.

"This pretty thing is yours," he said. "I understand so much from your son Arthur, who tells me you would be glad to have it again."

"Most cordially do I thank you," said the merchant. "The necklace is certainly mine; that is, the packet of which it formed the contents was under my charge; and it is at this moment of greater additional value to me than even its actual worth, since it serves as my pledge and token for the performance of an important mission. — And how, my young friend," he continued, addressing Sigismund, "have you been so fortunate as to recover what we have sought for hitherto in vain? Let me return my best

240

acknowledgments; and do not think me over-curious if I ask how it reached you?"

"For that matter," said Sigismund, "the story is soon told. I had planted myself as near the scaffold as I could, having never beheld an execution before; and I observed the executioner, who I thought did his duty very cleverly, just in the moment that he spread a cloth over the body of De Hagenbach, snatch something from the dead man's bosom, and huddle it hastily into his own; so, when the rumour arose that an article of value was amissing, I hurried in quest of the fellow. I found he had bespoke masses to the extent of a hundred crowns at the high altar of St. Paul's; and I traced him to the tavern of the village, where some ill-looking men were joyously drinking to him as a free citizen and a nobleman. So I stepped in amongst them with my partisan, and demanded of his lordship either to surrender to me what he had thus possessed himself of, or to try the weight of the weapon I carried. His lordship, my Lord Hangman, hesitated, and was about to make a brawl. But I was something peremptory, and so he judged it best to give me the parcel, which I trust you, Seignor Philipson, will find safe and entire as it was taken from you. And — and — I left them to conclude their festivities — and that is the whole of the story."

"Thou art a brave lad," said Philipson; "and with a heart always right, the head can seldom be far wrong. But the Church shall not lose its dues; and I take it on myself, ere I leave La Ferette, to pay for the masses which the man had ordered for the sake of De Hagenbach's soul, snatched from the world so unexpectedly."

Sigismund was about to reply; but Philipson, fearing he might bring out some foolery to diminish the sense which his fattier had so joyously entertained of his late conduct, immediately added, "Hie away, my good youth, and give to my son Arthur this precious casket."

With simple exultation at receiving applause to which he was little accustomed, Sigismund took his leave, and the council were once more left to their own privacy.

There was a moment's silence; for the Landamman could not overcome the feeling of exquisite pleasure at the sagacity which poor Sigismund, whose general conduct warranted no such expectations, had displayed on the present occasion. It was not, however, a feeling to which circumstances permitted him to give vent, and he reserved it for his own secret enjoyment, as a solace to the anxiety which he had hitherto entertained concerning the limited intellect of this simple-minded young man. When he spoke, it was to Philipson, with the usual candour and manliness of his character.

"Seignor Philipson," he said, "we will hold you bound by no offer which you made while these glittering matters were out of your possession; because a man may often think, that if he were in such and such a situation, he would be able to achieve certain ends, which, that position being attained, he may find himself unable to accomplish. But I now ask you, whether, having thus fortunately and unexpectedly regained possession of what you say will give you certain credence with the Duke of Burgundy, you conceive yourself entitled to mediate with him on our behalf, as you formerly proposed?"

All bent forward to hear the merchant's answer.

"Landamman," he replied, "I never spoke the word in difficulty which I was not ready to redeem when that difficulty was removed. You say, and I believe, that you had no concern with this storming of La Ferette. You say also, that the life of De Hagenbach was taken by a judicature over which you had no control, and exercised none — let a protocol be drawn up, averring these circumstances, and, as far as possible, proving them. Intrust it to me, — under seal if you will, — and if such points be established, I will pledge my word as a — as a — as an honest man and a true-born Englishman, that the Duke of Burgundy will neither detain nor offer you any personal injury. I also hope to show to Charles strong and weighty reasons why a league of friend-hip betwixt Burgundy and the United Cantons of Helvetia is, on his grace's part, a wise and generous measure. But it is possible I may fail in this last point; and if I do, I shall deeply grieve for it. In warranting your safe passage to the Duke's court, and your safe return from it to your own country, I think I cannot fail. If I do, my own life, and that of my beloved and only child, shall pay the ransom for my excess of confidence in the Duke's justice and honour."

The other deputies stood silent, and looked on the Landamman; but Rudolph Donnerhugel spoke.

"Are we then to trust our own lives, and, what is still dearer to us, that of our honoured associate, Arnold Biederman, on the simple word of a foreign trader? We all know the temper of the Duke, and how vindictively and relentlessly he has ever felt towards our country and its interests. Methinks this English merchant should express the nature of his interest at the court of Burgundy more plainly, if he expects us to place such implicit reliance in it."

"That, Seignor Rudolph Donnerhugel," replied the merchant, "I find myself not at liberty to do. I pry not into your secrets, whether they belong to you as a body or as individuals. My own are sacred. If I consulted my own safety merely, I should act most wisely to part company with you here. But the object of your mission is peace; and your sudden return, after what has chanced at La Ferette, will make war inevitable. I think I can assure you of a safe and free audience from the Duke, and I am willing, for the chance of securing the peace of Christendom, to encounter any personal peril which may attach to myself."

"Say no more, worthy Philipson," said the Landamman; "thy good faith is undoubted on our part, and ill-luck is his who cannot read it written on thy manly forehead. We go forward, then, prepared to risk our own safety at the hand of a despotic prince, rather than leave undischarged the mission which our country has intrusted us with. He is but half a brave man who will risk his life only in the field of battle. There are other dangers, to front which is equally honourable; and since the weal of Switzerland demands that we should encounter them, not one of us will hesitate to take the risk."

The other members of the mission bowed in assent, and the conclave broke up to prepare for their farther entrance into Burgundy.

CHAPTER XVII

Upon the mountain's heathery side,
The day's last lustre shone,
And rich with many a radiant hue,
Gleam'd gaily on the Rhone.

SOUTHEY.

The English merchant was now much consulted by the Swiss Commissioners in all their motions. He exhorted them to proceed with all dispatch on their journey, so as to carry to the Duke their own account of the affair of Brisach, and thus anticipate all rumours less favourable to their conduct on the occasion. For this purpose Philipson recommended that the Deputies, dismissing their escort, whose arms and numbers might give umbrage and suspicion, while they were too few for defence, should themselves proceed by rapid journeys on horseback towards Dijon, or wherever the Duke might chance to be for the time.

This proposal was, however, formally resisted by the very person who had hitherto been the most ductile of the party, and the willing echo of the Landamman's pleasure. On the present occasion, notwithstanding that Arnold Biederman declared the advice of Philipson excellent, Nicholas Bonstetten stood in absolute and insurmountable opposition; because, having hitherto trusted to his own limbs for transporting himself to and fro on all occasions, he could by no means be persuaded to commit himself to the discretion of a horse. As he was found obstinately positive on this subject, it was finally determined that the two Englishmen should press forward on their journey, with such speed as they might, and that the elder of them should make the Duke acquainted with so much as to the capture of La Ferette, as he had himself witnessed of the matter. The particulars which had attended the death of De Hagenbach, the Landamman assured him, would be sent to the Duke by a person of confidence, whose attestation on the subject could not be doubted.

This course was adopted, as Philipson expressed his confidence of getting an early and private audience with his grace of Burgundy.

"My best intercession," he said, "you have a good right to reckon upon; and no one can bear more direct testimony than I can, to the ungovernable cruelty and rapacity of De Hagenbach, of which I had so nearly been the victim. But of his trial and execution, I neither know nor can tell any thing; and as Duke Charles is sure to demand why execution was done upon his officer without an appeal to his own tribunal, it will be well that you either provide me with such facts as you have to state, or send forward, at least, as speedily as possible, the evidence which you have to lay before him on that most weighty branch of the subject."

The proposal of the merchant created some visible embarrassment on the countenance of the Swiss, and it was with obvious hesitation that Arnold Biederman, having led him aside, addressed him in a whisper —

"My good friend," he said, "mysteries are in general like the hateful mists which disfigure the noblest features of nature; yet, like mists, they will sometimes intervene when we most desire their absence — when we most desire to be plain and explicit. The manner of De Hagenbach's death, you saw — we will take care that the Duke is informed of the authority by which it was inflicted. This is all that I can at present tell you on the subject; and let me add, that the less you speak of it with any one, you will be the more likely to escape inconvenience."

"Worthy Landamman," said the Englishman, "I also am by nature, and from the habits of my country, a hater of mysteries. Yet, such is my firm confidence in your truth and honour, that you shall be my guide in these dark and secret transactions, even as amongst the mists and precipices of your native land, and I rest contented in either case to place unlimited confidence in your sagacity. Let me only recommend that your explanation with Charles be instant, as well as clear and candid. Such being the case, I trust my poor interest with the Duke may be reckoned for something in your favour. Here then we part, but, as I trust, soon to meet again."

The elder Philipson now rejoined his son, whom he directed to hire horses, together with a guide, to conduct them with all speed to the presence of the Duke of Burgundy. By various inquiries in the town, and especially among the soldiers of the slain De Hagenbach, they at length learned that Charles had been of late occupied in taking possession of Lorraine, and, being now suspicious of unfriendly dispositions on the part of the Emperor of Germany, as well as of Sigismund, Duke of Austria, had drawn a considerable part of his army together near Strasburg, in order to be prepared against any attempt of these princes, or of the Free Imperial Cities, which might interfere with his course of conquest. The Duke of Burgundy, at this period, well deserved his peculiar epithet of the Bold, since, surrounded by enemies, like one of the nobler animals of the chase, he yet astounded, by his stern and daring countenance, not only the princes and states we have mentioned, but even the King of France, equally powerful, and far more politic, than himself.

To his camp, therefore, the English travellers bent their way, each full of such deep and melancholy reflection, as, perhaps, prevented his bestowing much attention on the other's state of mind. They rode as men deeply immersed in their own thoughts, and with less intercourse than had been usual betwixt them on their former journeys. The nobleness of the elder Philipson's nature, and his respect for the Landamman's probity, joined with gratitude for his hospitality, had prevented him from separating his cause from that of the Swiss Deputies, nor did he now repent this generosity in adhering to them. But when he recollected the nature and importance of the personal affairs which he himself had to dispatch with a proud, imperious, and irritable prince, he could not but regret the circumstances which had involved his own particular mission, of so much consequence to himself and his friends, with that of persons likely to be so highly obnoxious to the Duke as Arnold Biederman and his companions; and, however grateful for the hospitality of Geierstein, he regretted, nevertheless, the circumstances which had obliged him to accept of it.

The thoughts of Arthur were no less anxious. He found himself anew separated from the object to which his thoughts were, almost against his own will, constantly returning. And this second separation had taken place after he had incurred an additional load of gratitude, and found new, as well as more mysterious food for his ardent imagination. How was he to reconcile the character and attributes of Anne of Geierstein, whom he had known so gentle, candid, pure, and simple, with those of the daughter of a sage, and of an elementary spirit, to whom night was as day, and an impervious dungeon the same as the open portico of a temple? Could they be identified as the same being? or, while strictly alike in shape and lineament, was the one a tenant of the earth, the other only a phantom, permitted to show itself among those of a nature in which she did not partake? Above all, must he never see her more, or receive from her own lips an explanation of the mysteries which were so awfully entwined with his recollections of her? Such were the questions which occupied the mind of the younger traveller, and prevented him from interrupting, or even observing, the reverie in which his father was plunged.

Had either of the travellers been disposed to derive amusement from the country through which their road lay, the vicinity of the Rhine was well qualified to afford it. The ground on the left bank of that noble river is indeed rather flat and tame; and the mountains of Alsace, a ridge of which sweeps along its course, do not approach so near as greatly to vary the level surface of the valley which divides them from its shores. But the broad stream itself, hurrying forward with dizzy rapidity, and rushing around the islets by which its course is interrupted, is one of the most majestic spectacles in nature. The right bank is dignified at once, and adorned, by the numerous eminences covered with wood, and interspersed with valleys, which constitute the district so well known by the name of the Black Forest, to which superstition attached so many terrors, and credulity such a variety of legends. Terrors, indeed, it had, of a real and existing character. The old castles, seen from time to time on the banks of the river itself, or on the ravines and large brooks which flow into it, were then no picturesque ruins, rendered interesting by the stories which were told about their former inhabitants, but constituted the real and apparently impregnable strongholds of that Robber-chivalry whom we have already frequently mentioned, and of whom, since Goethe, an author born to arouse the slumbering fame of his country, has dramatized the story of Goetz of Berlichingen, we have had so many spirit-stirring tales. The danger attending the vicinity of these fortresses was only known on the right, or German bank of the Rhine, for the breadth and depth of that noble stream effectually prevented any foray of their inhabitants from reaching Alsace. The former was in possession of the Cities or Free Towns of the Empire, and thus the feudal tyranny of the German lords was chiefly exerted at the expense of their own countrymen, who, irritated and exhausted with their rapine and oppression, were compelled to erect barriers against it, of a nature as interesting and extraordinary, as were the wrongs from which they endeavoured to protect themselves.

But the left bank of the river, over great part of which Charles of Burgundy exercised his authority, under various characters, was under the regular protection of the ordinary magistrates, who were supported in the discharge of their duty by large bands of mercenary soldiers. These were maintained by Charles out of his private revenue; he, as well as his rival Louis, and other princes of the period, having discovered that the feudal system gave an inconvenient degree of independence to their vassals, and thinking, of course, that it was better to substitute in its place a standing army, consisting of free companies, or soldiers by profession. Italy furnished most of these bands, which composed the strength of Charles's army, at least the part of it in which he most trusted.

Our travellers, therefore, pursued their way by the banks of the river, in as great a degree of security as could well be enjoyed in that violent and distracted time, until at length, the father, after having eyed for some time the person whom Arthur had hired to be their guide, suddenly asked of his son, who or what the man was. Arthur replied that he had been too eager to get a person who knew the road, and was willing to show it, to be very particular in inquiring into his station or occupation; but that he thought, from the man's appearance, he must be one of those itinerant ecclesiastics, who travel through the country with relics, pardons, and other religious trinkets, and were in general but slightly respected, excepting by the lower orders, on whom these vendors of superstitious wares were often accused of practising gross deceptions.

The man's appearance was rather that of a lay devotee, or palmer, bound on his pilgrimage to different shrines, than of a mendicant friar, or questionary. He wore the hat, scrip, staff, and coarse dalmatic, somewhat like the military cloak of the modern hussar, which were used by such persons on their religious peregrinations. Saint Peter's keys, rudely shaped out of some scarlet rag of cloth, appeared on the back of his mantle, placed, as heralds say, saltire wise. This devotee seemed a man of fifty and upwards, well made, and stout, for his age, with a cast of countenance which, though not positively ugly, was far from being well-favoured. There was shrewdness, and an alert expression in his eye and actions, which made some occasional contrast with the sanctimonious demeanour of the character he now bore. This difference betwixt his dress and physiognomy was by no means uncommon among persons of his description, many of whom embraced this mode of life, rather to indulge roving and idle habits, than from any religious call.

"Who art thou, good fellow?" said the elder Philipson; "and by what name am I to call thee while we are fellow-travellers?"

"Bartholomew, sir," said the man; "Brother Bartholomew — I might say Bartholomæus, but it does not become a poor lay brother like me to aspire to the honour of a learned termination."

"And whither does thy journey tend, good Brother Bartholomew?"

"In whichever direction your worship chooses to travel, and to require my services as guide," answered the palmer; "always premising, you allow me leisure for my devotions at such holy stations as we pass on our route."

"That is, thine own journey hath no professed or pressing object or end?" said the Englishman.

"None, as your worship says, peculiar," said the itinerant; "or I might rather say, that my journey, good sir, embraces so many objects, that it is matter of indifference to me which of them I accomplish first. My vow binds me for four years to travel from one shrine, or holy place, to another; but I am not directly tied to visit them by any precise rule of rotation."

"That is to say, thy vow of pilgrimage does not prevent thee from hiring thyself to wait upon travellers as their guide," replied Philipson.

"If I can unite the devotion I owe to the blessed saints whose shrines I visit, with a service rendered to a wandering fellow-creature who desires to be directed upon his journey, I do maintain," replied Bartholomew, "that the objects are easily to be reconciled to each other."

"Especially as a little worldly profit may tend to cement the two duties together, if otherwise incompatible," said Philipson.

"It pleases your honour to say so," replied the pilgrim; "but you yourself may, if you will, derive from my good company something more than the mere knowledge of the road in which you propose to travel. I can make your journey more edifying by legends of the blessed saints whose holy relics I have visited, and pleasing, by the story of the wonderful things which I have seen and heard in my travels. I can impart to you an opportunity of providing yourself with his Holiness's pardon, not only for the sins which you have committed, but also granting you indulgence for future errors."

"These things are highly available doubtless," replied the merchant; "but, good Bartholomew, when I desire to speak of them, I apply to my father confessor, to whom I have been uniformly regular in committing the charge of my conscience, and who must be, therefore, well acquainted with my state of mind, and best accustomed to prescribe what its case may require."

"Nevertheless," said Bartholomew, "I trust your worship is too religious a man and too sound a Catholic, to pass any hallowed station without endeavouring to obtain some share of the benefits which it is the means of dispensing to those who are ready and willing to deserve them. More especially as all men, of whatever trade and degree, hold respect to the holy saint who patronizeth his own mystery; so I hope you, being a merchant, will not pass the Chapel of Our Lady of the Ferry, without making some fitting orison."

"Friend Bartholomew," said Philipson, "I have not heard of the shrine which you recommend to me; and, is my business is pressing, it were better worth my while to make a pilgrimage hither on purpose to make mine homage at a litter season, than to delay my journey at present. This, God willing, I will not fail to do, so that I may be held excused for delaying my reverence till I can pay it more respectfully, and at greater leisure."

"May it please you not to be wroth," said the guide, "if I say that your behaviour in this matter is like that of a fool, who, finding a treasure by the roadside, omits to put it in his bosom and carry it along with him, proposing to return from a distance on a future day, of express purpose to fetch it."

Philipson, something astonished at the man's pertinacity, was about to answer hastily and angrily, but was prevented by the arrival of three strangers, who rode hastily up from behind them.

The foremost of these was a young female, most elegantly attired, and mounted upon a Spanish jennet, which she reined with singular grace and dexterity. She wore on her right hand such a glove as that which was used to carry hawks, and had a merlin perched upon it. Her head was covered with a montero cap, and, as was frequently the custom at the period, she wore on her face a kind of black silk vizard, which effectually concealed her features. Notwithstanding this disguise, Arthur Philipson's heart sprung high at the appearance of these strangers, for he was at once certain he recognised the matchless form of the Swiss maiden, by whom his mind was so anxiously occupied. Her attendants were a falconer with his hunting-pole, and a female, both apparently her domestics. The elder Philipson, who had no such accuracy of recollection as his son manifested upon the occasion, saw in the fair stranger only some dame or damsel of eminence engaged in the amusement of hawking, and, in return to a brief salutation, merely asked her, with suitable courtesy, as the case demanded, whether she had spent the morning in good sport.

"Indifferent, good friend," said the lady. "I dare not fly my hawk so near the broad river, lest he should soar to the other side, and so I might lose my companion. But I reckon on finding better game when I have crossed to the other side of the ferry, which we are now approaching."

"Then your ladyship," said Bartholomew, "will hear mass in Hans' Chapel, and pray for your success?"

"I were a heathen to pass the holy place without doing so," replied the damsel.

"That, noble damsel, touches the point we were but now talking of," said the guide Bartholomew; "for know, fair mistress, that I cannot persuade this worthy gentleman how deeply the success of his enterprise is dependent upon his obtaining the blessing of Our Lady of the Ferry."

"The good man," said the young maiden, seriously, and even severely, "must know little of the Rhine. I will explain to the gentleman the propriety of following your advice."

She then rode close to young Philipson, and spoke in Swiss, for she had hitherto used the German language, "Do not start, but hear me!" and the voice was that of Anne of Geierstein. "Do not, I say, be surprised — or at least show not your wonder — you are beset by dangers. On this road, especially, your business is known — your lives are laid in wait for. Cross over the river at the Ferry of the Chapel, or Hans' Ferry, as it is usually termed."

Here the guide drew so near to them, that it was impossible for her to continue the conversation without being overheard. At that same moment a woodcock sprung from some bushes, and the young lady threw off her merlin in pursuit.

"Sa ho — sa ho — wo ha!" hollowed the falconer, in a note which made the thicket ring again; and away he rode in pursuit. The elder Philipson and the guide himself followed the chase eagerly with their eyes, so attractive was the love of that brave sport to men of all ranks. But the voice of the maiden was a lure, which would have summoned Arthur's attention from matters more deeply interesting.

"Cross the Rhine," she again repeated, "at the Ferry to Kirch-hoff, on the other side of the river. Take your lodgings at the Golden Fleece, where you will find a guide to Strasburg. I must stay here no longer."

So saying, the damsel raised herself in her saddle, struck her horse lightly with the loose reins, and the mettled animal, already impatient at her delay, and the eager burst of its companions, flew forward at such a pace, as if he had meant to emulate the flight of the hawk, and of the prey he pursued. The lady and her attendants soon vanished from the sight of the travellers.

A deep silence for some time ensued, during which Arthur studied how to communicate the warning he had received, without awakening the suspicions of their guide.

But the old man broke silence himself, saying to Bartholomew, "Put your horse into more motion, I pray you, and ride onward a few yards; I would have some private conference with my son."

The guide obeyed, and, as if with the purpose of showing a mind too profoundly occupied by heavenly matters, to admit a thought concerning those of this transitory world, he thundered forth a hymn in praise of Saint Wendelin the Shepherd, in a strain so discordant, as startled every bird from every bush by which they passed. There was never a more unmelodious melody, whether sacred or profane, than that under protection of which the elder Philipson thus conferred with his son.

"Arthur," he said, "I am much convinced that this howling hypocritical vagrant has some plot upon us; and I had well-nigh determined, that the best mode to baffle it would be to consult my own opinion, and not his, as to our places of repose, and the direction of our journey."

"Your judgment is correct, as usual," said his son. "I am well convinced of yonder man's treachery from a whisper in which that maiden informed me that we ought to take the road to Strasburg, by the eastern side of the river, and for that purpose cross over to a place called Kirch-hoff, on the opposite bank."

"Do you advise this, Arthur?" replied his father.

"I will pledge my life for the faith of this young person," replied his son.

"What!" said his father, "because she sits her palfrey fairly, and shows a faultless shape? Such is the reasoning of a boy — and yet my own old and cautious heart feels inclined to trust her. If our secret is known in this land, there are doubtless many who may be disposed to think they have an interest in barring my access to the Duke of Burgundy, even by the most violent means; and well you know that I should on my side hold my life equally cheap, could I discharge mine errand at the price of laying it down. I tell thee, Arthur, that my mind reproaches me for taking hitherto over little care of ensuring the discharge of my commission, owing to the natural desire I had to keep thee in my company. There now lie before us two ways, both perilous and uncertain, by which we may reach the Duke's Court. We may follow this guide, and take the chance of his fidelity, or we may adopt the hint of yonder damsel-errant, and cross over to the other side of the Rhine, and again repass the river at Strasburg. Both roads are perhaps equally perilous. I feel it my duty to diminish the risk of the miscarriage of my commission, by sending thee across to the right bank, while I pursue my proposed course upon the left. Thus, if one of us be intercepted, the other may escape, and the important commission which he bears may be duly executed."

"Alas, my father!" said Arthur, "how is it possible for me to obey you, when by doing so I must leave you alone, to incur so many dangers, to struggle with so many difficulties, in which my aid might be at least willing, though it could only be weak? Whatever befall us in these delicate and dangerous circumstances, let us at least meet it in company."

"Arthur, my beloved son," said his father, "in parting from thee I am splitting mine own heart in twain; but the same duty which commands us to expose our bodies to death, as peremptorily orders us not to spare our most tender affections. We must part."

"Oh, then," replied his son eagerly, "let me at least prevail in one point. Do thou, my father, cross the Rhine, and let me prosecute the journey by the route originally proposed."

"And why, I pray you," answered the merchant, "should I go one of these roads in preference to the other?"

"Because," said Arthur eagerly, "I would warrant yonder maiden's faith with my life."

"Again, young man?" said his father; "and wherefore so confident in that young maiden's faith? Is it merely from the confidence which youth reposes in that which is fair and pleasing, or have you had farther acquaintance with her than the late brief conversation with her admitted?"

"Can I give you an answer?" — replied his son. "We have been long absent from lands of knights and ladies, and is it not natural that we should give to those who remind us of the honoured ties of chivalry and gentle blood, the instinctive credence which we refuse to such a poor wretch as this itinerant mountebank, who gains his existence by cheating, with false relics and forged legends, the poor peasants amongst whom he travels?"

"It is a vain imagination, Arthur," said his father; "not unbefitting, indeed, an aspirant to the honours of chivalry, who draws his ideas of life and its occurrences from the romances of the minstrels, but too visionary for a youth who has seen, as thou hast, how the business of this world is conducted. I tell thee, and thou wilt learn to know I say truth, that around the homely board of our host the Landamman, were ranged truer tongues, and more faithful hearts, than the *Cour plenière* of a monarch has to boast. Alas! the manly spirit of ancient faith and honour has fled even from the breast of kings and knights, where, as John of France said, it ought to continue to reside a constant inhabitant, if banished from all the rest of the world."

"Be that as it may, dearest father," replied the younger Philipson, "I pray you to be persuaded by me; and if we must part company, let it be by your taking the right bank of the Rhine, since I am persuaded it is the safest route."

"And if it be the safest," said his father, with a voice of tender reproach, "is that a reason why I should spare my own almost exhausted thread of life, and expose thine, my dear son, which has but begun its course?"

"Nay, father," answered the son with animation, "in speaking thus you do not consider the difference of our importance to the execution of the purpose which you have so long entertained, and which seems now so nigh being accomplished. Think how imperfectly I might be able to discharge it, without knowledge of the Duke's person, or credentials to gain his confidence. I might, indeed, repeat your words, but the circumstances would be wanting to attract the necessary faith, and of consequence, your scheme, for the success of which you have lived, and now are willing to run the risk of death, would miscarry along with me."

"You cannot shake my resolution," said the elder Philipson, "or persuade me that my life is of more importance than yours. You only remind me, that it is you, and not I, who ought to be the bearer of this token to the Duke of Burgundy. Should you be successful in reaching his court or camp, your possession of these gems will be needful to attach credit to your mission; a purpose for which they would be less necessary to me, who can refer to other circumstances under which I might claim credence, if it should please Heaven to leave me alone to acquit myself of this important commission, which, may Our Lady, in her mercy, forefend! Understand, therefore, that, should an opportunity occur by which you can make your way to the opposite side of the Rhine, you are to direct your journey so as again to cross to this bank at Strasburg, where you will inquire for news of me at the Flying Stag, a hostelry in that city, which you will easily discover. If you hear no tidings of me at that place, you will proceed to the Duke, and deliver to him this important packet."

Here he put into his son's hand, with as much privacy as possible, the case containing the diamond necklace.

"What else your duty calls on you to do," continued the elder Philipson, "you well know; only I conjure you, let no vain inquiries after my fate interfere with the great duty you have there to discharge. In the meantime, prepare to bid me a sudden farewell, with a heart as bold and confident as when you went before me, and courageously led the way amid the rocks and storms of Switzerland. Heaven was above us then, as it is over us now. Adieu, my beloved Arthur! Should I wait till the moment of separation, there may be but short time to speak the fatal word, and no eye save thine own must see the tear which I now wipe away."

The painful feeling which accompanied this anticipation of their parting, was so sincere on Arthur's part, as well as that of his father, that it did not at first occur to the former, as a source of consolation, that it seemed likely he might be placed under the guidance of the singular female, the memory of whom haunted him. True it was, that the beauty of Anne of Geierstein, as well as the striking circumstances in which she had exhibited herself, had on that very morning been the principal occupation of his mind; but they were now chased from it by the predominant recollection, that he was about to be separated in a moment of danger from a father, so well deserving of his highest esteem and his fondest affection.

Meanwhile, that father dashed from his eye the tear which his devoted stoicism could not suppress, and, as if afraid of softening his resolution by indulging his parental fondness, he recalled the pious Bartholomew, to demand of him how far they were from the Chapel of the Ferry.

"Little more than a mile," was the reply; and when the Englishman required further information concerning the cause of its erection, he was informed that an old boatman and fisherman, named Hans, had long dwelt at the place, who gained a precarious livelihood by transporting travellers and merchants from one bank of the river to the other. The misfortune, however, of losing first one boat and then a second, in the deep and mighty stream, with the dread inspired in travellers by the repetition of such accidents, began to render his profession an uncertain one. Being a good Catholic, the old man's distress took a devotional turn. He began to look back on his former life, and consider by what crimes he had deserved the misfortunes which darkened the evening of his days. His remorse was chiefly excited by the recollection that he had, on one occasion, when the passage was peculiarly stormy, refused to discharge his duty as a ferryman, in order to transport to the other shore a priest, who bore along with him an image of the Virgin, destined for the village of Kirchhoff, on the opposite or right bank of the Rhine. For this fault, Hans submitted to severe penance, as he was now disposed to consider as culpable his doubt of the Virgin's power of protecting herself, her priest, and the bark employed in her service; besides which, the offering of a large share of his worldly goods to the church of Kirch-hoff, expressed the truth of the old man's repentance. Neither did he ever again permit himself to interpose any delay in the journey of men of holy Church; but all ranks of the clergy, from the mitred prelate to the barefooted friar, might at any time of day or night have commanded the services of him and his boat.

While prosecuting so laudable a course of life, it became at length the lot of Hans to find, on the banks of the Rhine, a small image of the Virgin, thrown by the waves, which appeared to him exactly to resemble that which he had formerly ungraciously refused to carry across, when under charge of the sacristan of Kirch-hoff. He placed it in the most conspicuous part of his hut, and poured out his soul before it in devotion, anxiously inquiring for some signal by which he might discover whether he was to consider the arrival of her holy image as a pledge that his offences were forgiven. In the visions of the night, his prayers were answered, and Our Lady, assuming the form of the image, stood by his bed-side, for the purpose of telling him wherefore she had come hither.

"My trusty servant," she said, "men of Belial have burned my dwelling at Kirch-hoff, spoiled my chapel, and thrown the sacred image which represents me into the swoln Rhine, which swept me downward. Now, I have resolved to dwell no longer in the neighbourhood of the profane doers of this deed, or of the cowardly vassals who dared not prevent it. I am, therefore, compelled to remove my habitation, and, in despite of the opposing current, I determined to take the shore on this side, being resolved to fix my abode with thee, my faithful servant, that the land in which thou dwellest may be blessed, as well as thou and thy household."

As the vision spoke, she seemed to wring from her tresses the water in which they had been steeped, while her disordered dress and fatigued appearance was that of one who has been buffeting with the waves.

Next rooming brought intelligence, that, in one of the numerous feuds of that fierce period, Kirch-hoff had been sacked, the church destroyed, and the church treasury plundered.

In consequence of the fisherman's vision being thus remarkably confirmed, Hans entirely renounced his profession, and, leaving it to younger men to supply his place as ferryman, he converted his hut into a rustic chapel, and he himself, taking orders, attended upon the shrine as a hermit, or daily chaplain. The figure was supposed to work miracles, and the ferry became renowned from its being under the protection of the Holy Image of Our Lady, and her no less holy servant.

When Bartholomew had concluded his account of the Ferry and its Chapel, the travellers had arrived at the place itself.

CHAPTER XVIII

Upon the Rhine, upon the Rhine they cluster,
   The grapes of juice divine,
Which make the soldier's jovial courage muster;
   O, blessed be the Rhine!

DRINKING SONG.[9]

A cottage or two on the side of the river, beside which were moored one or two fishing-boats, showed the pious Hans had successors in his profession as a boatman. The river, which at a point a little lower was restrained by a chain of islets, expanded more widely, and moved less rapidly, than when it passed these cottages, affording to the ferryman a smoother surface, and a less heavy stream to contend with, although the current was even there too strong to be borne up against, unless the river was in a tranquil state.

On the opposite bank, but a good deal lower than the hamlet which gave name to the ferry, was seated on a small eminence, screened by trees and bushes, the little town of Kirch-hoff. A skiff departing from the left bank was, even on favourable occasions, carried considerably to leeward ere it could attain the opposite side of the deep and full stream of the Rhine, so that its course was oblique towards Kirch-hoff. On the other hand, a boat departing from Kirch-hoff must have great advantage both of wind and oars, in order to land its loading or crew at the Chapel of the Ferry, unless it were under the miraculous influence which carried the image of the Virgin in that direction. The communication, therefore, from the east to the west bank, was only maintained by towing boats up the stream, to such a height on the eastern side, that the leeway which they made during the voyage across might correspond with the point at which they desired to arrive, and enable them to attain it with ease. Hence, it naturally happened, that the passage from Alsace into Suabia being the most easy, the ferry was more used by those who were desirous of entering Germany, than by travellers who came in an opposite direction.

---

[9] This is one of the best and most popular of the German ditties: —
"Am Rhein, am Rhein, da wachsen unsere Reben
Gesegnet sei der Rhein," &c.

When the elder Philipson had by a glance around him ascertained the situation of the ferry, he said firmly to his son, —
"Begone, my dear Arthur, and do what I have commanded thee."

With a heart rent with filial anxiety, the young man obeyed,
and took his solitary course towards the cottages, near which the
barks were moored, which were occasionally used for fishing, as
well as for the purposes of the ferry.

"Your son leaves us?" said Bartholomew to the elder Philipson.

"He does for the present," said his father, "as he has certain
inquiries to make in yonder hamlet."

"If they be," answered the guide, "any matters connected
with your honour's road, I laud the Saints that I can better answer your inquiries than those ignorant boors, who hardly understand your language."

"If we find that their information needs thy commentary,"
said Philipson, "we will request it — meanwhile, lead on to the
chapel, where my son will join us."

They moved towards the chapel, but with slow steps, each
turning his looks aside to the fishing hamlet; the guide as if
striving to see whether the younger traveller was returning towards them, the father anxious to descry, on the broad bosom of
the Rhine, a sail unloosed, to waft his son across to that which
might be considered as the eater side. But though the looks of
both guide and traveller were turned in the direction of the river,
their steps carried them towards the chapel, to which the inhabitants, in memory of the founder, had given the title of Hans-
Chapelle.

A few trees scattered around gave an agreeable and silvan
air to the place; and the chapel, that appeared on a rising ground
at some distance from the hamlet, was constructed in a style of
pleasing simplicity, which corresponded with the whole scene.
Its small size confirmed the tradition, that it had originally been
merely the hut of a peasant; and the cross of fir-trees, covered
with bark attested the purpose to which it was now dedicated.
The chapel and all round it breathed peace and solemn tranquillity, and the deep sound of the mighty river seemed to impose
silence on each human voice which might presume to mingle
with its awful murmur.

When Philipson arrived in the vicinity, Bartholomew took

the advantage afforded by his silence to thunder forth two stanzas to the praise of the Lady of the Ferry, and her faithful worshipper Hans, after which he broke forth into the rapturous exclamation, — "Come hither, ye who fear wreck, here is your safe haven! — Come hither, ye who die of thirst, here is a well of mercy open to you! — Come those who are weary and far-travelled, this is your place of refreshment!" — And more to the same purpose he might have said, but Philipson sternly imposed silence on him.

"If thy devotion were altogether true," he said, "it would be less clamorous; but it is well to do what is good in itself, even if it is a hypocrite who recommends it. — Let us enter this holy chapel, and pray for a fortunate issue to our precarious travels."

The pardoner caught up the last words.

"Sure was I," he said, "that your worship is too well advised to pass this holy place without imploring the protection and influence of Our Lady of the Ferry. Tarry but a moment until I find the priest who serves the altar, that he may say a mass on your behalf."

Here he was interrupted by the door of the chapel suddenly opening, when an ecclesiastic appeared on the threshold. Philipson instantly knew the Priest of Saint Paul's, whom he had seen that morning at La Ferette. Bartholomew also knew him, as it would seem; for his officious hypocritical eloquence failed him in an instant, and he stood before the priest with his arms folded on his breast, like a man who waits for the sentence of condemnation.

"Villain," said the ecclesiastic, regarding the guide with a severe countenance, "dost thou lead a stranger into the houses of the Holy Saints, that thou mayst slay him, and possess thyself of his spoils? But Heaven will no longer bear with thy perfidy. Back, thou wretch, to meet thy brother miscreants, who are hastening hither-ward. Tell them thy arts were unavailing, and that the innocent stranger is under MY protection — under my protection, which those who presume to violate will meet with the reward of Archibald de Hagenbach!"

The guide stood quite motionless, while addressed by the priest in a manner equally menacing and authoritative; and no sooner did the latter cease speaking, than, without offering a word either in justification or reply, Bartholomew turned round,

and retreated at a hasty pace by the same road which had conducted the traveller to the chapel.

"And do you, worthy Englishman," continued the priest,
"enter into this chapel and perform in safety those devotions, by
means of which yonder hypocrite designed to detain you until his
brethren in iniquity came up. — But first, wherefore are you
alone? I trust nought evil hath befallen your young companion?"

"My son," said Philipson, "crosses the Rhine at yonder
ferry, as we had important business to transact on the other side."

As he spoke thus, a light boat, about which two or three
peasants had been for some time busy, was seen to push from the
shore, and shoot into the stream, to which it was partly compelled to give way, until a sail stretched along the slender yard,
and supporting the bark against the current, enabled her to stand
obliquely across the river.

"Now, praise be to God!" said Philipson, who was aware
that the bark he looked upon must be in the act of carrying his
son beyond the reach of the dangers by which he was himself
surrounded.

"Amen!" answered the priest, echoing the pious ejaculation
of the traveller. "Great reason have you to return thanks to
Heaven."

"Of that I am convinced," replied Philipson; "but yet from
you I hope to learn the special cause of danger from which I
have escaped?"

"This is neither time nor place for such an investigation,"
answered the priest of Saint Paul's. "It is enough to say, that
yonder fellow, well known for his hypocrisy and his crimes, was
present when the young Switzer, Sigismund, reclaimed from the
executioner the treasure of which you were robbed by Hagenbach. Thus Bartholomew's avarice was awakened. He undertook
to be your guide to Strasburg, with the criminal intent of detain-
ing you by the way till a party came up, against whose numbers
resistance would have been in vain. But his purpose has been
anticipated. — And now, ere giving vent to other worldly
thoughts, whether of hope or fear, — to the chapel, sir, and join
in orisons to Him who hath been your aid, and to those who have
interceded with him in your behalf."

Philipson entered the chapel with his guide, and joined in
returning thanks to Heaven and the tutelary power of the spot,

for the escape which had been vouchsafed to him.

When this duty had been performed, Philipson intimated his purpose of resuming his journey, to which the Black Priest replied, "That far from delaying him in a place so dangerous, he would himself accompany him for some part of the journey, since he also was bound to the presence of the Duke of Burgundy."

"You, my father! — you!" said the merchant, with some astonishment.

"And wherefore surprised?" answered the priest. "Is it so strange that one of my order should visit a prince's court? Believe me, there are but too many of them to be found there."

"I do not speak with reference to your order," answered Philipson, "but in regard of the part which you have this day acted, in abetting the execution of Archibald de Hagenbach. Know you so little of the fiery Duke of Burgundy, as to imagine you can dally with his resentment with more safety than you would pull the mane of a sleeping lion?"

"I know his mood well," said the priest; "and it is not to excuse, but to defend the death of De Hagenbach, that I go to his presence. The Duke may execute his serfs and bondsmen at his pleasure, but there is a spell upon my life, which is proof to all his power. But let me retort the question — You, Sir Englishman, knowing the conditions of the Duke so well — you, so lately the guest and travelling companion of the most unwelcome visitors who could approach him — you, implicated, in appearance at least, in the uproar at La Ferette — what chance is there of your escaping his vengeance? and wherefore will you throw yourself wantonly within his power?"

"Worthy father," said the merchant, "let each of us, without offence to the other, keep his own secret. I have, indeed, no spell to secure me from the Duke's resentment — I have limbs to suffer torture and imprisonment, and property which may be seized and confiscated. But I lave had in former days many dealings with the Duke; I may even say I have laid him under obligations, and hope my interest with him may in consequence be sufficient, not only to save me from the consequences of this day's procedure, but be of some avail to my friend the Landamman."

"But if you are in reality bound to the court of Burgundy as a merchant," said the priest, "where are the wares in which you traffic? Have you no merchandise save that which you carry on your person? I heard of a sumpter-horse with baggage, has yonder villain deprived you of it?"

This was a trying question to Philipson, who, anxious about the separation from his son, had given no direction whether the baggage should remain with himself, or should be transported to the other side of the Rhine. He was, therefore, taken at advantage by the priest's inquiry, to which he answered with some incoherence, — "I believe my baggage is in the hamlet — that is, unless my son has taken it across the Rhine with him."

"That we will soon learn," answered the priest.

Here a novice appeared from the vestiary of the chapel at his call, and received commands to inquire at the hamlet whether Philipson's bales, with the horse which transported them, had been left there, or ferried over along with his son.

The novice, being absent a few minutes, presently returned with the baggage-horse, which, with its burden, Arthur, from regard to his father's accommodation, had left on the western side of the river. The priest looked on attentively, while the elder Philipson, mounting his own horse, and taking the rein of the other in his hand, bade the Black Priest adieu in these words, — "And now, father, farewell! I must pass on with my bales, since there is little wisdom in travelling with them after nightfall, else would I gladly suit my pace, with your permission, so as to share the way with you."

"If it is your obliging purpose to do so, as indeed I was about to propose," said the priest, "know I will be no stay to your journey. I have here a good horse; and Melchior, who must otherwise have gone on foot, may ride upon your sumpter-horse. I the rather propose this course, as it will be rash for you to travel by night. I can conduct you to an hostelrie about five miles off, which we may reach with sufficient daylight, and where you will be lodged safely for your reckoning."

The English merchant hesitated a moment. He had no fancy for any new companion on the road, and although the countenance of the priest was rather handsome, considering his years, yet the expression was such as by no means invited confidence. On the contrary, there was something mysterious and gloomy which clouded his brow, though it was a lofty one, and a similar expression gleamed in his cold gray eye, and intimated severity and even harshness of disposition. But notwithstanding this repulsive circumstance, the priest had lately rendered Philipson a considerable service, by detecting the treachery of his hypocritical guide, and the merchant was not a man to be startled from his course by any imaginary prepossessions against the looks or manners of any one, or apprehensions of machinations against himself. He only revolved in his mind the singularity attending his destiny, which, while it was necessary for him to appear before the Duke of Burgundy in the most conciliatory manner, seemed to force upon him the adoption of companions who must needs be obnoxious to that prince; and such, be was too well aware, must be the case with the Priest of St. Paul's. Having reflected for an instant, he courteously accepted the offer of the priest to guide him to some place of rest and entertainment, which must be absolutely necessary for his horse before he reached Strasburg, even if he himself could have dispensed with it.

The party being thus arranged, the novice brought forth the priest's steed, which he mounted with grace and agility, and the neophyte, being probably the same whom Arthur had represented during his escape from La Ferette, took charge, at his master's command, of the baggage-horse of the Englishman; and, crossing himself, with an humble inclination of his head, as the priest passed him, he full into the rear, and seemed to pass the time, like the false brother Bartholomew, in telling his heads, with an earnestness which had perhaps more of affected than of real piety. The Black Priest of St. Paul's, to judge by the glance which he cast upon his novice, seemed to disdain the formality of the young man's devotion. He rode upon a strong black horse, more like a warrior's charger than the ambling palfrey of a priest, and the manner in which he managed him was entirely devoid of awkwardness and timidity. His pride, whatever was its character, was not certainly of a kind altogether professional, but had its origin in other swelling thoughts which arose in his mind, to mingle with and enhance the self-consequence of a powerful ecclesiastic.

As Philipson looked on his companion from time to time, his scrutinizing glance was returned by a haughty smile, which seemed to say, "You may gaze on my form and features, but you cannot penetrate my mystery."

The looks of Philipson, which were never known to sink before mortal man, seemed to retort, with equal haughtiness, "Nor shall you, proud priest, know that you are now in company with one whose secret is far more important than thine own can be."

At length the priest made some advance towards conversation, by allusion to the footing upon which, by a mutual understanding, they seemed to have placed their intercourse.

"We travel then," he said, "like two powerful enchanters, each conscious of his own high and secret purpose; each in his own chariot of clouds, and neither imparting to his companion the direction or purpose of his journey."

"Excuse me, father," answered Philipson, "I have neither asked your purpose, nor concealed my own, so far as it concerns you. I repeat, I am bound to the presence of the Duke of Burgundy, and my object, like that of any other merchant, is to dispose of my wares to advantage."

"Doubtless, it would seem so," said the Black Priest, "from the extreme attention to your merchandise, which you showed not above half an hour since, when you knew not whether your bales had crossed the river with your son, or were remaining in your own charge. Are English merchants usually so indifferent to the sources of their traffic?"

"When their lives are in danger," said Philipson, "they are sometimes negligent of their fortune."

"It is well," replied the priest, and again resumed his solitary musings; until another half-hour's travelling brought them to a dorff, or village, which the Black Priest informed Philipson was that where he proposed to stop for the night.

"The novice," he said, "will show you the inn, which is of good reputation, and where you may lodge with safety. For me, I have to visit a penitent in this village, who desires my ghostly offices; — perhaps I may see you again this evening, perhaps not till the next morning; — at any rate, adieu for the present."

So saying, the priest stopped his horse, while the novice, coming close up to Philipson's side, conducted him onward through the narrow street of the village, whilst the windows exhibited here and there a twinkling gleam, announcing that the hour of darkness was arrived. Finally, he led the Englishman through an archway into a sort of court-yard, where there stood a car or two of a particular shape, used occasionally by women when they travel, and some other vehicles of the same kind. Here the young man threw himself from the sumpter-horse, and placing the rein in Philipson's hand, disappeared in the increasing darkness, after pointing to a large but dilapidated building, along the front of which not a spark of light was to be discovered from any of the narrow and numerous windows, which were dimly visible in the twilight.

CHAPTER XIX

First Carrier. — What, ostler! — a plague on thee, hast never an eye in thy head? Canst thou not hear? An 'twere not as good a deed as drink to break the pate of thee, I am a very villain — Come, and be hanged — Hast thou no faith in thee?

Gadshill. — I pray thee, lend me thy lantern, to see my gelding in the stable.

Second Carrier. — Nay, soft, I pray you — I know a trick worth two of that.

Gadshill. — I prithee lend me thine.

Third Carrier. — Ay, when? Canst tell? — Lend thee my lantern, quotha! Marry, I'll see thee hanged first.

HENRY IV.

The social spirit peculiar to the French nation had already introduced into the inns of that country the gay and cheerful character of welcome, upon which Erasmus, at a later period, dwells with strong emphasis, as a contrast to the saturnine and sullen reception which strangers were apt to meet with at a German caravansera. Philipson was, therefore, in expectation of being received by the busy, civil, and talkative host — by the hostess and her daughter, all softness, coquetry, and glee, — the smiling and supple waiter — the officious and dimpled chambermaid. The better inns in France boast also separate rooms, where strangers could change or put in order their dress, where they might sleep without company in their bedroom, and where they could deposit their baggage in privacy and safety. But all these luxuries were as yet unknown in Germany; and in Alsace, where the scene now lies, as well as in the other dependencies of the Empire, they regarded as effeminacy every thing beyond such provisions as were absolutely necessary for the supply of the wants of travellers; and even these were coarse and indifferent, and, excepting in the article of wine, sparingly ministered.

The Englishman, finding that no one appeared at the gate, began to make his presence known by calling aloud, and finally by alighting, and smiting with all his might on the doors of the hostelrie for a long time, without attracting the least attention. At length the head of a grizzled servitor was thrust out at a small window, who, in a voice which sounded like that of one displeased at the interruption, rather than hopeful of advantage from the arrival of a guest, demanded what he wanted.

"Is this an inn?" replied Philipson.

"Yes," bluntly replied the domestic, and was about to withdraw from the window, when the traveller added, —

"And if it be, can I have lodgings?"

"You may come in," was the short and dry answer.

"Send some one to rake the horses," replied Philipson.

"No one is at leisure," replied this most repulsive of waiters; "you must litter down your horses yourself, in the way that likes you best."

"Where is the stable?" said the merchant, whose prudence and temper were scarce proof against this Dutch phlegm.

The fellow, who seemed as sparing of his words, as if, like the Princess in the fairy tale, he had dropped ducats with each of them, only pointed to a door in an outer building, more resembling that of a cellar than of a stable, and, as if weary of the conference, drew in his head, and shut the window sharply against the guest, as he would against an importunate beggar.

Cursing the spirit of independence which left a traveller to his own resources and exertions, Philipson, making a virtue of necessity, led the two nags towards the door pointed out as that of the stable, and was rejoiced at heart to see light glimmering through its chinks. He entered with his charge into a place very like the dungeon vault of an ancient castle, rudely fitted up with some racks and mangers. It was of considerable extent in point of length, and at the lower end two or three persons were engaged in tying up their horses, dressing them, and dispensing them their provender.

This last article was delivered by the ostler, a very old lame man, who neither put his hand to wisp or currycomb, but sat weighing forth hay by the pound, and counting out corn, as it seemed, by the grain, so anxiously did he bend over his task, by the aid of a blinking light enclosed within a horn lantern. He did not even turn his head at the noise which the Englishman made on entering the place with two additional horses, far less did he seem disposed to give himself the least trouble, or the stranger the smallest assistance.

In respect of cleanliness, the stable of Augeas bore no small resemblance to that of this Alsatian dorff; and it would have been an exploit worthy of Hercules to have restored it to such a state of cleanliness, as would have made it barely decent in the eyes, and tolerable to the nostrils, of the punctilious Englishman. But this was a matter which disgusted Philipson himself much more than those of his party which were principally concerned. They, *videlicet* the two horses, seeming perfectly to understand that the rule of the place was, "first come first served," hastened to occupy the empty stalls which happened to be nearest to them. In this one of them at least was disappointed, being received by a groom with a blow across the face with a switch.

"Take that," said the fellow, "for forcing thyself into the place taken up for the horses of the Baron of Randelsheim."

Never in the course of his life had the English merchant more pain to retain possession of his temper than at that moment. Reflecting, however, on the discredit of quarrelling with such a man in such a cause, he contented himself with placing the animal, thus repulsed from the stall he had chosen, into one next to that of his companion, to which no one seemed to lay claim.

The merchant then proceeded, notwithstanding the fatigue of the day, to pay all that attention to the mute companions of his journey, which they deserve from every traveller who has any share of prudence, to say nothing of humanity. The unusual degree of trouble which Philipson took to arrange his horses, although his dress, and much more his demeanour, seemed to place him above this species of servile labour, appeared to make an impression even upon the iron insensibility of the old ostler himself. He showed some alacrity in furnishing the traveller, who knew the business of a groom so well, with corn, straw, and hay, though in small quantity, and at exorbitant rates, which were instantly to be paid; nay, he even went as far as the door of the stable, that he might point across the court to the well, from which Philipson was obliged to fetch water with his own hands. The duties of the stable being finished, the merchant concluded that he had gained such an interest with the grim master of the horse, as to learn of him whether he might leave his bales safely in the stable.

"You may leave them if you will," said the ostler "but touching their safety, you will do much more wisely if you take them with you, and give no temptation to any one by suffering them to pass from under your own eyes

So saying, the man of oats closed his oracular jaws, nor could he be prevailed upon to unlock them again by any inquiry which his customer could devise.

In the course of this cold and comfortless reception, Philipson recollected the necessity of supporting the character of a prudent and wary trader, which he had forgotten once before in the course of the day; and, imitating what he saw the others do, who had been, like himself, engaged in taking charge of their horses, he took up his baggage, and removed himself and his property to the inn. Here he was suffered to enter, rather than admitted, into the general or public *stubé*, or room of entertainment, which, like the ark of the patriarch, received all ranks without distinction, whether clean or unclean.

The *stubé or* stove, of a German inn, derived its name from the great hypocaust, which is always strongly heated to secure the warmth of the apartment in which it is placed. There travellers of every age and description assembled — there their upper garments were indiscriminately hung up around the stove to dry or to air — and the guests themselves were seen employed in various acts of ablution or personal arrangement, which are generally, in modern times, referred to the privacy of the dressing-room.

The more refined feelings of the Englishman were disgusted with this scene, and he was reluctant to mingle in it. For this reason he inquired for the private retreat of the landlord himself, trusting that, by some of the arguments powerful among his tribe, he might obtain separate quarters from the crowd, and a morsel of food, to be eaten in private. A gray-haired Ganymede, to whom he put the question where the landlord was, indicated a recess behind the huge stove, where, veiling his glory in a very dark and extremely hot corner, it pleased the great man to obscure himself from vulgar gaze. There was something remarkable about this person. Short, stout, bandylegged, and consequential, he was in these respects like many brethren of the profession in all countries. But the countenance of the man, and still more his manners, differed more from the merry host of France or England, than even the experienced Philipson was prepared to expect. He knew German customs too well to expect the suppliant and serviceable qualities of the master of a French inn, or even the more blunt and frank manners of an English landlord. But such German innkeepers as he had yet seen, though indeed arbitrary and peremptory in their country fashions, yet, being humoured in these, they, like tyrants in their hours of relaxation, dealt kindly with the guests over whom their sway extended, and mitigated, by jest and jollity, the harshness of their absolute power. But this man's brow was like a tragic volume, in which you were as unlikely to find any thing of jest or amusement, as in a hermit's breviary. His answers were short, sudden, and repulsive, and the air and manner with which they were delivered was as surly as their tenor; which will appear from the following dialogue betwixt him and his guest: —

"Good host," said Philipson, in the mildest tone he could assume, "I am fatigued, and far from well — May I request to have a separate apartment, a cup of wine, and a morsel of food, in my private chamber?"

"You may," answered the landlord; but with a look strangely at variance with the apparent acquiescence which his words naturally implied.

"Let me have such accommodation, then, with your earliest convenience."

"Soft!" replied the innkeeper. "I have said that you may request these things, but not that I would grant them. If you would insist on being served differently from others, it must be at another inn than mine."

"Well, then," said the traveller, "I will shift without supper for a night — nay, more, I will be content to pay for a supper which I do not eat, if you will cause me to be accommodated with a private apartment?"

"Signior traveller," said the innkeeper, "every one here must be accommodated as well as you, since all pay alike. Whose comes to this house of entertainment, must eat as others eat, drink as others drink, sit at table with the rest of my guests, and go to bed when the company have done drinking."

"All this," said Philipson, humbling himself where anger would have been ridiculous, "is highly reasonable; and I do not oppose myself to your laws or customs. But," added he, taking his purse from his girdle, "sickness craves some privilege; and when the patient is willing to pay for it, methinks the rigour of your laws may admit of some mitigation?"

"I keep an inn, Signior, and not an hospital. If you remain here, you shall be served with the same attention as others, — if you are not willing to do as others do, leave my house and seek another inn."

On receiving this decisive rebuff, Philipson gave up the contest, and retired from the *sanctum sanctorum* of his ungracious host, to await the arrival of supper, penned up like a bullock in a pound amongst the crowded inhabitants of the *stubé*. Some of these, exhausted by fatigue, snored away the interval between their own arrival and that of the expected repast; others conversed together on the news of the country, and others again played at dice, or such games as might serve to consume the time. The company were of various ranks, from those who were apparently wealthy and well appointed, to some whose garments and manners indicated that they were but just beyond the grasp of poverty.

A begging friar, a man apparently of a gay and pleasant temper, approached Philipson, and engaged him in conversation. The Englishman was well enough acquainted with the world to be aware, that whatever of his character and purpose it was desirable to conceal, would be best hidden under a sociable and open demeanour. He, therefore, received the friar's approaches graciously, and conversed with him upon the state of Lorraine, and the interest which the Duke of Burgundy's attempt to seize that fief into his own hands was likely to create both in France and Germany. On these subjects, satisfied with hearing his fellow-traveller's sentiments, Philipson expressed no opinion of his own, but, after receiving such intelligence as the friar chose to communicate, preferred rather to talk upon the geography of the country, the facilities afforded to commerce, and the rules which obstructed or favoured trade.

While he was thus engaged in the conversation which seemed most to belong to his profession, the landlord suddenly entered the room, and, mounting on the head of an old barrel, glanced his eye slowly and steadily round the crowded apartment, and when he had completed his survey, pronounced, in a decisive tone, the double command, — "Shut the gates — Spread the table."

"The Baron St. Antonio be praised," said the friar, "our

landlord has given up hope of any more guests to-night, until which blessed time, we might have starved for want of food before he had relieved us. Ay, here comes the cloth, the old gates of the courtyard are now bolted fast enough, and when Ian Mengs has once said, 'Shut the gates,' the stranger may knock on the outside as he will, but we may rest assured that it shall not be opened to him."

"Meinherr Mengs maintains strict discipline in his house," said the Englishman.

"As absolute as the Duke of Burgundy," answered the friar. "After ten o'clock, no admittance — the 'seek another inn,' which is before that a conditional hint, becomes, after the clock has struck, and the watchmen have begun their rounds, an absolute order of exclusion. He that is without remains without, and he that is within must, in like manner, continue there until the gates open at break of day. Till then the house is almost like a beleaguered citadel, John Mengs its seneschal" —

"And we its captives, good father," said Philipson. "Well, content am I; a wise traveller must submit to the control of the leaders of the people, when he travels; and I hope a goodly fat potentate, like John Mengs, will be as clement as his station and dignity admit of."

While they were talking in this manner, the aged waiter, with many a weary sigh, and many a groan, had drawn out certain boards, by which a table, that stood in the midst of the *stubé*, had the capacity of being extended, so as to contain the company present, and covered it with a cloth, which was neither distinguished by extreme cleanliness nor fineness of texture. On this table, when it had been accommodated to receive the necessary number of guests, a wooden trencher and spoon, together with a glass drinking cup, were placed before each, he being expected to serve himself with his own knife for the other purposes of the table. As for forks, they were unknown until a much later period, all the Europeans of that day making the same use of the fingers to select their morsels and transport them to the mouth, which the Asiatics now practise.

The board was no sooner arranged, than the hungry guests hastened to occupy their seats around it; for which purpose the sleepers were awakened, the dicers resigned their game, and the idlers and politicians broke off their sage debates, in order to secure their station at the supper-table, and be ready to perform their part in the interesting solemnity which seemed about to take place. But there is much between the cup and the lip, and not less sometimes between the covering of a table and the placing food upon it. The guests sat in order, each with his knife drawn, already menacing the victuals which were still subject to the operations of the cook. They had waited with various degrees of patience, for full half an hour, when at length the old attendant before mentioned entered with a pitcher of thin Moselle wine, so light and so sharp-tasted, that Philipson put down his cup with every tooth in his head set on edge by the slender portion which he had swallowed. The landlord, John Mengs, who had assumed a seat somewhat elevated at the head of the table, did not omit to observe this mark of insubordination, and to animadvert upon it.

"The wine likes you not, I think, my master?" said he to the English merchant.

"For wine, no," answered Philipson; "but could I see any thing requiring such sauce, I have seldom seen better vinegar."

This jest, though uttered in the most calm and composed manner, seemed to drive the innkeeper to fury.

"Who are you," he exclaimed, "for a foreign pedlar, that ventures to quarrel with my wine, which has been approved of by so many princes, dukes, reigning dukes, graves, rhinegraves, counts, barons, and knights of the Empire, whose shoes you are altogether unworthy even to clean? Was it not of this wine that the Count Palatine of Nimmersatt drank six quarts before he ever rose from the blessed chair in which I now sit?"

"I doubt it not, mine host," said Philipson; "nor should I think of scandalizing the sobriety of your honourable guest, even if he had drunken twice the quantity."

"Silence, thou malicious railer!" said the host; "and let instant apology be made to me, and the wine which you have calumniated, or I will instantly command the supper to be postponed till midnight."

Here there was a general alarm among the guests, all abjuring any part in the censures of Philipson, and most of them proposing that John Mengs should avenge himself on the actual culprit, by turning him instantly out of doors, rather than involve so many innocent and famished persons in the consequences of his guilt. The wine they pronounced excellent; some two or three even drank their glass out, to make their words good; and they all offered, if not with lives and fortunes, at least with hands and feet, to support the ban of the house against the contumacious Englishman. While petition and remonstrance were assailing John Mengs on every side, the friar, like a wise counsellor, and a trusty friend, endeavoured to end the feud, by advising Philipson to submit to the host's sovereignty.

"Humble thyself, my son," he said; "bend the stubbornness of thy heart before the great lord of the spigot and butt. I speak for the sake of others as well as my own; for Heaven alone knows how much longer they or I can endure this extenuating fast!"

"Worthy guests," said Philipson, "I am grieved to have offended our respected host, and am so far from objecting to the wine, that I will pay for a double flagon of it, to be served all round to this honourable company — so only, they do not ask me to share of it."

These last words were spoken aside; but the Englishman could not fail to perceive, from the wry mouths of some of the party who were possessed of a nicer palate, that they were as much afraid as himself of a repetition of the acid potation.

The friar next addressed the company with a proposal, that the foreign merchant, instead of being amerced in a measure of the liquor which he had scandalized, should be mulcted in an equal quantity of the more generous wines which were usually produced after the repast had been concluded. In this, mine host, as well as the guests, found their advantage; and, as Philipson made no objection, the proposal was unanimously adopted, and John Mengs gave, from his seat of dignity, the signal for supper to be served.

The long-expected meal appeared, and there was twice as much time employed in consuming as there had been in expecting it. The articles of which the supper consisted, as well as the mode of serving them up, were as much calculated to try the patience of the company as the delay which had preceded its appearance. Messes of broth and vegetables followed in succession, with platters of meat sodden and roasted, of which each in its turn took a formal course around the ample table, and was specially subjected to every one in rotation. Black-puddings, hung beef, dried fish, also made the circuit, with various condiments, called Botargo, Caviare, and similar names, composed of the roes of fish mixed with spices, and the like preparations, calculated to awaken thirst and encourage deep drinking. Flagons of wine accompanied these stimulating dainties. The liquor was so superior in flavour and strength to the ordinary wine which had awakened so much controversy, that it might be objected to on the opposite account, being so heady, fiery, and strong, that, in spite of the rebuffs which his criticism had already procured, Philipson ventured to ask for some cold water to allay it.

"You are too difficult to please, sir guest," replied the landlord, again bending upon the Englishman a stern and offended brow; "if you find the wine too strong in my house, the secret to allay its strength is to drink the less. It is indifferent to us whether you drink or not, so you pay the reckoning of those good fellows who do." And he laughed a gruff laugh.

Philipson was about to reply, but the friar, retaining his character of mediator, plucked him by the cloak, and entreated him to forbear. "You do not understand the ways of the place," said he; "it is not here as in the hostelries of England and France, where each guest calls for what he desires for his own use, and where he pays for what he has required, and for no more. Here we proceed on a broad principle of equality and fraternity. No one asks for any thing in particular; but such provisions as the host thinks sufficient are set down before all indiscriminately; and as with the feast, so is it with the reckoning. All pay their proportions alike, without reference to the quantity of wine which one may have swallowed more than another; and thus the sick and infirm, nay, the female and the child, pay the same as the hungry peasant and strolling *lanz-knecht*."

"It seems an unequal custom," said Philipson; "but travellers are not to judge. So that when a reckoning is called, every one, I am to understand, pays alike?"

"Such is the rule," said the friar, — "excepting, perhaps, some poor brother of our own order, whom Our Lady and St. Francis send into such a scene as this, that good Christians may bestow their alms upon him, and so make a step on their road to Heaven."

The first words of this speech were spoken in the open and independent tone in which the friar had begun the conversation; the last sentence died away into the professional whine of mendicity proper to the convent, and at once apprized Philipson at what price he was to pay for the friar's counsel and mediation. Having thus explained the custom of the country, good Father Gratian turned to illustrate it by his example, and, having no objection to the new service of wine on account of its strength, he seemed well disposed to signalize himself amongst some stout topers, who, by drinking deeply, appeared determined to have full pennyworths for their share of the reckoning. The good wine gradually did its office, and even the host relaxed his sullen and grim features, and smiled to see the kindling flame of hilarity catch from one to another, and at length embrace almost all the numerous guests at the table d'hôte, except a few who were too temperate to partake deeply of the wine, or too fastidious to enter into the discussions to which it gave rise. On these the host cast, from time to time, a sullen and displeased eye.

Philipson, who was reserved and silent, both in consequence of his abstinence from the wine-pot, and his unwillingness to mix in conversation with strangers, was looked upon by the landlord as a defaulter in both particulars; and as he aroused his own sluggish nature with the fiery wine, Mengs began to throw out obscure hints about kill-joy, mar-company, spoil-sport, and such like epithets, which were plainly directed against the Englishman. Philipson replied, with the utmost equanimity, that he was perfectly sensible that his spirits did not at this moment render him an agreeable member of a merry company, and that, with the leave of those present, he would withdraw to his sleeping apartment, and wish them all a good evening, and continuance to their mirth.

But this very reasonable proposal, as it might have elsewhere seemed, contained in it treason against the laws of German compotation.

"Who are you," said John Mengs, "who presume to leave the table before the reckoning is called and settled? Sapperment der teufel! we are not men upon whom such an offence is to be put with impunity! You may exhibit your polite pranks in Rams-Alley if you will, or in East-cheap, or in Smithfield; but it shall not be in John Mengs's Golden Fleece; nor will I suffer one guest to go to bed to blink out of the reckoning, and so cheat me and all the rest of my company."

Philipson looked round, to gather the sentiments of the

company, but saw no encouragement to appeal to their judgment. Indeed, many of them had little judgment left to appeal to, and those who paid any attention to the matter at all, were some quiet old soakers, who were already beginning to think of the reckoning, and were disposed to agree with the host in considering the English merchant as a flincher, who was determined to evade payment of what might be drunk after he left the room so that John Mengs received the applause of the whole company, when he concluded his triumphant denunciation against Philipson.

"Yes, sir, you may withdraw if you please; but, poz element! it shall not be for this time to seek for another inn, but to the court-yard shall you go, and no further, there to make your bed upon the stable litter; and good enough for the man that will needs be the first to break up good company."

"It is well said, my jovial host," said a rich trader from Ratisbon; "and here are some six of us — more or less — who will stand by you to maintain the good old customs of Germany; and the — umph — laudable and — and praiseworthy rules of the Golden Fleece."

"Nay, be not angry, sir," said Philipson; "yourself and your three companions, whom the good wine has multiplied into six, shall have your own way of ordering the matter; and since you will not permit me to go to bed, I trust that you will take no offence if I fall asleep in my chair."

"How say you? what think you, mine host?" said the citizen from Ratisbon; "may the gentleman, being drunk, as you see he is, since he cannot tell that three and one make six — I say, may he, being drunk, sleep in the elbow-chair?"

This question introduced a contradiction on the part of the host, who contended that three and one made four, not six; and this again produced a retort from the Ratisbon trader. Other clamours rose at the same time, and were at length with difficulty silenced by the stanzas of a chorus song of mirth and good fellowship, which the friar, now become somewhat oblivious of the rule of St. Francis, thundered forth with better good-will than he ever sung a canticle of King David. Under cover of this tumult, Philipson drew himself a little aside, and though he felt it impossible to sleep, as he had proposed, was yet enabled to escape the reproachful glances with which John Mengs distinguished all those who did not call for wine loudly, and drink it lustily. His thoughts roamed far from the *stubé* of the Golden Fleece, and upon matter very different from that which was discussed around him, when his attention was suddenly recalled by a loud and continued knocking on the door of the hostelry.

"What have we here?" said John Mengs, his nose reddening with very indignation; "who the foul fiend presses on the Golden Fleece at such an hour, as if he thundered at the door of a bordel? To the turret window some one — Geoffrey, knave ostler, or thou, old Timothy, tell the rash man there is no admittance into the Golden Fleece save at timeous hours."

The men went as they were directed, and might be heard in the *stubé* vying with each other in the positive denial which they gave to the ill-fated guest, who was pressing for admission. They returned, however, to inform their master, that they were unable to overcome the obstinacy of the stranger, who refused positively to depart until he had an interview with Mengs himself.

Wroth was the master of the Golden Fleece at this ill-omened pertinacity, and his indignation extended, like a fiery exhalation, from his nose, all over the adjacent regions of his cheeks and brow. He started from his chair, grasped in his hand a stout stick, which seemed his ordinary sceptre or leading staff of command, and muttering something concerning cudgels for the shoulders of fools, and pitchers of fair or foul water for the drenching of their ears, he marched off to the window which looked into the court, and left his guests nodding, winking, and whispering to each other, in full expectation of hearing the active demonstrations of his wrath. It happened otherwise, however; for, after the exchange of a few indistinct words, they were astonished when they heard the noise of the unbolting and un-barring of the gates of the inn, and presently after the footsteps of men upon the stairs; and the landlord entering, with an appearance of clumsy courtesy, prayed those assembled to make room for an honoured guest, who came, though late, to add to their numbers. A tall dark form followed, muffled in a travelling cloak; on laying aside which, Philipson at once recognised his late fellow-traveller, the Black Priest of St. Paul's.

There was in the circumstance itself nothing at all surprising, since it was natural that a landlord, however coarse and insolent to ordinary guests, might yet show deference to an ecclesiastic, whether from his rank in the Church, or from his reputation for sanctity. But what did appear surprising to Philipson, was the effect produced by the entrance of this unexpected guest. He seated himself, without hesitation, at the highest place of the board, from which John Mengs had dethroned the aforesaid trader from Ratisbon, notwithstanding his zeal for ancient German customs, his steady adherence and loyalty to the Golden Fleece, and his propensity to brimming goblets. The priest took instant and unscrupulous possession of his seat of honour, after some negligent reply to the host's unwonted courtesy; when it seemed that the effect of his long black vestments, in place of the slashed and flounced coat of his predecessor, as well as of the cold gray eye with which he slowly reviewed the company, in some degree resembled that of the fabulous Gorgon, and if it did not literally convert those who looked upon it into stone, there was yet something petrifying in the steady unmoved glance with which he seemed to survey them, looking as if desirous of reading their very inmost souls, and passing from one to another, as if each upon whom he looked in succession was unworthy of longer consideration.

Philipson felt, in his turn, that momentary examination, in which, however, there mingled nothing that seemed to convey recognition. All the courage and composure of the Englishman could not prevent an unpleasant feeling while under this mysterious man's eye, so that he felt a relief when it passed from him and rested upon another of the company, who seemed in turn to acknowledge the chilling effects of that freezing glance. The noise of intoxicated mirth and drunken disputation, the clamorous argument, and the still more boisterous laugh, which had been suspended on the priest's entering the eating apartment, now, after one or two vain attempts to resume them, died away, as if the feast had been changed to a funeral, and the jovial guests had been at once converted into the lugubrious mutes who attend on such solemnities. One little rosy-faced man, who afterwards proved to be a tailor from Augsburg, ambitious, perhaps, of showing a degree of courage not usually supposed consistent with his effeminate trade, made a bold effort; and yet it was with a timid and restrained voice, that he called on the jovial friar to renew his song. But whether it was that he did not dare to venture on an uncanonical pastime in presence of a brother in orders, or whether he had some other reason for declining the invitation, the merry church-man hung his head, and shook it with such an expressive air of melancholy, that the tailor drew back as if he had been detected in cabbaging from a cardinal's robes, or cribbing the lace of some cope or altar gown. In short, the revel was hushed into deep silence, and so attentive were the company to what should arrive next, that the bells of the village church, striking the first hour after midnight, made the guests start as if they heard them rung backwards, to announce an assault or conflagration. The Black Priest, who had taken some slight and hasty repast, which the host had made no kind of objection to supplying him with, seemed to think the bells, which announced the service of lauds, being the first after midnight, a proper signal for breaking up the party.

"We have eaten," he said, "that we may support life; let us pray that we may be fit to meet death; which waits upon life as surely as night upon day, or the shadow upon the sunbeam, though we know not when or from whence it is to come upon us."

The company, as if mechanically, bent their uncovered heads, while the priest said, with his deep and solemn voice, a Latin prayer, expressing thanks to God for protection throughout the day, and entreating for its continuance during the witching hours which were to pass ere the day again commenced. The hearers bowed their heads in token of acquiescence in the holy petition; and, when they raised them, the Black Priest of St. Paul's had followed the host out of the apartment, probably to that which was destined for his repose. His absence was no sooner perceived, than signs, and nods, and even whispers, were exchanged between the guests; but no one spoke above his breath, or in such connected manner, as that Philipson could understand any thing distinctly from them. He himself ventured to ask the friar, who sat near him, observing at the same time the under-tone which seemed to be fashionable for the moment, whether the worthy ecclesiastic who had left them, was not the Priest of St. Paul's, on the frontier town of La Ferette.

"And if you know it is he," said the friar, with a countenance and a tone, from which all signs of intoxication were suddenly banished, "why do you ask of me?"

"Because," said the merchant, "I would willingly learn the spell which so suddenly converted so many merry tipplers into men of sober manners, and a jovial company into a convent of Carthusian friars?"

"Friend," said the friar, "thy discourse savoureth mightily of asking after what thou knowest right well. But I am no such silly duck as to be taken by a decoy. If thou knowest the Black Priest, thou canst not be ignorant of the terrors which attend his presence, and that it were safer to pass a broad jest in the holy House of Loretto, than where he shows himself."

So saying, and as if desirous of avoiding further discourse, he withdrew to a distance from Philipson.

At the same moment the landlord again appeared, and, with more of the usual manners of a publican than he had hitherto exhibited, commanded his waiter, Geoffrey, to hand round to the company a sleeping drink, or pillow-cup of distilled water, mingled with spices, which was indeed as good as Philipson himself had ever tasted. John Mengs, in the meanwhile, with somewhat of more deference, expressed to his guests a hope that his entertainment had given satisfaction; but this was in so careless a manner, and he seemed so conscious of deserving the affirmative which was expressed on all hands, that it became obvious there was very little humility in proposing the question. The old man, Timothy, was in the meantime mustering the guests, and marking with chalk on the bottom of a trencher the reckoning, the particulars of which were indicated by certain conventional hieroglyphics, while he showed on another the division of the sum total among the company, and proceeded to collect an equal share of it from each. When the fatal trencher, in which each man paid down his money, approached the jolly friar, his countenance seemed to be somewhat changed. He cast a piteous look towards Philipson, as the person from whom he had the most hope of relief; and our merchant, though displeased with the manner in which he had held back from his confidence, yet not unwilling in a strange country to incur a little expense, in the hope of making a useful acquaintance, discharged the mendicant's score as well as his own. The poor friar paid his thanks in many a blessing in good German and bad Latin, but the host cut them short; for, approaching Philipson with a candle in his hand, he offered his own services to show him where he might sleep, and even had the condescension to carry his mail, or portmanteau, with his own landlordly hands.

"You take too much trouble, mine host," said the merchant, somewhat surprised at the change in the manner of John Mengs, who had hitherto contradicted him at every word.

"I cannot take too much pains for a guest," was the reply, "whom my venerable friend, the Priest of St. Paul's, hath especially recommended to my charge."

He then opened the door of a small bedroom, prepared for the occupation of a guest, and said to Philipson, — "Here you may rest till to-morrow at what hour you will, and for as many days more as you incline. The key will secure your wares against theft or pillage of any kind. I do not this for every one; for, if my guests were every one to have a bed to himself, the next thing they would demand might be a separate table; and then there would be an end of the good old German customs, and we should be as foppish and frivolous as our neighbours."

He placed the portmanteau on the floor, and seemed about to leave the apartment, when, turning about, he began a sort of apology for the rudeness of his former behaviour.

"I trust there is no misunderstanding between us, my worthy guest. You might as well expect to see one of our bears come aloft and do tricks like a jackanapes, as one of us stubborn old Germans play the feats of a French or an Italian host. Yet I pray you to note. that if our behaviour is rude our charges are honest, and our articles what they profess to be. We do not expect to make Moselle pass for Rhenish, by dint of a bow and a grin, nor will we sauce your mess with poison, like the wily Italian, and call you all the time Illustrissimo and Magnifico."

He seemed in these words to have exhausted his rhetoric, for, when they were spoken, he turned abruptly and left the apartment.

Philipson was thus deprived of another opportunity to inquire who or what this ecclesiastic could be, that had exercised such influence on all who approached him. He felt, indeed, no desire to prolong a conference with John Mengs, though he had laid aside in such a considerable degree his rude and repulsive manners; yet he longed to know who this man could be, who had power with a word to turn aside the daggers of Alsatian banditti, habituated as they were, like most borderers, to robbery and pillage, and to change into civility the proverbial rudeness of a German innkeeper. Such were the reflections of Philipson, as he doffed his clothes to take his much-needed repose, after a day of fatigue, danger, and difficulty, on the pallet afforded by the hospitality of the Golden Fleece in the Rhein-Thal.

CHAPTER XX

Macbeth. — How now, ye secret, black, and midnight
hags, What is't ye do?

Witches. — A deed without a name.

MACBETH.

We have said in the conclusion of the last chapter, that, after
a day of unwonted fatigue and extraordinary excitation, the merchant, Philipson, naturally expected to forget so many agitating
passages in that deep and profound repose, which is at once the
consequence and the cure of extreme exhaustion. But he was no
sooner laid on his lowly pallet, than he felt that the bodily ma-
chine, over-laboured by so much exercise, was little disposed to
the charms of sleep. The mind had been too much excited, the
body was far too feverish, to suffer him to partake of needful
rest. His anxiety about the safety of his son, his conjectures concerning the issue of his mission to the Duke of Burgundy, and a
thousand other thoughts which recalled past events, or specu-
lated on those which were to come, rushed upon his mind like
the waves of a perturbed sea, and prevented all tendency to repose. He had been in bed about an hour, and sleep had not yet
approached his couch, when he felt that the pallet on which he
lay was sinking below him, and that he was in the act of descending along with it he knew not whither. The sound of ropes
and pullies was also indistinctly heard, though every caution had
been taken to make them run smooth; and the traveller, by feeling around him, became sensible that he and the bed on which he
lay had been spread upon a large trap-door, which was capable
of being let down into the vaults, or apartments beneath.

Philipson felt fear in circumstances so well qualified to produce it; for how could he hope a safe termination to an adventure
which had begun so strangely? But his apprehensions were those
of a brave, ready-witted man, who, even in the extremity of danger, which appeared to surround him, preserved his presence of
mind. His descent seemed to be cautiously managed, and he held
himself in readiness to start to his feet and defend himself, as
soon as he should be once more upon firm ground. Although
somewhat advanced in years, he was a man of great personal
vigour and activity, and unless taken at advantage, which no

doubt was at present much to be apprehended, he was likely to make a formidable defence. His plan of resistance, however, had been anticipated. He no sooner readied the bottom of the vault, down to which he was lowered, than two men, who had been waiting there till the operation was completed, laid hands on him from either side, and forcibly preventing him from starting up as he intended, cast a rope over his arms, and made him a prisoner as effectually as when he was in the dungeons of La Ferette. He was obliged, therefore, to remain passive and unresisting, and await the termination of this formidable adventure. Secured as he was, he could only turn his head from one side to the other; and it was with joy that he at length saw lights twinkle, but they appeared at a great distance from him.

From the irregular manner in which these scattered lights advanced, sometimes keeping a straight line, sometimes mixing and crossing each other, it might be inferred that the subterranean vault in which they appeared was of very considerable extent. Their number also increased; and as they collected more together, Philipson could perceive that the lights proceeded from many torches, borne by men muffled in black cloaks, like mourners at a funeral, or the Black Friars of Saint Francis's Order, wearing their cowls drawn over their heads so as to conceal their features. They appeared anxiously engaged in measuring off a portion of the apartment; and while occupied in that employment, they sung in the ancient German language, rhymes more rude than Philipson could well understand, but which may be imitated thus: —

> Measurers of good and evil,
> Bring the square, the line, the level, —
> Bear the altar, dig the trench,
> Blood both stone and ditch shall drench.
> Cubits six, from end to end,
> Must the fatal bench extend, —
> Cubits six, from side to side,
> Judge and culprit must divide.
> On the east the Court assembles,
> On the west the Accused trembles —
> Answer, brethren, all and one,
> Is the ritual rightly done?

A deep chorus seemed to reply to the question. Many voices

joined in it, as well of persons already in the subterranean vault, as of others who as yet remained without in various galleries and passages which communicated with it, and whom Philipson now presumed to be very numerous. The answer chanted run as follows: —

> On life and soul, on blood and bone,
> One for all, and all for one,
> We warrant this is rightly done.

The original strain was then renewed in the same manner as before —

> How wears the night? — Doth morning shine
> In early radiance on the Rhine?
> What music floats upon his tide?
> Do birds the tardy morning chide?
> Brethren, look out from hill and height,
> And answer true, how wears the night?

The answer was returned, though less loud than at first, and it seemed that those by whom the reply was given were at a much greater distance than before; yet the words were distinctly heard.

> The night is old; on Rhine's broad breast
> Glance drowsy stars which long to rest.
>   No beams are twinkling in the east
> There is a voice upon the flood,
> The stern still call of blood for blood;
>   'Tis time we listen the behest.

The chorus replied with many additional voices —

> Up, then, up! When day's at rest,
> 'Tis time that such as we are watchers;
> Rise to judgment, brethren, rise!
> Vengeance knows not sleepy eyes,
> He and night are matchers.

The nature of the verses soon led Philipson to comprehend that he was in presence of the Initiated, or the Wise Men; names which were applied to the celebrated Judges of the Secret Tribunal, which continued at that period to subsist in Suabia, Franconia, and other districts of the east of Germany, which was called, perhaps from the frightful and frequent occurrence of executions by command of those invisible judges, the Red Land. Philipson had often heard that the seat of a free Count, or chief of the Secret Tribunal, was secretly instituted even on the left bank of the Rhine, and that it maintained itself in Alsace, with the usual tenacity of those secret societies, though Duke Charles of Burgundy had expressed a desire to discover and discourage its influence, so far as was possible without exposing himself to danger from the thousands of poniards which that mysterious tribunal could put in activity against his own life; — an awful means of defence, which for a long time rendered it extremely hazardous for the sovereigns of Germany, and even the Emperors themselves, to put down by authority those singular associations.

So soon as this explanation flashed on the mind of Philipson, it gave some clew to the character and condition of the Black Priest of St. Paul's. Supposing him to be a president, or chief official of the secret association, there was little wonder that he should confide so much in the inviolability of his terrible office, as to propose vindicating the execution of De Hagenbach; that his presence should surprise Bartholomew, whom he had power to have judged and executed upon the spot; and that his mere appearance at supper on the preceding evening should have appalled the guests; for though every thing about the institution, its proceedings and its officers, was preserved in as much obscurity as is now practised in free-masonry, yet the secret was not so absolutely well kept as to prevent certain individuals from being guessed or hinted at as men initiated and intrusted with high authority by the Vehmegericht, or tribunal of the bounds. When such suspicion attached to an individual, his secret power, and supposed acquaintance with all guilt, however secret, which was committed within the society in which he was conversant, made him at once the dread and hatred of every one who looked on him; and he enjoyed a high degree of personal respect, on the same terms on which it would have been yielded to a powerful enchanter, or a dreaded genie. In conversing with such a person, it was especially necessary to abstain from all questions alluding, however remotely, to the office which he bore in the Secret Tribunal; and, indeed, to testify the least curiosity upon a subject so solemn and mysterious, was sure to occasion some misfortune to the inquisitive person.

All these things rushed at once upon the mind of the Englishman, who felt that he had fallen into the hands of an unsparing tribunal, whose proceedings were so much dreaded by those who resided within the circle of their power, that the friendless stranger must stand a poor chance of receiving justice at their hands, whatever might be his consciousness of innocence. While Philipson made this melancholy reflection, he resolved, at the same time, not to forsake his own cause, but defend himself as he best might; conscious as he was that these terrible and irresponsible judges were nevertheless governed by certain rules of right and wrong, which formed a check on the rigours of their extraordinary code.

He lay, therefore, devising the best means of obviating the present danger, while the persons whom he beheld glimmered before him, less like distinct and individual forms, than like the phantoms of a fever, or the phantasmagoria with which a disease of the optic nerves has been known to people a sick man's chamber. At length they assembled in the centre of the apartment where they had first appeared, and seemed to arrange themselves into form and order. A great number of black torches were successively lighted, and the scene became distinctly visible. In the centre of the hall, Philipson could now perceive one of the altars which are sometimes to be found in ancient subterranean chapels. But we must pause, in order briefly to describe, not the appearance only, but the nature and constitution of this terrible court.

Behind the altar, which seemed to be the central point, on which all eyes were bent, there were placed in parallel lines two benches covered with black cloth. Each was occupied by a number of persons, who seemed assembled as judges; but those who held the foremost bench were fewer, and appeared of a rank superior to those who crowded the seat most remote from the altar. The first seemed to be all men of some consequence, priests high in their order, knights or noblemen; and notwithstanding an appearance of equality which seemed to pervade this singular institution, much more weight was laid upon their opinion, or testimonies. They were called Free Knights, Counts, or whatever title they might bear, while the inferior class of the judges were only termed Free and worthy Burghers. For it must be observed, that the Vehmique Institution,[10] which was the name that it commonly bore, although its power consisted in a wide system of espionage, and the tyrannical application of force which acted upon it, was yet (so rude were the ideas of enforcing public law) accounted to confer a privilege on the country in which it was received, and only freemen were allowed to experience its influence. Serfs and peasants could neither have a place among the Free Judges, their assessors, or assistants; for there was in this assembly even some idea of trying the culprit by his peers.

Besides the dignitaries who occupied the benches, there were others who stood around, and seemed to guard the various entrances to the hall of judgment, or, standing behind the seats on which their superiors were ranged, looked prepared to execute their commands. These were members of the order, though not of the highest ranks. Schöppen is the name generally assigned to them, signifying officials, or sergeants of the Vehmique Court, whose doom they stood sworn to enforce, through good report and bad report, against their own nearest and most beloved, as well as in cases of ordinary malefactors.

The Schöppen, or Scahini, as they were termed in Latin, had another horrible duty to perform, that, namely, of denouncing to the tribunal whatever came under their observation, that might be construed as an offence falling under its cognizance; or, in their language, a crime against the Vehme. This duty extended to the judges as well as the assistants, and was to be discharged without respect of persons; so that, to know, and wilfully conceal, the guilt of a mother or brother, inferred, on the part of the unfaithful official, the same penalty as if he himself had committed the crime which his silence screened from punishment. Such an institution could only prevail at a time when ordinary means of justice were excluded by the hand of power, and when, in order to bring the guilty to punishment, it required all the influence and authority of such a confederacy. In no other country than one exposed to every species of feudal tyranny, and deprived of every ordinary mode of obtaining justice or redress, could such a

---

[10] The word Wehme, pronounced Vehme, is of uncertain derivation, but was always used to intimate this inquisitorial and secret Court. The members were termed Wissenden, or Initiated, answering to the modern phrase of Illuminati. Mr. Palgrave seems inclined to derive the word *Vehme* from *Ehme,* i. e. *Law,* and he is probably right.

system have taken root and nourished.

We must now return to the brave Englishman, who, though feeling all the danger he encountered from so tremendous a tribunal, maintained nevertheless a dignified and unaltered composure.

The meeting being assembled, a coil of ropes, and a naked sword, the well-known signals and emblems of Vehmique authority, were deposited on the altar; where the sword, from its being usually straight, with a cross handle, was considered as representing the blessed emblem of Christian Redemption, and the cord as indicating the right of criminal jurisdiction, and capital punishment. Then the President of the meeting, who occupied the centre seat on the foremost bench, arose, and laying his hand on the symbols, pronounced aloud the formula expressive of the duty of the tribunal, which all the inferior judges and assistants repeated after him, in deep and hollow murmurs.

"I swear by the Holy Trinity, to aid and coöperate, without relaxation, in the things belonging to the Holy Vehme, to defend its doctrines and institutions against father and mother, brother and sister, wife and children; against fire, water, earth, and air; against all that the sun enlightens; against all that the dew moistens; against all created things of heaven and earth, or the waters under the earth; and I swear to give information to this holy judicature, of all that I know to be true, or hear repeated by credible testimony, which, by the rules of the Holy Vehme, is deserving of animadversion or punishment; and that I will not cloak, cover, or conceal, such my knowledge, neither for love, friendship, or family affection, nor for gold, silver, or precious stones; neither will I associate with such as are under the sentence of this Sacred Tribunal, by hinting to a culprit his danger or advising him to escape, or aiding and supplying him with counsel, or means to that effect; neither will I relieve such culprit with fire, clothes, food, or shelter, though my father should require from me a cup of water in the heat of summer noon, or my brother should request to sit by my fire in the bitterest cold night of winter: And further, I vow and promise to honour this holy association, and do its behests speedily, faithfully, and firmly, in preference to those of any other tribunal whatsoever — so help me God, and his holy Evangelists."

When this oath of office had been taken, the President addressing the assembly, as men who judge in secret and punish in secret, like the Deity, desired them to say, why this "child of the cord"[11] lay before them bound and helpless? An individual rose from the more remote bench, and in a voice which, though altered and agitated, Philipson conceived that he recognized, declared himself the accuser, as bound by his oath, of the child of the cord, or prisoner, who lay before them.

"Bring forward the prisoner," said the President, "duly secured, as is the order of our secret law; but not with such severity as may interrupt his attention to the proceedings of the tribunal, or limit his power of hearing and replying."

Six of the assistants immediately dragged forward the pallet and platform of boards on which Philipson lay, and advanced it towards the foot of the altar. This done, each unsheathed his dagger, while two of them unloosed the cords by which the merchant's hands were secured, and admonished him in a whisper, that the slightest attempt to resist or escape, would be the signal to stab him dead.

"Arise!" said the President; "listen to the charge to be preferred against you, and believe you shall in us find judges equally just and inflexible."

Philipson, carefully avoiding any gesture which might indicate a desire to escape, raised his body on the lower part of the couch, and remained seated, clothed as he was in his under-vest and *caleçons*, or drawers, so as exactly to face the muffled President of the terrible court. Even in these agitating circumstances, the mind of the undaunted Englishman remained unshaken, and his eyelid did not quiver, nor his heart beat quicker, though he seemed, according to the expression of Scripture, to be a pilgrim in the Valley of the Shadow of Death, beset by numerous snares, and encompassed by total darkness, where light was most necessary for safety.

The President demanded his name, country, and occupation?

"John Philipson," was the reply; "by birth an Englishman, by profession a merchant."

"Have you ever borne any other name, and profession?"

---

[11] The term *Strick-kind,* or child of the cord, was applied to the person accused before these awful assemblies.

demanded the Judge.

"I have been a soldier, and, like most others, had then a name by which I was known in war."

"What was that name?"

"I laid it aside when I resigned my sword, and I do not desire again to be known by it. Moreover, I never bore it where your institutions have weight and authority," answered the Englishman.

"Know you before whom you stand?" continued the Judge.

"I may at least guess," replied the merchant.

"Tell your guess, then," continued the interrogator "Say who we are, and wherefore are you before us?"

"I believe that I am before the Unknown, or Secret Tribunal, which is called Vehmegericht."

"Then are you aware," answered the Judge, "that you would be safer if you were suspended by the hair over the Abyss of Schaffhausen, or if you lay below an axe, which a thread of silk alone kept back from the fall. What have you done to deserve such a fate?"

"Let those reply by whom I am subjected to it," answered Philipson, with the same composure as before.

"Speak, accuser," said the President, "to the four quarters of Heaven! — To the ears of the free judges of this tribunal, and the faithful executors of their doom! — And to the face of the child of the cord, who denies or conceals his guilt, make good the substance of thine accusation!"

"Most dreaded," answered the accuser, addressing the President, "this man hath entered the Sacred Territory, which is called the Red Land, — a stranger under a disguised name and profession. When he was yet on the eastern side of the Alps, at Turin, in Lombardy, and elsewhere, he at various times spoke of the Holy Tribunal in terms of hatred and contempt, and declared that were he Duke of Burgundy, he would not permit it to extend itself from Westphalia, or Suabia, into his dominions. Also, I charge him, that, nourishing this malevolent intention against the Holy Tribunal, he who now appears before the bench as child of the cord, has intimated his intention to wait upon the court of the Duke of Burgundy, and use his influence with him, which he boasts will prove effectual, to stir him up to prohibit the meetings of the Holy Vehme in his dominions, and to inflict on their officers, and the executors of their mandates, the punishment due to robbers and assassins."

"This is a heavy charge, brother!" said the President of the assembly, when the accuser ceased speaking — "How do you purpose to make it good?"

"According to the tenor of those secret statutes, the perusal of which is prohibited to all but the initiated," answered the accuser.

"It is well," said the President; "but I ask thee once more, What are those means of proof? — You speak to holy and to initiated ears."

"I will prove my charge," said the accuser, "by the confession of the party himself, and by my own oath upon the holy emblems of the Secret Judgment — that is, the steel and the cord."

"It is a legitimate offer of proof," said a member of the aristocratic bench of the assembly; "and it much concerns the safety of the system to which we are bound by such deep oaths, a system handed down to us from the most Christian and holy Roman Emperor, Charlemagne, for the conversion of the heathen Saracens, and punishing such of them as revolted again to their Pagan practices, that such criminals should be looked to. This Duke Charles of Burgundy hath already crowded his army with foreigners, whom he can easily employ against this Sacred Court, more especially with English, a fierce insular people, wedded to their own usages, and hating those of every other nation. It is not unknown to us, that the Duke hath already encouraged opposition to the officials of the Tribunal in more than one part of his German dominions; and that in consequence, instead of submitting to their doom with reverent resignation, children of the cord have been found bold enough to resist the executioners of the Vehme, striking, wounding, and even slaying those who have received commission to put them to death. This contumacy must be put an end to; and if the accused shall be proved to be one of those by whom such doctrines are harboured and inculcated, I say let the steel and cord do their work on him."

A general murmur seemed to approve what the speaker had said; for all were conscious that the power of the Tribunal depended much more on the opinion of its being deeply and firmly rooted in the general system, than upon any regard or esteem for an institution, of which all felt the severity. It followed, that those of the members who enjoyed consequence by means of their station in the ranks of the Vehme, saw the necessity of supporting its terrors by occasional examples of severe punishment; and none could be more readily sacrificed, than an unknown and wandering foreigner. All this rushed upon Philipson's mind, but did not prevent his making a steady reply to the accusation.

"Gentlemen," he said, "good citizens, burgesses, or by whatever other name you please to be addressed, know, that in my former days I have stood in as great peril as now, and have never turned my heel to save my life. Cords and daggers are not calculated to strike terror into those who have seen swords and lances. My answer to the accusation is, that I am an Englishman, one of a nation accustomed to yield and to receive open-handed and equal justice dealt forth in the broad light of day. I am, however, a traveller, who knows that he has no right to oppose the rules and laws of other nations, because they do not resemble those of his own. But this caution can only be called for in lands, where the system about which we converse is in full force and operation. If we speak of the institutions of Germany, being at the time in France or Spain, we may, without offence to the country in which they are current, dispute concerning them, as students debate upon a logical thesis in a university. The accuser objects to me, that at Turin, or elsewhere in the north of Italy, I spoke with censure of the institution under which I am now judged. I will not deny that I remember something of the kind; but it was in consequence of the question being in a manner forced upon me by two guests, with whom I chanced to find myself at table. I was much and earnestly solicited for an opinion ere I gave one."

"And was that opinion," said the presiding Judge, "favourable or otherwise to the Holy and Secret Vehmegericht? Let truth rule your tongue — remember, life is short, judgment is eternal!"

"I would not save my life at the expense of a falsehood. My opinion was unfavourable; and I expressed myself thus: — No laws or judicial proceedings can be just or commendable, which exist and operate by means of a secret combination. I said, that justice could only live and exist in the open air, and that when she ceased to be public, she degenerated into revenge and hatred. I said, that a system, of which your own jurists have said, *non frater a fratre, non hospes a hospite, tutus,* was too much adverse to the laws of nature, to be connected with or regulated by those of religion."

These words were scarcely uttered, when there burst a murmur from the Judges highly unfavourable to the prisoner, — "He blasphemes the Holy Vehme — Let his mouth be closed for ever!"

"Hear me," said the Englishman, "as you will one day wish to be yourselves heard! I say such were my sentiments, and so I expressed them — I say also, I had a right to express these opinions, whether sound or erroneous, in a neutral country, where this Tribunal neither did, nor could, claim any jurisdiction. My sentiments are still the same. I would avow them if that sword were at my bosom, or that cord around my throat. But I deny that I have ever spoken against the institutions of your Vehme, in a country where it had its course as a national mode of justice. Far more strongly, if possible, do I denounce the absurdity of the falsehood, which represents me, a wandering foreigner, as commissioned to traffic with the Duke of Burgundy about such high matters, or to form a conspiracy for the destruction of a system, to which so many seem warmly attached. I never said such a thing, and I never thought it."

"Accuser," said the presiding Judge, "thou hast heard the accused — What is thy reply?"

"The first part of the charge," said the accuser, "he hath confessed in this high presence, namely, that his foul tongue hath basely slandered our holy mysteries; for which he deserves that it should be torn out of his throat. I myself, on my oath of office, will aver, as use and law is, that the rest of the accusation, namely, that which taxes him as having entered into machinations for the destruction of the Vehmique institutions, are as true as those which he has found himself unable to deny."

"In justice," said the Englishman, "the accusation, if not made good by satisfactory proof, ought to be left to the oath of the party accused, instead of permitting the accuser to establish by his own deposition the defects in his own charge."

"Stranger," replied the presiding Judge, "we permit to thy ignorance a longer and more full defence than consists with our usual forms. Know that the right of sitting among these venerable judges confers on the person of him who enjoys it a sacredness of character, which ordinary men cannot attain to. The oath of one of the initiated must counterbalance the most solemn asseveration of every one that is not acquainted with our holy secrets. In the Vehmique court all must be Vehmique. The averment of the Emperor, he being uninitiated, would not have so much weight in our counsels as that of one of the meanest of these officials. The affirmation of the accuser can only be rebutted by the oath of a member of the same Tribunal, being of superior rank."

"Then, God be gracious to me, for I have no trust save in Heaven!" said the Englishman in solemn accents. "Yet I will not fall without an effort. I call upon thee, thyself, dark spirit, who presides! in this most deadly assembly — I call upon thyself, to declare on thy faith and honour, whether thou boldest me guilty of what is thus boldly averred by this false calumniator — I call upon thee by thy sacred character — by the name of' — —

"Hold!" replied the presiding Judge. "The name by which we are known in open air must not be pronounced in this subterranean judgment-seat."

He then proceeded to address the prisoner and the assembly, — "I, being called on in evidence, declare that the charge against thee is so far true as it is acknowledged by thyself, namely, that thou hast in other lands than the Red Soil,[12] spoken lightly of this holy institution of justice. But I believe in my soul, and will bear witness on my honour, that the rest of the accusation is incredible and false. And this I swear, holding my hand on the dagger and the cord. — What is your judgment, my brethren, upon the case which you have investigated?"

A member of the first-seated and highest class amongst the judges, muffled like the rest, but the tone of whose voice, and the stoop of whose person, announced him to be more advanced in years than the other two who had before spoken, arose with difficulty, and said with a trembling voice, —

"The child of the cord who is before us, has been convicted

---

[12] The parts of Germany subjected to the operation of the Secret Tribunal were called, from the blood which it spilt, or from some other reason, (Mr. Palgrave suggests the ground tincture of the ancient banner of the district,) the Red Soil. Westphalia, as the limits of that country were understood in the middle ages, which are considerably different from the present boundaries, was the principal theatre of the Vehme.

of folly and rashness in slandering our holy institution. But he spoke his folly to ears which had never heard our sacred laws — He has, therefore, been acquitted by irrefragable testimony, of combining for the impotent purpose of undermining our power, or stirring up princes against our holy association, for which death were too light a punishment — He hath been foolish, then, but not criminal; and as the holy laws of the Vehme bear no penalty save that of death, I propose for judgment that the child of the cord be restored without injury to society, and to the upper world, having been first duly admonished of his errors."

"Child of the cord," said the presiding Judge, "thou hast heard thy sentence of acquittal. But as thou desirest to sleep in an unbloody grave, let me warn thee, that the secrets of this night shall remain with thee, as a secret not to be communicated to father nor mother, to spouse, son, or daughter; neither to be spoken aloud nor whispered; to be told in words or written in characters to be carved or to be painted, or to be otherwise communicated, either directly, or by parable and emblem. Obey this behest, and thy life is in surety. Let thy heart then rejoice within thee, but let it rejoice with trembling. Never more let thy vanity persuade thee that thou art secure from the servants and Judges of the Holy Vehme. Though a thousand leagues lie between thee and the Red Land, and thou speakest in that where our power is not known; though thou shouldst be sheltered by thy native island, and defended by thy kindred ocean, yet, even there, I warn thee to cross thyself when thou dost so much as think of the Holy and Invisible Tribunal, and to retain thy thoughts within thine own bosom; for the Avenger may be beside thee, and thou mayst die in thy folly. Go hence, be wise, and let the fear of the Holy Vehme never pass from before thine eyes."

At the concluding words, all the lights were at once extinguished with a hissing noise. Philipson felt once more the grasp of the hands of the officials, to which he resigned himself as the safest course. He was gently prostrated on his pallet-bed, and transported back to the place from which he had been advanced to the foot of the altar. The cordage was again applied to the platform, and Philipson was sensible that his couch rose with him for a few moments, until a slight shock apprized him that he was again brought to a level with the floor of the chamber in which he had been lodged on the preceding night, or rather morning. He pondered over the events that had passed, in which he was sensible that he owed Heaven thanks for a great deliverance. Fatigue at length prevailed over anxiety, and he fell into a deep and profound sleep, from which he was only awakened by returning light. He resolved on an instant departure from so dangerous a spot, and without seeing any one of the household but the old ostler, pursued his journey to Strasburg, and reached that city without farther accident.

CHAPTER XXI

Away with these! — True Wisdom's world will be
Within its own creation, or in thine,
Maternal Nature! for who teems like thee
Thus on the banks of thy majestic Rhine?
There Harold gazes on a work divine,
A blending of all beauties, streams, and dells —
Fruit, foliage, crag, wood, cornfield, mountain, vine,
And chietless castles breathing stern farewells,
From gray but leafy walls, where ruin greenly dwells.

CHILDE HAROLD'S PILGRIMAGE, Canto III.

When Arthur Philipson left his father, to go on board the bark which was to waft him across the Rhine, he took but few precautions for his own subsistence, during a separation of which he calculated the duration to be very brief. Some necessary change of raiment, and a very few pieces of gold, were all which he thought it needful to withdraw from the general stock; the rest of the baggage and money he left with the sumpter-horse, which he concluded his father might need, in order to sustain his character as an English trader. Having embarked with his horse and his slender appointments on board a fishing skiff, she instantly raised her temporary mast, spread a sail across the yard, and, supported by the force of the wind against the downward power of the current, moved across the river obliquely in the direction of Kirch-hoff, which, as we have said, lies somewhat lower on the river than Hans-Chapelle. Their passage was so favourable, that they reached the opposite side in a few minutes, but not until Arthur, whose eye and thoughts were on the left bank, had seen his father depart from the Chapel of the ferry, accompanied by two horsemen, whom he readily concluded to be the guide Bartholomew, and some chance traveller who had joined him; but the second of whom was in truth the Black Priest of St. Paul's, as has been already mentioned.

This augmentation of his father's company was, he could not but think, likely to be attended with an increase of his safety, since it was not probable he would suffer a companion to be forced upon him, and one of his own choosing might be a protection, in case his guide should prove treacherous. At any rate, he had to rejoice that he had seen his father depart in safety from the spot where they had reason to apprehend some danger awaited him. He resolved, therefore, to make no stay at Kirchhoff, but to pursue his way, as fast as possible, towards Strasburg, and rest, when darkness compelled him to stop, in one of the dorffs, or villages, which were situated on the German side of the Rhine. At Strasburg, he trusted, with the sanguine spirit of youth, he might again be able to rejoin his father; and if he could not altogether subdue his anxiety on their separation, he fondly nourished the hope that he might meet him in safety. After some short refreshment and repose afforded to his horse, he lost no time in proceeding on his journey down the eastern bank of the broad river.

He was now upon the moat interesting side of the Rhine, walled in and repelled as the river is on that shore by the most romantic cliffs, now mantled with vegetation of the richest hue, tinged with all the variegated colours of autumn; now surmounted by fortresses, over whose gates were displayed the pennons of their proud owners; or studded with hamlets, where the richness of the soil supplied to the poor labourer the food, of which the oppressive hand of his superior threatened altogether to deprive him. Every stream which here contributes its waters to the Rhine, winds through its own tributary dell, and each valley possesses a varying and separate character, some rich with pastures, cornfields, and vineyards, some frowning with crags and precipices, and other romantic beauties.

The principles of taste were not then explained or analyzed as they have been since, in countries where leisure has been found for this investigation. But the feelings arising from so rich a landscape as is displayed by the valley of the Rhine, must have been the same in every bosom, from the period when our Englishman took his solitary journey through it, in doubt and danger, till that in which it heard the indignant Childe Harold bid a proud farewell to his native country in the vain search of a land in which his heart might throb less fiercely.

Arthur enjoyed the scene, although the fading daylight began to remind him, that, alone as he was, and travelling with a very valuable charge, it would be matter of prudence to look out for some place of rest during the night. Just as he had formed the resolution of inquiring at the next habitation he passed, which way he should follow for this purpose, the road he pursued descended into a beautiful amphitheatre filled with large tries, which protected from the heats of summer the delicate and tender herbage of the pasture. A large brook flowed through it and joined the Rhine. At a short mile up the brook, its waters made a crescent round a steep craggy eminence, crowned with flanking walls, and Gothic towers and turrets, enclosing a feudal castle of the first order. A part of the savannah that has been mentioned, had been irregularly cultivated for wheat, which had grown a plentiful crop. It was gathered in, but the patches of deep yellow stubble contrasted with the green of the undisturbed pasture land, and with the seared and dark-red foliage of the broad oaks which stretched their arms athwart the level space. There a lad, in a rustic dress, was employed in the task of netting a brood of partridges with the assistance of a trained spaniel; while a young woman, who had the air rather of a domestic in some family of rank, than that of an ordinary villager, sat on the stump of a decayed tree, to watch the progress of the amusement. The spaniel, whose duty it was to drive the partridges under the net, was perceptibly disturbed at the approach of the traveller; his attention was divided, and he was obviously in danger of marring the sport, by barking and putting up the covey, when the maiden quitted her seat, and advancing towards Philipson, requested him, for courtesy, to pass at a greater distance, and not interfere with their amusement.

The traveller willingly complied with her request.

"I will ride, fair damsel," he said, "at whatever distance you please. And allow me, in guerdon, to ask, whether there is convent, castle, or good man's house, where a stranger, who is belated and weary, might receive a night's hospitality?"

The girl, whose face he had not yet distinctly seen, seemed to suppress some desire to laugh, as she replied, "Hath not yon castle, think you," pointing to the distant towers, "some corner which might accommodate a stranger in such extremity?"

"Space enough, certainly," said Arthur; "but perhaps little inclination to grant it."

"I myself," said the girl, "being one, and a formidable part of the garrison, will be answerable for your reception. But as you parley with me in such hostile fashion, it is according to martial order that I should put down my visor."

So saying, she concealed her face under one of those riding

masks, which at that period women often wore when they went abroad, whether for protecting their complexion, or screening themselves from intrusive observation. But ere she could accomplish this operation, Arthur had detected the merry countenance of Annette Veilchen, a girl who, though her attendance on Anne of Geierstein was in a menial capacity, was held in high estimation at Geierstein. She was a bold wench, unaccustomed to the distinctions of rank, which were little regarded in the simplicity of the Helvetian hills, and she was ready to laugh, jest, and flirt with the young men of the Landamman's family. This attracted no attention, the mountain manners making little distinction between the degrees of attendant and mistress, further than that the mistress was a young woman who required help, and the maiden one who was in a situation to offer and afford it. This kind of familiarity would perhaps have been dangerous in other lands, but the simplicity of Swiss manners, and the turn of Annette's disposition, which was resolute and sensible, though rather bold and free, when compared to the manners of more civilized countries, kept all intercourse betwixt her and the young men of the family in the strict path of honour and innocence.

Arthur himself had paid considerable attention to Annette, being naturally, from his feelings towards Anne of Geierstein, heartily desirous to possess the good graces of her attendant; a point which was easily gained by the attentions of a handsome young man, and the generosity with which he heaped upon her small presents of articles of dress or ornament, which the damsel, however faithful, could find no heart to refuse.

The assurance that he was in Anne's neighbourhood, and that he was likely to pass the night under the same roof, both of which circumstances were intimated by the girl's presence and language, sent the blood in a hastier current through Arthur's veins; for though, since he had crossed the river, he had sometimes nourished hopes of again seeing her who had made so strong an impression on his imagination, yet his understanding had as often told him how slight was the chance of their meeting, and it was even now chilled by the reflection, that it could be followed only by the pain of a sudden and final separation. He yielded himself, however, to the prospect of promised pleasure, without attempting to ascertain what was to be its duration or its consequence. Desirous, in the meantime, to hear as much of

Anne's circumstances as Annette chose to tell, he resolved not to let that merry maiden perceive that she was known by him, until she chose of her own accord to lay aside her mystery.

While these thoughts passed rapidly through his imagination, Annette bade the lad drop his nets, and directed him that, having taken two of the best fed partridges from the covey, and carried them into the kitchen, he was to set the rest at liberty.

"I must provide supper," said she to the traveller, "since I am bringing home unexpected company."

Arthur earnestly expressed his hope that his experiencing the hospitality of the castle would occasion no trouble to the inmates, and received satisfactory assurances upon the subject of his scruples.

"I would not willingly be the cause of inconvenience to your mistress," pursued the traveller.

"Look you there," said Annette Veilchen, "I have said nothing of master or mistress, and this poor forlorn traveller has already concluded in his own mind that he is to be harboured in a lady's bower!"

"Why, did you not tell me," said Arthur, somewhat confused at his blunder, "that you were the person of second importance in the place? A damsel, I judged, could only be an officer under a female governor."

"I do not see the justness of the conclusion," replied the maiden. "I have known ladies bear offices of trust in lords' families; nay, and over the lords themselves."

"Am I to understand, fair damsel, that you hold so predominant a situation in the castle which we are now approaching, and of which I pray you to tell me the name?"

"The name of the castle is Arnheim," said Annette.

"Your garrison must be a large one," said Arthur, looking at the extensive building, "if you are able to man such a labyrinth of walls and towers."

"In that point," said Annette, "I must needs own we are very deficient. At present we rather hide in the castle than inhabit it; and yet it is well enough defended by the reports which frighten every other person who might disturb its seclusion."

"And yet you yourselves dare to reside in it?" said the Englishman, recollecting the tale which had been told by Rudolph Donnerhugel, concerning the character of the Barons of Arnheim, and the final catastrophe of the family.

"Perhaps," replied his guide, "we are too intimate with the cause of such fears to feel ourselves strongly oppressed with them — perhaps we have means of encountering the supposed terrors proper to ourselves — perhaps, and it is not the least likely conjecture, we have no choice of a better place of refuge. Such seems to be your own fate at present, sir, for the tops of the distant hills are gradually losing the lights of the evening; and if you rest not in Arnheim, well contented or not, you are likely to find no safe lodging for many a mile."

As she thus spoke she separated from Arthur, taking with the fowler who attended her, a very steep but short footpath, which ascended straight up to the site of the castle; at the same time motioning to the young Englishman to follow a horse-track, which, more circuitous, led to the same point, and, though less direct, was considerably more easy.

He soon stood before the south front of Arnheim Castle, which was a much larger building than he had conceived, either from Rudolph's description, or from the distant view. It had been erected at many different periods, and a considerable part of the edifice was less in the strict Gothic than in what has been termed the Saracenic style, in which the imagination of the architect is more florid than that which is usually indulged in the North, — rich in minarets, cupolas, and similar approximations to Oriental structures. This singular building bore a general appearance of desolation and desertion, but Rudolph had been misinformed when he declared that it had become ruinous. On the contrary, it had been maintained with considerable care; and when it fell into the hands of the Emperor, although no garrison was maintained within its precincts, care was taken to keep the building in repair; and though the prejudices of the country people prevented any one from passing the night within the fearful walls, yet it was regularly visited from time to time by a person having commission from the imperial chancery to that effect. The occupation of the domain around the castle was a valuable compensation for this official person's labour, and he took care not to endanger the loss of it by neglecting his duty. Of late this officer had been withdrawn, and now it appeared that the young Baroness of Arnheim had found refuge in the deserted towers of her ancestors.

The Swiss damsel did not leave the youthful traveller time

to study particularly the exterior of the castle, or to construe the meaning of emblems and mottoes, seemingly of an Oriental character, with which the outside was inscribed and which expressed in various modes, more or less directly, the attachment of the builders of this extensive pile to the learning of the Eastern sages. Ere he had time to take more than a general survey of the place, the voice of the Swiss maiden called him to an angle of the wall in which there was a projection, from whence a long plank extended over a dry moat, and was connected with a window in which Annette was standing.

"You have forgotten your Swiss lessons already," said she, observing that Arthur went rather timidly about crossing the temporary and precarious drawbridge.

The reflection that Anne, her mistress, might make the same observation, recalled the young traveller to the necessary degree of composure. He passed over the plank with the same *sang froid* with which he had learned to brave the far more terrific bridge, beneath the ruinous Castle of Geierstein. He had no sooner entered the window than Annette, taking off her mask, bade him welcome to Germany, and to old friends with new names.

"Anne of Geierstein," she said, "is no more; but you will presently see the Lady Baroness of Arnheim, who is extremely like her; and I, who was Annette Veilchen in Switzerland, the servant to a damsel who was not esteemed much greater than myself, am now the young Baroness's waiting woman, and make every body of less quality stand back."

"If, in such circumstances," said young Philipson, "you have the influence due to your consequence, let me beseech of you to tell the Baroness, since we must now call her so, that my present intrusion on her is occasioned by my ignorance."

"Away, away," said the girl, laughing, "I know better what to say in your behalf. You are not the first poor man and pedlar that has got the graces of a great lady; but I warrant you it was not by making humble apologies, and talking of unintentional intrusion. I will tell her of love, which all the Rhine cannot quench, and which has driven you hither, leaving you no other choice than to come or to perish!"

"Nay, but Annette, Annette" ——

"Fie on you for a fool, — make a shorter name of it, — cry Anne, Anne! and there will be more prospect of your being answered."

So saying, the wild girl ran out of the room, delighted, as a mountaineer of her description was likely to be, with the thought of having done as she would desire to be done by, in her benevolent exertions to bring two lovers together, when on the eve of inevitable separation.

In this self-approving disposition, Annette sped up a narrow turnpike stair to a closet, or dressing-room, where her young mistress was seated, and exclaimed, with open mouth, — "Anne of Gei ——, I mean my Lady Baroness, they are come — they are come!"

"The Philipsons?" said Anne, almost breathless as she asked the question.

"Yes — no —" answered the girl; "that is, yes, — for the best of them is come, and that is Arthur."

"What meanest thou, girl? Is not Signior Philipson, the father, along with his son?"

"Not he, indeed," answered Veilchen, "nor did I ever think of asking about him. He was no friend of mine, nor of any one else, save the old Landamman; and well met they were for a couple of wiseacres with eternal proverbs in their mouths, and care upon their brows."

"Unkind, inconsiderate girl, what hast thou done?" said Anne of Geierstein. "Did I not warn and charge thee to bring them both hither? and you have brought the young man alone to a place where we are nearly in solitude? What will he — what can he think of me?"

"Why, what should I have done?" said Annette, remaining firm in her argument. "He was alone, and should I have sent him down to the dorff to be murdered by the Rhingrave's Lanzknechts? All is fish, I trow, that comes to their net; and how is he to get through this country, so beset with wandering soldiers, robber barons, (I beg your ladyship's pardon,) and roguish Italians, flocking to the Duke of Burgundy's standard? — Not to mention the greatest terror of all, that is never in one shape or other absent from one's eye or thought."

"Hush, hush, girl! add not utter madness to the excess of folly; but let us think what is to be done. For our sake, for his own, this unfortunate young man must leave thin castle instantly."

"You must take the message yourself then, Anne — I beg pardon, most noble Baroness; — it may be very fit for a lady of high birth to send such a message, which, indeed, I have heard the minne-singers tell in their romances; but I am sure it is not a meet one for me, or any frank-hearted Swiss girl, to carry. No more foolery; but remember, if you were born Baroness of Arnheim, you have been bred and brought up in the bosom of the Swiss hills, and should conduct yourself like an honest and well-meaning damsel."

"And in what does your wisdom reprehend my folly, good Mademoiselle Annette?" replied the Baroness.

"Ay, marry! now our noble blood stirs in our veins. But remember, gentle my lady, that it was a bargain between us, when I left yonder noble mountains, and the free air that blows over them, to coop myself up in this land of prisons and slaves, that I should speak my mind to you as freely as I did when our heads lay on the same pillow."

"Speak, then," said Anne, studiously averting her face as she prepared to listen; "but beware that you say nothing which it is unfit for me to hear."

"I will speak nature and common sense; and if your noble ears are not made fit to hear and understand these, the fault lies in them, and not in my tongue. Look you, you have saved this youth from two great dangers, — one at the earth-shoot at Geierstein, the other this very day, when his life was beset. A handsome young man he is, well spoken, and well qualified to gain deservedly a lady's favour. Before you saw him, the Swiss youth were at least not odious to you. You danced with them, — you jested with them, — you were the general object of their admiration, — and, as you well know, you might have had your choice through the Canton — Why, I think it possible a little urgency might have brought you to think of Rudolph Donnerhugel as your mate."

"Never, wench, never!" exclaimed Anne.

"Be not so very positive, my lady. Had he recommended himself to the uncle in the first place, I think, in my poor sentiment, he might at some lucky moment have carried the niece. But since we have known this young Englishman, it has been little less than contemning, despising, and something like hating, all the men whom you could endure well enough before."

"Well, well," said Anne, "I will detest and hate thee more than any of them, unless you bring your matters to an end."

"Softly, noble lady, fair and easy go far. All this argues you love the young man, and let those say that you are wrong, who think there is any thing wonderful in the matter. There is much to justify you, and nothing that I know against it."

"What, foolish girl! Remember my birth forbids me to love a mean man — my condition to love a poor man — my father's commands to love one whose addresses are without his consent — above all, my maidenly pride forbids me fixing my affections on one who cares not for me, — nay, perhaps, is prejudiced against me by appearances."

"Here is a fine homily!" said Annette; "but I can clear every point of it as easily as Father Francis does his text in a holiday sermon. Your birth is a silly dream, which you have only learned to value within these two or three days, when, having come to German soil, some of the old German weed, usually called family pride, has begun to germinate in your heart. Think of such folly as you thought when you lived at Geierstein, that is, during all the rational part of your life, and this great terrible prejudice will sink into nothing. By condition, I conceive you mean estate. But Philipson's father, who is the most free-hearted of men, will surely give his son as many zecchins as will stock a mountain farm. You have firewood for the cutting, and land for the occupying, since you are surely entitled to part of Geierstein, and gladly will your uncle put you in possession of it. You can manage the dairy, Arthur can shoot, hunt, fish, plough, harrow, and reap."

Anne of Geierstein shook her head, as if she greatly doubted her lover's skill in the last of the accomplishments enumerated.

"Well, well, he can learn, then," said Annette Veilchen; "and you will only live the harder the first year or so. Besides, Sigismund Biederman will aid him willingly, and he is a very horse at labour; and I know another besides, who is a friend" —

"Of thine own, I warrant," quoth the young Baroness.

"Marry, it is my poor friend, Martin Sprenger; and I'll never be so false-hearted as to deny my bachelor."

"Well, well, but what is to be the end of all this?" said the Baroness, impatiently.

"The end of it, in my opinion," said Annette, "is very simple. Here are priests and prayer-books within a mile — go down to the parlour, speak your mind to your lover, or hear him speak his mind to you; join hands, go quietly back to Geierstein in the character of man and wife, and get every thing ready to receive your uncle on his return.

This is the way that a plain Swiss wench would cut off the romance of a German Baroness" ——

"And break the heart of her father," said the young lady, with a sigh.

"It is more tough than you are aware of," replied Annette; "he hath not lived without you so long, but that he will be able to spare you for the rest of his life, a great deal more easily than you, with all your new-fan-glad ideas of quality, will be able to endure his schemes of wealth and ambition, which will aim at making you the wife of some illustrious Count, like De Hagenbach, whom we saw not long since make such an edifying end, to the great example of all Robber-Chivalry upon the Rhine."

"Thy plan is naught, wench; a childish vision of a girl, who never knew more of life than she has heard told over her milking-pail. Remember that my uncle entertains the highest ideas of family discipline, and that, to act contrary to my father's will, would destroy us in his good opinion. Why else am I here? wherefore has he resigned his guardianship? and why am I obliged to change the habits that are dear to me, and assume the manners of a people that are strange, and therefore unpleasing to me?"

"Your uncle," said Annette, firmly, "is Landamman of the Canton of Unterwalden; respects its freedom, and is the sworn protector of its laws, of which, when you, a denizen of the Confederacy, claim the protection, he cannot refuse it to you."

"Even then," said the young Baroness, "I should forfeit his good opinion, his more than paternal affection; but it is needless to dwell upon this. Know, that although I could have loved the young man, whom I will not deny to be as amiable as your partiality paints him — know," — she hesitated for a moment, — "that he has never spoken a word to me on such a subject as you, without knowing either his sentiments or mine, would intrude on my consideration."

"Is it possible?" answered Annette. "I thought — I believed, though I have never pressed on your confidence — that you must — attached as you were to each other — have spoken together, like true maid and true bachelor, before now. I have done wrong, when I thought to do for the best. — Is it possible! — such things have been heard of even in our Canton — is it possible he can have harboured so unutterably base purposes, as that Martin of Brisach, who made love to Adela of the Sundgau, enticed her to folly — the thing, though almost incredible, is true, — fled — fled from the country and boasted of his villainy, till her cousin Raymund silenced for ever his infamous triumph, by beating his brains out with his club, even in the very street of the villain's native town? By the Holy Mother of Einsiedlen! could I suspect this Englishman of meditating such treason, I would saw the plank across the moat till a fly's weight would break it, and it should be at six fathom deep that he should abye the perfidy which dared to meditate dishonour against an adopted daughter of Switzerland."

As Annette Veilchen spoke, all the fire of her mountain courage flashed from her eyes, and she listened reluctantly while Anne of Geierstein endeavoured to obliterate the dangerous impression which her former words had impressed on her simple but faithful attendant.

"On my word" — she said, "on my soul — you do Arthur Philipson injustice — foul injustice in intimating such a suspicion; — his conduct towards me has ever been upright and honourable — a friend to a friend — a brother to a sister — could not, in all he has done and said, have been more respectful, more anxiously affectionate, more undeviatingly candid. In our frequent interviews and intercourse he has indeed seemed very kind — very attached. But had I been disposed — at times I may have been too much so — to listen to him with endurance," — the young lady here put her hand on her forehead, but the tears streamed through her slender fingers. — "he has never spoken of any love — any preference; if he indeed entertains any, some obstacle, insurmountable on his part, has interfered to prevent him."

"Obstacle?" replied the Swiss damsel. "Ay, doubtless — some childish bashfulness — some foolish idea about your birth being so high above his own — some dream of modesty pushed to extremity which considers as impenetrable the ice of a spring frost. This delusion may be broken by a moment's encouragement, and I will take the task on myself to spare your blushes, my dearest Anne."

"No, no; for heaven's sake, no, Veilchen!" answered the Baroness, to whom Annette had so long been a companion and confidant, rather than a domestic. "You cannot anticipate the nature of the obstacles which may prevent his thinking on what you are so desirous to promote. Hear me — My early education, and the instructions of my kind uncle, have taught me to know something more of foreigners and their fashions, than I ever could have learned in our happy retirement of Geierstein; I am well-nigh convinced that these Philipsons are of rank, as they are of manners and bearing, far superior to the occupation which they appear to hold. The father is a man of deep observation, of high thoughts and pretension, and lavish of gifts, far beyond what consists with the utmost liberality of a trader."

"That is true," said Annette; "I will say for myself that the silver chain he gave me weighs against ten silver crowns, and the cross which Arthur added to it, the day after the long ride we had together up towards Mons Pilatre, is worth, they tell me, as much more. There is not the like of it in the Cantons. Well, what then? They are rich, so are you. So much the better."

"Alas! Annette, they are not only rich, but noble. I am persuaded of this; for I have observed often, that even the father retreated, with an air of quiet and dignified contempt, from discussions with Donnerhugel and others, who, in our plain way, wished to fasten a dispute upon him. And when a rude observation or blunt pleasantry was pointed at the son, his eye flashed, his cheek coloured, and it was only a glance from his father which induced him to repress the retort of no friendly character which rose to his lips."

"You have been a close observer," said Annette. "All this may be true, but I noted it not. But what then, I say once more? If Arthur has some fine noble name in his own country, are not you yourself Baroness of Arnheim? And I will frankly allow it as something of worth, if it smooths the way to a match, where I think you must look for happiness — I hope so, else I am sure it should have no encouragement from me."

"I do believe so, my faithful Veilchen; but, alas! how can you, in the state of natural freedom in which you have been bred, know, or even dream, of the various restraints which this gilded or golden chain of rank and nobility hangs upon those whom it fetters and encumbers, I fear, as much as it decorates? In every country, the distinction of rank binds men to certain duties. It may carry with it restrictions, which may prevent alliances in foreign countries — it often may prevent them from consulting their inclinations when they wed in their own. It leads to alliances in which the heart is never consulted, to treaties of marriage, which are often formed when the parties are in the cradle, or in leading strings, but which are not the less binding on them in honour and faith. Such may exist in the present case. These alliances are often blended and mixed up with state policy; and if the interest of England, or what he deems such, should have occasioned the elder Philipson to form such an engagement, Arthur would break his own heart — the heart of any one else — rather than make false his father's word."

"The more shame to them that formed such an engagement!" said Annette. "Well, they talk of England being a free country; but if they can bar young men and women of the natural privilege to call their hands and hearts their own, I would as soon be a German serf. — Well, lady, you are wise, and I am ignorant. But what is to be done? I have brought this young man here, expecting, God knows, a happier issue to your meeting. But it is clear you cannot marry him without his asking you. Now, although I confess that, if I could think him willing to forfeit the hand of the fairest maid of the Cantons, either from want of manly courage to ask it, or from regard to some ridiculous engagement, formed betwixt his father and some other nobleman of their island of noblemen, I would not in either case grudge him a ducking in the moat; yet it is another question, whether we should send him down to be murdered among those cut-throats of the Rhingrave; and unless we do so, I know not how to get rid of him."

"Then let the boy William give attendance on him here, and do you see to his accommodation. It is best we do not meet."

"I will," said Annette; "yet what am I to say for you? Unhappily, I let him know that you were here."

"Alas, imprudent girl! Yet why should I blame thee," said Anne of Geierstein, "when the imprudence has been so great on my own side. It is myself, who, suffering my imagination to rest too long upon this young man and his merits, have led me into this entanglement. But I will show thee that I can overcome this folly, and I will not seek in my own error a cause for evading the duties of hospitality. Go, Veilchen, get some refreshment ready. Thou shalt sup with us, and thou must not leave us. Thou shalt see me behave as becomes both a German lady and a Swiss maiden. Get me first a candle, however, my girl, for I must wash these tell-tales, my eyes, and arrange my dress."

To Annette this whole explanation had been one scene of astonishment, for, in the simple ideas of love and courtship in which she had been brought up amid the Swiss mountains, she had expected that the two lovers would have taken the first opportunity of the absence of their natural guardians, and have united themselves for ever; and she had even arranged a little secondary plot, in which she herself and Martin Sprenger, her faithful bachelor, were to reside with the young couple as friends and dependents. Silenced, therefore, but not satisfied, by the objections of her young mistress, the zealous Annette retreated murmuring to herself, — "That little hint about her dress is the only natural and sensible word she has said in my hearing. Please God, I will return and help her in the twinkling of an eye. That dressing my mistress is the only part of a waiting-lady's life that I have the least fancy for — it seems so natural for one pretty maiden to set off another — in faith we are but learning to dress ourselves at another time."

And with this sage remark Annette Veilchen tripped down stairs.

CHAPTER XXII

Tell me not of it — I could ne'er abide
The mummery of all that forced civility.
"Pray, seat yourself, my lord." With cringing hams
The speech is spoken, and, with bended knee,
Heard by the smiling courtier. — "Before you, sir?
It must be on the earth then." Hang it all!
The pride which cloaks itself in such poor fashion
Is scarcely fit to swell a beggar's bosom.

OLD PLAY.

UP stairs and down stairs tripped Annette Veilchen, the soul of all that was going on in the only habitable corner of the huge castle of Arnheim. She. was equal to every kind of service, and therefore popped her head into the stable to be sure that William attended properly to Arthur's horse, looked into the kitchen to see that the old cook, Marthon, roasted the partridges in due time, (an interference for which she received little thanks,) rummaged out a flask or two of Rhine wine from the huge Dom Daniel of a cellar, and, finally, just peeped into the parlour to see how Arthur was looking; when, having the satisfaction to see he had in the best manner he could sedulously arranged his person, she assured him that he should shortly see her mistress, who was rather indisposed, yet could not refrain from coming down to see so valued an acquaintance.

Arthur blushed when she spoke thus, and seemed so handsome in the waiting-maid's eye, that she could not help saying to herself, as she went to her young lady's room — "Well, if true love cannot manage to bring that couple together, in spite of all the obstacles that they stand boggling at, I will never believe that there is such a thing as true love in the world, let Martin Sprenger say what he will, and swear to it on the gospels."

When she reached the young Baroness's apartment, she found, to her surprise, that instead of having put on what finery she possessed, that young lady's choice had preferred the same simple kirtle which she had worn during the first day that Arthur had dined at Geierstein. Annette looked at first puzzled and doubtful, then suddenly recognised the good taste which had dictated the attire, and exclaimed — "You are right — you are right — it is best to meet him as a free-hearted Swiss maiden."

Anne also smiled as she replied — "But at the same time, in the walls of Arnheim, I must appear in some respect as the daughter of my father. — Here, girl, aid me to put this gem upon the riband which binds my hair."

It was an aigrette, or plume, composed of two feathers of a vulture, fastened together by an opal, which changed to the changing light with a variability which enchanted the Swiss damsel, who had never seen any thing resembling it in her life.

"Now, Baroness Anne," said she, "if that pretty thing be really worn as a sign of your rank, it is the only thing belonging to your dignity that I should ever think of coveting; for it doth shimmer and change colour after a most wonderful fashion, even something like one's own cheek when one is fluttered."

"Alas, Annette!" said the Baroness, passing her hand across her eyes, "of all the gauds which the females of my house have owned, this perhaps hath been the most fatal to its possessors."

"And why then wear it?" said Annette. "Why wear it now of all days in the year?"

"Because it best reminds me of my duty to my father and family. And now, girl, look thou sit with us at table, and leave not the apartment; and see thou fly not to and fro to help thyself or others with any thing on the board, but remain quiet and seated till William helps you to what you have occasion for."

"Well, that is a gentle fashion, which I like well enough," said Annette, "and William serves us so debonairly, that it is a joy to see him; yet, ever and anon, I feel as I were not Annette Veilchen herself, but only Annette Veilchen's picture, since I can neither rise, sit down, run about, or stand still, without breaking some rule of courtly breeding. It is not so, I dare say, with you, who are always mannerly."

"Less courtly than thou seemest to think," said the high-born maiden; "but I feel the restraint more on the greensward, and under heaven's free air, than when I undergo it closed within the walls of an apartment."

"Ah, true — the dancing," said Annette; "that was something to be sorry for indeed."

"But most am I sorry, Annette, that I cannot tell whether I act precisely right or wrong in seeing this young man, though it must be for the last time. Were my father to arrive? — Were Ital Schreckenwald to return" ——

"Your father is too deeply engaged on some of his dark and mystic errands," said the flippant Swiss; "sailed to the mountains of the Brockenberg, where witches hold their sabbath or gone on a hunting-party with the Wild Huntsman."

"Fie, Annette, how dare you talk thus of my father?"

"Why, I know little of him personally," said the damsel, "and you yourself do not know much more. And how should that be false which all men say is true?"

"Why, fool, what do they say?"

"Why, that the Count is a wizard — that your grandmother was a will-of-wisp, and old Ital Schreckenwald a born devil incarnate; and there is some truth in that, whatever comes of the rest."

"Where is he?"

"Gone down to spend the night in the village, to see the Rhingrave's men quartered, and keep them in some order, if possible; for the soldiers are disappointed of pay which they had been promised; and when this happens, nothing resembles a Lanz-knecht except a chafed bear."

"Go we down then, girl; it is perhaps the last night which we may spend for years, with a certain degree of freedom."

I will not pretend to describe the marked embarrassment with which Arthur Philipson and Anne of Geierstein met; neither lifted their eyes, neither spoke intelligibly, as they greeted each other, and the maiden herself did not blush more deeply than her modest visitor; while the good-humoured Swiss girl, whose ideas of love partook of the freedom of a more Arcadian country and its customs, looked on with eyebrows a little arched, much in wonder, and a little in contempt, at a couple, who, as she might think, acted with such unnatural and constrained reserve. Deep was the reverence and the blush with which Arthur offered his hand to the young lady, and her acceptance of the courtesy had the same character of extreme bashfulness, agitation, and embarrassment. In short, though little or nothing intelligible passed between this very handsome and interesting couple, the interview itself did not on that account lose any interest. Arthur handed the maiden, as was the duty of a gallant of the day, into the next room, where their repast was prepared; and Annette, who watched with singular attention every thing which occurred, felt with astonishment, that the forms and ceremonies of the higher orders of society had such an influence, even over her free-born mind, as the rites of the Druids over that of the Roman general, when he said,

"I scorn them, yet they awe me."

"What can have changed them?" said Annette; "when at Geierstein, they looked but like another girl and bachelor, only that Anne is so very handsome; but now they move in time and manner as if they were leading a stately pavin, and behave to each other with as much formal respect as if he were Landamman of the Unterwalden, and she the first lady of Berne. 'Tis all very fine, doubtless, but it is not the way that Martin Sprenger makes love."

Apparently, the circumstances in which each of the young people were placed, recalled to them the habits of lofty, and somewhat formal courtesy, to which they might have been accustomed in former days; and while the Baroness felt it necessary to observe the strictest decorum, in order to qualify the reception of Arthur into the interior of her retreat, he, on the other hand, endeavoured to show, by the profoundness of his respect, that he was incapable of misusing the kindness with which he had been treated. They placed themselves at table, scrupulously observing the distance which might become a "virtuous gentleman and maid." The youth William did the service of the entertainment with deftness and courtesy, as one well accustomed to such duty; and Annette, placing herself between them, and endeavouring as closely as she could, to adhere to the ceremonies which she saw them observe, made practice of the civilities which were expected from the attendant of a baroness. Various, however, were the errors which she committed. Her demeanour in general was that of a greyhound in the slips, ready to start up every moment; and she was only withheld by the recollection that she was to ask for that which she had far more mind to help herself to.

Other points of etiquette were transgressed in their turn, after the repast was over, and the attendant had retired. The waiting damsel often mingled too unceremoniously in the conversation, and could not help calling her mistress by her Christian name of Anne, and, in defiance of all decorum, addressed her, as well as Philipson, with the pronoun *thou*, which then, as well as now, was a dreadful solecism in German politeness. Her blunders were so far fortunate, that by furnishing the young lady and Arthur with a topic foreign to the peculiarities of their own situation, they enabled them to withdraw their attentions from its embarrassments, and to exchange smiles at poor Annette's expense. She was not long of perceiving this, and half nettled, half availing herself of the apology to speak her mind, said, with considerable spirit, "You have both been very merry, forsooth, at my expense, and all because I wished rather to rise and seek what I wanted, than wait till the poor fellow, who was kept trotting between the board and beauffet, found leisure to bring it to me. You laugh at me now, because I call you by your names, as they were given to you in the blessed church at your christening; and because I say to you *thee* and *thou*, addressing my Juncker and my Yungfrau as I would do if I were on my knees praying to Heaven. But for all your new-world fancies, I can tell you, you are but a couple of children, who do not know your own minds, and are jesting away the only leisure given you to provide for your own happiness. Nay, frown not, my sweet Mistress Baroness; I have looked at Mount Pilatre too often, to fear a gloomy brow."

"Peace, Annette," said her mistress, "or quit the room."

"Were I not more your friend than I am my own," said the headstrong and undaunted Annette, "I would quit the room, and the castle to boot, and leave you to hold your house here, with your amiable seneschal, Ital Schreckenwald."

"If not for love, yet for shame, for charity, be silent, or leave the room."

"Nay," said Annette, "my bolt is shot, and I have but hinted at what all upon Geierstein Green said, the night when the bow of Buttisholz was bended. You know what the old saw says" —
—

"Peace! peace, for Heaven's sake, or I must needs fly!" said the young Baroness.

"Nay, then," said Annette, considerably changing her tone, as if afraid that her mistress should actually retire, "if you must fly, necessity must have its course. I know no one who can follow. This mistress of mine, Signior Arthur, would require for her attendant, not a homely girl of flesh and blood like myself, but a waiting woman with substance composed of gossamer, and breath supplied by the spirit of ether. Would you believe it — It is seriously held by many, that she partakes of the race of spirits of the elements, which makes her so much more bashful than maidens of this everyday world."

Anne of Geierstein seemed rather glad to lead away the conversation from the turn which her wayward maiden had given to it, and to turn it on more indifferent subjects, though these were still personal to herself.

"Signior Arthur," she said, "thinks, perhaps, he has some room to nourish some such strange suspicion as your heedless folly expresses, and some fools believe, both in Germany and Switzerland. Confess, Signior Arthur, you thought strangely of me when I passed your guard upon the bridge of Graffs-lust, on the night last past."

The recollection of the circumstances which had so greatly surprised him at the time, so startled Arthur, that it was with some difficulty he commanded himself, so as to attempt an answer at all; and what he did say on the occasion was broken and unconnected.

"I did hear, I own — that is, Rudolph Donnerhugel reported — But that I believed that you, gentle lady, were other than a Christian maiden" ——

"Nay, if Rudolph were the reporter," said Annette, "you would hear the worst of my lady and her lineage, that is certain. He is one of those prudent personages who depreciate and find fault with the goods he has thoughts of purchasing, in order to deter other offerers. Yes, he told you a fine goblin story, I warrant you, of my lady's grandmother; and truly, it so happened, that the circumstances of the case gave, I dare say, some colour in your eyes to" ——

"Not so, Annette," answered Arthur; "whatever might be said of your lady that sounded uncouth and strange, fell to the ground as incredible."

"Not quite so much so, I fancy," interrupted Annette, without heeding sign or frown. "I strongly suspect I should have had much more trouble in dragging you hither to this castle, had you known you were approaching the haunt of the Nymph of the Fire, the Salamander, as they call her, not to mention the shock of again seeing the descendant of that Maiden of the Fiery Mantle."

"Peace, once more, Annette," said her mistress; "since Fate has occasioned this meeting, let us not neglect the opportunity to disabuse our English friend, of the absurd report he has listened to with doubt and wonder perhaps, but not with absolute incredulity."

"Signior Arthur Philipson," she proceeded, "it is true my grandfather, by the mother's side, Baron Herman of Arnheim, was a man of great knowledge in abstruse sciences. He was also a presiding judge of a tribunal of which you must have heard, called the Holy Vehme. One night a stranger, closely pursued by the agents of that body, which (crossing herself) it is not safe even to name, arrived at the castle and craved his protection, and the rights of hospitality. My grandfather, finding the advance which the stranger had made to the rank of Adept, gave him his protection, and became bail to deliver him to answer the charge against him, for a year and a day, which delay he was, it seems, entitled to require on his behalf. They studied together during that term, and pushed their researches into the mysteries of nature, as far, in all probability, as men have the power of urging them. When the fatal day drew nigh on which the guest must part from his host, he asked permission to bring his daughter to the castle, that they might exchange a last farewell. She was introduced with much secrecy, and after some days, finding that her father's fate was so uncertain, the Baron, with the sage's consent, agreed to give the forlorn maiden refuge in his castle, hoping to obtain from her some additional information concerning the languages and the wisdom of the East. Dannischemend, her father, left this castle, to go to render himself up to the Vehmegericht at Fulda. The result is unknown; perhaps he was saved by Baron Arnheim's testimony, perhaps he was given up to the steel and the cord. On such matters, who dare speak?

"The fair Persian became the wife of her guardian and protector. Amid many excellences, she had one peculiarity allied to imprudence. She availed herself of her foreign dress and manners, as well as of a beauty, which was said to have been marvellous, and an agility seldom equalled, to impose upon and terrify the ignorant German ladies, who, hearing her speak Persian and Arabic, were already disposed to consider her as over closely connected with unlawful arts. She was of a fanciful and imaginative disposition, and delighted to place herself in such colours and circumstances as might confirm their most ridiculous suspicions, which she considered only as matter of sport. There was no end to the stories to which she gave rise. Her first appearance in the castle was said to be highly picturesque, and to have inferred something of the marvellous. With the levity of a child, she had some childish passions, and while she encouraged the growth and circulation of the most extraordinary legends amongst some of the neighbourhood, she entered into disputes with persons of her own quality concerning rank and precedence, on which the ladies of Westphalia have at all times set great store. This cost her life; for, on the morning of the christening of my poor mother, the Baroness of Arnheim died suddenly, even while a splendid company was assembled in the castle chapel to witness the ceremony. It was believed that she died of poison, administered by the Baroness Steinfeldt, with whom she was engaged in a bitter quarrel, entered into chiefly on behalf of her friend and companion, the Countess Waldstetten."

"And the opal gem? — and the sprinkling with water?" said Arthur Philipson.

"Ah!" replied the young Baroness, "I see you desire to hear the real truth of my family history, of which you have yet learned only the romantic legend. — The sprinkling of water was necessarily had recourse to, on my ancestress's first swoon. As for the opal, I have heard that it did indeed grow pale, but only because it is said to be the nature of that noble gem, on the approach of poison. Some part of the quarrel with the Baroness Steinfeldt was about the right of the Persian maiden to wear this stone, which an ancestor of my family won in battle from the Soldan of Trebizond. All these things were confused in popular tradition, and the real facts turned into a fairy tale."

"But you have said nothing," suggested Arthur Philipson, "on — on" ——

"On what?" said his hostess.

"On your appearance last night."

"Is it possible," said she, "that a man of sense, and an Englishman, cannot guess at the explanation which I have to give, though not, perhaps, very distinctly? My father, you are aware, has been a busy man in a disturbed country, and has incurred the hatred of many powerful persons. He is, therefore, obliged to move in secret, and avoid unnecessary observation. He was, besides, averse to meet his brother, the Landamman. I was therefore told, on our entering Germany, that I was to expect a signal where and when to join him — the token was to be a small crucifix of bronze, which had belonged to my poor mother. In my apartment at Graffs-lust I found the token, with a note from my father, making me acquainted with a secret passage proper to such places, which, though it had the appearance of being blocked up, was in fact very slightly barricaded. By this I was instructed to pass to the gate, make my escape into the woods, and meet my father at a place appointed there."

"A wild and perilous adventure," said Arthur.

"I have never been so much shocked," continued the maiden, "as at receiving this summons, compelling me to steal away from my kind and affectionate uncle, and go I knew not whither. Yet compliance was absolutely necessary. The place of meeting was plainly pointed out. A midnight walk, in the neighbourhood of protection, was to me a trifle; but the precaution of posting sentinels at the gate might have interfered with my purpose, had I not mentioned it to some of my elder cousins, the Biedermans, who readily agreed to let me pass and repass unquestioned. But you know my cousins; honest and kind hearted, they are of a rude way of thinking, and as incapable of feeling a generous delicacy as — some other persons." — (Here there was a glance towards Annette Veilchen.) — "They exacted from me, that I should conceal myself and my purpose from Sigismund; and as they are always making sport with the simple youth, they insisted that I should pass him in such a manner as might induce him to believe that I was a spiritual apparition, and out of his terrors for supernatural beings, they expected to have much amusement. I was obliged to secure their connivance at my escape on their own terms; and, indeed, I was too much grieved at the prospect of quitting my kind uncle, to think much of any thing else. Yet my surprise was considerable, when, contrary to expectation, I found you on the bridge as sentinel, instead of my cousin Sigismund. Your own ideas I ask not for."

"They were those of a fool," said Arthur, "of a thrice-sodden fool. Had I been aught else, I would have offered my escort. My sword" ——

"I could not have accepted your protection," said Anne, calmly. "My mission was in every respect a secret one. I met my father — some intercourse had taken place betwixt him and Rudolph Donnerhugel, which induced him to alter his purpose of carrying me away with him last night. I joined him, however, early this morning, while Annette acted for a time my part amongst the Swiss pilgrims. My father desired that it should not be known when or with whom I left my uncle and his escort. I need scarce remind you that I saw you in the dungeon."

"You were the preserver of my life," said the youth — "the restorer of my liberty."

"Ask me not the reason of my silence. I was then acting under the agency of others, not under mine own. Your escape was effected, in order to establish a communication betwixt the Swiss without the fortress and the soldiers within. After the alarm at La Ferette, I learned from Sigismund Biederman that a party of banditti were pursuing your father and you, with a view to pillage and robbery. My father had furnished me with the means of changing Anne of Geierstein into a German maiden of quality. I set out instantly, and glad I am to have given you a hint which might free you from danger."

"But my father?" said Arthur.

"I have every reason to hope he is well and safe," answered the young lady. "More than I were eager to protect both you and him — poor Sigismund amongst the first. — And now, my friend, these mysteries explained, it is time we part, and for ever."

"Part! — and for ever!" repeated the youth, in a voice like a dying echo.

"It is our fate," said the maiden. "I appeal to you if it is not your duty — I tell you it is mine. You will depart with early dawn to Strasburg — and — and — we never meet again."

"With an ardour of passion which he could not repress, Arthur Philipson threw himself at the feet of the maiden, whose faltering tone had clearly expressed that she felt deeply in uttering the words. She looked round for Annette, but Annette had disappeared at this most critical moment; and her mistress for a second or two was not perhaps sorry for her absence.

"Rise," she said, "Arthur — rise. You must not give way to feelings that might be fatal to yourself and me."

"Hear me, lady, before I bid you adieu, and for ever — the word of a criminal is heard, though he plead the worst cause — I am a belted knight, and the son and heir of an Earl, whose name has been spread throughout England and France, and wherever valour has had fame."

"Alas!" said she, faintly, "I have but too long suspected what you now tell me. — Rise, I pray you, rise."

"Never till you hear me," said the youth, seizing one of her hands, which trembled, but hardly could be said to struggle in his grasp. — "Hear me," he said, with the enthusiasm of first love, when the obstacles of bashfulness and diffidence are surmounted — "My father and I are — I acknowledge it — bound on a most hazardous and doubtful expedition. You will very soon learn its issue for good or bad. If it succeed, you shall hear of me in my own character — If I fall, I must — I will — I do claim a tear from Anne of Geierstein. If I escape, I have yet a horse, a lance, and a sword; and you shall hear robly of him whom you have thrice protected from imminent danger."

"Arise — arise, repeated the maiden, whose tears began to flow fast, as, struggling to raise her lover, they fell thick upon his head and face. "I have heard enough — to listen to more were indeed madness, both for you and myself."

"Yet one single word," added the youth; "while Arthur has a heart, it beats for you — while Arthur can wield an arm, it strikes for you, and in your cause."

Annette now rushed into the room.

"Away, away!" she cried — "Schreckenwald has returned from the village with some horrible tidings, and I fear me he comes this way."

Arthur had started to his feet at the first signal of alarm.

"If there is danger near your lady, Annette, there is at least one faithful friend by her side."

Annette looked anxiously at her mistress.

"But Schreckenwald," she said — "Schreckenwald, your father's steward — his confidant. — O, think better of it — I can hide Arthur somewhere."

The noble-minded girl had already resumed her composure, and replied with dignity — "I have done nothing," she said, "to offend my father. If Schreckenwald be my father's steward, he is my vassal. I hide no guest to conciliate him. Sit down," (addressing Arthur,) "and let us receive this man. — Introduce him instantly, Annette, and let us hear his tidings — and bid him remember, that when he speaks to me he addresses his mistress."

Arthur resumed his seat still more proud of his choice from the noble and fearless spirit displayed by one who had so lately shown herself sensible to the gentlest feelings of the female sex.

Annette, assuming courage from her mistress's dauntless demeanour, clapped her hands together as she left the room, saying, but in a low voice, "I see that after all it is something to be a Baroness, if one can assert her dignity conformingly. How could I be so much frightened for this rude man!"

CHAPTER XXIII

———— Affairs that walk
(As they say spirits do) at midnight, have
In them a wilder nature, than the business
That seeks dispatch by day.

HENRY VIII. *Act* 5.

The approach of the steward was now boldly expected by the little party. Arthur, flattered at once and elevated by the firmness which Anne had shown when this person's arrival was announced, hastily considered the part which he was to act in the approaching scene, and prudently determined to avoid all active and personal interference, till he should observe from the demeanour of Anne, that such was likely to be useful or agreeable to her. He resumed his place, therefore, at a distant part of the board, on which their meal had been lately spread, and remained there, determined to act in the manner Anne's behaviour should suggest as most prudent and fitting, — veiling, at the same time, the most acute internal anxiety, by an appearance of that deferential composure, which one of inferior rank adopts when admitted to the presence of a superior. Anne, on her part, seemed to prepare herself for an interview of interest. An air of conscious dignity succeeded the extreme agitation which she had so lately displayed, and, busying herself with some articles of female work, she also seemed to expect with tranquillity the visit, to which her attendant was disposed to attach so much alarm.

A step was heard upon the stair, hurried and unequal, as that of some one in confusion as well as haste; the door flew open, and Ital Schreckenwald entered.

This person, with whom the details given to the elder Philipson by the Landamman Biederman have made the reader in some degree acquainted, was a tall, well-made, soldierly-looking man. His dress, like that of persons of rank at the period in Germany, was more varied in colour, more cut and ornamented, slashed and jagged, than the habit worn in France and England. The never-failing hawk's feather decked his cap, secured with a medal of gold, which served as a clasp. His doublet was of buff, for defence, but *laid down*, as it was called in the tailor's craft, with rich lace on each seam, and displaying on the breast a golden chain, the emblem of his rank in the Baron's household. He entered with rather a hasty step, and busy and offended look, and said, somewhat rudely, — "Why, how now, young lady — wherefore this? Strangers in the castle at this period of night!"

Anne of Geierstein, though she had been long absent from her native country, was not ignorant of its habits and customs, and knew the haughty manner in which all who were noble exerted their authority over their dependents.

"Are you a vassal of Arnheim, Ital Schreckenwald, and do you speak to the Lady of Arnheim in her own castle with an elevated voice, a saucy look, and bonneted withal? Know your place; and, when you have demanded pardon for your insolence, and told your errand in such terms as befit your condition and mine. I may listen to what you have to say."

Schreckenwald's hand, in spite of him, stole to his bonnet, and uncovered his haughty brow.

"Noble lady," he said, in a somewhat milder tone, "excuse me if my haste be unmannerly, but the alarm is instant. The soldiery of the Rhingrave have mutinied, plucked down the banners of their master, and set up an independent ensign, which they call the pennon of St. Nicholas, under which they declare that they will maintain peace with God, and war with all the world. This castle cannot escape them, when they consider that the first course to maintain themselves, must be to take possession of some place of strength. You must up then, and ride with the very peep of dawn. For the present, they are busy with the wine-skins of the peasants; but when they wake in the morning, they will unquestionably march hither; and you may chance to fall into the hands of those who will think of the terrors of the castle of Arnheim as the figments of a fairy-tale, and laugh at its mistress's pretensions to honour and respect."

"Is it impossible to make resistance? The castle is strong," said the young lady, "and I am unwilling to leave the house of my fathers without attempting somewhat in our defence."

"Five hundred men," said Schreckenwald, "might garrison Arnheim, battlement and tower. With a less number it were madness to attempt to keep such an extent of walls; and how to get twenty soldiers together, I am sure I know not. — So, having now the truth of the story, let me beseech you to dismiss this guest, — too young, I think, to be the inmate of a lady's bower, — and I will point to him the nighest way out of the castle for this is a strait in which we must all be contented with looking to our own safety."

"And whither is it that you propose to go?" said the Baroness, continuing to maintain, in respect to Ital Schreckenwald, the complete and calm assertion of absolute superiority, to which the seneschal gave way with such marks of impatience, as a fiery steed exhibits under the management of a complete cavalier.

"To Strasburg I propose to go, — that is, if it so please you, — with such slight escort as I can get hastily together by daybreak. I trust we may escape being observed by the mutineers; or, if we fall in with a party of stragglers, I apprehend but little difficulty in forcing my way."

"And wherefore do you prefer Strasburg as a place of asylum?"

"Because I trust we shall there meet your excellency's father, the noble Count Albert of Geierstein."

"It is well," said the young lady. — "You also, I think, Signior Philipson, spoke of directing your course to Strasburg. If it consist with your convenience, you may avail yourself of the protection of my escort as far as that city, where you expect to meet your father."

It will readily be believed, that Arthur cheerfully bowed assent to a proposal which was to prolong their remaining in society together; and might possibly, as his romantic imagination suggested, afford him an opportunity, on a road beset with dangers, to render some service of importance.

Ital Schreckenwald attempted to remonstrate.

"Lady! — lady!" — he said, with some marks of impatience.

"Take breath and leisure, Schreckenwald," said Anne, "and you will be more able to express yourself with distinctness, and with respectful propriety."

The impatient vassal muttered an oath betwixt his teeth, and answered with forced civility, — "Permit me to state, that our case requires we should charge ourselves with the care of no one but you. We shall be few enough for your defence, and I cannot permit any stranger to travel with us."

"If," said Arthur, "I conceived that I was to be a useless encumbrance on the retreat of this noble young lady, worlds, Sir

Squire, would not induce me to accept her offer. But I am neither child nor woman — I am a full-grown man, and ready to show such good service as manhood may in defence of your lady."

"If we must not challenge your valour and ability, young sir," said Schreckenwald, "who shall answer for your fidelity?"

"To question that elsewhere," said Arthur, "might be dangerous."

But Anne interfered between them. "We must straight to rest, and remain prompt for alarm, perhaps even before the hour of dawn. Schreckenwald, I trust to your care for due watch and ward — You have men enough at least for that purpose. — And hear and mark — It is my desire and command, that this gentleman be accommodated with lodgings here for this night, and that he travel with us to-morrow. For this I will be responsible to my father, and your part, is only to obey my commands. I have long had occasion to know both the young man's father and himself, who were ancient guests of my uncle, the Landamman. On the journey you will keep the youth beside you, and use such courtesy to him as your rugged temper will permit."

Ital Schreckenwald intimated his acquiescence with a look of bitterness, which it were vain to attempt to describe. It expressed spite, mortification, humbled pride and reluctant submission. He did submit, however, and ushered young Philipson into a decent apartment with a bed, which the fatigue and agitation of the preceding day rendered very acceptable.

Notwithstanding the ardour with which Arthur expected the rise of the next dawn, his deep repose, the fruit of fatigue, held him until the reddening of the east, when the voice of Schreckenwald exclaimed, "Up, Sir Englishman, if you mean to accomplish your boast of loyal service. It is time we were in the saddle, and we shall tarry for no sluggards."

Arthur was on the floor of the apartment, and dressed in almost an instant, not forgetting to put on his shirt of mail, and assume whatever weapons seemed most fit to render him an efficient part of the convoy. He next hastened to seek out the stable, to have his horse in readiness; and descending for that purpose into the under story of the lower mass of buildings, he was wandering in search of the way which led to the offices, when the voice of Annette Veilchen softly whispered, "This way, Signior Philipson; I would speak with you."

The Swiss maiden, at the same time, beckoned him into a small room, where he found her alone.

"Were you not surprised," she said, "to see my lady queen it so over Ital Schreckenwald, who keeps every other person in awe with his stern looks and cross words? But the air of command seems so natural to her, that, instead of being a baroness, she might have been an empress. It must come of birth, I think, after all, for I tried last night to take state upon me, after the fashion' of my mistress, and, would you think it, the brute Schreckenwald threatened to throw me out of the window? But if ever I see Martin Sprenger again, I'll know if there is strength in a Swiss arm, and virtue in a Swiss quarter-staff. — But here I stand prating, and my lady wishes to see you for a minute ere we take to horse."

"Your lady?" said Arthur, starting, "why did you lose an instant? — why not tell me before?"

"Because I was only to keep you here till she came, and — here she is."

Anne of Geierstein entered, fully attired for her journey. Annette, always willing to do as she would wish to be done by, was about to leave the apartment, when her mistress, who had apparently made up her mind concerning what she had to do or say, commanded her positively to remain.

"I am sure," she said, "Signior Philipson will rightly understand the feelings of hospitality — I will say of friendship — which prevented my suffering him to be expelled from my castle last night, and which have determined me this morning to admit of his company on the somewhat dangerous road to Strasburg. At the gate of that town we part, I to join my father, you to place yourself under the direction of yours. From that moment intercourse between us ends, and our remembrance of each other must be as the thoughts which we pay to friends deceased."

"Tender recollections," said Arthur, passionately, "more dear to our bosoms than all we have surviving upon earth."

"Not a word in that tone," answered the maiden. "With night delusion should end, and reason awaken with dawning. One word more — Do not address me on the road; you may, by doing so, expose me to vexatious and insulting suspicion, and yourself to quarrels and peril. — Farewell, our party is ready to take horse."

She left the apartment, where Arthur remained for a moment deeply bewildered in grief and disappointment. The patience, nay, even favour, with which Anne of Geierstein had, on the previous night, listened to his passion, had not prepared him for the terms of reserve and distance which she now adopted towards him. He was ignorant that noble maids, if feeling or passion has for a moment swayed them from the strict path of principle and duty, endeavour to atone for it, by instantly returning, and severely adhering, to the line from which they have made a momentary departure. He looked mournfully on Annette, who, as she had been in the room before Anne's arrival, took the privilege of remaining a minute after her departure; but he read no comfort in the glances of the confidant, who seemed as much disconcerted as himself.

"I cannot imagine what hath happened to her," said Annette; "to me she is kind as ever, but to every other person about her she plays countess and baroness with a witness; and now she is begun to tyrannize over her own natural feelings — and — if this be greatness, Annette Veilchen trusts always to remain the penniless Swiss girl; she is mistress of her own freedom, and at liberty to speak with her bachelor when she pleases, so as religion and maiden modesty suffer nothing in the conversation. Oh, a single daisy twisted with content into one's hair, is worth all the opals in India, if they bind us to torment ourselves and other people, or hinder us from speaking our mind, when our heart is upon our tongue. But never fear, Arthur; for if she has the cruelty to think of forgetting you, you may rely on one friend who, while she has a tongue, and Anne has ears, will make it impossible for her to do so."

So saying, away tripped Annette, having first indicated to Philipson the passage by which he would find the lower court of the castle. There his steed stood ready among about twenty others. Twelve of these were accoutred with war saddles and frontlets of proof, being intended for the use of as many cavaliers, or troopers, retainers of the family of Arnheim, whom the seneschal's exertions had been able to collect on the spur of the occasion. Two palfreys, somewhat distinguished by their trappings, were designed for Anne of Geierstein and her favourite female attendant. The other menials, chiefly boys and women servants, had inferior horses. At a signal made, the troopers took their lances and stood by their steeds, till the females and menials were mounted and in order; they then sprang into their saddles and began to move forward, slowly and with great precaution. Schreckenwald led the van, and kept Arthur Philipson close beside him. Anne and her attendant were in the centre of the little body, followed by the unwarlike train of servants, while two or three experienced cavaliers brought up the rear with strict orders to guard against surprise.

On their being put into motion, the first thing which surprised Arthur was, that the horses' hoofs no longer sent forth the sharp and ringing sound arising from the collision of iron and flint, and as the morning light increased, he could perceive, that the fetlock and hoof of every steed, his own included, had been carefully wrapped around with a sufficient quantity of wool, to prevent the usual noise which accompanied their motions. It was a singular thing to behold the passage of the little body of cavalry down the rocky road which led from the castle, unattended with the noise, which we are disposed to consider as inseparable from the motions of horse, the absence of which seemed to give a peculiar and almost an unearthly appearance to the cavalcade.

They passed in this manner the winding path which led from the castle of Arnheim to the adjacent village, which, as was the ancient feudal custom, lay so near the fortress, that its inhabitants, when summoned by their lord, could instantly repair for its defence. But it was at present occupied by very different inhabitants, the mutinous soldiers of the Rhingrave. When the party from Arnheim approached the entrance of the village, Schreckenwald made a signal to halt, which was instantly obeyed by his followers. He then rode forward in person to reconnoitre, accompanied by Arthur Philipson, both moving with the utmost steadiness and precaution. The deepest silence prevailed in the deserted streets. Here and there a soldier was seen, seemingly designed for a sentinel, but uniformly fast asleep.

"The swinish mutineers!" said Schreckenwald; "a fair nightwatch they keep, and a beautiful morning's rouse would I treat them with, were not the point to protect yonder peevish wench. — Halt thou here, stranger, while I ride back and bring them on — there is no danger."

Schreckenwald left Arthur as he spoke, who, alone in the street of a village filled with banditti, though they were lulled into temporary insensibility, had no reason to consider his case as very comfortable. The chorus of a wassel-song, which some reveller was trolling over in his sleep; or, in its turn, the growling of some village cur, seemed the signal for an hundred ruffians to start up around him. But in the space of two or three minutes, the noiseless cavalcade, headed by Ital Schreckenwald, again joined him, and followed their leader, observing the utmost precaution not to give an alarm. All went well till they reached the farther end of the village, where, although the Baaren-hauter[13] who kept guard was as drunk as his companions on duty, a large shaggy dog which lay beside him was more vigilant. As the little troop approached, the animal sent forth a ferocious yell, loud enough to have broken the rest of the Seven Sleepers, and which effectually dispelled the slumbers of its master. The soldier snatched up his carabine and fired, he knew not well at what, or for what reason. The ball, however, struck Arthur's horse under him, and, as the animal fell, the sentinel rushed forward to kill or make prisoner the rider.

"Haste on, haste on, men of Arnheim! care for nothing but the young lady's safety," exclaimed the leader of the band.

"Stay, I command you; — aid the stranger, on your lives!" — said Anne, in a voice which, usually gentle and meek, she now made heard by those around her, like the note of a silver clarion. "I will not stir till he is rescued."

Schreckenwald had already spurred his horse for flight; but perceiving Anne's reluctance to follow him, he dashed back, and seizing a horse, which, bridled and saddled, stood picqueted near him, he threw the reins to Arthur Philipson; and pushing his own horse, at the same time, betwixt the Englishman and the soldier, he forced the latter to quit the hold he had on his person. In an instant Philipson was again mounted, when, seizing a battle-axe which hung at the saddle-bow of his new steed, he struck down the staggering sentinel, who was endeavouring again to seize upon him. The whole troop then rode off at a gallop, for the alarm began to grow general in the village; some soldiers were seen coming out of their quarters, and others were beginning to get upon horseback. Before Schreckenwald and his party had

---

[13] *Baaren-hauter,* — he of the Bear's hide, — a nickname for a German private soldier.

ridden a mile, they heard more than once the sound of bugles; and when they arrived upon the summit of an eminence commanding a view of the village, their leader, who, during the retreat, had placed himself in the rear of his company, now halted to reconnoitre the enemy they had left behind them. There was bustle and confusion in the street, but there did not appear to be any pursuit; so that Schreckenwald followed his route down the river, with speed and activity indeed, but with so much steadiness at the same time, as not to distress the slowest horse of his party.

When they had ridden two hours or more, the confidence of their leader was so much augmented, that he ventured to command a halt at the edge of a pleasant grove, which served to conceal their number, whilst both riders and horses took some refreshment, for which purpose forage and provisions had been borne along with them. Ital Schreckenwald having held some communication with the Baroness, continued to offer their travelling companion a sort of surly civility. He invited him to partake of his own mess, which was indeed little different from that which was served out to the other troopers, but was seasoned with a glass of wine from a more choice flask.

"To your health, brother," he said; "if you tell this day's story truly, you will allow that I was a true comrade to you two hours since, in riding through the village of Arnheim."

"I will never deny it, fair sir," said Philipson, "and I return you thanks for your timely assistance; alike, whether it sprang from your mistress's order, or your own good-will."

"Ho! ho! my friend," said Schreckenwald, laughing, "you are a philosopher, and can try conclusions while your horse lies rolling above you, and a Baaren-hauter aims his sword at your throat? — Well, since your wit hath discovered so much, I care not if you know, that I should not have had much scruple to sacrifice twenty such smooth-faced gentlemen as yourself, rather than the young Baroness of Arnheim had incurred the slightest danger."

"The propriety o f the sentiment," said Philipson, "is so undoubtedly correct, that I subscribe to it, even though it is something discourteously expressed towards myself."

In making this reply, the young man, provoked at the insolence of Schreckenwald's manner, raised his voice a little. The circumstance did not escape observation, for, on the instant, Annette Veilchen stood before them, with her mistress's commands on them both to speak in whispers, or rather to be altogether silent.

"Say to your mistress that I am mute," said Philipson.

"Our mistress, the Baroness, says," continued Annette, with an emphasis on the title, to which she began to ascribe some talismanic influence, — "the Baroness, I tell you, says, that silence much concerns our safety, for it were most hazardous to draw upon this little fugitive party the notice of any passengers who may pass along the road during the necessary halt; and so, sirs, it is the Baroness's request that you will continue the exercise of your teeth as fast as you can, and forbear that of your tongues till you are in a safer condition."

"My lady is wise," answered Ital Schreckenwald, "and her maiden is witty. I drink, Mistress Annette, in a cup of Rudersheimer, to the continuance of her sagacity, and of your amiable liveliness of disposition. Will it please you, fair mistress, to pledge me in this generous liquor?"

"Out, thou German wine-flask! — Out, thou eternal swill-flagon! — Heard you ever of a modest maiden who drank wine before she had dined?"

"Remain without the generous inspiration then," said the German, "and nourish thy satirical vein on sour cider or acid whey."

A short space having been allowed to refresh themselves, the little party again mounted their horses, and travelled with such speed, that long before noon they arrived at the strongly fortified town of Kehl, opposite to Strasburg, on the eastern bank of the Rhine.

It is for local antiquaries to discover, whether the travellers crossed from Kehl to Strasburg by the celebrated bridge of boats which at present maintains the communication across the river, or whether they were wafted over by some other mode of transportation. It is enough that they passed in safety, and had landed on the other side, where — whether she dreaded that he might forget the charge she had given him, that here they were to separate, or whether she thought that something more might be said in the moment of parting — the young Baroness, before remounting her horse, once more approached Arthur Philipson, who too truly guessed the tenor of what she had to say.

"Gentle stranger," she said, "I must now bid you farewell. But first let me ask if you know whereabouts you are to seek your father?"

"In an inn called the Flying Stag," said Arthur, dejectedly; "but where that is situated in this large town, I know not."

"Do you know the place, Ital Schreckenwald?"

"I, young lady? — Not I — I know nothing of Strasburg and its inns. I believe most of our party are as ignorant as I am."

"You and they speak German, I suppose," said the Baroness, dryly, "and can make inquiry more easily than a foreigner? Go, sir, and forget not that humanity to the stranger is a religious duty."

With that shrug of the shoulders which testifies a displeased messenger, Ital went to make some inquiry, and, in his absence, brief as it was, Anne took an opportunity to say apart, — "Farewell! — Farewell! Accept this token of friendship, and wear it for my sake. May you be happy!"

Her slender fingers dropped into his hand a very small parcel. He turned to thank her, but she was already at some distance; and Schreckenwald, who had taken his place by his side, said in his harsh voice, "Come, Sir Squire, I have found out your place of rendezvous, and I have but little time to play the gentleman-usher."

He then rode on; and Philipson, mounted on his military charger, followed him in silence to the point where a large street joined, or rather crossed, that which led from the quay on which they had landed.

"Yonder swings the Flying Stag," said Ital, pointing to an immense sign, which, mounted on a huge wooden frame, crossed almost the whole breadth of the street. "Your intelligence can, I think, hardly abandon you, with such a guide-post in your eye."

So saying, he turned his horse without further farewell, and rode back to join his mistress and her attendants.

Philipson's eyes rested on the same group for a moment, when he was recalled to a sense of his situation by the thoughts of his father; and, spurring his jaded horse down the cross street, he reached the hostelrie of the Flying Stag.

CHAPTER XXIV

——— I was, I must confess,
Great Albion's Queen in former golden days;
But now mischance hath trode my title down,
And with dishonour laid me on the ground;
Where I must take like seat unto my fortune,
And to my humble scat conform myself.
                                        HENRY IV. *Part III.*

The hostelrie of the Flying Stag, in Strasburg, was, like every inn in the empire at that period, conducted much with the same discourteous inattention to the wants and accommodation of the guests, as that of John Mengs. But the youth and good looks of Arthur Philipson, circumstances which seldom or never fail to produce some effect where the fair are concerned, prevailed upon a short, plump, dimpled, blue-eyed, fair-skinned yungfrau, the daughter of the landlord of the Flying Stag, (himself a fat old man, pinned to the oaken-chair in the *stubé,)* to carry herself to the young Englishman with a degree of condescension, which, in the privileged race to which she belonged, was little short of degradation. She not only put her light buskins and her pretty ankles in danger of being soiled by tripping across the yard to point out an unoccupied stable, but, on Arthur's inquiry after his father, condescended to recollect, that such a guest as he described had lodged in the house last night, and had said he expected to meet there a young person, his fellow-traveller.

"I will send him out to you, fair sir," said the little yungfrau, with a smile, which, if things of the kind are to be valued by their rare occurrence, must have been reckoned inestimable.

She was as good as her word. In a few instants the elder Philipson entered the stable, and folded his son in his arms.

"My son — my dear son!" said the Englishman, his usual stoicism broken down and melted by natural feeling and parental tenderness, — "Welcome to me at all times — welcome, in a period of doubt and danger — and most welcome of all, in a moment which forms the very crisis of our fate. In a few hours I shall know what we may expect from the Duke of Burgundy. — Hast thou the token?"

Arthur's hand first sought that which was nearest to his heart, both in the literal and allegorical sense, the small parcel, namely, which Anne had given him at parting. But he recollected himself in the instant, and presented to his father the packet, which had been so strangely lost and recovered at La Ferette.

"It hath run its own risk since you saw it," he observed to his father, "and so have I mine. I received hospitality at a castle last night, and behold a body of *lanz-knechts* in the neighbourhood began in the morning to mutiny for their pay. The inhabitants fled from the castle to escape their violence, and as we passed their leaguer in the gray of the morning, a drunken Baaren-hauter shot my poor horse, and I was forced, in the way of exchange, to take up with his heavy Flemish animal, with its steel saddle, and its clumsy chaffron."

"Our road is beset with perils," said his father. "I too have had my share, having been in great danger" (he told not its precise nature) "at an inn, where I rested last night. But I left it in the morning, and proceeded hither in safety. I have at length, however, obtained a safe escort to conduct me to the Duke's camp near Dijon; and I trust to have an audience of him this evening. Then if our last hope should fail, we will seek the seaport of Marseilles, hoist sail for Candia or for Rhodes, and spend our lives in defence of Christendom, since we may no longer fight for England."

Arthur heard these ominous words without reply; but they did not the less sink upon his heart, deadly as the doom of the judge which secludes the criminal from society and all its joys, and condemns him to an eternal prison-house. The bells from the cathedral began to toll at this instant, and reminded the elder Philipson of the duty of hearing mass, which was said at all hours in some one or other of the separate chapels which he contained in that magnificent pile. His son followed on an intimation of his pleasure.

In approaching the access to this superb cathedral, the travellers found it obstructed, as is usual in Catholic countries, by the number of mendicants of both sexes, who crowded round the entrance to give the worshippers an opportunity of discharging the duty of alms-giving, so positively enjoined as a chief observance of their church. The Englishmen extricated themselves from their importunity by bestowing, as is usual on such occasions, a donative of small coin upon those who appeared most needy, or most deserving of their charity. One tall woman stood on the steps close to the door, and extended her hand to the elder Philipson, who, struck with her appearance exchanged for a piece of silver the copper coins which he had been distributing amongst others.

"A marvel!" she said, in the English language, but in a tone calculated only to be heard by him alone, although his son also caught the sound and sense of what she said, — "Ay, a miracle! — An Englishman still possesses a silver piece, and can afford to bestow it on the poor!"

Arthur was sensible that his father started somewhat at the voice or words, which bore, even in his ear, something of deeper import than the observation of an ordinary mendicant. But after a glance at the female who thus addressed him, his father passed onwards into the body of the church, and was soon engaged in attending to the solemn ceremony of the mass, as it was performed by a priest at the altar of a chapel, divided from the main body of the splendid edifice, and dedicated, as it appeared from the image over the altar, to Saint George; that military Saint, whose real history is so obscure, though his popular legend rendered him an object of peculiar veneration during the feudal ages. The ceremony was begun and finished with all customary forms. The officiating priest, with his attendants, withdrew, and though some of the few worshippers who had assisted at the solemnity remained telling their beads, and occupied with the performance of their private devotions, far the greater part left the chapel, to visit other shrines, or to return to the prosecution of their secular affairs.

But Arthur Philipson remarked, that whilst they dropped off one after another, the tall woman who had received his father's alms continued to kneel near the altar; and he was yet more surprised to see that his father himself, who, he had many reasons to know, was desirous to spend in the church no more time than the duties of devotion absolutely claimed, remained also on his knees, with his eyes resting on the form of the veiled devotee, (such she seemed from her dress,) as if his own motions were to be guided by hers. By no idea which occurred to him, was Arthur able to form the least conjecture as to his father's motives — he only knew that he was engaged in a critical and dangerous negotiation, liable to influence or interruption from various quarters; and that political suspicion was so generally awake both in

France, Italy, and Flanders, that the most important agents were often obliged to assume the most impenetrable disguises, in order to insinuate themselves without suspicion into the countries where their services were required. Louis XI. in particular, whose singular policy seemed in some degree to give a character to the age in which he lived, was well known to have disguised his principal emissaries and envoys in the fictitious garbs of mendicant monks, minstrels, gipsies, and other privileged wanderers of the meanest description.

Arthur concluded, therefore, that it was not improbable that this female might, like themselves, be something more than her dress imported; and he resolved to observe his father's deportment towards her, and regulate his own actions accordingly. A bell at last announced that mass, upon a more splendid scale, was about to be celebrated before the high altar of the cathedral itself, and its sound withdrew from the sequestered chapel of St. George the few who had remained at the shrine of the military saint, excepting the father and son, and the female penitent who kneeled opposite to them. When the last of the worshippers had retired, the female arose and advanced towards the elder Philipson, who, folding his arms on his bosom, and stooping his head, in an attitude of obeisance which his son had never before seen him assume, appeared rather to wait what she had to say, than to propose addressing her.

There was a pause. Four lamps, lighted before the shrine of the saint, cast a dim radiance on his armour and steed, represented as he was in the act of transfixing with his lance the prostrate dragon, whose outstretched wings and writhing neck were in part touched by their beams. The rest of the chapel was dimly illuminated by the autumnal sun, which could scarce find its way through the stained panes of the small lanceolated window, which was its only aperture to the open air. The light fell doubtful and gloomy, tinged with the various hues through which it passed, upon the stately, yet somewhat broken and dejected form of the female, and on those of the melancholy and anxious father, and his son, who, with all the eager interest of youth, suspected and anticipated extraordinary consequences from so singular an interview.

At length the female approached to the same side of the shrine with Arthur and his father, as if to be more distinctly heard, without being obliged to raise the slow solemn voice in which she had spoken.

"Do you here worship," she said, "the St. George of Burgundy, or the St. George of merry England, the flower of chivalry?"

"I serve," said Philipson, folding his hands humbly on his bosom, "the saint to whom this chapel is dedicated, and the Deity with whom I hope for his holy intercession, whether here or in my native country."

"Ay — you," said the female, "even you can forget — you, even you, who have been numbered among the mirror of knighthood — can forget that you have worshipped in the royal fane of Windsor — that you have there bent a *gartered* knee, where kings and princes kneeled around you — you can forget, this, and make your orisons at a foreign shrine, with a heart undisturbed with the thoughts of what you have been, — praying, like some poor peasant, for bread and life during the day that passes over you."

"Lady," replied Philipson, "in my proudest hours, I was, before the Being to whom I preferred my prayers, but as a worm in the dust — In His eyes I am now neither less nor more, degraded as I may be in the opinion of my fellow-reptiles."

"How canst thou think thus?" said the devotee; "and yet it is well with thee that thou canst. But what have thy losses been, compared to mine!"

She put her hand to her brow, and seemed for a moment overpowered by agonizing recollections.

Arthur pressed to his father's side, and inquired, in a tone of interest which could not be repressed, "Father, who is this lady? — Is it my mother?"

"No, my son," answered Philipson; — "peace, for the sake of all you hold dear or holy!"

The singular female, however, heard both the question and answer, though expressed in a whisper.

"Yes," she said, "young man — I am — I should say I was — your mother; the mother, the protectress, of all that was noble in England — I am Margaret of Anjou."

Arthur sank on his knees before the dauntless widow of Henry the Sixth, who so long, and in such desperate circumstances, upheld, by unyielding courage and deep policy, the sinking cause of her feeble husband; and who, if she occasionally abused victory by cruelty and revenge, had made some atonement by the indomitable resolution with which she had supported the fiercest storms of adversity. Arthur had been bred in devoted adherence to the now dethroned line of Lancaster, of which his father was one of the most distinguished supporters; and his earliest deeds of arms, which, though unfortunate, were neither obscure nor ignoble, had been done in their cause. With an enthusiasm belonging to his age and education, he in the same instant flung his bonnet on the pavement, and knelt at the feet of his ill-fated sovereign.

Margaret threw back the veil which concealed those noble and majestic features, which even yet, — though rivers of tears had furrowed her cheek, — though care, disappointment, domestic grief, and humbled pride, had quenched the fire of her eye, and wasted the smooth dignity of her forehead, — even yet showed the remains of that beauty which once was held unequalled in Europe. The apathy with which a succession of misfortunes and disappointed hopes had chilled the feelings of the unfortunate Princess, was for a moment melted by the sight of the fair youth's enthusiasm. She abandoned one hand to him, which he covered with tears and kisses, and with the other stroked with maternal tenderness his curled locks, as she endeavoured to raise him from the posture he had assumed. His father, in the meanwhile, shut the door of the chapel, and placed his back against it, withdrawing himself thus from the group, as if for the purpose of preventing any stranger from entering, during a scene so extraordinary.

"And thou, then," said Margaret, in a voice where female tenderness combated strangely with her natural pride of rank, and with the calm, stoical indifference induced by the intensity of her personal misfortunes; "thou, fair youth, art the last scion of the noble stem, so many fair boughs of which have fallen in our hapless cause. Alas, alas! what can I do for thee? Margaret has not even a blessing to bestow! So wayward is her fate, that her benedictions are curses, and she has but to look on you and wish you well, to ensure your speedy and utter ruin. I — I have been the fatal poison-tree, whose influence has blighted and destroyed all the fair plants that arose beside and around me, and brought death upon every one, yet am myself unable to find it!"

"Noble and royal mistress," said the elder Englishman, "let not your princely courage, which has borne such extremities, be dismayed, now that they are passed over, and that a chance at least of happier times is approaching to you and to England."

"To England, to *me*, noble Oxford!" said the forlorn and widowed Queen. — "If to-morrow's sun could place me once more on the throne of England, could it give back to me what I have lost? I speak not of wealth or power — they are as nothing in the balance — I speak not of the hosts of noble friends who have fallen in defence of me and mine — Somersets, Percys, Staffords, Cliffords — they have found their place in fame, in the annals of their country — I speak not of my husband, he has exchanged the state of a suffering saint upon earth for that of a glorified saint in Heaven — But O, Oxford! my son — my Edward! — Is it possible for me to look on this youth, and not remember that thy countess and I on the same night gave birth to two fair boys? How oft we endeavoured to prophesy their future fortunes, and to persuade ourselves that the same constellation which shone on their birth, would influence their succeeding life, and hold a friendly and equal bias till they reached some destined goal of happiness and honour! Thy Arthur lives but, alas! my Edward, born under the same auspices, fills a bloody grave!"

She wrapped her head in her mantle, as if to stifle the complaints and groans which maternal affection poured forth at these cruel recollections. Philipson, or the exiled Earl of Oxford, as we may now term him, distinguished in those changeful times by the steadiness with which he had always maintained his loyalty to the line of Lancaster, saw the imprudence of indulging his sovereign in her weakness.

"Royal mistress," he said, "life's journey is that of a brief winter's day, and its course will run on, whether we avail ourselves of its progress or no. My sovereign is, I trust, too much mistress of herself to suffer lamentation for what is passed to deprive her of the power of using the present time. I am here in obedience to your command; I am to see Burgundy forthwith, and if I find him pliant to the purpose to which we would turn him, events may follow which will change into gladness our present mourning. But we must use our opportunity with speed as well as zeal. Let me know then, madam, for what reason your Majesty hath come hither, disguised and in danger? Surely it was not merely to weep over this young man that the high-minded Queen Margaret left her father's court, disguised herself in mean attire, and came from a place of safety to one of doubt at least, if not of danger?"

"You mock me, Oxford," said the unfortunate Queen, "or you deceive yourself, if you think you still serve that Margaret whose word was never spoken without a reason, and whose slightest action was influenced by a motive. Alas! I am no longer the same firm and rational being. The feverish character of grief, while it makes one place hateful to me, drives me to another in very impotence and impatience of spirit. My father's residence, thou sayst, is safe; but is it tolerable for such a soul as mine? Can one who has been deprived of the noblest and richest kingdom of Europe — one who has lost hosts of noble friends — one who is a widowed consort, a childless mother — one upon whose head Heaven hath poured forth its last vial of unmitigated wrath — can she stoop to be the companion of a weak old man, who, in sonnets and in music, in mummery and folly, in harping and rhyming, finds a comfort for all that poverty has that is distressing; and what is still worse, even a solace in all that is ridiculous and contemptible?"

"Nay, with your leave, madam," said her counsellor, "blame not the good King René, because, persecuted by fortune, he has been able to find out for himself humbler sources of solace, which your prouder spirit is disposed to disdain. A contention among his minstrels, has for him the animation of a knightly combat; and a crown of flowers, twined by his troubadours, and graced by their sonnets, he accounts a valuable compensation for the diadems of Jerusalem, of Naples, and of both Sicilies, of which he only possesses the empty titles."

"Speak not to me of the pitiable old man," said Margaret; "sunk below even the hatred of his worst enemies, and never thought worthy of any thing more than contempt. I tell thee, noble Oxford, I have been driven nearly mad with my forced residence at Aix, in the paltry circle which he calls his court. My ears, tuned as they now are only to sounds of affliction, are not so weary of the eternal tinkling of harps, and squeaking of rebecks, and snapping of castanets; — my eyes are not so tired of the beggarly affectation of court ceremonial, which is only respectable alien it implies wealth and expresses power — as my very soul is sick of the paltry ambition which can find pleasure in spangles, tassels, and trumpery, when the reality of all that is great and noble hath passed away. No, Oxford, if I am doomed to lose the last cast which fickle fortune seems to offer me, I will retreat into the meanest convent in the Pyrencan hills, and at least escape the insult of the idiot gaiety of my father. — Let him pass from our memory as from the page of history, in which his name will never be recorded. I have much of more importance both to hear and to tell. — And now, my Oxford, what news from Italy? Will the Duke of Milan afford us assistance with his counsels, or with his treasures?"

"With his counsels willingly, madam; but how you will relish them I know not, since he recommends to us submission to our hapless fate, and resignation to the will of Providence."

"The wily Italian! Will not, then, Galeasso advance any part of his hoards, or assist a friend, to whom he hath in his time full often sworn faith?"

"Not even the diamonds which I offered to deposit in his hands," answered the Earl, "could make him unlock his treasury to supply us with ducats for our enterprise. Yet he said, if Charles of Burgundy should think seriously of an exertion in our favour, such was his regard for that great prince, and his deep sense of your majesty's misfortunes, that he would consider what the state of his exchequer, though much exhausted, and the condition of his subjects, though impoverished by taxes and talliages, would permit him to advance in your behalf."

"The double-faced hypocrite!" said Margaret. "If the assistance of the princely Burgundy lends us a chance of regaining what is our own, then he will give us some paltry parcel of crowns, that our restored prosperity may forget his indifference to our adversity! — But what of Burgundy? I have ventured hither to tell you what I have learned, and to hear report of your proceedings — a trusty watch provides for the secrecy of our interview. My impatience to see you brought me hither in this mean disguise. I have a small retinue at a convent a mile beyond the town — I have had your arrival watched by the faithful Lambert — and now I come to know your hopes or your fears, and to tell you my own."

"Royal lady," said the Earl, "I have not seen the Duke. You know his temper to be wilful, sudden, haughty, and unpersuadable. If he can adopt the calm and sustained policy which the times require, I little doubt his obtaining full amends of Louis, his sworn enemy, and even of Edward, his ambitious brother-in-law. But if he continues to yield to extravagant fits of passion, with or without provocation, he may hurry into a quarrel with the poor but hardy Helvetians, and is likely to engage in a perilous contest, in which he cannot be expected to gain any thing, while he undergoes a chance of the most serious losses."

"Surely," replied the Queen, "he will not trust the usurper Edward, even in the very moment when he is giving the greatest proof of treachery to his alliance?"

"In what respect, madam?" replied Oxford. "The news you allude to has not reached me."

"How, my lord? Am I then the first to tell you, that Edward of York has crossed the sea with such an army, as scarce even the renowned Henry V., my father-in-law, ever transported from France to Italy?"

"So much I have indeed heard was expected," said Oxford; "and I anticipated the effect as fatal to our cause."

"Edward is arrived," said Margaret, "and the traitor and usurper hath sent defiance to Louis of France, and demanded of him the crown of that kingdom as his own right — that crown which was placed on the head of my unhappy husband, when he was yet a child in the cradle."

"It is then decided — the English are in France!" answered Oxford, in a tone expressive of the deepest anxiety. — "And whom brings Edward with him on this expedition?"

"All — all the bitterest enemies of our house and cause — The false, the traitorous, the dishonoured George, whom he calls Duke of Clarence — the blood-drinker, Richard — the licentious Hastings — Howard — Stanley — in a word, the leaders of all those traitors whom I would not name, unless by doing so my curses could sweep them from the face of the earth."

"And — I tremble to ask," said the Earl — "Does Burgundy prepare to join them as a brother of the war, and make common cause with this Yorkish host against King Louis of France?"

"By my advices," replied the Queen, "and they are both private and sure, besides that they are confirmed by the bruit of common fame — No, my good Oxford, no!"

"For that may the Saints be praised!" answered Oxford.

"Edward of York — I will not malign even an enemy — is a bold and fearless leader — But he is neither Edward the Third, nor the heroic Black Prince — nor is he that fifth Henry of Lancaster, under whom I won my spurs, and to whose lineage the thoughts of his glorious memory would have made me faithful, had my plighted TOWS of allegiance ever permitted me to entertain a thought of varying, or of defection. Let Edward engage in war with Louis without the aid of Burgundy, on which he has reckoned. Louis is indeed no hero, but he is a cautious and skilful general, more to be dreaded, perhaps, in these politic days, than if Charlemagne could again raise the Oriflamme, surrounded by Roland and all his paladins. Louis will not hazard such fields as those of Cressy, of Poictiers, or of Agincourt. With a thousand lances from Hainault, and twenty thousand crowns from Burgundy, Edward shall risk the loss of England, while he is engaged in a protracted struggle for the recovery of Normandy and Guienne. But what are the movements of Burgundy?"

"He has menaced Germany," said Margaret, "and his troops are now employed in overrunning Lorraine, of which he has seized the principal towns and castles."

"Where is Ferrand de Vaudemont — a youth, it is said, of courage and enterprise, and claiming Lorraine in right of his mother, Yolande of Anjou, the sister of your Grace?"

"Fled," replied the Queen, "into Germany or Helvetia."

"Let Burgundy beware of him," said the experienced Earl; "for should the disinherited youth obtain confederates in Germany, and allies among the hardy Swiss, Charles of Burgundy may find him a far more formidable enemy than he expects. We are strong for the present, only in the Duke's strength, and if it is wasted in idle and desultory efforts, our hopes, alas! vanish with his power, even if he should be found to have the decided will to assist us. My friends in England are resolute not to stir without men and money from Burgundy."

"It is a fear," said Margaret, "but not our worst fear I dread more the policy of Louis, who, unless my espials have grossly deceived me, has even already proposed a secret peace to Edward, offering with large sums of money to purchase England to the Yorkists, and a truce of seven years."

"It cannot be," said Oxford. "No Englishman, commanding such an army as Edward must now lead, dares for very shame to retire from France without a manly attempt to recover his lost provinces."

"Such would have been the thoughts of a rightful prince," said Margaret, "who left behind him an obedient and faithful kingdom. Such may not be the thoughts of this Edward, mis-named Plantagenet, base perhaps in mind as in blood, since they say his real father was one Blackburn, an archer of Middle-ham — usurper, at least, if not bastard — such will not be his thoughts.[14] Every breeze that blows from England will bring with it apprehensions of defection amongst those over whom he has usurped authority. He will not sleep in peace till he returns to England with those cut-throats, whom he relies upon for the de-fence of his stolen crown. He will engage in no war with Louis, for Louis will not hesitate to soothe his pride by humiliation — to gorge his avarice and pamper his voluptuous prodigality by sums of gold — and I fear much we shall soon hear of the Eng-lish army retiring from France with the idle boast, that they have displayed their banners once more, for a week or two, in the provinces which were formerly their own."

"It the more becomes us to be speedy in moving Burgundy to decision," replied Oxford; "and for that purpose I post to Di-jon. Such an army as Edward's cannot be transported over the narrow seas in several weeks. The probability is, that they must winter in France, even if they should have truce with King Louis. With a thousand Hainault lances from the eastern part of Flanders, I can be soon in the North, where we have many friends, besides the assurance of help from Scotland. The faithful west will rise at a signal — a Clifford can be found, though the mountain mists have hid him from Edward's researches — the Welsh will assemble at the rallying word of Tudor — the Red Rose raises its head once more — and so, God save King Henry!"

"Alas!" said the Queen — "But no husband — no friend of mine — the son but of my mother-in-law by a Welsh chief-tain — cold, they say, and crafty — But be it so — let me only see Lancaster triumph, and obtain revenge upon York, and I will die contented!"

---

[14] The Lancastrian party threw the imputation of bastardy, (which was totally unfounded,) upon Edward IV.

"It is then your pleasure that I should make the proffers expressed by your Grace's former mandates, to induce Burgundy to stir himself in our cause? If he learns the proposal of a truce betwixt France and England, it will sting sharper than aught I can say."

"Promise all, however," said the Queen. "I know his inmost soul — it is set upon extending the dominions of his House in every direction. For this he has seized Gueldres — for this he now overruns and occupies Lorraine — for this he covets such poor remnants of Provence as my father still calls his own. With such augmented territories, he proposes to exchange his ducal diadem for an arched crown of independent sovereignty. Tell the Duke, Margaret can assist his views — tell him, that my father René shall disown the opposition made to the Duke's seizure of Lorraine — He shall do more — he shall declare diaries his heir in Provence, with my ample consent — tell him, the old man shall cede his dominions to him upon the instant that his Hainaulters embark for England, some small pension deducted to maintain a concert of fiddlers, and a troop of morrice-dancers. These are René's only earthly wants. Mine are still fewer — Revenge upon York, and a speedy grave! — For the pall-y gold which we may need, thou hast jewels to pledge — For the other conditions, security if required."

"For these, madam, I can pledge my knightly word, in addition to your royal faith; and if more is required, my son shall be a hostage with Burgundy."

"Oh, no — no!" exclaimed the dethroned Queen, touched by perhaps the only tender feeling, which repeated and extraordinary misfortunes had not chilled into insensibility, — "Hazard not the life of the noble youth — he that is the last of the loyal and faithful House of Vere — he that should have been the brother in arms of my beloved Edward — he that had so nearly been his companion in a bloody and untimely grave! Do not involve this poor child in these fatal intrigues, which have been so baneful to his family. Let him go with me. Him at least I will shelter from danger whilst I live, and provide for when I am no more."

"Forgive me, madam," said Oxford, with the firmness which distinguished him. "My son, as you deign to recollect, is a De Vere, destined, perhaps, to be the last of his name. Fall, he may, but it must not be without honour. To whatever dangers his duty and allegiance call him, be it from sword or lance, axe or gibbet, to these he must expose himself frankly, when his doing so can mark his allegiance. His ancestors have shown him how to brave them all."

"True, true," exclaimed the unfortunate Queen, raising her arms wildly, — "All must perish — all that have honoured Lancaster — all that have loved Margaret, or whom she has loved! The destruction must be universal — the young must fall with the old — not a lamb of the scattered Hock shall escape!"

"For God's sake, gracious madam," said Oxford, "compose yourself! — I hear them knock on the chapel door."

"It is the signal of parting," said the exiled Queen, collecting herself. "Do not fear, noble Oxford, I am not often thus; but how seldom do I see those friends, whose faces and voices can disturb the composure of my despair! Let me tie this relic about thy neck, good youth, and fear not its evil influence, though you receive it from an ill-omened hand. It was my husband's, blessed by many a prayer, and sanctified by many a holy tear; even my unhappy hands cannot pollute it. I should have bound it on my Edward's bosom on the dreadful morning of Tewkesbury fight; but he armed early — went to the field without seeing me, and all my purpose was vain."

She passed a golden chain round Arthur's neck as she spoke, which contained a small gold crucifix of rich but barbarous manufacture. It had belonged, said tradition, to Edward the Confessor. The knock at the door of the chapel was repeated.

"We must not tarry," said Margaret; "let us part here — you for Dijon — I to Aix, my abode of unrest in Provence. Farewell — we may meet in a better hour — yet how can I hope it? Thus I said on the morning before the fight of St. Albans — thus on the dark dawning of Towton — thus on the yet more bloody field of Tewkesbury — and what was the event? Yet hope is a plant which cannot be rooted out of a noble breast, till the last heart-string crack as it is pulled away."

So saying, she passed through the chapel door, and mingled in the miscellaneous assemblage of personages who worshipped or indulged their curiosity, or consumed their idle hours amongst the aisles of the cathedral.

Philipson and his son, both deeply impressed with the singular interview which had just taken place, returned to their inn, where they found a pursuivant, with the Duke of Burgundy's badge and livery, who informed them, that if they were the English merchants who were carrying wares of value to the court of the Duke, he had orders to afford them the countenance of his escort and inviolable character. Under his protection they set out from Strasburg; but such was the uncertainty of the Duke of Burgundy's motions, and such the numerous obstacles which occurred to interrupt their journey, in a country disturbed by the constant passage of troops and preparation for war, that it was evening on the second day ere they readied the plain near Dijon, on which the whole, or great part of his power, lay encamped.

CHAPTER XXV

Thus said the Duke — thus dill the Duke infer.

RICHARD III.

The eyes of the elder traveller were well accustomed to sights of martial splendour, yet even he was dazzled with the rich and glorious display of the Burgundian camp, in which, near the walls of Dijon, Charles, the wealthiest prince in Europe, had displayed his own extravagance, and encouraged his followers to similar profusion. The pavilions of the meanest officers were of silk and samite, while those of the nobility and great leaders glittered with cloth of silver, cloth of gold, variegated tapestry, and other precious materials, which in no other situation would have been employed as a cover from the weather, but would themselves have been thought worthy of the most careful protection. The horsemen and infantry who mounted guard, were arrayed in the richest and most gorgeous armour. A beautiful and very numerous train of artillery was drawn up near the entrance of the camp, and in its commander, Philipson (to give the Earl the travelling name to which our readers are accustomed) recognised Henry Colvin, an Englishman of inferior birth, but distinguished (or his skill in conducting these terrible engines, which had of late come into general use in war. The banners and pennons which were displayed by every knight, baron, and man of rank, floated before their tents, and the owners of these transitory dwellings sat at the door half-armed, and enjoyed the military contests of the soldiers, in wrestling, pitching the bar, and other athletic exercises.

Long rows of the noblest horses were seen at picquet, prancing and tossing their heads, as impatient of the inactivity to which they were confined, or were heard neighing over the provender, which was spread plentifully before them. The soldiers formed joyous groups around the minstrels and strolling jugglers, or were engaged in drinking parties at the sutlers' tent; others strolled about with folded arms, casting their eyes now and then to the sinking sun, as if desirous that the hour should arrive which would put an end to a day unoccupied, and therefore tedious.

At length the travellers reached, amidst the dazzling varieties of this military display, the pavilion of the Duke himself, before which floated heavily in the evening breeze, the broad and rich banner, in which glowed the armorial bearings and quarterings of a prince, Duke of six provinces, and Count of fifteen counties, who was, from his power, his disposition, and the success which seemed to attend his enterprises, the general dread of Europe. The pursuivant made himself known to some of the household, and the Englishmen were immediately received with courtesy, though not such as to draw attention upon them, and conveyed to a neighbouring tent, the residence of a general officer, which they were given to understand was destined for their accommodation, and where their packages accordingly were deposited, and refreshments offered them.

"As the camp is filled," said the domestic who waited upon them, "with soldiers of different nations and uncertain dispositions, the Duke of Burgundy, for the safety of your merchandise, has ordered you the protection of a regular sentinel. In the meantime, be in readiness to wait on his Highness, seeing you may look to be presently sent for."

Accordingly, the elder Philipson was shortly after summoned to the Duke's presence, introduced by a back entrance into the ducal pavilion, and into that part of it which, screened by close curtains and wooden barricades, formed Charles's own separate apartment. The plainness of the furniture, and the coarse apparatus of the Duke's toilet, formed a strong contrast to the appearance of the exterior of the pavilion; for Charles, whose character was in that as in other things, far from consistent, exhibited in his own person during war an austerity, or rather coarseness of dress, and sometimes of manners also, which was more like the rudeness of a German lanz-knecht, than the bearing of a prince of exalted rank; while, at the same time, he encouraged and enjoined a great splendour of expense and display amongst his vassals and courtiers, as if to be rudely attired, and to despise every restraint, even of ordinary ceremony, were a privilege of the sovereign alone. Yet when it pleased him to assume state in person and manners, none knew better than Charles of Burgundy how he ought to adorn and demean himself.

Upon his toilet appeared brushes and combs, which might have claimed dismissal as past the term of service, over-worn hats and doublets, dog-leashes, leather-belts, and other such paltry articles; amongst which lay at random, as it seemed, the great diamond called Sanci, — the three rubies termed the Three Brothers of Antwerp, — another great diamond called the Lamp of Flanders, and other precious stones of scarcely inferior value and rarity. This extraordinary display somewhat resembled the character of the Duke himself, who mixed cruelty with justice, magnanimity with meanness of spirit, economy with extravagance, and liberality with avarice; being, in fact, consistent in nothing excepting in his obstinate determination to follow the opinion he had once formed, in every situation of things, and through all variety of risks.

In the midst of the valueless and inestimable articles of his wardrobe and toilet, the Duke of Burgundy called out to the English traveller, "Welcome, Herr Philipson — welcome, you of a nation whose traders are princes, and their merchants the mighty ones of the earth. What new commodities have you brought to gull us with? You merchants, by St. George, are a wily generation."

"Faith, no new merchandise I, my lord," answered the elder Englishman; "I bring but the commodities which I showed your Highness the last time I communicated with you, in the hope of a poor trader, that your Grace may find them more acceptable upon a review, than when you first saw them."

"It is well, Sir — Philipville, I think they call you? — you are a simple trader, or you take me for a silly purchaser, that you think to gull me with the same wares which I fancied not formerly. Change of fashion, man — novelty — is the motto of commerce; your Lancaster wares have had their day, and I have bought of them like others, and was like enough to have paid dear for them too. York is all the vogue now."

"It may be so among the vulgar," said the Earl of Oxford; "but for souls like your Highness, faith, honour, and loyalty, are jewels which change of fancy, or mutability of taste, cannot put out of fashion."

"Why, it may be, noble Oxford," said the Duke, "that I preserve in my secrct mind some veneration for these old-fashioned qualities, else how should I have such regard for your person, in which they have ever been distinguished? But my situation is painfully urgent, and should I make a false step at this crisis, I might break the purposes of my whole life. Observe me, Sir

Merchant. Here has come over your old competitor, Blackburn, whom some call Edward of York and of London, with a commodity of bows and bills such as never entered France since King Arthur's time; and he offers to enter into joint adventure with me, or, in plain speech, to make common cause with Burgundy, till we smoke out of his earths the old fox Louis, and nail his hide to the stable-door. In a word, England invites me to take part with him against my most wily and inveterate enemy, the King of France; to rid myself of the chain of vassalage, and to ascend into the rank of independent princes; — how think you, noble Earl, can I forego this seducing temptation?"

"You must ask this of some of your counsellors of Burgundy," said Oxford; "it is a question fraught too deeply with ruin to my cause, for me to give a fair opinion on it."

"Nevertheless," said Charles, "I ask thee as an honourable man, what objections you see to the course proposed to me? Speak your mind, and speak it freely."

"My lord, I know it is in your Highness's nature to entertain no doubts of the facility of executing any thing which you have once determined shall be done. Yet, though this prince-like disposition may in some cases prepare for its own success, and has often done so, there are others, in which persisting in our purpose, merely because we have once willed it, leads not to success, but to ruin. Look, therefore, at this English army; winter is approaching, where are they to be lodged? how are they to be victualled? by whom are they to be paid? Is your Highness to take all the expense and labour of fitting them for the summer campaign? for, rely on it, an English army never was, nor will be, fit for service, till they have been out of their own island long enough to accustom them to military duty. They are men, I grant, the fittest for soldiers in the world; but they are not soldiers as yet, and must be trained to become such at your Highness's expense."

"Be it so," said Charles; "I think the Low Countries can find food for the beef-consuming knaves for a few weeks, and villages for them to lie in, and officers to train their sturdy limbs to war, and provost-marshals enough to reduce their refractory spirit to discipline."

"What happens next?" said Oxford. "You march to Paris, add to Edward's usurped power another kingdom; restore to him all the possessions which England ever had in France, Normandy, Maine, Anjou, Gascony, and all besides. — Can you trust this Edward when you shall have thus fostered his strength, and made him far stronger than this Louis whom you have united to pull down?"

"By St. George, I will not dissemble with you! It is in that very point that my doubts trouble me. Edward is indeed my brother-in-law, but I am a man little inclined to put my head under my wife's girdle."

"And the times," said Philipson, "have too often shown the inefficiency of family alliances, to prevent the most gross breaches of faith."

"You say well, Earl. Clarence betrayed his father-in-law; Louis poisoned his brother — Domestic affections, pshaw! they sit warm enough by a private man's fireside, but they cannot come into fields of battle, or princes' halls, where the wind blows cold. No, my alliance with Edward by marriage were little succour to me in time of need. I would as soon ride an unbroken horse, with no better bridle than a lady's garter. But what then is the result? He wars on Louis; whichever gains the better, I, who must be strengthened in their mutual weakness, receive the advantage — The Englishmen slay the French with their cloth-yard shafts, and the Frenchmen, by skirmishes, waste, weaken, and destroy the English. With spring I take the field with an army superior to both, and then, St. George for Burgundy!"

"And if, in the meanwhile, your Highness will deign to assist, even in the most trifling degree, a cause the most honourable that ever knight laid lance in rest for, — a moderate sum of money, and a small body of Hainault lances, who may gain both fame and fortune by the service, may replace the injured heir of Lancaster in the possession of his native and rightful dominion."

"Ay, marry, Sir Earl," said the Duke, "you come roundly to the point; but we hare seen, and indeed partly assisted at, so many turns betwixt York and Lancaster, that we have some doubt which is the side to which Heaven has given the right, and the inclinations of the people the effectual power; we are surprised into absolute giddiness by so many extraordinary revolutions of fortune as England has exhibited."

"A proof, my lord, that these mutations are not yet ended, and that your generous aid may give to the better side an effectual turn of advantage."

"And lend my cousin, Margaret of Anjou, my arm to de-throne my wife's brother? Perhaps he deserves small good-will at my hands, since he and his insolent nobles have been urging me with remonstrances, and even threats, to lay aside all my own important affairs, and join Edward, forsooth, in his knight-errant expedition against Louis. I will march against Louis at my own time, and not sooner; and, by St. George! neither island king, nor island noble, shall dictate to Charles of Burgundy. You are fine conceited companions, you English of both sides, that think the matters of your own bedlam island are as interesting to all the world as to yourselves. But neither York nor Lancaster; neither brother Blackburn, nor cousin Margaret of Anjou, not with John de Vere to back her, shall gull me. Men lure no hawks with empty hands."

Oxford, familiar with the Duke's disposition, suffered him to exhaust himself in chafing, that any one should pretend to dictate his course of conduct, and, when he was at length silent, replied with calmness — "Do I live to hear the noble Duke of Burgundy, the mirror of European chivalry, say, that no reason has been shown to him for an adventure where a helpless queen is to be redressed — a royal house raised from the dust? Is there not immortal *los* and honour — the trumpet of fame to proclaim the sovereign, who, alone in a degenerate age, has united the du-ties of a generous knight with those of a princely sovereign" — —

The Duke interrupted him, striking him at the same tine on the shoulder — "And King Rune's five hundred fiddlers to tune their cracked violins in my praise? and King René himself to listen to them, and say, 'Well fought Duke — well played fid-dler!' I tell thee, John of Oxford, when thou and I wore maiden armour, such words as fame, honour, *los*, knightly glory, lady's love, and so forth, were good mottoes for our snow-white shields, and a fair enough argument for splintering lances — Ay, and in tilt-yard, though somewhat old for these fierce follies, I would jeopard my person in such a quarrel yet, as becomes a knight of the order. But when we come to paying down of crowns, and embarking of large squadrons, we must have to pro-pose to our subjects some substantial excuse for plunging them in war; some proposal for the public good — or, by St. George!

for our own private advantage, which is the same thing. This is the course the world runs, and, Oxford, to tell the plain truth, I mean to hold the same bias."

"Heaven forbid that I should expect your Highness to act otherwise than with a view to your subjects' welfare — the increase, that is, as your Grace happily expresses it, of your own power and dominion. The money we require is not in benevolence, but in loan; and Margaret is willing to deposit these jewels, of which I think your Grace knows the value, till she shall repay the sum which your friendship may advance in her necessity."

"Ha, ha!" said the Duke, "would our cousin make a pawnbroker of us, and have us deal with her like a Jewish usurer with his debtor? — Yet, in faith, Oxford, we may need the diamonds, for if this business were otherwise feasible, it is possible that I myself must become a borrower to aid my cousin's necessities. I have applied to the States of the Duchy, who are now sitting, and expect, as is reasonable, a large supply. But there are restless heads and close hands among them, and they may be niggardly — So place the jewels on the table in the meanwhile. — Well, say I am to be no sufferer in purse by this feat of knighterrantry which you propose to me, still princes enter not into war without some view of advantage?"

"Listen to me, noble sovereign. You are naturally bent to unite the great estates of your father, and those you have acquired by your own arms, into a compact and firm dukedom" —

"Call it kingdom," said Charles; "it is the worthier word."

"Into a kingdom, of which the crown shall sit as fair and even on your Grace's brow as that of France on your present suzerain, Louis."

"It needs not such shrewdness as yours to descry that such is my purpose," said the Duke; "else, wherefore am I here with helm on my head, and sword by my side? And wherefore are my troops seizing on the strong places in Lorraine, and chasing before them the beggarly De Vaudemont, who has the insolence to claim it as his inheritance? Yes, my friend, the aggrandizement of Burgundy is a theme for which the duke of that fair province is bound to fight, while he can put foot in stirrup."

"But think you not," said the English Earl, "since you allow me to speak freely with your Grace, on the footing of old acquaintanceship, think you not that in this chart of your dominions, otherwise so fairly bounded, there is something on the southern frontier which might be arranged more advantageously for a King of Burgundy?"

"I cannot guess whither you would lead me," said the Duke, looking at a map of the Duchy and his other possessions, to which the Englishman had pointed his attention, and then turning his broad keen eye upon the face of the banished Earl.

"I would say," replied the latter, "that, to so powerful a prince as your Grace, there is no safe neighbour but the sea. Here is Provence, which interferes betwixt you and the Mediterranean; Provence, with its princely harbours, and fertile cornfields and vineyards. Were it not well to include it in your map of sovereignty, and thus touch the middle sea with one hand, while the other rested on the sea-coast of Flanders?"

"Provence, said you?" — replied the Duke, eagerly; "why, man, my very dreams are of Provence. I cannot smell an orange but it reminds me of its perfumed woods and bowers, its olives, citrons, and pomegranates. But how to frame pretensions to it? Shame it were to disturb René, the harmless old man, nor would it become a near relation. Then he is the uncle of Louis; and most probably, failing his daughter Margaret, or perhaps in preference to her, he hath named the French King his heir."

"A better claim might be raised up in your Grace's own person," said the Earl of Oxford, "if you will afford Margaret of Anjou the succour she requires by me."

"Take the aid thou requirest," replied the Duke; "take double the amount of it in men and money! Let me but have a claim upon Provence, though thin as a single thread of thy Queen Margaret's hair, and let me alone for twisting it into the tough texture of a quadruple cable. — But I am a fool to listen to the dreams of one who, ruined himself, can lose little by holding forth to others the most extravagant hopes."

Charles breathed high, and changed complexion as he spoke.

"I am not such a person, my Lord Duke," said the Earl. "Listen to me — René is broken with years, fond of repose, and too poor to maintain his rank with the necessary dignity; too good-natured, or too feeble-minded, to lay farther imposts on his subjects; weary of contending with bad fortune, and desirous to resign his territories" ——

"His territories!" said Charles.

"Yes, all he actually possesses; and the much more extensive dominions which he has claim to, but which have passed from his sway."

"You take away my breath!" said the Duke. "René resign Provence! and what says Margaret — the proud, the high-minded Margaret — will she subscribe to so humiliating a proceeding?"

"For the chance of seeing Lancaster triumph in England, she would resign, not only dominion, but life itself. And in truth, the sacrifice is less than it may seem to be. It is certain that, when René dies, the King of France will claim the old man's county of Provence as a male fief, and there is no one strong enough to back Margaret's claim of inheritance, however just it may be."

"It is just," said Charles; "it is undeniable! I will not hear of its being denied or challenged — that is, when once it is established in our own person. It is the true principle of the war for the public good, that none of the great fiefs be suffered to revert again to the crown of France, least of all while it stands on a brow so astucious and unprincipled as that of Louis. Burgundy joined to Provence — a dominion from the German Ocean to the Mediterranean! Oxford — thou art my better angel!"

"Your Grace must, however, reflect," said Oxford, "that honourable provision must be made for King René."

"Certainly, man, certainly; he shall have a score of fiddlers and jugglers to play, roar, and recite to him from morning till night. He shall have a court of Troubadours, who shall do nothing but drink, flute, and fiddle to him. and pronounce *arrests* of *love,* to be confirmed or reversed by an appeal to himself, the supreme *Roi d'Amour.* And Margaret shall also be honourably sustained, in the manner you may point out."

"That will be easily settled," answered the English Earl. "If our attempts on England succeed, she will need no aid from Burgundy. If she fails, she retires into a cloister, and it will not be long that she will need the honourable maintenance which, I am sure, your Grace's generosity will willingly assign her."

"Unquestionably," answered Charles; "and on a scale which will become us both; — but, by my halidome, John of Vere, the abbess into whose cloister Margaret of Anjou shall retire, will have an ungovernable penitent under her charge. Well do I know her; and, Sir Earl, I will not clog our discourse by expressing any doubts, that, if she pleases, she can compel her father to resign his estates to whomsoever she will. She is like my brache, Gorgon, who compels whatsoever hound is coupled with her to go the way she chooses, or she strangles him if he resists. So has Margaret acted with her simple-minded husband, and I am aware that her father, a fool of a different cast, must of necessity be equally tractable. I think *I* could have matched her, — though my very neck aches at the thought of the struggles we should have had for mastery. But you look grave, because I jest with the pertinacious temper of my unhappy cousin."

"My lord," said Oxford, "whatever are or have been the defects of my mistress, she is in distress, and almost in desolation. She is my sovereign, and your Highness's cousin not the less."

"Enough said, Sir Earl," answered the Duke. "Let us speak seriously. Whatever we may think of the abdication of King René, I fear we shall find it difficult to make Louis XI. see the matter as favourably as we do. He will hold that the county of Provence is a male fief, and that neither the resignation of René, nor the consent of his daughter, can prevent its reverting to the crown of France, as the King of Sicily, as they call him, hath no male issue."

"That, may it please your Grace, is a question for battle to decide; and your Highness has successfully braved Louis for a less-important stake. All I can say is, that if your Grace's active assistance enables the young Earl of Richmond to succeed in his enterprise, you shall have the aid of three thousand English archers, if old John of Oxford, for want of a better leader, were to bring them over himself."

"A noble aid," said the Duke; "graced still more by him who promises to lead them. Thy succour, noble Oxford, were precious to me, did you but come with your sword by your side, and a single page at your back. I know you well, both heart and head. But let us to this gear; exiles, even the wisest, are privileged in promises, and sometimes — excuse me, noble Oxford — impose on themselves as well as on their friends. What are the hopes on which you desire me again to embark on so troubled and uncertain an ocean, as these civil contests of yours?"

The Earl of Oxford produced a schedule, and explained to

the Duke the plan of his expedition to be backed by an insurrection of the friends of Lancaster, of which it is enough to say, that it was bold to the verge of temerity; but yet so well compacted and put together, as to bear in those times of rapid revolution, and under a leader of Oxford's approved military skill and political sagacity, a strong appearance of probable success.

While Duke Charles mused over the particulars of an enterprise attractive and congenial to his own disposition, — while he counted over the affronts which he had received from his brother-in-law, Edward IV., the present opportunity for taking a signal revenge, and the rich acquisition which he hoped to make in Provence by the cession in his favour of René of Anjou and his daughter, the Englishman failed not to press on his consideration the urgent necessity of suffering no time to escape.

"The accomplishment of this scheme," he said, "demands the utmost promptitude. To have a chance of success, I must be in England, with your Grace's auxiliary forces, before Edward of York can return from France with his army."

"And, having come hither," said the Duke, "our worthy brother will be in no hurry to return again. He will meet with black-eyed French women and ruby-coloured French wine, and brother Blackburn is no man to leave such commodities in a hurry."

"My Lord Duke, I will speak truth of my enemy. Edward is indolent and luxurious when things are easy around him, but let him feel the spur of necessity, and he becomes as eager as a pampered steed. Louis, too, who seldom fails in finding means to accomplish his ends, is bent upon determining the English King to recross the sea — therefore speed, noble Prince — speed is the soul of your enterprise."

"Speed!" said the Duke of Burgundy, — "Why, I will go with you and see the embarkation myself; and tried, approved soldiers you shall have, such as are nowhere to be found save in Artois and Hainault."

"But pardon yet, noble Duke, the impatience of a drowning wretch urgently pressing for assistance. — When shall we to the coast of Flanders, to order this important measure?"

"Why, in a fortnight, or perchance a week, or, in a word, so soon as I shall have chastised to purpose a certain gang of thieves and robber, who, as the scum of the caldron will always be uppermost, have got up into the fastnesses of the Alps, and from thence annoy our frontiers by contraband traffic, pillage, and robbery."

"Your Highness means the Swiss Confederates?"

"Ay, the peasant churls give themselves such a name. They are a sort of manumitted slaves of Austria, and, like a ban-dog, whose chain is broken, they avail themselves of their liberty to annoy and rend whatever comes in their way."

"I travelled through their country from Italy," said the exiled Earl, "and I heard it was the purpose of the Cantons to send envoys to solicit peace of your Highness."

"Peace!" exclaimed Charles. — "A proper sort of peaceful proceedings those of their embassy have been! Availing themselves of a mutiny of the burghers of La Ferette, the first garrison town which they entered, they stormed the walls, seized on Archibald de Hagenbach, who commanded the place on my part, and put him to death in the market-place. Such an insult must be punished, Sir John de Vere; and if you do not see me in the storm of passion which it well deserves, it is because I have already given orders to hang up the base runagates who call themselves ambassadors."

"For God's sake, noble Duke," said the Englishman, throwing himself at Charles's feet — "for your own character, for the sake of the peace of Christendom, revoke such an order if it is really given!"

"What means this passion?" said Duke Charles. — "What are these men's lives to thee, excepting that the consequences of a war may delay your expedition for a few days?"

"May render it altogether abortive," said the Earl; "nay, *must* needs do so. — Hear me, Lord Duke. I was with these men on a part of their journey."

"You!" said the Duke — "you a companion of the paltry Swiss peasants? Misfortune has sunk the pride of English nobility to a low ebb, when you selected such associates."

"I was thrown amongst them by accident," said the Earl. "Some of them are of noble blood, and are, besides, men for whose peaceable intentions I ventured to constitute myself their warrant."

"On my honour, my Lord of Oxford, you graced them highly, and me no less, in interfering between the Swiss and myself! Allow me to say that I condescend, when, in deference to past friendship, I permit you to speak to me of your own English affairs. Methinks you might well spare me your opinion upon topics with which you have no natural concern."

"My Lord of Burgundy," replied Oxford, "I followed your banner to Paris, and had the good luck to rescue you in the fight at Mont L'Hery, when you were beset by the French men-at-arms" ——

"We have not forgot it," said Duke Charles; "and it is a sign that we keep the action in remembrance, that you have been suffered to stand before us so long, pleading the cause of a set of rascals, whom we are required to spare from the gallows, that groans for them, because forsooth they have been the fellow-travellers of the Earl of Oxford!"

"Not so, my lord. I ask their lives, only because they are upon a peaceful errand, and the leaders amongst them, at least, have no accession to the crime of which you complain."

The Duke traversed the apartment with unequal steps in much agitation, his large eyebrows drawn down over his eyes, his hands clenched, and his teeth set, until at length he seemed to take a resolution. He rung a hand-bell of silver, which stood upon his table.

"Here, Contay," he said to the gentleman of his chamber, who entered, "are these mountain fellows yet executed?"

"No, may it please your Highness; but the executioner waits them so soon as the priest hath confessed them."

"Let them live," said the Duke. "We will hear tomorrow in what manner they propose to justify their proceedings towards us."

Contay bowed and left the apartment; then turning to the Englishman, the Duke said, with an indescribable mixture of haughtiness with familiarity and even kindness, but having his brows cleared, and his looks composed, — "We are now clear of obligation, my Lord of Oxford — you have obtained life for life — nay, to make up some inequality which there may be betwixt the value of the commodities bestowed, you have obtained six lives for one. I will, therefore, pay no more attention to you, should you again upbraid me with the stumbling horse at Mont L'Hery, or your own achievements on that occasion. Most princes are contented with privately hating such men as have rendered them extraordinary services — I feel no such disposition — I only detest being reminded of having had occasion for them. — Pshaw! I am half-choked with the effort of foregoing my own fixed resolution. — So ho! who waits there? Bring me to drink."

An usher entered, bearing a large silver flagon, which, instead of wine, was filled with tisanne, slightly flavoured by aromatic herbs.

"I am so hot and choleric by nature," said the Duke, "that our leeches prohibit me from drinking wine. But you, Oxford, are bound by no such regimen. Get thee to thy countryman, Colvin, the general of our artillery. We commend thee to his custody and hospitality till to-morrow, which must be a busy day, since I expect to receive the answer of these wiseacres of the Dijon assembly of estates; and have also to hear (thanks to your lordship's interference) these miserable Swiss envoys, as they call themselves. Well, no more on't. — Good night. You may communicate freely with Colvin, who is, like yourself, an old Lancastrian. — But hark ye, not a word respecting Provence — not even in your sleep. — Contay, conduct this English gentleman to Colvin's tent. He knows my pleasure respecting him."

"So please your Grace," answered Contay, "I left the English gentleman's son with Monsieur de Colvin."

"What! thine own son, Oxford? And with thee here? Why did you not tell me of him? Is he a true scion of the ancient tree?"

"It is my pride to believe so, my lord. He has been the faithful companion of all my dangers and wanderings."

"Happy man!" said the Duke with a sigh. "You, Oxford, have a son to share your poverty and distress — I have none to be partner and successor to my greatness."

"You have a daughter, my lord," said the noble De Vere, "and it is to be hoped she will one day wed some powerful prince, who may be the stay of your Highness's house."

"Never! By Saint George, never!" answered the Duke, sharply and shortly. "I will have no son-in-law, who may make the daughter's bed a stepping-stone to teach the father's crown. Oxford, I have spoken more freely than I am wont, perhaps more freely than I ought — but I hold some men trustworthy, and believe you, Sir John de Vere, to be one of them."

The English nobleman bowed, and was about to leave his presence, but the Duke presently recalled him.

"There is one thing more, Oxford. — The cession of Provence is not quite enough. René and Margaret must disavow this hot-brained Ferrand de Vaudemont, who is making some foolish stir in Lorraine, in right of his mother Yolande."

"My lord," said Oxford, "Ferrand is the grandson of King René, the nephew of Queen Margaret; but yet" ——

"But yet, by Saint George, his rights, as he calls them, on Lorraine, must positively be disowned. You talk of their family feelings, while you are urging me to make war on my own brother-in-law!"

"René's best apology for deserting his grandson," answered Oxford, "will be his total inability to support and assist him. I will communicate your Grace's condition, though it is a hard one."

So saying, he left the pavilion.

CHAPTER XXVI

I humbly thank your Highness;
And am right glad to catch this good occasion
Most throughly to be winnowed, where my chaff
And corn shall fly asunder.

KING HENRY VIII.

Colvin, the English officer, to whom the Duke of Burgundy, with splendid pay and appointments, committed the charge of his artillery, was owner of the tent assigned for the Englishman's lodging, and received the Earl of Oxford with the respect due to his rank, and to the Duke's especial orders upon that subject. He had been himself a follower of the Lancaster faction, and of course was well disposed towards one of the very few men of distinction whom he had known personally, and who had constantly adhered to that family through the train of misfortunes by which they seemed to be totally overwhelmed. A repast, of which his son had already partaken, was offered to the Earl by Colvin, who omitted not to recommend, by precept and example, the good wine of Burgundy, from which the sovereign of the province was himself obliged to refrain.

"His Grace shows command of passion in that," said Colvin. "For, sooth to speak, and only conversing betwixt friends, his temper grows too headlong to bear the spur which a cup of cordial beverage gives to the blood, and he, therefore, wisely restricts himself to such liquid as may cool rather than inflame his natural fire of disposition."

"I can perceive as much," said the Lancastrian noble. "When I first knew the noble Duke, who was then Earl of Charolois, his temper, though always sufficiently fiery, was calmness to the impetuosity which he now displays on the smallest contradiction. Such is the course of an uninterrupted flow of prosperity. He has ascended, by his own courage and the advantage of circumstances, from the doubtful place of a feudatory and tributary prince, to rank with the most powerful sovereigns in Europe, and to assume independent majesty. But I trust the noble starts of generosity, which atoned for his wilful and wayward temper, are not more few than formerly?"

"I have good right to say that they are not," replied the soldier of fortune, who understood generosity in the restricted sense of liberality. "The Duke is a noble and open-handed master."

"I trust his bounty is conferred on men who are as faithful and steady in their service as you, Colvin, have ever been. But I see a change in your army. I know the banners of most of the old houses in Burgundy — How is it that I observe so few of them in the Duke's camp? I see flags, and pennons, and pennoncelles; but even to me, who have been so many years acquainted with the nobility both of France and Flanders, their bearings are unknown."

"My noble Lord of Oxford," answered the officer, "it ill becomes a man who lives on the Duke's pay to censure his conduct; but his Highness hath of late trusted too much, as it seems to me, to the hired arms of foreign levies, and too little to his own native subjects and retainers. He holds it better to take into his pay large bands of German and Italian mercenary soldiers, than to repose confidence in the knights and squires, who are bound to him by allegiance and feudal faith. He uses the aid of his own subjects but as the means of producing him sums of money, which he bestows on his hired troops. The Germans are honest knaves enough while regularly paid; but Heaven preserve me from the Duke's Italian bands, and that Campo-Basso their leader, who waits but the highest price to sell his Highness like a sheep for the shambles!"

"Think you so ill of him?" demanded the Earl.

"So very ill indeed, that I believe," replied Colvin, "there is no sort of treachery which the heart can devise, or the arm perpetrate, that hath not ready reception in his breast, and prompt execution at his hand. It is painful, my lord, for an honest Englishman like me to serve in an army where such traitors have command. But what can I do, unless I could once more find me a soldier's occupation in my native country? I often hope it will please merciful Heaven again to awaken those brave civil wars in my own dear England, where all was fair fighting, and treason was unheard of."

Lord Oxford gave his host to understand, that there was a possibility that his pious wish of living and dying in his own country, and in the practice of his profession, was not to be despaired of. Meantime he requested of him, that early on the next morning he would procure him a pass and an escort for his son, whom he was compelled to dispatch forthwith to Nancy, the residence of King René.

"What!" said Colvin, "is my young Lord of Oxford to take a degree in the Court of Love, for no other business is listened to at King René's capital, save love and poetry?"

"I am not ambitious of such distinction for him, my good host," answered Oxford; "but Queen Margaret is with her father, and it is but fitting that the youth should kiss her hand."

"Enough spoken," said the veteran Lancastrian. "I trust, though winter is fast approaching, the Red Rose may bloom in spring."

He then ushered the Earl of Oxford to the partition of the tent which he was to occupy, in which there was a couch for Arthur also — their host, as Colvin might be termed, assuring them, that, with peep of day, horses and faithful attendants should be ready to speed the youth on his journey to Nancy.

"And now, Arthur," said his father, "we must part once more. I dare give thee, in this land of danger, no written communication to my mistress, Queen Margaret; but say to her, that I have found the Duke of Burgundy wedded to his own views of interest, but not averse to combine them with hers. Say, that I have little doubt that he will grant us the required aid, but not without the expected resignation in his favour by herself and King René. Say, I would never have recommended such? sacrifice for the precarious chance of overthrowing the House of York, but that I am satisfied that France and Burgundy are hanging like vultures over Provence, and that the one or other, or both princes, are ready, on her father's demise, to pounce on such possessions as they have reluctantly spared to him during his life. An accommodation with Burgundy may therefore, on the one hand, ensure his active coöperation in the attempt on England; and, on the other, if our high-spirited princess complies not with the Duke's request, the justice of her cause will give no additional security to her hereditary claims on her father's dominions. Bid Queen Margaret, therefore, unless she should have changed her views, obtain King René's formal deed of cession, conveying his estates to the Duke of Burgundy, with her Majesty's consent. The necessary provisions to the King and to herself may be filled up at her Grace's pleasure, or they may be left blank. I can trust to the Duke's generosity to their being suitably arranged. All that I fear is, that Charles may embroil himself" —

"In some silly exploit, necessary for his own honour and the safety of his dominions," answered a voice behind the lining of the tent; "and, by doing so, attend to his own affairs more than to ours? Ha, Sir Earl!"

At the same time the curtain was drawn aside, and a person entered, in whom, though clothed with the jerkin and bonnet of a private soldier of the Walloon guard, Oxford instantly recognised the Duke of Burgundy's harsh features and fierce eyes, as they sparkled from under the fur and feather with which the cap was ornamented.

Arthur, who knew not the Prince's person, started at the intrusion, and laid his hand on his dagger; but his father made a signal which staid his hand, and he gazed with wonder on the solemn respect with which the Earl received the intrusive soldier. The first word informed him of the cause.

"If this masking be done in proof of my faith, noble Duke, permit me to say it is superfluous."

"Nay, Oxford," answered the Duke, "I was a courteous spy; for I ceased to play the eavesdropper, at the very moment when I had reason to expect you were about to say something to anger me."

"As I am a true Knight, my Lord Duke, if you had remained behind the arras, you would only have heard the same truths which I am ready to tell in your Grace's presence, though it may have chanced they might have been more bluntly expressed."

"Well, speak them then, in whatever phrase thou wilt — they lie in their throats that say Charles of Burgundy was ever offended by advice from a well-meaning friend."

"I would then have said," replied the English Earl, "that all which Margaret of Anjou had to apprehend, was that the Duke of Burgundy, when buckling on his armour to win Provence for himself, and to afford to her his powerful assistance to assert her rights in England, was likely to be withdrawn from such high objects by an imprudently eager desire to avenge himself of imaginary affronts, offered to him, as he supposed, by certain confederacies of Alpine mountaineers, over whom it is impossible to gain any important advantage, or acquire reputation, while, on the contrary, there is a risk of losing both. These men dwell amongst rocks and deserts which are almost inaccessible, and subsist in a manner so rude, that the poorest of your subjects would starve if subjected to such diet. They are formed by nature to be the garrison of the mountain fortresses in which she has placed them; — for Heaven's sake meddle not with them, but follow forth your own nobler and more important objects, without stirring a nest of hornets, which, once in motion, may sting you into madness."

The Duke had promised patience, and endeavoured to keep his word; but the swoln muscles of his face, and his flashing eyes, showed how painful to him it was to suppress his resentment.

"You are misinformed, my lord," he said; "these men lire not the inoffensive herdsmen and peasants you are pleased to suppose them. If they were, I might afford to despise them. But, flushed with some victories over the sluggish Austrians, they have shaken off all reverence for authority, assume airs of independence, form leagues, make inroads, storm towns, doom and execute men of noble birth at their pleasure. — Thou art dull, and look'st as if thou dost not apprehend me. To rouse thy English blood, and make thee sympathize with my feelings to these mountaineers, know that these Swiss are very Scots to my dominions in their neighbourhood; poor, proud, ferocious; easily offended, because they gain by war; ill to be appeased, because they nourish deep revenge; ever ready to seize the moment of advantage, and attack a neighbour when he is engaged in other affairs. The same unquiet, perfidious, and inveterate enemies that the Scots are to England, are the Swiss to Burgundy and to my allies. What say you? Can I undertake any thing of consequence till I have crushed the pride of such a people? It will be but a few days' work. I will grasp the mountain-hedgehog, prickles and all, with my steel-gauntlet."

"Your Grace will then have shorter work with them," replied the disguised nobleman, "than our English Kings have had with Scotland. The wars there have lasted so long, and proved so bloody, that wise men regret we ever began them."

"Nay," said the Duke, "I will not dishonour the Scots by comparing them in all respects to these mountain-churls of the Cantons. The Scots have blood and gentry among them, and we have seen many examples of both; these Swiss are a mere brood of peasants, and the few gentlemen of birth they can boast must hide their distinction in the dress and manners of clowns. They will, I think, scarce stand against a charge of Hainaulters."

"Not if the Hainaulters find ground to ride upon. But" ——

"Nay, to silence your scruples," said the Duke, interrupting him, "know that these people encourage, by their countenance and aid, the formation of the most dangerous conspiracies in my dominions. Look here — I told you that my officer, Sir Archibald de Hagenbach, was murdered when the town of Brisach was treacherously taken by these harmless Switzers of yours. And here is a scroll of parchment, which announces that my servant was murdered by doom of the Vehmegericht, a band of secret assassins, whom I will not permit to meet in any part of my dominions. O, could I but catch them above ground as they are found lurking below, they should know what the life of a nobleman is worth! Then, look at the insolence of their attestation."

The scroll bore, with the day and date adjected, that judgment had been done on Archibald de Hagenbach, for tyranny, violence, and oppression, by order of the Holy Vehme, and that it was executed by their officials, who were responsible for the same to their tribunal alone. It was countersigned in red ink, with the badges of the Secret Society, a coil of ropes and a drawn dagger.

"This document I found stuck to my toilet with a knife," said the Duke; "another trick by which they give mystery to their murderous jugglery."

The thought of what he had undergone in John Mengs's house, and reflections upon the extent and omnipresence of these Secret Associations, struck even the brave Englishman with an involuntary shudder.

"For the sake of every saint in Heaven," he said, "forbear, my lord, to speak of these tremendous societies, whose creature's are above, beneath, and around us. No man is secure of his life, however guarded, if it be sought by a man who is careless of his own. You are surrounded by Germans, Italians, and other strangers — How many amongst these may be bound by the secret ties which withdraw men from every other social bond, to unity them together in one inextricable, though secret compact? Beware, noble Prince, of the situation on which your throne is placed, though it still exhibits all the splendour of power, and all the solidity of foundation that belongs to so august a structure. I — the friend of thy house — were it with my dying breath —

must needs tell thee, that the Swiss hang like an avalanche over thy head; and the Secret Associations work beneath thee like the first throes of the coming earthquake. Provoke not the contest, and the snow will rest undisturbed on the mountain-side — the agitation of the subterranean vapours will be hushed to rest; but a single word of defiance, or one flash of indignant scorn, may call their terrors into instant action."

"You speak," said the Duke, "with more awe of a pack of naked churls, and a band of midnight assassins, than I have seen you show for real danger. Yet I will not scorn your counsel — I will hear the Swiss envoys patiently, and I will not, if I can help it, show the contempt with which I cannot but regard their pretensions to treat as independent states. On the Secret Associations I will be silent, till time gives me the means of acting in combination with the Emperor, the Diet, and the Princes of the Empire, that they may be driven from all their burrows at once. — Ha, Sir Earl, said I well?"

"It is well thought, my lord, but it may be unhappily spoken. You are in a position, where one word overheard by a traitor, might produce death and ruin."

"I keep no traitors about me," said Charles. "If I thought there were such in my camp, I would rather die by them at once, than live in perpetual terror and suspicion."

"Your Highness's ancient followers and servants," said the Earl, "speak unfavourably of the Count of Campo-Basso, who holds so high a rank in your confidence."

"Ay," replied the Duke, with composure, "it is easy to decry the most faithful servant in a court by the unanimous hatred of all the others. I warrant me your bull-headed countryman, Colvin, has been railing against the Count like the rest of them, for Campo-Basso sees nothing amiss in any department, but he reports it to me without fear or favour. And then his opinions are cast so much in the same mould with my own, that I can hardly get him to enlarge upon what he best understands, if it seems in any respect different from my sentiments. Add to this, a noble person, grace, gaiety, skill in the exercises of war, and in the courtly arts of peace — such is Campo-Basso; and being such, is he not a gem for a prince's cabinet?"

"The very materials out of which a favourite is formed," answered the Earl of Oxford, "but something less adapted for making a faithful counsellor."

"Why, thou mistrustful fool," said the Duke, "must I tell thee the very inmost secret respecting this man, Campo-Basso, and will nothing short of it stay these imaginary suspicions which thy new trade of an itinerant merchant hath led thee to entertain so rashly?"

"If your Highness honours me with your confidence," said the Earl of Oxford, "I can only say that my fidelity shall deserve it."

"Know, then, thou misbelieving mortal, that my good friend and brother, Louis of France, sent me private information, through no less a person than his famous barber, Oliver le Diable, that Campo-Basso had for a certain sum offered to put my person into his hands, alive or dead. — You start!"

"I do indeed — recollecting your Highness's practice of riding out lightly armed, and with a very small attendance, to reconnoitre the ground, and visit the outposts, and therefore how easily such a treacherous device might be carried into execution."

"Pshaw!" answered the Duke. — "Thou seest the danger as if it were real, whereas nothing can be more certain than that, if my cousin of France had ever received such an offer, he would have been the last person to have put me on my guard against the attempt. No — he knows the value I set on Campo-Basso's services, and forged the accusation to deprive me of them."

"And yet, my lord," replied the English Earl, "your Highness, by my counsel, will not unnecessarily or impatiently fling aside your armour of proof, or ride without the escort of some score of your trusty Walloons."

"Tush, man, thou wouldst make a carbonado of a fever-stirred wretch like myself, betwixt the bright iron and the burning sun. But I will be cautious though I jest thus — and you, young man, may assure my cousin, Margaret of Anjou, that I will consider her affairs as my own. And remember, youth, that the secrets of princes are fatal gifts, if he to whom they are imparted blaze them abroad; but if duly treasured up, they enrich the bearer. And thou shall have cause to say so, if thou canst bring back with thee from Aix the deed of resignation, of which thy father hath spoken. — Good-night — good-night!"

He left the apartment.

"You have just seen," said the Earl of Oxford to his son, "a sketch of this extraordinary prince, by his own pencil. It is easy to excite his ambition or thirst of power, but well-nigh impossible to limit him to the just measures by which it is most likely to be gratified. He is ever like the young archer, startled from his mark by some swallow crossing his eye, even careless as he draws the string. Now irregularly and offensively suspicious — now unreservedly lavish of his confidence — not long since the enemy of the line of Lancaster, and the ally of her deadly foe — now its last and only stay and hope. God mend all! — it is a weary thing to look on the game and see how it might be won, while we are debarred by the caprice of others from the power of playing it according to our own skill. How much must depend on the decision of Duke Charles upon the morrow, and how little do I possess the power of influencing him, either for his own safety or our advantage! Good-night my son, and let us trust events to Him who alone can control them."

CHAPTER XXVII

My blood hath been too cold and temperate,
Unapt to stir at these indignities,
And you have found me; for, accordingly,
You tread upon my patience.

HENRY IV.

The dawn of morning roused the banished Earl of Oxford and his son, and its lights were scarce abroad on the eastern heaven, ere their host, Colvin, entered with an attendant, bearing some bundles, which he placed on the floor of the tent, and instantly retired. The officer of the Duke's ordnance then announced, that he came with a message from the Duke of Burgundy.

"His Highness," he said, "has sent four stout yeomen, with a commission of credence to my young master of Oxford, and an ample purse of gold, to furnish his expenses to Aix, and while his affairs may detain him there. Also a letter of credence to King René, to ensure his reception, and two suits of honour for his use, as for an English gentleman, desirous to witness the festive solemnities of Provence, and in whose safety the Duke deigns to take deep interest. His farther affairs there, if he hath any, his Highness recommends to him to manage with prudence and secrecy. His Highness hath also sent a couple of horses for his use, — one an ambling jennet for the road, and another a strong barbed horse of Flanders, in case he hath aught to do. It will be fitting that my young master change his dress, and assume attire more near his proper rank. His attendants know the road, and have power, in case of need, to summon, in the Duke's name, assistance from all faithful Burgundians. I have but to add, the sooner the young gentleman sets forward, it will be the better sign of a successful journey."

"I am ready to mount, the instant that I have changed my dress," said Arthur.

"And I," said his father, "have no wish to detain him on the service in which he is now employed. Neither he nor I will say more than God be with you. How and where we are to meet again, who can tell?"

"I believe," said Colvin, "that must rest on the motions of the Duke, which, perchance, are not yet determined upon; but his

Highness depends upon your remaining with him, my noble lord, till the affairs of which you come to treat may be more fully decided. Something I have for your lordship's private ear, when your son hath parted on his journey."

While Colvin was thus talking with his father, Arthur, who was not above half dressed when he entered the tent, had availed himself of an obscure corner, in which he exchanged the plain garb belonging to his supposed condition as a merchant, for such a riding suit as became a young man of some quality attached to the Court of Burgundy. It was not without a natural sensation of pleasure, that the youth resumed an apparel suitable to his birth, and which no one was personally more fitted to become; but it was with much deeper feeling that he hastily, and as secretly as possible, flung round his neck, and concealed under the collar and folds of his ornamented doublet, a small thin chain of gold, curiously linked in what was called Morisco work. This was the contents of the parcel which Anne of Geierstein had indulged his feelings, and perhaps tier own, by putting into his hands as they parted. The chain was secured by a slight plate of gold, on which a bodkin, or a point of a knife, had traced on the one side, in distinct though light characters, ADIEU FOR EVER! while, on the reverse, there was much more obscurely traced, the word REMEMBER! — A. VON G.

All who may read this are, have been, or will be, lovers; and there is none, therefore, who may not be able to comprehend why this token was carefully suspended around Arthur's neck, so that the inscription might rest on the region of his heart, without the interruption of any substance which could prevent the pledge from being agitated by every throb of that busy organ.

This being hastily ensured, a few minutes completed the rest of his toilet; and he kneeled before his father to ask his blessing, and his further commands for Aix.

His father blessed him almost inarticulately, and then said, with recovered firmness, that he was already possessed of all the knowledge necessary for success on his mission.

"When you can bring me the deeds wanted," he whispered with more firmness, "you will find me near the person of the Duke of Burgundy."

They went forth of the tent in silence, and found before it the four Burgundian yeomen, tall and active-looking men, ready mounted themselves, and holding two saddled horses — the one accoutred for war, the other a spirited jennet, for the purposes of the journey. One of them led a sumpter-horse, on which Colvin informed Arthur he would find the change of habit necessary when he should arrive at Aix; and at the same time delivered to him a heavy purse of gold.

"Thiebault," he continued, pointing out the eldest of the attendant troopers, "may be trusted — I will be warrant for his sagacity and fidelity. The other three are picked men, who will not fear their skin-cutting."

Arthur vaulted into the saddle with a sensation of pleasure, which was natural to a young cavalier who had not for many months felt a spirited horse beneath him. The lively jennet reared with impatience. Arthur, sitting firm on his seat, as if he had been a part of the animal, only said, "Ere we are long acquainted, thy spirit, my fair roan, will be something more tamed."

"One word more, my son," said his father, and whispered in Arthur's ear, as he stooped from the saddle; "if you receive a letter from me, do not think yourself fully acquainted with the contents till the paper has been held opposite to a hot fire."

Arthur bowed, and motioned to the elder trooper to lead the way, when all, giving rein to their horses, rode off through the encampment at a round pace, the young leader signing an adieu to his father and Colvin.

The Earl stood like a man in a dream, following his son with his eyes, in a kind of reverie, which was only broken when Colvin said, "I marvel not, my lord, that you are anxious about my young master; he is a gallant youth, well worth a father's caring for, and the times we live in are both false and bloody."

"God and St. Mary be my witness," said the Earl, "that if I grieve, it is not for my own house only; — if I am anxious, it is not for the sake of my own son alone; — but it is hard to risk a last stake in a cause so perilous. — What commands brought you from the Duke?"

"His Grace," said Colvin, "will get on horseback after he has breakfasted. He sends you some garments, which, if not fitting your quality, are yet nearer to suitable apparel than those you now wear, and he desires that, observing your incognito as an English merchant of eminence, you will join him in his cavalcade to Dijon, where he is to receive the answer of the Restates of Burgundy concerning matters submitted to their consideration, and thereafter give public audience to the Deputies from Switzerland. His Highness has charged me with the care of finding you suitable accommodation during the ceremonies of the day, which, he thinks, you will, as a stranger, be pleased to look upon. But he probably told you all this himself, for I think you saw him last night in disguise — Nay, look as strange as you will — the Duke plays that trick too often to be able to do it with secrecy; the very horse-boys know him while he traverses the tents of the common soldiery, and sutler women give him the name of the spied spy. If it were only honest Harry Colvin who knew this, it should not cross his lips. But it is practised too openly, and too widely known. Come, noble lord, though I must teach my tongue to forego that courtesy, will you along to breakfast?"

The meal, according to the practice of the time, was a solemn and solid one; and a favoured officer of the great Duke of Burgundy, lacked no means, it may be believed, of rendering due hospitality to a guest having claims of such high respect. But ere the breakfast was over, a clamorous flourish of trumpets announced that the Duke, with his attendants and retinue, were sounding to horse. Philipson, as he was still called, was, in the name of the Duke, presented with a stately charger, and with his host mingled in the splendid assembly which began to gather in front of the Duke's pavilion. In a few minutes, the Prince himself issued forth, in the superb dress of the Order of the Golden Fleece, of which his father Philip had been the founder, and Charles was himself the patron and sovereign. Several of his courtiers were dressed in the same magnificent robes, and with their followers and attendants, displayed so much wealth and splendour of appearance, as to warrant the common saying, that the Duke of Burgundy maintained the most magnificent court in Christendom. The officers of his household attended in their order, together with heralds and pursuivants, the grotesque richness of whose habits had a singular effect among those of the high clergy in their albes and dalmatiques, and of the knights and crown vassals who were arrayed in armour. Among these last, who were variously equipped, according to the different character of their service, rode Oxford, but in a peaceful habit, neither so plain as to be out of place amongst such splendour, nor so rich as to draw on him a special or particular degree of attention. He rode by the side of Colvin, his tall muscular figure, and deep-marked features, forming a strong contrast to the rough, almost ignoble, cast of countenance, and stout thick-set form, of the less distinguished soldier of fortune.

Ranged into a solemn procession, the rear of which was closed by a guard of two hundred picked arquebusiers, a description of soldiers who were just then coming into notice, and as many mounted men-at-arms; the Duke and his retinue, leaving the barriers of the camp, directed their march to the town, or rather city, of Dijon, in those days the capital of all Burgundy.

It was a town well secured with walls and ditches, which last were filled by means of a small river, named Dousche, which combines its waters for that purpose with a torrent called Suson. Four gates, with appropriate barbicans, outworks, and drawbridges, corresponded nearly to the cardinal points of the compass, and gave admission to the city. The number of towers, which stood high above its walls, and defended them at different angles, was thirty-three; and the walls themselves, which exceeded in most places the height of thirty feet, were built of stones hewn and squared, and were of great thickness. This stately city was surrounded on the outside with hills covered with vineyards, while from within its walls rose the towers of many noble buildings, both public and private, as well as the steeples of magnificent churches, and of well-endowed convents, attesting the wealth and devotion of the House of Burgundy.

When the trumpets of the Duke's procession had summoned the burgher guard at the gate of St. Nicholas, the drawbridge fell, the portcullis rose, the people shouted joyously, the windows were hung with tapestry, and as, in the midst of his retinue, Charles himself came riding on a milkwhite steed, attended only by six pages under fourteen years old, with each a gilded partisan in his hand, the acclamations with which he was received on all sides, showed that, if some instances of misrule had diminished his popularity, enough of it remained to render his reception into his capital decorous at least, if not enthusiastic. It is probable that the veneration attached to his father's memory counteracted for a long time the unfavourable effect which some of his own actions were calculated to produce on the public mind.

The procession halted before a large Gothic building in the centre of Dijon. This was then called Maison du Due, as, after the union of Burgundy with France, it was termed Maison du Roy. The Maire of Dijon attended on the steps before this palace, accompanied by his official brethren, and escorted by a hundred able-bodied citizens, in black velvet cloaks, bearing half pikes in their hands. The Maire kneeled to kiss the stirrup of the Duke, and at the moment when Charles descended from his horse, every bell in the city commenced so thundering a peal, that they might almost have awakened the dead who slept in the vicinity of the steeples, which rocked with their clangour. Under the influence of this stunning peal of welcome, the Duke entered the great ball of the building, at the upper end of which were erected a throne for the sovereign, seats for his more distinguished officers of state and higher vassals, with benches behind for persons of less note. On one of these, but in a spot from which he might possess a commanding view of the whole assembly, as well as of the Duke himself, Colvin placed the noble Englishman; and Charles, whose quick stern eye glanced rapidly over the party when they were seated, seemed, by a nod so slight as to be almost imperceptible to those around him, to give his approbation of the arrangement adopted.

When the Duke and his assistants were seated and in order, the Maire, again approaching, in the most humble manner, and kneeling on the lowest step of the ducal throne, requested to know if his Highness's leisure permitted him to hear the inhabitants of his capital express their devoted zeal to his person, and to accept the benevolence which, in the shape of a silver cup filled with gold pieces, he had the distinguished honour to place before his feet, in name of the citizens and community of Dijon.

Charles, who at no time affected much courtesy, answered, briefly and bluntly, with a voice which was naturally harsh and dissonant, "All things in their order, good Master Maire. Let us first hear what the Estates of Burgundy have to say to us; we will then listen to the burghers of Dijon."

The Maire rose and retired, bearing in his hand the silver cup, and experiencing probably some vexation, as well as surprise, that its contents had not secured an instant and gracious acceptance.

"I expected," said Duke Charles, "to have met at this hour and place our Estates of the duchy of Burgundy, or a deputation of them, with an answer to our message conveyed to them three days since by our chancellor. Is there no one here on their part?"

The Maire, as none else made any attempt to answer, said that the members of the Estates had been in close deliberation the whole of that morning, and doubtless would instantly wait upon his Highness, when they heard that he had honoured the town with his presence.

"Go, Toison d'Or," said the Duke to the herald of the Order of the Golden Fleece,[15] "bear to these gentlemen the tidings that we desire to know the end of their deliberations; and that neither in courtesy nor in loyalty can they expect us to wait long. Be round with them, Sir Herald, or we shall be as round with you."

While the herald was absent on his mission, we may remind our readers, that in all feudalized countries, (that is to say, in almost all Europe during the middle ages,) an ardent spirit of liberty pervaded the constitution; and the only fault that could be found was, that the privileges and freedom for which the great vassals contended did not sufficiently descend to the lower orders of society, or extend protection to those who were most likely to need it. The two first ranks in the state, the nobles and clergy, enjoyed high and important privileges; and even the third estate, or citizens, had this immunity in peculiar, that no new duties, customs, or taxes of any kind, could be exacted from them save by their own consent.

The memory of Duke Philip, the father of Charles, was dear to the Burgundians; for during twenty years that sage prince had maintained his rank amongst the sovereigns of Europe with much dignity, and had accumulated treasure without exacting or receiving any great increase of supplies from the rich countries which he governed. But the extravagant schemes and immoderate expense of Duke Charles had already excited the suspicion of his Estates; and the mutual good-will betwixt the prince and people began to be exchanged for suspicion and distrust on the one side, and defiance on the other. The refractory disposition of the Estates had of late increased; for they had disapproved of various wars in which their Duke had needlessly embarked; and from his levying such large bodies of mercenary troops, they came to suspect he might finally employ the wealth voted to him by his subjects, for the undue extension of his royal prerogative,

---

[15] The chief order of knighthood in the state of Burgundy.

and the destruction of the liberties of the people.

At the same time the Duke's uniform success in enterprises which appeared desperate as well as difficult, esteem for the frankness and openness of his character, and dread of the obstinacy and headstrong tendency of a temper which could seldom bear persuasion, and never endured opposition, still threw awe and terror around the throne, which was materially aided by the attachment of the common people to the person of the present Duke, and to the memory of his father. It had been understood, that upon the present occasion there was strong opposition amongst the Estates to the system of taxation proposed on the part of the Duke, and the issue was expected with considerable anxiety by the Duke's counsellors, and with fretful impatience by the sovereign himself.

After a space of about ten minutes had elapsed, the Chancellor of Burgundy, who was Archbishop of Vienne, and a prelate of high rank, entered the hall with his train; and passing behind the ducal throne to occupy cue of the most distinguished places in the assembly, he stopped for a moment to urge his master to receive the answer of his Estates in a private manner, giving him at the same time to understand, that the result of the deliberations had been by no means satisfactory.

"By Saint George of Burgundy, my Lord Archbishop," answered the Duke, sternly and aloud, "we are not a prince of a mind so paltry that we need to shun the moody looks of a discontented and insolent faction. If the Estates of Burgundy send a disobedient and disloyal answer to our paternal message, let them deliver it in open court, that the assembled people may learn how to decide between their Duke and those petty yet intriguing spirits, who would interfere with our authority."

The Chancellor bowed gravely, and took his seat; while the English Earl observed, that most of the members of the assembly, excepting such as in doing so could not escape the Duke's notice, passed some observations to their neighbours, which were received with a half-expressed nod, shrug, or shake of the head, as men treat a proposal upon which it is dangerous to decide. At the same time, Toison d'Or, who acted as master of the ceremonies, introduced into the hall a committee of the Estates, consisting of twelve members, four from each branch of the Estates, announced as empowered to deliver the answer of that assembly to the Duke of Burgundy.

When the deputation entered the hall, Charles arose from his throne, according to ancient custom, and taking from his head his bonnet, charged with a huge plume of feathers, "Health and welcome," he said, "to my good subjects of the Estates of Burgundy!" All the numerous train of courtiers rose and uncovered their heads with the same ceremony. The members of the states then dropt on one knee, the four ecclesiastics, among whom. Oxford recognized the Black Priest of St. Paul's, approaching nearest to the Duke's person, the nobles kneeling behind them, and the burgesses in the rear of the whole.

"Noble Duke," said the Priest of St. Paul's, "will it best please you to hear the answer of your good and loyal Estates of Burgundy by the voice of one member speaking for the whole, or by three persons, each delivering the sense of the body to which he belongs?"

"As you will," said the Duke of Burgundy.

"A priest, a noble, and a free burgher," said the churchman, still on one knee, "will address your Highness in succession. For though, blessed be the God who leads brethren to dwell together in unity! we are agreed in the general answer, yet each body of the Estates may have special and separate reasons to allege for the common opinion."

"We will hear you separately," said Duke Charles, casting his hat upon his head, and throwing himself carelessly back into his seat. At the same time, all who were of noble blood, whether in the committee or amongst the spectators, vouched their right to be peers of their sovereign by assuming their bonnets, and a cloud of waving plumes at once added grace and dignity to the assembly.

When the Duke resumed his seat, the deputation arose from their knees, and the Black Priest of St. Paul's, again stepping forth, addressed him in these words: —

"My Lord Duke, your loyal and faithful clergy have considered your Highness's proposal to lay a talliage on your people, in order to make war on the Confederate Cantons in the country of the Alps. The quarrel, my liege lord, seems to your clergy an unjust and oppressive one on your Highness's part; nor can they hope that God will bless those who arm in it. They are therefore compelled to reject your Highness's proposal."

The Duke's eye lowered gloomily on the deliverer of this unpalatable message. He shook his head with one of those stern and menacing looks which the harsh composition of his features rendered them peculiarly qualified to express. "You have spoken, Sir Priest," was the only reply which he deigned to make.

One of the four nobles, the Sire de Myrebeau, then expressed himself thus: —

"Your Highness has asked of your faithful nobles to consent to new imposts and exactions, to be levied through Burgundy, for the raising of additional bands of hired soldiers for the maintenance of the quarrels of the state. My lord, the swords of the Burgundian nobles, knights, and gentlemen, have been ever at your Highness's command, as those of our ancestors have been readily wielded for your predecessors. In your Highness's just quarrel we will go farther, and fight firmer, than any hired fellows who can be procured, whether from France, or Germany, or Italy. We will not give our consent that the people should be taxed for paying mercenaries to discharge that military duty which it is alike our pride and our exclusive privilege to render."

"You have spoken, Sire de Myrebeau," were again the only words of the Duke's reply. He uttered them slowly and with deliberation, as if afraid lest some phrase of imprudent violence should escape along with what he purposed to say. Oxford thought he cast a glance towards him before he spoke, as if the consciousness of his presence was some additional restraint on his passion. "Now, Heaven grant," he said to himself, "that this opposition may work its proper effect, and induce the Duke to renounce an imprudent attempt, so hazardous and so unnecessary!"

While he muttered these thoughts, the Duke made a sign to one of the *tiers état*, or commons, to speak in his turn. The person who obeyed the signal was Martin Block, a wealthy butcher and grazier of Dijon. His words were these: — "Noble Prince, our fathers were the dutiful subjects of your predecessors; we are the same to you; our children will be alike the liegemen of your successors. But touching the request your chancellor has made to us, it is such as our ancestors never complied with; such as we are determined to refuse, and such as will never be conceded by the Estates of Burgundy, to any prince whatsoever, even to the end of time."

Charles had borne with impatient silence the speeches of the two former orators, but this blunt and hardy reply of the third Estate, excited him beyond what his nature could endure. He gave way to the impetuosity of his disposition, stamped on the floor till the throne shook, and the high vault rung over their heads, and overwhelmed the bold burgher with reproaches. "Beast of burden," he said, "am I to be stunned with thy braying, too? The nobles may claim leave to speak, for they can fight; the clergy may use their tongues, for it is their trade; but thou, that hast never shed blood, save that of bullocks, less stupid than thou art thyself — must thou and thy herd come hither, privileged, forsooth, to bellow at a prince's footstool? Know, brute as thou art, that steers are never introduced into temples but to be sacrificed, or butchers and mechanics brought before their sovereign, save that they may have the honour to supply the public wants from their own swelling hoards!"

A murmur of displeasure, which even the terror of the Duke's wrath could not repress, ran through the audience at these words; and the burgher of Dijon, a sturdy plebeian, replied, with little reverence, — "Our purses, my Lord Duke, are our own — we will not put the strings of them into your Highness's hands, unless we are satisfied with the purposes to which the money is to be applied; and we know well how to protect our persons and our goods against foreign ruffians and plunderers."

Charles was on the point of ordering the deputy to be arrested, when, having cast his eye towards the Earl of Oxford, whose presence, in despite of himself, imposed a certain degree of restraint upon him, he exchanged that piece of imprudence for another.

"I see," he said, addressing the committee of Estates, "that you are all leagued to disappoint my purposes, and doubtless to deprive me of all the power of a sovereign, save that of wearing a coronet, and being served on the knee like a second Charles the Simple, while the Estates of my kingdom divide the power among them. But you shall know that you have to do with Charles of Burgundy, a prince, who, though he has deigned to consult you, is fully able to fight battles without the aid of his nobles, since they refuse him the assistance of their swords — to defray the expense without the help of his sordid burghers — and, it may be, to find out a path to Heaven without the assistance of an ungrateful priesthood. I will show all that are here present, how little my mind is affected, or my purpose changed, by your seditious reply to the message with which I honoured you. — Here, Toison d'Or, admit into our presence these men from the confederated towns and cantons, as they call themselves, of Switzerland."

Oxford, and all who really interested themselves in the Duke's welfare, heard, with the utmost apprehension, his resolution to give an audience to the Swiss Envoys, prepossessed as he was against them, and in the moment when his mood was chafed to the uttermost by the refusal of the Estates to grant him supplies. They were aware that obstacles opposed to the current of his passion, were like rocks in the bed of a river, whose course they cannot interrupt, while they provoke it to rage and foam. All were sensible that the die was cast, but none who were not endowed with more than mortal prescience, could have imagined how deep was the pledge which depended upon it. Oxford, in particular, conceived that the execution of his plan of a descent upon England, was the principal point compromised by the Duke in his rash obstinacy; but he suspected not — he dreamed not of supposing — that the life of Charles himself, and the independence of Burgundy as a separate kingdom, hung quivering in the same scales.

CHAPTER XXVIII

Why, 'tis a boisterous and cruel style,
A style for challengers. Why, she defies us,
Like Turk to Christian.

AS YOU LIKE IT.

The doors of the hall were now opened to the Swiss Deputies, who for the preceding hour had been kept in attendance on the outside of the building, without receiving the slightest of those attentions, which among civilized nations are universally paid to the representatives of a foreign state. Indeed, their very appearance, dressed in coarse gray frocks, like mountain hunters or shepherds, in the midst of an assembly blazing with divers-coloured garments, gold and silver lace, embroidery, and precious stones, served to confirm the idea that they could only have come hither in the capacity of the most humble petitioners.

Oxford, however, who watched closely the deportment of his late fellow-travellers, failed not to observe that they retained each in his own person the character of firmness and indifference which formerly distinguished them. Rudolph Donnerhugel preserved his bold and haughty look; the Banneret the military indifference which made him look with apparent apathy on all around him; the burgher of Soleure was as formal and important as ever; nor did any of the three show themselves affected in the slightest degree by the splendour of the scene around them, or embarrassed by the consideration of their own comparative inferiority of appointments. But the noble Landamman, on whom Oxford chiefly bent his attention, seemed overwhelmed with a sense of the precarious state in which his country was placed; fearing from the rude and unhonoured manner in which they were received, that war was unavoidable, while, at the same time, like a good patriot, he mourned over the consequences of ruin to the freedom of his country by defeat, or injury to her simplicity and virtuous indifference of wealth, by the introduction of foreign luxuries and the evils attending on conquest.

Well acquainted with the opinions of Arnold Biederman, Oxford could easily explain his sadness, while his comrade Bonstetten, less capable of comprehending his friend's feelings, looked at him with the expression which may be seen in the countenance of a faithful dog, when the creature indicates sympathy with his master's melancholy, though unable to ascertain or appreciate its cause. A look of wonder now and then glided around the splendid assembly on the part of all the forlorn group, excepting Donnerhugel and the Landamman; for the indomitable pride of the one, and the steady patriotism of the other, could not for even an instant be diverted by external objects from their own deep and stern reflections.

After a silence of nearly five minutes, the Duke spoke, with the haughty and harsh manner which he might imagine belonged to his place, and which certainly expressed his character.

"Men of Berne, of Schwitz, or of whatever hamlet and wilderness you may represent, know that we had not honoured you, rebels as you are to the dominion of your lawful superiors, with an audience in our own presence, but for the intercession of a well-esteemed friend, who has sojourned among your mountains, and whom you may know by the name of Philipson, an Englishman, following the trade of a merchant, and charged with certain valuable matters of traffic to our court. To his intercession we have so far given way, that instead of commanding you, according to your demerits, to the gibbet and the wheel in the Place de Morimont, we have condescended to receive you into our own presence, sitting in our *cour plénière*, to hear from you such submission as you can offer for your outrageous storm of our town of La Ferette, the slaughter of many of our liegemen, and the deliberate murder of the noble knight, Archibald of Hagenbach, executed in your presence, and by your countenance and device. Speak — if you can say aught in defence of your felony and treason, either to deprecate just punishment, or crave undeserved mercy."

The Landamman seemed about to answer; but Rudolph Donnerhugel, with his characteristic boldness and hardihood, took the task of reply on himself. He confronted the proud Duke with an eye unappalled, and a countenance as stern as his own.

"We came not here," he said, "to compromise our own honour, or the dignity of the free people whom we represent, by pleading guilty in their name, or our own, to crimes of which we are innocent. And when you term us rebels, you must remember, that a long train of victories, whose history is written in the noblest blood of Austria, has restored to the confederacy of our communities the freedom, of which an unjust tyranny in vain attempted to deprive us. While Austria was a just and beneficent mistress, we served her with our lives; — when she became oppressive and tyrannical, we assumed independence. If she has aught yet to claim from us, the descendants of Tell, Faust, and Staufbaucher, will be as ready to assert their liberties as their fathers were to gain them. Your Grace — if such be your title — has no concern with any dispute betwixt us and Austria. For your threats of gibbet and wheel, we are here defenceless men, on whom you may work your pleasure; but we know how to die, and our countrymen know how to avenge us."

The fiery Duke would have replied by commanding the instant arrest, and probably the immediate execution, of the whole deputation. But his chancellor, availing himself of the privilege of his office, rose, and doffing his cap with a deep reverence to the Duke, requested leave to reply to the misproud young man, who had, he said, so greatly mistaken the purpose of his Highness's speech.

Charles feeling perhaps at the moment too much irritated to form a calm decision, threw himself back in his chair of state, and with an impatient and angry nod, gave his chancellor permission to speak.

"Young man," said that high officer, "you have mistaken the meaning of the high and mighty sovereign, in whose presence you stand. Whatever be the lawful rights of Austria over the revolted villages which have flung off their allegiance to their native superior, we have no call to enter on that argument. But that for which Burgundy demands your answer, is, wherefore, coming here in the guise, and with the character, of peaceful envoys, on affairs touching your own communities and the rights of the Duke's subjects, you have raised war in our peaceful dominions, stormed a fortress, massacred its garrison, and put to death a noble knight, its commander? — all of them actions contrary to the law of nations, and highly deserving of the punishment with which you have been justly threatened, but with which I hope our gracious sovereign will dispense, if you express some sufficient reason for such outrageous insolence, with an offer of due submission to his Highness's pleasure, and satisfactory reparation for such a high injury."

"You are a priest, grave sir?" answered Rudolph Donnerhugel, addressing the Chancellor of Burgundy. "If there be a soldier in this assembly who will avouch your charge, I challenge him to the combat, man to man. We did not storm the garrison of La Ferette — we were admitted into the gates in a peaceful manner, and were there instantly surrounded by the soldiers of the late Archibald de Hagenbach, with the obvious purpose of assaulting and murdering us on our peaceful mission. I promise you there had been news of more men dying than us. But an uproar broke out among the inhabitants of the town, assisted, I believe, by many neighbours, to whom the insolence and oppression of Archibald de Hagenbach had become odious, as to all who were within his reach. We rendered them no assistance; and, I trust, it was not expected that we should interfere in the favour of men who had stood prepared to do the worst against us. But not a pike or sword belonging to us or our attendants was dipped in Burgundian blood. Archibald de Hagenbach perished, it is true, on a scaffold, and I saw him die with pleasure, under a sentence pronounced by a competent court, such as is recognised in Westphalia, and its dependencies on this side of the Rhine. I am not obliged to vindicate their proceedings; but I aver, that the Duke has received full proof of his regular sentence; and, in fine, that it was amply deserved by oppression, tyranny, and foul abuse of his authority, I will uphold against all gainsayers, with the body of a man. There lies my glove."

And, with an action suited to the language he used, the stern Swiss flung his right-hand glove on the floor of the hall. In the spirit of the age, with the love of distinction in arms which it nourished, and perhaps with the desire of gaining the Duke's favour, there was a general motion among the young Burgundians to accept the challenge, and more than six or eight gloves were hastily doffed by the young knights present, those who were more remote flinging them over the heads of the nearest, and each proclaiming his name and title as he proffered the gage of combat.

"I set at all," said the daring young Swiss, gathering the gauntlets as they fell clashing around him. "More, gentlemen, more! a glove for every finger! come on, one at once — fair lists, equal judges of the field, the combat on foot, and the weapons two-handed swords, and I will not budge for a score of you."

"Hold, gentlemen; on your allegiance, hold!" said the Duke, gratified at the same time, and somewhat appeased, by the zeal which was displayed in his cause — moved by the strain of reckless bravery evinced by the challenger, with a hardihood akin to his own — perhaps also not unwilling to display, in the view of his *cour plénière*, more temperance than he had been at first capable of. "Hold, I command you all. — Toison d'Or, gather up these gauntlets, and return them each to its owner. God and St. George forbid that we should hazard the life of even the least of our noble Burgundian gentry against such a churl as this Swiss peasant, who never so much as mounted a horse, and knows not a jot of knightly courtesy, or the grace of chivalry. — Carry your vulgar brawls elsewhere, young man, and know that, on the present occasion, the Place Morimont were your only fitting lifts, and the hangman your meet antagonist. And you, sirs, his companions — whose behaviour in suffering this swaggerer to take the lead amongst you, seems to show that the laws of nature, as well as of society, are inverted, and that age is preferred to youth, as gentry to peasants — you while-bearded men, I say, is there none of you who can speak your errand in such language as it becomes a sovereign prince to listen to?"

"God forbid else," said the Landamman, stepping forward and silencing Rudolph Donnerhugel, who was commencing an answer of defiance — "God forbid," he said, "Noble Duke, that we should not be able to speak so as to be understood before your Highness, since, I trust, we shall speak the language of truth, peace, and justice. Nay, should it incline your Highness to listen to us the more favourably for our humility, I am willing to humble myself rather than you should shun to hear us. For my own part, I can truly say, that though I have lived, and by free choice have resolved to die, a husbandman and a hunter on the Alps of the Unterwald, I may claim by birth the hereditary right to speak before Dukes and Kings, and the Emperor himself. There is no one, my Lord Duke, in this proud assembly, who derives his descent from a nobler source than Geierstein."

"We have heard of you," said the Duke. "Men call you the peasant-count. Your birth is your shame; or perhaps your mother's, if your father had happened to have a handsome ploughman, the fitting father of one who has become a willing serf."

"No serf, my Lord," answered the Landamman, "but a freeman, who will neither oppress others, nor be himself tyrannized over. My father was a noble lord, my mother a most virtuous lady. But I will not be provoked, by taunt or scornful jest, to refrain from stating with calmness what my country has given me ill charge to say. The inhabitants of the bleak and inhospitable regions of the Alps desire, mighty sir, to remain at peace with all their neighbours, and to enjoy the government they have chosen, as best fitted to their condition and habits, leaving all other states and countries to their free-will in the same respects. Especially, they desire to remain at peace and in unity with the princely House of Burgundy, whose dominions approach their possessions on so many points. My lord, they desire it, they entreat it, they even consent to pray for it. We have been termed stubborn, intractable, and insolent contemners of authority, and headers of sedition and rebellion. In evidence of the contrary, my Lord Duke, I, who never bent a knee but to Heaven, feel no dishonour in kneeling before your Highness, as before a sovereign prince in the *cour plénière* of his dominions, where he has a right to exact homage from his subjects out of duty, and from strangers out of courtesy. No vain pride of mine," said the noble old man, his eyes swelling with tears, as he knelt on one knee, "shall prevent me from personal humiliation, when peace — that blessed peace, so dear to God, so inappreciably valuable to man — is in danger of being broken off."

The whole assembly, even the Duke himself, were affected by the noble and stately manner in which the brave old man made a genuflection, which was obviously dictated by neither meanness nor timidity. "Arise, sir," said Charles; "if we have said aught which can wound your private feelings, we retract it as publicly as the reproach was spoken, and sit prepared to hear you as a fair-meaning envoy."

"For that, my noble Lord, thanks; and I shall hold it a blessed day, if I can find words worthy of the cause I have to plead. My Lord, a schedule in your Highness's hands has stated the sense of many injuries received at the hand of your Highness's officers, and those of Romont Count of Savoy, your strict ally and adviser, we have a right to suppose, under your Highness's countenance. For Count Romont — he has already felt with whom he has to contend; but we have as yet taken no measures to avenge injuries, affronts, interruptions to our commerce, from those who have availed themselves of your Highness's authority to intercept our countrymen, spoil our goods, impress their persons, and even, in some instances, take their lives. The affray at La Ferette — I can vouch for what I saw — had no origin or abettance from us; nevertheless, it is impossible an independent nation can suffer the repetition of such injuries, and free and independent we are determined to remain, or to die in defence of our rights. What then must follow, unless your Highness listens to the terms which I am commissioned to offer? War, a war to extermination; for so long as one of our Confederacy can wield a halberd, so long, if this fatal strife once commences, there will be war betwixt your powerful realms and our poor and barren states. And what can the noble Duke of Burgundy gain by such a strife? — is it wealth and plunder? Alas, my Lord, there is more gold and silver on the very bridle-bits of your Highness's household troops, than can be found in the public treasures or private hoards of our whole Confederacy. Is it fame and glory you aspire to? There is little honour to be won by a numerous army over a few scattered bands, by men clad in mail over half-armed husbandmen and shepherds — of such conquest small were the glory. But if, as all Christian men believe, and as it is the constant trust of my countrymen, from memory of the times of our fathers, — if the Lord of Hosts should cast the balance in behalf of the fewer numbers and worse-armed party, I leave it with your Highness to judge, what would, in that event, be the diminution of worship and fame. Is it extent of vassalage and dominion your Highness desires, by warring with your mountain neighbours? Know that you may, if it be God's will, gain our barren and rugged mountains; but, like our ancestors of old, we will seek refuge in wilder and more distant solitudes, and when we have resisted to the last, we will starve in the icy wastes of the Glaciers. Ay, men, women, and children, we will be frozen into annihilation together, ere one free Switzer will acknowledge a foreign master."

The speech of the Landamman made an obvious impression on the assembly. The Duke observed it, and his hereditary obstinacy was irritated by the general disposition which he saw entertained in favour of the ambassador. This evil principle overcame some impression which the address of the noble Biederman had not failed to make upon him. He answered with a lowering brow, interrupting the old man as he was about to continue his speech, — "You argue falsely, Sir Count, or Sir Landamman, or by whatever name you call yourself, if you think we war on you from any hope of spoil, or any desire of glory. We know as well as you can tell us, that there is neither profit nor fame to be achieved by conquering you. But sovereigns, to whom Heaven has given the power, must root out a band of robbers, though there is dishonour in measuring swords with them; and we hunt to death a herd of wolves, though their flesh is carrion, and their skins are nought."

The Landamman shook his gray head, and replied, without testifying emotion, and even with something approaching to a smile, — "I am an older woodsman than you, my Lord Duke — and, it may be, a more experienced one. The boldest, the hardiest hunter, will not safely drive the wolf to his den. I have shown your Highness the poor chance of gain, and the great risk of loss, which even you, powerful as you are, must incur by risking a war with determined and desperate men. Let me now tell what we are willing to do to secure a sincere and lasting peace with our powerful neighbour of Burgundy. Your Grace is in the act of engrossing Lorraine, and it seems probable, under so vigorous and enterprising a Prince, your authority may be extended to the shores of the Mediterranean — be our noble friend and sincere ally, and our mountains, defended by warriors familiar with victory, will be your barriers against Germany and Italy. For your sake we will admit the Count of Savoy to terms, and restore to him our conquests, on such conditions as your Highness shall yourself judge reasonable. Of past subjects of offence on the part of your lieutenants and governors upon the frontier, we will be silent, so we have assurance of no such aggressions in future. Nay, more, and it is my last and proudest offer, we will send three thousand of our youth to assist your Highness in any war which you may engage in, whether against Louis of France, or the Emperor of Germany. They are a different set of men — proudly and truly may I state it — from the scum of Germany and Italy, who form themselves into mercenary bands of soldiers. And, if Heaven should decide your Highness to accept our offer, there will be one corps in your army which will leave their carcasses on the field ere a man of them break their plighted troth."

A swarthy, but tall and handsome man, wearing a corslet

richly engraved with arabesque work, started from his seat with the air of one provoked beyond the bounds of restraint. This was the Count de Campo-Basso, commander of Charles's Italian mercenaries, who possessed, as has been alluded to, much influence over the Duke's mind, chiefly obtained by accommodating himself to his master's opinions and prejudices, and placing before the Duke specious arguments to justify him for following his own way.

"This lofty presence must excuse me," he said, "if I speak in defence of my honour, and those of my bold lances, who have followed my fortunes from Italy to serve the bravest Prince in Christendom. I might, indeed pass over without resentment the outrageous language of this gray-haired churl, whose words cannot affect a knight and a nobleman more than the yelling of a peasant's mastiff. But when I hear him propose to associate his bands of mutinous misgoverned ruffians, with your Highness's troops, I must let him know that there is not a horse-boy in my ranks who would fight in such fellowship. No, even I myself, bound by a thousand ties of gratitude, could not submit to strive abreast with such comrades. I would fold up my banners, and lead five thousand men to seek, — not a nobler master, for the world has none such, — but wars in which we might not be obliged to blush for our assistants."

"Silence, Campo-Basso," said the Duke, "and be assured you serve a prince who knows your worth too well to exchange it for the untried and untrustful services of those, whom we have only known as vexatious and malignant neighbours."

Then addressing himself to Arnold Biederman, he said coldly and sternly, "Sir Landamman, we have heard you fairly. We have heard you, although you come before us with hands dyed deep in the blood of our servant, Sir Archibald de Hagenbach; for, supposing he was murdered by a villainous association, — which, by Saint George! shall never, while we live and reign, raise its pestilential head on this side of the Rhine, — yet it is not the less undeniable and undenied, that you stood by in arms, and encouraged the deed the assassins performed under your countenance. Return to your mountains, and be thankful that you return in life. Tell those who sent you, that I will be presently on their frontiers. A deputation of your most notable persons, who meet me with halters round their necks, torches in their left hands, in their right their swords held by the point, may learn on what conditions we will grant you peace."

"Then farewell peace, and welcome war," said the Landamman; "and be its plagues and curses on the heads of those who choose blood and strife rather than peace and union. We will meet you on our frontiers with our naked swords, but the hilts, not their points, shall be in our grasp. Charles of Burgundy, Flanders, and Lorraine, Duke of seven dukedoms, Count of seventeen earldoms, I bid you defiance; and declare war against you in the name of the Confederated Cantons, and such others as shall adhere to them. There," he said, "are my letters of defiance."

The herald took from Arnold Biederman the fatal denunciation.

"Road it not, Toison d'Or!" said the haughty Duke. 'Let the executioner drag it through the streets at his horse's tail, and nail it to the gibbet, to show in what account we hold the paltry scroll, and those who sent it. — Away, sirs," speaking to the Swiss, "trudge back to your wildernesses with such haste as your feet can use. When we next meet, you shall better know whom you have offended. — Get our horse ready — the council is broken up."

The Maire of Dijon, when all were in motion to leave the hall, again approached the Duke, and timidly expressed some hopes that his Highness would deign to partake of a banquet which the magistracy had prepared, in expectation he might do them such an honour.

"No, by Saint George of Burgundy, Sir Maire," said Charles, with one of the withering glances, by which he was wont to express indignation mixed with contempt, — "you have not pleased us so well with our breakfast as to induce us to trust our dinner to the loyalty of our good town of Dijon."

So saying, he rudely turned off from the mortified chief magistrate, and, mounting his horse, rode back to his camp, conversing earnestly on the way with the Count of Campo-Basso.

"I would offer you dinner, my Lord of Oxford," said Colvin to that nobleman, when he alighted at his tent, "but I foresee, ere you could swallow a mouthful, you will be summoned to the Duke's presence; for it is our Charles's way, when he has fixed on a wrong course, to wrangle with his friends and counsellors, in order to prove it is a right one. Marry, he always makes a convert of yon supple Italian."

Colvin's augury was speedily realized; for a page almost immediately summoned the English merchant, Philipson, to attend the Duke. Without waiting an instant, Charles poured forth an incoherent tide of reproaches against the Estates of his dukedom, for refusing him their countenance in so slight a matter, and launched out in explanations of the necessity which he alleged there was for punishing the audacity of the Swiss. "And thou, too, Oxford," he concluded, "art such an impatient fool as to wish me to indulge in a distant war with England, and transport forces over the sea, when I have such insolent mutineers to chastise on my own frontiers?"

When he was at length silent, the English Earl laid before him, with respectful earnestness, the danger that appeared to be involved in engaging with a people, poor indeed, but universally dreaded, from their discipline and courage, and that under the eye of so dangerous a rival as Louis of France, who was sure to support the Duke's enemies underhand, if he did not join them openly. On this point the Duke's resolution was immovable. "It shall never," he said, "be told of me, that I uttered threats which I dared not execute. These boors have declared war against me, and they shall learn whose wrath it is that they have wantonly provoked; but I do not, therefore, renounce thy scheme, my good Oxford. If thou canst procure me this same cession of Provence, and induce old René to give up the cause of his grandson, Ferrand of Vaudemont, in Lorraine, thou wilt make it well worth my while to send thee brave aid against my brother Blackburn, who, while he is drinking healths pottle-deep in France, may well come to lose his lands in England. And be not impatient because I cannot at this very instant send men across the seas. The march which I am making towards Neufchatel, which is, I think, the nearest point where I shall find these churls, will be but like a morning's excursion. I trust you will go with us, old companion. I should like to see if you have forgotten, among yonder mountains, how to back a horse and lay a lance in rest."

"I will wait on your Highness," said the Earl, "as is my duty, for my motions must depend on your pleasure. But I will not carry arms, especially against those people of Helvetia, from whom I have experienced hospitality, unless it be for my own personal defence."

"Well," replied the Duke, "e'en be it so; we shall have in you an excellent judge, to tell us who best discharges his devoir against the mountain clowns."

At this point in the conversation there was a knocking at the entrance of the pavilion, and the Chancellor of Burgundy presently entered in great haste and anxiety. "News, my Lord — news of France and England," said the prelate, and then observing the presence of a stranger, he looked at the Duke, and was silent.

"It is a faithful friend, my Lord Bishop," said the Duke; "you may tell your news before him."

"It will soon be generally known," said the chancellor — "Louis and Edward are fully accorded." Both the Duke and the English Earl started.

"I expected this," said the Duke, "but not so soon."

"The Kings have met," answered his minister.

"How — in battle?" said Oxford, forgetting himself in his extreme eagerness.

The chancellor was somewhat surprised, but as the Duke seemed to expect him to give an answer, he replied, "No, Sir Stranger, not in battle, but upon appointment, and in peace and amity."

"The sight must have been worth seeing," said the Duke; "when the old fox Louis, and my brother Black — I mean my brother Edward — met. Where held they their rendezvous?"

"On a bridge over the Seine, at Picquigny."

"I would thou hadst been there," said the Duke, looking to Oxford, "with a good axe in thy hand, to strike one fair blow for England, and another for Burgundy. My grandfather was treacherously slain at just such a meeting, at the Bridge of Montereau, upon the Yonne."

"To prevent a similar chance," said the chancellor, "a strong barricade, such as closes the cages in which men keep wild beasts, was raised in the midst of the bridge, and prevented the possibility of their even touching each other's hands."

"Ha, ha! By Saint George, that smells of Louis's craft and caution; for the Englishman, to give him his due, is as little acquainted with fear as with policy. But what terms have they made? Where do the English army winter? What towns, fortresses, and castles are surrendered to them, in pledge, or in perpetuity?"

"None, my liege," said the chancellor. "The English army returns into England, as fast as shipping can be procured to transport them; and Louis will accommodate them with every sail and oar in his dominions, rather than they should not instantly evacuate France."

"And by what concessions has Louis bought a peace so necessary to his affairs?"

"By fair words," said the chancellor, "by liberal presents, and by some five hundred tuns of wine."

"Wine!" exclaimed the Duke — "Heard'st thou ever the like, Signior Philipson? Why, your countrymen are little better than Esau, who sold his birthright for a mess of pottage. Marry, I must confess I never saw an Englishman who loved a dry-lipped bargain."

"I can scarce believe this news," said the Earl of Oxford. "If this Edward were content to cross the sea with filly thousand Englishmen merely to return again, there are in his camp both proud nobles and haughty commons enough to resist his disgraceful purpose."

"The money of Louis," said the statesman, "has found noble hands willing to clutch it. The wine of France has flooded every throat in the English army — the riot and uproar was unbounded — and at one time the town of Amiens, where Louis himself resided, was full of so many English archers, all of them intoxicated, that the person of the King of France was almost in their hands. Their sense of national honour has been lost in the universal revel, and those amongst them who would be more dignified and play the wise politicians say, that having come to France by connivance of the Duke of Burgundy, and that prince having failed to join them with his forces, they have done well, wisely, and gallantly, considering the season of the year, and the impossibility of obtaining quarters, to take tribute of France, and return home in triumph."

"And leave Louis," said Oxford, "at undisturbed freedom to attack Burgundy with all his forces?"

"Not so, friend Philipson," said Duke Charles; "know, that there is a truce betwixt Burgundy and France for the space of seven years, and had not this been granted and signed, it is probable that we might have found some means of marring the treaty betwixt Edward and Louis, even at the expense of affording those voracious islanders beef and beer during the winter months. — Sir Chancellor, you may leave us, but be within reach of a hasty summons."

When his minister left the pavilion, the Duke, who with his rude and imperious character united much kindness, if it could not be termed generosity of disposition, came up to the Lancastrian lord, who stood like one at whose feet a thunderbolt has just broken, and who is still appalled by the terrors of the shock.

"My poor Oxford," he said, "thou art stupefied by this news, which thou canst not doubt must have a fatal effect on the plan which thy brave bosom cherishes with such devoted fidelity. I would for thy sake I could have detained the English a little longer in France; but had I attempted to do so, there were an end of my truce with Louis, and of course to my power to chastise these paltry Cantons, or send forth an expedition to England. As matters stand, give me but a week to punish these mountaineers, and you shall have a larger force than your modesty has requested of me for your enterprise; and, in the meanwhile, I will take care that Blackburn and his cousin-archers have no assistance of shipping from Flanders. Tush, man, never fear it — thou wilt be in England long ere they; and, once more, rely on my assistance — always, thou knowest, the cession of Provence being executed, as in reason. Our cousin Margaret's diamonds we must keep for a time; and perhaps they may pass as a pledge, with some of our own, for the godly purpose of setting at freedom the imprisoned angels of our Flemish usurers, who will not lend even to their sovereign, unless on good current security. To such straits has the disobedient avarice of our estates for the moment reduced us."

"Alas! my Lord," said the dejected nobleman, "I were ungrateful to doubt the sincerity of your good intentions. But who can presume on the events of war, especially when time presses for instant decision? You are pleased to trust me. Let your Highness extend your confidence thus far; I will take my horse and ride after the Landamman, if he hath already set forth. I have little doubt to make such an accommodation with him that you may be secure on all your south-eastern frontiers. You may then with security work your will in Lorraine and Provence."

"Do not speak of it," said the Duke, sharply; "thou forget'st thyself and me, when thou supposest that a prince, who has pledged his word to his people, can recall it like a merchant chaffering for his paltry wares. Go to — we will assist you, but we will be ourselves judge of the time and manner. Yet, having both kind will to our distressed cousin of Anjou, and being your good friend, we will not linger in the matter. Our host have orders to break up this evening and direct their march against Neufchatel, where these proud Swiss shall have a taste of the fire and sword which they have provoked."

Oxford sighed deeply, but made no farther remonstrance; in which he acted wisely, since it was likely to have exasperated the fiery temper of the sovereign to whom it was addressed, while it was certain that it would not in the slightest degree alter his resolution.

He took farewell of the Duke, and returned to Colvin, whom he found immersed in the business of his department, and preparing for the removal of the artillery, an operation which the clumsiness of the ordnance, and the execrable state of the roads, rendered at that time a much more troublesome operation than at present, though it is even still one of the most laborious movements attending the march of an army. The Master of the Ordnance welcomed Oxford with much glee, and congratulated himself on the distinguished honour of enjoying his company during the campaign, and acquainted him, that, by the especial command of the Duke, he had made fitting preparations for his accommodation, suitable to the disguised character which he meant to maintain, but in every other respect as convenient as a camp could admit of.

CHAPTER XXIX

A mirthful man he was — the snows of age
Fell, but they did not chill him. Gaiety,
Even in life's closing, touch'd his teeming brain
With such wild visions as the setting sun
Raises in front of some hoar glacier,
Painting the bleak ice with a thousand hues.

OLD PLAY.

Leaving the Earl of Oxford in attendance on the stubborn Duke of Burgundy during an expedition, which the one represented as a brief excursion more resembling a hunting party than a campaign, and which the other considered in a much graver and more perilous light, we return to Arthur de Vere, or the younger Philipson, as he continued to be called, who was conducted by his guide with fidelity and success, but certainly very slowly, upon his journey into Provence.

The state of Lorraine, overrun by the Duke of Burgundy's army, and infested at the same time by different scattered bands, who took the field, or held out the castles, as they alleged, for the interest of Count Ferrand de Vaudemont, rendered journeying so dangerous, that it was often necessary to leave the main road, and to take circuitous tracks, in order to avoid such unfriendly encounters as travellers might otherwise have met with.

Arthur, taught by sad experience to distrust strange guides, found himself, nevertheless, in this eventful and perilous journey, disposed to rest considerable confidence in his present conductor, Thiebault, a Provençal by birth, intimately acquainted with the roads which they took, and, as far as he could judge, disposed to discharge his office with fidelity. Prudence alike, and the habits which he had acquired in travelling, as well as the character of a merchant which he still sustained, induced him to waive the *morgue,* or haughty superiority of a knight and noble towards an inferior personage, especially as he rightly conjectured that free intercourse with this man, whose acquirements seemed of a superior cast, was likely to render him a judge of his opinions and disposition towards him. In return for his condescension, he obtained a good deal of information concerning the province which he was approaching.

As they drew near the boundaries of Provence, the communications of Thiebault became more fluent and interesting. He could not only tell the name and history of each romantic castle which they passed, in their devious and doubtful route, but had at his command the chivalrous history of the noble knights and barons to whom they now pertained, or had belonged in earlier days, and could recount their exploits against the Saracens, by repelling their attacks upon Christendom, or their efforts to recover the Holy Sepulchre from Pagan hands. In the course of such narrations, Thiebault was led to speak of the Troubadours, a race of native poets of Provençal origin, differing widely from the minstrels of Normandy, and the adjacent provinces of France, with whose tales of chivalry, as well as the numerous translations of their works into Norman-French and English, Arthur, like most of the noble youth of his country, was intimately acquainted and deeply imbued. Thiebault boasted that his grandsire, of humble birth indeed, but of distinguished talent, was one of this gifted race, whose compositions produced so great an effect on the temper and manners of their age and country. It was, however, to be regretted, that inculcating as the prime duty of life a fantastic spirit of gallantry, which sometimes crossed the Platonic bound prescribed to it, the poetry of the Troubadours was too frequently used to soften and seduce the heart, and corrupt the principles.[16]

---

[16] The smoothness of the Provençal dialect, partaking strongly of the Latin, which had been spoken for so many ages in what was called for distinction's sake the Roman Province of Gaul, and the richness and fertility of a country abounding in all that could delight the senses and soothe the imagination, naturally disposed the inhabitants to cultivate the art of poetry, and to value and foster the genius of those who distinguished themselves by attaining excellence in it. Troubadours, that is, *finders,* or *inventors,* equivalent to the northern term of *makers,* arose in every class, from the lowest to the highest, and success in their art dignified men of the meanest rank, and added fresh honours to those who were born in the Patrician file of society. War and love, more especially the latter, were dictated to them by the chivalry of the times as the especial subjects of their verse. Such, too, were the themes of our northern minstrels. But whilst the latter confined themselves in general to those well-known metrical histories in which scenes of strife and combat mingled with adventures of enchantment, and fables of giants and monsters subdued by valiant champions, such as best attracted the ears of the somewhat duller and more barbarous warriors of northern France, of Britain, and of Germany — the more lively Troubadours produced poems which turned on human passion, and on love, affection, and dutiful observance, with which the faithful knight was

Arthur's attention was called to this peculiarity, by Thiebault sinking, which he could do with good skill, the history of a Troubadour, named William Cabestainy, who loved, *par amours*, a noble and beautiful lady, Margaret, the wife of a baron called Raymond de Rousillon. The jealous husband obtained proof of his dishonour, and having put Cabestainy to death by assassination, he took his heart from his bosom, and causing it to be dressed like that of an animal, ordered it to be served up to his lady; and when she had eaten of the horrible mess, told her of

---

bound to regard the object of his choice, and the honour and respect with which she was bound to recompense his faithful services.

Thus far it cannot be disputed, that the themes selected by the Troubadours were those on which poetry is most naturally exerted, and with the best chance of rising to excellence. But it usually happens, that when any one of the fine arts is cultivated exclusively, the taste of those who practise and admire its productions loses sight of nature, simplicity, and true taste, and the artist endeavours to discover, while the public learn to admire, some more complicated system, in which pedantry supersedes the dictates of natural feeling, and metaphysical ingenuity is used instead of the more obvious qualifications of simplicity and good sense. Thus, with the unanimous approbation of their hearers, the Troubadours framed for themselves a species of poetry describing and inculcating a system of metaphysical affection as inconsistent with nature as the minstrel's tales of magicians and monsters; with this evil to society, that it was calculated deeply to injure its manners and its morals. Every Troubadour, or good Knight, who took the maxims of their poetical school for his rule, was bound to choose a lady-love, the fairest and noblest to whom he had access, to whom he dedicated at once his lyre and his sword, and who, married or single, was to be the object to whom his life, words, and actions, were to be devoted. On the other hand, a lady thus honoured and distinguished, was bound, by accepting the services of such a gallant, to consider him as her lover, and on all due occasions to grace him as such with distinguished marks of personal favour. It is true, that according to the best authorities, the intercourse betwixt her lover and herself was to be entirely of a Platonic character, and the loyal swain was not to require, or the chosen lady to grant, any thing beyond the favour she might in strict modesty bestow. Even under this restriction, the system was like to make wild work with the domestic peace of families, since it permitted, or rather enjoined, such familiarity betwixt the fair dame and her poetical admirer; and very frequently human passions, placed in such a dangerous situation, proved too strong to be confined within the metaphysical bounds prescribed to them by so fantastic and perilous a system. The injured husbands on many occasions avenged themselves with severity, and even with dreadful cruelty, on the unfaithful ladies, and the musical skill and chivalrous character of the lover proved no protection to his person. But the real spirit of the system was seen in this, that in the poems of the other Troubadours, by whom such events are recorded, their pity is all bestowed on the hapless lovers, while, without the least allowance for just provocation, the injured husband is held up to execration.

what her banquet was composed. The lady replied, that since she had been made to partake of food so precious, no coarser morsel should ever after cross her lips. She persisted in her resolution, and thus starved herself to death. The Troubadour, who celebrated this tragic history, had displayed in his composition a good deal of poetic art. Glossing over the error of the lovers as the fault of their destiny, dwelling on their tragical fate with considerable pathos, and finally, execrating the blind fury of the husband with the full fervour of poetical indignation, he recorded, with vindictive pleasure, how every bold knight and true lover in the south of France assembled to besiege the baron's castle, stormed it by main force, left not one stone upon another, and put the tyrant himself to an ignominious death. Arthur was interested in the melancholy tale, which even beguiled him of a few tears; but as he thought further on its purport, he dried his eyes, and said, with some sternness — "Thiebault, sing me no more such lays. I have heard my father say, that the readiest mode to corrupt a Christian man, is to bestow upon vice the pity and the praise which are due only to virtue. Your Baron of Roussillon is a monster of cruelty; but your unfortunate lovers were not the less guilty. It is by giving fair names to foul actions, that those who would start at real vice are led to practise its lessons, under the disguise of virtue."

"I would you knew, Signior," answered Thiebault, "that this Lay of Cabestainy, and the Lady Margaret of Roussillon, is reckoned a masterpiece of the joyous science. Fie, sir, you are too young to be so strict a censor of morals. What will you do when your head is gray, if you are thus severe when it is scarcely brown?"

"A head which listens to folly in youth, will hardly be honourable in old age," answered Arthur.

Thiebault had no mind to carry the dispute farther.

"It is not for me to contend with your worship. I only think, with every true son of chivalry and song, that a knight without a mistress is like a sky without a star."

"Do I not know that?" answered Arthur; "but yet better remain in darkness than be guided by such false lights as shower down vice and pestilence."

"Nay, it may be your seignorie is right," answered the guide. "It is certain, that even in Provence here we have lost much of our keen judgment on matters of love, — its difficulties, its intricacies, and its errors, since the Troubadours are no longer regarded as usual, and since the High and Noble Parliament of Love[17] has ceased to hold its sittings."

"But in these latter days," continued the Provençal, "kings, dukes, and sovereigns, instead of being the foremost and most faithful vassals of the Court of Cupid, are themselves the slaves of selfishness, and love of gain. Instead of winning hearts by breaking lances in the lists, they are breaking the hearts of their impoverished vassals by the most cruel exactions — instead of attempting to deserve the smile and favours of their lady-loves, they are meditating how to steal castles, towns, and provinces from their neighbours. But long life to the good and venerable King René! While he has an acre of land left, his residence will be the resort of valiant knights, whose only aim is praise in arms, of true lovers, who are persecuted by fortune, and of high-toned harpers, who know how to celebrate faith and valour."

Arthur, interested in learning something more precise than common fame had taught him on the subject of this prince, easily induced the talkative Provençal to enlarge upon the virtues of his old sovereign's character, as just, joyous, and debonair, a friend to the most noble exercises of the chase and the tilt-yard, and still more so to the joyous science of Poetry and Music; who gave away more revenue than he received, in largesses to knights-errant and itinerant musicians, with whom his petty court

---

[17] In Provence, during the flourishing time of the Troubadours, Love was esteemed so grave and formal a part of the business of life, that a Parliament or High Court of Love was appointed for deciding such questions. This singular tribunal was, it may be supposed, conversant with more of imaginary than of real suits; but it is astonishing with what cold and pedantic ingenuity the Troubadours of whom it consisted set themselves to plead and to decide, upon reasoning which was not less singular and able than out of place, the absurd questions which their own fantastic imaginations had previously devised. There, for example, is a reported case, of much celebrity, where a lady sitting in company with three persons, who were her admirers, listened to one with the most favourable smiles, while she pressed the hand of the second, and touched with her own the foot of the third. It was a case much agitated and keenly contested in the l'arliament of Love, which of these rivals had received the distinguishing mark of the lady's favour. Much ingenuity was wasted on this and similar cases, of which there is a collection, in all judicial form of legal proceedings, under the title of *Arrets d'Amour* (Adjudged cases of the Court of Love).

was crowded, as one of the very few in which the ancient hospitality was still maintained.

Such was the picture which Thiebault drew of the last minstrel-monarch; and though the eulogium was exaggerated, perhaps the facts were not overcharged.

Born of royal parentage, and with high pretensions, René had at no period of his life been able to match his fortunes to his claims. Of the kingdoms to which he asserted right, nothing remained in his possession but the county of Provence itself, a fair and fertile principality, but diminished by the many claims which France had acquired upon portions of it by advances of money to supply the personal expenses of its master, and by other portions, which Burgundy, to whom René had been a prisoner, held in pledge for his ransom. In his youth he engaged in more than one military enterprise, in the hope of attaining some part of the territory of which he was styled sovereign. His courage is not impeached, but fortune did not smile on his military adventures; and he seems at last to have become sensible, that the power of admiring and celebrating warlike merit, is very different from possessing that quality. In fact, René was a prince of very moderate parts, endowed with a love of the fine arts, which he carried to extremity, and a degree of good humour, which never permitted him to repine at fortune, but rendered its possessor happy, when a prince of keener feelings would have died of despair. This insouciant, light-tempered, gay, and thoughtless disposition, conducted René, free from all the passions which embitter life, and often shorten it, to a hale and mirthful old age. Even domestic losses, which often affect those who are proof against mere reverses of fortune, made no deep impression on the feelings of this cheerful old monarch. Most of his children had died young; René took it not to heart. His daughter Margaret's marriage with the powerful Henry of England was considered a connexion much above the fortunes of the King of the Troubadours. But in the issue, instead of René deriving any splendour from the match, he was involved in the misfortunes of his daughter, and repeatedly obliged to impoverish himself to supply her ransom. Perhaps in his private soul the old king did not think these losses so mortifying, as the necessity of receiving Margaret into his court and family. On fire when reflecting on the losses she had sustained, mourning over friends slain and kingdoms lost, the proudest and most passionate of princesses was ill suited to dwell with the gayest and best-humoured of sovereigns, whose pursuits she contemned, and whose lightness of temper, for finding comfort in such trifles, she could not forgive. The discomfort attached to her presence, and vindictive recollections, embarrassed the good-humoured old monarch, though it was unable to drive him beyond his equanimity.

Another distress pressed him more sorely. — Yolande, a daughter of his first wife, Isabella, had succeeded to his claims upon the Duchy of Lorraine, and transmitted them to her son, Ferrand, Count of Vaudemont, a young man of courage and spirit, engaged at this time in the apparently desperate undertaking of making his title good against the Duke of Burgundy, who, with little right, but great power, was seizing upon and overrunning this rich Duchy, which he laid claim to as a male fief. And to conclude, while the aged king on one side beheld his dethroned daughter in hopeless despair, and on the other his disinherited grandson, in vain attempting to recover part of their rights, he had the additional misfortune to know, that his nephew, Louis of France, and his cousin, the Duke of Burgundy, were secretly contending which should succeed him in that portion of Provence which he still continued to possess; and that it was only jealousy of each other which prevented his being despoiled of this last remnant of his territory. Yet amid all this distress, René feasted and received guests, danced, sung, composed poetry, used the pencil or brush with no small skill, devised and conducted festivals and processions, and studying to promote, as far as possible, the immediate mirth and good-humour of his subjects, if he could not materially enlarge their more permanent prosperity, was never mentioned by them, excepting as *Le bon Roi René,* a distinction conferred on him down to the present day, and due to him certainly by the qualities of his heart, if not by those of his head.

Whilst Arthur was receiving from his guide a full account of the peculiarities of King René, they entered the territories of that merry monarch. It was late in the autumn, and about the period when the south-eastern counties of France rather show to least advantage. The foliage of the olive-tree is then decayed and withered; and as it predominates in the landscape, and resembles the scorched complexion of the soil itself, an ashen and arid hue is given to the whole. Still, however, there were scenes in the hilly and pastoral parts of the country, where the quantity of evergreens relieved the eye even in this dead season.

The appearance of the country, in general, had much in it that was peculiar.

The travellers perceived at every turn some marks of the King's singular character. Provence as the part of Gaul which first received Roman civilisation, and as having been still longer the residence of the Grecian colony who founded Marseilles, is more full of the splendid relics of ancient architecture than any other country in Europe, Italy and Greece excepted. The good taste of the King René had dictated some attempts to clear out and restore these memorials of antiquity. Was there a triumphal arch, or an ancient temple — huts and hovels were cleared away from its vicinity, and means were used at least to retard the approach of ruin. Was there a marble fountain, which superstition had dedicated to some sequestered naiad — it was surrounded by olives, almond, and orange trees — its cistern was repaired, and taught once more to retain its crystal treasures. The huge amphitheatres, and gigantic colonnades, experienced the same anxious care, attesting that the noblest specimens of the fine arts found one admirer and preserver in King René, even during the course of those which are termed the dark and barbarous ages.

A change of manners could also be observed in passing from Burgundy and Lorraine, where society relished of German bluntness, into the pastoral country of Provence, where the influence of a fine climate and melodious language, joined to the pursuits of the romantic old monarch, with the universal taste for music and poetry, had introduced a civilisation of manners, which approached to affectation. The shepherd literally marched abroad in the morning, piping his flocks forth to the pasture, with some love sonnet, the composition of an amorous Troubadour; and his "fleecy care" seemed actually to be under the influence of his music, instead of being ungraciously insensible to its melody, as is the case in colder climates. Arthur observed, too, that the Provençal sheep, instead of being driven before the shepherd, regularly followed him, and did not disperse to feed until the swain, by turning his face round to them, remaining stationary, and executing variations on the air which he was playing, seemed to remind them that it was proper to do so. While in motion, his huge dog, of a species which is trained to face the wolf, and who is respected by the sheep as their guardian, and not feared as their tyrant, followed his master with his ears pricked, like the chief critic and prime judge of the performance, at some tones of which he seldom failed to intimate disapprobation; while the flock, like the generality of an audience, followed in unanimous though silent applause. At the hour of noon, the shepherd had sometimes acquired an augmentation to his audience, as some comely matron or blooming maiden, with whom he had rendezvoused by such a fountain as we have described, and who listened to the husband's or lover's chalumeau, or mingled her voice with his in the duets, of which the songs of the Troubadours have left so many examples. In the cool of the evening, the dance on the village green, or the concert before the hamlet door; the little repast of fruits, cheese, and bread, which the traveller was readily invited to share, gave new charms to the illusion, and seemed in earnest to point out Provence as the Arcadia of France.

But the greatest singularity was, in the eyes of Arthur, the total absence of armed men and soldiers in this peaceful country. In England, no man stirred without his long-bow, sword, and buckler. In France, the hind wore armour even when he was betwixt the stilts of his plough. In Germany, you could not look along a mile of highway, but the eye was encountered by clouds of dust, out of which were seen, by fits, waving feathers and flashing armour. Even in Switzerland, the peasant, if he had a journey to make, though but of a mile or two, cared not to travel without his halberd and two-handed sword. But in Provence all seemed quiet and peaceful, as if the music of the land had lulled to sleep all its wrathful passions. Now and then a mounted cavalier might pass them, the harp at whose saddle-bow, or carried by one of his attendants, attested the character of a Troubadour, which was affected by men of all ranks; and then only a short sword on his left thigh, borne for show rather than use, was a necessary and appropriate part of his equipment.

"Peace," said Arthur, as he looked around him, "is an inestimable jewel; but it will be soon snatched from those who are not prepared with heart and hand to defend it."

The sight of the ancient and interesting town of Aix, where King René held his court, dispelled reilections of a general character, and recalled to the young Englishman the peculiar mission on which he was engaged.

He then required to know from the Provençal, Thiebault, whether his instructions were to leave him, now that he had successfully attained the end of his journey.

"My instructions," answered Thiebault, "are to remain in Aix while there is any chance of your seignorie's continuing there, to be of such use to you as you may require, either as a guide or an attendant, and to keep these men in readiness to wait upon you when you have occasion for messengers or guards. With your approbation, I will see them disposed of in fitting quarters, and receive my farther instructions from your seignorie wherever you please to appoint me. I propose this separation, because I understand it is your present pleasure to be private."

"I must go to court," answered Arthur, "without any delay. Wait for me in half an hour by that fountain in the street, which projects into the air such a magnificent pillar of water, surrounded, I would almost swear, by a vapour like steam, serving as a shroud to the jet which it envelopes."

"The jet is so surrounded," answered the Provençal, "because it is supplied by a hot-spring rising from the bowels of the earth, and the touch of frost on this autumn morning makes the vapour more distinguishable than usual. — But if it is good King René whom you seek, you will find him at this time walking in his chimney. Do not be afraid of approaching him, for there never was a monarch so easy of access, especially to good-looking strangers like you, seignorie."

"But his ushers," said Arthur, "will not admit me into his hall."

"His hall!" repeated Thiebault — "Whose hall?"

"Why, King René's, I apprehend. If he is walking in a chimney, it can only be in that of his hall, and a stately one it must be to give him room for such exercise."

"You mistake my meaning," said the guide, laughing. — "What we call King René's chimney is the narrow parapet yonder; it extends between these two towers, has an exposure to the south, and is sheltered in every other direction. Yonder it is his pleasure to walk and enjoy the beams of the sun, on such cool mornings as the present. It nurses, he says, his poetical vein. If you approach his promenade he will readily speak to you, unless, indeed, he is in the very act of a poetical composition."

Arthur could not forbear smiling at the thoughts of a king, eighty years of age, broken down with misfortunes and beset with dangers, who yet amused himself with walking in an open parapet, and composing poetry in presence of all such of his loving subjects as chose to look on.

"If you will walk a few steps this way," said Thiebault, "you may see the good King, and judge whether or not you will accost him at present. I will dispose of the people, and await your orders at the fountain in the Corso."

Arthur saw no objection to the proposal of his guide, and was not unwilling to have an opportunity of seeing something of the good King René, before he was introduced to his presence.

CHAPTER XXX

Ay, this is he who wears the wreath of bays
Wove by Apollo and the Sisters Nine,
Which Jove's dread lightning scathes not. He hath doft
The cumbrous helm of steel, and flung aside
The yet more galling diadem of gold;
While, with a leafy circlet round his brows,
He reigns the King of Lovers and of Poets.

A cautious approach to the chimney, that is, the favourite walk of the King, who is described by Shakspeare as bearing

—— the style of King of Naples,
Of both the Sicilies, and Jerusalem,
Yet not so wealthy as an English yeoman,

gave Arthur the perfect survey of his Majesty in person. He saw an old man, with locks and beard, which, in amplitude and whiteness, nearly rivalled those of the envoy from Schwitz, but with a fresh and ruddy colour in his cheek, and an eye of great vivacity. His dress was showy to a degree almost inconsistent with his years; and his step, not only firm but full of alertness and vivacity, while occupied in traversing the short and sheltered walk, which he had chosen, rather for comfort than for privacy, showed juvenile vigour still animating an aged frame. The old King carried his tablets and a pencil in his hand, seeming totally abstracted in his own thoughts, and indifferent to being observed by several persons from the public street beneath his elevated promenade.

Of these, some, from their dress and manner, seemed themselves Troubadours; for they held in their hands rebecks, rotes, small portable harps, and other indications of their profession. Such appeared to be stationary, as if engaged in observing and recording their remarks on the meditations of their Prince. Other passengers, bent on their own more serious affairs, looked up to the King as to some one whom they were accustomed to see daily, but never passed without doffing their bonnets, and expressing, by a suitable obeisance, a respect and affection towards his person, which appeared to make up in cordiality of feeling what it wanted in deep and solemn deference.

René, in the meanwhile, was apparently unconscious both of

the gaze of such as stood still, or the greeting of those who passed on, his mind seeming altogether engrossed with the apparent labour of some arduous task in poetry or music. He walked fast or slow as best suited the progress of composition. At times he stopped to mark hastily down on his tablets something which seemed to occur to him as deserving of preservation; at other times he dashed out what he had written, and flung down the pencil as if in a sort of despair. On these occasions, the Sibylline leaf was carefully picked up by a beautiful page, his only attendant, who reverently observed the first suitable opportunity of restoring it again to his royal hand. The same youth bore a viol, on which, at a signal from his master, he occasionally struck a few musical notes, to which the old King listened, now with a soothed and satisfied air, now with a discontented and anxious brow. At times, his enthusiasm rose so high, that he even hopped and skipped with an activity which his years did not promise; at other times his motions were extremely slow, and occasionally he stood still, like one wrapped in the deepest and most anxious meditation. When he chanced to look on the group which seemed to watch his motions, and who ventured even to salute him with a murmur of applause, it was only to distinguish them with a friendly and good-humoured nod; a salutation with which, likewise, he failed not to reply to the greeting of the occasional passengers, when his earnest attention to his task, whatever it might be, permitted him to observe them.

At length the royal eye lighted upon Arthur, whose attitude of silent observation, and the distinction of his figure, pointed him out as a stranger. René beckoned to his page, who, receiving his master's commands in a whisper, descended from the royal chimney, to the broader platform beneath, which was open to general resort. The youth, addressing Arthur with much courtesy, informed him the King desired to speak with him. The young Englishman had no alternative but that of approaching, though pondering much in his own mind how he ought to comport himself towards such a singular specimen of royalty.

When he drew near, King René addressed him in a tone of courtesy not unmingled with dignity, and Arthur's awe in his immediate presence was greater than he himself could have anticipated from his previous conception of the royal character.

"You are, from your appearance, fair sir," said King René,

"a stranger in this country. By what name must we call you, and to what business are we to ascribe the happiness of seeing you at our court?"

Arthur remained a moment silent, and the good old man imputing it to awe and timidity, proceeded in an encouraging tone.

"Modesty in youth is ever commendable; you are doubtless an acolyte in the noble and joyous science of Minstrelsy and Music, drawn hither by the willing welcome which we afford to the professors of those arts, in which — praise be to Our Lady and the Saints! — we have ourself been deemed a proficient."

"I do not aspire to the honours of a Troubadour," answered Arthur.

"I believe you," answered the King, "for your speech smacks of the northern, or Norman-French, such as is spoken in England and other unrefined nations. But you are a minstrel, perhaps, from these ultramontane parts. Be assured we despise not their efforts; for we have listened, not without pleasure and instruction, to many of their bold and wild romaunts, which, though rude in device and language, and therefore far inferior to the regulated poetry of our Troubadours, have yet something in their powerful and rough measure, which occasionally rouses the heart like the sound of a trumpet."

"I have felt the truth of your Grace's observation, when I have heard the songs of my country," said Arthur; "but I have neither skill nor audacity to imitate what I admire — My latest residence has been in Italy."

"You are perhaps then a proficient in painting," said René; "an art which applies itself to the eye as poetry and music do to the ear, and is scarce less in esteem with us. If you are skilful in the art, you have come to a monarch who loves it, and the fair country in which it is practised."

"In simple truth, Sire, I am an Englishman, and my hand has been too much welk'd and hardened by practice of the bow, the lance, and the sword, to touch the harp or even the pencil."

"An Englishman!" said René, obviously relaxing in the warmth of his welcome; "and what brings you here? England and I have long had little friendship together."

"It is even on that account that I am here," said Arthur. "I come to pay my homage to your Grace's daughter, the Princess Margaret of Anjou, whom I and many true Englishmen regard still as our Queen, though traitors have usurped her title."

"Alas, good youth," said René, "I must grieve for you, while I respect your loyalty and faith. Had my daughter Margaret been of my mind, she had long since abandoned pretensions, which have drowned in seas of blood the noblest and bravest of her adherents."

The King seemed about to say more, but checked himself.

"Go to my palace," he said; "inquire for the Seneschal Hugh de Saint Cyr, he will give thee the means of seeing Margaret — that is, if it be her will to see thee. If not, good English youth, return to my palace, and thou shalt have hospitable entertainment; for a King who loves minstrelsy, music, and painting, is ever most sensible to the claims of honour, virtue, and loyalty; and I read in thy looks thou art possessed of these qualities, and willingly believe thou mayst, in more quiet times, aspire to share the honours of the joyous science. But if thou hast a heart to be touched by the sense of beauty and fair proportion, it will leap within thee at the first sight of my palace, the stately grace of which may be compared to the faultless form of some high-bred dame, or the artful, yet seemingly simple modulations of such a tune as we have been now composing."

The King seemed disposed to take his instrument, and indulge the youth with a rehearsal of the strain he had just arranged; but Arthur at that moment experienced the painful internal feeling of that peculiar species of shame, which well-constructed minds feel when they see others express a great assumption of importance, with a confidence that they are exciting admiration, when in fact they are only exposing themselves to ridicule. Arthur, in short, took leave, "in very shame," of the King of Naples, both the Sicilies, and Jerusalem, in a manner somewhat more abrupt than ceremony demanded. The King looked after him, with some wonder at this want of breeding, which, however, he imputed to his visitor's insular education, and then again began to twangle his viol.

"The old fool!" said Arthur; "his daughter is dethroned, his dominions crumbling to pieces, his family on the eve of becoming extinct, his grandson driven from one lurking-place to another, and expelled from his mother's inheritance, — and he can find amusement in these fopperies! I thought him, with his long white beard, like Nicholas Bonstetten; but the old Swiss is a

Solomon compared with him."

As these and other reflections, highly disparaging to King René, passed through Arthur's mind, he reached the place of rendezvous, and found Thiebault beneath the steaming fountain, forced from one of those hot springs which had been the delight of the Romans from an early period. Thiebault, having assured his master that his retinue, horse and man, were so disposed as to be ready on an instant's call, readily undertook to guide him to King René's palace, which, from its singularity, and indeed its beauty of architecture, deserved the eulogium which the old monarch had bestowed upon it. The front consisted of three towers of Roman architecture, two of them being placed on the angles of the palace, and the third, which served the purpose of a mausoleum, forming a part of the group, though somewhat detached from the other buildings. This last was a structure of beautiful proportions. The lower part of the edifice was square, serving as a sort of pedestal to the upper part, which was circular, and surrounded by columns of massive granite. The other two towers at the angles of the palace were round, and also ornamented with pillars, and with a double row of windows. In front of, and connected with, these Roman remains, to which a date had been assigned as early as the fifth or sixth century, arose the ancient palace of the Counts of Provence, built a century or two later, but where a rich Gothic or Moorish front contrasted, and yet harmonized, with the more regular and massive architecture of the lords of the world. It is not more than thirty or forty years since this very curious remnant of antique art was destroyed to make room for new public buildings, which have never yet been erected.

Arthur really experienced some sensation of the kind which the old King had prophesied, and stood looking with wonder at the ever-open gate of the palace, into which men of all kinds seemed to enter freely. After looking around for a few minutes, the young Englishman ascended the steps of a noble portico, and asked of a porter, as old and as lazy as a great man's domestic ought to be, for the seneschal named to him by the King. The corpulent janitor, with great politeness, put the stranger under the charge of a page, who ushered him to a chamber, in which he found another aged functionary of higher rank, with a comely face, a clear composed eye, and a brow which, having never been knit into gravity, intimated that the seneschal of Aix was a proficient in the philosophy of his royal master. He recognised Arthur the moment he addressed him.

"You speak northern French, fair sir; you have lighter hair and a fairer complexion than the natives of this country — You ask after Queen Margaret — By all these marks I read you English — Her Grace of England is at this moment paying a vow at the monastery of Mont Saint Victoire, and if your name be Arthur Philipson, I have commission to forward you to her presence immediately, — that is, as soon as you have tasted of the royal provision."

The young man would have remonstrated, but the seneschal left him no leisure.

"Meat and mass," he said, "never hindered work — it is perilous to youth to journey too far on an empty stomach — he himself would take a mouthful with the Queen's guest, and pledge him to boot in a flask of old Hermitage."

The board was covered with an alacrity which showed that hospitality was familiarly exercised in King René's dominions. Pasties, dishes of game, the gallant boar's head, and other delicacies, were placed on the table, and the seneschal played the merry host, frequently apologizing (unnecessarily) for showing an indifferent example, as it was his duty to carve before King René, and the good King was never pleased unless he saw him feed lustily as well as carve featly.

"But for you, sir guest, eat freely, since you may not gee food again till sunset; for the good Queen takes her misfortunes so to heart that sighs are her food, and her tears a bottle of drink, as the Psalmist hath it. But I bethink me you will need steeds for yourself and your equipage to reach Mont Saint Victoire, which is seven miles from Aix."

Arthur intimated that he had a guide and horses in attendance, and begged permission to take his adieu. The worthy seneschal, his fair round belly graced with a gold chain, accompanied him to the gate with a step, which a gentle fit of the gout had rendered uncertain, b it which, he assured Arthur, would vanish before three days' use of the hot springs. Thiebault appeared before the gate, not with the tired steeds from which they had dismounted an hour since, but with fresh palfreys from the stable of the King.

"They are yours from the moment you have put foot in stirrup," said the seneschal; "the good King René never received back as his property a horse which he had lent to a guest; and that is perhaps one reason why his Highness and we of his household must walk often a-foot."

Here the seneschal exchanged greetings with his young visitor, who rode forth to seek Queen Margaret's place of temporary retirement at the celebrated monastery of Saint Victoire. He demanded of his guide in which direction it lay, who pointed, with an air of triumph, to a mountain three thousand feet and upwards in height, which arose at five or six miles' distance from the town, and which its bold and rocky summit rendered the most distinguished object of the landscape. Thiebault spoke of it with unusual glee and energy, so much so as to lead Arthur to conceive that his trusty squire had not neglected to avail himself of the lavish hospitality of *Le bon Roi René.* Thiebault, however, continued to expatiate on the fame of the mountain and monastery. They derived their name, he said, from a great victory which was gained by a Roman general, named Caio Mario, against two large armies of Saracens with ultramontane names, (the Teutones probably and Cimbri,) in gratitude to Heaven for which victory Caio Mario vowed to build a monastery on the mountain for the service of the Virgin Mary, in honour of whom he had been baptized. With all the importance of a local connoisseur, Thiebault proceeded to prove his general assertion by specific facts.

"Yonder," he said, "was the camp of the Saracens, from which, when the battle was apparently decided, their wives and women rushed, with horrible screams, dishevelled hair, and the gestures of furies, and for a time prevailed in stopping the flight of the men." He pointed out too the river, for access to which, cut off by the superior generalship of the Romans, the barbarians, whom he called Saracens, hazarded the action, and whose streams they empurpled with their blood. In short, he mentioned many circumstances which showed how accurately tradition will preserve the particulars of ancient events, even whilst forgetting, misstating, and confounding dates and persons.

Perceiving that Arthur lent him a not unwilling ear, — for it may be supposed that the education of a youth bred up in the heat of civil wars, was not. well qualified to criticise his account of the wars of a distant period, — the Provençal, when he had exhausted this topic, drew up close to his master's side, and asked, in a suppressed tone, whether he knew, or was desirous of being made acquainted with, the cause of Margaret's having left Aix, to establish herself in the monastery of Saint Victoire?

"For the accomplishment of a vow," answered Arthur; "all the world knows it."

"All Aix knows the contrary," said Thiebault; "and I can tell you the truth, so I were sure it would not offend your seignorie."

"The truth can offend no reasonable man, so it be expressed in the terms of which Queen Margaret must be spoken in the presence of an Englishman."

Thus replied Arthur, willing to receive what information he could gather, and desirous, at the same time, to check the petulance of his attendant.

"I have nothing," replied his follower, "to state in disparagement of the gracious Queen, whose only misfortune is, that, like her royal father, she has more titles than towns. Besides, I know well that you Englishmen, though you speak wildly of your sovereigns yourselves, will not permit others to fail in respect to them."

"Say on, then," answered Arthur.

"Your seignorie must know, then," said Thiebault, "that the good King René has been much disturbed by the deep melancholy which afflicted Queen Margaret, and has bent himself with all his power to change it into a gayer humour. He made entertainments in public and in private; he assembled minstrels and troubadours, whose music and poetry might have drawn smiles from one on his death-bed. The whole country resounded with mirth and glee, and the gracious Queen could not stir abroad in the most private manner, but before she had gone a hundred paces, she lighted on an ambush, consisting of some pretty pageant, or festivous mummery, composed often by the good King himself, which interrupted her solitude, in purpose of relieving her heavy thoughts with some pleasant pastime. But the Queen's deep melancholy rejected all these modes of dispelling it, and at length she confined herself to her own apartments, and absolutely refused to see even her royal father, because he generally brought into her presence those whose productions he thought likely to soothe her sorrow. Indeed, she seemed to hear the harpers with loathing, and, excepting one wandering English-man, who sung a rude and melancholy ballad, which threw her into a flood of tears, and to whom she gave a chain of price, she never seemed to look at or be conscious of the presence of any one. And at length, as I have had the honour to tell your seignorie, she refused to see even her royal father unless he came alone; and that he found no heart to do."

"I wonder not at it," said the young man; "by the White Swan, I am rather surprised his mummery drove her not to frenzy."

"Something like it indeed took place," said Thiebault; "and I will tell your seignorie how it chanced. You must know that good King René, unwilling to abandon his daughter to the foul fiend of melancholy, bethought him of making a grand effort. You must know further, that the King, powerful in all the craft of Troubadours and Jongleurs, is held in peculiar esteem for con-ducting mysteries, and other of those gamesome and delightful sports and processions, with which our holy Church permits her graver ceremonies to be relieved and diversified, to the cheering of the hearts of all true children of religion. It is admitted that no one has ever been able to approach his excellence in the ar-rangement of the Fête-Dieu; and the tune to which the devils cudgel King Herod, to the great edification of all Christian spectators, is of our good King's royal composition. He hath danced at Tarsaconne in the ballet of Saint Martha and the Dragon, and was accounted in his own person, the only actor competent to present the Tarrasque. His Highness introduced also a new ritual into the consecration of the Boy Bishop, and composed an entire set of grotesque music for the Festival of Asses. In short, his Grace's strength lies in those pleasing and becoming festivities which strew the path of edification with flowers, and send men dancing and singing on their way to Heaven.

"Now the good King René, feeling his own genius for such recreative compositions, resolved to exert it to the utmost, in the hope that he might thereby relieve the melancholy in which his daughter was plunged, and which infected all that approached her. It chanced, some short time since, that the Queen was absent for certain days, I know not where or on what business, but it gave the good King time to make his preparations. So when his daughter returned, he with much importunity prevailed on her to make part of a religious procession to Saint Sauveur, the principal church in Aix. The Queen, innocent of what was intended, decked herself with solemnity, to witness and partake of what she expected would prove a work of grave piety. But no sooner had she appeared on the esplanade in front of the palace, than more than an hundred masks, dressed up like Turks, Jews, Saracens, Moors, and I know not whom besides, crowded around to offer her their homage, in the character of the Queen of Sheba; and a grotesque piece of music called them to arrange themselves for a ludicrous ballet, in which they addressed the Queen in the most entertaining manner, and with the most extravagant gestures. The Queen, stunned with the noise, and affronted with the petulance of this unexpected onset, would have gone back into the palace; but the doors had been shut by the King's order so soon as she set forth; and her retreat in that direction as cut off. Finding herself excluded from the palace, the Queen advanced to the front of the façade, and endeavoured by signs and words to appease the hubbub, but the maskers, who had their instructions, only answered with songs, music, and shouts."

"I would," said Arthur, "there had been a score of English yeomen in presence, with their quarter-staves, to teach the bawling villains respect for one that has worn the crown of England!"

"All the noise that was made before was silence and soft music," continued Thiebault, "till that when the good King himself appeared, grotesquely dressed in the character of King Solomon" ——

"To whom, of all princes, he has the least resemblance," said Arthur ——

"With such capers and gesticulations of welcome to the Queen of Sheba, as, I am assured by those who saw it, would have brought a dead man alive again, or killed a living man with laughing. Among other properties, he had in his hand a truncheon, somewhat formed like a fool's bauble" ——

"A most fit sceptre for such a sovereign," said Arthur ——

"Which was headed," continued Thiebault, "by a model of the Jewish Temple, finely gilded and curiously cut in pasteboard. He managed this with the utmost grace, and delighted every spectator by his gaiety and activity, excepting the Queen, who, the more he skipped and capered, seemed to be the more incensed, until, on his approaching her to conduct her to the procession, she seemed roused to a sort of frenzy, struck the truncheon out of his hand, and breaking through the crowd, who felt as if a tigress had leapt amongst them from a showman's cart, rushed into the royal court-yard. Ere the order of the scenic representation, which her violence had interrupted, could be restored, the Queen again issued forth, mounted and attended by two or three English cavaliers of her Majesty's suite. She forced her way through the crowd, without regarding either their safety or her own, flew like a hail-storm along the streets, and never drew bridle till she was as far up this same Mont Saint Victoire as the road would permit. She was then received into the convent, and has since remained there; and a vow of penance is the pretext to cover over the quarrel betwixt her and her father."

"How long may it be," said Arthur, "since these things chanced?"

"It is but three days since Queen Margaret left Aix in the manner I have told you. — But we are come as far up the mountain as men usually ride. See, yonder is the monastery rising betwixt two huge rocks, which form the very top of Mont Saint Victoire. There is no more open ground than is afforded by the cleft, into which the convent of Saint Mary of Victory is, as it were, niched; and the access is guarded by the most dangerous precipices. To ascend the mountain, you must keep that narrow path which, winding and turning among the cliffs, leads at length to the summit of the hill, and the gate of the monastery."

"And what becomes of you and the horses?" said Arthur.

"We will rest," said Thiebault, "in the hospital maintained by the good fathers at the bottom of the mountain, for the accommodation of those who attend on pilgrims; — for I promise you the shrine is visited by many who come from afar, and are attended both by man and horse. — Care not for me, — I shall be first under cover; but there muster yonder in the west some threatening clouds, from which your seignorie may suffer inconvenience, unless you reach the convent in time. I will give you an hour to do the feat, and will say you are as active as a chamois hunter, if you reach it within the time."

Arthur looked around him, and did indeed remark a mustering of clouds in the distant west, which threatened soon to change the character of the day, which had hitherto been brilliantly clear, and so serene that the falling of a leaf might have been heard. He therefore turned him to the steep and rocky path which ascended the mountain, sometimes by scaling almost precipitous rocks, and sometimes by reaching their tops by a more circuitous process. It winded through thickets of wild boxwood and other low aromatic shrubs, which afforded some pasture for the mountain goats, but were a bitter annoyance to the traveller who had to press through them. Such obstacles were so frequent, that the full hour allowed by Thiebault had elapsed before he stood on the summit of Mont Saint Victoire, and in front of the singular convent of the same name.

We have already said, that the crest of the mountain, consisting entirely of one bare and solid rock, was divided by a cleft or opening into two heads or peaks, between which the convent was built, occupying all the space between them. The front of the building was of the most ancient and sombre cast of the old Gothic, or rather, as it has been termed, the Saxon; and in that respect corresponded with the savage exterior of the naked cliffs, of which the structure seemed to make a part, and by which it was entirely surrounded, excepting a small open space of more level ground, where, at the expense of much toil, and by carrying earth up the hill, from different spots where they could collect it in small quantities, the good fathers had been able to arrange the accommodations of a garden.

A bell summoned a lay-brother, the porter of this singularly situated monastery, to whom Arthur announced himself as an English merchant, Philipson by name, who came to pay his duty to Queen Margaret. The porter, with much respect, showed the stranger into the convent, and ushered him into a parlour, which, looking towards Aix, commanded an extensive and splendid prospect over the southern and western parts of Provence. This was the direction in which Arthur had approached the mountain from Aix; but the circuitous path by which he had ascended had completely carried him round the hill. The western side of the monastery, to which the parlour looked, commanded the noble view we have mentioned; and a species of balcony, which, connecting the two twin crags, at this place not above four or five yards asunder, ran along the front of the building, and appeared to be constructed for the purpose of enjoying it. But on stepping from one of the windows of the parlour upon this battlemented bartizan, Arthur became aware that the wall on which the parapet rested stretched along the edge of a precipice, which sunk sheer down five hundred feet at least from the foundations of the convent. Surprised and startled at finding himself on so giddy a verge, Arthur turned his eyes from the gulf beneath him to admire the distant landscape, partly illumined, with ominous lustre, by the now westerly sun. The setting beams showed in dark red splendour a vast variety of hill and dale, champaign and cultivated ground, with towns, churches, and castles, some of which rose from among trees, while others seemed founded on rocky eminences; others again lurked by the side of streams or lakes, to which the heat and drought of the climate naturally attracted them.

The rest of the landscape presented similar objects when the weather was serene, but they were now rendered indistinct, or altogether obliterated, by the sullen shade of the approaching clouds, which gradually spread over great part of the horizon, and threatened altogether to eclipse the sun, though the lord of the horizon still struggled to maintain his influence, and, like a dying hero, seemed most glorious even in the moment of defeat. Wild sounds, like groans and howls, formed by the wind in the numerous caverns of the rocky mountain, added to the terrors of the scene, and seemed to foretell the fury of some distant storm, though the air in general was even unnaturally calm and breathless. In gazing on this extraordinary scene, Arthur did justice to the monks who had chosen this wild and grotesque situation, from which they could witness Nature in her wildest and grandest demonstrations, and compare the nothingness of humanity with her awful convulsions.

So much was Arthur awed by the scene before him, that he had almost forgotten, while gazing from the bartizan, the important business which had brought him to this place, when it was suddenly recalled by finding himself in the presence of Margaret of Anjou, who, not seeing him in the parlour of reception, had stept upon the balcony, that she might meet with him the sooner.

The Queen's dress was black, without any ornament except a gold coronal of an inch in breadth, restraining her long black tresses, of which advancing years, and misfortunes, had partly altered the hue. There was placed within the circlet a black plume with a red rose, the last of the season, which the good father who kept the garden had presented to her that morning, as the badge of her husband's house. Care, fatigue, and sorrow, seemed to dwell on her brow and her features. To another messenger, she would in all probability have administered a sharp rebuke, for not being alert in his duty to receive her as she entered; but Arthur's age and appearance corresponded with that of her loved and lost son. He was the son of a lady whom Margaret had loved with almost sisterly affection, and the presence of Arthur continued to excite in the dethroned Queen the same feelings of maternal tenderness which had been awakened on their first meeting in the Cathedral of Strasburg. She raised him as he kneeled at her feet, spoke to him with much kindness, and encouraged him to detail at full length his father's message, and such other news as his brief residence at Dijon had made him acquainted with.

She demanded which way Duke Charles had moved with his army.

"As I was given to understand by the master of his artillery," said Arthur, "towards the Lake of Neufchatel, on which side he proposes his first attack on the Swiss."

"The headstrong fool!" said Queen Margaret, — "he resembles the poor lunatic, who went to the summit of the mountain, that he might meet the rain half way. — Does thy father then," continued Margaret, "advise me to give up the last, remains of the extensive territories, once the dominions of our royal House, and for some thousand crowns, and the paltry aid of a few hundred lances, to relinquish what is left of our patrimony to our proud and selfish kinsman of Burgundy, who extends his claim to our all, and affords so little help, or even promise of help, in return?"

"I should have ill discharged my father's commission," said Arthur, "if I had left your Highness to think that he recommends so great a sacrifice. He feels most deeply the Duke of Burgundy's grasping desire of dominion. Nevertheless, he thinks that Provence must, on King René's death, or sooner, fall either to the share of Duke Charles, or to Louis of France, whatever opposition your Highness may make to such a destination; and it may be that my father, as a knight and a soldier, hopes much from obtaining the means to make another attempt on Britain.

But the decision must rest with your Highness."

"Young man," said the Queen, "the contemplation of a question so doubtful almost deprives me of reason!"

As she spoke, she sunk down as one who needs rest, on a stone seat placed on the very verge of the balcony, regardless of the storm, which now began to rise with dreadful gusts of wind, the course of which being intermitted and altered by the crags round which they howled, it seemed as if in very deed Boreas, and Eurus, and Caurus, unchaining the winds from every quarter of heaven, were contending for mastery around the convent of our Lady of Victory. Amid this tumult, and amid billows of mist which concealed the bottom of the precipice, and masses of clouds which racked fearfully over their heads, the roar of the descending waters rather resembled the fall of cataracts than the rushing of torrents of rain. The seat on which Margaret had placed herself was in a considerable degree sheltered from the storm, but its eddies, varying in every direction, often tossed aloft her dishevelled hair; and we cannot describe the appearance of her noble and beautiful, yet ghastly and wasted features, agitated strongly by anxious hesitation, and conflicting thoughts, unless to those of our readers who have had the advantage of having seen our inimitable Siddons in such a character as this. Arthur, confounded by anxiety and terror, could only beseech her Majesty to retire before the fury of the approaching storm, into the interior of the convent.

"No," she replied with firmness; "roofs, and walls have ears, and monks, though they have forsworn the world, are not the less curious to know what passes beyond their cells. It is in this place you must hear what I have to say; as a soldier you should scorn a blast of wind or a shower of rain; and to me, who have often held counsel amidst the sound of trumpets and clash of arms, prompt for instant fight, the war of elements is an unnoticed trifle. I tell thee, young Arthur Vere, as I would to your father — as I would to my son — if indeed Heaven had left such a blessing to a wretch forlorn" ——

She paused, and then proceeded.

"I tell thee, as I would have told my beloved Edward, that Margaret, whose resolutions were once firm and immovable as these rocks among which we are placed, is now doubtful and variable as the clouds which are drifting around us. I told your father, in the joy of meeting once more a subject of such inappreciable loyalty, of the sacrifices I would make to assure the assistance of Charles of Burgundy, to so gallant an undertaking as that proposed to him by the faithful Oxford. But since I saw him, I have had cause of deep reflection. I met my aged father only to offend, and, I say it with shame, to insult the old man in presence of his people. Our tempers are as opposed as the sunshine, which a short space since gilded a serene and beautiful landscape, differs from the tempests which are now wasting it. I spurned with open scorn and contempt what he, in his mistaken affection, had devised for means of consolation, and, disgusted with the idle follies which he had devised for curing the melancholy of a dethroned Queen, a widowed spouse — and, alas! a childless mother, — I retired hither from the noisy and idle mirth, which was the bitterest aggravation of my sorrows. Such and so gentle is René's temper, that even my unfilial conduct will not diminish my influence over him; and if your father had announced, that the Duke of Burgundy, like a knight and a sovereign, had cordially and nobly entered into the plan of the faithful Oxford, I could have found it in my heart to obtain the cession of territory his cold and ambitious policy requires, in order to ensure the assistance, which he now postpones to afford till he has gratified his own haughty humour by settling needless quarrels with his unoffending neighbours. Since I have been here, and calmness and solitude have given me time to reflect, I have thought on the offences I have given the old man, and on the wrongs I was about to do him. My father, let me do him justice, is also the father of his people. They have dwelt under their vines and fig-trees, in ignoble ease, perhaps, but free from oppression and exaction, and their happiness has been that of their good King. Must I change all this? — Must I aid in turning over these contented people to a fierce, headlong, arbitrary prince? — May I not break even the easy and thoughtless heart of my poor old father, should I succeed in urging him to do so? — These are questions which I shudder even to ask myself. On the other hand, to disappoint the toils, the venturous hopes of your father, to forego the only opportunity which may ever again offer itself, of revenue on the bloody traitors of York, and restoration of the House of Lancaster! — Arthur, the scene around us is not so convulsed by the fearful tempest and the driving clouds, as my mind is by doubt and uncertainty."

"Alas!" replied Arthur, "I am too young and inexperienced to be your Majesty's adviser in a case so arduous. I would my father had been in presence himself."

"I know what he would have said," replied the Queen; "but knowing all. I despair of aid from human counsellors — I have sought others, but they also are deaf to my entreaties. Yes, Arthur, Margaret's misfortunes have rendered her superstitious. Know, that beneath these rocks, and under the foundation of this convent, there runs a cavern, entering by a secret and defended passage a little to the westward of the summit, and running through the mountain, having an opening to the south, from which, as from this bartizan, you can view the landscape so lately seen from this balcony, or the strife of winds and confusion of clouds which we now behold. In the middle of this cavernous thoroughfare is a natural pit, or perforation, of great, but unknown depth. A stone dropped into it is heard to dash from side to side, until the noise of its descent, thundering from cliff to cliff, dies away in distant and faint tinkling, less loud than that of a sheep's bell at a mile's distance. The common people, in their jargon, call this fearful gulf, Lou Garagoule; and the traditions of the monastery annex wild and fearful recollections to a place in itself sufficiently terrible. Oracles, it is said, spoke from thence in pagan days, by subterranean voices, arising from the abyss; and from these the Roman general is said to have heard, in strange and uncouth rhymes, promises of the victory which gives name to this mountain. These oracles, it is averred, may be yet consulted after performance of strange rites, in which heathen ceremonies are mixed with Christian acts of devotion. The abbots of Mont Saint Victoire have denounced the consultation of Lou Garagoule, and the spirits who reside there, to be criminal. But as the sin may be expiated by presents to the Church, by masses, and penances, the door is sometimes opened by the complaisant fathers to those whose daring curiosity leads them, at all risks, and by whatever means, to search into futurity. Arthur, I have made the experiment, and am even now returned from the gloomy cavern, in which, according to the traditional ritual, I have spent six hours by the margin of the gulf, a place so dismal, that after its horrors even this tempestuous scene is refreshing."

The Queen stopped, and Arthur the more struck with the wild tale, that it reminded him of his place of imprisonment at La Ferette, asked anxiously if her inquiries had obtained any answer.

"None whatever," replied the unhappy princess. "The demons of Garagoule, if there be such, are deaf to the suit of an unfortunate wretch like me, to whom neither friends nor fiends will afford counsel or assistance. It is my father's circumstances which prevent my instant and strong resolution. Were my own claims on this piping and paltry nation of Troubadours alone interested, I could, for the chance of once more setting my foot in merry England, as easily and willingly resign them, and their paltry coronet, as I commit to the storm this idle emblem of the royal rank which I have lost."

As Margaret spoke, she tore from her hair the sable feather and rose which the tempest had detached from the circlet in which they were placed, and tossed them from the battlement with a gesture of wild energy. They were instantly whirled off in a bickering eddy of the agitated clouds, which swept the feather far distant into empty space, through which the eye could not pursue it. But while that of Arthur involuntarily strove to follow its course, a contrary gust of wind caught the red rose, and drove it back against his breast, so that it was easy for him to catch hold of and retain it.

"Joy, joy, and good fortune, royal mistress!" he said, returning to her the emblematic flower; "the tempest brings back the badge of Lancaster to its proper owner."

"I accept the omen," said Margaret; "but it concerns yourself, noble youth, and not me. The feather which is borne away to waste and desolation, is Margaret's emblem. My eyes will never see the restoration of the line of Lancaster. But you will live to behold it, and to aid to achieve it, and to dye our red rose deeper yet in the blood of tyrants and traitors. My thoughts are so strangely poised, that a feather or a flower may turn the scale. But my head is still giddy, and my heart sick. — To-morrow you shall see another Margaret, and till then adieu."

It was time to retire, for the tempest began to be mingled with fiercer showers of rain. When they re-entered the parlour, the Queen clapped her hands, and two female attendants entered.

"Let the Father Abbot know," she said, "that it is our desire that this young gentleman receive for this night such hospitality as befits an esteemed friend of ours. — Till to-morrow, young sir, farewell."

With a countenance which betrayed not the late emotion of her mind, and with a stately courtesy, that would have become her when she graced the halls of Windsor, she extended her hand, which the youth saluted respectfully. After her leaving the parlour, the Abbot entered, and in his attention to Arthur's entertainment and accommodation for the evening, showed his anxiety to meet and obey Queen Margaret's wishes.

CHAPTER XXXI

—— Want you a man
Experienced in the world and its affairs?
Here he is for your purpose. He's a monk.
He hath forsworn the world and all its work —
The rather that he knows it passing well,
Special the worst of it, for he's a monk.

OLD PLAY.

While the dawn of the morning was yet gray, Arthur was awakened by a loud ringing at the gate of the monastery, and presently afterwards the porter entered the cell which had been allotted to him for his lodgings, to tell him, that, if his name was Arthur Philipson, a brother of their order had brought him dispatches from his father. The youth started up, hastily attired himself, and was introduced, in the parlour, to a Carmelite monk, being of the same order with the community of Saint Victoire.

"I have ridden many a mile, young man, to present you with this letter," said the monk, "having undertaken to your father that it should be delivered without delay. I came to Aix last night during the storm, and learning at the palace that you had ridden hither, I mounted as soon as the tempest abated, and here I am."

"I am beholden to you, father," said the youth, "and if I could repay your pains with a small donative to your convent" ——

"By no means," answered the good father; "I took my personal trouble out of friendship to your father, and mine own errand led me this way. The expenses of my long journey have been amply provided for. But open your packet, I can answer your questions at leisure."

The young man accordingly stepped into an embrasure of the window, and read as follows: —

"SON ARTHUR, — Touching the state of the country, in so tar as concerns the safety of travelling, know that the same is precarious. The Duke hath taken the towns of Brie and Granson, and put to death five hundred men, whom he made prisoners in garrison there. But the Confederates are approaching with a large force, and God will judge for the right. Howsoever the game may go, these are sharp wars, in which little quarter is spoken of on either side, and therefore there is no safety for men of our profession, till something decisive shall happen. In the meantime, you may assure the widowed lady that our correspondent continues well disposed to purchase the property which she has in hand; but will scarce be able to pay the price till his present pressing affairs shall be settled, which I hope will be in time to permit us to embark the funds in the profitable adventure I told our friend of. I have employed a friar, travelling to Provence, to carry this letter, which I trust will come safe. The bearer may be trusted.

"Your affectionate father,

"JOHN PHILIPSON."

Arthur easily comprehended the latter part of the epistle, and rejoiced he had received it at so critical a moment. He questioned the Carmelite on the amount of the Duke's army, which the monk stated to amount to sixty thousand men, while he said the Confederates, though making every exertion, had not yet been able to assemble the third part of that number. The young Ferrand de Vaudemont was with their army, and had received, it was thought, some secret assistance from France; but as he was little known in arms, and had few followers, the empty title of General which he bore, added little to the strength of the Confederates. Upon the whole, he reported, that every chance appeared to be in favour of Charles, and Arthur, who looked upon his success as presenting the only chance in favour of his father's enterprise, was not a little pleased to find it ensured, as far as depended on a great superiority of force. He had no leisure to make farther inquiries, for the Queen at that moment entered the apartment, and the Carmelite, learning her quality, withdrew from her presence in deep reverence.

The paleness of her complexion still bespoke the fatigues of the day preceding; but as she graciously bestowed on Arthur the greetings of the morning, her voice was firm, her eye clear, and her countenance steady. "I meet you," she said, "not as I left you, but determined in my purpose. I am satisfied, that if René does not voluntarily yield up his throne of Provence, by some step like that which we propose, he will be hurled from it by violence, in which, it may be, his life will not be spared. We will, therefore, to work with all speed — the worst is, that I cannot leave this convent till I have made the necessary penances for having visited the Garagoule, without performing which, I were no Christian woman. When you return to Aix, inquire at the palace for my secretary, with whom this line will give you credence. I have, even before this door of hope opened to me, endeavoured to form an estimate of King René's situation, and collected the documents for that purpose. Tell him to send me, duly sealed, and under fitting charge, the small cabinet hooped with silver. Hours of penance for past errors may be employed to prevent others; and, from the contents of that cabinet, I shall learn whether I am, in this weighty matter, sacrificing my father's interests to my own half-desperate hopes. But of this I have little or no doubt. I can cause the deeds of resignation and transference to be drawn up here under my own direction, and arrange the execution of them when I return to Aix, which shall be the first moment after my penance is concluded."

"And this letter, gracious madam," said Arthur, "will inform you what events are approaching, and of what importance it may be to take time by the forelock. Place me but in possession of these momentous deeds, and I will travel night and day till I reach the Duke's camp. I shall find him most likely in the moment of victory, and with his heart too much open to refuse a boon to the royal kinswoman who is surrendering to him all. We will — we must — in such an hour, obtain princely succours; and we shall soon see if the licentious Edward of York, the savage Richard, the treacherous and perjured Clarence, are hereafter to be lords of merry England, or whether they must give place to a more rightful sovereign and better man. But O! royal madam, all depends on haste."

"True — yet a few days may — nay, must — cast the die between Charles and his opponents; and, ere making so great a surrender, it were as well to be assured that he whom we would propitiate, is in capacity to assist us. All the events of a tragic and varied life have led me to see there is no such thing as an inconsiderable enemy. I will make haste, however, trusting in the interim we may have good news from the banks of the lake at Neufchatel."

"But who shall be employed to draw these most important deeds?" said the young man.

Margaret mused ere she replied — "The Father Guardian is complaisant, and I think faithful; but I would not willingly repose confidence in one of the Provençal monks. Stay, let me think — your father says the Carmelite who brought the letter may be trusted — he shall do the turn. He is a stranger, and will be silent for a piece of money. Farewell, Arthur de Vere. — You will be treated with all hospitality by my father. If thou dost receive farther tidings, thou wilt let me know them; or, should I have instructions to send, thou wilt hear from me. — So, benedicite."

Arthur proceeded to wind down the mountain at a much quicker pace than he had ascended on the day before. The weather was now gloriously serene, and the beauties of vegetation, in a country where it never totally slumbers, were at once delicious and refreshing. His thoughts wandered from the crags of Mont Saint Victoire, to the cliff of the canton of Unterwalden, and fancy recalled the moments when his walks through such scenery were not solitary, but when there was a form by his side, whose simple beauty was engraved on his memory. Such thoughts were of a preoccupying nature; and I grieve to say, that they entirely drowned the recollection of the mysterious caution given him by his father, intimating that Arthur might not be able to comprehend such letters as he should receive from him, till they were warmed before a fire.

The first thing which reminded him of this singular caution, was the seeing a chafing dish of charcoal in the kitchen of the hostelrie at the bottom of the mountain, where he found Thiebault and his horses. This was the first fire which he had seen since receiving his father's letter, and it reminded him not unnaturally of what the Earl had recommended. Great was his surprise to see, that after exposing the paper to the fire as if to dry it, a word emerged in an important passage of the letter, and the concluding words now read — "The bearer may *not* be trusted." Well-nigh choked with shame and vexation, Arthur could think of no other remedy than instantly to return to the convent, and acquaint the Queen with this discovery, which he hoped still to convey to her in time to prevent any risk being incurred by the Carmelite's treachery.

Incensed at himself, and eager to redeem his fault, he bent his manly breast against the steep hill, which was probably never scaled in so short time as by the young heir of De Vere; for, within forty minutes from his commencing the ascent, he stood breathless and panting in the presence of Queen Margaret, who was alike surprised at his appearance and his exhausted condition.

"Trust not the Carmelite!" he exclaimed — "You are betrayed, noble Queen, and it is by my negligence. Here is my dagger — bid me strike it into my heart!"

Margaret demanded and obtained a more special explanation, and when it was given, she said, "It is an unhappy chance; but your father's instructions ought to have been more distinct. I have told yonder Carmelite the purpose of the contracts, and engaged with him to draw them. He has but now left me to serve at the choir. There is no withdrawing the confidence I have inhappily placed; but I can easily prevail with the Father Guardian to prevent the monk from leaving the convent till we are indifferent to his secrecy. It is our best chance to secure it, and we will take care that what inconvenience he sustains by his detention shall be well recompensed. Meanwhile, rest thou, good Arthur, and undo the throat of thy mantle. Poor youth, thou art well-nigh exhausted with thy haste."

Arthur obeyed, and sat down on a seat in the parlour; for the speed which he had exerted rendered him almost incapable of standing.

"If I could but see," he said, "the false monk, I would find a way to charm him to secrecy!"

"Better leave him to me," said the Queen; "and in a word, I forbid you to meddle with him. The coif can treat better with the cowl than the casque can do. Say no more of him. I joy to see you wear around your neck the holy relic I bestowed on you; — but what Moorish charmlet is that you wear beside it? Alas! I need not ask. Your heightened colour, almost as deep as when you entered a quarter of an hour hence, confesses a true-love token. Alas! poor boy, hast thou not only such a share of thy country's woes to bear, but also thine own load of affliction, not the less poignant now that future time will show thee how fantastic it is! Margaret of Anjou could once have aided wherever thy affections were placed; but now she can only contribute to the misery of her friends, not to their happiness. But this lady of the charm, Arthur, is she fair — is she wise and virtuous — is she of noble birth — and does she love?" — She perused his countenance with the glance of an eagle, and continued, "To all, thou wouldst answer Yes, if shamefacedness permitted thee.

Love her then in turn, my gallant boy, for love is the parent of brave actions. Go, my noble youth — high-born and loyal, valorous and virtuous, enamoured and youthful, to what mayest thou nut rise? The chivalry of ancient Europe only lives in a bosom like thine. Go, and let the praises of a Queen fire thy bosom with the love of honour and achievement. In three days we meet at Aix."

Arthur, highly gratified with the Queen's condescension, once more left her presence.

Returning down the mountain with a speed very different from that which he had used in the ascent, he again found his Provençal squire, who had remained in much surprise at witnessing the confusion in which his master had left the inn, almost immediately after he had entered it without any apparent haste or agitation. Arthur explained his hasty return by alleging he had forgot his purse at the convent. "Nay, in that case," said Thiebault, "considering what you left and where you left it, I do not wonder at your speed; though, Our Lady save me, as I never saw living creature, save a goat with a wolf at his heels, make his way over crag and briers with half such rapidity as you did."

They reached Aix after about an hour's riding, and Arthur lost no time in waiting upon the good King René, who gave him a kind reception, both in respect of the letter from the Duke of Burgundy, and in consideration of his being an Englishman, the avowed subject of the unfortunate Margaret. The placable monarch soon forgave his young guest the want of complaisance with which he had eschewed to listen to his compositions; and Arthur speedily found, that to apologize for his want of breeding in that particular, was likely to lead to a great deal more rehearsing than he could find patience to tolerate. He could only avoid the old King's extreme desire to recite his own poems, and perform his own music, by engaging him in speaking of his daughter Margaret. Arthur had been sometimes induced to doubt the influence which the Queen boasted herself to possess over her aged father; but on being acquainted with him personally, he became convinced that her powerful understanding and violent passions inspired the feeble-minded and passive King with a mixture of pride, affection, and fear, which united to give her the most ample authority over him.

Although she had parted with him but a day or two since,

and in a manner so ungracious on her side, René was as much overjoyed at hearing of the probability of her speedy return, as the fondest father could have been at the prospect of being reunited to the most dutiful child, whom he had not seen for years. The old King was impatient as a boy for the day of her arrival, and, still strangely unenlightened on the difference of her taste from his own, he was with difficulty induced to lay aside a project of meeting her in the character of old Palemon, —

"The prince of shepherds, and their pride,"

at the head of an Arcadian procession of nymphs and swains, to inspire whose choral dances and songs, every pipe and tambourine in the country was to be placed in requisition. Even the old seneschal, however, intimated his disapprobation of this species of *joyeuse entrée*; so that René suffered himself at length to be persuaded that the Queen was too much occupied by the religious impressions to which she had been of late exposed, to receive any agreeable sensation from sights or sounds of levity. The King gave way to reasons which he could not sympathize with; and thus Margaret escaped the shock of welcome, which would perhaps have driven her in her impatience back to the mountain of Saint Victoire, and the sable cavern of Lou Garagoule.

During the time of her absence, the days of the court of Provence were employed in sports and rejoicings of every description; tilting at the barrier with blunted spears, riding at the ring, parties for hare-hunting and falconry, frequented by the youth of both sexes, in the company of whom the King delighted, while the evenings were consumed in dancing and music.

Arthur could not but be sensible, that not long since all this would have made him perfectly happy; but the last months of his existence had developed his understanding and passions. He was now initiated in the actual business of human life, and looked on its amusements with an air of something like contempt; so that among the young and gay noblesse, who composed this merry court, he acquired the title of the youthful philosopher, which was not bestowed upon him, it may be supposed, as inferring any thing of peculiar compliment.

On the fourth day news were received, by an express messenger, that Queen Margaret would enter Aix before the hour of noon, to resume her residence in her father's palace. The good King René seemed, as it drew nigh, to tear the interview with his daughter as much as he had previously desired it, and contrived to make all around him partake of his fidgety anxiety. He tormented his steward and cooks to recollect what dishes they had ever observed her to taste of with approbation — he pressed the musicians to remember the tunes which she approved, and when one of them boldly replied he had never known her Majesty endure any strain with patience, the old monarch threatened to turn him out of his service for slandering the taste of his daughter. The banquet was ordered to be served at half-past eleven, as if accelerating it would have had the least effect upon hurrying the arrival of the expected guests; and the old King, with his napkin over his arm, traversed the hall from window to window, wearying every one with questions, whether they saw any thing of the Queen of England. Exactly as the bells tolled noon, the Queen, with a very small retinue, chiefly English, and in mourning habits like herself, rode into the town of Aix. King René, at the head of his court, failed not to descend from the front of his stately palace, and move along the street to meet his daughter. Lofty, proud, and jealous of incurring ridicule, Margaret was not pleased with this public greeting in the market-place. But she was desirous at present to make amends for her late petulance, and therefore she descended from her palfrey; and although something shocked at seeing René equipped with a napkin, she humbled herself to bend the knee to him, asking at once his blessing and forgiveness.

"Thou hast — thou hast nay blessing, my suffering dove," said the simple King to the proudest and most impatient princess that ever wept for a lost crown. — "And for thy pardon, how canst thou ask it, who never didst me an offence since God made me father to so gracious a child? — Rise, I say rise — nay, it is for me to ask thy pardon — True, I said in my ignorance, and thought within myself, that my heart had indited a goodly thing — but it vexed thee. It is therefore for me to crave pardon." — — And down sunk good King René upon both knees; and the people, who are usually captivated with any thing resembling the trick of the scene, applauded with much noise, and some smothered laughter, a situation in which the royal daughter and her parent seemed about to rehearse the scene of the Roman

Charity.

Margaret, sensitively alive to shame, and fully aware that her present position was sufficiently ludicrous in its publicity at least, signed sharply to Arthur, whom she saw in the King's suite, to come to her; and using his arm to rise, she muttered to him aside, and in English, — "To what saint shall I vow myself, that I may preserve patience when I so much need it!"

"For pity's sake, royal madam, recall your firmness of mind and composure," whispered her esquire, who felt at the moment more embarrassed than honoured by his distinguished office, for he could feel that the Queen actually trembled with vexation and impatience.

They at length resumed their route to the palace, the father and daughter arm in arm, a posture most agreeable to Margaret, who could bring herself to endure her father's effusions of tenderness, and the general tone of his conversation, so that he was not overheard by others. In the same manner, she bore with laudable patience the teasing attentions which he addressed to her at table, noticed some of his particular courtiers, inquired after others, led the way to his favourite subjects of conversation on poetry, painting, and music, till the good King was as much delighted with the unwonted civilities of his daughter, as ever was lover with the favourable confessions of his mistress, when, after years of warm courtship, the ice of her bosom is at length thawed. It cost the haughty Margaret an effort to bend herself to play this part — her pride rebuked her for stooping to flatter her father's foibles, in order to bring him over to the resignation of his dominions — yet having undertaken to do so, and so much having been already hazarded upon this sole remaining chance of success in an attack upon England, she saw, or was willing to see, no alternative.

Betwixt the banquet, and the ball by which it was to be followed, the Queen sought an opportunity of speaking to Arthur.

"Bad news, my sage counsellor," she said. "The Carmelite never returned to the convent after the service was over. Having learned that you had come back in great haste, he had, I suppose, concluded he might stand in suspicion, so he left the convent of Mont Saint Victoire."

"We must hasten the measures which your Majesty has resolved to adopt," answered Arthur.

"I will speak with my father to-morrow. Meanwhile, you must enjoy the pleasures of the evening, for to you they may be pleasures. — Young Lady of Boisgelin, I give you this cavalier to be your partner for the evening."

The black-eyed and pretty Provençale curtesied with due decorum, and glanced at the handsome young Englishman with an eye of approbation; but whether afraid of his character as a philosopher, or his doubtful rank, added the saving clause, — "If my mother approves."

"Your mother, damsel, will scarce, I think, disapprove of any partner whom you receive from the hands of Margaret of Anjou. Happy privilege of youth," she added with a sigh, as the youthful couple went off to take their place in the *bransle*,[18] "which can snatch a flower even on the roughest road."

Arthur acquitted himself so well during the evening, that perhaps the young Countess was only sorry that so gay and handsome a gallant limited his compliments and attentions within the cold bounds of that courtesy enjoined by the rules of ceremony.

---

[18] Bransle, in English, brawl, — a species of dance.

CHAPTER XXXII

For I have given here my full consent,
To undeck the pompous body of a king,
Make glory base, and sovereignty a slave,
Proud Majesty a subject, state a peasant.

RICHARD II.

The next day opened a grave scene. King René had not forgotten to arrange the pleasures of the day, when, to his horror and discomfiture, Margaret demanded an interview upon serious business. If there was a proposition in the world which René from his soul detested, it was any that related to the very name of business.

"What was it that his child wanted?" he said. "Was it money? He would give her whatever ready sums he had, though he owned his exchequer was somewhat bare; yet he had received his income for the season. It was ten thousand crowns. How much should he desire to be paid to her? — the half — three parts — or the whole? All was at her command."

"Alas, my dear father," said Margaret, "it is not my affairs, but your own, on which I desire to speak with you."

"If the affairs are mine," said René, "I am surely master to put them off to another day — to some rainy dull day, fit for no better purpose. See, my love, the hawking party are all on their steeds and ready — the horses are neighing; and pawing — the gallants and maidens mounted, and ready with hawk on fist — the spaniels struggling in the leash. It were a sin, with wind and weather to friend, to lose so lovely a morning."

"Let them ride their way," said Queen Margaret, "and find their sport; for the matter I have to speak concerning involves honour and rank, life and means of living."

"Nay, but I have to hear and judge between Calezon and John of Acqua Mortis, the two most celebrated Troubadours."

"Postpone their cause till to-morrow," said Margaret, "and dedicate an hour or two to more important affairs."

"If you are peremptory," replied King René, "you are aware, my child, I cannot say you nay."

And with reluctance he gave orders for the hawkers to go on and follow their sport, as he could not attend them that day.

The old King then suffered himself, like an unwilling greyhound withheld from the chase, to be led into a separate apartment. To ensure privacy, Margaret stationed her secretary, Mordaunt, with Arthur, in an antechamber, giving them orders to prevent all intrusion.

"Nay, for myself, Margaret," said the good-natured old man, "since it must be, I consent to be put au secret; but why keep old Mordaunt from taking a walk in this beautiful morning; and why prevent young Arthur from going forth with the rest? I promise you, though they term him a philosopher, yet he showed as light a pair of heels last night with the young Countess de Boisgelin, as any gallant in Provence."

"They are come from a country," said Margaret, "in which men are trained from infancy to prefer their duty to their pleasure."

The poor King, led into the council closet, saw with internal shuddering, the fatal cabinet of ebony, bound with silver, which had never been opened but to overwhelm him with weariness, and dolefully calculated how many yawns he must strangle ere he sustained the consideration of its contents. They proved, however, when laid before him, of a kind that excited even his interest, though painfully.

His daughter presented him with a short and clear view of the debts which were secured on his dominions, and for which they were mortgaged in various pieces and parcels. She then showed him, by another schedule, the large claims of which payment was instantly demanded, to discharge which no funds could be found or assigned. The King defended himself like others in his forlorn situation. To every claim of six, seven, or eight thousand ducats, he replied by the assertion, that he had ten thousand crowns in his chancery, and showed some reluctance to be convinced, till repeatedly urged upon him, that the same sum could not be adequate to the discharge of thirty times the amount.

"Then," said the King, somewhat impatiently, "why not pay off those who are most pressing, and let the others wait till receipts come round?"

"It is a practice which has been too often resorted to," replied the Queen, "and it is but a part of honesty to pay creditors who have advanced their all in your Grace's service."

"But are we not," said René, "King of both the Sicilies,

Naples, Arragon, and Jerusalem? And why is the monarch of such fair kingdoms to be pushed to the wall, like a bankrupt yeoman, for a few bags of paltry crowns."

"You are indeed monarch of these kingdoms," said Margaret; "but is it necessary to remind your Majesty that it is but as I am Queen of England, in which I have not an acre of land, and cannot command a penny of revenue? You have no dominions which are a source of revenue, save those which you see in this scroll, with an exact list of the income they afford. It is totally inadequate, you see, to maintain your state and to pay the large engagements incurred to former creditors."

"It is cruel to press me to the wall thus," said the poor King. "What can I do? If I am poor, I cannot help it. I am sure I would pay the debts you talk of, if I knew the way."

"Royal father, I will show it you. — Resign your useless and unavailing dignity, which, with the pretensions attending it, serves but to make your miseries ridiculous. Resign your rights as a sovereign, and the income which cannot be stretched out to the empty excesses of a beggarly court, will enable you to enjoy, in ease and opulence, all the pleasures you most delight in as a private baron."

"Margaret, you speak folly," answered René, somewhat sternly. "A king and his people are bound by ties which neither can sever without guilt. My subjects are my flock, I am their shepherd. They are assigned to my governance by Heaven, and I dare not renounce the charge of protecting them."

"Were you in condition to do so," answered the Queen, "Margaret would bid you fight to the death. But don your harness, long disused — mount your war-steed — cry, René for Provence! and see if a hundred men will gather round your standard. Your fortresses are in the hands of strangers; army you have none; your vassals may have good-will, but they lack all military skill and soldier-like discipline. You stand but the mere skeleton of monarchy, which France or Burgundy may prostrate on the earth, whichever first puts forth his arm to throw it down."

The tears trickled fast down the old King's cheeks, when this unflattering prospect was set before him, and he could not forbear owning his total want of power to defend himself, and his dominions, and admitting that he had often thought of the necessity of compounding for his resignation with one of his powerful neighbours.

"It was thy interest, Margaret, harsh and severe as you are, which prevented my entering, before now, into measures most painful to my feelings, but perhaps best calculated for my advantage. But I had hoped it would hold on for my day; and thou, my child, with the talents Heaven has given thee, wouldst, I thought, have found remedy for distresses, which I cannot escape, otherwise than by shunning the thoughts of them."

"If it is in earnest you speak of my interest," said Margaret, "know, that your resigning Provence will satisfy the nearest, and almost the only wish that my bosom can form; but, so judge me Heaven, as it is on your account, gracious sire, as well as mine, that I advise your compliance."

"Say no more on't, child; give me the parchment of resignation, and I will sign it: I see thou hast it ready drawn; let us sign it, and then we will overtake the hawkers. We must suffer woe, but there is little need to sit down and weep for it."

"Do you not ask," said Margaret, surprised at his apathy, "to whom you cede your dominions?"

"What boots it," answered the King, "since they must be no more my own? It must be either to Charles of Burgundy, or my nephew Louis — both powerful and politic princes. God send my poor people may have no cause to wish their old man back again, whose only pleasure was to see them happy and mirthful."

"It is to Burgundy you resign Provence," said Margaret.

"I would have preferred him," answered René; "he is fierce, but not malignant. One word more — are my subjects' privileges and immunities fully secured?"

"Amply," replied the Queen; "and your own wants of all kinds honourably provided for. I would not leave the stipulations in your favour in blank, though I might perhaps have trusted Charles of Burgundy, where money alone is concerned."

"I ask not for myself — with my viol and my pencil, René the Troubadour will be as happy as ever was René the King."

So saying, with practical philosophy he whistled the burden of his last composed ariette, and signed away the rest of his royal possessions without pulling off his glove, or even reading the instrument.

"What is this?" he said, looking at another and separate parchment, of much briefer contents. "Must my kinsman Charles have both the Sicilies, Catalonia, Naples, and Jerusalem, as well as the poor remainder of Provence? Methinks, in decency, some greater extent of parchment should have been allowed to so ample a cession."

"That deed," said Margaret, "only disowns and relinquishes all countenance of Ferrand de Vaudemont's rash attempt on Lorraine, and renounces all quarrel on that account against Charles of Burgundy."

For once Margaret miscalculated the tractability of her father's temper. René positively started, coloured, and stammered with passion, as he interrupted her. — "*Only* disown — *only* relinquish — *only* renounce the cause of my grandchild, the son of my dear Yolande — his rightful claims on his mother's inheritance! — Margaret, I am ashamed for thee. Thy pride is an excuse for thy evil temper; but what is pride worth which can stoop to commit an act of dishonourable meanness? To desert, nay, disown my own flesh and blood, because the youth is a bold knight under shield, and disposed to battle for his right — I were worthy that harp and horn rung out shame on me, should I listen to thee."

Margaret was overcome in some measure by the old man's unexpected opposition. She endeavoured, however, to show that there was no occasion, in point of honour, why René should engage in the cause of a wild adventurer, whose right, be it good be it bad, was only upheld by some petty and underhand supplies of money from France, and the countenance of a few of the restless banditti who inhabit the borders of all nations. But ere René could answer, voices, raised to an unusual pitch, were heard in the antechamber, the door of which was flung open by an armed knight, covered with dust, who exhibited all the marks of a long journey.

"Here I am," he said, "father of my mother — behold your grandson — Ferrand de Vaudemont; the son of your lost Yolande kneels at your feet, and implores a blessing on him and his enterprise."

"Thou hast it," replied René, "and may it prosper with thee, gallant youth, image of thy sainted mother — my blessings, my prayers, my hopes, go with you!"

"And you, fair aunt of England," said the young knight, addressing Margaret, "you who are yourself dispossessed by traitors, will you not own the cause of a kinsman who is struggling for his inheritance?"

"I wish all good to your person, fair nephew," answered the Queen of England, "although your features are strange to me. But to advise this old man to adopt your cause, when it is desperate in the eyes of all wise men, were impious madness."

"Is my cause then so desperate?" said Ferrand; "forgive me if I was not aware of it. And does my aunt Margaret say this, whose strength of mind supported Lancaster so long, after the spirits of her warriors had been quelled by defeat? What — forgive me, for my cause must be pleaded — what would you have said had my mother Yolande been capable to advise her father to disown your own Edward, had God permitted him to reach Provence in safety?"

"Edward," said Margaret, weeping as she spoke, "was incapable of desiring his friends to espouse a quarrel that was irremediable. His, too, was a cause for which mighty princes and peers laid lance in rest."

"Yet Heaven blessed it not" — said Vaudemont.

"Thine," continued Margaret, "is but embraced by the robber nobles of Germany, the upstart burghers of the Rhine cities, the paltry and clownish Confederates of the Cantons."

"But Heaven *has blessed it*," replied Vaudemont. "Know, proud woman, that I come to interrupt your treacherous intrigues; no petty adventurer, subsisting and maintaining warfare by sleight rather than force, but a conqueror from a bloody field of battle, in which Heaven has tamed the pride of the tyrant of Burgundy."

"It is false!" said the Queen, starting; "I believe it not."

"It is true," said De Vaudemont, "as true as heaven is above us. — It is four days since I left the field of Granson, heaped with Burgundy's mercenaries — his wealth, his jewels, his plate, his magnificent decorations, the prize of the poor Swiss, who scarce can tell their value. Know you this, Queen Margaret?" continued the young soldier, showing the well-known jewel which decorated the Duke's order of the Golden Fleece; "think you not the lion was closely hunted when he left such trophies as these behind him?"

Margaret looked with dazzled eyes and bewildered thoughts, upon a token which confirmed the Duke's defeat, and the extinction of her last hopes. Her father, on the contrary, was struck with the heroism of the young warrior, a quality which, except as it existed in his daughter Margaret, had, he feared, taken leave of his family. Admiring in his heart the youth who exposed himself to danger for the need of praise, almost as much as he did the poets by whom the warrior's fame is rendered immortal, he hugged his grandson to his bosom, bidding him "gird on his sword in strength," and assuring him, if money could advance his affairs, he, King René, could command ten thousand crowns, any part, or the whole of which, was at Ferrand's command; thus giving proof of what had been said of him, that his head was incapable of containing two ideas at the same time.

We return to Arthur, who, with the Queen of England's secretary, Mordaunt, had been not a little surprised by the entrance of the Count de Vaudemont, calling himself Duke of Lorraine, into the anteroom, in which they kept a kind of guard, followed by a tall strong Swiss, with a huge halberd over his shoulder. The prince naming himself, Arthur did not think it becoming to oppose his entrance to the presence of his grandfather and aunt, especially as it was obvious that his opposition must have created an affray. In the huge staring halberdier, who had sense enough to remain in the anteroom, Arthur was not a little surprised to recognise Sigismund Biederman, who, after staring wildly at him for a moment, like a dog which suddenly recognises a favourite, rushed up to the young Englishman with a wild cry of gladness, and in hurried accents, told him how happy he was to meet with him, and that he had matters of importance to tell him. It was at no time easy for Sigismund to arrange his ideas, and now they were altogether confused by the triumphant joy which he expressed for the recent victory of his countrymen over the Duke of Burgundy; and it was with wonder that Arthur heard his confused and rude, but faithful tale.

"Look you, King Arthur, the Duke had come up with his huge army as far as Granson, which is near the outlet of the great lake of Neufchatel. There were five or six hundred Confederates in the place, and they held it till provisions failed, and then you know they were forced to give it over. But though hunger is hard to bear, they had better have borne it a day or two longer, for the butcher Charles hung them all up by the neck, upon trees round the place, — and there was no swallowing for them, you know, after such usage as that. Meanwhile all was busy on our hills, and every man that had a sword or lance accoutred himself with it. We met at Neufchatel, and some Germans joined us with the noble Duke of Lorraine. Ah, King Arthur, there is a leader! — we all think him second but to Rudolph of Donnerhugel — you saw him even now — it was he that went into that room — and you saw him before, — it is he that was the Blue Knight of Bâle; but we called him Laurenz then, for Rudolph said his presence among us must not be known to our father, and I did not know myself at that time who he really was. Well, when we came to Neufchatel we were a goodly company; we were fifteen thousand stout Confederates, and of others, Germans and Lorraine men, I will warrant you five thousand more. We heard that the Burgundian was sixty thousand in the field; but we heard at the same time that Charles had hung up our brethren like dogs, and the man was not among us — among the Confederates, I mean — who would stay to count heads, when the question was to avenge them. I would you could have heard the roar of fifteen thousand Swiss demanding to be led against the butcher of their brethren! My father himself, who, you know, is usually so eager for peace, now gave the first voice for battle; so, in the gray of the morning, we descended the lake towards Granson, with tears in our 'eyes and weapons in our hands, determined to have death or vengeance. We came to a sort of strait, between Vauxmoreux and the lake; there were horse on the level ground between the mountain and the lake, and a large body of infantry on the side of the hill. The Duke of Lorraine and his followers engaged the horse, while we climbed the hill to dispossess the infantry. It was with us the affair of a moment. Every man of us was at home among the crags, and Charles's men were stuck among them as thou wert, Arthur, when thou didst first come to Geierstein. But there were no kind maidens to lend them their hands to help them down. No, no — There were pikes, clubs, and halberds, many a one, to dash and thrust them from places where they could hardly keep their feet had there been no one to disturb them. So the horsemen, pushed by the Lorrainers, and seeing us upon their flanks, fled as fast as their horses could carry them. Then we drew together again on a fair field, which is *buon campagna,* as the Italian says, where the hills retire from the lake. But to you, we had scarce arrayed our ranks, when we heard such a din and clash of instruments, such a trample of their great horses, such a shouting and crying of men, as if all the soldiers, and all the minstrels in France and Germany, were striving which should make the loudest noise. Then there was a huge cloud of dust approaching us, and we began to see we must do or die, for this was Charles and his whole army come to support his vanguard. A blast from the mountain dispersed the dust, for they had halted to prepare for battle. O, good Arthur! you would have given ten years of life but to have seen the sight. There were thousands of horse, all in complete array, glancing against the sun, and hundreds of knights with crowns of gold and silver on their helmets, and thick masses of spears on foot, and cannon, as they call them. I did not know what things they were, which they drew on heavily with bullocks and placed before their army, but I knew more of them before the morning was over. Well, we were ordered to draw up in a hollow square, as we are taught at exercise, and before we pushed forwards, we were commanded, as is the godly rule and guise of our warfare, to kneel down and pray to God, Our Lady, and the blessed saints; and we afterwards learned that Charles, in his arrogance, thought we asked for mercy — Ha! ha! ha! a proper jest. If my father once knelt to him, it was for the sake of Christian blood and godly peace; but on the field of battle, Arnold Biederman would not have knelt to him and his whole chivalry, though he had stood alone with his sons on that field. Well, but Charles, supposing we asked grace, was determined to show us that we had asked it at a graceless face, for he cried, 'Fire my cannon on the coward slaves; it is all the mercy they have to expect from me!' — Bang — bang — bang — off went the things I told you of, like thunder and lightning, and some mischief they did, but the less that we were kneeling; and the saints doubtless gave the huge balls a hoist over the heads of those who were asking grace from them, but from no mortal creatures. So we had the signal to rise and rush on, and I promise you there were no sluggards. Every man felt ten men's strength. My halberd is no child's toy — if you have forgotten it, there it is — and yet it trembled in my grasp as if it had been a willow-wand to drive cows with. On we went, when suddenly the cannon were silent, and the earth shook with another and continued growl and battering, like thunder under ground. It was the men-at-arms rushing to charge us. But our leaders knew their trade, and had seen such a sight before — It was, Halt, halt — kneel down in the front — stoop in the second rank — close shoulder to shoulder like brethren, lean all spears forward and receive them like an iron wall! On they rushed, and there was a rending of lances that would have served the Unterwalden old women with splinters of firewood for a twelvemonth. Down went armed horse — down went accoutred knight — down went banner and bannerman — down went peaked boot and crowned helmet, and of those who fell not a man escaped with life. So they drew off in confusion, and were getting in order to charge again, when the noble Duke Ferrand and his horsemen dashed at them in their own way, and we moved onward to support him. Thus on we pressed, and the foot hardly waited for us, seeing their cavalry so handled. Then if you had seen the dust and heard the blows! the noise of a hundred thousand thrashers, the flight of the chaff which they drive about, would be but a type of it. On my word, I almost thought it shame to dash about ray halberd, the rout was so helplessly piteous. Hundreds were slain unresisting, and the whole army was in complete flight."

"My father — my father!" exclaimed Arthur; "in such a rout, what can have become of him?"

"He escaped safely," said the Swiss; "fled with Charles."

"It must have been a bloody field ere he fled," replied the Englishman.

"Nay," answered Sigismund, "he took no part in the fight, but merely remained by Charles; and prisoners said it was well for us, for that he is a man of great counsel and action in the wars. And as to flying, a man in such a matter must go back if he cannot press forward, and there is no shame in it, especially if you be not engaged in your own person."

As he spoke thus, their conversation was interrupted by Mordaunt, with "Hush, hush — the King and Queen come forth."

"What am I to do?" said Sigismund, in some alarm. "I care not for the Duke of Lorraine; but what am I to do when Kings and Queens enter?"

"Do nothing but rise, unbonnet yourself, and be silent."

Sigismund did as he was directed.

King René came forth arm in arm with his grandson and

Margaret followed, with deep disappointment and vexation on her brow. She signed to Arthur as she passed, and said to him — "Make thyself master of the truth of this most unexpected news, and bring the particulars to me. Mordaunt will introduce thee."

She then cast a look on the young Swiss, and replied courteously to his awkward salutation. The royal party then left the room, René bent on carrying his grandson to the sporting-party, which had been interrupted, and Margaret to seek the solitude of her private apartment, and await the confirmation of what she regarded as evil tidings.

They had no sooner passed, than Sigismund observed, — "And so that is a King and Queen! — Peste! the King looks somewhat like old Jacomo, the violer, that used to scrape on the fiddle to us when he came to Geierstein in his rounds. But the Queen is a stately creature. The chief cow of the herd, who carries the bouquets and garlands, and leads the rest to the chalet, has not a statelier pace. And how deftly you approached her and spoke to her! I could not have done it with so much grace — but it is like that you have served apprentice to the court trade?"

"Leave that for the present, good Sigismund," answered Arthur, "and tell me more of this battle."

"By Saint Mary, but I must have some victuals and drink first," said Sigismund, "if your credit in this fine place reaches so far."

"Doubt it not, Sigismund," said Arthur; and, by the intervention of Mordaunt, he easily procured, in a more retired apartment, a collation and wine, to which the young Biederman did great honour, smacking his lips with much gusto after the delicious wines, to which, in spite of his father's ascetic precepts, his palate was beginning to be considerably formed and habituated. When be found himself alone with a flask of *cote roti* and a biscuit, and his friend Arthur, he was easily led to continue his tale of conquest.

"Well — where was I — Oh, where we broke their infantry — well — they never rallied, and fell into greater confusion at every step — and we might have slaughtered one half of them, had we not stopt to examine Charles's camp. Mercy on us, Arthur, what a sight was there! Every pavilion was full of rich clothes, splendid armour, and great dishes and flagons, which some men said were of silver; but I knew there was not so much silver in the world, and was sure they must be of pewter, rarely burnished. Here there were hosts of laced lacqueys, and grooms, and pages, and as many attendants as there were soldiers in the army; and thousands, for what I knew, of pretty maidens. By the same token, both menials and maidens placed themselves at the disposal of the victors; but I promise you that my father was right severe on any who would abuse the rights of war. But some of our young men did not mind him, till he taught them obedience with the staff of his halberd. Well, Arthur, there was fine plundering, for the Germans and French that were with us rifled every thing, and some of our men followed the example — it is very catching — So I got into Charles's own pavilion, where Rudolph and some of his people were trying to keep out every one, that he might have the spoiling of it himself, I think; but neither he, nor any Bernese of them all, dared lay truncheon over my pate; so I entered, and saw them putting piles of pewter-trenchers, so clean as to look like silver, into chests and trunks. I pressed through them into the inner-place, and there was Charles's pallet-bed — I will do him justice, it was the only hard one in his camp — and there were fine sparkling stones and pebbles lying about among gauntlets, boots, vambraces, and such like gear — So I thought of your father and you, and looked for something, when what should I see but my old friend here," (here he drew Queen Margaret's necklace from his bosom,) "which I knew, because you remember I recovered it from the Scharfgeriechter at Brisach. — 'Oho! you pretty sparklers,' said I, 'you shall be Burgundian no longer, but go back to my honest English friends,' and therefore" ——

"It is of immense value," said Arthur, "and belongs not to my father or to me, but to the Queen you saw but now."

"And she will become it rarely," answered Sigismund. "Were she but a score, or a score and a half years younger, she were a gallant wife for a Swiss landholder. I would warrant her to keep his household in high order."

"She will reward thee liberally for recovering her property," said Arthur, scarce suppressing a smile at the idea of the proud Margaret becoming the housewife of a Swiss shepherd.

"How — reward!" said the Swiss. "Bethink thee, I am Sigismund Biederman, the son of the Landamman of Unterwalden — I am not a base *lanz-knecht*, to be paid for courtesy with piastres. Let her grant me a kind word of thanks, or the matter of a kiss, and I am well contented."

"A kiss of her hand, perhaps," said Arthur, again smiling at his friend's simplicity.

"Umph, the hand! Well! it may do for a Queen of some fifty years and odd, but would be poor homage to a Queen of May."

Arthur here brought back the youth to the subject of his battle, and learned that the slaughter of the Duke's forces in the flight had been in no degree equal to the importance of the action.

"Many rode off on horseback," said Sigismund; "and our German *reiters* flew on the spoil when they should have followed the chase. And, besides, to speak truth, Charles's camp delayed our very selves in the pursuit; but had we gone half a mile further, and seen our friends hanging on trees, not a Confederate would have stopped from the chase while he had limbs to carry him in pursuit."

"And what has become of the Duke?"

"Charles has retreated into Burgundy, like a boar who has felt the touch of the spear, and is more enraged than hurt; but is, they say, sad and sulky. Others report that he has collected all his scattered army, and immense forces besides, and has screwed his subjects to give him money, so that we may expect another brush. But all Switzerland will join us after such a victory."

"And my father is with him?" said Arthur.

"Truly he is, and has in a right godly manner tried to set afoot a treaty of peace with my own father. But it will scarce succeed. Charles is as mad as ever; and our people are right proud of our victory, and so they well may. Nevertheless, my father for ever preaches that such victories, and such heaps of wealth, will change our ancient manners, and that the ploughman will leave his labour to turn soldier. He says much about it; but why money, choice meat and wine, and fine clothing, should do so much harm, I cannot bring my poor brains to see — And many better heads than mine are as much puzzled — Here's to you, friend Arthur — This is choice liquor!"

"And what brings you and your General, Prince Ferrand, post to Nancy?" said the young Englishman.

"Faith, you are yourself the cause of our journey."

"I the cause?" said Arthur. — "Why, how could that be?"

"Why, it is said you and Queen Margaret are urging this old fiddling King René to yield up his territories to Charles, and to disown Ferrand in his claim upon Lorraine. And the Duke of Lorraine sent a man that you know well — that is, you do not know *him*, but you know some of his family, and he knows more of you than you wot — to put a spoke in your wheel, and prevent your getting for Charles the county of Provence, or preventing Ferrand being troubled or traversed in his natural rights over Lorraine."

"On my word, Sigismund, I cannot comprehend you," said Arthur.

"Well," replied the Swiss, "my lot is a hard one. All our house say that I can comprehend nothing, and I shall be next told that nobody can comprehend me. — Well, in plain language, I mean, my uncle, Count Albert, as he calls himself, of Geierstein — my father's brother."

"Anne of Geierstein's father?" echoed Arthur.

"Ay, truly; I thought we should find some mark to make you know him by."

"But I never saw him."

"Ay, but you have though — An able man he is, and knows more of every man's business than the man does himself. Oh! it was not for nothing that he married the daughter of a Salamander!"

"Pshaw, Sigismund, how can you believe that nonsense?" answered Arthur.

"Rudolph told me you were as much bewildered as I was that night at Graffs-lust," answered the Swiss.

"If I were so, I was the greater ass for my pains," answered Arthur.

"Well, but this uncle of mine has got some of the old conjuring books from the library at Arnheim, and they say he can pass from place to place with more than mortal speed; and that he is helped in his designs by mightier counsellors than mere men. Always, however, though so ably and highly endowed, his gifts, whether coming from a lawful or unlawful quarter, bring him no abiding advantage. He is eternally plunged into strife and danger."

"I know few particulars of his life," said Arthur, disguising as much as he could his anxiety to hear more of him; "but I have heard that he left Switzerland to join the Emperor."

"True," answered the young Swiss, "and married the young Baroness of Arnheim — but afterwards he incurred my namesake's imperial displeasure, and not less that of the Duke of Austria. They say you cannot live in Rome and strive with the Pope; so my uncle thought it best to cross the Rhine, and betake himself to Charles's court, who willingly received noblemen from all countries, so that they had good sounding names, with the title of Count, Marquis, Baron, or suchlike, to march in front of them. So my uncle was most kindly received; but within this year or two all this friendship has been broken up. Uncle Albert obtained a great lead in some mysterious societies of which Charles disapproved, and set so hard at my poor uncle, that he was fain to take orders and shave his hair, rather than lose his head. But though he cut off his hair, his brain remains as busy as ever; and although the Duke suffered him to be at large, yet he found him so often in his way, that all men believed he waited but an excuse for seizing upon him and putting him to death. But my uncle persists that he fears not Charles; and that, Duke as he is, Charles has more occasion to be afraid of him. — And so you saw how boldly he played his part at La Ferette."

"By Saint George of Windsor!" exclaimed Arthur, "the Black Priest of St. Paul's!"

"Oh, ho! you understand me now. Well, he took it upon him that diaries would not dare to punish him for his share in De Hagenbach's death; and no more did he, although uncle Albert sat and voted in the Estates of Burgundy, and stirred them up all he could to refuse giving Charles the money he asked of them. But when the Swiss war broke out, uncle Albert became assured his being a clergyman would be no longer his protection, and that the Duke intended to have him accused of corresponding with his brother and countrymen; and so he appeared suddenly in Ferrand's camp at Neufchatel, and sent a message to Charles that he renounced his allegiance, and bid him defiance."

"A singular story of an active and versatile man," said the young Englishman.

"Oh, you may seek the world for a man like uncle Albert. Then he knows every thing; and he told Duke Ferrand what you were about here, and offered to go and bring more certain information — ay, though he left the Swiss camp but five or six days before the battle, and the distance between Arles and Neufchatel be four hundred miles complete, yet he met him on his return, when Duke Ferrand, with me to show him the way, was hastening hitherward, having set off from the very field of battle."

"Met him!" said Arthur — "Met whom? — Met the Black Priest of St. Paul's?"

"Ay, I mean so," replied Sigismund; "but he was habited as a Carmelite monk."

"A Carmelite!" said Arthur, a sudden light flashing on him; "and I was so blind as to recommend his services to the Queen! I remember well that he kept his face much concealed in his cowl — and I, foolish beast, to fall so grossly into the snare! — And yet perhaps it is as well the transaction was interrupted, since I fear, if carried successfully through, all must have been disconcerted by this astounding defeat."

Their conversation had thus far proceeded, when Mordaunt appearing, summoned Arthur to his royal mistress's apartment. In that gay palace, a gloomy room, whose windows looked upon some part of the ruins of the Roman edifice, but excluded every other object, save broken walls and tottering columns, was the retreat which Margaret had chosen for her own. She received Arthur with a kindness more touching, that it was the inmate of so proud and fiery a disposition, — of a heart assailed with many woes, and feeling them severely.

"Alas, poor Arthur!" she said, "thy life begins where thy father's threatens to end, in useless labour to save a sinking vessel. The rushing leak pours in its waters faster than human force can lighten or discharge. All — all goes wrong, when our unhappy cause becomes connected with it — Strength becomes weakness, wisdom folly, and valour cowardice. The Duke of Burgundy, hitherto victorious in all his bold undertakings, has but to entertain the momentary thought of yielding succour to Lancaster, and behold his sword is broken by a peasant's flail; and his disciplined army, held to be the finest in the world, flies like chaff before the wind; while their spoils are divided by renegade German hirelings, and barbarous Alpine shepherds! — What more hast thou learned of this strange tale?"

"Little, madam, but what you have heard. The worst additions are, that the battle was shamefully coward-like, and completely lost, with every advantage to have won it — the best, that the Burgundian army has been rather dispersed than destroyed, and that the Duke himself has escaped, and is rallying his forces in Upper Burgundy."

"To sustain a new defeat, or engage in a protracted and doubtful contest, fatal to his reputation as defeat itself. Where is thy father?"

"With the Duke, madam, as I have been informed," replied Arthur.

"Hie to him, and say I charge him to look after his own safety, and care no farther for my interests. This last blow has sunk me — I am without an ally, without a friend, without treasure" ——

"Not so, Madam," replied Arthur. "One piece of good fortune has brought back to your Grace this inestimable relic of your fortunes." — And producing the precious necklace, he gave the history of its recovery.

"I rejoice at the chance which has restored these diamonds," said the Queen, "that in point of gratitude, at least, I may not be utterly bankrupt. Carry them to your father, — tell him my schemes are over — and my heart, which so long clung to hope, is broken at last. — Tell him the trinkets are his own, and to his own use let him apply them. They will but poorly repay the noble earldom of Oxford, lost in the cause of her who sends them."

"Royal madam," said the youth, "be assured my father would sooner live by service as a *schwarsreiter*, than become a burden on your misfortunes."

"He never yet disobeyed command of mine," said Margaret; "and this is the last I will lay upon him. If he is too rich or too proud to benefit by his Queen's behest, he will find enough of poor Lancastrians who have fewer means or fewer scruples."

"There is yet a circumstance I have to communicate," said Arthur, and recounted the history of Albert of Geierstein, and the disguise of a Carmelite monk.

"Are you such a fool," answered the Queen, "as to suppose this man has any supernatural powers to aid him in his ambitious projects and his hasty journeys?"

"No, madam — but it is whispered that the Count Albert of Geierstein, or this Black Priest of St. Paul's, is a chief amongst the Secret Societies of Germany, which even princes dread whilst they hate them; for the man that can command a hundred daggers, must be feared even by those who rule thousands of swords."

"Can this person," said the Queen, "being now a churchman, retain authority amongst those who deal ill life and death? It is contrary to the canons."

"It would seem so, royal madam; but every thing in these dark institutions differs from what is practised in the light of day. Prelates are often heads of a Vehmique bench, and the Archbishop of Cologne exercises the dreadful office of their chief as Duke of Westphalia, the principal region in which these societies flourish.[19] Such privileges attach to the secret influence of the chiefs of this dark association, as may well seem supernatural to those who are unapprised of circumstances, of which men shun to speak in plain terms."

"Let him be wizard or assassin," said the Queen, "I thank him for having contributed to interrupt my plan of the old man's cession of Provence, which, as events stand, would have stripped René of his dominions, without furthering our plan of invading England. — Once more, be stirring with the dawn, and bend thy way back to thy father, and charge him to care for himself and think no more of me. Bretagne, where the heir of Lancaster resides, will be the safest place of refuge for its bravest followers. Along the Rhine, the Invisible Tribunal, it would seem, haunts both shores, and to be innocent of ill is no security; even here the proposed treaty with Burgundy may take air, and the Provençaux carry daggers as well as crooks and pipes. But I hear the horses fast returning from the hawking party, and the silly old man forgetting all the eventful proceedings of the day, whistling as he ascends the steps. Well, we will soon part, and my removal will be, I think, a relief to him. Prepare for banquet and ball, for noise and nonsense — above all, to bid adieu to Aix with morning dawn."

---

[19] The Archbishop of Cologne was recognised as head of all the Free Tribunals (*i. e.,* the Vehmique benches) in Westphalia, by a writ of privilege granted in 1335, by the Emperor Charles IV. Winceslaus confirmed this act by a privilege dated 1382, in which the Archbishop is termed Grand Master of the Vehme, or Grand Inquisitor. And this prelate and other priests were encouraged to exercise such office, by Pope Boniface III., whose ecclesiastical discipline permitted them in such cases to assume the right of judging in matters of life and death.

be elegant; his dancing, for Count Sigismund failed not to dance, was the bounding and gamboling of a young elephant; yet they were preferred to the handsome proportions and courtly movements of the youthful Englishman, even by the black-eyed Countess, in whose good graces Arthur had made some progress on the preceding evening. Arthur thus thrown into the shade, felt as Mr. Pepys afterwards did when he tore his camlet cloak, — the damage was not great, but it troubled him.

Nevertheless, the passing evening brought him some revenge. There are some works of art, the defects of which are not seen till they are injudiciously placed in too strong a light, and such was the case with Sigismund the Simple. The quick-witted, though fantastic Provençaux, soon found out the heaviness of his intellect, and the extent of his good-nature, and amused themselves at his expense, by ironical compliments and well-veiled raillery. It is probable they would have been less delicate on the subject, had not the Swiss brought into the dancing-room along with him his eternal halberd, the size, and weight, and thickness of which boded little good to any one whom the owner might detect in the act of making merry at his expense. But Sigismund did no further mischief that night, except that, in achieving a superb *entrechat*, he alighted with his whole weight on the miniature foot of his pretty partner, which he well-nigh crushed to pieces.

Arthur had hitherto avoided looking towards Queen Margaret during the course of the evening, lest he should disturb her thoughts from the channel in which they were rolling, by seeming to lay a claim on her protection. But there was something so whimsical in the awkward physiognomy of the mal-adroit Swiss, that he could not help glancing an eye to the alcove where the Queen's chair of state was placed, to see if she observed him. The very first view was such as to rivet his attention. Margaret's head was reclined on the chair, her eyes scarcely open, her features drawn up and pinched, her hands closed with effort. The English lady of honour who stood behind her, — old, deaf, and dim-sighted, — had not discovered any thing in her mistress's position more than the abstracted and indifferent attitude with which the Queen was wont to be present in body and absent in mind, during the festivities of the Provençal court. But when Arthur, greatly alarmed, came behind the seat to press her attention to her mistress, she exclaimed, after a minute's investigation, "Mother of Heaven, the Queen is dead!" And it was so. It seemed that the last fibre of life, in that fiery and ambitious mind, had, as she herself prophesied, given way at the same time with the last thread of political hope.

CHAPTER XXXIII

Toll, toll the bell!
Greatness is o'er,
The heart has broke,
To ache no more;
An unsubstantial pageant all —
Drop o'er the scene the funeral-pall.

OLD POEM.

The commotion and shrieks of fear and amazement which
were excited among the ladies of the court by an event so singular and shocking, had begun to abate, and the sighs, more serious
though less intrusive, of the few English attendants of the deceased Queen began to be heard, together with the groans of old
King René, whose emotions were as acute as they were
shortlived. The leeches had held a busy but unavailing consultation, and the body that was once a Queen's, was delivered to the
Priest of St. Sauveur, that beautiful church in which the spoils of
Pagan temples have contributed to fill up the magnificence of the
Christian edifice. The stately pile was duly lighted up, and the
funeral provided with such splendour as Aix could supply. The
Queen's papers being examined, it was found, that Margaret, by
disposing of jewels and living at small expense, had realized the
means of making a decent provision for life, for her very few
English attendants. Her diamond necklace, described in her last
will, as in the hands of an English merchant named John Philipson, or his son, or the price thereof, if by them sold or pledged,
she left to the said John Philipson and his son Arthur Philipson,
with a view to the prosecution of the design which they had been
destined to advance, or if that should prove impossible, to their
own use and profit. The charge of her funeral rites was wholly
intrusted to Arthur, called Philipson, with a request that they
should be conducted entirely after the forms observed in England. This trust was expressed in an addition to her will, signed
the very day on which she died.

Arthur lost no time in dispatching Thiebault express to his
father, with a letter, explaining in such terms as he knew would
be understood, the tenor of all that had happened since he came
to Aix, and, above all, the death of Queen Margaret.

Finally, he requested directions for his motions, since the

necessary delay occupied by the obsequies of a person of such eminent rank must detain him at Aix till he should receive them.

The old King sustained the shock of his daughter's death so easily, that on the second day after the event, he was engaged in arranging a pompous procession for the funeral, and composing an elegy, to be sung to a tune also of his own composing, in honour of the deceased Queen, who was likened to the goddesses of heathen mythology, and to Judith, Deborah, and all the other holy women, not to mention the saints of the Christian dispensation. It cannot be concealed, that when the first burst of grief was over, King René could not help feeling that Margaret's death cut a political knot which he might have otherwise found it difficult to untie, and permitted him to take open part with his grandson, so far indeed as to afford him a considerable share of the contents of the Provençal treasury, which amounted to no larger sum than ten thousand crowns. Ferrand having received the blessing of his grandfather, in a form which his affairs rendered most important to him, returned to the resolutes whom he commanded; and with him, after a most loving farewell to Arthur, went the stout but simple-minded young Swiss, Sigismund Biederman.

The little court of Aix were left to their mourning. King René, for whom ceremonial and show, whether of a joyful or melancholy character, was always matter of importance, would willingly have bestowed in solemnizing the obsequies of his daughter Margaret what remained of his revenue, but was prevented from doing so, partly by remonstrances from his ministers, partly by the obstacles opposed by the young Englishman, who, acting upon the presumed will of the dead, interfered to prevent any such fantastic exhibitions being produced at the obsequies of the Queen, as had disgusted her during her life.

The funeral, therefore, after many days had been spent in public prayers, and acts of devotion, was solemnized with the mournful magnificence due to the birth of the deceased, and with which the Church of Rome so well knows how to affect at once the eye, ear, and feelings.

Amid the various nobles who assisted on the solemn occasion, there was one who arrived just as the tolling of the great bells of St. Sauveur had announced that the procession was already on its way to the Cathedral. The stranger hastily exchanged his travelling dress for a suit of deep mourning, which was made after the fashion proper to England. So attired, he repaired to the Cathedral, where the noble mien of the cavalier imposed such respect on the attendants, that he was permitted to approach close to the side of the bier; and it was across the coffin of the Queen for whom he had acted and suffered so much, that the gallant Earl of Oxford exchanged melancholy glance with his son. The assistants, especially the English servants of Margaret, gazed on them both with respect and wonder, and the elder cavalier, in particular, seemed to them no unapt representative of the faithful subjects of England, paying their last duty at the tomb of her who had so long swayed the sceptre, if not faultlessly, yet always with a bold and resolved hand.

The last sound of the solemn dirge had died away, and almost all the funeral attendants had retired, when the father and son still lingered in mournful silence beside the remains of their Sovereign. The clergy at length approached, and intimated they were about to conclude the last duties, by removing the body which had been lately occupied and animated by so haughty and restless a spirit, to the dust, darkness, and silence of the vault, where the long-descended Counts of Provence awaited dissolution. Six priests raised the bier on their shoulders, others bore huge waxen torches before and behind the body, as they carried it down a private staircase which yawned in the floor to admit their descent. The last notes of the requiem, in which the churchmen joined, had died away along the high and fretted arches of the Cathedral, the last flash of light which arose from the mouth of the vault had glimmered and disappeared, when the Earl of Oxford, taking his son by the arm, led him in silence forth into a small cloistered court behind the building, where they found themselves alone. They were silent for a few minutes, for both, and particularly the father, were deeply affected. At length the Earl spoke.

"And this, then, is her end," said he. "Here, royal lady, all that we have planned and pledged life upon falls to pieces with thy dissolution! The heart of resolution, the head of policy is gone; and what avails it that the limbs of the enterprise still have motion and life? Alas, Margaret of Anjou! may Heaven reward thy virtues, and absolve thee from the consequence of thine errors! Both belonged to thy station, and if thou didst hoist too high a sail in prosperity, never lived there princess who defied more proudly the storms of adversity, or bore up against them with such dauntless nobility of determination. With this event the drama has closed, and our parts, my son, are ended."

"We bear arms, then, against the infidels, my lord?" said Arthur, with a sigh that was, however, hardly audible.

"Not," answered the Earl, "until I learn that Henry of Richmond, the undoubted heir of the House of Lancaster, has no occasion for my services. In these jewels, of which you wrote me, so strangely lost and recovered, I may be able to supply him with resources more needful than either your services or mine. But I return no more to the camp of the Duke of Burgundy; for in him there is no help."

"Can it be possible that the power of so great a sovereign has been overthrown in one fatal battle?" said Arthur.

"By no means," replied his father. "The loss at Granson was very great; but to the strength of Burgundy it is but a scratch on the shoulders of a giant. It is the spirit of Charles himself, his wisdom at least, and his foresight, which have given way under the mortification of a defeat, by such as he accounted inconsiderable enemies, and expected to have trampled down with a squadrons of his men-at-arms. Then his temper is become froward, peevish, and arbitrary, devoted to those who flatter, and, as there is too much reason to believe, betray him; and suspicious of those counsellors who give him wholesome advice. Even I have had my share of distrust. Thou knowest I refused to bear arms against our late hosts the Swiss; and he saw in that no reason for rejecting my attendance on his march. But since the defeat of Granson, I have observed a strong and sudden change, owing, perhaps, in some degree to the insinuations of Campo-Basso, and not a little to the injured pride of the Duke, who was unwilling that an indifferent person in my situation, and thinking as I do, should witness the disgrace of his arms. He spoke in my hearing of lukewarm friends, cold-blooded neutrals, — of those who, not being with him, must be against him. I tell thee, Arthur de Vere, the Duke has said that which touched my honour so nearly, that nothing but the commands of Queen Margaret, and the interests of the House of Lancaster, could have made me remain in his camp. That is over — My royal mistress has no more occasion for my poor services — the Duke can spare no aid to our cause — and if he could, we can no longer dispose of the only bribe which might have induced him to afford us succours. The power of seconding his views on Provence is buried with Margaret of Anjou."

"What, then, is your purpose?" demanded his son.

"I propose," said Oxford, "to wait at the court of King René until I can hear from the Earl of Richmond, as we must still call him. I am aware that banished men are rarely welcome at the court of a foreign prince; but I have been the faithful follower of his daughter Margaret. I only propose to reside in disguise, and desire neither notice nor maintenance; so methinks King René will not refuse to permit me to breathe the air of his dominions, until I learn in what direction fortune or duty shall call me."

"Be assured he will not," answered Arthur. "René is incapable of a base or ignoble thought; and if he could despise trifles as he detests dishonour, he might be ranked high in the list of monarchs."

This resolution being adopted, the son presented his father at King René's court, whom he privately made acquainted that he was a man of quality, and a distinguished Lancastrian. The good King would in his heart have preferred a guest of lighter accomplishments and gayer temper, to Oxford, a statesman and a soldier of melancholy and grave habits. The Earl was conscious of this, and seldom troubled his benevolent and light-hearted host with his presence. He had, however, an opportunity of rendering the old King a favour of peculiar value. This was in conducting an important treaty betwixt René and Louis XI. of France, his nephew. Upon that crafty monarch, René finally settled his principality, for the necessity of extricating his affairs by such a measure was now apparent even to himself, every thought of favouring Charles of Burgundy in the arrangement having died with Queen Margaret. The policy and wisdom of the English Earl, who was intrusted with almost the sole charge of this secret and delicate measure, were of the utmost advantage to good King Rend, who was freed from personal and pecuniary vexations, and enabled to go piping and labouring to his grave. Louis did not fail to propitiate the plenipotentiary, by throwing out distant hopes of aid to the efforts of the Lancastrian party in England. A faint and insecure negotiation was entered into upon the subject; and these affairs, which rendered two journeys to Paris necessary on the part of Oxford and his son, in the spring and summer of the year 1476, occupied them until that year was half spent.

In the meanwhile, the wars of the Duke of Burgundy with the Swiss Cantons and Count Ferrand of Lorraine, continued to rage. Before midsummer, 1476, Charles had assembled a new army of at least sixty thousand men, supported by one hundred and fifty pieces of cannon, for the purpose of invading Switzerland, where the warlike mountaineers easily levied a host of thirty thousand Switzers, now accounted almost invincible, and called upon their confederates, the Free Cities on the Rhine, to support them with a powerful body of cavalry. The first efforts of Charles were successful. He overran the Pays de Vaud, and recovered most of the places which he had lost after the defeat at Granson. But instead of attempting to secure a well-defended frontier, or what would have been still more politic, to achieve a peace upon equitable terms with his redoubtable neighbours, this most obstinate of princes resumed the purpose of penetrating into the recesses of the Alpine mountains, and chastising the mountaineers even within their own strongholds, though experience might have taught him the danger, nay desperation, of the attempt. Thus the news received by Oxford and his son, when they returned to Aix in midsummer, was, that Duke Charles had advanced to Morat, (or Murten,) situated upon a lake of the same name, at the very entrance of Switzerland. Here report said, that Adrian de Bubenberg, a veteran knight of Berne, commanded, and maintained the most obstinate defence, in expectation of the relief which his countrymen were hastily assembling.

"Alas, my old brother-in-arms!" said the Earl to his son, on hearing these tidings, "this town besieged, these assaults repelled, this vicinity of an enemy's country, this profound lake, these inaccessible cliffs, threaten a second part of the tragedy of Granson, more calamitous perhaps than even the former."

On the last week of July, the capital of Provence was agitated by one of those unauthorized, yet generally received rumours, which transmit great events with incredible swiftness, as an apple flung from hand to hand by a number of people will pass a given space infinitely faster than if borne by the most rapid series of expresses. The report announced a second defeat of the Burgundians, in terms so exaggerated, as induced the Earl of Oxford to consider the greater part, if not the whole, as a fabrication.

CHAPTER XXXIV

And is the hostile troop arrived,
And have they won the day?
It must have been a bloody field
Ere Darwent fled away!

THE ETTRICK SHEPHERD

Sleep did not close the eyes of the Earl of Oxford or his son; for although the success or defeat of the Duke of Burgundy could not now be of importance to their own private or political affairs, yet the father did not cease to interest himself in the fate of his former companion in arms; and the son, with the fire of youth, always eager after novelty,[20] expected to find something to advance or thwart his own progress in every remarkable event which agitated the world.

Arthur had risen from his bed, and was in the act of attiring himself, when the tread of a horse arrested his attention. He had no sooner looked out of the window, than exclaiming, "News, my father, news from the army!" he rushed into the street, where a cavalier, who appeared to have ridden very hard, was inquiring for the two Philipsons, father and son. He had no difficulty in recognizing Colvin, the master of the Burgundian ordnance. His ghastly look bespoke distress of mind; his disordered array and broken armour, which seemed rusted with rain, or stained with blood, gave the intelligence of some affray in which he had probably been worsted; and so exhausted was his gallant steed, that it was with difficulty the animal could stand upright. The condition of the rider was not much better. When he alighted from his horse to greet Arthur, he reeled so much that he would have fallen without instant support. His horny eye had lost the power of speculation; his limbs possessed imperfectly that of motion, and it was with a half suffocated voice that he muttered, "Only fatigue — want of rest and of food."

Arthur assisted him into the house, and refreshments were procured; but he refused all except a bowl of wine, after tasting which he set it down, and looking at the Earl of Oxford with an eye of the deepest affliction, he ejaculated, "The Duke of Burgundy!"

---

[20] Cupidus novarum rerum.

"Slain?" replied the Earl; "I trust not!"

"It might have been better if he were," said the Englishman; "but dishonour has come before death."

"Defeated, then?" said Oxford.

"So completely and fearfully defeated," answered the soldier, "that all that I have seen of loss before was slight in comparison."

"But how, or where?" said the Earl of Oxford; "you were superior in numbers, as we were informed."

"Two to one at least," answered Colvin; "and when I speak of our encounter at this moment, I could rend my flesh with my teeth for being here to tell such a tale of shame. We had sat down for about a week before that paltry town of Murten, or Morat, or whatever it is called. The governor, one of those stubborn mountain bears of Berne, bade us defiance. He would not even condescend to shut his gates, but when we summoned the town, returned for answer, we might enter if we pleased — we should be suitably received. I would have tried to bring him to reason by a salvo or two of artillery, but the Duke was too much irritated to listen to good counsel. Stimulated by that black traitor, Campo-Basso, he deemed it better to run forward with his whole force upon a place, which, though I could soon have battered it about their German ears, was yet too strong to be carried by swords, lances, and hagbuts. We were beaten off with great loss, and much discouragement to the soldiers. We then commenced more regularly, and my batteries would have brought these mad Switzers to their senses. Walls and ramparts went down before the lusty cannoneers of Burgundy; we were well secured also by intrenchments against those whom we heard of as approaching to raise the siege. But on the evening of the twentieth of this month, we learned that they were close at hand, and Charles, consulting only his own bold spirit, advanced to meet them, relinquishing the advantage of our batteries and strong position. By his orders, though against my own judgment I accompanied him with twenty good pieces, and the flower of my people. We broke up on the next morning, and had not advanced far before we saw the lances and thick array of halberds and two-handed swords which crested the mountain. Heaven, too, added its terrors — A thunder-storm, with all the fury of those tempestuous climates, descended on both armies, but did most annoyance to ours, as our troops, especially the Italians, were more sensible to the torrents of rain which poured down, and the rivulets, which swelled into torrents, inundated and disordered our position. The Duke for once saw it necessary to alter his purpose of instant battle. He rode up to me, and directed me to defend with the cannon the retreat which he was about to commence, adding, that he himself would in person sustain me with the men-at-arms. The order was given to retreat. But the movement gave new spirit to an enemy already sufficiently audacious. The ranks of the Swiss instantly prostrated themselves in prayer — a practice on the field of battle which I have ridiculed — but I will do so no more. When, after five minutes they sprung again on their feet, and began to advance rapidly, sounding their horns and crying their war-cries with all their usual ferocity — behold, my lord, the clouds of heaven opened, shedding on the Confederates the blessed light of the returning sun, while our ranks were still in the gloom of the tempest. My men were discouraged. The host behind them was retreating; the sudden light thrown on the advancing Switzers showed along the mountains a prolusion of banners, a glancing of arms, giving to the enemy the appearance of double the numbers that had hitherto bee a visible to us. I exhorted my followers to stand fast, but in doing so I thought a thought, and spoke a word, which was a grievous sin. 'Stand fast, my brave cannoneers,' I said, 'we will presently let them hear louder thunders, and show them more fatal lightnings, than their prayers have put down!' — My men shouted — But it was an impious thought — a blasphemous speech — and evil came after it. We levelled our guns on the advancing masses as fairly as cannon were ever pointed — I can vouch it, for I laid the Grand Duchess of Burgundy myself — Ah, poor Duchess! what rude hands manage thee now! — The volley was fired, and ere the smoke spread from the muzzles, I could see many a man, and many a banner, go down. It was natural to think such a discharge should have checked the attack, and whilst the smoke hid the enemy from us, I made every effort again to load our cannon, and anxiously endeavoured to look through the mist to discover the state of our opponents. But ere our smoke was cleared away, or the cannon again loaded, they came headlong down on us, horse and foot, old men and boys, men-at-arms and varlets, charging up to the muzzle of the guns, and over them, with total disregard to their lives. My brave fellows were cut down, pierced through, and overrun, while they were again loading their pieces, nor do I believe that a single cannon was fired a second time."

"And the Duke?" said the Earl of Oxford, "did he not support you?"

"Most loyally and bravely," answered Colvin, "with his own body-guard of Walloons and Burgundians. But a thousand Italian mercenaries went off, and never showed face again. The pass, too, was cumbered with the artillery, and in itself narrow, bordering on mountains and cliffs, a deep lake close beside. In short, it was a place totally unfit for horsemen to act in. In spite of the Duke's utmost exertions, and those of the gallant Flemings who fought around him, all were borne back in complete disorder. I was on foot, fighting as I could, without hopes of my life, or indeed thoughts of saving it, when I saw the guns taken and my faithful cannoneers slain. But I saw Duke Charles hard pressed, and took my horse from my page that held him — Thou, too, art lost, my poor orphan boy! I could only aid Monseigneur de la Croye and others to extricate the Duke. Our retreat became a total rout, and when we reached our rear-guard, which we had left strongly encamped, the banners of the Switzers were waving on our batteries, for a large division had made a circuit, through mountain-passes known only to themselves, and attacked our camp, vigorously seconded by that accursed Adrian de Bubenberg, who sallied from the beleaguered town, so that our intrenchments were stormed on both sides at once. — I have more to say, but having ridden day and night to bring you these evil tidings, my tongue clings to the roof of my mouth, and I feel that I can speak no more. The rest is all flight and massacre, disgraceful to every soldier that shared in it. For my part, I confess my contumelious self-confidence and insolence to man, as well as blasphemy to Heaven. If I live, it is but to hide my disgraced head in a cowl, and expiate the numerous sins of a licentious life."

With difficulty the broken-minded soldier was prevailed upon to take some nourishment and repose, together with an opiate, which was prescribed by the physician of King René, who recommended it as necessary to preserve even the reason of his patient, exhausted by the events of the battle, and subsequent fatigue.

The Earl of Oxford, dismissing other assistance, watched alternately with his son at Colvin's bedside. Notwithstanding the draught that had been administered, his repose was far from sound. Sudden starts, the perspiration which sprung from his brow, the distortions of his countenance, and the manner in which he clenched his fists and flung about his limbs, showed that in his dreams he was again encountering the terrors of a desperate and forlorn combat. This lasted for several hours; but about noon fatigue and medicine prevailed over nervous excitation, and the defeated commander fell into a deep and untroubled repose till evening. About sunset he awakened, and, after learning with whom and where he was, he partook of refreshments, and without any apparent consciousness of having told them before, detailed once more all the particulars of the battle of Murten.

"It were little wide of truth," he said, "to calculate that one half of the Duke's army fell by the sword, or were driven into the lake. Those who escaped are great part of them scattered, never again to unite. Such a desperate and irretrievable rout was never witnessed. We fled like deer, sheep, or any other timid animals, which only remain in company because they are afraid to separate, but never think of order or of defence."

"And the Duke?" said the Earl of Oxford.

"We hurried him with us," said the soldier, "rather from instinct than loyalty, as men flying from a conflagration snatch up what they have of value without knowing what they are doing. Knight and knave, officer and soldier, fled in the same panic, and each blast of the horn of Uri in our rear added new wings to our flight."

"And the Duke?" repeated Oxford.

"At first he resisted our efforts, and strove to turn back on the foe; but when the flight became general, he galloped along with us, without a word spoken or a command issued. At first we thought his silence and passiveness, so unusual in a temper so fiery, were fortunate for securing his personal safety. But when we rode the whole day, without being able to obtain a word of reply to all our questions, — when he sternly refused refreshments of every kind, though he had tasted no food all that disastrous day, — when every variation of his moody and uncertain temper was sunk into silent and sullen despair, we took counsel what was to be done, and it was by the general voice that I was despatched to entreat that you, for whose counsels alone Charles has been known to have had some occasional deference, would come instantly to his place of retreat, and exert all your influence to awaken him from this lethargy, which may otherwise terminate his existence."

"And what remedy can I interpose?" said Oxford. "You know how he neglected my advice, when following it might have served my interest as well as his own. You are aware that my life was not safe among the miscreants that surrounded the Duke, and exercised influence over him."

"Most true," answered Colvin; "but I also know he is your ancient companion-in-arms, and it would ill become me to teach the noble Earl of Oxford what the laws of chivalry require. For your lordship's safety, every honest man in the army will give willing security."

"It is for that I care least," said Oxford, indifferently; "and if indeed my presence can be of service to the Duke, — if I could believe that he desired it" ——

"He does — he does, my lord!" said the faithful soldier, with tears in his eyes. "We heard him name your name, as if the words escaped him in a painful dream."

"I will go to him, such being the case," said Oxford. — "I will go instantly. Where did he purpose to establish his headquarters?"

"He had fixed nothing for himself on that or other matters; but Monsieur de Contay named La Rivière, near Salins, in Upper Burgundy, as the place of his retreat."

"Thither, then, will we, my son, with all haste of preparation. Thou, Colvin, hadst better remain here, and see some holy man, to be assoilzied for thy hasty speech on the battle-field of Morat. There was offence in it without doubt, but it will be ill-atoned for by quitting a generous master when he hath most need of your good service; and it is but an act of cowardice to retreat into the cloister, till we have no longer active duties to perform in this world."

"It is true," said Colvin, "that should I leave the Duke now, perhaps not a man would stay behind that could stell a cannon properly. The sight of your lordship cannot but operate favourably on my noble master, since it has waked the old soldier in myself. If your lordship can delay your journey till to-morrow, I will have my spiritual affairs settled, and my bodily health sufficiently restored, to be your guide to La Rivière; and, for the cloister, I will think of it when I have regained the good name which I have lost at Murten. But I will have masses said, and these right powerful, for the souls of my poor cannoneers."

The proposal of Colvin was adopted, and Oxford, with his son, attended by Thiebault, spent the day in preparation, excepting the time necessary to take formal leave of King René, who seemed to part with them with regret. In company with the ordnance officer of the discomfited Duke, they traversed those parts of Provence, Dauphiné, and Franche Compté, which lie between Aix and the place to which the Duke of Burgundy had retreated; but the distance and inconvenience of so long a route consumed more than a fortnight on the road, and the month of July 1476 was commenced, when the travellers arrived in Upper Burgundy, and at the Castle of La Rivière, about twenty miles to the south of the town of Salins. The castle, which was but of small size, was surrounded by very many tents, which were pitched in a crowded, disordered, and unsoldierlike manner, very unlike the discipline usually observed in the camp of Charles the Bold. That the Duke was present there, however, was attested by his broad banner, which, rich with all its quarterings, streamed from the battlements of the castle. The guard turned out to receive the strangers, but in a manner so disorderly, that the Earl looked to Colvin for explanation. The master of the ordnance shrugged up his shoulders, and was silent.

Colvin having sent in notice of his arrival, and that of the English Earl, Monsieur de Contay caused them presently to be admitted, and expressed much joy at their arrival.

"A few of us," he said, "true servants of the Duke, are holding council here, at which your assistance, my noble Lord of Oxford, will be of the utmost importance. Messieurs De la Croye, De Craon, Rubempré, and others, nobles of Burgundy, are now assembled to superintend the defence of the country at this exigence."

They all expressed delight to see the Earl of Oxford, and had only abstained from thrusting their attentions on him the last time he was in the Duke's camp, as they understood it was his wish to observe incognito.

"His Grace," said De Craon, "has asked after you twice, and on both times by your assumed name of Philipson."

"I wonder not at that, my Lord of Craon," replied the English nobleman; "the origin of the name took its rise in former days, when I was here during my first exile. It was then said, that we poor Lancastrian nobles must assume other names than our own, and the good Duke Philip said, as I was brother-in-arms to his son Charles, I must be called after himself, by the name of Philipson. In memory of the good sovereign, I took that name when the day of need actually arrived, and I see that the Duke thinks of our early intimacy by his distinguishing me so. — How fares his Grace?"

The Burgundians looked at each other, and there was a pause.

"Even like a man stunned, brave Oxford," at length De Contay replied. "Sieur d'Argentin, you can best inform the noble Earl of the condition of our sovereign."

"He is like a man distracted," said the future historian of that busy period. "After the battle of Granson, he was never, to my thinking, of the same sound judgment as before. But then, he was capricious, unreasonable, peremptory, and inconsistent, and resented every counsel that was offered, as if it had been meant in insult; was jealous of the least trespass in point of ceremonial, as if his subjects were holding him in contempt. Now there is a total change, as if this second blow had stunned him, and suppressed the violent passions which the first called into action. He is silent as a Carthusian, solitary as a hermit, expresses interest in nothing, least of all in the guidance of his army. He was, you know, anxious about his dress; so much so, that there was some affectation even in the rudenesses which he practised in that matter. But, woe's me, you will see a change now; he will not suffer his hair or nails to be trimmed or arranged. He is totally heedless of respect or disrespect towards him, takes little or no nourishment, uses strong wines, which, however, do not seem to affect his understanding; he will hear nothing of war or state affairs, as little of hunting or of sport. Suppose an anchorite brought from a cell to govern a kingdom, you see in him, except in point of devotion, a picture of the fiery active Charles of Burgundy."

"You speak of a mind deeply wounded, Sieur d'Argentin,"

replied the Englishman. "Think you it fit I should present myself before the Duke?"

"I will inquire," said Contay; and leaving the apartment, returned presently, and made a sign to the Earl to follow him.

In a cabinet, or closet, the unfortunate Charles reclined in a large arm-chair, his legs carelessly stretched on a footstool, but so changed that the Earl of Oxford could have believed what he saw to be the ghost of the once fiery Duke. Indeed, the shaggy length of hair which, streaming from his head, mingled with his beard; the hollowness of the caverns, at the bottom of which rolled his wild eyes; the falling in of the breast, and the advance of the shoulders, gave the ghastly appearance of one who has suffered the final agony which takes from mortality the signs of life and energy. His very costume (a cloak flung loosely over him) increased his resemblance to a shrouded phantom. De Contay named the Earl of Oxford; but the Duke gazed on him with a lustreless eye, and gave him no answer.

"Speak to him, brave Oxford," said the Burgundian in a whisper; "he is even worse than usual, but perhaps he may know your voice."

Never, when the Duke of Burgundy was in the most palmy state of his fortunes, did the noble Englishman kneel to kiss his hand with such sincere reverence. He respected in him, not only the afflicted friend, but the humbled sovereign, upon whose tower of trust the lightning had so recently broken. It was probably the falling of a tear upon his hand which seemed to awake the Duke's attention, for he looked towards the Earl, and said, "Oxford — Philipson — my old — my only friend, hast thou found me out in this retreat of shame and misery?"

"I am not your only friend, my lord," said Oxford. "Heaven has given you many affectionate friends among your natural and loyal subjects. But though a stranger, and saving the allegiance I owe to my lawful sovereign, I will yield to none of them in the respect and deference which I have paid to your Grace in prosperity, and now come to render to you in adversity."

"Adversity, indeed!" said the Duke; "irremediable, intolerable adversity! I was lately Charles of Burgundy, called the Bold — now am I twice beaten by a scum of German peasants; my standard taken, my men-at-arms put to flight, my camp twice plundered, and each time of value more than equal to the price of all Switzerland fairly lost; myself hunted like a caitiff goat or chamois — The utmost spite of hell could never accumulate more shame on the head of a sovereign!"

"On the contrary, my lord," said Oxford, "it is a trial of Heaven, which calls for patience and strength of mind. The bravest and best knight may lose the saddle; he is but a laggard who lies rolling on the sand of the lists after the accident has chanced."

"Ha, laggard, sayst thou?" said the Duke, some part of his ancient spirit awakened by the broad taunt; "Leave my presence, sir, and return to it no more, till you are summoned thither" ——

"Which I trust will be no later than your Grace quits your dishabille, and disposes yourself to see your vassals and friends with such ceremony as befits you and them," said the Earl composedly.

"How mean you by that, Sir Earl? You are unmannerly."

"If I be, my lord, I am taught my ill-breeding by circumstances. I can mourn over fallen dignity; but I cannot honour him who dishonours himself by bending, like a regardless boy, beneath the scourge of evil fortune."

"And who am I that you should term me such?" said Charles, starting up in all his natural pride and ferocity "or who are you but a miserable exile, that you should break in upon my privacy with such disrespectful upbraiding?"

"For me," replied Oxford, "I am, as you say, an unrespected exile; nor am I ashamed of my condition, since unshaken loyalty to my king and his successors has brought me to it. But in you, can I recognise the Duke of Burgundy in a sullen hermit, whose guards are a disorderly soldiery, dreadful only to their friends; whose councils are in confusion for want of their sovereign, and who himself lurks, like a lamed wolf in its den, in an obscure castle, waiting but a blast of the Switzer's horn to fling open its gates, which there are none to defend; who wears not a knightly sword to protect his person, and cannot even die like a stag at bay, but must be worried like a hunted fox?"

"Death and hell, slanderous traitor!" thundered the Duke, glancing a look at his side, and perceiving himself without a weapon, — "It is well for thee I have no sword, or thou shouldst never boast of thine insolence going unpunished. — Contay, step forth like a good knight and confute the calumniator. Say, are not my soldiers arrayed, disciplined, and in order?"

"My lord," said Contay, trembling (brave as he was in battle) at the frantic rage which Charles exhibited, "there are a numerous soldiery yet under your command, but they are in evil order, and in worse discipline, I think, than they were wont."

"I see it — I see it," said the Duke; "idle and evil counsellors are ye all. — Hearken, Sir of Contay, what have you and the rest of you been doing, holding as you do large lands and high fiefs of us, that I cannot stretch my limbs on a sick-bed, when my heart is half broken, but my troops must fall into such scandalous disorder as exposes me to the scorn and reproach of each beggarly foreigner?"

"My lord," replied Contay more firmly, "we have done what we could. But your Grace has accustomed your mercenary generals and leaders of Free Companies, to take their orders only from your own mouth, or hand. They clamour also for pay, and the treasurer refuses to issue it without your Grace's order, as he alleges it might cost him his head; and they will not be guided and restrained, either by us or those who compose your council."

The Duke laughed sternly, but was evidently somewhat pleased with the reply.

"Ha, ha!" he said, "it is only Burgundy who can ride his own wild horses, and rule his own wild soldiery. Hark thee, Contay — To-morrow I ride forth to review the troops — for what disorder has passed allowance shall be made. Pay also shall be issued — but woe to those who shall have offended too deeply! Let my grooms of the chamber know to provide me fitting dress and arms. I have got a lesson," (glancing a dark look at Oxford,) "and I will not again be insulted without the means of wreaking my vengeance. Begone, both of you. And, Contay, send the treasurer hither with his accounts, and woe to his soul if I find aught to complain of! Begone, I say, and send him hither."

They left the apartment with suitable obeisance. As they retired, the Duke said abruptly, "Lord of Oxford, a word with you. Where did you study medicine? In your own famed university, I suppose. Thy physic hath wrought a wonder. Yet, Doctor Philipson, it might have cost thee thy life."

"I have ever thought my life cheap," said Oxford, "when the object was to help my friend."

"Thou art indeed a friend," said Charles, "and a fearless

one. But go — I have been sore troubled, and thou hast tasked my temper closely. To-morrow we will speak further; meantime, I forgive thee, and I honour thee."

The Earl of Oxford retired to the Council-hall, where the Burgundian nobility, aware of what had passed, crowded around him with thanks, compliments, and congratulations. A general bustle now ensued; orders were hurried off in every direction. Those officers who had duties to perform which had been neglected, hastened to conceal or to atone for their negligence. There was a general tumult in the camp, but it was a tumult of joy; for soldiers are always most pleased when they are best in order for performing their military service; and license or inactivity, however acceptable at times, are not, when continued, so agreeable to their nature, as strict discipline and a prospect of employment.

The treasurer, who was, luckily for him, a man of sense and method, having been two hours in private with the Duke, returned with looks of wonder, and professed, that never in Charles's most prosperous days, had he showed himself more acute in the department of finance, of which he had but that morning seemed totally incapable; and the merit was universally attributed to the visit of Lord Oxford, whose timely reprimand had, like the shot of a cannon, dispersing foul mists, awakened the Duke from his black and bilious melancholy.

On the following day, Charles reviewed his troops with his usual attention, directed new levies, made various dispositions of his forces, and corrected the faults of their discipline by severe orders, which were enforced by some deserved punishments, (of which the Italian mercenaries of Campo-Basso had a large share,) and rendered palatable by the payment of arrears, which was calculated to attach them to the standard under which they served.

The Duke also, after consulting with his council, agreed to convoke meetings of the States in his different territories, redress certain popular grievances, and grant some boons which he had hitherto denied; and thus began to open a new account of popularity with his subjects, in place of that which his rashness had exhausted.

CHAPTER XXXV

— Here's a weapon now,
Shall shake a conquering general in his tent,
A monarch on his throne, or reach a prelate,
However holy he his offices,
E'en while he serves the altar.

OLD PLAY.

From this time all was activity in the Duke of Burgundy's court and army. Money was collected, soldiers were levied, and certain news of the Confederates' motions only were wanting to bring on the campaign. But although Charles was, to all outward appearance, as active as ever, yet those who were more immediately about his person were of opinion that he did not display the soundness of mind, or the energy of judgment, which had been admired in him before these calamities. He was still liable to fits of moody melancholy, similar to those which descended upon Saul, and was vehemently furious when aroused out of them. Indeed, the Earl of Oxford himself seemed to have lost the power which he had exercised over him at first. Nay, though in general Charles was both grateful and affectionate towards him, he evidently felt humbled by the recollection of his having witnessed his impotent and disastrous condition, and was so much afraid of Lord Oxford being supposed to lead his counsels, that he often repelled his advice, merely, as it seemed, to show his own independence of mind.

In these froward humours, the Duke was much encouraged by Campo-Basso. That wily traitor now saw his master's affairs tottering to their tall, and he resolved to lend his lever to the work, so as to entitle him to a share of the spoil. He regarded Oxford as one of the most able friends and counsellors who adhered to the Duke; he thought he saw in his looks that he fathomed his own treacherous purpose, and therefore he hated and feared him. Besides, in order perhaps to colour over, even to his own eyes, the abominable perfidy he meditated, he affected to be exceedingly enraged against the Duke for the late punishment of marauders belonging to his Italian bands. He believed that chastisement to have been inflicted by the advice of Oxford; and he suspected that the measure was pressed with the hope of discovering that the Italians had not pillaged for their own emolument only, but for that of their commander. Believing that Oxford was thus hostile to him, Campo-Basso would have speedily found means to take him out of his path, had not the Earl himself found it prudent to observe some precautions; and the lords of Flanders and Burgundy, who loved him for the very reasons for which the Italian abhorred him, watched over his safety with a vigilance, of which he himself was ignorant, but which certainly was the means of preserving his life.

It was not to be supposed that Ferrand of Lorraine should have left his victory so long unimproved, but the Swiss Confederates, who were the strength of his forces, insisted that the first operations should take place in Savoy and the Pays de Vaud, where the Burgundians had many garrisons, which, though they received no relief, yet were not easily or speedily reduced. Besides, the Switzers being, like most of the national soldiers of the time, a kind of militia, most of them returned home, to get in their harvest, and to deposit their spoil in safety. Ferrand, therefore, though bent on pursuing his success with all the ardour of youthful chivalry, was prevented from making any movement in advance until the month of December, 1476. In the mean time, the Duke of Burgundy's forces, to be least burdensome to the country, were cantoned in distant places of his dominions, where every exertion was made to perfect the discipline of the new levies. The Duke, if left to himself, would have precipitated the struggle by again assembling his forces, and pushing forward into the Helvetian territories; but though he inwardly foamed at the recollection of Granson and Murten, the memory of these disasters was too recent to permit such a plan of the campaign. Meantime, weeks glided past, and the month of December was far advanced, when one morning, as the Duke was sitting in council, Campo-Basso suddenly entered, with a degree of extravagant rapture in his countenance, singularly different from the cold, regulated, and subtle smile which was usually his utmost advance towards laughter. "*Guantes,*"[21] he said, "*Guantes,* for luck's sake, if it please your Grace."

"And what of good fortune comes nigh us?" said the Duke, — "Methought she had forgot the way to our gates."

---

[21] *Guantes,* used by the Spanish as the French say étrennes, or the English handsell or luckpenny — phrases used by inferiors to their patrons as the bringers of good news.

"She has returned to them, please your Highness, with her cornucopia full of choicest gifts, ready to pour her fruit, her flowers, her treasures, on the head of the sovereign of Europe most worthy to receive them."

"The meaning of all this?" said Duke Charles; "riddles are for children."

"The harebrained young madman Ferrand, who calls himself of Lorraine, has broken down from the mountains, at the head of a desultory army of scapegraces like himself; and what think you, — ha! ha! ha! — they are over running Lorraine, and have taken Nancy — ha! ha! ha!"

"By my good faith, Sir Count," said Contay, astonished at the gay humour with which the Italian treated a matter so serious, "I have seldom heard a fool laugh more gayly at a more scurvy jest than you, a wise man, laugh at the loss of the principal town of the province we are fighting for."

"I laugh," said Campo-Basso, "among the spears, as my war-horse does — ha! ha! — among the trumpets. I laugh also over the destruction of the enemy, and the dividing of the spoil, as eagles scream their joy over the division of their prey; I laugh" ——

"You laugh," said the Lord of Contay, waxing impatient, "when you have all the mirth to yourself, as you laughed after our losses at Granson and Murten."

"Peace, sir!" said the Duke. "The Count of Campo-Basso has viewed the case as I do. This young knight-errant ventures from the protection of his mountains; and Heaven deal with me as I keep my oath, when I swear that the next fair field on which we meet shall see one of us dead! It is now the last week of the old year, and before Twelfth-Day we will see whether he or I shall find the bean in the cake. — To arms, my lords; let our camp instantly break up, and our troops move forward towards Lorraine. Send off the Italian and Albanian light cavalry, and the Stradiots, to scour the country in the van — Oxford, thou wilt bear arms in this journey, wilt thou not?"

"Surely," said the Earl. "I am eating your Highness's bread; and when enemies invade, it stands with my honour to fight for your Grace as if I was your born subject. With your Grace's permission, I will dispatch a pursuivant, who shall carry letters to my late kind host, the Landamman of Unterwalden, acquainting him with my purpose."

The Duke having given a ready assent, the pursuivant was dismissed accordingly, and returned in a few hours, so near had the armies approached to each other. He bore a letter from the Landamman, in a tone of courtesy and even kindness, regretting that any cause should have occurred for bearing arms against his late guest, for whom he expressed high personal regard. The same pursuivant also brought greetings from the family of the Biedermans to their friend Arthur, and a separate letter, addressed to the same person, of which the contents ran thus: —

"Rudolph Donnerhugel is desirous to give the young merchant, Arthur Philipson, the opportunity of finishing the bargain which remained unsettled between them in the castle-court of Geierstein. He is the more desirous of this, as he is aware that the said Arthur has done him wrong, in seducing the affections of a certain maiden of rank, to whom he, Philipson, is not, and cannot be, any thing beyond an ordinary acquaintance. Rudolph Donnerhugel will send Arthur Philipson word, when a fair and equal meeting can take place on neutral ground. In the mean time, he will be as often as possible in the first rank of the skirmishers."

Young Arthur's heart leapt high as he read the defiance, the piqued tone of which showed the state of the writer's feelings, and argued sufficiently Rudolph's disappointment on the subject of Anne of Geierstein, and his suspicion that she had bestowed her affections on the youthful stranger. Arthur found means of dispatching a reply to the challenge of the Swiss, assuring him of the pleasure with which he would attend his commands, either in front of the line or elsewhere, as Rudolph might desire.

Meantime the armies were closely approaching to each other, and the light troops sometimes met. The Stradiots from the Venetian territory, a sort of cavalry resembling that of the Turks, performed much of that service on the part of the Burgundian army, for which, indeed, if their fidelity could have been relied on, they were admirably well qualified. The Earl of Oxford observed, that these men, who were under the command of Campo-Basso, always brought in intelligence that the enemy were in indifferent order, and in full retreat. Besides, information was communicated through their means, that sundry individuals, against whom the Duke of Burgundy entertained peculiar personal dislike, and whom he specially desired to get into his hands, had taken refuge in Nancy. This greatly increased the Duke's ardour for retaking that place, which became perfectly ungovernable when he learned that Ferrand and his Swiss allies had drawn off to a neighbouring position called Saint Nicholas, on the news of his arrival. The greater part of the Burgundian counsellors, together with the Earl of Oxford, protested against his besieging a place of some strength, while an active enemy lay in the neighbourhood to relieve it. They remonstrated on the smallness of his army, on the severity of the weather, on the difficulty of obtaining provisions, and exhorted the Duke, that having made such a movement as had forced the enemy to retreat, he ought to suspend decisive operations till spring. Charles at first tried to dispute and repel these arguments; but when his counsellors reminded him that he was placing himself and his army in the same situation as at Granson and Murten, he became furious at the recollection, foamed at the mouth, and only answered by oaths and imprecations, that he would be master of Nancy before Twelfth-Day.

Accordingly, the army of Burgundy sat down before Nancy, in a strong position, protected by the hollow of a watercourse, and covered with thirty pieces of cannon, which Colvin had under his charge.

Having indulged his obstinate temper in thus arranging the campaign, the Duke seemed to give a little more heed to the advice of his counsellors touching the safety of his person, and permitted the Earl of Oxford, with his son, and two or three officers of his household, men of approved trust, to sleep within his pavilion, in addition to the usual guard.

It wanted three days of Christmas when the Duke sat down before Nancy, and on that very evening a tumult happened which seemed to justify the alarm for his personal safety. It was midnight, and all in the ducal pavilion were at rest, when a cry of treason arose. The Earl of Oxford, drawing his sword and snatching up a light which burned beside him, rushed into the Duke's apartment, and found him standing on the floor totally undressed, but with his sword in his hand, and striking around him so furiously, that the Earl himself had difficulty in avoiding his blows. The rest of his officers rushed in, their weapons drawn, and their cloaks wrapped around their left arms. When the Duke was somewhat composed, and found himself surrounded by his friends, he informed them with rage and agitation, that the officers of the Secret Tribunal had, in spite of the vigilant precautions taken, found means to gain entrance into his chamber, and charged him, under the highest penalty, to appear before the Holy Vehmé upon Christmas night.

The bystanders heard this story with astonishment, and some of them were uncertain whether they ought to consider it as a reality or a dream of the Duke's irritable fancy. But the citation was found on the Duke's toilet, written, as was the form, upon parchment, signeted with three crosses, and stuck to the table with a knife. A slip of wood had been also cut from the table. Oxford read the summons with attention. It named as usual a place, where the Duke was cited to come unarmed and unattended, and from which it was said he would be guided to the seat of judgment.

Charles, after looking at the scroll for some time, gave vent to his thoughts.

"I know from what quiver this arrow comes," he said. "It is shot by that degenerate noble, apostate priest, and accomplice of sorcerers, Albert of Geierstein. We have heard that he is among the motley group of murderers and outlaws, whom the old fiddler of Provence's grandson has raked together. But, by Saint George of Burgundy! neither monk's cowl, soldier's casque, nor conjuror's cap, shall save him after such an insult as this. I will degrade him from knighthood, hang him from the highest steeple in Nancy, and his daughter shall choose between the meanest herdboy in my army, and the convent of *filles repentées!*"

"Whatever are your purposes, my lord," said Contay, "it were surely best be silent, when, from this late apparition, we may conjecture that more than we wot of may be within hearing."

The Duke seemed struck with this hint, and was silent, or at least only muttered oaths and threats betwixt his teeth, while the strictest search was made for the intruder on his repose. But it was in vain.

Charles continued his researches, incensed at a flight of audacity higher than ever had been ventured upon by these Secret Societies, who, whatever might be the dread inspired by them, had not as yet attempted to cope with sovereigns. A trusty party of Burgundians were sent on Christmas night to watch the spot, (a meeting of four cross roads,) named in the summons, and make prisoners of any whom they could lay hands upon; but no suspicious persons appeared at or near the place. The Duke not the less continued to impute the affront he had received to Albert of Geierstein. There was a price set upon his head; and Campo-Basso, always willing to please his master's mood, undertook that some of his Italians, sufficiently experienced in such feats, should bring the obnoxious baron before him, alive or dead. Colvin, Contay, and others, laughed in secret at the Italian's promises.

"Subtle as he is," said Colvin, "he will lure the wild vulture from the heavens before he gets Albert of Geierstein into his power."

Arthur, to whom the words of the Duke had given subject for no small anxiety, on account of Anne of Geierstein, and of her father for her sake, breathed more lightly on hearing his menaces held so cheaply.

It was the second day after this alarm that Oxford felt a desire to reconnoitre the camp of Ferrand of Lorraine, having some doubts whether the strength and position of it were accurately reported. He obtained the Duke's consent for this purpose, who at the same time made him and his son a present of two noble steeds of great power and speed, which he himself highly valued.

So soon as the Duke's pleasure was communicated to the Italian Count, he expressed the utmost joy that he was to have the assistance of Oxford's age and experience upon an exploratory party, and selected a chosen band of a hundred Stradiots, whom he said he had sent sometimes to skirmish up to the very beards of the Switzers. The Earl showed himself much satisfied with the active and intelligent manner in which these men performed their duty, and drove before them and dispersed some parties of Ferrand's cavalry. At the entrance of a little ascending valley, Campo-Basso communicated to the English noblemen, that if they could advance to the farther extremity they would have a full view of the enemy's position. Two or three Stradiots then spurred on to examine this defile, and, returning back, communicated with their leader in their own language, who, pronouncing the passage safe, invited the Earl of Oxford to accompany him. They proceeded through the valley without seeing an enemy, but on issuing upon a plain at the point intimated by

Campo-Basso, Arthur, who was in the van of the Stradiots, and separated from his father, did indeed see the camp of Duke Ferrand within half a mile's distance; but a body of cavalry had that instant issued from it, and were riding hastily towards the gorge of the valley, from which he had just emerged. He was about to wheel his horse and ride off, but, conscious of the great speed of the animal, he thought he might venture to stay for a moment's more accurate survey of the camp. The Stradiots who attended him did not wait his orders to retire, but went off, as was indeed their duty, when attacked by a superior force.

Meantime, Arthur observed that the knight, who seemed leader of the advancing squadron, mounted on a powerful horse that shook the earth beneath him, bore on his shield the Bear of Berne, and had otherwise the appearance of the massive frame of Rudolph Donnerhugel. He was satisfied of this when he beheld the cavalier halt his party and advance towards him alone, putting his lance in rest, and moving slowly, as if to give him time for preparation. To accept such a challenge, in such a moment, was dangerous, but to refuse it was disgraceful; and while Arthur's blood boiled at the idea of chastising an insolent rival, he was not a little pleased at heart that their meeting on horseback gave him an advantage over the Swiss, through his perfect acquaintance with the practice of the tournay, in which Rudolph might be supposed more ignorant.

They met, as was the phrase of the time, "manful under shield." The lance of the Swiss glanced from the helmet of the Englishman, against which it was addressed, while the spear of Arthur, directed right against the centre of his adversary's body, was so justly aimed, and so truly seconded by the full fury of the career, as to pierce, not only the shield which hung round the ill-fated warrior's neck, but a breastplate, and a shirt of mail which he wore beneath it. Passing clear through the body, the steel point of the weapon was only stopped by the back-piece of the unfortunate cavalier, who fell headlong from his horse, as if struck by lightning, rolled twice or thrice over on the ground, tore the earth with his hands, and then lay prostrate a dead corpse.

There was a cry of rage and grief among those men-at-arms whose ranks Rudolph had that instant left, and many couched their lances to avenge him; but Ferrand of Lorraine, who was present in person, ordered them to make prisoner, but not to harm the successful champion. This was accomplished, for Arthur had not time to turn his bridle for flight, and resistance would have been madness.

When brought before Ferrand, he raised his visor, and said, "Is it well, my lord, to make captive an adventurous Knight, for doing his devoir against a personal challenger?"

"Do not complain, Sir Arthur of Oxford," said Ferrand, "before you experience injury — You are free, Sir Knight. Your father and you were faithful to my royal aunt Margaret, and although she was my enemy, I do justice to your fidelity in her behalf; and from respect to her memory, disinherited as she was like myself, and to please my grandfather, who I think had some regard for you, I give you your freedom. But I must also care for your safety during your return to the camp of Burgundy. On this side of the hill we are loyal and true-hearted men, on the other, they are traitors and murderers. — You, Sir Count, will, I think, gladly see our captive placed in safety."

The Knight to whom Ferrand addressed himself, a tall stately man, put himself in motion to attend on Arthur, while the former was expressing to the young Duke of Lorraine the sense he entertained of his chivalrous conduct. "Farewell, Sir Arthur de Vere," said Ferrand. "You have slain a noble champion, and to me a most useful and faithful friend. But it was done nobly and openly, with equal arms, and in the front of the line; and evil befall him who entertains feud first!" Arthur bowed to his saddlebow. Ferrand returned the salutation, and they parted.

Arthur and his new companion had ridden but a little way up the ascent, when the stranger spoke thus: —

"We have been fellow-travellers before, young man, yet you remember me not."

Arthur turned his eyes on the cavalier, and observing that the crest which adorned his helmet was fashioned like a vulture, strange suspicions began to cross his mind, which were confirmed, when the Knight, opening his helmet, showed him the dark and severe features of the Priest of Saint Paul's.

"Count Albert of Geierstein!" said Arthur.

"The same," replied the Count, "though thou hast seen him in other garb and headgear. But tyranny drives all men to arms, and I have resumed, by the license and command of my superiors, those which I had laid aside. A war against cruelty and oppression is holy as that waged in Palestine, in which priests bear armour."

"My Lord Count," said Arthur, eagerly, "I cannot too soon entreat you to withdraw to Sir Ferrand of Lorraine's squadron. Here you are in peril, where no strength or courage can avail you. The Duke has placed a price on your head; and the country betwixt this and Nancy swarms with Stradiots and Italian light horsemen."

"I laugh at them," answered the Count. "I have not lived so long in a stormy world, amid intrigues of war and policy, to fall by the mean hand of such as they — besides, thou art with me, and I have seen but now that thou canst bear thee nobly."

"In your defence, my lord," said Arthur, who thought of his companion as the father of Anne of Geierstein, "I should try to do my best."

"What, youth!" replied Count Albert with a stern sneer, that was peculiar to his countenance; "wouldst thou aid the enemy of the lord under whose banner thou servest, against his waged soldiers?"

Arthur was somewhat abashed at the turn given to his ready offer of assistance, for which he had expected at least thanks; but he instantly collected himself, and replied, "My Lord Count Albert, you have been pleased to put yourself in peril to protect me from partisans of your party — I am equally bound to defend you from those of our side."

"It is happily answered," said the Count; — "yet I think there is a little blind partisan of whom troubadours and minstrels talk, to whose instigation I might, in case of need, owe the great zeal of my protector."

He did not allow Arthur, who was a good deal embarrassed time to reply, but proceeded: "Hear me, young man — Thy lance has this day done an evil deed to Switzerland, to Berne, and Duke Ferrand, in slaying their bravest champion. But to me, the death of Rudolph Donnerhugel is a welcome event. Know that he was, as his services grew more indispensable, become importunate in requiring Duke Ferrand's interest with me for my daughter's hand. And the Duke himself, the son of a princess, blushed not to ask me to bestow the last of my house — for my brother's family are degenerate mongrels — upon a presumptuous young man, whose uncle was a domestic in the house of my wife's father, though they boasted some relationship, I believe, through an illegitimate channel, which yonder Rudolph was wont to make the most of, as it favoured his suit."

"Surely," said Arthur, "a match with one so unequal in birth, and far more in every other respect, was too monstrous to be mentioned?"

"While I lived," replied Count Albert, "never should such union have been formed, if the death both of bride and bridegroom by my dagger could have saved the honour of my house from violation. But when I — I whose days, whose very hours are numbered — shall be no more, what could prevent an undaunted suitor, fortified by Duke Ferrand's favour, by the general applause of his country, and perhaps by the unfortunate prepossession of my brother Arnold, from carrying his point against the resistance and scruples of a solitary maiden?"

"Rudolph is dead," replied Arthur, "and may Heaven assoilzie him from guilt! But were he alive, and urging his suit on Anne of Geierstein, he would find there was a combat to be fought" ——

"Which has been already decided," answered Count Albert. "Now, mark me, Arthur de Vere! My daughter has told me of the passages betwixt you and her. Your sentiments and conduct are worthy of the noble house you descend from, which I well know ranks with the most illustrious in Europe. You are indeed disinherited, but so is Anne of Geierstein, save such pittance as her uncle may impart to her of her paternal inheritance. If you share it together till better days, (always supposing your noble father gives his consent, for my child shall enter no house against the will of its head,) my daughter knows that she has my willing consent and my blessing. My brother shall also know my pleasure. He will approve my purpose; for though dead to thoughts of honour and chivalry, he is alive to social feelings, loves his niece, and has friendship for thee and for thy father. What say'st thou, young man, to taking a beggarly Countess to aid thee in the journey of life? I believe — nay, I prophesy, (for I stand so much on the edge of the grave, that methinks I command a view beyond it,) that a lustre will one day, after I have long ended my doubtful and stormy life, beam on the coronets of De Vere and Geierstein."

De Vere threw himself from his horse, clasped the hand of Count Albert, and was about to exhaust himself in thanks; but the Count insisted on his silence.

"We are about to part," he said. "The time is short — the place is dangerous. You are to me, personally speaking, less than nothing. Had any one of the many schemes of ambition which I have pursued led me to success, the son of a banished Earl had not been the son-in-law I had chosen. Rise and remount your horse — thanks are unpleasing when they are not merited."

Arthur arose, and, mounting his horse, threw his raptures into a more acceptable form, endeavouring to describe how his love for Anne, and efforts for her happiness, should express his gratitude to her father, and observing that the Count listened with some pleasure to the picture he drew of their future life, he could not help exclaiming, — "And you, my lord — you who have been the author of all this happiness, will you not be the witness and partaker of it? Believe me, we will strive to soften the effect of the hard blows which fortune has dealt to you, and should a ray of better luck shine upon us, it will be the more welcome that you can share it."

"Forbear such folly," said the Count Albert of Geierstein. "I know my last scene is approaching. — Hear and tremble. The Duke of Burgundy is sentenced to die, and the Secret and Invisible Judges, who doom in secret, and avenge in secret, like the Deity, have given the cord and the dagger to my hand!"

"Oh, cast from you these vile symbols!" exclaimed Arthur, with enthusiasm; "let them find butchers and common stabbers to do such an office, and not dishonour the noble Lord of Geierstein!"

"Peace, foolish boy!" answered the Count. "The oath by which I am sworn is higher than that clouded sky, more deeply fixed than those distant mountains. Nor think my act is that of an assassin, though for such I might plead the Duke's own example. I send not hirelings, like these base Stradiots, to hunt his life, without imperilling mine own. I give not his daughter — innocent of his offences — the choice betwixt a disgraceful marriage and a discreditable retreat from the world. No, Arthur de Vere, I seek Charles with the resolved mind of one, who, to take the life of an adversary, exposes himself to certain death."

"I pray you speak no farther of it," said Arthur, very anxiously. "Consider I serve for the present the Prince whom you threaten" ——

"And art bound," interrupted the Count, "to unfold to him what I tell you. I desire you should do so; and though he hath already neglected a summons of the Tribunal, I am glad to have this opportunity of sending him personal defiance. Say to Charles of Burgundy, that he has wronged Albert of Geierstein. He who is injured in his honour loses all value for his life, and who-ever does BO has full command over that of another man. Bid him keep himself well from me, since if he see a second sun of the approaching year rise over the distant Alps, Albert of Geier-stein is forsworn. — And now begone, for I see a party approach under a Burgundian banner. They will ensure your safety, but, should I remain longer, would endanger mine."

So saying, the Count of Geierstein turned his horse and rode off.

CHAPTER XXXVI

Faint the din of battle bray'd
  Distant down the heavy wind;
War and terror fled before,
  Wounds and death were left behind.

MICKLE.

Arthur, left alone, and desirous perhaps to cover the retreat of Count Albert, rode towards the approaching body of Burgundian cavalry, who were arrayed under the Lord Contay's banner.

"Welcome, welcome," said that nobleman, advancing hastily to the young knight. "The Duke of Burgundy is a mile hence, with a body of horse to support the reconnoitring party. It is not half an hour since your father galloped up, and stated that you had been led into an ambuscade by the treachery of the Stradiots, and made prisoner. He has impeached Campo-Basso of treason, and challenged him to the combat. They have both been sent to the camp, under charge of the Grand-Marshal, to prevent their fighting on the spot, though I think our Italian showed little desire to come to blows. The Duke holds their gages, and they are to fight upon Twelfth-Day."

"I doubt that day will never dawn for some who look for it," said Arthur; "but if it do, I will myself claim the combat, by my father's permission."

He then turned with Contay, and met a still larger body of cavalry under the Duke's broad banner. He was instantly brought before Charles. The Duke heard, with some apparent anxiety, Arthur's support of his father's accusations against the Italian, in whose favour he was so deeply prejudiced. When assured that the Stradiots had been across the hill, and communicated with their leader just before he encouraged Arthur to advance, as it proved, into the midst of an ambush, the Duke shook his head, lowered his shaggy brows, and muttered to himself, — "Ill will to Oxford, perhaps — these Italians are vindictive." — Then raising his head, he commanded Arthur to proceed.

He heard with a species of ecstasy the death of Rudolph Donnerhugel, and, taking a ponderous gold chain from his own neck, flung it over Arthur's.

"Why, thou hast forestalled all our honours, young Arthur — this was the biggest bear of them all — the rest are but suckling whelps to him! I think I have found a youthful David to match their huge thick-headed Goliath. But the idiot, to think his peasant hand could manage a lance! Well, my brave boy — what more? How earnest thou off? By some wily device or agile stratagem, I warrant."

"Pardon me, my lord," answered Arthur. "I was protected by their chief, Ferrand, who considered my encounter with Rudolph Donnerhugel as a personal duel; and desirous to use fair war, as he said, dismissed me honourably, with my horse and arms."

"Umph!" said Charles, his bad humour returning; "your Prince Adventurer must play the generous — Umph — well, it belongs to his part, but shall not be a line for me to square my conduct by. Proceed with your story, Sir Arthur de Vere."

As Arthur proceeded to tell how and under what circumstances Count Albert of Geierstein named himself to him, the Duke fixed on him an eager look, and trembled with impatience as he fiercely interrupted him with the question — "And you — you struck him with your poniard under the fifth rib, did you not?"

"I did not, my Lord Duke — we were pledged in mutual assurance to each other."

"Yet you knew him to be my mortal enemy?" said the Duke. "Go, young man, thy lukewarm indifference has cancelled thy merit. The escape of Albert of Geierstein hath counterbalanced the death of Rudolph Donnerhugel."

"Be it so, my lord," said Arthur, boldly. "I neither claim your praises, nor deprecate your censure. I had to move me in either case motives personal to myself, — Donnerhugel was my enemy, and to Count Albert I owe some kindness."

The Burgundian nobles who stood around, were terrified for the effect of this bold speech. But it was never possible to guess with accuracy how such things would affect Charles. He looked around him with a laugh — "Hear you this English cockerel, my lords — what a note will he one day sound, that already crows so bravely in a prince's presence!"

A few horsemen now came in from different quarters, recounting that the Duke Ferrand and his company had retired into their encampment, and the country was clear of the enemy.

"Let us then draw back also," said Charles, "since there is

no chance of breaking spears to-day. And thou, Arthur de Vere, attend me closely."

Arrived in the Duke's pavilion, Arthur underwent an examination, in which he said nothing of Anne of Geierstein, or her father's designs concerning him, with which he considered Charles as having nothing to do; but he frankly conveyed to him the personal threats which the Count had openly used. The Duke listened with more temper, and when he heard the expression, "That a man who is desperate of his own life might command that of any other person," he said, "But there is a life beyond this, in which he who is treacherously murdered, and his base and desperate assassin, shall each meet their deserts." He then took from his bosom a gold cross, and kissed it, with much appearance of devotion. "In this," said he, "I will place my trust. If I fail in this world, may I find grace in the next — Ho, Sir Marshal!" he exclaimed — "Let your prisoners attend us."

The Marshal of Burgundy entered with the Earl of Oxford, and stated that his other prisoner, Campo-Basso, had desired so earnestly that he might be suffered to go and post his sentinels on that part of the camp intrusted to the protection of his troops, that he, the Marshal, had thought fit to comply with his request.

"It is well," said Burgundy, without further remark — "Then to you, my Lord Oxford, I would present your son, had you not already locked him in your arms. He has won great *los* and honour, and done me brave service. This is a period of the year when good men forgive their enemies; — I know not why, — my mind was little apt to be charged with such matters, — but I feel an unconquerable desire to stop the approaching combat betwixt you and Campo-Basso. For my sake, consent to be friends, and to receive back your gage of battle, and let me conclude this year — perhaps the last I may see — with a deed of peace."

"My lord," said Oxford, "it is a small thing you ask of me, since your request only enforces a Christian duty. I was enraged at the loss of my son. I am grateful to Heaven and your Grace for restoring him. To be friends with Campo-Basso is to me impossible. Faith and treason, truth and falsehood, might as soon shake hands and embrace. But the Italian shall be to me no more than he has been before this rupture; and that is literally nothing. I put my honour in your Grace's hands; — if he receives back his gage, I am willing to receive mine. John de Vere needs not be apprehensive that the world will suppose that he fears Campo-Basso."

The Duke returned sincere thanks, and detained the officers to spend the evening in his tent. His manners seemed to Arthur to be more placid than he had ever seen them before, while to the Earl of Oxford they recalled the earlier days in which their intimacy commenced, ere absolute power and unbounded success had spoiled Charles's rough, but not ungenerous disposition. The Duke ordered a distribution of provisions and wine to the soldiers, and expressed an anxiety about their lodgings, the cure of the wounded, and the health of the army, to which he received only unpleasing answers. To some of his counsellors, apart, he said, "Were it not for our vow, we would relinquish this purpose till spring, when our poor soldiers might take the field with less of suffering."

Nothing else remarkable appeared in the Duke's manner, save that he inquired repeatedly after Campo-Basso, and at length received accounts that he was indisposed, and that his physician had recommended rest; he had therefore retired to repose himself, in order that he might be stirring on his duty at peep of day, the safety of the camp depending much on his vigilance.

The Duke made no observation on the apology, which be considered as indicating some lurking disinclination, on the Italian's part, to meet Oxford. The guests at the ducal pavilion were dismissed an hour before midnight.

When Oxford and his son were in their own tent, the Earl full into a deep reverie, which lasted nearly ten minutes. At length, starting suddenly up, he said, "My son, give orders to Thiebault and thy yeomen to have our horses before the tent by break of day, or rather before it; and it would not be amiss if you ask our neighbour Colvin to ride along with us. I will visit the outposts by daybreak."

"It is a sudden resolution, my lord," said Arthur.

"And yet it may be taken too late," said his father. "Had it been moonlight, I would have made the rounds to-night."

"It is dark as a wolf's threat," said Arthur. "But wherefore, my lord, can this night in particular excite your apprehensions?"

"Son Arthur, perhaps you will hold your father credulous.

But my nurse, Martha Nixon, was a northern woman, and full of superstitions. In particular, she was wont to say, that any sudden and causeless change of a man's nature, as from license to sobriety, from temperance to indulgence, from avarice to extravagance, from prodigality to love of money, or the like, indicates an immediate change of his fortunes — that some great alteration of circumstances, either for good or evil, (and for evil most likely, since we live in an evil world,) is impending over him whose disposition is so much altered. This old woman's fancy has recurred so strongly to my mind, that I am determined to see with mine own eyes, ere to-morrow's dawn, that all our guards and patrols around the camp are on the alert."

Arthur made the necessary communications to Colvin and to Thiebault, and then retired to rest.

It was ere daybreak of the first of January, 1474, a period long memorable for the events which marked it, that the Earl of Oxford, Colvin, and the young Englishman, followed only by Thiebault and two other servants, commenced their rounds of the Duke of Burgundy's encampment. For the greater part of their progress, they found sentinels and guards all on the alert and at their posts. It was a bitter morning. The ground was partly covered with snow, — that snow had been partly melted by a thaw, which had prevailed for two days, and partly congealed into ice by a bitter frost, which had commenced the preceding evening, and still continued. A more dreary scene could scarcely be witnessed.

But what were the surprise and alarm of the Earl of Oxford and his companions, when they came to that part of the camp which had been occupied the day before by Campo-Basso and his Italians, who, reckoning men-at-arms and Stradiots, amounted to nigh two thousand men — not a challenge was given — not a horse neighed — no steeds were seen at picquet — no guard on the camp. They examined several of the tents and huts — they were empty.

"Let us back to alarm the camp," said the Earl of Oxford; "here is treachery."

"Nay, my lord," said Colvin, "let us not carry back imperfect tidings. I have a battery an hundred yards in advance, covering the access to this hollow way; let us see if my German cannoneers are at their post, and I think I can swear that we shall find them so. The battery commands a narrow pass, by which alone the camp can be approached; and if my men are at their duty, I will pawn my life that we make the pass good till you bring up succours from the main body."

"Forward, then, in God's name!" said the Earl of Oxford.

They galloped, at every risk, over broken ground, slippery with ice in some places, encumbered with snow in others. They came to the cannon, judiciously placed to sweep the pass, which rose towards the artillery on the outward side, and then descended gently from the battery into the lower ground. The waning winter moon mingling with the dawning light, showed them that the guns were in their places, but no sentinel was visible.

"The villains cannot have deserted!" said the astonished Colvin — "But see, there is light in their cantonment. — Oh, that unhallowed distribution of wine! Their usual sin of drunkenness has beset them. I will soon drive them from their revelry."

He sprung from his horse, and rushed into the tent from whence the light issued. The cannoneers, or most of them, were still there, but stretched on the ground, their cups and flagons scattered around them; and so drenched were they in wassail, that Colvin could only, by commands and threats, awaken two or three, who, staggering, and obeying him rather from instinct than sense, reeled forward to man the battery. A heavy rushing sound, like that of men marching fast, was now heard coming up the pass.

"It is the roar of a distant avalanche," said Arthur.

"It is an avalanche of Switzers, not of snow," said Colvin. — "Oh, these drunken slaves! — The cannon are deeply loaded, and well pointed — this volley must check them if they were fiends, and the report will alarm the camp sooner than we can do. — But, oh, these drunken villains!"

"Care not for their aid," said the Earl; "my son and I will each take a linstock, and be gunners for once."

They dismounted, and bade Thiebault and the grooms look to the horses, while the Earl of Oxford and his son took each a linstock from one of the helpless gunners, three of whom were just sober enough to stand by their guns.

"Bravo!" cried the bold Master of Ordnance, "never was a battery so noble. Now, my mates — your pardon, my lords, for there is no time for ceremony — and you, ye drunken knaves, take heed not to fire till I give the word, and, were the ribs of these tramplers as flinty as their Alps, they shall know how old Colvin loads his guns."

They stood breathless, each by his cannon. The dreaded sound approached nearer and more near, till the imperfect light showed a dark and shadowy but dense column of men, armed with long spears, pole-axes, and other weapons, amidst which banners dimly floated. Colvin suffered them to approach to the distance of about forty yards, and then gave the word, Fire! But his own piece alone exploded; a slight flame flashed from the touch-hole of the others, which had been spiked by the Italian deserters, and left in reality disabled, though apparently fit for service. Had they been all in the same condition with that fired by Colvin, they would probably have verified his prophecy; for even that single discharge produced an awful effect, and made a long lane of dead and wounded through the Swiss column, in which the first and leading banner was struck down.

"Stand to it yet," said Colvin, "and aid me if possible to re-load the piece."

For this, however, no time was allowed. A stately form, conspicuous in the front of the staggered column, raised up the fallen banner, and a voice as of a giant exclaimed, "What, coun-trymen! have you seen Murten and Granson, and are you daunted by a single gun? — Berne — Uri — Schwitz — banners forward! Unterwalden, here is your standard! — Cry your war-cries, wind your horns; Unterwalden, follow your Landamman!"

They rushed on like a raging ocean, with a roar as deafen-ing, and a course as impetuous. Colvin, still labouring to reload his gun, was struck down in the act. Oxford and his son were overthrown by the multitude, the closeness of which prevented any blows being aimed at them. Arthur partly saved himself by getting under the gun he was posted at; his father, less fortunate, was much trampled upon, and must have been crushed to death but for his armour of proof. The human inundation, consisting of at least four thousand men, rushed down into the camp, continu-ing their dreadful shouts, soon mingled with shrill shrieks, groans, and cries of alarm.

A broad red glare rising behind the assailants, and putting to shame the pallid lights of the winter morning, first recalled Arthur to a sense of his condition. The camp was on fire in his rear, and resounded with all the various shouts of conquest and terror that are heard in a town which is stormed. Starting to his feet, he looked around him for his father. He lay near him senseless, as were the gunners, whose condition prevented their attempting an escape. Having opened his father's casque, he was rejoiced to see him give symptoms of reanimation.

"The horses, the horses!" said Arthur. "Thiebault, where art thou?"

"At hand, my lord," said that trusty attendant, who had saved himself and his charge by a prudent retreat into a small thicket, which the assailants had avoided that they might not disorder their ranks.

"Where is the gallant Colvin?" said the Earl; "get him a horse, I will not leave him in jeopardy."

"His wars are ended, my lord," said Thiebault; "he will never mount steed more."

A look and a sigh as he saw Colvin, with the ramrod in his hand, before the muzzle of the piece, his head cleft by a Swiss battle-axe, was all the moment permitted.

"Whither must we take our course?" said Arthur to his father.

"To join the Duke," said the Earl of Oxford. "It is not on a day like this that I will leave him."

"So please you," said Thiebault, "I saw the Duke, followed by some half score of his guards, riding at full speed across this hollow watercourse, and making for the open country to the northward. I think I can guide you on the track."

"If that be so," replied Oxford, "we will mount and follow him. The camp has been assailed on several places at once, and all must be over since he has fled."

With difficulty they assisted the Earl of Oxford to his horse, and rode as fast as his returning strength permitted, in the direction which the Provençal pointed out. Their other attendants were dispersed or slain.

They looked back more than once on the camp, now one great scene of conflagration, by whose red and glaring light they could discover on the ground the traces of Charles's retreat. About three miles from the scene of their defeat, the sound of which they still heard, mingled with the bells of Nancy, which were ringing in triumph, they reached a half-frozen swamp, round which lay several dead bodies. The most conspicuous was that of Charles of Burgundy, once the possessor of such unlimited power — such unbounded wealth. He was partly stripped and plundered, as were those who lay round him. His body was pierced with several wounds, inflicted by various weapons. His sword was still in his hand, and the singular ferocity which was wont to animate his features in battle, still dwelt on his stiffened countenance. Close behind him, as if they had fallen in the act of mutual fight, lay the corpse of Count Albert of Geierstein; and that of Ital Schreckenwald, the faithful though unscrupulous follower of the latter, lay not far distant. Both were in the dress of the men-at-arms composing the Duke's guard, a disguise probably assumed to execute the fatal commission of the Secret Tribunal. It is supposed that a party of the traitor Campo-Basso's men had been engaged in the skirmish in which the Duke fell, for six or seven of them, and about the same number of the Duke's guards, were found near the spot.

The Earl of Oxford threw himself from his horse, and examined the body of his deceased brother-in-arms, with all the sorrow inspired by early remembrance of his kindness. But as he gave way to the feelings inspired by so melancholy an example of the fall of human greatness, Thiebault, who was looking out on the path they had just pursued, exclaimed, "To horse, my lord! here is no time to mourn the dead, and little to save the living — the Swiss are upon us."

"Fly thyself, good fellow," said the Earl; "and do thou, Arthur, fly also, and save thy youth for happier days. I cannot and will not fly farther. I will render me to the pursuers; if they take me to grace, it is well; if not, there is ONE above that will receive me to His."

"I will not fly," said Arthur, "and leave you defenceless; I will stay and share your fate."

"And I will remain also," said Thiebault; "the Switzers make fair war when their blood has not been heated by much opposition, and they have had little enough to day."

The party of Swiss which came up proved to be Sigismund, with his brother Ernest, and some of the youths of Unterwalden. Sigismund kindly and joyfully received them to mercy; and thus, for the third time, rendered Arthur an important service, in return for the kindness he had expressed towards him.

"I will take you to my father," said Sigismund, "who will be right glad to see you; only that he is ill at ease just now for the death of brother Rudiger, who fell with the banner in his hand, by the only cannon that was fired this morning; the rest could not bark; Campo-Basso had muzzled Colvin's mastiffs, or we should many more of us have been served like poor Rudiger. But Colvin himself is killed."

"Campo-Basso then was in your correspondence?" said Arthur.

"Not in ours — we scorn such companions — but some dealing there was between the Italian and Duke Ferrand; and having disabled the cannon, and filled the German gunners soundly drunk, he came off to our camp with fifteen hundred horse, and offered to act with us. 'But no, no!' said my father, — 'traitors come not into our Swiss host;' and so, though we walked in at the door which he left open, we would not have his company. So he marched with Duke Ferrand to attack the other extremity of the camp, where he found them entrance by announcing them as the return of a reconnoitring party."

"Nay, then," said Arthur, "a more accomplished traitor never drew breath, nor one who drew his net with such success."

"You say well," answered the young Swiss. "The Duke will never, they say, be able to collect another army?"

"Never, young man," said the Earl of Oxford, "for he lies dead before you."[22]

---

[22] The following very striking passage is that in which Philip de Commines sums up the last scene of Charles the Bold, whose various fortunes he had long watched with a dark anticipation that a character so reckless, and capable of such excess, must sooner or later lead to a tragical result: —

"As soon as the Count de Campo-Basso arrived in the Duke of Lorrain's army, word was sent him to leave the camp immediately, for they would not entertain, nor have any communication with such traytors. Upon which message he retir'd with his party to a Castle and Pass not far off, where he fortified himself with carts and other things as well as he could, in hopes, that if the Duke of Burgundy was routed, he might have an opportunity of coming in for a share of the plunder, as he did afterwards. Nor was this practice with the Duke of Lorrain the most execrable action that Campo-Basso was guilty of; but before he left the army he conspir'd with several other officers (finding it was impracticable to attempt any thing against the Duke of Burgundy's person) to leave him just as they came to charge, for at that time he suppos'd it would put the Duke into the greatest terror and consternation, and if he fled, he was sure he could not escape alive, for he had order'd thirteen or fourteen sure men, some to run as soon as the Germans came up to charge 'em, and others to watch the Duke of Burgundy, and kill him in the rout, which was well enough contrived; I myself have seen two or three of those who were employed to kill the Duke. Having thus settled his conspiracy at home, he went over to the Duke of Lorrain upon the approach of the German army; but finding they would not entertain him, he retired to Conde.

"The German army march'd forward, and with 'em a considerable body of French horse, whom the King had given leave to be present at that action. Several parties lay in ambush not far off, that if the Duke of Burgundy was routed, they might surprise some person of quality, or take some considerable booty. By this every one may see into what a deplorable condition this poor Duke had brought himself, by his contempt of good counsel. Both armies being joyn'd, the Duke of Burgundy's forces having been twice beaten before, and by consequence weak and dispirited, and ill provided besides, were quickly broken and entirely defeated: Many sav'd themselves and got off; the rest were either taken or kill'd: and among 'em the Duke of Burgundy himself was kill'd on the spot. One Monsieur Claude of Bausmont, Captain of the Castle of Dier in Lorrain, kill'd the Duke of Burgundy. Finding his army routed, he mounted a swift horse, and endeavouring to swim a little river in order to make his escape, his horse fell with him, and overset him: The Duke cry'd out for quarter to this gentleman who was pursuing him, but he being deaf, and not hearing him, immediately kill'd and stripp'd him, not knowing who he was, and left him naked in the ditch, where his body was found the next day after the battle; which the Duke of Lorrain (to his eternal honour) buried with great pomp and magnificence in St. George's Church, in the old town of Nancy, himself and all his nobility, in deep mourning, attending the corpse to the grave. The following epitaph was sometime afterwards ingrav'd on his tomb: —

'Carolus hoc busto Burgundæ gloria gentis
Conditur, Europæ qui fuit ante timor.'

I saw a seal ring of his, since his death, at Milan, with his arms cut curiously upon a sardonix that I have seen him often wear in a ribbon at his breast, which was sold at Milan for two ducats, and had been stolen from him by a rascal that waited on him in his chamber. I have often seen the Duke dress'd and undress'd in great state and formality, and attended by very great persons; but at his death all this pomp and magnificence ceas'd, and his family was involved in the same ruin with himself, and very likely as a punishment for his having deliver'd up the Constable not long before, out of a base and avaricious principle; but God forgive him. I have known him a powerful and honourable Prince, in as great esteem, and as much courted by his neighbours, (when his affairs were in a prosperous condition,) as any Prince in Europe, and perhaps more; and I cannot conceive what should provoke God Almighty's displeasure so highly against him, unless it was his self-love and arrogance, in appropriating all the success of his enterprises, and all the renown he ever acquir'd, to his own wisdom and conduct, without attributing any thing to God. Yet to speak truth, he was master of several good qualities: No Prince ever had a greater ambition to entertain young noblemen than he, nor was more careful of their education: His presents and bounty were never profuse and extravagant, because he gave to many, and had a mind everybody should taste of it. No Prince was ever more easie of access to his servants and subjects. Whilst I was in his service he was never cruel, but a little before his death be took up that humour, which was an infallible sign of the shortness of his life. He was very splendid and curious in his dress, and in every thing else, and indeed a little too much. He paid great honours to all ambassadors and foreigners, and entertain'd them nobly: His ambitious desire of fame was insatiable, and it was that which induced him to be eternally in wars, more than any other motive. He ambitiously desired to imitate the old Kings and Heroes of antiquity, whose actions still shine in History, and are so much talked of in the world, and his courage was equal to any Prince's of his time.

"But all his designs and imaginations were vain and extravagant, and turn'd afterwards to his own dishonour and confusion, for 'tis the conquerors and not the conquer'd that purchase to themselves renown. I cannot easily determine towards whom God Almighty show'd his anger most, whether towards him who died suddenly without pain or sickness in the field of battle, or towards his subjects who never enjoy'd peace after his death, but were continually involv'd in wars, against which they were not able to maintain themselves, upon account of the civil dissensions and cruel animosities that arose among 'em; and that which was the most insupportable, was, that the very people, to whom they were now obliged for their defence and preservation, were the Germans, who were strangers, and not long since their profess'd enemies. In short, after the Duke's death, there was not a neighbouring state that wish'd them to prosper, nor even Germany that defended 'em. And by the management of their affairs, their understanding seem'd to be as much infatuated as their master's, for they rejected all good counsel, and pursued such methods as directly tended to their destruction; and they are still in such a condition, that though they have at present some little ease and relaxation from their sorrows, yet it is with great danger of a relapse, and 'tis well if it turns not in the end to their utter ruin.

"I am partly of their opinion who maintain, that God gives Princes, as he in his wisdom thinks fit, to punish or chastise the subjects; and he disposes the affection of subjects to their Princes, as he has determin'd to raise or depress 'em. Just so it has pleas'd him to deal with the House of Burgundy; for after a long series of riches and prosperity, and six-and-twenty years' peace under three Illustrious Princes, predecessors to this Charles, (all of 'em excellent persons, and of great prudence and discretion,) it pleased God to send this Duke Charles, who involv'd them in bloody wars, as well winter as summer, to their great affliction and expense, in which most of their richest and stoutest men were either killed or utterly undone. Their misfortunes continu'd successively to the very hour of his death; and after such a manner, that at the last, the whole strength of their country was destroy'd, and all kill'd or taken prisoners who had any zeal or affection for the House of Burgundy, and had power to defend the state and dignity of that family; so that in a manner their losses were equal to, if not over-balanc'd their former prosperity; for as I have seen those Princes heretofore puissant, rich, and honourable, so it fared the same with their subjects; for I think I have seen and known the greatest part of Europe; yet I never knew any province, or country, tho' perhaps of a larger extent, so abounding in

Sigismund started; for he had an inherent respect, and somewhat of fear, for the lofty name of Charles the Bold, and could hardly believe that the mangled corpse which now lay before him, was once the personage he had been taught to dread. But his surprise was mingled with sorrow, when he saw the body of his uncle, Count Albert of Geierstein.

"Oh, my uncle!" he said — "my dear uncle Albert! has all your greatness and your wisdom brought you to a death, at the side of a ditch, like any crazed beggar? — Come, this sad news must be presently told to my father, who will be concerned to hear of his brother's death, which will add gall to bitterness, coming on the back of poor Rudiger's. It is some comfort, however, that father and uncle never could abide each other."

With some difficulty they once more assisted the Earl of Oxford to horseback, and were proceeding to set forward when the English lord said, — "You will place a guard here, to save these bodies from farther dishonour, that they may be interred with due solemnity."

"By Our Lady of Einsiedlen! I thank you for the hint," said Sigismund. "Yes, we should do all that the Church can for uncle Albert. It is to be hoped he has not gambled away his soul beforehand, playing with Satan at odds and evens. I would we had a priest to stay by his poor body; but it matters not, since no one ever heard of a demon appearing just before breakfast."

They proceeded to the Landamman's quarters through sights and scenes which Arthur, and even his father, so well accustomed to war in all its shapes, could not look upon without shuddering. But the simple Sigismund, as he walked by Arthur's side, contrived to hit upon a theme so interesting as to divert his sense of the horrors around them.

"Have you farther business in Burgundy, now this Duke of yours is at an end?"

---

money, so extravagantly fine in furniture for their horses, so sumptuous in their buildings, so profuse in their expenses, so luxurious in their feasts and entertainments, and so prodigal in all respects, as the subjects of these Princes, in my time; but it has pleased God at one blow to subvert and ruin this illustrious family. Such changes and revolutions in states and kingdoms, God in his providence has wrought before we were born, and will do again when we are in our graves; for this is a certain maxim, that the prosperity or adversity of Princes are wholly at his disposal." — COMMINES, Book V. Chap. 9.

"My father knows best," said Arthur; "but I apprehend we have none. The Duchess of Burgundy, who must now succeed to some sort of authority in her late husband's dominion, is sister to this Edward of York, and a mortal enemy to the House of Lancaster, and to those who have stood by it faithfully. It were neither prudent nor safe to tarry where she has influence."

"In that case," said Sigismund, "my plan will fadge bravely. You shall go back to Geierstein and take up your dwelling with us. Your father will be a brother to mine, and a better one than uncle Albert, whom he seldom saw or spoke with; while with your father he will converse from morning till night, and leave us all the work of the farm. And you, Arthur, you shall go with us, and be a brother to us all, in place of poor Rudiger, who was, to be sure, my real brother, which you cannot be; nevertheless, I did not like him so well, in respect he was not so good-natured. And then Anne — cousin Anne — is left all to my father's charge, and is now at Geierstein — and you know, King Arthur, we used to call her Queen Guenover."

"You spoke great folly then," said Arthur.

"But it is great truth — For, look you, I loved to tell Anne tales of our hunting, and so forth, but she would not listen a word till I threw in something of King Arthur, and then I warrant she would sit still as a heath-hen when the hawk is in the heavens. And now Donnerhugel is slain, you know you may marry my cousin when you and she will, for nobody hath interest to prevent it."

Arthur blushed with pleasure under his helmet, and almost forgave that new-year's morning all its complicated distresses.

"You forget," he replied to Sigismund, with as much indifference as he could assume, "that I may be viewed in your country with prejudice on account of Rudolph's death."

"Not a whit, not a whit; we bear no malice for what is done in fair fight under shield. It is no more than if you had beat him in wrestling or at quoits — only it is a game cannot be played over again."

They now entered the town of Nancy; the windows were hung with tapestry, and the streets crowded with tumultuous and rejoicing multitudes, whom the success of the battle had relieved from great alarm for the formidable vengeance of Charles of Burgundy.

The prisoners were received with the utmost kindness by the Landamman, who assured them of his protection and friendship. He appeared to support the death of his son Rudiger with stern resignation.

"He had rather," he said, "his son fell in battle, than that he should live to despise the old simplicity of his country, and think the object of combat was the gaining of spoil. The gold of the dead Burgundy," he added, "would injure the morals of Switzerland more irretrievably than ever his sword did their bodies."

He heard of his brother's death without surprise, but apparently with emotion.

"It was the conclusion," he said, "of a long tissue of ambitious enterprises, which often offered fair prospects, but uniformly ended in disappointment."

The Landamman farther intimated, that his brother had apprized him that he was engaged in an affair of so much danger, that he was almost certain to perish in it, and had bequeathed his daughter to her uncle's care, with instructions respecting her.

Here they parted for the present, but shortly after, the Landamman inquired earnestly of the Earl of Oxford, what his motions were like to be, and whether he could assist them.

"I think of choosing Bretagne for my place of refuge," answered the Earl, "where my wife has dwelt since the battle of Tewkesbury expelled us from England."

"Do not so," said the kind Landamman, "but come to Geierstein with the Countess, where, if she can, like you, endure our mountain manners and mountain fare, you are welcome as to the house of a brother, to a soil where neither conspiracy nor treason ever flourished. Bethink you, the Duke of Bretagne is a weak prince, entirely governed by a wicked favourite, Peter Landais. He is as capable — I mean the minister — of selling brave men's blood, as a butcher of selling bullock's flesh; and you know, there are those, both in France and Burgundy, that thirst after yours."

The Earl of Oxford expressed his thanks for the proposal, and his determination to profit by it, if approved of by Henry of Lancaster, Earl of Richmond, whom he now regarded as his sovereign.

To close the tale, about three months after the battle of Nancy, the banished Earl of Oxford resumed his name of Philipson, bringing with his lady some remnants of their former wealth, which enabled them to procure a commodious residence near to Geierstein; and the Landamman's interest in the state procured for them the right of denizenship. The high blood, and the moderate fortunes, of Anne of Geierstein and Arthur de Vere, joined to their mutual inclination, made their marriage in every respect rational; and Annette with her bachelor took up their residence with the young people, not as servants, but mechanical aids in the duties of the farm; for Arthur continued to prefer the chase to the labours of husbandry, which was of little consequence, as his separate income amounted, in that poor country, to opulence. Time glided on, till it amounted to five years since the exiled family had been inhabitants of Switzerland. In the year 1482, the Landamman Biederman died the death of the righteous, lamented universally, as a model of the true and valiant, simple-minded and sagacious chiefs, who ruled the ancient Switzers in peace, and headed them in battle. In the same year, the Earl of Oxford lost his noble Countess.

But the star of Lancaster, at that period, began again to culminate, and called the banished lord and his son from their retirement, to mix once more in politics. The treasured necklace of Margaret was then put to its destined use, and the produce applied to levy those bands which shortly after fought the celebrated battle of Bosworth, in which the arms of Oxford and his son contributed so much to the success of Henry VII. This changed the destinies of De Vere and his lady. Their Swiss farm was conferred on Annette and her husband; and the manners and beauty of Anne of Geierstein attracted as much admiration at the English Court as formerly in the Swiss Chalet.

Printed in Great Britain by
Amazon.co.uk, Ltd.,
Marston Gate.